THE QUEEN'S HEIR

KATHRYN OSCAR

 Formatted with Vellum

Author's Note:

This is a work of fiction. Unless otherwise indicated, all the names, characters, businesses, places, events and incidents in this book are either the product of the author's imagination or used in a fictitious manner. Any resemblance to actual persons, living or dead, or actual places or events is purely coincidental.

The Queen's Heir contains subject matter that might be difficult for some readers. It is an adult fantasy romance with themes that may not be suitable for all audiences. Reader discretion is advised.

Content warnings can be a spoilers for some. If you do not need them, please feel free to skip the next paragraph. If you are someone who needs the heads up to protect your mental health, continue on.

Content Warning: This book contains violence and death (on page), explicit language, sexual acts (on-page), alcohol consumption, character eluding to non-consensual acts, brief mention of suicidal thoughts, and other mental health issues (including anxiety and references to panic attacks).

Dedication

This book is dedicated to the readers who have ever questioned their self worth. You are more than enough. I hope you can see just how special you are.

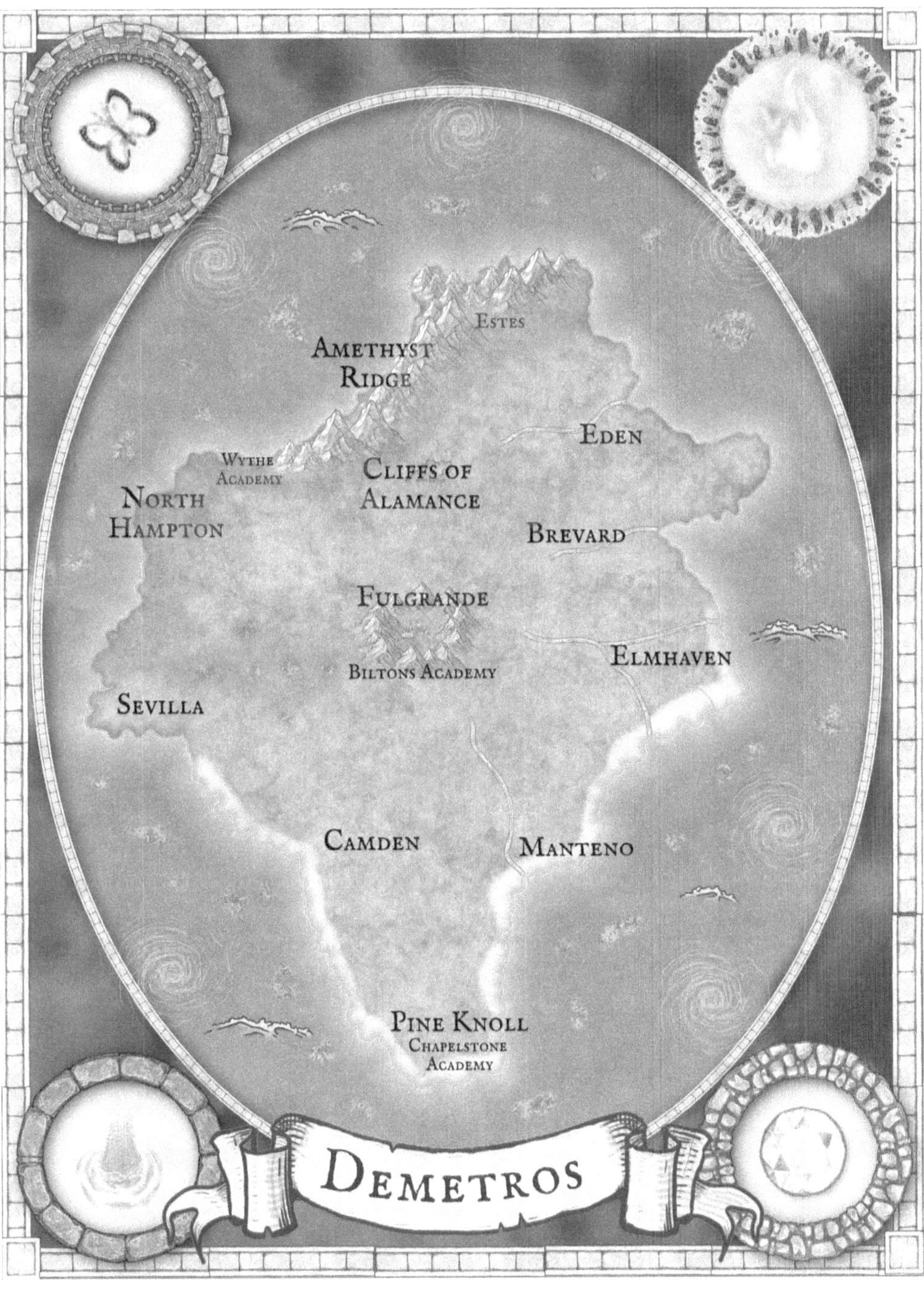

Estes
Amethyst Ridge
Eden
Wythe Academy
Cliffs of Alamance
North Hampton
Brevard
Fulgrande
Elmhaven
Biltons Academy
Sevilla
Camden
Manteno
Pine Knoll
Chapelstone Academy
Demetros

A Note Abut the Following Map

The map on the next page may contain spoilers for the first chunk of the book. If you do not wish to have anything spoiled, skip over the next page and come back to it when you have read enough to feel comfortable viewing it (you will know when this happens). Otherwise, please enjoy.

THE DARK KINGDOM
IREDELL
FALKLAND
TVERNESS
MARITUK
ELMAS
AMBERDEEN
THE WESTERN LANDS
LOCHMERE
WOLVESDEN
THE VIOLET FOREST
THE VIOLET FOREST
THE EMERALD ISLE
THE LIGHT KINGDOM

One

drenaline and fear propelled me away from Biltons Academy and the capital city of Fulgrande, but it couldn't sustain me forever. No amount of training could have prepared me for the exhaustion of traveling all night, and I found myself grateful the horse beneath me seemed to hold some level of cognitive thought because I had drifted asleep more than once, and we remained on the right path to Eden.

Even with the sparsest of information from Ryana, the mere mention of my mother's boots underneath the chair in our family cottage had me trusting her words and heeding her warning to flee. It had seemed right in the moment, with her revealing that crucial detail of my past, but the further I got away from the academy, the more I spiraled about the events that had led me here. Puzzle pieces that didn't quite fit, a disjointed image of chaos and tragedy.

Finding that sheet with the designation Operarius beside my name had been devastating, and although Ryana had disregarded that fact as fiction, she hadn't given me anything else substantial to make me believe I wasn't powerless.

Cade had chosen the support of his family over our relationship. Even if it turned out that I had access to a greater power, I wasn't sure I could forgive how willing he was to choose them over us when he believed me to be nothing.

Mr. Higgins, my botany instructor, had revealed himself as my anonymous donor. The man had admitted, with an uncomfortable amount of glee, that he had only entered into our agreement because he had known I would be marked powerless. It begged the question: How had I already been flagged as powerless before I had even stepped foot inside the academy walls? Furthermore, how could I be certain that Mr. Higgins wouldn't go after my father in my absence?

For the short term, Ryana had assured me she could deliver a potion to the instructor that was potent enough to erase our last interaction. Even if I believed that such a thing existed, it did little to dampen my anxiety. It wouldn't stop him from eventually coming to collect his debt.

Magical contract or not, I had signed what I still assumed to be a legally binding document, and Ryana hadn't made it sound like she'd be erasing anything but recent memories. With Berit Murdock, his other investment, dead, surely, Mr. Higgins wouldn't let my escape go with calm indifference. The reminder of Berit's ire—of his attack—was enough to send a fresh wave of shivers racing down my spine but it was the probability of Mr. Higgins' impending request for me to fulfill my end of the bargain that made me want to turn South to Elmhaven rather than continue my quest North.

If Ryana hadn't promised to alert my dad, hadn't indicated that he had planned for this eventuality too, I wouldn't have even attempted to venture North. So, it was an equal mixture of hope and curiosity that propelled me forward, rather than down the moonlit path that would lead me home, even as I was already drifting to sleep again.

With an impatient snort from the horse, my view instantly shifted from a wooded trail to a cluster of buildings as I jolted awake once more. We had already passed so many towns that the sight of another sign hardly gave me any cause for excitement, but I peered over at the slab of wood all the same. Stunning white ornate lettering had been hand-carved into the board, which was mounted on two sturdy legs.

Welcome to Eden

A shuddering sigh tumbled from my lips as I fought against the sudden urge to cry. Instead, I leaned over, patting the horse's neck in appreciation for his aid in getting me this far. "Thank you, boy," I muttered to the beast, not caring who heard or saw me conversing with an animal. At this late hour, all were probably asleep anyhow.

Now, all I had to do was locate the Barker Inn, find someone named Skylar—who would preferably be awake—and then throw myself into any available bed.

The task turned out to be more difficult than I expected, as I had wrongfully assumed the establishment, like most other venues designated for rest, would be at the center of the town. I passed storefronts and even other inns, but nothing with the correct name. Just as I considered slipping into a different inn and starting fresh again the next morning, a building caught my eye at the far side of the town.

It was the opposite of everything I had expected, but I had already woven through the streets of Eden too many times to think I had somehow passed The Barker Inn amongst the buildings clustered in the city center.

Hesitantly, I approached the manor-like structure, tying Ryana's scarf tighter around my neck as I shivered against the frigid night air. The building before me, nestled on a riverbed at the edge of the settlement, was alive with flickering candles in every window, neither quaint nor inconspicuous.

The wooden boards of the exterior of the home were painted a crisp white, lifted on red-bricked arches tall enough to walk underneath. The house boasted three additional floors on top, each with its own expansive porch.

Strands of evergreen garlands were draped against the rails that spanned all six columns holding up the multi-level porch. Dozens of flickering candles illuminated the building, drawing even more attention to it. It struck me with a sudden pang in my chest that the building had been decorated for the solstice.

Three hefty brick chimneys emitted dark smoke into the star-streaked sky, a sign someone inside was awake. A tidy but small sign had been mounted close to the steps, and my body nearly buckled with exhaustion as I read the name of my destination.

The Barker Inn

"Thank the gods," I muttered, despite not actually practicing the old religion. None of us did, but that didn't keep me from lifting silent prayers on the off chance it actually worked.

My dismount was sloppy as I landed on shaky legs, but I kept moving, tying the horse up to the post out front and climbing the grand white staircase. The bronze lion head knocker was ice cold against my ungloved hands as I used it to bang at the entrance to the establishment. After several moments with no response, my brain finally connected that this was a place of business, not a home.

Slipping through the unlocked door, a completely unoccupied entryway greeted me. No one was sitting at the paint-chipped desk where I would have expected someone to be welcoming potential patrons, even though it was a late hour.

It was eerily silent with the exception of a faint humming coming from a nearby hallway. Tilting my head in that direction, I picked up on what sounded like a gathering.

Meandering down the dimly lit passageway, I followed the muffled hums as the racket grew louder and louder. Surely there was someone back there who could help situate me in a room.

The end of the hallway spilled out into a large pub that might have been considered cozy had it not been overtaken by rowdy depravity.

In one corner, a woman in a red dress played loudly on a piano, singing off-tune songs with a handful of the other patrons. A few men were clustered at tables, cards splayed wide in their grips as they stared at one another with hopeful grins.

Others were enjoying the party in different ways. My cheeks flamed as my eyes caught sight of a trio nestled in an alcove that boasted a rather large couch. Sheer curtains blocked some of my view of them, but not all.

The man, who had short golden hair and a smirk playing across his lips, was leaning back against the couch cushions. One arm was casually bent behind his head as the two women in front of him danced suggestively, shaking their scantly covered hips as they swayed to a beat only in their own minds, having nothing in common with the sharp banging of the woman at the piano.

He looked so content there, so pleased to be the center of attention as he sipped from a low glass of amber liquid. The brunette woman dipped low, grinding her ass against his crotch, throwing her head back against his shoulder as she let her weight fall on him. Just as the man's hand began roaming her hips, I averted my gaze ahead, bringing my focus back to the task at hand.

Find Skylar.

Code dragonfire.

My eyes locked on the only person in the room who appeared sober, a woman who stood behind a waist-height counter, preparing drinks for the patrons. She wore an apron over her plain navy tunic, so it was likely she knew the person who could check me in.

Weaving my way through the crowd, I slid onto an unoccupied stool, resting my elbows on the smooth wood of the countertop as I leaned forward to get the attention of the barkeep.

"What can I get you tonight? Obviously, everapple wine is on special," the woman said, gesturing at the sweaty, pulsing bodies in the room.

A forced laugh left my throat as I scanned the crowd. Everapple wine was said to make people more suggestible, but I had never experienced its effects firsthand. It wasn't until witnessing the chaos around me that I believed there might be some merit to the rumors.

My gaze shifted back to the barkeep, and I realigned my body to assess her with more intent. She looked to be a few inches over five feet tall. Petite but muscular. Her hair was a shade of pink usually reserved for spring flowers, like the tulips I could find in my father's garden.

It was difficult to be sure in the flickering candlelight illuminating the room, but there was a glow about her that seemed almost bronze, dappled with dark brown freckles that spanned the bridge of her nose. Other than the freckles, her skin tone was similar to Cade's, and I felt my heart constrict in my chest at the reminder of him. A burning sensation swept over my eyes, but I pushed through the heavy emotion. "I'm here to meet someone."

Two pink eyebrows rose to the woman's hairline. "Honey, if you're meeting someone here, he's probably already upstairs with someone else, but I'll see if I can help you find him." She started scanning the pub for patrons that I assumed she knew personally. "What's his name?"

"It's a woman, actually," I said, still distracted by the sensuality surrounding me.

The barkeep cleared offered me an apologetic smile. "My mistake. I shouldn't have assumed."

She turned her attention back to the crowd but tossed a fist to her hip when her eyes locked on the threesome. "But she's also probably already with someone else, too. I hope it's not Gabriella. She has been known to double-book when he's in town unexpectedly."

Immediately, my eyes moved to the trio again. Now the man was more upright in his seat and shirtless. The blonde woman was behind him, rubbing his shoulders while the brunette straddled him, still twisting her hips to a slow and steady rhythm.

As if sensing my attention, the man's gaze snapped to mine, our eyes locking. Another smirk curled his lip, his hands skimming the ribs of the woman on his lap as we held the prolonged contact. He drew the bottom half of his quirked lips between his teeth, winking directly at me.

My face was suddenly crimson, and I practically fell off the stool as I fought to reorient myself to the woman behind the bar. "No, it's not like that," I choked out, entirely too flustered by that interaction. "I was sent here by a friend. I'm looking for Skylar."

At the mention of the name, the woman paused what she was doing, spine stiffening as she almost dropped the glass in her hand. She leaned across the bar, so our faces were inches away from touching. "Who sent you?" Her once jovial tone had disappeared, ushering in a rising concern that concentrated behind her eyes.

"My friend Ryana sent me," I answered. "Are you Skylar?" I couldn't even hold back the hopefulness in my tone. Gods, I needed this ordeal to be over, and I longed for a soft mattress and the warm embrace of a blanket.

The woman's eyes squinted like she was truly trying to take me in now. "I am," she admitted, and then her voice got so low I could barely hear it over the sounds of the party raging on around us. "Do you have a message for me?"

My voice dropped to her level. "Dragonfire?"

At the mention of the code word, the woman blew out a long breath. "You need to follow me." Quickly, Skylar stepped around the counter and practically dragged me into an open doorway.

At the end of the hallway, she slipped inside what appeared to be a storage closet, beckoning for me to trail behind her. Just when I thought we'd hit a wall, she pulled down a wooden broom handle, and a small opening appeared, only big enough for one body at a time.

From there, she weaved through a dark, narrow passageway and up a steep set of stairs until we reached a landing with a blue-painted door that was almost shorter than me and covered in various chips and scrapes.

Ducking inside, she brought her voice down to a whisper as she looked over her shoulder to speak to me. "Just a little further." We traversed the rest of the narrow passageway in silence.

She finally stopped at an unmarked door, allowing it to swing inwards when she opened it. "It's not much, but you can stay here and get some rest until someone is prepared to enact the rest of the protocol."

My confusion must have been palpable on my features, because the woman's face scrunched as she offered me an apologetic smile. "There's a basin in the corner. Someone will bring you fresh water to wash off. Is that your horse I saw out front?"

I nodded, too exhausted to clarify I had borrowed him from the academy. My eyelids were already drooping at the sight of the bed.

Her expression turned contemplative. "Okay. That's fine. I will send someone to tend to the animal and put him in the stables for tonight." Her gaze fell back on me. "You won't be able to take the horse with you. Did you steal it, or do we need to figure out how to return it?"

My head tilted as I faced her because I hadn't realized I'd be leaving the Barker Inn until I reunited with my father. "When do I leave, and where am I going?"

If I hadn't already been looking at the woman, I would have missed the shadow or her wince. "As soon as possible, and I don't know your final destination. It's part of the arrangement."

"And where I'm going next, I can't take the horse?" Really, bringing the animal with me was the least of my problems, but if I truly was leaving the inn, wouldn't I need transportation?

Momentarily avoiding my question, Skylar moved around the room, lighting a small fire in the hearth with a flick of her wrist. She was Ignus. I had been too distracted with the task of finding her to look at her brand when we had spoken, but as I peeked at her forearm, I found it covered in the gauzy sleeves of her top.

She frowned as our eyes met again. "We can't have whoever you stole the horse from tracing him back here. It could jeopardize our setup. And he won't fit on the boat."

My body, as fatigued as it was, allotted my brain just enough energy to snag on that word. "What boat?"

She eyed me warily. "The boat to the Emerald Isle. It's your next stop. You said dragonfire, right?"

It was entirely too late for me to continue like this with her, so I just said, "Ryana didn't have a chance to tell me anything. I don't know where I'm going or why."

Skylar's expression turned more empathetic then. "When the next contact comes, you will be sent to board a boat to the Emerald Isle."

A grimace twisted my features as I recalled the name of that location from my father's stories of his travels. "One of the barrier islands? Why?"

She just patted my arm. "I don't know what path you take once you leave my Inn. They keep the logistics of the next steps a secret from each of us. That way, if we are ever caught, there is almost no one who knows the entire plan."

There was that we again, and something about it sparked along the edges of my senses, but I was too exhausted to ask more.

A young girl, maybe aged twelve or thirteen, walked into the room with a pitcher in her hands. I couldn't fathom why someone of her age would be at a place like this, but the thought was quickly dismissed as I considered how good that water would feel against my skin. Silently, the girl placed a chunk of soap on the table next to the basin and fled the room as quickly as possible.

A tired sigh escaped Skylar's lips. "Get cleaned up and try to get some rest. I'll leave some clothes outside the door for you to change into when it's time to leave."

"Thank you," I replied, somehow holding onto some semblance of my manners.

Not for the first time tonight, the woman's gaze ran from my toes to my face. This time, the resulting smile was strained. "Goodnight," she offered.

She hadn't exactly inquired about my name, but it felt rude not to exchange pleasantries. "It's Ashton."

Her body froze mid-motion toward the door, eyes cutting to me from over her shoulder. "It's best if I don't know anything else." She paused. "But let me know if you need anything. A bell will sound in my quarters if you open that door," she said, pointing toward the threshold we had just walked through.

Numbly, I offered her a small nod, which was all she needed to exit the room and leave me completely alone.

As much as I wanted to puzzle this all out, my body had other thoughts. With hands trembling from exhaustion, I shed my coat and Ryana's scarf, dropping them both in a heap on the ground. With only a quick pass of the wet cloth against my face, I practically tossed myself into the bed, remembering nothing past that moment until I woke.

Two

The sound of a boot tapping against wood drew me awake. Shifting only slightly, I grabbed the pillow beneath my head, rearing back to toss it at Jemma, when the feel of the scratchy material against my fingertips jostled me back into reality.

Memories of the previous evening flooded me in a strange, violent haze, both jarring and somehow slightly out of reach.

With a start, I scrambled to get myself upright and into some semblance of a defensive position. Out of the corner of my eye, I glimpsed black leather boots, and even if I had held any modicum of hope that it was Jemma aggravating me from her perch beneath my bunk, the sheer size of them eliminated that as an option.

My focus narrowed onto the broad chest of the man sitting in the corner of the room, my body half-crouched on the mattress. "What do you want?" My gaze flickered all around the space, now illuminated in the early morning light, searching for anything that could be used as a weapon. The nightstand didn't even boast a heavy candlestick, just a cylinder of half-melted wax sitting on a plate too small to do any damage.

A chuckle brought my attention back to the would-be assassin, but all I found when I finally let my eyes drift to his face was the blonde-haired man from the previous night's threesome.

The familiarity did nothing to soothe my nerves, and he still hadn't answered me. "Who are you?" I demanded, heart racing at the presence of the strange man in my room. If Ryana had sent me to The Barker Inn and he had been here when I arrived, I had to assume that he wasn't specifically here for me, but that didn't mean he wasn't a threat.

His cold, grey eyes roamed my entire form with an almost bored assessment. A swatch of golden hair swept across his forehead, falling in short waves down the side of his neck, not quite reaching his shoulders. "Well, good morning, Princess," he drawled from his chair. The cleft in his chin now more prominent with his full lips cocked into a quarter smile.

It was almost as if he were soaking in my evident fear to fuel his own amusement, forcing me to battle the impulse to growl at him in response. He wasn't the first man who translated my fear into pleasure, and he probably wouldn't be the last, but unlike with Berit, I had not yet lost the upper hand. I held my stance.

He raked a hand through his hair, revealing thick eyebrows arched over those steely eyes. A scar ran from the middle of his right eyebrow to the top of the same cheek, splitting from there into two white lines that continued to his jawline like a lightning strike. Whatever had caused the wound had barely missed the eye itself.

The man stared at me as if waiting for me to do something, like I was already failing some test he had set forth even though I wasn't given the rules. Slowly, I stepped toward my pack, thinking if I could get to it, I could access the knife I kept within its compartments since I had fled without the one that I usually kept strapped to my boot or thigh.

Keeping my eyes pinned to the man, ensuring he wasn't about to make any quick movements, I said, "I asked you what you wanted with me and who you were, neither of which has been answered."

It was then that I caught sight of the daggers holstered in the belt across his waist. The leather harness that spanned his chest was free of the broadsword I suspected it typically carried, but that did not mean it was not nearby.

I was woefully outmatched.

He leaned back in the chair, one ankle resting on his other knee, observing me with a careless ease that for some reason made me want to punch the expression off his face. Catching my stare, his head tilted to the side. "What I want from you is for you to be awake and ready. So, thank you for finally doing me the honor of rising. You snore, by the way."

An incredulous breath hitched from my lungs, but I caught myself before I could fully scoff at this stranger, not wanting to draw too much attention to my movements. "And you are?" My arms folded over my chest to appear less bothered than I truly was.

My question, or perhaps my new stance, seemed to deepen the man's smirk. "I am your escort for the next leg of the journey."

Some garbled sound escaped my throat as I did my absolute best to neutralize my features. "No." The word came out in a clipped, biting tone. There was no way I was going to entrust my life or my father's life in the hands of this pompous party boy.

His scarred brow pitched into the sky. "No?"

I shook my head. "You are not qualified."

A barking laugh tumbled from his lips. "You don't even know why you're here and you can somehow deduce that I am not qualified to escort you to our next stop?" Obviously, he had spoken to Skylar, but that didn't make him trustworthy.

My chin lifted into the air as I ground my teeth together. There was some merit in his words, but he had woken me up from a fitful few hours of sleep and he wasn't even trying to help me understand.

It was entirely possible that I was releasing a bit of the frustrations from the past twenty-four hours out on him, but whether cognitively or as a side effect from my predicament, I let my irritation coil like a snake before striking. "You seem more apt to *entertaining* the guests than taking a job seriously. I am not trusting my life in your hands." For added effect, I let my focus drop to his palms. The same fingertips I had seen trailing the ribs of the brunette the night before.

When my eyes flashed back to his face, his teeth had slid over his plump lower lip as if he were biting back a full-blown grin. "Did you like what you saw last night?"

My traitorous skin flamed, but I didn't dare lower my chin, keeping my stare locked with his. "It hardly qualifies you to escort me."

He moved then, standing to full height and stepping toward me with all the grace and elegance of a jungle cat. It caused me to reach for the dagger that was not strapped to the edges of my skirts, my fingertips finding the fragile jewel-crusted fabric instead.

Those steely eyes caught the movement of my hand, flickering back up to meet my gaze. "Smart girl. You would do well not to trust me blindly."

For a moment, I thought he might close the gap between us to strangle me. Instead, he simply turned, walking to a different chair to procure a small canvas bag from its seat.

My eyes shot to the door, wondering if I could make it to Skylar before he caught me. Maybe I could demand another traveling companion.

The low rumble of his laugh distracted me from my plans of escape.

"Take this," he said, passing me the bag. "There are some clothes in there for our journey unless you want to stay in your pretty ball gown."

There was condescension in his tone, but that wasn't what weighed down the corners of my lips. Last night, the dress had felt beautiful, magical even. Now, it just seemed dull and dirty, like broken promises and shattered dreams, ready to be tossed in a rubbish bin.

"Thanks," I said flatly, snatching the bag from his grip and backing away from him once more.

He sighed heavily, as if this was all some inconvenience for him. "Please hurry. We are already late because you decided to sleep in instead of readying yourself."

With no desire to fight back, I neglected to inform him that I had been traveling for hours before I got here and wasn't told to wake at a particular time to move along. At any point, he could have woken me up, but I kept that comment close to my chest as well.

"Fine," I snapped. "But you still haven't given me a reason to trust you." Not that I required some grand gesture, I just wanted him to try to make me feel better about this decision, and thus far, our interactions hadn't made me any more agreeable to leaving with him.

He bared his teeth in an expression that might have been considered a smile under different circumstances. "If I had wanted to harm you, I would have already slit your throat and left you for dead. I certainly wouldn't be offering you fresh clothes and a multitude of patience."

The noise that came from me was some blend of a scoff and a gasp. He made a decent point, but my sleep-addled mind was too stubborn to lose any ground. "You could be waiting for another time to strike."

He pinned those cold eyes on me; the mirth draining from his features. In two long strides, he was directly in front of me, staring down with icy indifference. "What would be a better time than this?" Our chests were millimeters from touching; the bag clutched in my hand was the only flimsy barrier between us.

A mortifying squeak came from somewhere in my throat and I scrambled to step back. He followed. Again, and again until my spine was pressed against the farthest wall.

My neck had to crane backwards to catch his glare. He was tall, possibly even surpassing Dante in stature. Certainly a few inches taller than Cade.

He dipped his chin down so that he was eye level with me, forcing our gazes to meld together. My pulse was erratic beneath my ribs. His breath was a hot gust against my face. "You were sleeping, unarmed, and dressed like you'd be better suited to dance than fight back." His attention meandered down to my heaving chest, sliding back up with a satisfied smirk. "You're not even trying to fight back now. What would I need to wait for?"

Grinding my molars together against the insinuation that I was somehow incompetent, I slid my hand to the hilt of the dagger strapped along his waist. With one fluid motion, I unsheathed the weapon, keeping my eyes locked on his as I carefully pressed the sharp tip against the pulse point at his neck.

My hands didn't betray me by trembling, but I hoped that I wouldn't have to use the blade to kill this man. I would if I had to, though. If Berit had taught me anything, it was that not all disagreements could be mended with words. Not all people were working within the confines of logic and reason.

The brows of the man before me raised for the fraction of a second that shock filtered across his features. Just when I thought I might have gained some leverage, or at least credit, he lobbed me with a wolfish grin.

"Good," he remarked, stepping back. In the same smooth movement, he snatched the dagger from my grip, placing it back into the holster.

He could have used it to harm me, just as he could have simply killed me in my sleep, so his actions earned him a sliver of my trust. That didn't mean I was keen to spend any more time with the insufferable brute than I had to.

"Get out," I seethed, pointing toward the door. My eyes narrowed to slits as I tracked his retreat into the hallway, unable to miss the shake of his shoulders as he left.

"Tick, tock," he called over his shoulder.

The second the door shut behind him, I unfolded the clothing from the bag. Plain cotton pants and a mismatched tunic in a similar fabric stared back at me. Skylar, or whoever had sent the bag, had even considered packing a bralette but had unfortunately left out other undergarments.

At the idea that I'd be forced to wear the strappy gold underwear, I sighed heavily. It was a memento of my horrible evening that I hadn't wanted to keep, but I supposed would be preferable to nothing.

My arm bent behind my back as I reached for the buttons along my spine, realizing with abject horror that I couldn't get the gown off without help.

A maniacal laugh clawed its way up my throat because of course this was how I would spend my solstice. Twenty-four hours ago, I had expected to wake up on this morning with the man of my dreams lying next to me. In another version of reality, I would have gotten my powers today and been one step closer to achieving my lifelong goal of being inducted into the Select Guard.

Instead, the universe had seen fit to make an utter mockery of everything I had ever wanted, imploding my life in the most dramatic way possible. Then, it had the audacity to gift me with the resident rake to be my escort all while I was trapped in the dress that symbolized all I left behind. *Great.*

My laughter died down abruptly and with a steadying inhale, I paced across the room and swung open the door in search of Skylar. Maybe she, or the teenager from the previous night, could help me rid myself of this gown, and everything it stood for, once and for all.

Instead of finding a blissfully empty hall, I discovered my escort, propped up against the wall, staring at me with another aggravated grimace. "That's not exactly getting dressed, Princess."

He pushed himself upright and heaved a sigh. "But if you want to keep on the fancy dress, that's fine with me." He turned his back to me as if I were just going to follow him down the hallway, shoeless in a filthy, tattered ball gown.

"Is Skylar still here?" I bit out the question like he owed me the answer.

He shifted his stance to face me once more and observed me for a heartbeat before he answered. "She's busy. Is there something I can help you with?"

Of course she was. "What about the young girl who works here?"

Thick arms, that I tried not to notice were corded with muscle, crossed over his chest. "Whatever it is, you're going to have to ask me for it. We are on a tight timeline, and everyone else is occupied right now." Then, before I could say anything further, he added, "If it's about your cycle, I know where Skylar keeps her stash of —"

"No!" I interrupted. "It's not that." Thank the gods, it wasn't that.

He propped himself back against the wall. "In that case, you're down to three minutes to change."

A shaky breath filtered from between my lips, making a noise more equine than human as I expelled my irritation. Much to my chagrin, I hadn't been left with a multitude of options here. My jaw remained clenched as I spoke through a sugary smile that I knew wasn't fooling anyone. "I can't reach the clasps of my dress."

The escort pressed his tongue into the side of his cheek, and his eyes glittered with unvarnished joy. I didn't even know him, and yet I hated him.

He motioned with his head toward my open door. "Go on, I'll help."

I wondered briefly if I could get the dress off by just ripping it apart instead of asking him for his aid, but I conceded that the quickest way to see my dad again—and maybe even get some answers about all of this—was to trudge forward. "Fine," I muttered as I stepped back over the threshold. I might loathe him already, but I was fairly confident that he wasn't going to harm me.

He left the door wide open, and I wasn't sure if it was to keep me comfortable or the fact that he clearly didn't care about nudity, considering I had witnessed him in the midst of being undressed in the pub last night. Briefly, I wondered how much farther the trio had taken their tryst before banishing that image from my mind.

Pausing in the center of the room, I turned, offering him my back. The floor creaked as he approached me. When he stopped, the heat from his body radiated against my spine even though it hadn't sounded like he should be close enough to share that level of warmth.

With a tenderness I had not expected, he moved my hair out of the way, the sentiment in opposition to his previous behavior. His breath tickled my neck as he effectively undid every clasp in a matter of seconds without once grazing the skin along my back. He was probably used to doing such things, if his show the previous night was any indication.

"All done," he said, already walking back through the doorway.

"Thank you," I whispered over my shoulder, my voice embarrassingly breathy.

He stilled at the threshold. "Please try to hurry. We want to make it to our next stop before nightfall." His voice was even, showing no signs of any reaction to my bare skin or our proximity. Meanwhile, I felt as undone as the back of my gown.

"Yeah, okay," I replied, loathing how my voice seemed to betray those ruffled emotions.

He shut the door behind him, and I shimmied the rest of the way out of the golden dress, donning the borrowed attire with haste.

Once dressed, I completed my new outfit with Ryana's scarf, noticing for the first time that she had sewn her lynx patch at the exact same location as mine. My smile was melancholy as I stroked my fingertips against the embroidered cat.

Looking down, I double checked that my mother's ring was still securely on my finger. That was the only silver lining to the fact that I had fled in my solstice eve ball attire. Sadly, I had left behind the necklace that Jemma had given me. There was no way to communicate with Ryana now, but I hoped that she brought my things with her when she came.

With nimble fingers, I brushed through my tangled hair, braiding the limp, matted curls as best I could. Then, I shouldered my bag and headed out the door, leaving behind the gemstone-encrusted gown in a pile of golden fabric in the center of the room without a second glance.

To my utter astonishment, my escort wasn't waiting for me in the hallways when I emerged. So, using the best of my foggy memories from the previous night, I followed the vaguely familiar pathway all the way back to the dimly lit pub.

Several patrons were spread out across couches and chairs in the room, some still sleeping from the night before, others holding steaming mugs of liquid. The piano was blessedly silent, although the woman who had been playing it was draped over its bench, sleeping soundly as if it were a fluffy mattress.

"Coffee?" Skylar asked me from behind the counter, stealing my attention from my surroundings long enough for me to see her gesturing to the open seat in front of her.

Inwardly, my stomach flipped with the sort of pleasure I only reserved for caffeine. And Cade, but I wasn't going to let myself think of him right now. "Yes, please."

After sliding a mug across the counter, she pointed to the far edge of the bar top. "Sugar and cream are over there. Help yourself."

The spoon clanked against the ceramic cup as I stirred in the additives and watched my beverage turn a lovely shade of beige. The moment the warm liquid touched my lips, I nearly curled into the cup to hug it. Although the brew was bitter and perhaps a tad too cool for my liking, this was the best thing that had happened to me in the last twenty-four hours.

"I heard you met Beckett," Skylar said, her lips quirked upward.

So that was his name. Amazingly, my features remained neutral even though internally I was cringing. "The man set to escort me?"

She dipped her chin once, a knowing smirk on her face. "Unfortunately."

The barkeep laughed, a light and airy sound that contained more than subtle hints of mirth. "He's really not so bad." She took one look at my face and added, "Once you get to know him."

My eyes narrowed at her in a tentative glare. "I hope we are not together long enough for me to find out if that is true."

There was a gleam in her eyes, something I might have deciphered if I knew her better. Then, her stare flickered over my shoulder, and the smile dropped. "Either way, I think he's about to leave you."

Twisting my head toward the pub's entrance, I glimpsed Beckett's brooding figure darkening the opening. His fist lifted toward the ceiling, and two of his fingers curled out and in, in slow motion. Beckoning me like a dog.

With mildly restrained irritation, I closed my eyes and sucked in the deepest, longest breath that my lungs would allow. On the exhale, I reminded myself he was the key to reaching my dad. The only thing that mattered was seeing my father again. As my thoughts slipped to him once more, worry began to gnaw at me all over again.

Would he even be able to make the journey here in his condition? The thought left a pit in the center of my stomach and instantly I regretted not going to get him myself.

Before I could spiral too deeply into those thoughts, Beckett's eyebrows lifted, an expression of irritation passing along his features.

"There isn't anyone else who can take me?" I asked, knowing full well it was ridiculous to be picky in my situation, but doing it all the same. There had to be someone, anyone, who would be better than this man.

Skylar's expression held pity as she shook her head. "He's honestly your best bet."

Releasing another pained exhale, I forced a smile to my lips. "Then, thank you for your hospitality. The clothes. The coffee." I eyed the unfinished mug longingly but didn't linger on what I was losing. "I appreciate your kindness, even if it was about whatever the hell *dragon-fire* means."

She gifted me with another one of her shrewd grins. "Beckett can probably tell you more about that if you ask him."

My responding grimace only elicited a breathy chuckle from Skylar in response. "Seriously, Ashton, it was no trouble at all."

All I could assemble was a weak curl of my lips in return, finding no humor in my predicament. If this was a place that Beckett liked to frequent, I could almost promise I'd never return, probably never see Skylar again. Instead of voicing those thoughts, I muttered a quick goodbye as I slipped from the stool.

With that, I left the Barker Inn, hopefully for the last time.

Three

"We should be lovers," Beckett said as we made our way to the docks. "I am a romantic, and we need privacy on a secluded island so that I may ravish you properly."

The disbelieving scoff left my mouth before I could hold it back. I had agreed to follow him but not enjoy his company, much less fake a relationship. "Absolutely not. You can be my brother," I replied sharply.

We were hashing out the story that we were going to tell the boat captain as to why we had hired him to take us to the private island at the last minute, and it was an effort to keep my voice even.

"Then it will be strange for me to have my hands all over you," he said, smirking. He seemed to always be making that stupid expression, and if I had a weapon, I would bet anything that I could find a way to slice it off his face. It alarmed me how easily my thoughts had shifted to violence in his presence, but not enough for my tone to soften.

My lips flattened into a line. "All the more reason for you to be my brother."

The retort didn't dampen his delight as I had hoped. His mouth remained twisted in a lopsided grin. He was enjoying this. "Fine, what is our story, then?"

I attempted to let an exhale blow away my indignation, although it failed miserably. "Our mother is dead, and we are going to her favorite island to scatter her ashes."

He snorted. "Okay. And what excuse could we have for not needing a ride back?"

My arms crossed over my chest for the thousandth time since we had met, as my eyes narrowed in his direction. "What excuse were you going to use if we were lovers?"

"I hadn't gotten that far," he admitted, his smirk shifting into a full-blown grin.

A huff of disapproval fell from my mouth. "Is this not supposed to be your responsibility? How had you not already thought of this?" Furthermore, what kind of operation was this that they didn't have even the rough idea of plans in place? My voice was rising, garnering the attention of the few people who had already left their homes, presumably on their way to their place of work or perhaps the bustling market.

He shrugged nonchalantly. "Sometimes I have to improvise, and I want to make sure all participants are on the same page."

His answer placated me enough that some, but not all, of my ire receded.

The next turn put us in the path of a bakery window, the pastries and treats behind the glass left my mouth watering but I didn't dare ask to stop. I refused to give him any more reasons to call me a *princess* again or insinuate that I was somehow spoiled. Instead, I pondered our predicament. "What if our brother had been delayed and he will join us with his own boat later today?"

Beckett pressed his tongue against his cheek. "It seems reasonable enough. Although, I'd still be happy to be your lover..." One eyebrow raised again. A question.

"I don't think it would be a believable story," I quipped. "It also seems wildly inappropriate for you to behave that way with someone you are supposed to be escorting to safety. For your job?" The questioning tone was bait that he unfortunately did not take.

He kept facing the docks ahead of us, but his eyes slid to mine. "If you're sure, I guess I am your brother, dutifully carrying his mother's ashes to the Emerald Isle for a burial at sea. I imagine the captain has heard far stranger tales."

"Good." My chin dipped once. "Then it's settled. You are my older brother who balks at any sort of physical touch and refuses to even hold my hand during the mourning process." Despite my consistent irritation, I found the corner of my mouth twitching upward, so I banished it away with a roll of my lips.

Beckett's only answer was a low chuckle.

It turned out that what Skylar had referred to as a boat was actually a small fishing vessel. While I had pictured that we would be traveling on the massive barges that surrounded our actual ride to the island, what floated before me was only the size of a ferryboat. One designed to cross a narrow river, not an ocean.

"We require a ferry, good sir," Beckett said as we approached the dock next to the vessel.

The captain, a gentleman that I would put in his late sixties, bobbed his head up and down, a hint of confusion marring his brow. "Right. Come aboard."

There was no discussion of coin, which had me wondering if this man regularly ferried people at a flat rate, but I was glad he agreed to take us. "Thank you for agreeing to this on such short notice." My palm pressed against my sternum. "Our mother loved the Emerald Isle so much; she would be happy to know we were taking her there one last time. Her ultimate resting place." Personally, I was proud of the single genuine-sounding sniffle I produced for added effect.

The captain eyed me warily. He looked over at Beckett with apprehension spreading, tangling with the confusion already there. "Excuse me? I wasn't aware I'd be transporting a dead body."

"It's just her ashes," I said, patting my bag. "My brother and I really appreciate the ride." Determination spurred my rapid blinking as I willed dampness to form at my lash line.

The captain hummed. "I didn't know you had a sister, Beckett. I thought this was one of your normal requests. I'm so sorry for your loss." The man's voice had become solemn.

Beckett burst out laughing at the same moment that realization dawned on me. He had made the whole thing up for his own twisted amusement.

Glaring at him, I pushed past his outstretched hand to board the boat. "That was not polite."

"But it was humorous," he said, his smile growing.

My teeth dug into the flesh at the inside of my cheek. "I thought you were supposed to be a professional." At least that was the assumption I made when he was given this task. Skylar had seemed to indicate that he was my best bet. I would hate to come into contact with my other options if this was the *best* they had to offer.

He brushed off the obvious insult. "I'm not usually called in for this," he said, gesturing at me. "I just happened to be heading this way."

That did not instill confidence in me. "Should we not wait for someone more qualified then?" Maybe if I waited, I'd meet my Dad here, rather than wherever we were going.

Beckett only shrugged. "Not if you want to leave quickly."

Truly, I wanted nothing more than to reunite with my father, and I wasn't even sure that his path would lead him through Eden, so I continued on without another word.

When both of us were fully boarded, the captain made himself scarce, pulling lines from the dock and pushing the boat out into the quiet waters of the marina.

Finding a spot at the bow, I took a seat, resting my legs through the metal rails. The salty wind whipped stray hairs across my face as we began to move, and I turned my attention to the water beneath my feet. It took impressive levels of my willpower to keep from glaring at Beckett, even if I was acutely aware he had begun to help the captain prepare for our voyage.

Without a single sail or oar, the boat picked up speed, moving swiftly out of the harbor, water rippling in our wake. The boat captain had to be Flumen then. It would take sails to utilize Caelum powers.

Just as I had let myself relax, Beckett sat down next to me, the tension returning to my stiff muscles tenfold. It wasn't as if his presence worried me, like Berit had, I was just so emotionally drained. So tired, in general, I didn't even want to make polite conversation with him. If he was even capable.

That, and I had not forgiven him for this joke.

Surprisingly, he instigated nothing, opting instead to stare out at the sea ahead. The only noise for the longest time was the lapping of the waves against the wooden hull of our vessel and the humming of the captain, who was content to ignore us.

About halfway into what we were told would be a two-hour ride, I broke our silence. "Can you tell me anything about where we will go after we reach the Emerald Isle?"

Beckett twisted so that he could glance at the captain over his shoulder before turning back to me. "Not with present company."

Through the foggy haze of my sleepy memories, I did recall Skylar telling me that hardly anyone knew the entire route. Perhaps the captain was only aware of this portion as his services were required. So, I decided to let it go, opting to ask a question that didn't pertain to the journey. Anything to keep my mind from reeling about my father's health and the utter abyss of unknowns I found myself surrounded by. "Where are you from, Beckett?" I asked, brushing a stray hair back behind my ear as I glanced at my escort.

He eyed me with his usual levity, and I wondered if he had noted that I used the name he hadn't given me yet. His focus slid back to the horizon. "The North."

This blew my theory on him being closed off around present company out of the water. I wasn't sure why Skylar thought he'd answer me about what dragonfire meant when he wouldn't even tell me basic information about himself. My fingernails slid against my palm as I convinced myself to be the bigger person. "Which town?"

"You wouldn't know it."

All of my patience drained from my body in a single fluid motion. "I know this might be difficult for you to believe, but I have traveled all over the Kingdom of Demetros with my dad. I've studied its geography for years, and I had to know the map of the continent like the back of my hand to compete in challenges to touch that stupid Ice Trophy. So, I bet you that I do."

He waited until I finished my monologue, face aggravatingly neutral, before he grinned. "Trust me, you really wouldn't."

The garbled noise I released through my teeth was so loud that I swore I heard the boat captain clear his throat with discomfort.

"Hey Princess," Beckett said to me in a calming tone. Like maybe he was done using our interactions as some sort of entertainment for himself. "Don't be so aggravated. We have protocols in place that prevent me from telling you some things." He jerked his head toward the captain. "And at this point, I don't think you'd believe the answers I gave you for the other questions I could answer. Not without the context of that first bit."

If he hadn't been so frustrating every moment we had been together since I woke up this morning, I might have found some logic in his response. In this moment, though, I was struggling not to feel anything but rage.

"But you do know Ryana, right?" I really needed the reassurance that I hadn't made a colossal mistake following a stranger onto a boat.

His eyes flicked to mine, regarding me with something that almost looked like concern before returning to the sea. "We've worked together for a while now." Beckett appeared to be in his late twenties, maybe early thirties, but Ryana was my age, so his admission seemed odd.

Creases formed on my forehead, and my nose scrunched. "How long?"

That amused smirk returned to his face. "That's classified, Princess."

"Is there anything you *can* tell me?" I hated how flustered I sounded. "And please, quit calling me that."

Beckett's eyes roamed over my body, his lips breaking apart into a ridiculous grin. "I can tell you plenty, *kitten*."

Air was pulled into my lungs through gritted teeth. I expelled the exhale like I was blowing out a candle, trying to rid myself of the urge to punch him in his smug face. "May I ask, why kitten? My name is Ashton, by the way."

He pointed to the lynx patch on my scarf. "You clearly like the animals. You seem so aggressive, but you probably have the bite of a kitten…" His fingertip tapped lightly on the end of my nose. "You're cute."

Cute was an interesting moniker for someone who had recently held a blade to his throat. Shoving the patch toward his face, I countered, "This is a lynx."

I could have sworn that I saw a twinkle in the silver swirls of his irises. "And a lynx is part of what kind of animal family?"

My lower lip stung as I bit down on it to hold back my indignation.

He chuckled. "It's okay if you don't know, kitten. They're part of the cat family."

His taunts were shoving me dangerously close to showing him exactly how cute I could be with his dagger, but I bit my tongue. My focus returned to the sea as I twisted my neck in the opposite direction of my escort. At most, I had an hour to continue to suffer in his presence, and I had no intention of talking to him again. Murdering him seemed like overkill for a blessedly temporary problem.

For his part, Beckett allowed me that terse silence for the remainder of the ride, and I almost let myself forget he was breathing the same air as me until the first island came into view. The land mass was just a speck of green on an endless glittering aquamarine horizon.

The closer we drew to its shores, the more obvious it became how the island had gotten its name. Three peaks shot up from the sea, all covered in lush vegetation that gave the mountains an appearance of a multifaceted emerald. It was an odd sight to find this far north on the first day of winter.

The island was curved like a crescent moon on its side, with one large peak on the left and two smaller ones on the right. The edges of the moon-shaped land opened to a circular beach with a lone dock in the center. The tide was barely high enough to allow us passage to its rickety old boards.

"Well, enjoy spreading out your mom," the captain said as he lazily dropped a looped rope over a post on the dock. The obvious attempt at humor—at my expense—left me cringing.

"Thank you for the ride," I said to him, refusing to meet his or Beckett's cheerful stares.

My grip tightened on the straps of my pack as I disembarked from the vessel. Before I could even offer a more formal goodbye to the captain, he had flipped the boat around, sputtering away and leaving me alone with Beckett.

Four

Begrudgingly, I turned to Beckett for instructions on how to proceed. Instead of providing any information, he sauntered right past me, heading toward the smooth sandy beaches and the lush jungle beyond. With balled fists, I drew in my inhale slowly, like I was a smoker savoring my last rolled stick and forced myself to follow him.

Half running, half speed walking, I finally caught up to his long strides. "Can you tell me where we are going now? When do you pass me off to the next person?" Glancing over at the empty dock and the captain's retreating form, I added, "And how do you even get back to Eden now?"

He paused his trek, only to study me for a fleeting moment, before delight washed over his features. "I'm not going back to Eden; I'm taking you all the way to our destination."

There was nothing I could do to halt my face from falling. "How long will that take? And where are we going?"

His fingers raked through his golden hair as he shook his head. "So many questions." He dropped his hand to his side. "We are going to a place called Lochmere, and it should take a few days. You will have all the answers you need supplied to you shortly after our arrival."

My jaw dropped. The name of the place he mentioned was no more familiar to me than the strangers we had passed in the streets of Eden. Perhaps there was some merit to his insinuation that I wouldn't know where he was from, although that seemed ridiculous given the amount of time I had studied the maps in preparation for the second challenge of the Ice Games.

"Where is that?" I asked in a whisper.

"North." His words were clipped, not out of aggravation necessarily, but likely because there was nothing else he intended to say on the matter. He began walking again, and I trailed closely behind, dodging branches and foliage as we moved into the thick, almost tropical vegetation.

Armed with the sudden realization that this was not a short-term situation, my remaining patience over the ordeal eddied from my body. "Is there anything useful you can tell me?" Sensing the dampness collected at the edges of my eyes, I gritted the words out through my clenched jaw as if sheer force would keep the tears at bay.

Beckett at least had the decency not to meet my state with more of his sarcasm. He sighed heavily, but whatever he saw in my expression prompted him to answer, casting his voice over his shoulder as he moved through the forest. "The code *dragonfire* means that you're important. The fact that you don't know why is surprising to me. All of the people they've sent over the years know *something* about their situation, so I have to assume there is a good reason you've been kept in the dark, and I can't relay anything else to you until I confirm with Ryana."

Steel grey eyes searched my face as he slowed just enough to make the assessment, probably determining how much of my ignorance was truth or feigned. My expression must have struck him as genuine, or at least desperate, as he finally offered me a morsel of something useful. "I cannot tell you the details of where we are going, and, as I have said, I doubt you'd believe me without witnessing it firsthand. But I am duty-bound to keep you safe. I am loyal to my kingdom, and they want you alive and well."

My eyes widened as a panic slithered its way, low and steady, to the bottom of my stomach, coiling there like a scaled beast. I skidded to a stop like I had slammed into an invisible brick wall; a feat that would have seemed comical if not for the grave situation I had found myself in. The organ in my chest shuddered as I swallowed hard against a suddenly dry throat. "Am I a captive?"

Beckett stilled, twisting his body to face mine. The smirk returned to his mouth, providing a wholly unsettling response to my question. "I'll only tie you up if you ask me to." His eyebrow lifted as if that was a genuine offer of services.

"That's not an answer," I replied, backing away slowly even though there was nowhere to run. Once again, I had gifted my upper hand to an assailant. This time I had done so willingly. We were on an island. The boat's captain was too far away for me to hail him, and that said nothing about his propensity to aid my escape. Realistically, I was trapped.

My eyes widened as my heart hammered away in my chest.

Beckett narrowed his eyes at me as the smirk fell. "Do you feel you are a captive? Neither your hands nor feet are bound. We have fed and clothed you. Are you feeling unsafe?"

More of his non-answers had my teeth clenching. "Could you just respond clearly to a single gods-damned question that I ask you?"

Beckett simply rolled those silver eyes at me. He resumed his walk into the forest, and for some stupid reason, I followed him.

"Answer me," I demanded, keeping a safe distance between us.

A muscle flexed in his jaw. "You are not a prisoner, and if you would like to go back at any point, I will escort you to the shores of Eden myself." His movements through the forest were sure enough that he could glance in my direction as he walked with confidence in where he was heading. As if he had done this a thousand times, even though there was no pathway marked into the jungle that we pushed through. No dirt laden trail that led the way.

"The code word you gave us gets you out of Demetros quickly, but you will not be forced out," he added, almost as an afterthought.

There was so much to unpack in that sentence. "What do you mean, out of Demetros? There is only Demetros?" The last sentence should have been a statement, but in lieu of his words, it felt like a question. Ryana had said I needed to get out, and my brain simply hadn't latched onto it hard enough at the time to give any merit to the meaning behind her words. Now, hearing it stated plainly, I was forced to give it more thought.

Beckett's shoulders climbed to his ears and then dropped back down. This man was an amalgamation of shrugs and smirks. "Yes, and no. I'll show you." He arched an eyebrow at me. "If you agree to continue following me, that is."

At the tail end of that statement, we arrived at a dense patch of foliage clinging to the base of a rocky mountain. With an outstretched hand, he pulled back on a thick curtain of vines before us, revealing a small opening in the stone wall. It appeared to lead to a dark tunnel, but it was so void of light I couldn't tell what lay beyond.

Hesitation paused my movements. "Is this where you plan to kill me? This is a lot of trouble for someone to go through when you could have just done it this morning." It was my nervous attempt at a joke, although there was a real question buried beneath the feigned mirth. He only laughed in response rather than answering me.

Maybe I should have turned around and taken my chances with the ocean, but I stepped past the vines and into the unknown like I didn't possess a single ounce of common sense or self-preservation. Propelled forward by curiosity and a healthy dose of fear for what I had left behind. The smallest thread of hope that this was my best chance at reuniting with my father tethered me to my decision.

A flash of light and the feeling of warmth washed over me as Beckett produced a fiery orb above his open palm, just like I had seen Cade do in the passageways to our meadow.

"Follow me," was all he uttered as he passed me, making his way deeper into the tunnel.

It was tall enough for even Beckett to stand at full height in most areas, but we still found ourselves squeezing around larger boulders as we ventured deeper into the underground terrain. At least I assumed we were going underground.

The walls were damp, dark-brown, packed dirt. The surrounding air was stale, and it might have been my imagination, or maybe adrenaline, but I felt like my lungs were struggling to cling to what little oxygen lingered here.

I was thankful for the light Beckett's fire produced, though, not just for the proof that oxygen remained, but also because without it we would have been thrust into total darkness. The sunlight filtering through the curtained vines had long since faded behind us.

With nothing else to focus on, the fire resting in Beckett's upturned palm entranced me. "You're Ignus."

Beckett didn't look back at me as he remained solely focused on getting us through the rocky passageways, even though there seemed to be only one direction to go. "We don't classify our magic like that."

It was lost on me why every answer from him had to be so cryptic. Trying again, I rephrased my statement into a question. "You have fire power?"

His lip quirked up the side of his face. "Obviously."

It was impossible to tell if I was more frustrated with his response or myself for asking the question in that way. Obviously, he had fire power, so why wasn't he just admitting that he was Ignus?

The sleeves of his black tunic had been unrolled, blocking any evidence of the marking that I could use to satisfy my curiosity. It was a brand I knew so well. A brand I had traced my fingertips against on Cade's forearm, more times than I could count.

It was difficult not to let my thoughts wander back to Cade. I was angry with him, not just for the obvious rejection, but also a little because he had told me he loved me too, when he clearly didn't love me in the way I wanted. Unconditionally.

Maybe I had little experience with serious romantic relationships, but I understood love. Through my dad, Jemma, Marjorie, and maybe even Ryana, I had come to learn what it felt like when it didn't require conditions to be met to offer it freely. I knew that no matter if I was powerless or not; I deserved it.

A part of me wished Cade had never spoken those words to me because it felt like, instead of actually meaning them, he liked *the idea* of meaning them. Before I was deemed powerless, anyway.

You're not worthy, the voice said, clawing its way back into my brain like a parasite, ready to feast on my insides.

I'd spent my whole life hoping I would amount to something, a fruitless attempt at lessening the guilt I felt at having taken my mother's place in the world. Not once did I expect to be working class. Certainly,

I hadn't imagined a scenario where the first man I truly allowed myself to love like that would tell me I wasn't worthy because of it.

"You're not going to cry again, are you?" I heard Beckett ask, shaking me out of my thoughts.

Roughly, I swallowed down the pitiful emotions scraping up my throat. "I haven't cried yet," I snapped, pulling my jacket tighter around my body. The further we walked, the colder it got. We were definitely going underground.

"*Yet* does not give me confidence here," he said, his eyes sliding back to me only briefly.

My exhale did little to hide my displeasure. "I'm not going to cry. I'm fine."

"Fine, is what women say when they mean they are not fine."

There wasn't really a choice here. I had to be fine, so I would be. Scoffing, I glared at the back of Beckett's head. "And you have so much experience with women?"

It was a rhetorical question that I had meant regarding their emotions, but unfortunately, it garnered a response, nonetheless. Beckett halted abruptly, almost causing me to slam against his back. He whipped around, letting his fiery orb rest between our faces, allowing me an intimate view of the mirth glittering in his stare. "You seemed keen to observe me last night. What do you think?" That damned scarred eyebrow rose up his forehead again.

I was glad that his orb was a soft, warm glow, because I felt my face go hot, likely the brightest red imaginable. My folded arms squeezed tightly against my ribcage. "Knowing the inner workings of a woman's mind and fucking her are not the same thing."

He dropped the orb slightly, bringing his face closer to mine. "So, you admit that you were watching me?" His voice was gravelly. Rough like Cade's was whenever he whispered sweet nothings to me in our meadow.

Being forcefully reminded of Cade against my will just made me angry again. My smile turned saccharine. "Seemed like an effect of the everapple wine to me."

Beckett didn't take the bait, and he didn't look annoyed at my obvious dig, which deflated me a little. He just turned around and kept walking through the tunnels, that infuriating smirk plastered on his face.

We traveled in silence for a few more minutes before a gentle breeze blew the stray hairs across my face. The air had gone from musty and stale to sweet and crisp, like a winter's wind blowing across a summer field of wildflowers.

A pale blue light shimmered from further up the path, beckoning me closer.

We rounded the corner, and the tunnel opened into an enormous cavern. Stalactites and stalagmites littered the cave ceiling and floor, reaching for each other like fingertips made of stone. The rocky claws were blanketed in a glowing moss, creating a luminous iridescent glow. It was so bright in this pocket of the cave that I hadn't even noticed that Beckett had extinguished his flame.

Numerous pools filled with semi-opaque turquoise water were scattered along the damp stone floor. Some were only large enough for one person to get in, but others were big enough to host a multitude of swimmers. In the back of the cavern was a waterfall with the same almost milky blue liquid, dumping into one of the larger reservoirs.

"Can you swim?" Beckett asked me as we approached the pool with the waterfall.

Confusion knotted my eyebrows. "Yes."

Beckett gestured to a large boulder a few feet from where we stood. "Take your clothes off and put everything over there behind that rock. You'll see where others have placed their items."

"Excuse me?" I sputtered, eyes wide and disbelieving at the audacity of this man. "No."

He scrubbed his palm over the stubble along his jaw. "We have to go through the falls to get to where we are going. There are clothes on the other side."

A narrowed-eyed, incredulous glare was all he received from me.

His hand waved over my body. "You can keep your undergarments on if you're concerned about your modesty. I assume they are cotton?"

The words felt like a taunt, or at the very least something I should be offended by. My arms tightened in their position across my chest.

"Look, I know it seems strange to ask you to do this, but please trust me on this. The magic won't allow us to pass through if there is too much Demetros on you," he said, dragging his fingertip down the length of my body in the air. "And it's not great for our wards."

Before I could even ask what he was talking about, his eyes flicked over to my backpack. "Do you have anything of value in there?"

The glittering orange stone of my mother's ring winked at me in the glow of the cavern. "I don't need anything in the pack."

He studied my ring for a moment but didn't mention it. "Good, then strip down and let's go."

My arms remained folded over my chest as I stood firmly in place, like my boots were rooted to the ground. "Is this another one of your pranks?"

He grinned as if the idea of that amused him greatly. "Nope," he replied, as he unfastened the belt of weapons from around his waist, letting the whole thing fall to the cavern floor with a clatter.

A wink was the only warning I got before he gripped the edges of his tunic and ripped it over his head.

"Fine," I sputtered, scurrying to the rock formation he had pointed out and hiding behind it quickly before I was forced to watch a show.

Just as he had indicated, there were a collection of other items that had been left behind. Boots, packs, and even towels and blankets were nestled in shelves that had been carved from the rock itself. Drawing in a deep breath, I resigned myself to continue on, allowing my racing heart to slow a bit before I stripped away my clothing and added it to the shelves in an empty slot. Perhaps I would need them again.

With much apprehension, I stepped around the boulder, trying and failing to keep my eyes trained on the waterfall, if for no other reason than I wanted to bolt if this turned out to be another inappropriate joke.

Beckett's back was facing me as he watched the water cascade over the boulders and into the pool, and I found myself relieved that he had decided to keep on his undergarments as well. The tight shorts hugged his figure that I attempted not to notice as I cleared my throat and stepped next to him at the water's edge.

Without even shifting his attention to me, he said, "No need to be modest. It's just a body, and I've seen plenty of those." There was no mocking in his tone, and I genuinely wondered if he was trying to comfort me. Although the idea of not measuring up to the other bodies he had seen had a wave of shame burning my cheeks. Why did I even care what he thought of me?

Regardless of the heat creeping up my neck, I lifted my chin, releasing the hold my arms had across my chest. I wouldn't give him the satisfaction of knowing his assessment of my figure affected me in any way. "I'm ready," I whispered, my stare cutting to my escort if only to wait for my instruction.

His steely irises flashed with a silvery light as he momentarily glanced my way, before jerking his attention abruptly back to the tumbling sky-blue water, clearing his throat before mumbling, "This way."

We entered the pool, which was surprisingly warm, and I walked forward until the water lapped against my throat.

Beckett turned to face me then, with significantly more of his upper body above the waterline. "You will need to swim to the waterfall and go under it. It will feel counterintuitive at first, but keep swimming until you can touch again. The cave on the other side is a match to this one."

He disappeared before me, and I gave it to the count of five to follow him. Doing what I was told, I swam forward until I reached the waterfall. It only took a second for me to contemplate whether this was a good idea before a silent internal force urged me along. Ducking under the warm, flowing waters, I held my breath as I pushed my way through the murky liquid.

After a few strokes, my toes scraped against the rocky pool floor and I stood, instantly sucking in a breath. With a bit of disbelief, I made my way to the stone-covered edge of the pool, taking in the views of the new cave, which was equally illuminated by the same glowing moss. In fact, this cave, even down to the location of the miniature puddle-sized lakes scattered around, looked like a mirror image of the one we had left.

I was almost completely out of the water when I slipped on a smooth stone. Rough, calloused hands caught me at my waist and righted my stance, twisting me into an embrace. My breasts, which I suddenly had an unhealthy awareness of beneath the thin, sopping wet, cotton of the bralette, pressed against Beckett's muscular abdomen. With my ear flattened awkwardly against his chest, I could hear the beating of his heart, not entirely slow and steady as I had expected.

There was a warmth emanating from his body, everywhere we connected, but I was absolutely on fire where his hand rested at the base of my spine. An involuntary sense of pleasure warmed at my core.

"Careful, kitten," he purred into my ear.

The sound of his voice startled me into awareness. I hastily pushed him away, squaring my shoulders and collecting what remained of my dignity.

My traitorous chest still heaved slightly with my labored breathing. His eyes darkened as the frantic movements drew his attention to the motion, and I refused to look down to see what the water had done to the flimsy fabric.

Twisting to block his view, I muttered, "You said there were clothes?"

He was silent for several heartbeats, and when I turned my head in his direction, ready to tell him off for another bout of unprofessionalism, he had already faced the other way.

"It's a mirror image of the other cave," he said roughly. "Head behind the same rock, and there should be plenty to choose from. Probably even a towel or two."

There were dry clothes but no undergarments, which really felt like poor planning on the part of whoever set this up. Especially if the crossing could, and possibly should, be done naked.

A rough burgundy towel was all I could find to wipe off most of the dampness from my body, and I wrung out my bralette and underwear the best I could before donning them.

After some time spent rummaging through the clothing piled along the boulder's edge, I settled on an all-black ensemble. By some stroke of luck, I even discovered socks and a pair of leather boots that were only a half size too big.

When I crept around the corner, I found Beckett dressed in an identical outfit to the one he had on before. "Do you have clothes on both sides?" I asked him, inspecting his attire.

"I left some on my way to Demetros, knowing I'd be coming back." Yet another answer that just left me with more questions.

My head tilted in his direction. "You come this way often?"

That eyebrow arched up his forehead again. "Often enough."

My mouth snapped shut as I resigned myself to ignoring him for the rest of the journey.

Beckett began walking down another passageway, so sure that I was trailing behind him, he didn't even look back to check.

Even though my fists were clenched at my sides, I made my feet move, traveling down the tunnel in absolute silence as we left the cave behind.

When we reached a curtain of vines, Beckett pulled it to the side just as he had done on the Emerald Isle. "After you," he said, breaking the modicum of peace I had gained while basking in our shared quiet.

I stepped forward, reminding myself that soon I would see my dad and this nightmare would be over. At least, I told myself it was the only possible outcome. I couldn't accept anything else.

My boots hit the sand, and beams from the sun bathed me in a light so intense I squinted against the brightness, throwing my hand over my eyes so that I could get a better view of my surroundings.

It took several blinks for me to register what I was seeing, certain that the light had damaged my retinas with the sudden shift from the cavern's dark, damp passageways, that it was tinting the foliage around me. Except, everything else was as it should be. The sand was a glittering tan; the rolling waves a shimmering blue. It was just the trees that were off. Both on the strip of beach we had emerged onto and the land I could see across the narrow waterway, every single plant was painted in stunning shades of purple.

If I hadn't believed him before, I certainly considered his statement about taking me away from Demetros probable now, because I was confident I had never seen a violet oasis on any map in the kingdom I knew like the back of my hand. We were not in Demetros anymore.

Five

"How?" I sputtered, taking in the plethora of purple-hued plants before me.

"Better save that nugget for the debrief, if you are allowed one," he replied, stepping around me to stand by the water's edge. With practiced motions, he held his palm out to the sea, and the remaining questions died in my throat as I watched stone structures emerge from the waters like a slow-moving whale coming to the surface to breathe. The rocky formation continued to rise until a bridge formed between the sandy shore of this beach and the land across the narrow waterway.

Astonishment bled into curiosity as I watched him. He could harness the power of earth *and* fire. He was Saxum *and* Ignus, and I had never heard of anyone who had multiple elemental gifts other than the Elemental Queen. It was the sole reason she had gotten her name and likely her seat.

"How did you do that?" I asked, practically stuttering.

Beckett cocked his head to the side as if the question itself was puzzling. "Magic," he replied flatly. "Let's go."

My feet refused to move as I gestured wildly at the bridge before us.

"I can see that it's magic. How do you have fire and earth powers? Only the Elemental Queen has multi-elemental gifts."

As if it were the single most ignorant statement anyone had ever made, he scoffed. "That is simply not true." He stepped forward onto the rocky platform as if he had done it a thousand times before.

Then, he paused, shaking his head almost at himself. "I almost forgot..." He didn't finish his sentence, he just snapped his fingers, and everything I was wearing, including my damp braid, was completely dry.

There was no heat to indicate fire magic, which meant... my eyes widened again. "You have Flumen powers too?"

"I do," He replied, eyeing me cautiously before continuing his passage across the damp walkway.

Despite my hesitation, I followed him, treading carefully across the wet, uneven terrain. I was more concerned with his ability to answer my questions than the likelihood of him still being my kidnapper now, but a hint of that fear still remained as I left some space between us. As if I could run now.

"Who are you?" I asked as I stepped around a particularly large puddle. Was it possible that he was the Elemental Queen's son? She had no heir, but she had been missing from public gatherings for years.

"I am Beckett Astor, and if you didn't notice, I am your escort on this little adventure we've found ourselves on."

My lips pursed. "That's not what I meant. I remember your name."

"Do you? What a relief," he deadpanned.

I could sense that he was purposefully changing the subject, or at the very least evading my questions, and I would not allow that. "Do you have the Caelum powers, too?"

A breeze ripped through my hair, causing my tunic to billow in its wake. Beckett turned back to me, and it ceased completely.

My glare homed in on his smug features. "You could have just answered yes."

"And where would the fun in that be?" he drawled, raking his gaze over the entire length of my body before landing on my face. "When you are so fun to antagonize, *kitten*." The last word came out as two sharp syllables.

Rage boiled within me, my face flushing with my anger. I hated that he called me that, even if by all accounts it wasn't inherently rude. "Have you already forgotten *my* name? You seem like the type." There was something about this man that brought out the worst in me, but I couldn't seem to stop myself.

Beckett closed the space between us, causing me to immediately freeze as his chest practically pressed against mine. Heat pulsed between us, as if it was ignoring the barrier of the cotton tunic that should have shielded me from that sensation, and I stared up at him with wide, startled eyes. I didn't fear that he was planning to hurt me, but I didn't know him either, and that gave me pause.

Why was he so close to me? Why wasn't I moving away? Had I learned nothing from Berit?

He craned his neck down, pulling my chin up with a single finger beneath my jaw and forcing me to face him in a familiar gesture. Although, this felt worlds different from the times Cade had done the same thing out of affection. This was less reassuring and more reminiscent of a predator warning its prey that it was about to become a meal.

My heart pounded an unsteady rhythm. Why wasn't I taking a step back?

"I have not forgotten your name, Ashton." His voice rumbled against my chest. Whatever emotion had overtaken his expression was quickly washed away by his rising smirk.

He pulled away, drawing his eyes skyward to the gathering fluffy white clouds. "We are wasting valuable time with all of this. Unless you want to sleep outside tonight, we need to hurry." With that, he spun on his heel, and I could have almost sworn he picked up his pace as if this was another test I had to pass to gain the information I needed.

Somehow, I kept up with his stride, moving my legs as quickly as I could to remain on his heels without running. Once by his side again, I abandoned my resolution to remain silent. There was simply too much to learn. "Where are we going now?" He had mentioned heading to Lochmere—wherever that was—but had alluded to the trip taking days. I wasn't sure if Lochmere was our final destination or our first stop, and I was eager to learn everything about my surroundings that I could.

He didn't even spare me a glance. "To the other side of the bridge."

Red hot violence slashed across my vision, and I wished for nothing more than to have magic so that I could put him in his place and make him give me answers. "And what awaits me there?"

His reply was curt. He was growing as weary of my questions as I was of his useless responses. "The Violet Forest."

I had been so focused on throwing daggers at the back of his head with my mind that I hadn't noticed that we had approached the end of the magical walkway. As soon as I stepped off the stone structure and onto the tan sand of this land's shores, Beckett swung around.

Instinctually, I flinched at his sudden approach, finally showing some semblance of logic. In response, he just sighed and stepped around me. Again, he held his hand to the sea, this time palm down, as the bridge groaned and sank back into its watery resting place.

He didn't acknowledge me, or his multi-elemental power, as he trudged past me and into the incredibly stunning and very purple forest. Where the beach we had left had some sparse foliage, this area was dense with the violet vegetation that must have given it its name. For a moment, I let myself get lost in its beauty, abandoning my need for answers momentarily so that I could study the plants around me.

Tall oak trees lined the woods, but instead of bright green leaves, every tree was blanketed in purple. Underneath the branches of these violet giants were smaller trees I recognized as dogwoods, with lilac blooms instead of their usual white foliage. Wisteria hung between branches and cascaded, like a waterfall, to the ground. The forest floor was even covered with purple grass, adorned with tiny amethyst daisies, no bigger than my pinky nail.

"It's beautiful," I whispered, fully expecting Beckett to ignore me.

"Welcome to the Light Kingdom," Beckett replied, wholly unaffected by this view.

My breath hitched. The voice that finally escaped me didn't belong to me. It was low and cracked with the effort of what I was saying. "The Light Kingdom? We aren't in Demetros anymore?"

He shot me a glance that reminded me he had told me we would leave Demetros. That we had traveled across what was clearly some kind of secret entrance to get here. That I should have known better than to ask such a stupid question. "No, we are not."

He had said the words, my eyes had witnessed the journey to this land, and I knew I had never seen or heard of a violet forest before, and yet everything about what he was saying felt so impossible. "This is a joke," I stuttered. It had to be. Another prank meant to make me look stupid, like he had on the boat with the captain.

"This would be a very poor joke and an incredible waste of magical resources," Beckett replied, his tone flat. "I do not possess the ability to wield illusions."

Gazing at the violet forest before me, I tried again to rationalize how I had ended up in another part of Demetros, a location which I had just never heard of before. A place I had already determined I had never seen on any maps that I had vigorously studied at the academy. In my own mind, prior to his statement, I had already come to the same realization and yet I struggled to fully believe him.

I tried to match Beckett's words and the visuals before me to my current reality, but I couldn't seem to make them blend. Even as I considered that this would explain why Demetros citizens had been trained for war—at least if someone else knew about this Light Kingdom—my brain simply wouldn't accept it. My heart rate elevated, higher even than when I considered that I was being kidnapped, and I sensed my limbs beginning to shake.

"Do you need a minute?" Beckett asked, his tone almost soothing. Convincing myself that the care I heard in his voice was an effect of the muffling pulse banging along in my ears, I ignored his question, leaving him hanging as I peered up into the tall violet oak trees as if they could provide me some answer the man before me could not.

Would my father truly find me in another kingdom? Did he actually know this existed? Once again, I cursed myself for not taking the fork in the road to Elmhaven rather than Eden when I had the chance. My dad could have helped me, and if he had known about this place, he could have brought me here, if that was actually what he wanted. Furthermore, I could have helped him travel here, versus leaving him to fend for himself. I had been so focused on getting away from Biltons, I hadn't even considered his physical state.

My breaths came in uneven pants, and without giving it a second thought, I lowered myself to the ground, burying my face in my palms as I tried, and failed, to steady my racing heart. My chest tightened almost painfully, my fingertips tingling with the impending numbness. I hadn't felt this way since the hand-to-hand combat portion of the Ice Games, and I cursed my body for betraying me again.

"Ashton," Beckett said, his tone still softened by the ringing in my ears.

It wasn't until I felt his hands on my wrists, flinching at the contact, that I looked up at him. He had lowered himself to a crouching position, so his face was nearly even with mine. There was a level of earnest in his expression that gave me enough pause not to skitter away from him.

"Deep breath in," he commanded, though his voice was quiet, almost kind. He mimicked the motion, taking in an exaggerated breath himself, and I begrudgingly followed his instruction, allowing the crisp forest air to enter my lungs.

"Again," he said in that same calming tone.

So, I did, over and over again, until the ringing in my ears had stopped and my breaths were even and less shallow. The pressure in my chest had loosened some and the feeling had mostly returned to my fingertips.

"Now," Beckett offered, standing up and offering me his hand. "Let's stand up and talk about this."

Slipping my fingers against his, I let him pull me to standing, snatching my hand away as quickly as possible to brush my palm off against my borrowed pants.

He turned to face me, keeping a respectable distance between us. "We are in another Kingdom, one that is not Demetros."

I nodded, uncertain what else to say to those words, unsure if I even believed him, even with the evidence in front of me.

"You provided a code that enacted a protocol designed to get you out of Demetros as quickly as possible."

Again, I let my chin dip once.

He sighed, rubbing his fingertips along his jaw as if giving himself time to search for the words he needed to say. "I said it before, and I will say it again. You are not going to be forced out. I don't know why Ryana didn't debrief you before she sent you away, and it's a large part of the reason I haven't been forthcoming about details because that is unusual." He paused, eyeing me as if I could provide some explanation for Ryana's choices.

When I didn't speak, he continued. "However, if you do not want to be here, if this is all too much, I will return you to Demetros."

My eyes widened, uncertainty flooding my veins.

"I will take you all the way to your home if that is what you desire, and we can pretend this never happened." Those steely grey eyes glanced up at the sky again, hidden partially behind all the violet foliage. "At this point, the memory potion would probably clear the majority of this entire sordid series of events."

His stare fell to me as if he expected me to say something further and when I still didn't respond he blew out a breath. "Do you want me to take you home?"

Something was genuine about his expression, something I wanted desperately to believe. "Ryana told me that my father knew about this. That he would join me wherever I was going as soon as he knew I was heading there. I don't want to leave if he's already on his way."

Confusion filtered across Beckett's features and this time he didn't try to smooth them away with indifference or boredom. "I know nothing about that. I can only guide you to Lochmere and wait with you until Ryana informs us both of her plans."

There was nothing reassuring about the series of statements he had made, other than the promise that I wasn't being forced out. Perhaps Ryana ranked higher above Beckett in whatever organization this was, and he simply didn't know part of the information he wasn't providing.

Furthermore, it didn't seem as though Ryana had expected to have to get me out. It was entirely possible that she hadn't been able to inform Beckett of the change in plans, the addition of another person fleeing Demetros.

"What awaits me in Lochmere?" I asked, determining that maybe I just wasn't asking the right questions in the correct way.

Pity flashed across Beckett's silver stare, and I wondered if that was the reason he released a fragment more information than he had already given up. "Oldenberg."

My eyes pinched as we fell into a familiar dance. "Is that a person or a place? Is that your organization? A leader?"

His expression relaxed. "I've already given up too much, if you'd like to know the answer to that you will have to come with me."

Looking back across the water, I considered the options I had before me. Return to Demetros and unknown danger, where Mr. Higgins was still very much alive and my father might already be on his way to me or follow this stranger into what was likely a new kingdom, toward a place I had never been that may or may not be teaming with enemies of my own kingdom.

"You are asking me to choose between two very difficult scenarios without all the information I need to make a decision," I replied.

He shrugged, some of the mannerisms of the man I had initially met already returning. A wry smirk spread across his face, and, for the first time, I noted something about it might be sinister.

Had I made a mistake blindly trusting Ryana? Was my father even on the way? I began to back away, toward the crystal blue water and the bridge that was no longer there.

"Ashton," Beckett said, holding his hand toward me as if he were going to grab me before he thought better of it and let it drop by his side. "This is your choice. I cannot make it for you."

Something about that statement calmed me in a way his words hadn't before. "And you will take me to Demetros if I decide to go back? No questions asked? No complaining?"

He huffed a little breath that might have been a laugh. "There may be a little complaining, after all, this whole ordeal has shortened my vacation time."

My eyes narrowed on him as I spared another quick glance toward the beach we had come from, violet palms swaying in the wind. If I could wrap my brain around the fact that this was another kingdom, and if I trusted that my father knew about this, my best course of action would be to continue to trudge ahead to Lochmere or Oldenberg or whatever awaited me, whatever place that would give me answers.

I slid my attention back to my escort. "Are there healers in The Light Kingdom?"

My inquiry seemed to momentarily surprise him, an expression he dusted off rather quickly. "Yes. There are many people who can heal a variety of ailments, both natural and magical."

Hope swelled in my chest.

"Would they treat us?" I didn't want to give too much away by telling him which of us was sick, but I needed to know that my father had a chance. "Even if we don't have much coin?"

Beckett assessed me with a curiosity he did not put a voice too, his eyes trailing over my body, presumably looking for a hint of injury. "You will be healed, free of charge. We are not in the habit of leaving people ill for the sake of it."

It took great effort to conceal my sigh of relief and resulting smile that threatened to curl my lips. Not only would my father be healed, but he would be treated free of charge. It was almost too good to be true, but Beckett seemed oddly sincere.

There was much unknown about this new kingdom, and plenty of curiosities that I wished to examine, but the reassurance that I hadn't thrown away any chance to heal my father spurred me on more than anything else. More than my fear of returning and the consequences that might await me. More than my trepidation at continuing to follow this stranger into an unfamiliar land.

Some might have called it naivety, and I could come to regret my choice, but I clung to that new found hope like it was my only life raft in the sea of so much that had gone wrong. Anything to heal my father. "Okay," I whispered.

The scarred eyebrow rose, amusement glittering in his stare. "Okay?"

"I'll go with you," I said, adjusting my posture to that of someone with confidence, the entire movement at odds with the twisting in my stomach.

"Good," he replied, turning on his heel and resuming his forward march to Lochmere or Oldenberg, or whatever awaited us next.

With a resigned sigh, I turned my back toward the Emerald Isle and followed Beckett's retreating form.

This was not what I had expected when I enrolled in Biltons Academy or when I had signed that contract in a last-ditch effort to save my father from his illness, but I had always been curious about the way the kingdom worked, and something told me I might finally get some answers to those questions that had plagued me for so long.

I might finally see my goal of healing my father become a reality.

I just had to hope that I hadn't traded one terrible deal for another.

Six

The silence between us stretched as we meandered down paths that seemed to be visible only to Beckett. Rather than ask any more questions, that likely would never be answered, I took note of the foliage around us. The vegetation had lost the purple hues about an hour back, as we seemingly left the Violet Forest behind us. What remained was something familiar and yet different all the same.

Vibrant flowers I had never seen before bloomed in clusters along the forest floor, clinging to the waning sunlight that streamed through the canopy in soft bands. It wasn't so completely rare to have a blossom that appeared in the winter, but in Demetros they were never so bright. The yellow of the petals evoked images of the roses in Dad's garden and at the reminder of him, my heart clenched.

Had my father already seen these flowers before? Had he once walked the same path I was taking now? It was confusing to consider that he had kept something like this—another kingdom—from me and I brushed the thought aside, too uncomfortable with inspecting it any further.

When we stepped from a particularly thick patch of the forest, Beckett halted, glancing up at the sky with furrowed brows. He turned to me, speaking his first words in hours. "We should make it to Wolvesden a little after sunset."

Wolvesden was clearly another town in this kingdom that I had never heard of. Another snippet of proof that I was, in fact, no longer in Demetros, and yet I still struggled to comprehend the entirety of that information. It was so disorienting, having all but accepted this as a reality, and still my mind warred with the possibility even as I witnessed it unfolding before me. I had always questioned the stories taught to us as history, but I had never once considered questioning the accuracy of the maps.

"Did you hear me?" Beckett asked, cutting through the tumultuous thoughts in my mind.

Clearing my throat, I turned to face him. "I'm sorry, no. What did you say?"

"We should get moving, we don't want to be out here too long after dark."

A shiver traced the line of my spine. "Why? Is it dangerous?" My hands gripped the opposite arm, as if that was enough to shield myself from the unknown horrors.

Beckett squinted at me, a smirk playing along his lips. "No, you are with me, there is no danger to you in these woods. I just don't want to miss dinner at the inn."

My stomach growled, as if in agreement with him, and I blew out a nervous breath. "Lead the way," I said, still resigning myself to following him, if for no other reason than I was forcing myself to trust that my father would be reunited with me shortly. And healed.

The next town came into view within thirty minutes of losing the light from the sun. It wasn't even as large as Elmhaven, but the architecture was similar. The streets were paved in grey cobblestones. Flickering lanterns mounted to iron poles cast shadows against the various buildings that appeared to be a mix of residences and shops. Some rooms were illuminated from within, the light showcasing the outline of the residents inside going about their nightly routines.

Beckett marched toward a building constructed of thick slabs of stone. It was quaint, just like I imagined an inn in a small settlement might be. A wooden plaque hung next to the door, with light blue lettering in handwritten but neat scrawl that was just visible underneath the glow of a nearby lamp.

The Wolf Inn in Wolvesden

The name of the establishment twisted my tongue, even as I read it in my mind. Another flicker of the flames, had me catching the obviously late addition of "*and pub*" stenciled crookedly beneath it.

My eyes slid to the entry, the dark stained wooden door boasting another sign in its window—this one removable—that said *closed*.

Though disappointment instantly sagged my shoulders, Beckett was undeterred by the declaration. He pounded his fist against the door, three times in quick succession, followed by a brief pause and then a fourth and final knock. Within seconds a crack formed, revealing a handsome man, maybe a little older than I was, with raven hair and black stubble shadowing his jaw.

The host eyed me warily at first until his gaze snagged on Beckett's face and his expression shifted to something akin to pure joy. He swung the door wide open, gesturing for us to enter as he exclaimed "Welcome back Becks! I wasn't expecting you for another few days."

Crossing the threshold first gave me unfettered access to the visual of the small but tidy receiving area. There was a coat rack and a simple table on one side which I assumed was used to intake guests. On the other side, past a widened opening, was a pub like space which hosted six or so patrons scattered about the mix-matched tables.

It took me no time at all to note that all of them were men. Instinctively I stepped backwards toward Beckett, and he didn't startle like I did as my back made purchase with his chest.

He placed one palm against my shoulder as he dipped his head next to mine and lowered his voice. "No one is going to hurt you here."

Dutifully, I ignored the tenderness in his tone that did not match the majority of the rest of my interactions with him. Other than when I had momentarily lost it in the Violet forest. These were likely anomalies.

The man who had led us inside the Wolf Inn, jutted his hand out in the space between us. "I'm Harris by the way."

"Ashton," I replied hesitantly as I offered him my palm in a shake which he dropped quickly, but not rudely, in favor of speaking to Beckett again.

"Usual table?"

My escort only grunted which somehow prompted Harris to lead us toward a booth-like structure at the back of the pub. There was enough privacy to block out the majority of the other patron's curious stares, but I slid into the farthest bench to give myself visual access to anyone approaching.

Without warning, Beckett joined me, forcing me to slide all the way to the wall to accommodate his size. Either he didn't see me or didn't care to acknowledge the glare I offered him in return, because he continued to treat me with silence.

Harris stood patiently by the end of the table while we settled and the moment Beckett noticed the man lingering, he stated, "The usual tonight, Harris."

Harris' honeyed brown eyes flickered in my direction and Beckett only hummed like he was just realizing I was still beside him. "Better make it two," Beckett stated.

With no menu to peruse and Harris deciding that Beckett's word was law, I had no way to confirm the selection. Not that I had been on a multitude of dates—or that this was anything close to a romantic evening—but even then, I did not appreciate having food ordered for me. In all things, I desired choice.

Even my deep, slow inhale did nothing to ebb my mounting irritation. "I can order for myself, you know."

When he didn't reply, I refocused my glare on my escort, but he was preoccupied with the patrons of the bar, examining each person with severe scrutiny. His silver-hued gaze continued to roam as he spoke. "The options are ale and soup of the day. Did you want food without drink or drink without food?" He smirked—of course he did—as his eyes slid slowly to mine.

"Oh," I said, setting my hands into my lap.

"Oh," he echoed, eyebrow lifted.

Harris returned a couple minutes later with two mugs of ale and two bowls of steaming liquid propped upon a large wooden tray. He set the tray down at the end of our table, passing me my dishes before placing Beckett's in front of him.

Skeptically, I peered over the edge of the ceramic dish to find that the *soup* inside was white, chalky even, and a bit lumpy with unidentifiable shapes floating in the thick liquid. My stomach grumbled just as I was considering skipping out on the meal.

Beckett dug in without a second thought, and with no other options, I made the reluctant decision to give it a try. Slowly, I raised the chowder to my lips and took a tentative sip. It was surprisingly delicious, salty and creamy with just a hint of a familiar seafood flavor. Something I thought I recognized from the eastern coast.

It wasn't until my own moan lifted to my ears that I realized how hungry I had been.

Beckett cocked his head in my direction, one eyebrow arched, amusement dancing in the grey of his eyes like swirling smoke over a campfire. "I take it you like it?"

My hunger was too rampant to be embarrassed over a few careless sounds emanating from my lips. "Yes, I do," I responded, shoveling another bite into my mouth, but reining in the noises more carefully this time.

He sniffed a laugh, bringing another spoonful of the chowder to his own lips while he watched me curiously.

Obviously, I didn't know him that well, but Beckett seemed more relaxed here. Not as *carefree* as I had seen him in the pub in the Barker Inn, but there was a calmness about him. Maybe it was just the ale, but I saw my opportunity and took it.

"Skylar said that normally, people who use the code word I gave know more information going into it..."

A hum of acknowledgement escaped his lips. "And?"

It wasn't an immediate shutdown, so I proceeded. "There has to be something I'm allowed to know. Something Ryana would have normally told the others like me if I hadn't been forced to leave so quickly. That is the only reason she didn't tell me more."

Hope swelled within my chest as Beckett paused mid-bite, dropping his spoon into his bowl at the same moment his eyes locked with mine.

"I've already explained that I won't be giving you any more details until I speak with Ryana."

Disappointment sagged my shoulders.

"But," he added with something like regret shimmering on the edge of his voice, "I will answer any questions you have about me."

It was hardly a concession, but I welcomed the distraction. "Okay," I began, before I was cut off by Beckett's voice.

"This is going to be a tradeoff," he said. "I'll tell you what you want to know if you answer my questions as well."

My nose scrunched in distaste. "A question for a question?'"

"An answer for an answer," he replied, as he resumed scanning the crowd.

Straightening in my seat, I placed my spoon delicately back in the bowl, silently promising to return to it. "I'll go first then," I remarked before he could beat me to it.

The side of his lip quirked, but he didn't comment.

"Where are you actually from?"

The smirk shifted to the beginnings of a smile. "Falkland. It is in the northern region of the Light Kingdom."

This explained why he didn't give me the answer while the boat captain was present, leaving me to wonder how much the man knew about The Light Kingdom at all. "How far north?" I asked, forgetting our little arrangement already.

Beckett shook his head. "Ah, ah," he chided. "My turn." He turned to face me, curiosity brimming in those silver-clad eyes. "What were you doing in a ball gown?"

A ghost of a laugh tumbled from my chest. There were any number of things that he could have asked me about, and it seemed a waste to question my attire. "It was the solstice eve ball at the academy that Ryana and I attended."

"That explains the strappy underwear," he stated almost under his breath, but not quiet enough for me to miss it.

My cheeks flushed, and I turned my attention to my soup, blurting out my next question before I could spend any more of my time thinking about how he noticed my undergarments. "Do you have any siblings?"

A light chuckle pushed past his lips, as if he were humored by my quick change in subject. "No. Did you have a date?"

The muscles beneath my jaw flexed at the reminder of Cade and what had transpired at the ball. "I did," I responded flatly, realizing I had very little left that I wanted to ask him if I couldn't get answers about why I was being brought here.

Chewing on my lip, I considered my next question carefully, finally landing on, "Where do you live now, when you aren't stealing away to pubs in Demetros?"

Beckett sniffed a laugh. "I split my time between Lochmere and Falkland when I'm not on assignment.

With a grin, Beckett's large hand curled around his mug, but he didn't lift it to his mouth. He watched me instead. "What happened with your date?"

His query shouldn't have been surprising, considering the rest of his questions, but something about this one struck a chord, blaring an off-key note that reverberated between my ribs. The truth wasn't a simple answer, and I found myself swallowing back the emotions it produced that were threatening to turn into tears. After another large gulp of my ale, I set the mug down on the table with a clatter. "He found out I was powerless and decided I wasn't worth his time."

The entirety of our relationship and the events of that horrid night were whittled down to a single sentence, and yet the weight of it remained a constant pressure in my chest, only marginally lessened by the fact that I was finally sharing it, even if it was with Beckett. The realization that the man escorting me from my home was my only confidant at the moment tasted a little bitter on my tongue, and I glanced at him cautiously, knowing I would find an amused smirk on his face.

Instead, what I discovered was almost akin to confusion. Two lines had formed between his eyebrows. "You are not powerless."

I sniffed a humorless laugh. "Ryana mentioned something similar, but since you refuse to tell me anything, I have no way to confirm that. All I know is that Biltons Academy marked me as powerless from the moment I applied to go there, and that was what the sheet said and—"

"You are not powerless," Beckett repeated, this time a little more sternly. "If you are code dragonfire, it means you have multiple elements at your disposal."

A rough swallow lodged itself in my throat as I gazed down to where my brand would have rested if that sentiment had been true. Then my mind snagged on a single detail. "You said elements?"

Seven

My lips parted on an inhale as I waited for Beckett to respond to my question. Before he could answer, if he even would have, I noticed the approach of a woman out of the corner of my eye. Normally, a stranger approaching wouldn't have derailed my thoughts so thoroughly, especially not on the current topic, but at first glance, this woman looked exactly like Connally Owens.

Suddenly, she was close enough that I could catch the subtle differences in their appearances. Her blonde hair was several shades darker than Connally's, her skin slightly less tanned. The stranger was at least a few inches taller than my not-quite-friend and almost nemesis, and although they both carried themselves in an assured manner, the woman before me had bright blue eyes. Eyes that were pinned to Beckett.

She stopped abruptly in front of our booth and then, with a dainty fingertip, slid Beckett's bowl of chowder out of the way so she could hoist herself upon the table. Without even deigning to look in my direction, her chin dipped, and her voice lowered as she spoke in smoky tones to Beckett. "Good to see you again, Becks." Her words came out more of a purr than a whisper, which was why I hardly registered her saying, "The inn is full tonight, but there is always room in my bed."

Those delicate fingers walked a line up the center of his chest, prowling for his chin, which he allowed her to lift so their eyes met. In response, her spine arched as she pressed her breasts against his chest. "I've missed you."

Per usual, Beckett seemed nonplussed, as if this was a normal occurrence and not an invasion of his space. But he did lean away, prompting a wave of confused irritation to pass along the woman's features. Only then did she glance my way with narrowed eyes.

Then, Beckett sighed heavily, drawing both of our attention back to him. "As you can see, Natasha, I have company tonight." He brought his hands behind his head, his elbows splayed out behind him in a movement that came very close to knocking me in the head.

Ducking, I caught sight of her face flushing pink. She wasn't difficult to read, her expression held mild contempt rather than embarrassment as she brought her fists to her hips. "If this is a job, I'm sure one of the boys over there could entertain her for a bit." The woman's thumb hiked over her shoulder, and I was grateful that the position of the booth kept me from being able to see the men she was suggesting.

The quirk of Beckett's lips had my stomach clenching until he shook his head. "This is a special *job*."

Given that I had a slim grasp over what the code *dragonfire* even related to, there was no way for me to gauge how common an occurrence this was. Though I did not miss the way he emphasized the word as if *job* and *chore* were synonymous for me.

Those icy blue eyes flashed with understanding, but the realization didn't make her any more agreeable. She pursed her lips and stood to leave, brushing her skirts down as she did. "Suit yourself," she huffed, taking several strides away before she paused and tilted her chin, so her lips were visible over her shoulder. "Room 114 if you change your mind." With that, she was gone in a flurry of lace and sass.

My eyes flared as I dipped my spoon into my chowder. "Don't avoid your fun on my account."

"Harris!" Beckett called, completely disregarding my comment.

The man quickly left a patron at a neighboring table and hurried over to Beckett's side, looking more than a little flustered at the summons. "Sir."

Beckett frowned. "Natasha tells me that the inn is full tonight. Do we need to find somewhere else to stay?"

Not for the first time today, nervousness settled in my gut. I had seen enough of this tiny settlement to be certain that there was not another inn, and I did not relish the idea of sleeping outside when I didn't know anything about the creatures that roamed in the shadows of the night.

Harris' returned grin was too nervous for my liking. "Uh, well, I'm sorry, Astor. Your usual suite is taken tonight."

Beckett ran a palm across his face. "Harris," he interjected. "Spit it out."

Harris' eyes cut to me before returning to Beckett. "We have a room that will be fine for you and your companion."

This seemed to satisfy Beckett, his only parting comment was to request more ale.

When Harris brought the beverages, he handed my escort a key with a tiny tag attached to it that I could not read.

Beckett might have been content with that, but my mind was stuck on the word *room*—and the singular key—which did not imply that there would be two, and he hadn't mentioned a suite, which might have expelled some of my nerves on the subject.

The bubbles in the beverage burned my throat as I chugged my second drink. As if he had been waiting for my cup to empty, Beckett turned to me the moment it hit the table. "Ready for bed?"

Despite knowing full well that there was no alternative meaning to his words, something warm seeped from my chest, slowly moving its way down my body until...

"Yes," I stated, abruptly cutting those thoughts away like a bruise from an apple. The second cup of ale had been a mistake.

This seemed to satisfy Beckett, and he stood, giving me room to get out of the bench before he waltzed from the dining area. I followed him as he walked to the nearby hall, up a flight of steps, and down a narrow corridor until we stopped in front of room 113. My eyes rolled of their own volition when I realized that we very likely shared a wall with Natasha, but I kept my theories to myself as I stepped over the threshold and into the room.

A fireplace was already lit and crackling by a small settee. A moderately sized bed was tucked with its headboard pressed against a window, on the other side of the room. It was more spacious than my bunk at the academy, so I was pleased.

There were homey touches that felt lived-in and cozy in a way I hadn't expected for an inn. A small clock with golden feet resting on the mantle. A handful of books were stacked on top of a dresser next to an ornately carved wooden box that looked like it might hold trinkets. Paintings that appeared to have been collected over years rather than commissioned by a single artist hung along the walls.

Beckett dropped into a half-bow next to a separate doorway, extending his arm out as if he were offering me first passage. "Your bath is that way, my lady. If you desire to freshen up."

My smile was terse. Of course, the idea of a bath, of washing away the grime of our travels, was appealing, but as I peered down at my attire, I grimaced.

"Is there a problem?" Beckett asked, the gentleness from earlier all but dissipated.

Rolling my lips together, I melded our stares. "Is there soap available so that I may wash these clothes?" I gestured down at my tunic and the large smear of dirt slashed across the front that made no sense, considering I hadn't fallen. "Unless your magic can do that too?"

He shook his head. "My powers are not so practical," he replied. "I could get rid of them, but I assume you'd like them back eventually."

My throat worked through a swallow when I realized that I did not have backup clothes here. "Is this like the Barker Inn? Do you have a stash of spare clothes? Something for me to sleep in?"

Beckett had propped himself against the doorframe during our exchange, pushing himself off to glide back into the hallway. "I'll go talk to Harris."

He returned several minutes later with a folded lump of fabric in his hands. Thrusting what appeared to be a sack toward my other hand, he said, "Put your soiled clothing in the bag and I will take them to the laundry."

His sudden accommodating behavior set me on high alert, until I realized he was likely keeping me busy so he could run off with Natasha.

Grabbing the fabric, I scurried to the bathing chambers, closing the door behind me and stripping out of the dirty attire almost the instant that the latch clicked into place. Once my clothing had been crammed into the sack, I cracked the door open just wide enough to shove it all through, muttering "Here you go" seconds before I slammed it shut again.

The rumble of his laugh was unmistakable, and I heard the shuffle of fabric as he grabbed the bag. My breath stilled in my lungs as I pressed my ear to the wooden planks, listening for footfalls leaving the suite. When I was confident that I was alone, I allowed my focus to fall to the bathtub, already steaming with deliciously warm water.

Slipping into the tub, my muscles relaxed, and the scent of whatever oil had already been added to the water wafted toward my nose. It was masculine and earthy with just a hint of lavender.

That aroma was the last thing I remembered being conscious of before I startled at the sound of a knock against the door, the movement sloshing warm water over the rim of the tub and onto the tiled floor with a dramatic splash.

"Shit," I muttered, righting myself in the tub and craning my neck toward the doorway. "Hello?"

The knob turned and the door cracked slightly, but Beckett didn't enter. His voice sounded far away, like he was facing the other direction. "Are you almost done in there?"

Rolling my eyes gave me a few moments to calm my racing heart as I replied. "Be out in a minute." As soon as the door clicked shut again, I stood, grabbing a nearby towel and drying off as best I could before I procured the spare outfit I had been given.

Within seconds of unfolding it, I immediately regretted not inspecting it further before I handed away all my clothes. The *garment* was not a traditional sleeping dress, as I had assumed, but a satin sapphire colored robe.

It was this poor excuse for appropriate clothing or be naked. So, with much reluctance, I donned the silky attire and glanced at my reflection in the mirror. A strangled noise left my throat as I caught how much was not left to the imagination, but I swallowed it down. With a deep breath, I forced myself to leave the bathing chamber before I lost the nerve.

Instead of a locating a pile of freshly laundered clothes, I discovered Beckett lounging on the settee by the fire. "About time," he said flatly.

The water was still warm when I left it, so it couldn't have been that—

My eyes narrowed on the clock above the mantle. It had been over an hour, and heat crept up my neck as my gaze fell back to Beckett. He had been warming the water with his magic, and the smirk on his face told me that he had witnessed the exact moment I put two and two together.

Straightening my spine, I lifted my chin ever so slightly. "My apologies."

He hummed some noncommittal noise, then came to full height, striding into the bathing chamber without another word.

Twenty minutes later, from my perch on the settee, I watched as Beckett emerged from the doorway with fresh clothing that I hadn't even noticed him carrying in. It was so unfair that he had spare respectable options, while I was sitting here in one step up from lingerie.

My feet were stretched out to a nearby footstool, a throw tossed over my lap as I skimmed over the book I had found on the side table.

My skin prickled with awareness, and I looked up just in time to catch Beckett's eyes roaming the length of my body before coming to rest lazily upon my face. "Comfortable?"

"Not particularly," I replied honestly, folding the book into my lap. "I would appreciate my clothes."

A hint of a grin feathered along Beckett's lips. "I'll go check." Again, with that obliging temperament that felt so out of place.

He was back in a few minutes, this time wearing an amused glint along his expression like flashy jewelry. "Do you want the good news or the bad news?"

Nothing about the way his mouth lifted on one side gave me any confidence that either bit of news would be considered *good*. "Bad first. Then, theoretically," I said suspiciously, "the mood can be brightened with the good news."

The other side of his mouth curled, putting an unsettling grin on his face. "The bad news is your clothes are not done."

My eyebrows climbed up my forehead. Surely it couldn't have taken more than an hour to wash the clothes. And, after witnessing him wield all four elements, I knew for a fact that he could dry them in record time. I had seen my father do it countless times.

Narrowing my gaze to slits, I tightened the rope around my waist as I glared at him. "And the good news?"

"The good news is, I was able to procure a sleeping gown that you can have," Beckett said, tossing another silky sapphire-hued scrap of fabric in my direction. When I caught it midair, I held it up by a single thin strap, inspecting it for the half second it took to determine it was no better than the robe.

My face scrunched in disgust as I took in the sight of the delicate fabric. "I don't need any of Natasha's old lingerie, thank you." Was this his idea of another joke?

He shrugged. "I didn't take you for the type, but don't let me stop you if you'd rather sleep naked."

A new wave of heat flushed across my chest, and I covered what I could by crossing my arms and pulling the edges of the robe further in. "Is there a particular reason my clothes aren't ready? You've shown me that you have the ability to dry them, and unless you are grossly misusing your position to try to take advantage of a person you are escorting, I cannot think of another reason you wouldn't be helping me with this situation."

His expression grew pensive, that smirk, that I had already grown to despise, wiped from his features. "Believe it or not, Princess, I don't need to use tricks on the women who end up naked in my bed."

With a fresh rebuttal on the tip of my tongue, I opened my mouth to speak, only to be cut off by Beckett's sharp words.

"Harris is the only employee on shift tonight, so he is also tasked with washing your clothes, something he cannot do until the bar patrons retire for the evening." Those cold silver eyes constricted with indignation. "As soon as he's done, I will happily dry your clothes and return them to you."

"I—"

There was something detached in his stare, something icy in his tone as he cut me off again. "Either put the clean and brand-new garment on and sleep in it or sleep naked. I do not care because I do not intend to be here."

So, he was planning to be with Natasha after all. "Good," I bit out. "See you in the morning."

A slight curl lifted on corner of Beckett's mouth. "Don't ask me how I know, but I do believe the walls in this establishment are quite thin, if you care to observe."

It was everything I could do to keep his stare and stop my eyes from rolling. It didn't matter where he was as long as I was alone in my bed and safe.

Except that a certain unease had begun to climb up my limbs, settling around my chest.

Beckett was already twisting the doorknob when I called out, "Wait." I loathed how frightened my voice sounded, but I continued anyway. Getting to wherever I was going alive was more important than whatever scrap of my dignity was left. "Is it safe for me here?" The question could have meant any number of things. Was I safe in Wolvesden? In the inn? In the room alone?

Beckett didn't seem to be bothered by any of the possibilities. A sigh rattled loose from his chest. "You will be fine." He spoke the words flatly, then immediately stalked from the room.

The slam of the door set my heartbeat galloping in my chest like a herd of wild horses. Panic raced through my bloodstream as I considered that I had no weapon, no way to identify a safe place to run, much less anyone I could trust, and the one person who knew why I was here and where I should be going had just abandoned me. My limbs trembled as I fisted the silky scrap of fabric, staring at the door like I might actually want him to return.

Eight

Silence reigned heavy in the moments after Beckett left the room, interrupted by jabs of my stuttering heartbeat. With a deep breath, I reminded myself that I was trained in hand-to-hand combat, and I was not powerless, even without a weapon or magic. Sighing the adrenaline out of my shaky limbs, I ambled to the bathing chamber to abandon the robe and change into the slip.

The fabric felt delicious against my skin, both cool and soft, providing a slight balm to my nerves. Although when I left the chamber and returned to the room, that unease surged again because Beckett was still missing. How had I gone from being irritated with his company to being so worried in his absence?

Padding over to the door, I locked it, providing myself a scrap of comfort before I made my way to the bed, slipping beneath the sheets with my eyes still darting to the door as if an assailant would just barge right in at any moment and attack me. I had been given no reason to believe I would not be safe inside these walls, but I had been fooled before. The very same instructor who had treated me with kindness and compassion during our in-person lessons, and especially during the first challenge, had been the same man who had tricked me into a deal he knew I could never win. The reminder that danger could be hiding in plain sight did nothing but settle heavily on my bones.

Unable to properly fall asleep, I scanned my surroundings once more. The room was still lit by the numerous sconces, their flames dancing behind foggy glass, giving me a view of every inch of the space. My lungs rose and fell on slow, silent breaths as I listened for any sound of an approach. It felt like being in the woods during the second challenge, holding my breath so I wouldn't miss the noises of Berit's attack.

A scoff eased its way from my parted lips. What a waste of my energy that had been. Berit had found me alone anyway.

The creaking of floorboards outside the door snapped my focus to the threshold. My eyes squeezed shut and I angled my head in that direction as I tried to determine if they were approaching my room or just a nearby suite. The question was answered immediately as metal scraped against metal, my lock rendered useless as the door blew wide open with hardly even a hint of the doorknob turning.

My attention flew to the intruder. A scowl rested on Beckett's face, but his eyes did not meet mine. Instead, he threw his hands out around him, blowing out all the candles in one fell swoop, pitching the room into near total darkness. Only a sliver of moonlight crested the crack in the thick curtains.

Relief spilled through me in a way that I was not ready to unpack or dissect, and I quickly rolled over, offering Beckett a view of my spine as I closed my eyes and attempted to appear asleep. If he hadn't bothered to look at me, it was possible he hadn't noticed my level of consciousness.

Boots paced the small space, stomping against the wood floors, followed quickly by the sound of cloth sliding against skin. Before I could consider what that meant, the mattress dipped behind me, and a wall of heated muscle pushed against my back. Either the size of him, or the force of his movements as he flopped himself into the bed, slid me toward the far edge of the mattress.

Whatever worry I had accumulated in his absence drained from my body. It wasn't like with Berit where I feared for my life and my wellbeing, but my heart thundered all the same, nudged faster by confusion and irritation. "Why are you here?"

Beckett huffed a little laugh that had his ribcage jolting against my back. "I didn't think it wise to leave you alone."

A deep breath drew a lungful of air through my nose, bringing with it the scent of night-blooming jasmine. There was something else there, too, something crisp like freshly fallen snow and an undertone of some smoky scent that could either be from partaking in rolled sticks or nights spent by a campfire. The aroma of ale had been replaced by the burning smell of liquor. None of them particularly went together, but somehow blended into something surprisingly pleasing, nonetheless.

"Do you think I am not safe here?" My voice came out as a cracked whisper, and I shoved a bit more bravado into it as I added, "Enough so that you needed to join me in the bed?"

The grumble he let out vibrated against me in all the places we touched. "I have no intention of sleeping on the ground, or I would have kept to the woods. That preference extends to a wooden floor."

Finding it ridiculous to continue to have a conversation while I faced the dying embers of the fire, I rolled over. "You could have stayed with Natasha."

He shifted so that our eyes were nearly aligned. "I told you; it would be unwise to leave you alone." There was something metallic in his gaze, like the band of moonlight hit them just right to illuminate them with quicksilver.

We were going in circles, and while I found the bed situation unnecessary, I did feel safer with him in the room. My chin dropped so that I was staring at the hard, bare planes of his chest rather than those intense eyes. "Who would be after me if no one knows who I am or why I'm here?"

Beckett's hand came to rest along my shoulders, and he squeezed lightly. So lightly, it was at odds with the heat pouring from his skin and the ferocity in his eyes. "There is no imminent danger to you. It is simply my job to ensure it stays that way, and I cannot do it from another suite."

The heat from his palm had a pulse of its own as it traveled down my body, distracting me from his words. "Why are you so hot?" I whispered.

There was just enough light to catch the glint of his smirk.

"No," I corrected sharply, rolling my eyes as I rested my hand along his chest. "You're burning up. Are you feverish?"

The smirk dropped along with his hand. "I'm just hot-natured."

My fingertips traced a path over his pectorals, finding the warmth comforting, ignoring the fact that I was touching him at all. "I had a friend who was Ignus. He was never this warm, though."

The corner of his mouth resumed its earlier lifted position. "Were you lying half-naked in bed with him?" He hadn't meant to land so close to the truth, I could tell by the way his expression turned to surprise as my frown collapsed the beginnings of what had been a tentative smile.

One golden eyebrow notched up. "Was that your date to the ball?"

"What happened with Natasha?" I asked, changing the subject rapidly away from Cade and that entire sordid disaster. My pain was too raw to confess anything more than I already had.

He snorted, eyes glittering with mischief. "Nothing."

The rumble of his voice sent shock waves up my finger that was somehow idly trailing circles down his chest and abdomen. A tight breath sucked back into my lungs as I retracted my hand like he had burned me. I needed to do something, anything, to feel like I had some semblance of control. "After all that, she turned you down?" My smile was honeyed.

A hum of a laugh slipped into the space between us. "No."

"Shame," I countered, omitting the way relief still coursed through my veins.

His brows furrowed like he had only just recognizing that he had slipped into the bed with me. "Do you still want me to leave?" It was as if he had a window to my inner thoughts, prying the truth out of me by carefully placed questions.

My eyes fell to his lips, full and soft. Then to my hand, already pressed against the ridges along his abdomen. What the fuck was wrong with me? Again, I yanked it back, eyes blazing a trail to his.

Beckett's face was indecipherable, unblinking even, as he took me in. "I asked you a question."

Those silver eyes seemed to pin me in place, and in the dark, I could almost forget why he drove me so mad. A part of me, the reckless part that was scrambling for control, considered just closing my eyes and pretending he was Cade. Jemma had always said that the best way to get over someone was to get under them. Beckett would be a beautiful distraction from my heartbreak and dread.

"No," I whispered.

A muscle feathered in his jaw. "No, what?"

Swallowing down the final vestiges of my distress, I let our gazes meet. "Don't go." My voice sounded so meek, even though I wasn't afraid of the man before me. Curious, yes, but terrified? No. And if he could help me leave behind that girl, I had been the night of the solstice eve ball, the one in the glittering golden ball gown, drowning in the hope of a happily ever after, then maybe I could tolerate his company after all.

Beckett's face remained undecipherable. "You want me to stay in this bed? With you? Even though it is—in your words—wildly unprofessional?" Nothing about his expression or inflection betrayed a hint of what he was thinking. For all I knew, this was another prank, and he was about to laugh in my face.

My fingertips were already grazing the line down the center of his abdomen, so it wasn't as if I could pretend my lust wasn't there. "Yes. Stay."

There was no braying laugh or sparks of amusement in Beckett's eyes as he moved. Fingertips rubbed small circles from my shoulder to my elbow, his touch meandering down my forearm before it ducked underneath the blanket. His grip tightened when he reached my hip, pulling me closer to him.

Instinctively, like we had done this a hundred times before, my hand curled around the base of his neck, and I pressed into him, soaking in every ounce of the warmth that radiated from him like the rays of a summer sun.

Beckett dipped his chin, his lips so close to mine that I could feel his breath on them. It was not fear that ratcheted my heart rate when I made to close the gap, but it was surprise that kept me from reaching him when a knock sounded at the door.

The jarring noise broke me from my trance, instantly reminding me

I probably wasn't as safe as I thought, just because my escort was with me.

Beckett, on the other hand, ignored the noise, his calloused palm already roaming further down my hips, slipping beneath the flimsy fabric of the gown to cup my ass.

Internally, I warred with the desire to figure out exactly what he would be doing with those hands and needing to address who was at the door because the knock came again, this time more urgent.

"Oh, for fucks sake," Beckett cursed under his breath, removing his hands from me and abruptly standing. The absence of his heat made me shiver as goosebumps dappled my skin.

In his thin shorts, Beckett practically charged the door, his irritation unfurling from his body like smoke. He threw it open with a few more curse words. "This better be serious, Harris," he grumbled.

Light from the hallway spilled into the room, illuminating the person who had interrupted us. It wasn't Harris at the door, though; it was Natasha.

Her eyes bulged as her gaze blazed a trail down his body. "Good, you're ready for me." She pushed him back into the room with her hands on his chest, slamming the door behind her with a flick of her wrist in the air.

She must be Caelum, I thought to myself, completely missing what was happening in front of me until it was too late. Beckett hardly had the wherewithal to catch himself as Natasha shoved him onto the bed. Thankfully, he landed in a halfway seated position, just narrowly missing squashing me beneath him.

There wasn't even enough time to blink when Natasha had fallen to her knees between his, clawing at the waistband of his shorts. If he hadn't appeared just as dumbfounded as I was, I would have considered that he had planned this as another elaborate joke at my expense.

"What the fuck?" I stammered, trying to get out of the bed while still clutching the blanket to my chest.

Natasha popped up, looking at me with a fury in her eyes before her attention snapped back to Beckett. "You know I don't like to share," she said pointedly. Then, she poked out her full bottom lip and added, "But if this is what you want tonight, she can go second".

Horror consumed me, and I sat there frozen in my retreat, unable to move an inch away, like my brain was screaming at me to do. As if I weren't even in the room, Natasha shrugged and dropped her face back toward Beckett's lap.

With a firm grasp on her shoulders, Beckett stopped her mid-air and guided her away from him. "Natasha, you should leave." His voice was stern, more serious than I had heard it before.

She scowled, still on her knees. "You're giving up a night with this," she waved her hands over her body, "for this?" Her hands gestured wildly at me, indignation written plainly on her features.

A muscle pulsed in Beckett's jaw as he rolled it. "I told you. I'm doing a job. I can't entertain you tonight."

She picked herself off the floor and stormed out of the room, slamming the door behind her with enough force to rattle the paintings on the wall beside it, and surely waking up whatever patrons had already fallen asleep.

Relief washed over me in waves. Partially because she had finally left, but also because she had inadvertently stopped me from doing whatever was about to happen with Beckett. With her sobering departure, I was forced to face how much of a mistake that might have been.

Beckett was my escort into a kingdom where I had no friends or allies. Complicating that relationship just because I was spiraling could have dire consequences. Not to mention that I wasn't even sure I liked him half of the time. Or most of the time.

My gaze slid over to Beckett, who was still seated on the edge of the bed, facing away from me. He finally moved, only to rake his fingers through his hair, acknowledging me without glancing in my direction. "I'm sorry, Ashton. That was... intense." The sound of my real name, foreign on his lips, took me aback and left me in a stunned silence.

His chest expanded slowly, then contracted on a long exhale. "I can find somewhere else to sleep tonight, if you'd like."

The air whooshed from my lungs. It had been a relief that we had been stopped, but somehow the idea of him leaving caused an uncomfortable sensation to build in my chest. Like my heart was being squeezed at the prospect of losing his presence. His safety.

"No, that's okay," I heard myself say, "Let's just get some rest."

Dropping back to the mattress, I turned around, settling beneath the quilt again, letting my eyes flutter closed.

It hit me at once. How close I had come to being intimate with someone new. How I hadn't had to work up to it in the same way I needed to with Cade after Berit's assault. I couldn't decipher what it meant other than to postulate that my brain was trying to get me to move on. Because while my thoughts had briefly strayed to the House Wyvern leader, I had mostly been thinking about Beckett.

A part of me had known Cade and I were done the moment he hesitated to tell me he loved me. Even if he had changed his mind eventually, his gut reaction and his initial rejection of me couldn't be taken back. I'd never forget the look on his face. The words he had said when he essentially called me unworthy of being introduced to his parents, of being a part of his life.

It had been the thing that I feared the most—being found less than—and he had taken that insecurity and brought it to the surface, shoving it into my face. Sadness clawed at my heart and chilled whatever heat was left from my infuriation turned lust toward my escort.

Unaware of the tears gathering in my lashes, Beckett stood from the bed, grabbing the pillow beside me before crossing the small space to the settee by the fire. He propped himself awkwardly on the cushions, his body obviously too big to comfortably sleep on the piece of furniture. Nevertheless, he bent and folded in an attempt to confine himself to its surface.

Neither of us said a word about it.

He obviously thought our union would have been a mistake, too, or he wouldn't have left the bed.

It was for the best.

"Goodnight," he whispered over his shoulder.

I paused, wondering if there would be more. But the steady rise and fall of his chest told me that he wasn't coming back.

"Goodnight," I replied to the darkness.

Nine

The next morning, I woke to an odd chirping noise I couldn't quite place. It, for the most part, sounded like a bird—it was probably a bird—but the notes were unfamiliar to me. As if whatever divided the two kingdoms had divided the branches of each species into something new, or at least different, even if they originated from a joint but now distant cousin.

Staring at the ceiling, I listened to the bird-like calls. Anything to avoid getting out of bed, which was adequate at best. Still, the faint yellow glow pouring into the window over my head told me that it was likely past time to leave.

With one final sigh that I heaved with all the force of a gale wind, I committed to getting out of the bed. My arms stretched out as far as they could go, finding the space beside me empty. Just as it had been when I fell asleep.

This time, a more practical sigh escaped my lips as I peeled the covers back and slid off the mattress. Taking my time, I padded to the bathing chamber where I took care of my business slowly, washing my hands and face in the lukewarm water left in the basin. The robe I had worn the night before was still hanging on the hook where I had left it, and I threw it on over the slip, stepping back into the suite. This time, I allowed myself a quick glance at the settee.

It was empty, save for the throw which was folded neatly on top of the pillow Beckett had taken from the bed last night. Next to that was a pile of what I hoped were freshly laundered clothes with a note on top. Unfolding the paper, I read the neat scrawling handwriting.

Your clean clothes, as promised. Be ready by 9. -BA

Based on a quick glance at the clock above the mantle, it was eight in the morning, meaning I had a few minutes to spare. Under normal circumstances, I might consider hiding in the room, embarrassed from whatever had almost happened last night, but I found myself more eager to have my questions answered, and my father's healing bartered for, than avoid an uncomfortable situation with Beckett.

In the light of day, I was mildly ashamed of my behavior, though. Allowing myself to succumb to the idea that being under Beckett might somehow erase my feelings for Cade was out of character for me, and more than that, it would ultimately be futile. The more logical part of my brain knew that I'd have to sit through the heartbreak and pain of my rejection before I could process it. Before I could truly move past it. No matter how many times I wished to be more like her, I was not Jemma.

Furthermore, I didn't even like Beckett. He was intolerable, at best. Arrogant. Conceited. The only thing he had going for him—besides the swath of women throwing themselves his way, which indicated that he *might* be a good time—was that he hadn't yet failed at keeping me safe. Even if we had come across no danger, he was technically doing his job, and I felt secure with him.

My eyes lingered back to the bed that we had almost shared, the blankets ruffled as if we had. More of me than I would be willing to admit aloud was at least mildly curious about what it would be like with him. His rough hands on my body, his dominating tone telling me exactly what to do. He'd probably smirk the entire time.

My breath slowed at my entirely too vivid daydream, and I dug my nails into my palms to drag myself out of my thoughts. I desperately needed to get a grip because this complicated attraction would bring nothing but disaster. The last time I had fostered a crush on someone, it had ended horribly. There was no need for a repeat of that.

Snatching up the pile of clothes, I walked back to the bathroom, stopping at the edge of the counter so I could stare at my reflection in the mirror. The purple bags forming below my eyelids had receded with last night's rest, but I still looked like I had been through hell. Maybe that had been what Natasha had meant when she articulated her outrage that Beckett had chosen to spend the night with me instead of her. Taking in the entirety of the mirror image of myself, I wasn't sure why he had either.

With that bit of self-loathing, I freshened up as best I could, and when I hazarded a glance back in the mirror, I did seem to look marginally better. No miracles had been performed, but I was a slightly less tragic version of the girl I had been in the Barker Inn two nights ago. Nodding at my image as if I had given myself a pep talk, I left the bathing chamber, walking straight out into the hallway, knowing that I wasn't going to find any of the answers to the questions that plagued me, contemplating my life choices in room 113.

As I headed down the creaking steps, I couldn't stop myself from being hopeful that someone had prepared breakfast. My stomach growled as if to verbally agree with the sentiment. Cheese and stale bread weren't nearly enough to sustain me, and the bowl of chowder from last night had long worked its way through my system.

Just as I crossed over the threshold of the dining area, I heard the sounds of smoked meats and eggs frying in a pan, contributing to the mouth-watering aroma in the air as I made my way to the booth that Beckett and I had shared the night before. Of course, he wasn't anywhere to be seen, but the other tables were blessedly empty.

Before I had even fully settled in, Harris approached me, grinning like I was already a familiar face to him. "What can I get you, miss?"

His formality made me stifle a laugh. Never mind that we were practically the same age. At most, he had a few years on me, which only made the way he spoke more comical. My eyes met his, a gold-flecked chocolate brown, and I offered him a warm smile. "Do you have a menu?"

At this, he chuckled, scrubbing his hand over the dark stubble that had grown even thicker overnight. It was clear that there was no formal menu in this place, but he obliged as best he could, listing off items in random order. "Bacon, eggs, sausage, toast with butter and jam, and seasonal fruit."

My smile broadened. "I'll take bacon and eggs. Can you scramble them?" I grimaced, realizing I was being horribly picky for someone who was on the run. "Or, actually... just —"

"We can do that, miss," Harris replied. "Is there anything else?"

My cringe seemed to add tension to the muscles in my shoulders, and I simply shook my head in response, prompting Harris to scurry back to the kitchens to relay my order.

Maybe my time at Biltons Academy had changed me, or at least made me accustomed to having an assortment to choose from every day. It hadn't been like that in Elmhaven, where we had to grow the majority of our food because—

Gasping, I realized all too late that I had placed an order, forgetting completely that I was in another kingdom. My money probably wasn't good here. Although, I had no idea. If I had any bills accumulated from my journey here, I hadn't been the one paying them.

The blood drained from my face. Would they let me wash dishes to pay off my debt? I didn't have anything else of value to trade except... My fingers stilled over my mother's ring, and my heart plummeted into my stomach. I'd give up anything except that.

As if my racing thoughts had conjured him, Beckett strode into the space from gods knew where, my attention drawn to him like I was a moth, and he was the brightest flame. I couldn't take my eyes off him, but it wasn't his enormous height or broad shoulders that kept my attention. He was sporting a rather unfortunate scowl on his face that I already knew spelled trouble for our travels today.

Without even making eye contact with me, Beckett crossed the room on long strides, sliding into the bench opposite mine this time. My eyes narrowed onto his hands, where he clutched a steaming mug of coffee.

"Good morning, Ashton," he said calmly, with none of the hints of amusement, sarcasm, or mockery that his voice typically held. Even my name sounded dull and lifeless on his tongue.

Begrudgingly lifting my focus from his coffee to meet his stare, I smiled. "Good morning, Beckett." I almost sang the words, positive that if I pretended like everything was normal, we could just go back to annoying each other. It was far preferable to this strange coldness that I did not think I deserved. While I was thankful for the interruption, Natasha had been the one to break up our union. His ire was better directed toward her, if that was what this was even about.

Instead of reacting to my tone in any way, he began scrutinizing the patrons who were just starting to mosey their way into the dining hall. Like I wasn't even there at all.

My mouth remained shut even as I internally bristled at the shift in atmosphere between us.

Harris returned with my food, turning to Beckett almost eagerly. "Can I get you some food, sir?"

"Actually," I interrupted, "I would love a cup of coffee. And maybe cream? And sugar?" If Beckett had coffee, it was safe to assume the inn had coffee.

Finally, Beckett's silver glare cut to me, but I quickly turned back to Harris, who was now fumbling over his words. "Su-sure thing, miss," he stuttered, turning his beet-red face back to Beckett. "Your usual?"

Beckett made an indiscernible noise, and Harris practically tripped over himself to get away from our table, something that I couldn't fully understand. Sure, my escort was in a foul mood, and he wasn't exactly hiding it, but he wasn't being aggressive. Unless Harris knew something I didn't.

Within far fewer minutes than should have been possible, Harris had returned with my coffee and Beckett's plate of food. "I hope you two were comfortable last night," Harris mumbled, clearly looking to make small talk but hopelessly oblivious to how the night had actually gone.

Avoiding answering altogether, I took a tentative sip of my coffee, relieved when I found it to be the perfect blend of sweet and bitter.

Harris was being promoted to my favorite person in the Light Kingdom, effective immediately.

Beckett's mug slammed to the table with a crash, jolting me from my pleasant thoughts. "Next time I come through on a job, I will require my usual rooms," he seethed. "Do you understand?"

Harris visibly flinched, his shoulders slumping. "Of course, s-sir. It's just been a while since you came through on official—"

Beckett raised a hand to cut him off. "If I need to reserve it year-round, I will."

"Yes, sir," Harris muttered, dropping in a slight bow before scrambling from the table.

For several long seconds, I gawked at Beckett, my eyes blown wide the entire time. Not once did he meet my glare, seemingly more content to focus on a knot on the wood tabletop with an intensity that threatened murder.

"What was that about?" I snapped at him, abandoning all pretenses of turning his mood around. "And don't tell me it's classified. I've had enough of that."

He finally lifted his steely glower to me. "That was about my expectations when I'm traveling on behalf of..." He stopped himself, pausing a moment as if he needed to swallow. "Oldenberg."

That narrowed it down. Oldenberg was either a person or an organization. Certainly not a place. One of my eyebrows lifted as I kept his stare. "And working on behalf of *Oldenberg* requires that you have two rooms? Requires that you snap at poor Harris when the Inn was full? He couldn't have possibly known you were coming through. You didn't even know you were coming through until I showed up at the Barker Inn two nights ago."

He gritted his teeth. "This whole situation should have been more professional."

The snort that left my nose was neither ladylike nor kind. "Oh please! When we met you were basically participating in an orgy in the middle of a pub."

Cold grey eyes narrowed in my direction, but I wasn't done with him.

"And last night was certainly not professional." My tone was drenched in accusation, even though I knew I was complicit in the act.

Beckett leaned forward, his elbows resting on the table between us. "What about last night?"

It was my turn to utilize the silence, letting it stretch between us. Slow blinks gave me several more moments to stall in my response.

"Exactly," he stated, pulling the mug to his lips and unwittingly snagging my attention there. "You just got carried away." Those words came out taunting.

My irritation flared, burning out whatever embarrassment I might have felt. "If I recall, you were the one about to kiss me before your little girlfriend interrupted."

This time, Beckett set his mug down gently, his face the pinnacle of neutrality. "You had your hands all over me, Princess. What did you want me to do?"

Recoiling at the nickname, I inhaled deeply through my nose, closing my eyes in the process on the off chance that whatever magic he promised I had wouldn't flare up and strike him down with my icy glare before I could be delivered to the healers that could save my father. When the breath was sufficiently exhaled, and my rage was somewhat contained to the tension in my chest, I opened my eyes again. "What I want you to do is take me to our destination so that we can be rid of each other for good."

"Fine," he bit out.

With that, I took my own mug into my hands and brought it delicately to my lips, as if whatever spat had just transpired didn't bother me in the slightest. As if his words didn't feel like another rejection.

My eyes closed when the sensation of the most perfect cup of coffee hit my tongue again, and I could almost forget how aggravating the man in front of me was. Almost.

Gingerly, I dropped the mug back to the table, keeping my palm curled around its ceramic surface, if for no other reason than I wasn't ready to be parted with it. With a careful smile, I asked, "Care to elaborate on where we are going now?"

"We will make it to Lochmere today," he replied, his neck stiff as he seemingly forced his attention on nothing in the distance.

Lochmere. My final destination, at least if what he had already told me was to be believed. "And then you will tell me what I need to know?" My voice was entirely too hopeful.

A heavy sigh released from his parted lips. "You will be debriefed as soon as I have a chance to speak with Ryana about why she sent you like this."

I nodded, as if he had given me something useful, rather than the same spiel again. Something about knowing I would make it to Lochmere today, and my father hopefully only a day behind me, filled me with such reassurance that I almost let a smile form along my lips.

I gave myself the time it took to take on more gulp of the perfectly concocted coffee before I dropped the mug to the table with a resigned sigh. "So, when are we leaving?"

Ten

After we finished our terse breakfast, Beckett and I left Wolvesden on foot, and I was shocked to learn there were no grand roads connecting the towns, as there were in Demetros. Here, in The Light Kingdom, there were hardly even well-worn paths that marked our way. Instead of using the cobblestones or dirt trails to prompt me, I followed Beckett's surefooted steps in near silence, taking in as much of the surroundings as I could while keeping the pace.

Eventually, my thoughts grew so loud that I had no choice but to attempt to get more information out of him. "You said I had multiple elements," I stated, peering over at him with what I hoped was a neutral face.

He grumbled an irritated sigh. "Right. The code dragonfire indicates multiple elemental powers. Perhaps even a gift."

Either I had sufficiently worn him down, or it was possible I had finally begun to ask the right questions to garner a useful response. "So, I might have four like you? What is a gift?"

Instantly, his expression changed to one of mild regret. Like he had been inconvenienced by having to explain his own statement. Momentarily, his gaze drifted over to me as if he were puzzling out exactly how this needed to go to save himself from being reprimanded by revealing too much information. "We are close enough to Lochmere that I can give you a memory potion if this goes poorly, so..." He threw his hands in the air as if the gesture concluded the sentence. "The Light Kingdom is home to the Fae."

My mouth fell open. Obviously, I had heard fairytales of the Fae growing up. The origins of our magic were whispered to have been Fae. But, yet again, I was surprised by the statement. "You're kidding?"

Those silver eyes rolled dramatically in a move that reminded me instantly of Jemma. "I prefer the immediate satisfaction of my humor, not a long game. You can choose to believe me or not, but you'll get the same information from Ryana when she arrives."

My teeth grazed along the inside of my cheek. "And what does this have to do with my elemental gifts?"

"The majority of the Fae that reside in the Light Kingdom are elemental. Most of them have four elements at their disposal." His tone was almost bored, like he was reciting history for a class rather than to a person who was struggling to keep up with all the new information she was receiving.

"I don't see how this relates to me," I confessed, nearly stuttering. "Why am I here?"

Beckett scrubbed a hand over his face. "Humans do not possess magic. Only those who are part Fae have elemental magic. Therefore..." His pause was expectant as if he were anticipating that I'd finish his sentence.

My brows drew together almost painfully. "You think I'm part Fae?"

"There she is. Clever girl," he remarked, sarcasm dripping from his tone.

I blew out a frustrated breath. "How did Fae get into Demetros? How is all of this even—"

"I'm going to stop you right there," Beckett stated, holding up a hand but never dragging his stare from the path ahead. "The how of it all needs to be saved for the debrief."

"But you just said you could give me a memory potion and—"

"No. This is the most I am comfortable discussing until I speak to Ryana." His words were final, his tone bordering on harsh.

I fought back the urge to flinch, but I was determined to learn everything I could, and the questions had become a nice distraction. "So, what are gifts?"

A flash of amusement registered across his face. "Most elemental Fae, the ones who possess all four elements," he corrected, "have a gift as well. Some magical ability that is *more*."

"Like what?" I pressed, eager to soak in the knowledge of this foreign placc. Perhaps, information about my own lineage.

"Some can heal," he began. At that, I grew excited. Magical healing had to be better than whatever we had in Demetros.

"Some can grow plants," he continued, unaware of the grin overtaking my face. "Some have illusions. It really is very specific to the individual and their lineage."

"So, it's genetic?" I probed. "Passed down like eye color?"

"Sometimes," he answered in that unhelpful way of his.

I expelled another frustrated puff of air, this time moving a few stray hairs out of my face. "What is your gift? I assume you have one since you have all four elements?"

The smirk that lifted the corner of his mouth should have been my first indication that the answer would be unexpected.

"Arousal," he answered casually, the boredom in his voice clashing with his expression.

I almost sputtered. "I'm sorry, what?"

"Arousal," he repeated. "I have the ability to enhance arousal with a partner."

My mouth went dry. "Did you use that on me?" Admittedly, my tone was a bit accusatory as I was trapped somewhere between shock and indignation at the idea that perhaps my reaction to him in the Wolf Inn was magically induced. I had the sudden urge to back away from him.

Beckett's stare cut to mine halting my retreat, his eyes darker than I remembered. "No. I only use my gift on willing participants." His cocky expression told me that it was likely he practiced his magic on *many* willing participants, but I couldn't bring myself to ask anything further even though curiosity piqued my interest. Since for some strange reason I found myself believing him, I wouldn't give him the satisfaction of inquiring more about his use of that particular gift again because his head was already large enough.

Luckily, I wasn't given an opportunity to fill the silence with any of those lingering questions because as we entered a clearing, Beckett frowned, face tipping to the sky. A deep rumble sounded off in the distance, shaking the ground beneath our feet.

The canopy of trees had blocked the majority of the horizon from our view until this moment, but now that they were gone, I could see menacing dark grey clouds swirling in the sky above our heads. Demetros had rain but rarely storms that looked so intense. It should have been frightening, but there was something beautiful about the artistry of the clouds and the subtle hum of energy in the air, surrounding us like mist.

Beckett sighed as he took in the sight before us. "We will probably be at Lochmere in the next hour if we continue walking, but the air feels off." His gaze arced from the sky to my own stare. "We can find somewhere to wait it out or we can run. What do you prefer?"

Mulling over my options, which seemed far and few between, I made my decision quickly. The only way I would be getting any answers was to get to Lochmere, and perhaps Oldenberg, as quickly as possible. "Let's run for it."

Beckett only spared me a mischievous grin before he bolted from the clearing. I took off a heartbeat behind him, dodging tree trunks and the occasional shrubbery as I went. He was fast, due in no small part to his long, muscular legs, but thanks to my extra training with Ryana, I wasn't winded as I matched him stride for stride.

We jogged alongside each other as we traversed the unfamiliar land. The ground before us began to rise and fall in the shape of hills, and in the distance, I could see a body of water, grey beneath the ominous clouds that loomed overhead.

We had made it to a high point when I spied the first evidence of a building along the coast. There had been nothing between Wolvesden and this place, a realization that sparked more curiosity about how the Light Kingdom operated and its number of citizens than anything else.

Despite my curiosity, my attention remained on the man-made structure in the distance. The first part of the building that came into focus was fortress walls, solid and comprised of what appeared to be hefty gray slabs. Beyond the smooth stone surface, I could just make out a line of windows that belonged to an interior building. Moss climbed its way up the outer perimeter, reaching for a charcoal-hued roof that was a near match to the angry churning sky.

"Almost there," Beckett said smoothly, as if he hadn't been running anywhere near his limit.

My focus swiftly returned to our destination. Flags whipped atop several spires, but I couldn't discern color or images from this far away. Not that I would recognize the symbols of a foreign nation.

Just when I was starting to think we were going to beat the storm, a massive crack of lightning filled the sky, slicing the air apart just over the fortress. As if it had been signaling the start of the weather event, the clouds above us broke open like eggs. Fat raindrops splattered against my face and clothes, dropping in quick succession as another roll of thunder shook the ground.

"Better hurry," Beckett called over his shoulder as he sped off in front of me.

By the time I caught up with him, he had already lodged himself in a small alcove at the base of the outer walls, rather than walking through the front gates.

Beckett's blonde hair was soaking wet, turned almost brown in this condition. Water droplets fell off his nose and face as he padded his palm against the bricks to his right, looking for something specific rather than drying himself off with his magic.

He pressed against some unknown marker on the wall that he kept shielded with his hand and the sound of stone-on-stone grinding together echoed in the small space. A slab had shifted to reveal a set of rocky steps. It almost felt like déjà vu, except I wasn't in Demetros, and this man certainly wasn't Cade leading me to our meadow.

A flick of Beckett's wrist lit the torchlights on the wall of the hidden staircase, and he began to ascend without further conversation.

The stairs were an unwelcome sight, considering how hard I was still panting after attempting to keep up with Beckett, but even I could admit they were preferable to the storm beyond that had only intensified since we had ducked into the alcove. Thick balls of ice had already started to fall before I had made it to safety. And they had stung.

Beckett shut the door, blocking out the view of the storm raging beyond, then turned to me, waving his hand over me like he was tracing my curves from several inches away. Before I could protest, the water vanished from my clothes and skin, the pulse of magic offering him the same reprieve.

"Thank you," I murmured, still a little awestruck at the blatant display of magic after so many months away from seeing it regularly. Outside of Cade's ball of flame...

My head shook as I physically tried to dislodge the images from my mind.

As if catching the internal exchange, Beckett's eyes narrowed in my direction, but he didn't ask anything further as he began to climb the stairs.

Our boots echoed loudly in the stone stairwell as I hurried to catch up to him, not wanting to be left behind in this strange place. My legs were burning by the time we reached a nondescript door that Beckett paused at, stalling only momentarily before he pushed it open without any hesitation over who might be beyond it. Like he owned the place or at least expected it to be empty. It was curious.

The hinges screeched in protest, and I winced as I followed Beckett through the threshold and into a completely empty hallway. It was sparsely decorated, with only a few equally spaced lanterns hanging on the grey stone walls. My attention snagged on them, though, because they were already lit, and instead of being the warm glow of a flickering fire, the flame danced in an eerie blue color. The movement and cold light cast a shadow over Beckett's features that made him look downright wicked.

"Follow me," he murmured, the smirk long gone.

We arrived at another arched doorway, and again he crossed the threshold without knocking. Rather than being empty, we were deposited into a bustling kitchen. People dressed in plain grey garb and cream-colored aprons were rushing around in every direction, grabbing ingredients from shelves and cupboards and chopping vegetables with silver-edged knives.

People with decidedly pointed ears. Until this moment, I had forgotten about that detail in the depictions of the Fae.

A woman, maybe in her forties, caught my attention immediately as she stood in the middle of the chaos with a clipboard, yelling out commands to the people around her. Her stance reminded me instantly of Katarina, even though this woman had no other physical attributes in common with my house leader. The woman before me had thick black wavy hair in place of Katarina's blonde, and smooth tawny skin.

When her focus filtered over us, her eyes flared in shock but then quickly shifted to something warm. She hurried over to where we had stopped, and I was certain she was about to detain me when she wrapped her arms around Beckett.

"Welcome back, Becks," she whispered lovingly as she embraced him in a fierce hug. Then, she pulled away, smacking him playfully across the chest. "You weren't supposed to be back for a day or more, we aren't prepared."

He smiled down at the woman, admiration glowing on his face, and I had to wonder if they were somehow related, despite such different features. "I had to come early; we had a *dragonfire* on our hands." He motioned over to me with his thumb. "Josaphine, meet Ashton, the reason I had to cut my *vacation* short."

She took my hand in hers, shaking it gently as she looked me up and down. Her facial expression showed her wariness of my presence, but her tone was kind. "Nice to meet you, Miss Ashton, I'm sure this is all a bit of a shock."

"I'm afraid I don't know enough to be shocked," I confessed to Josaphine, her reassuring presence somehow putting me at ease.

She slapped her palm against Beckett's arm this time, the sound dying on the fabric of his tunic. "You don't have to be such a brute. If the girl is here for the spell, then there should be nothing off limits to her."

Instantly, that one word snagged my attention. Spell? "What spell?" I asked, suddenly skeptical of the true motivations behind bringing me here.

Beckett spared me a glance before turning back to the woman named Josaphine. "She doesn't know *anything*, Josy," Beckett said, giving her a look that practically spelled out the words *be careful*. His emphasis on the word *anything* had hair rising on the back of my neck.

Josaphine huffed, shaking her head at him, acting far too casual for the exchange. "You said code dragonfire and..." Beckett cleared his throat, and her words evaporated to nothing as she took me in with a strange expression. "Very well," she offered, giving me a smile that didn't reach her eyes. "But if she is here, I'm sure I can give her the tour. She's already inside the castle."

Given the most recent revelation, the last thing I cared about was being shown around the castle by another stranger. "What spell, Beckett?"

Rather than answering me, he turned his attention to Josaphine as if I hadn't spoken at all. "Is Oldenberg here yet?"

With a sad expression, Josaphine shook her head. "Oldenberg has been detained in Iverness," she replied. "Border issues again," she added with a shrug.

I might not get an immediate answer about the spell, but at least I had deduced that Oldenberg was a person. Someone who clearly had the authority to tell me whatever information Ryana had left out. Probably the person who could authorize my father's treatment.

Beckett turned to me, shrugging with more of that indifference. "You'll have to wait for Ryana to get here then." Before I could argue with him again, he turned to Josaphine. "Can you show her to her rooms? I have somewhere to be."

Once again, I considered disputing his mention of having *somewhere to be*, considering he shouldn't even be here if his own statement was to be believed, but I kept my lips pressed in a firm line as I watched Josaphine smile sweetly at my escort.

"Of course," she replied, shifting her attention to me. "You must be starving; I'm sure Becks didn't feed you properly. He doesn't usually handle transport of people. Anymore anyway. Not since—"

"Josy," Beckett interrupted. "Just feed her and take her to her room. No need to spill all the kingdom's secrets."

Josaphine snorted a laugh, moving me toward a cart at the edge of the kitchens. She poured steaming brown liquid into a dainty cup, passing it to me before snatching a scone from a nearby table and placing it on a napkin, which she also shoved in front of my face. With my hands full of what appeared to be tea and a pastry with what I hoped were chunks of blueberry, I followed the eager woman from the room, leaving Beckett behind to attend to his plans.

"Well, Beckett introduced me as Josaphine, but I am also the estate manager for the property when," she paused as if needed to conjure the name again, "Oldenberg is away." It was almost as if the moniker was as unused as the path between Wolvesden and Castle Lochmere had been.

I eyed her curiously, wondering if she was easier to crack than Beckett. "So, about this spell," I said, trying to sound indifferent as I pushed my luck.

Rather than annoyance, her expression only twisted with pity as she continued to lead me down a narrow hallway. "If Beckett is not comfortable with sharing that information, I am afraid I cannot."

"He's in charge here?" I asked, wondering about the dynamic between Ryana and Beckett.

Josaphine's face scrunched with more of that uncomfortable commiseration. "I would love to tell you about the castle. Some of the artwork around us?"

My eyes scanned the hallway. Wherever Beckett had been leading me through before had not been the main passageways of the castle because everything around us was decorated in finery I had only seen in Biltons Academy and the Elemental Queen's castle. The stone beneath our feet had morphed into intricate wooden boards, and the blocked walls were all but covered up behind artwork and stunning carved inlay.

Lifelike oil paintings lined the walls, all depicting scenes of nature, but I didn't really care to know anything about that. "The décor is lovely," I replied lamely.

My escort only smiled, as if she wasn't offended at all by my dismissal of the decorations lining the halls, and we continued on in relative silence.

We scaled a grand staircase with marble slab steps and golden handrails that were propped up by scrolling iron panels. The wall along the stairwell, nearly three stories tall, boasted a tapestry that almost completely spanned its height. It was clearly an emblem of the house that this estate belonged to, or maybe even the Light Kingdom itself.

The majority of the fabric was a creamy ivory. In the center was the profile of a lion, embroidered in rich oranges, rusts, and chocolate brown. At the lion's muzzle was what appeared to be the sun, woven with marigold and lemon hues. Splitting the sun and the lion's face was a sword, the only color other than the greys of steel was the vibrant purple stone embedded into the pommel. It seemed important somehow, but without any reference as to what it meant and no desire to have a history lesson when I really needed answers, I moved on without asking about it.

We exited at a random landing and Josaphine took the first left, which sent us down another never-ending hall, full of the same style artwork and decorations that had adorned the rest of the castle.

At the fifth door, she stopped and produced a set of skeleton keys from the deep pocket in her full crimson skirts, sliding one into the lock with a click. She swung the door open and motioned me inside.

It was an elegant space, which was wholly unsurprising considering the halls we had just traversed. Dark oak planks lined the floor, covered by a plush minty green floral rug that took up half the room. Pristine white furniture filled most of the space. The bed was draped in gorgeous pink linens that complemented the velvet armchairs that bracketed the floor-to-ceiling windows on the opposite wall.

When my focus swept away from the inviting room and back to Josaphine, her brown eyes were watching me. Her silent attention held no assessment—like Beckett's so frequently had— she was merely giving me the time to take in my surroundings.

Josaphine smiled, her expression radiating kindness. "This is your room, please make yourself at home."

"Thank you," I replied, surprised to find a frown forming along her lips.

She fought with it for a moment, trying and failing to recall her previous grin. "Unfortunately, you have arrived prior to Oldenberg, and because of that, it is policy to have you stay in your rooms until you have been properly vetted."

Swallowing down the emotion that felt too much like fear, I regarded my situation in a different light. For the first time since Beckett had reassured me that I wasn't being taken against my will, I started to question my decision to leave.

My lashes fluttered furiously as I blinked back the moisture gathering along my eyelids.

"Oh no, dear," Josaphine corrected, "there is nothing to be concerned with. In fact, this has never happened before," she admitted, almost sheepishly. "It's just a precaution."

Even as I bobbed my head as if I understood, my limbs began to tremble.

The estate manager pointed toward the door at the far side of the room. "Just beyond that door is your bathing chamber. There is soap already inside and someone will bring fresh clothes to you shortly. Is there anything else you need?"

She was being so kind, but something was wrong about this. It was a luxurious suite that I was being kept in, but it was a prison, nonetheless. My head jerked back and forth, and I fought to form words that wouldn't reveal the emotions that accompanied that thought. "No, thank you," I finally whispered.

Josaphine spared me one final pitiful glance before she inclined her head and waltzed toward the door. "Ring that bell if you need anything," she added, motioning her hand toward a rope dangling to the left of the doorframe.

All I could do was nod, as I stared at my feet like a scolded child.

"Goodbye, dear," she offered before she closed the door behind her.

Eleven

Meals were delivered by Josaphine several times over the course of the following day, but she never lingered long after she brought my food. It was probably the scowl on my face that kept her away and the fact that the only thing I had found to do in the room they had sequestered me to was stare out the window, waiting for any sign of my father's approach. I hadn't exactly been friendly when she came, and I certainly wasn't up for idle chit chat.

But as the sun began to set on my second day in Castle Lochmere, my restless mind began to churn. How far behind did they expect Ryana? If she left immediately after the ceremony, and made quicker time than Beckett and I had, she might already be here. Although I had seen no sign of approach while holding my vigil at the windows, that didn't mean I was even facing the right way.

Pushing myself up from the pink velvet chair I was holding court in, I made my way to the door, ready to bang it down, demand to be released, and insist upon getting real answers that I knew Beckett had. Out of habit, or maybe a subconscious idea, I tried the handle first, finding that it turned easily.

Cautiously, I peered around the doorframe, half relieved and half flabbergasted that there was no one guarding the outside of my door.

Had I been free to roam this entire time? I thought back to Josaphine's words, considering that she had only asked me to stay in my suite, and I suddenly felt very silly for assuming the worst.

Then again, I was in a wholly unfamiliar place, and I had no idea what the Fae were capable of or why they even wanted me in the first place. The reminder of Josaphine's mention of a spell kept me on high alert as I listened for the noises of an impending approach.

When none came, I tiptoed in the direction I had been led from the day prior, only briefly considering my option to ring the bell and simply ask Josaphine to call for Beckett. Then again, whatever the hierarchy was here, she certainly wouldn't get him if he had told her not to. If I wanted to confront the man who had brought me here, I'd have to find him myself.

The estate manager hadn't exactly given me a tour of the castle, only took me on the direct path to my room, so finding my way to wherever Beckett would be, wasn't obvious. Despite my uncertainty in where I was going, I was more steadfast than ever about leaving that room behind.

On steady feet, I kept moving, across corridors and down plush carpeted stairs, my footsteps nearly silent as I traveled past floral paintings and ornately gilded walls. When I reached the massive stairway and the tapestry of the lion, I counted the flights down until I was certain I'd made it to the landing I had been brought from the first day. Slowly, I crept down the connecting hallway, almost instantaneously sure that I had never seen this particular passage before.

The breath in my lungs stilled when I heard the trickle of voices coming from a nearby room, recognizing the male voice like it was something familiar to me, and not a sound that had only been in my life for the span of a few days.

I sent a silent thank you to Josaphine for gifting me with silk-bottomed slippers, as I silently made my way to the open doorway where Beckett was discussing something with the estate manager. Perhaps it was impolite of me to listen, but I had a gut feeling that if I kept quiet, I would likely learn far more than I could garner from simply asking.

Josaphine's voice was raised, but not necessarily angry. "You can't just shut her up in there forever."

A gasp threatened to slip through my lips, and I covered my mouth with my hand to stop it, angling my head closer to the opening to hear Beckett's response more clearly. They were definitely talking about me.

"I don't intend to," Beckett replied, his tone heightened. "As soon as Vissorri gets here and I figure out what the hell is going on, she will be debriefed properly and allowed to roam free until she attempts to break the spell."

A million thoughts filtered through my mind, none of them comforting. Who was Vissorri? Was this yet another person who would hold my fate in their hands? Or, perhaps more troubling, what was this spell, and why was I the one who was intended to break it?

A female scoff in the room stole my attention once more, forcing me to plaster my spine and hands against the wall, praying I wasn't already caught before I heard the rest of this horrid, but enlightening, conversation.

"You know just as well as I do that you can do whatever you want to," Josaphine retorted. "Show the girl some compassion. Walk her around the castle. Treat her like a person."

The estate manager raised a good point. Why hadn't he done that if it sounded like he had the authority to?

One of Beckett's incredulous laughs split the air. "You want me to make her my friend? So that what?" He paused, clearly blowing out a frustrated breath. "So that I can be the one to tell her that breaking the spell will kill her?"

The words stole the air from my lungs. No wonder he didn't want Josaphine to talk to me about the spell. No wonder they were leaving me sequestered in my room with no information. No wonder they brought me here without giving me the slightest hint as to what they needed me for.

My mind raced as I considered how quickly I had grown to trust Ryana, so assured by her boldly stating that she had known my father, so comforted by her knowing the details of my mother's boots. What a fool I had been because there wasn't a world where my father would have agreed to sending me to any place that would lead to my death.

With my pulse thundering in my ears, I pushed away from the wall, already preparing to run as far away from this place as I could get, when another voice caught my attention.

"Ashton!" Ryana called from further down the hall. "I'm so glad you made it. I've been worried sick."

The blood drained from my face. Not only had I been found out before I could leave, but my captor, who had once played the role of friend, was pretending that she cared about me.

My stare remained on her as I backed away slowly, wondering if I could find another point of egress than the way I had come. "Don't pretend like you didn't just bring me here to have me die over that spell." The hurt seeped through my words, even if I tried to morph it into something less pathetic.

Beckett and Josaphine appeared in the doorway, perched halfway between where Ryana and I stood.

"What the fuck are you telling her, Beckett?" Ryana hissed as she glowered at him.

Beckett pinched the bridge of his nose. "I didn't tell her anything. The little vagrant was sneaking around when she should have been in her room." His glare shifted to Josaphine.

"You're not even going to deny it?" I asked all of them at once.

"This is why I don't explain these things to the people that my subordinates collect," Beckett muttered to no one in particular. He gestured over at me without looking in my direction. "I have no idea what kind of magic you sensed or why you thought to send the girl ahead with no information."

I took a few tentative steps backwards. Maybe they wouldn't notice my exit if they were bickering amongst themselves at whose responsibility that it should have been to inform me of my ultimate demise.

Ryana turned to me first; palms raised in the air between us. "You are not going to die breaking this spell."

Beckett groaned. "You cannot promise her that. If she is capable of breaking it, it will take all of her magic and kill her. This is the only thing we know for certain."

Ryana's marbled brown eyes remained locked on mine as she replied to him. "No. Ashton will not be attempting to break the spell." She seemed so confident that I wanted to believe her, if for no other reason than it would mean I could live. That I might see my father again. Even if I was currently questioning the existence of these healers I had been promised.

Beckett stepped further into the hallway; head reared back at Ryana as if she had just slapped him. "I'm sorry, Vissorri. I hardly think that it is your call to make."

"Vissorri?" I whispered, sure, based on the natural way that Beckett said it, that it was her surname. But I had only known her as Ryana Vance.

Ryana finally tore her gaze from Beckett to give me another pleading look. "I will explain everything if you just stop trying to run away. Okay?"

Beckett's jaw had grown tense, his arms folded rigidly over his abdomen. "Please tell me why you think you will have more say than I in this matter?" If tone alone could have cut, his would have sliced her to the bone.

Ryana shifted her stare to Beckett, and although he was easily over a foot taller than her, she stared up at him as if she didn't care a bit, and I almost smiled at the reminder of her ferocity during the Ice Games. Almost. "It won't be your call to make when Oldenberg returns either."

So, whoever this Oldenberg was, they were a person, and obviously Beckett's superior too.

Another menacing laugh huffed from Beckett's mouth, his tongue pressing against the inside of his cheek. "Are you privy to some information that the General of the Light Kingdom somehow does not know?"

It was so obvious that he was talking about himself, which meant that Beckett was a general in this kingdom. If he hadn't been anticipating me, what was he doing in Demetros?

Ryana crossed her arms over her chest, a smug look of satisfaction on her face. "Actually, yes."

Even Josaphine, who had remained silently standing within the confines of the doorframe, flinched with surprise.

"Excuse me?" Beckett forced out through his clenched jaw.

Josaphine straightened herself and walked calmly between the two of them, a palm raised at both of their chests. "I think it is clear that we need to calm down until Oldenberg arrives to settle this herself."

Beckett was still seething, but as he glanced down at the woman before him, I could tell that some of the tension had receded, and Josaphine grinned as if she had noticed the same thing. "If Ryana has returned, I imagine that she has come with Grethe, and I, for one, am dying to see my boy."

My eyes widened as I looked to Ryana for confirmation that Grethe was also part of this. How deep did her, or their, deception go? Before I could determine what was true, I heard Beckett say, "We should return her to her room until Oldenberg arrives."

Fear latched onto my lungs, freezing them in place. Now that I knew about the consequences of breaking the spell they had brought me here for, that sounded like a good way for me to be trapped in my room until I was marched to my slaughter.

With careful, measured steps, I began to slowly back away from the group. The movement was noticed almost immediately by Ryana, who held her hands out like she was attempting to be less threatening to a wild animal.

"You don't need to run," Ryana said, the calmness in her tone a juxtaposition to her wide, nearly frantic eyes. "You are not going to break that spell, and you are not going to be locked in your room."

"Vissorri," Beckett drawled, irritation lining his tone again. "You cannot make such promises. We have a protocol—"

"I'm on orders from the Queen," Ryana interrupted, garnering the undivided attention from everyone in the hallway.

"Then I think it's time for that debrief," Beckett stated, throwing a thumb over his shoulder to point further down the hall.

"I'll fetch some snacks," Josaphine offered before hastily adding, "and send Grethe your way."

"Gianna's back too," Ryana replied, giving the estate manager a warm smile. "Better send her in as well." Her head swung to face me as she took a measured step toward me. "Let's give you that debrief, yeah?"

Twelve

"Where is my father?" I blurted out, my feet rooted to the spot. Josaphine had already left to go retrieve Grethe, whoever Gianna was, and food for us to snack on, but neither Beckett nor Ryana had seen fit to move until I did, the former eying me with an extra helping of skepticism.

Beckett dragged his palm across his face. "You invited a parent to The Light Kingdom? Ry…"

Ryana only rolled her eyes, letting them fall to me. "I sent someone from the network to deliver the message to him, but I would like to ask for Gianna's aid in confirming his approach."

"Vissorri," Beckett warned, narrowing his silver eyes in her direction. A repetition of that name I had never heard her use.

"Astor," she quipped, offering him a placating grin, "Don't worry, all will be revealed." It seemed lighthearted, but there was something troublesome in her expression, as if there might be a legitimate reason to have concern.

Ryana quickly brushed that comment off and all but bounded over to me, halting abruptly when she caught my scowl. Her face fell, but she mustered a half smile. "If you would follow me, we are going to take you to the meeting room. We cannot risk anyone overhearing these details."

Spurred on by curiosity and a need to confirm that Ryana was, in fact, going to ask whoever Gianna was for aid in finding my father, I silently agreed, offering her a small dip of my chin.

Ryana spun on her heel, glancing over her shoulder to make sure I was trailing her, before walking down the hall and toward the large stairwell. Beckett took his place behind me, and I tried not to consider that he had done so to thwart any chance of escape, but my heart pounded all the same as if the organ didn't quite believe that.

We ascended a flight of stairs before veering off down an unfamiliar hallway lined with more ornate paintings and plush, expensive rugs. The extravagance in this place was nothing short of extraordinary, and I wondered if I would come to learn more of how it came to be. Despite my curiosity, I kept my jaw clamped tightly shut as we meandered through the castle. My priority was my father.

We reached a door spaced away from the others, and Ryana entered without knocking. I followed her, stopping far enough inside to allow Beckett passage without committing fully to the room. Where I thought I might find devices of torture, I was met with what was indeed a meeting room.

A long ebony table spanned the majority of the space, bracketed by leather-clad chairs. In the far corner, a small, equally dark hutch stood watch, presumably prepared to host whatever food Josaphine was planning to bring us. The walls were painted a cream color that was a stark contrast to the borderline pitch-black furniture and wrought iron chandelier hanging overhead, but other than the minuscule hint of yellow in the paint, the room was void of any other color. There was no artwork on the wall or even a plush rug beneath the table. It was almost clinical.

"Please have a seat," Ryana said, gesturing to a chair two spaces away from the head seat. Maybe that was reserved for Gianna? Oldenberg? Perhaps the Queen she had mentioned.

Silently, I slipped into the leather chair, ignoring the way it creaked beneath my weight. Beckett took the seat next to mine, likely another precaution to deter my escape, and Ryana slid into the space directly across from me.

Before I could even open my mouth, Grethe's voice sounded from the doorway. "Mom, I promise I'm fine. I didn't even break a sweat in the last challenge."

Swiveling to face him, I caught the familiar sight of a lopsided smile and a mop of unruly blonde hair. Grethe's green eyes shifted to mine, and his grin almost became symmetrical. "Ashton! You made it!"

Josaphine pushed past him, placing a tray of snacks on the hutch in the corner, but I abandoned my investigation of those in favor of speaking to Grethe. "You're here too?" I asked, uncertain of whether I should be concerned that Biltons Academy has seemingly been infiltrated by... my eyes squinted, peering at Grethe's perfectly rounded ears.

He shrugged, plopping into the chair on the other side of Ryana, leaving the one beside the head open. "Surprise!" he said cheerfully.

This did nothing to appease my concern. For all I knew, he and Ryana were still wearing whatever masks they had worn when tricking me into being their friends.

Another figure walked into the room, closing the door behind her with a click, making me startle in my chair again, swinging around once more to face them. This woman was middle-aged, likely a similar age to Josaphine. She had bright blonde hair, tied at the nape of her neck in a tight bun, although a few wavy pieces had come loose. Her green eyes were almost hauntingly familiar.

"Mom!" Grethe called out as the woman approached the table.

She flicked her attention over to Grethe, giving him a terse smile that did not speak of the familiarity of that moniker. "Alcides," she said, nodding her chin in his direction before moving onto Ryana, "Vissorri. I hear we have a guest."

Without waiting for the response, the unnamed woman took the seat between the head of the table and Ryana, sweeping her gaze momentarily over mine before adding, "Is there a reason I am being called into this particular meeting?"

I had no reason to believe this, nor did I know her enough to assume with any evidence to support it, but something about the way she articulated her question made me feel like the woman suspected that I had been causing problems, rather than aiding in their quest to break this mysterious spell.

Ryana cleared her throat, dropping her hands into her lap. "Since you are all here, I'd like to start by saying that the circumstances that brought Ashton here were unusual and even I cannot reveal all the details until Oldenberg is present, so please do not ask me."

Everyone at the table seemed to pin Ryana with confused stares. Some, like Beckett, were sharper than others. Even Grethe appeared to be left out of whatever secret information Ryana possessed, causing him to be thoroughly put out, although not angry or skeptical in the way the unknown woman and my former escort looked.

Josaphine quietly dropped small plates of food in front of each of us, causing me to lose sight of Ryana as she continued. "Based on my assessment, it was imperative that Ashton be removed from Demetros quickly, so I called a code dragonfire to ensure her immediate escape."

"Right," the blonde woman said, already pushing away from the table as if she had been dismissed.

"Except," Ryana started, facing the woman now. "I hadn't had a chance to debrief her yet. At all."

The words hung there for a moment as the woman soaked them in. She raised a slender, pale eyebrow. "At all?"

"No," Ryana said, although her features were anything but sheepish. "And furthermore, her father will be joining us, and I was hoping you would send the swallows to confirm his whereabouts and—"

"Vissorri, this is way out of line," the woman snapped. "Bringing an unvetted girl into the kingdom? Offering refuge to her family? What has gotten into you? She has to be well past the timeframe to deliver a memory potion. This is incredibly reckless."

"My thoughts exactly, Alcides," Beckett muttered under his breath, but loud enough for me to hear every syllable.

The woman's face was becoming red and blotchy. Her mouth flew open as if to continue laying into Ryana when Josaphine placed a hand on her shoulder. "Gianna, why don't you give her some time to explain. I'm sure whatever she did on the Queen's orders was for good reason."

This gave the woman, presumably Gianna, pause. She rolled her lips together, her throat bobbing with an exaggerated swallow. "Please proceed," she muttered.

Ryana's head jerked down and back up, as if the sentence had been a command. "The Queen sent me on a mission in addition to my primary task in Demetros that she will have to explain herself. I was under strict orders not to tell a soul," she offered Grethe an apologetic smile. "And the details surrounding that are to remain classified until she returns."

Beside me, Beckett drew in a lung full of air. "Is there something you can tell us?"

The irony of his statement was almost enough to make me laugh. Now, he knew what that felt like.

But Ryana didn't share my humor. She only shook her head. "I called Gianna in to ask for the use of her swallows. Otherwise, I only intended this to be the debrief that I never got to have."

The woman, Gianna, stood from her chair slowly and part of me considered that she had done so in order to be looking down at Ryana when she said, "Forgive me for not blindly trusting your word but I will need confirmation from her majesty before I send my swallows to intercept an unvetted individual on his way to our kingdom."

Gianna made a face I couldn't see to Josaphine, before the two of them strode from the room together.

"Well, that could have gone better," Grethe said, a bit of his own humor returning. "I can't wait to hear all about this secret mission you were on though."

"Yeah," Beckett said wryly. "Me, either."

"All in due time," Ryana mumbled, staring at the door. She blinked a few times before her eyes came back into focus in my direction. "But first, let's do that debrief."

Thirteen

Ryana faced me, making sure to hold our eye contact. "I always start at the beginning," she said.

Beckett sniffed a laugh. "As opposed to?"

Although a scoff filtered through Ryana's lips, the accompanying rolling of her eyes was almost playful. She ignored him in favor of turning her attention fully on me. "With you, I think I might need to take a slightly different approach."

Beckett leaned back in his chair, folding his arms over one another. "Instead of starting at the beginning?" There was amusement in his tone, a teasing that came off oddly friendly.

I had to admit, even I was curious as to why she wouldn't start from the beginning, but instead of voicing those thoughts as inelegantly as Beckett had, I simply nodded.

"I'm Ryana Vissorri," she stated proudly, waving at me from across the table. "I adopted the use of Vance in order to ensure no one recognized my true last name. Which I usually get to later in the story, but I didn't want there to be any confusion."

I jerked my chin again, as if the whole thing made perfect sense, even though I was adequately confused.

"And I am Grethe Alcides," Grethe commented, with that typical lop-sided grin. "Alexander is my undercover name for the same reason."

My chin dipped once. "And you are undercover because?"

Ryana's chest expanded on a deep breath. "As you can see, Demetros is cut off from the rest of the continent, except, what you are taught is a natural occurrence and rough seas is actually due to a spell."

There was the mention of that spell again. My ears perked up along with my pulse. "The spell I am expected to die to break?" I asked flatly.

"Yes," she replied, eyes widening before she quickly corrected herself. "No. You won't be breaking that spell, but the reason for that is part of the classified information I cannot give."

An exasperated breath blew from Beckett's lips, drawing Ryana's attention to him. "Actually, what did you tell her?"

His returned glare was narrow-eyed. "I mentioned that Fae live in these lands, and that the code indicated she had multiple elements, but nothing more."

She turned to me for confirmation, and yet again, I bobbed my head lamely.

"Right," Ryana said slowly, as if she was calculating how to proceed. "So, what you need to know is that there are Fae and humans. We will get into the specifics of each Fae species at a later time, but the gist of it is that two hundred years ago, a human uprising caused war to rage across the continent."

My eyes flared wide. "The Great Conflict?"

"Yes," Ryana answered cautiously. "Only, what you know as a civil war spanned all three kingdoms."

This caught my attention. "Three kingdoms?"

With an almost nonchalant wave, Ryana swatted her hand at the air between us. "You'll learn all about the Dark Kingdom later. For now, just know that the war was ugly and came from the humans' desire to take Fae power."

I recalled what Beckett had said about the Fae who possessed all the elements and even a gift, remembering that he thought I might have Fae lineage considering the code and my alleged magic. "Power that you think I possess?" My tone was almost hopeful.

"Yes," she replied, with no elaboration. "When the humans lost, they, along with the Guides and the Elemental Queen, were banished by a powerful spell that stripped any remaining magic and their memories."

"It was a really powerful spell," Grethe chimed in. "It rewrote your history tomes and erased any mention of Demetros' true connection to the outside world."

I considered the fairytales I had read as a child, the mentions of Fae and other magical creatures as something obviously fantastical. The spell might have altered the texts, but it hadn't removed those ties completely. "And no one remembered anything?" I asked.

Ryana's marbled brown eyes cast downwards, almost as if she were ashamed of the confession. Like it was her burden to bear. "For a long time, we believed that Demetros was operating under leadership with no memories of their former lives. At least not in regard to the Light Kingdom. The spell tampered enough with the memories so that all mentions of other kingdoms should have been removed or altered."

My mind raced with the adrenaline that accompanied all this new information. "So, the Elemental Queen is truly that old? All the stories about her were true?" A shocked breath rippled from my chest. My eyes darted over the grooves of the wood beneath my palms until my thoughts skidded to a halt, my head snapping to Ryana's location. "You think that they remember, don't you?"

"Teams have been sent to monitor the situation in Demetros for many years; however, it is recently that we've come to suspect foul play," she replied, her stare falling to my forearm. "Demetros had been left to its exile for decades before anyone thought to check on it with more scrutiny. The Light Queen was new and eager to leave behind the evidence of the war."

I didn't realize I was gripping the table until the edge of it bit into my stomach as I leaned forward. "What's going on? What does this have to do with me?"

Ryana offered me a smile. "I'm getting there," she teased, before her expression returned to a more serious look. "More recently, it has come to our attention that the brands might not just be unlocking the bind on the citizens' powers but stealing them."

The air whooshed from my lungs as I sat back down in my seat, getting the sense that my face looked as dumbstruck as I felt.

"That's why they sent us," Grethe added, reminding me that he was still in the room. "We were meant to infiltrate the academy and determine the purpose of the brands. As well as try to get closer to the Elemental Queen by being named her heir."

My voice was hardly a whisper. "What did you find out?"

"That, I'm afraid, is classified," Beckett stated from beside me. I granted him one glower before twisting to confirm his decree with Ryana.

She gave me a wince of a smile before continuing. "But what I can tell you is that you should not be Operarius." Instantly, her features scrunched. "Although I am uncertain why they planned to brand you as such. It was the entire reason I had to get you out. It felt like you were being targeted..." Her words trailed off, surprise lined her expression as if she had accidentally said too much. Even though, from my perspective, she hadn't revealed anything I didn't already know.

Frustration was building up along my muscles again, and I had to cross my arms, squeezing tightly, in order to expel the tension somewhere other than my tone. "And my supposed power level has to do with the spell, because?"

"The spell has to be broken," Beckett replied. "It's pulling entirely too much from the land. Pure blooded Elemental Fae are being born without gifts, some even without all of the elements."

It made sense from a logical standpoint. I could conceptualize that a spell of that magnitude needed a source, and that it could hypothetically pull from the land or from its people, although I still didn't understand why I was crucial to this need. "And I am important..." My words trailed off because I didn't feel important. I still felt like that girl labeled Operarius in the ballroom, abandoned by one of the people I thought to be closest to me on the planet. Unloved and unworthy.

"You meet the criteria to break the spell," Beckett replied at the same time Ryana reiterated, "That will not be your concern."

Both of their heads snapped to each other in a synchronous, jarring movement.

Exasperation flared in Ryana's face. "I already told you; I have orders from the Queen."

"If she's the key to breaking the spell, I doubt the Queen will see any reason not to let her try," Beckett countered, those silver eyes constricted in Ryana's direction, rather than mine, the topic of his statement.

"Why would I be the key?" I asked, a bit impatiently. I needed to know what I was up against if I was going to decide if running was still my best option, especially with Gianna's refusal to send whatever a swallow was to find my father.

Ryana and Beckett were still having some sort of standoff with their eyes, so Grethe was the one who finally answered me. "The spell can only be broken by a child of both worlds."

"Human and Fae?" I surmised, suspecting they didn't truly mean another world was out there. I had only marginally accepted the idea of a singular other kingdom being within reach, I'd never wrap my mind around the concept of life beyond the stars.

Grethe moved his chin up and down to confirm my guess. "I think the idea was that if we had garnered enough peace to procreate again, then the spell could be lifted."

My brows furrowed as I contemplated my next words, although Ryana beat me to them.

"The magic of the spell needs a source to counter it. Records from those who helped put the spell in place have indicated the counter spell would deplete the source." Ryana's tone was far too calm for the news she just delivered.

I didn't realize I was standing until a warm palm was resting on my elbow. "Sit," Beckett commanded, although his voice was too gentle to be meant to be intimidating. It didn't matter; I was already shaking.

My hurt gaze found Ryana's, rather than give any of my attention to the man beside me. He didn't know me. He hadn't befriended me and earned my trust only to bring me here to die. He had only been following orders and escorting a stranger. Ryana on the other hand... "You brought me here to die?"

"No," Ryana replied, voice and eyes pleading.

The hand around my elbow squeezed, lowering me back into the chair with a slight pressure. "Those who are asked to break the spell are given a choice." Beckett's tone was steady and even, just as it had been in the Violet Forest. "We will not force anyone to do so against their will. Usually, people know all of this before they opt to cross the border."

I glanced over at him only to find that he was shooting daggers in Ryana's direction, adding to the insinuation in his pointed statement.

"Astor," Ryana warned.

"Ryana," Beckett countered, making me think that this was about more than orders. Were these people friends?

Clearing my throat, I kept my skeptical glare on Beckett until he turned back to face me. "So, you aren't going to force me to my death? Even if I am the key, as you say?"

Beckett's expression softened, but his lips remained a thin line, not even the hint of a bend present. "No. We will not force your hand, but you must understand how important this is." He let his stare momentarily flicker to Ryana before adding, "If the Guides and the Elemental Queen are scheming, it won't be long before we have another uprising on our hands. This says nothing of the draining of the magic in the lands and the issues ongoing on our northern border."

My mouth popped open to ask about that other border, presumably one shared with the previously mentioned Dark Kingdom, but Beckett continued before I had the chance. "No one is going to make you do this, but you would be saving countless lives if you considered it. You would be honoring the entire continent with your sacrifice."

The breath seemed to shudder in my lungs, coming out in a shaky gasp. My entire life, I had wanted to be worthy of my mother's sacrifice, and this—saving the continent from losing its magic and thwarting whatever schemes the Guides and the Elemental Queen were believed to be up to—might be the one thing I could actually do to make a difference.

"I'll consider it," I replied, ignoring Ryana's not-so-silent protests that I would not be asked to do this. "Under three conditions."

Beckett raised an eyebrow at me, shock filtering across his features as if he truly had not expected to win me over.

"I won't make any decision until I see my father," I said, holding my chin up regardless of the fear that blossomed within my chest at the mention of the man I had left behind. "And when he arrives, he is going to have the best healers available to him."

"And?" Beckett drawled, not exactly agreeing to my first two demands.

"I want to know everything, including whatever classified information Ryana found out in Biltons Academy. If I am going to sacrifice myself, I need to know as much information as I can before I make that decision." I thought my words came off as stern, maybe even harsh, so Ryana's sigh of relief was entirely out of place.

Beckett didn't look to Ryana for confirmation, leading me to solidify my suspicions that amongst them, he was in charge. A general, as he had already insinuated, didn't need permission from his subordinates to strike a deal. "I accept your terms," he said calmly, although something unreadable flashed in those silver eyes.

Only after I silently gestured my agreement did he turn his attention to Ryana and Grethe. "I'd like to hear the information from the two of you without her present. We will reconvene in the morning."

I opened my mouth in protest, but my words were stopped by Beckett's cold stare. "It's this or nothing," he supplied as if he held all the cards, and I was only here by his good graces.

His chin angled down as he peered at me. "I will talk to Gianna about sending her swallows as a show of good faith," he added, and tears of relief nearly sprang to my eyes. Banishing them away with several harsh blinks, I bit out the word, "Fine."

"In that case," Beckett said, pushing away from the table, "I will see you all tomorrow."

He didn't wait for goodbyes before leaving the room like a shadow pouring through the door.

"You took all of that surprisingly well," Grethe commented from the other side of the table, dragging my attention away from the empty threshold.

A shrug bounced my shoulders. "I never trusted the history of Demetros anyway."

That lopsided grin returned as Grethe tilted his head to the side. "Yeah, but that's a lot of information to just believe. And you seem so calm."

A humorless huff left my lips. "I never said I trusted you, just that I was willing to hear you out."

At my casual tone over my serious statement, the beginnings of a smile began to lift Ryana's lips. She stood, dragging Grethe to his feet as well. "I always knew you were a smart one," she said, offering me a smile that for the life of me felt genuine. I couldn't piece together a fragment of it that seemed out of place or worn like a mask. "How about we chat about less classified information over dinner?"

There it was again, that offer of answers that had me almost brimming with hope. My curiosity won out over my fears as I pushed away from the table and joined them in the hallway.

Ryana didn't loop her arm in mine, even though I could tell that she wanted to by the slight twitch in her fingers, but she did stand by my side as we traversed the hallway in silence. All the while, I compiled a list of questions that I desperately needed answers to.

Fourteen

ESTELLA

The memories that had returned to Estella were agonizingly clear. They made way for feelings that the Elemental Queen hadn't experienced in what felt like ages.

She was no longer nameless, but she felt like she was stranded in an unforgiving sea of all the emotions that accompanied her recollections.

Loneliness. Grief. Despair. Anger. Hate.

Surprisingly, joy was sprinkled in there too. She could finally remember being truly happy. Not just the memory of the emotion, but that aching feeling of longing that took over her chest when she recounted an unlocked memory. Longing to be back inside the images, to be that girl once again.

It felt like breathing fresh mountain air after living in a damp cave for years.

The mirth that flooded her in those moments was shadowed with another emotion. Fear.

The Elemental Queen had been born in an age when her magic had not been a threat. The kingdoms all lived in harmony, and she hadn't been considered an abomination in her youth. She was the product of a half-human father and a Fae mother. In retrospect, it was possible that she just hadn't noticed under the perception of a carefree child.

She had elemental powers and a gift, rare for those in Demetros, but not completely unheard of. In the beginning, she thought her magic had been revered, cherished even.

It wasn't until she had gotten older that she could finally recognize the tension lacing those youthful memories. Instead of bright smiles, she began receiving angry glares as she passed neighbors and former friends on the street.

She couldn't recall the moment that the atmosphere shifted around her, but her adolescence had been plagued with this unrest. A growing hatred between the Fae and humans. She was neither and both at the same time, and this had confused her.

Even now, she did not understand how fear had morphed into hate, but eventually she became obsessed with it. Looking for it on every face she passed.

Because of that, she had spent too much time watching the shadows for an attack when she should have been watching her friends and her supposed allies. For it was not an enemy with a sharpened blade that had taken her freedom from her, but a companion with a comforting smile.

The returned memories did nothing to indicate how much time had been lost since her initial imprisonment. So much of her days since being sequestered into this room had been a blur of loneliness and sporadic visits from her captors.

Those visits were becoming more frequent, now. Even with a loose concept of time, she knew this with certainty.

They had tried to talk to her without removing the bind on her voice but had left flustered and irritated each time. She knew it was only a matter of a few more discouraging *conversations* before they were forced to let her speak.

They were clearly up to something and while she knew she held minimal power here, she had just enough to gain a foothold. That's all she needed. Information could be just as powerful as magic.

A man barged into her room, causing the door to bang against the wall as the two collided. He held a small vial in his gnarled, spotted hands. "I brought you something," the man said politely, although she knew that it would not be a kindness.

Estella shook her head, not even able to utter a hum of disagreement at the prospect. Sighs and gasps could escape her lungs, but her vocal cords refused to react to the same movement of air.

"I've known you a long time," the man said, still traversing the room with that vial in his hand. "I can tell that your view of me has shifted. It is obvious that your memories are returning."

Of course they had altered her perception of him. She remembered every agonizing minute that he had carved his blade against her flesh, marking her with the runes that stole her magic and left her powerless. She didn't want to feel powerless again.

Wide-eyed, Estella scrambled off her settee, not wanting to lose the fragile hold she had on her past. She glanced over her shoulder at the balcony doors. In all her time here, she had never considered flinging herself to the rocks below, but the idea of giving up a single inch of the advantage that had presumably taken her years to gain back was inconceivable.

"Relax, Estella," the man said, obviously noting her train of thought. "This will only aid in your compliance. It is imperative that you recall your past."

Her eyes narrowed almost imperceptibly at him. For a moment, she considered that he might be trying to help her, but she had recalled more than just one instance of his betrayal, and she refused to back down.

Her slippers slid silently on the bare floor as she made to take another step back.

The man sighed heavily. "Freeze," he commanded. Her body obeyed, even as her mind thrashed at the words.

He shook his head as if having to use this magic on her was an inconvenience.

Estella's body leaned on her back foot, leaving her fearful that she might topple over, but she feared the man before her more.

He slowed his steps, as if he were purposefully drawing out the experience for her. He didn't stand in front of her, where her eyes might have caught his expression. Instead, he lingered outside of her periphery.

Clammy fingertips brushed along her lips, and her stomach heaved inside her body. "Open," he commanded, and her jaw hinged to oblige him.

Her lips separated, and the glass rim of the vial pressed against her mouth. The contents poured down the back of her throat.

"Swallow." His words brushed against her neck as her throat bobbed against her will.

Whatever was inside that vial made her feel lucid. Her vision went hazy as if she was gliding through a dense fog, and her limbs felt on the edge of numbness.

If she hadn't been frozen and mute, she would have screamed.

He waited until her eyelids slammed shut before he spoke. "You may move again."

Her body slumped to the floor in a heap, too weak to drag herself to the nearby settee.

"I hate to have to use this on you," the man admitted, although even in her haze, Estella doubted the validity of that. Another sigh rattled through his chapped lips. "Unfortunately, I don't have the power to force the truth from you. Only to make small physical commands, so we will continue like this until we find what you have been hiding."

There were several bits of information that Estella picked up on through his statements, none of which he had meant to give her. One, he didn't have the power to force her to tell the truth, which meant she could lie. Additionally, and perhaps most important of all, her captors needed something from her.

The swish of a robe indicated the man was walking away, his voice growing more distant as he spoke. "We will be back, and hopefully, you will be more compliant when we return."

The earth seemed to tilt beneath her, even though she was still lying on the ground, so she clamped her eyes shut. It didn't change how easily she felt her captor's words, like an unwanted finger tracing the line of her spine.

The shuffling of retreating feet paused, and even with her eyelids closed, she sensed the man's attention on her. "There is someone we need to ask you about."

She didn't know what he could possibly mean, but it felt monumental. More so than the other tidbits he had let slip. She gripped onto that word; certain it was crucial somehow.

Someone. Someone. Someone.

The word repeated itself in her mind like a chant or a prayer, drumming up a hope in her that when she opened her eyes again, she'd remember that there was someone out there waiting for her.

Someone.

Fifteen

Because Biltons Academy was the closest I had ever been to a castle's dining hall, I had expected something similar from Castle Lochmere. A vast open space, filled with tables and void of décor. What I found instead was a room that, despite its large size, felt cozy and lived in.

There were enough tables to host about half the number of people that Biltons could accommodate, and every single one of them was lined with emerald runners and decorated with evergreen branches and warm, flickering candles.

The room itself boasted thick wooden columns, carved with intricate leaves and vines that climbed to the ceiling where the foliage met grand arching beams. A gilded chandelier hung from the center of the room, surrounded by a halo of smaller replicas, all of them laden with glittering gemstones in shades of green that reminded me of a lush garden.

"This is the dining hall," Grethe offered, as if I needed the confirmation. It was possible that he was just trying to fill the silence that I had created, so I smiled at him anyway.

Ryana and Grethe walked to a table toward the center of the room, which was somewhat smaller than the others but somehow felt important because of its differing size. Around us, only two other tables had occupants at all, and as my gaze passed over them, I considered it odd that a room of this grandeur had so few people gathering at what I could only assume was a mealtime.

I was not introduced to any of the strangers as Ryana ushered me to a seat before walking to the other side of the table to take the chair opposite mine. Grethe followed her, brushing against her shoulder as he sat, and I moved my question relating to the two of them slightly higher amongst my growing lists.

Servers in solid grey attire scuttled from the shadows of the far edge of the room, some holding goblets and others carrying pitchers. In the blink of an eye, I had both water and wine to choose from, and the workers had disappeared before I could utter a thank you.

Choosing the water, I turned my attention back to Ryana, considering how I might word my first question for a moment before I spoke. "Is there an update on the botany instructor?"

She knew what I was asking, and I hoped it didn't cross over into that classified information I had to wait until tomorrow to learn. Mr. Higgins was, to my knowledge, the biggest threat to my father's safety. If he were contained, at least I'd collect a modicum of comfort around my father's lack of presence within the castle.

A sigh sawed its way from Ryana's mouth before her stare arced around us. The servers were nestled back into the shadows at the perimeter of the room, and the handful of people seated at the surrounding tables were far enough away that I didn't think they would overhear our conversation, even if one of them, a curly haired boy a few years my junior, was staring at me.

"The potion kept him from recalling your altercation," Ryana replied. "That should be enough for now."

This was not the news I had wanted to hear, and the precise reason I had asked this question first. "What do you mean, that *should* be enough?"

"There are other things at play right now," Ryana hissed, leaning across the table so as not to garner any more attention than we already had.

My arms folded over my chest. "Other things? More important than the safety of my father?"

"Classified things," She replied, her eyes practically begging me to drop it.

There was no way I was letting this go. I was already pushing to standing, ready to leave the entire castle behind, when Grethe blurted out, "Berit was important."

At the sound of my attacker's name, I stilled. Cold dread coursed through my veins. It didn't matter how hard I had worked to move past what had happened to me in the woods, the reminder of him caught me off guard, practically thrusting me back into that moonlit slice of the forest. Twigs snapping beneath me, leaves plastered in my hair.

"His family really was important, and someone anonymous let slip that he and Mr. Higgins were in communications," Grethe added, careful not to say Berit's name again. The fact that Grethe had noted my reaction was enough to shame me into lowering my eyes to the floor.

"I destroyed the evidence of your interactions with the instructor so nothing can be traced back to you, but we thought it was better to distract him than take him out," Ryana said, her voice almost a whisper.

Only with her confession did I let my gaze slide back to her as I slipped back into my chair. "He's going to pay for his crimes?"

Ryana's throat bobbed with a rough swallow. "That is the hope. And you will be left out of it, so no one goes looking for you. He would only be incriminating himself to bring you up. Especially since you are technically missing."

Ryana's words seemed to ring true, and her logic was sound. It would be far too suspicious to have an instructor go missing rather than have him so bogged down by an investigation that he wouldn't have the time to pursue my father. At least not until it was too late.

Her last sentence was a perfect segue into my next question, considering there wasn't much else I could tease from the Mr. Higgins situation. "What does the school think? About my departure?"

My change of subject didn't seem to faze either of them, but it was Grethe who replied first, as if they had rehearsed this inevitable question. "The headmaster made a general announcement that some of the students labeled Operarius on that sheet had opted to return home rather than be branded."

I had heard stories that in the earlier days of the branding, powerless individuals could opt to remain unmarred, as the ink served mostly as a symbol of their lack of magic, but I hadn't met anyone over the age of twenty whose skin had not been marked by those triangles. Somewhere along the line, the monarchy had decided to keep the class designation a secret until after the ceremony. Meaning, everyone would be branded, and you wouldn't know your class until you gained consciousness again afterwards.

Still, my brows pinched together as I considered the full picture. "And no one seemed confused by that statement? They haven't let people go unbranded in decades, maybe even centuries."

"The branding ceremony stole most of the attention," Ryana replied swiftly. "But we didn't catch any rumblings that the story of your departure wasn't believed by the academy instructors or the headmaster. In fact, I doubt they send anyone to search for you. It didn't seem like a big deal."

Relief was not the emotion coursing through my veins, but I wasn't sure how to put into words what else I wanted to know without sounding pathetic. Had Jemma or even Cade thought to worry about my sudden disappearance? Perhaps the latter might have considered that I would leave without saying goodbye, but my best friend should have known better.

Toying with the stem of my wine glass, I let my gaze fall to that movement instead of meeting anyone's stare. "Jemma didn't seem bothered?"

The pause between my question and Ryana's response was far too long, and I peered at her from over the edge of the wine glass only to find her face contorted in a frown. "It appeared that she believed the story. She said she knew how much it meant for you to be powerful, and she supposed she didn't blame you for leaving."

The answer sounded plausible but also rehearsed. Like there was something more I was missing. My eyes constricted as I searched Ryana's face for a sign as to what she might be hiding, but the movement of Grethe's hand, resting on top of her shoulder, snagged my attention away.

There was no time like the present to move away from the depressing thoughts of Jemma's reaction and onto my third question on the list. "What are you two to each other?" My gaze lingered on Ryana. "You said you had a boyfriend back home, but the two of you were always sneaking around."

A braying laugh sounded from Grethe's lips. "I thought we were more inconspicuous than that," he confessed, the apples of his cheeks splotched with the slightest hint of pink.

My head shook back and forth. "Not really, no," I replied. "Although, now I'm wondering if it was all schemes and not an affair."

Grethe laughed again. "Can you even have an affair with your bonded?" There was so much affection behind the look he gave Ryana that I considered averting my gaze to give them a moment of privacy.

Instead, I tilted my head. "Bonded?"

Grethe's expression turned almost sheepish as he shrugged. "It's kind of like being married for humans but magically."

"You're married?" I sputtered, wondering what else I had yet to learn about them.

Ryana rolled those marbled brown eyes before pinning them to me. "It's not the same, but yes, our life forces are bound together."

A grimace twisted my features. "I know little of the magic here, but that sounds... painful?"

A lilting laugh tumbled from Ryana's parted lips. "It wasn't. Not for us, anyway."

"It's incredibly over the top and completely unnecessary," a familiar voice said, before occupying the chair beside me. Beckett's presence seemed to suck the air from my lungs. Not really fear but perhaps worry that his sudden appearance was going to keep me from having my questions answered.

As if his entrance triggered the servants to move, plates of food were placed in front of us, stealing my moment to ask him what he meant.

Rather than try to see my way around the flurry of motion, I focused on my plate. The design on the porcelain dish was covered by the mounds of beans, some sort of fowl, and what I believed to be purple carrots. With the closest fork, I pushed the carrot suspiciously around on the plate before committing to try it, chewing slowly until I determined that I did, in fact, appreciate the flavors.

"Not all of us see it as a death sentence like you," Grethe said when the plates had all been set down and the grey-clad staff had all returned to the perimeter. Surprisingly, there was a teasing in his tone that told me that he hadn't truly taken offense at Beckett's statement.

"So, what is the point of it?" I asked. "Why not just get married?" A blush instantly crept up my throat and over my cheeks as I realized that I knew nothing about their culture and that might have been wildly offensive.

If it was, Grethe took it in stride, letting his grin lift at the corners of his mouth as he looked to Ryana, rather than to me, to answer the question. "I wanted to be tied to her in every way I could be. There was no part of me that I wouldn't share with her, and it just felt right."

I half expected Beckett to scoff, but he only took a bite of his food as if he wasn't moved by that declaration. Maybe it wasn't the first time he had heard it, but for me, something in my chest swelled.

"That's romantic," I said, although my tone betrayed a bit of my jealousy, despite my efforts not to let it show. "Is that the norm here, rather than simply exchanging vows?"

"No," Beckett said, shaking his head. "Only for those who are fools."

My head whipped in Beckett's direction, ready to chastise him for the rude comment, but a smile was lifting the corner of his lips.

Grethe scoffed. "It comes with some pretty cool perks though," he countered, turning to me. "We can share our magic, and I get to sense her emotions when they're heightened. It's like having a mood ring for her in here." He shoved his pointer finger against his chest.

"You can share magic?" I asked, pushing past the absolutely smitten look on Grethe's face when he mentioned sharing emotions. That seemed far too intimate to ask anything further on.

"Not fully," Grethe replied, "But at least partially."

My eyes squinted as I took them in. "Are you both Fae?"

Momentarily, Ryana looked confused, until her fingers moved

along the upper curve of her ear. "Oh, that." In a blink, her ears were pointed again. "Yes, Grethe and I both have elemental powers and a gift."

Suddenly, I wasn't able to look at the man beside me, knowing full well what his gift was and not wanting to draw any more attention to my thoughts on the matter. Instead, I cleared my throat, begging my voice not to betray me. "What are your gifts?"

Grethe puffed his chest in the air. "Mine is strength!" A wince threatened to twist my expression as I recalled the sound of snapping bones during Grethe's last match in the challenge. His confession seemed to be corroborated by that memory.

"I have the ability to detect and manipulate energy," Ryana stated, "Which is why I was sent to Biltons Academy. Once we figured out something was going on with those brands—"

"Vissorri," Beckett interjected, almost lazily reminding her that this was classified information.

My shoulders slumped at the realization that my concerns about Beckett's presence had come to fruition.

"She's going to be cleared," Ryana replied, somewhat defiantly.

"That's up to me to decide after I hear whatever information you need to relay," Beckett stated with a firm tone.

Ryana gifted Beckett with a placating smile.

"Anyway," Ryana continued around a bite of her fowl. "I can sense power levels from a distance, which is how I knew you would be powerful, but I do need to be closer to determine the individual magic. Usually through touch."

"That's really fascinating," I replied, truly in awe and unable to even wrap my mind around what to ask on the subject. Magic outside of the elemental powers I knew in Demetros was so foreign to me, I couldn't even fathom the limitations.

My focus shifted to Grethe as I considered their shared powers. "Do you have that same ability?"

A shrug lifted both of Grethe's shoulders in unison. "It's not as intense as Ry's, and she's had a lot more years to practice, but I get a little tingle when someone nearby is incredibly powerful."

"So, I make you tingle?" Beckett asked, his smirk on full display.

Grethe pointed his fork in Beckett's direction. "This is not about you; we are teaching Ashton about our Kingdom and our powers."

"Just admit it, Alcides. You tingle when I walk into the room." Beckett was practically gloating, and I let myself grin at their exchange. He was so different with Ryana and Grethe than he had been with just me, but perhaps that just spoke to their familiarity.

Grethe rolled his eyes, spearing some beans onto the fork with exaggerated stabs. "I can feel you the same as I can feel her," he replied, nodding his head in my direction. "You're not that special, Astor."

Beckett slid his palm to his chest. "And here I was thinking you only perked up for me. I am wounded."

"I'm sure your pride will survive the blow," Ryana deadpanned.

"Anyway," Grethe interrupted, that lopsided grin tilting his smile. "There is one other cool part about the bond."

I wanted to soak in everything I could learn about this place and the magic that I might one day have. So, although I tried to keep the excitement from my tone, I knew the moment the words came out that I had failed. My elbows dug into the table, my fork long abandoned, as I leaned forward to collect whatever information Grethe was about to offer. "What's that?"

"If she dies," Grethe said, throwing a thumb over his shoulder, "the bond can save her life."

The magic of the Light Kingdom was all so new that none of it should have surprised me. But this, what sounded like resurrection magic, was incredibly fascinating, almost to the point of being terrifying. "How?" I asked, nearly breathless.

"I mean, there are *rules* to it," Grethe said in a huff, as if said rules or resurrecting someone from the dead were nothing more than a slight annoyance. He started raising fingers as he spoke, like each rule had its own assigned number. "First, I, or the surviving partner, cannot be mortally wounded."

"Second," he added, with a grimace, "There has to be an intact body to return to."

A horrified expression crossed my face. "What?"

"She can't be burned to death or chopped up into little pieces or—"

"I get it," I interrupted, not wanting to picture anyone I knew in that condition. I hadn't even had the courage to give a once over to Berit's dead body, and he had tried to kill me. Arguably, he had deserved his fate, but that hadn't meant I wanted to see the outcome of his karma.

"That's it though," Grethe said, nonchalantly. "As long as those conditions are met, she can't die while bonded to me."

"That's... wow," I muttered, collecting my thoughts. "That is intense."

"See," Beckett stated, taking a turn to point his empty fork at Grethe. "Unnecessary."

"I didn't say that," I argued, not wanting to offend the couple. "I think for their line of work, it makes perfect sense."

"Really?" That scarred eyebrow rose to Beckett's hairline. "You would bond yourself to someone else. Be forced to live in the swamp of their feelings?" He said the last word like it was a bitter thing in his mouth, even his lips twisted.

There had been someone I had considered sharing a life with, even allowed myself to visualize it when I had assumed it to be a real possibility. Maybe Beckett knew that, sensed it from the little bits of information I had given about Cade during our journey here. If that was true, his statement was almost cruel.

"I think that if they love each other and see those things as benefits, then it's beautiful," I said, glancing sideways at Ryana, uncertain if I was defending her more or my own ridiculous belief in the idea of love. The possibility that there might be someone out there for me who looked to me the way Grethe just gazed at Ryana. The way my father must have looked at my mother.

"The resurrection thing is arguably amazing," I added, letting my glare fall back on Beckett, daring him to mock them further.

When I found a curious expression on his face rather than the smirk I had suspected I'd find, I averted my attention back to my purple carrots, taking another tentative bite.

"Well, I'll leave that kind of connection for the romantics," Beckett said, and I didn't miss the insinuation in his tone nor his inflection on the word *romantics* like we—like they—were some diseased group.

"Good thing you'll never have to be put in such a position," Grethe countered, one edge of his lips tilted upwards. "I'd hate for you to enjoy whatever union Ebus and Onyx see fit for you in the future."

It wasn't difficult to conclude that those people were likely his parents, but it seemed invasive for me to ask about it. To them, I was here to break a spell, and for me I just wanted to learn as much information as I could so that I could make a decision on that front when my father arrived.

Ryana must have caught something in my expression because she added, "Ebus and Onyx are Beckett's parents." There was a look on her face that told me all I needed to know about the couple. If I could still read Ryana as well as I once had, I was certain she was not a fan.

Beside her, Grethe cringed. "The Astors will likely arrange a marriage for Becks over here." He shook his head, pity lining his features. "Poor girl."

Despite myself, I burst out laughing, clapping my hand over my mouth to muffle the sound.

Ignoring my outburst, Beckett smiled warmly toward Grethe. "Watch yourself, Alcides, you almost sound jealous." He winked in Grethe's direction, which only brightened both of their smiles.

"They're always like this," Ryana said to me in a commiserative tone. "You get used to it eventually."

There was much about their hierarchy here that I didn't understand, but it was clearer than ever that these people had a relationship outside of their organization. "You are friends?" I asked all of them, and none of them in particular.

"Those two have been friends most of their lives," Ryana replied before either of the men could respond. "They met when they were young, teenagers maybe? It was a while ago."

Considering I had been a teenager only two years prior, the statement struck me as odd. "How old are you?" My attention shifted to Beckett, either by habit or some subconscious notion that he was the holder of the information, the final say in whether or not I got to learn it.

"Beckett is really old," Grethe blurted out. "Like, ancient." His eyed widened almost comically as a pleased smirk was lobbed in Beckett's direction.

My attention snapped back to Beckett just as he groaned. His eyes closed and his head shook, but he did not elaborate on Grethe's statement further.

I took in the sharp lines of his face, his full lips, that scar that bisected his eyebrow, yet didn't seem to be flanked by any wrinkles. At most, I'd put him in his early thirties, but even that was a stretch as there were no grays in his beard or hair. Only the silver of his eyes, which were pinned on me.

"He's like two hundred years old," Grethe said through a laugh.

Beckett's eyes left mine to cut to Grethe. "I'm hardly much older than you," he replied flatly.

Grethe chuckled, clearly pleased with himself. "He's one hundred and seventy-two," he stated, smiling at me before swinging his focus back to Beckett. "Or is it one hundred and seventy-three?"

I expected to turn to Beckett to find him rolling his eyes, but when I peeked at him, he had returned to collecting some chicken on his fork. "Somewhere around there."

"You're serious?" I stammered. If playing jokes on me was going to be a regular occurrence, and Grethe was planning to be a part of it, I was going to find myself scarce at these gatherings.

Those quicksilver eyes turned to me as Beckett chewed on his latest bite. When he swallowed, he took one gulp of his wine, and only then did he deign to reply. "My parents aren't big on celebrating birthdays, so I'm a little fuzzy on the year. I usually round down because it makes me feel better," he said, casting a dirty look to Grethe.

"Ha ha ha," I said, mocking laughter. "Nice try. I am done falling for your games."

"He's not lying," Ryana interjected. "Fae live a really long time. I'm one hundred and thirty-two."

My jaw hinged open.

"And I'm one hundred and sixty-eight," Grethe stated, practically beaming as if it were some accomplishment. Perhaps it was.

"But you all look so young?" My statement came out as more of a question as my eyes darted around the room.

"Well, Fae age slower once they reach maturity," Ryana stated. "Our lifespans vary with numerous factors, but it would not be uncommon for Fae to live to three or four hundred years old. Longer if they are related to the old monarchs."

"The Gods," Beckett corrected. "They are the reason that the Elemental Fae have gifts."

"It is a popular belief that there were immortal monarchs from long ago that gifted the Fae their magic," Ryana said, almost cautiously. "The royal lines that descend from those immortals do live longer, but it could just be genetic since the crowns pass by blood."

"Like our old gods in Demetros?" I inquired, wondering how much of those texts had been altered by the spell.

Beckett only shrugged in response as if he didn't care either way.

"One and the same," Ryana replied.

Considering this new piece of information as fact, I turned it over in my mind. If I was supposed to have Fae blood in order to break the spell, and there had been others like me, then... "But no one in Demetros lives that long except the Elemental Queen and her Guides."

"Your Queen is part Fae, and her crown must have protected her from the aging aspect of the spell," Beckett replied almost carelessly. "Her Guides are an abomination."

My curiosity was multiplying like the mice in Elmhaven that could take over the grain stores and consume everything in sight. With a deep breath, my mouth flew open, a fresh wave of questions sitting on the tip of my tongue which were halted when Beckett said, "That's enough history lessons for tonight."

There was a hint of a warning in his tone, like maybe I was teetering too close to that classified information I wasn't supposed to know again, and only because we were in a public gathering hall did I hold my tongue.

I finished my meal, the three of them making small talk while my mind whirled. My thoughts kept circling around that one word: abomination. It told me that there was still so much more I had left to learn about not only the magic of the Light Kingdom, but the magic of the entire world outside of Demetros. So much had been hidden from us, and there was so much left to uncover.

Sixteen

When I was asked to stay in my rooms for the morning while Beckett had his official debrief with Ryana and Grethe, I nearly growled in frustration. That was, until Ryana handed me a worn book that I recognized instantly. Emotion clogged my throat as I glanced down at one of the tomes that I had taken with me to Biltons Academy. Back when I had been worried that I'd need to reread the words for the hundredth time to provide myself comfort during my first true separation from my father.

"I couldn't get them all," she confessed with a frown. "But I got the one on top. I thought it wouldn't be too suspicious if you ran off in the middle of the night with one book in tow."

"Did you bring anything else?" I asked, hopeful she had also grabbed the necklace Jemma had gifted me. My heart still ached at the thought of leaving that crescent pendant, and her, behind.

Ryana shook her head, and although it looked like she might have had more to say, the only words that came from her mouth were, "No. I'm sorry."

"Don't be," I replied. "I'm grateful for this." To prove the statement, I curled my arms around the book like I was giving it the hug I so desperately needed.

"I thought this could keep you company while we wrap up. You're not confined to the room, but without a guide, I don't know how much fun it will be to roam around the castle." Her tone was light-hearted, but I suspected that it would be more trouble if I chose to wander.

With the promise she'd return as soon as possible, we shared good-byes and Ryana departed. By the time she came back for me, Josaphine had brought me lunch, and I had skimmed through the majority of my book. I had been expecting to have this formal talk in the same meeting room from the previous day, instead, Ryana led me to a new much cozier space.

The walls on the far side had enormous wooden shelves, heavy with books. Leather-clad sofas had been placed atop a plush green rug with various flowers woven into its surface. Oversized chairs faced an ornate fireplace against one wall, and across the room, a nook played host to a hexagonal table where Beckett and Grethe were playing a friendly game of cards.

Even from an outsider's perspective, it all looked like a typical Demetros afternoon. The only thing out of place in all of this was the almost agreeable expression plastered on Beckett's face.

"Hi, boys," Ryana said, not even bothering to pause before she crossed the room and plopped into a vacant seat.

Attempting to act nonchalant, I followed suit, slipping into the last open chair while Beckett laid a card onto the middle of the table. It was a crimson dragon, curling around a blood red moon. This was a game I had never seen before.

"Game," Beckett announced.

Grethe grumbled, and he tossed his remaining cards to the pile beside Beckett's dragon, as a series of mutterings too quiet to decipher spilled from his lips.

"Perfect timing then," Ryana said, amusement lilting her tone.

It was only with this disruption that Beckett finally gave her his full attention. "You want to play in the next round?"

She offered him a look that said he knew exactly why she was there. "Nice try, but I think it's time to have the rest of that discussion with Ashton."

Beckett's nostrils flared as if the idea of that was bothersome to him, but he turned his focus to me. "I suppose so."

For a moment, all I could do was blink at him, waiting for him to say anything else.

Sensing this or just recognizing I didn't know what to ask, he sighed. "I have spoken to Gianna, and she has agreed to send the swallows to your cottage. Ryana has already relayed the necessary details, and they have departed. They should return in a few days with news of your father."

The confirmation that someone would be looking for my dad made me happy, but I was still confused. "What are the swallows?"

Ryana's mouth fell open like she planned to reply to me, but Beckett cut her off. "All you need to know is that they are members of the team that can quickly get in and out of Demetros to relay news and messages. Past that, it has nothing to do with you."

My lips remained pressed together because, although I wanted to know more, I would rather learn the information that did pertain to me than be shut out because I pushed my luck to satisfy my curiosity.

"Luckily for all of us," Beckett stated, "the swallows should return around the same time Oldenberg is expected to arrive. Therefore, we should *all* be getting the answers to our questions at the same time."

I thought he might be done, but he lobbed Ryana with a scathing glare. "I'm so interested to learn why the Queen sent my subordinate on a secret mission without my knowledge."

Ryana replied with a hesitant smile as if she wasn't confident that Beckett would get exactly what he wanted from his interaction with Oldenberg, but all she said was, "Okay."

Beckett's eyes narrowed like he had drawn the same conclusion but rather than halting the conversation, he waived his hand in the air. "Go on."

I could sense something was still off by the way Ryana nervously shuffled the cards while she spoke, but it was easy to chalk it up to the topic when she said, "There's no easy way to say this, but we believe that the brands are siphons."

She paused her speech and the shuffling of the cards to meet my stare. "It is the reason I did not go to your father myself. I had to see where the energy stream led." Her eyes were heavy with an apology that she did not voice, but given the insight to what they had discovered, I couldn't say I didn't understand why her priority had not been my father.

In fact, nothing I had learned in this meeting seemed like information an outsider should know, so I drank it in, thankful they appeared to be holding up their end of the bargain. If I was being asked to sacrifice myself for the greater good, this was the kind of knowledge that would sway my decision. "What do you mean by siphons?" I asked, understanding the basic principle, but not how it related to our brands.

There was no hesitation as Ryana answered. "The brands are said to unlock your magic, but a spell can do that," Ryana replied. "The brands themselves seem to be part of a permanent spell that, for lack of a better word, sucks the magic from the host and sends it elsewhere."

I gaped at her. "All of the brands?"

Ryana gave me a reluctant smile. "Based on the energies I sensed at Biltons, I believe that a large portion of the students have multiple elemental powers. Some may even possess a gift. Once the brands were in place, I could still sense them, but they were all considerably weakened."

A breath whooshed from my lungs as my fingertips instinctively traced a line over the spot where my brand would have been if I had stayed in Demetros. Realization felt like a slap across the face as I trained my stare to the location under the table where Ryana's arms were resting. "Did they brand you?"

"Yes," she replied, holding up her arm to reveal a Flumen symbol. In the next blink, the brand was gone and all I could do was stare at her speechless.

Ryana smiled, recognizing my panic. "I broke the spell after I followed the trail of the siphoned magic to the Elemental castle. I put this in place afterwards." Before my eyes, the Fluman brand returned, as if I had imagined its disappearance.

My brows furrowed. "I thought you could only detect energies. Or manipulate them. You have illusions too?"

With that same quarter smile, Ryana shook her head, gesturing toward her forearm. "Well, technically, it's just manipulation of minerals and water. Over time, you find different ways to utilize the elemental gifts."

Immediately, my thoughts went back to my father and his unusual use of Flumen abilities. Was it possible that he had access to more? That his ingenuity with water was just a sleight of hand?

Mentally, I shook myself away from those thoughts, focusing on the ones I could ask. It was hard to decide exactly where to go next, but the destination of the stolen magic seemed like a good place. "The magic led you to the Elemental castle?"

Grethe replied in Ryana's place. "We believe that the Guides and the Elemental Queen have been stealing magic from the people for centuries."

The brands had been around for almost as long as our history books had reported the tales of our past. Although, based on recent events, I knew that those tomes couldn't be entirely trusted, no one alive remembered a time when they were not part of our ability to utilize our powers. Knowing what I knew about the exile spell and it being the genesis of Demetros citizens being blocked from their magic, it wasn't difficult to leap to conclusions. "Do you believe the Queen and her Guides never lost their memories?"

Ryana seemed pleased with my assessment, offering Beckett an expression I couldn't ascertain. "That is the current theory. It explains why the brands appeared almost immediately after the exile began."

I frowned, not even giving myself a moment to relish in being correct because the truth of it was so distressing. "What is the Elemental Queen even doing with all that magic?"

"That's why we have to go back," Grethe began before Beckett cleared his throat pointedly. Whatever Grethe was about to say, was, once again, teetering toward the line I wasn't allowed to cross.

"I still can't believe she would do this to her own people," I said, letting my gaze fall back to my arm. "Does this mean my powers are trapped until I return to Demetros? Will I have to go back to the academy?" My skin itched where the brand should be, as if my confined magic was pressing along the surface, begging to be released at the mention of it.

"That, I can help with," Ryana stated proudly. In fact, the smile along her face was bordering on giddy. "We can remove it today, if you'd like."

For unknown reasons, my focus shifted to Beckett, surprise widening my eyes. "You're letting me have my magic?"

"You'll need your magic for a counter spell," he replied, flatly. Even his silver eyes looked dulled as he spoke, and I couldn't help but wonder what was going through his mind. Was he angry that he had been left out of the Queen's plans? Was there something else about me that was bothering him? It was like I was getting two sides of him—the rogue in Demetros and the General in the Light Kingdom—and I wasn't sure which I preferred. Which I should prefer.

Attempting to shift my focus away from his mercurial moods, I forced my gaze back to Ryana. "When?"

Grethe hit his hands on the table, eyes alight with glee. "I have an idea."

Ryana laughed, and out of the corner of my eye, I caught the edge of Beckett's mouth twitch.

"We can do it tonight. At the pools!" Grethe exclaimed, his gaze darting around the table as he waited for the rest of us to join in on his exuberance.

Beckett rolled his eyes but said nothing.

Ryana shook her head and huffed another laugh through a full smile. "Fine. She needs to eat first anyway." Her stare slid to mine. "It can be draining. It's why they send you home after the ceremonies in Demetros."

"Is it draining because the ceremony—or spell," I corrected, "is painful?"

An uncomfortable look passed over Ryana's features. "Unfortunately, I don't remember the ceremony at all. Whatever they gave us to block our memories of it are better than the memory potions we use."

My brows knitted together as I considered that. "You knew that you wouldn't be aware of what was happening to you, and you did the ceremony anyway? Weren't you worried about being discovered?"

The Guides had to have a method to determine which elemental gift a person possessed. By Ryana's own admission, not everyone had access to all four and the Elemental Queen's advisors certainly wouldn't be planting power where it did not already exist if they intended to steal it.

"We planned for that," Beckett drawled, as if my question had been an offensive attack on his character.

"We take a suppressant so that only one elemental power presents," Grethe offered. "Once we take the antidote, we have our magic back and it's just a matter of removing the brand."

"Which is no different than breaking a spell, except I don't use Gothi magic," Ryana added.

My head was drowning with information. "Gothi magic?"

"Natural magic," Ryana answered. "Think of them as witches and wizards, like from your stories, but all part of a specific society. Here, the special sect is called Gothi, although not all witches and wizards align with that order."

"It's irrelevant to what you're asking," Beckett interrupted. "Ryana has removed binds and brands enough to know it won't hurt you, if that's what you're concerned about."

It was on the tip of my tongue to tease him about being worried over my wellbeing when I remembered that we didn't do that in front of present company.

"Don't worry, Ash," Grethe said, "We will catch you up to speed on everything eventually. You don't have to learn it all tonight. There are no quizzes here."

An unexpected huff of a laugh tumbled from my lips. "Thank the gods for that."

Beckett offered me a strange look, like he was trying to puzzle me out, but rather than voice his thoughts, he stood from the table. "I believe you have gotten all the information relevant to your request. If you will excuse me, I'll see you after dinner."

In what I was learning was typical Beckett fashion; he strolled from the room without a formal goodbye.

Smirks, shrugs, and exiting rooms without farewells were the norm for this man and yet, learning that didn't bring me any closer to under-standing him. Perhaps I never would.

My focus remained trained to the door long after he had disap-peared into the hall beyond it. Once again, it left me feeling like I was a moth and he was a flame and no matter how many times he infuriated or confounded me, I couldn't quite bring myself to look away. As if I was destined to find him first in rooms, searching for a pair of silver eyes that never revealed the essence of the man behind them.

"Ignore him," Ryana said, in such a way that felt like she was reading my thoughts. "He's testy when he's left out of plans and doesn't know all the information."

I snorted a laugh, but my gaze remained pinned to the empty threshold. "How ironic."

Seventeen

For the next several hours, Ryana and Grethe attempted, and spectacularly failed, at teaching me the game of cards that I had seen when I walked into what I was dubbing the game room. It was far more complicated than it looked because each match wasn't won outright by a higher-ranking card but took into account the cards already in play from previous rounds as well as whatever each opponent might play in the current one.

For instance, I thought I had gotten lucky by drawing Beckett's crimson dragon moon, but Grethe ended up playing something that was a weakness to my card, and I lost the round to a mushroom. I couldn't keep up with all the rules, and after what felt like the hundredth round, I blew out a frustrated breath and tossed my hand to the table. "I think I'm done. I used to think I was fairly intelligent, but now I know it was only by human standards."

Grethe chuckled, one side of his mouth lifting higher than the other. "It will just take practice. A few rounds to understand how the cards work together. You'll get it soon enough."

My head hit the back of the chair as I looked up to the ceiling. "I thought the dragon would win; I was so excited." My head snapped up, eyes narrowing at Grethe. "You can't see my cards, right? You don't have foresight or telepathy?"

This time his laugh was barked. "No. As far as we know, mind-reading is not a gift bestowed upon us from the Gods. Although"—he tilted his head toward Ryana—"it would be super cool."

Ryana cringed. "It would be incredibly dangerous."

"My thoughts exactly," I replied, mimicking her face of discomfort just as my stomach grumbled.

After glancing over her shoulder toward the clock on the mantle, Ryana huffed a laugh. "Right on cue, Ash. It's time for dinner."

Attempting not to let my excitement bleed through my expression, I dampened my smile. "Great," I replied, hoping to sound level. Although I was hungry, I was more excited for what came after dinner. My bind was going to be removed, and I'd finally have access to the magic that had been blocked from me for my whole life.

In unison, we stood, making our way to the door at the same time, only to find it swinging open before we reached it.

Without even realizing it had happened, my gaze had fallen on a pair of grey eyes. Beckett looked startled to find me there but rather than speak about the thoughts running through his mind, he simply cleared his throat, averting his gaze from mine and finding Grethe instead. "I came to find you because I am not going in there alone."

"It's already started then?" Grethe asked, blowing raspberries between his lips as he rolled his eyes. The three of us stepped into the hall and began our trek to the dining hall.

"What is it?" I asked, my vision instinctively going to the man who had brought me here yet again.

"Just another game of political nonsense," Beckett replied in that way he liked to, which told me absolutely nothing.

Ryana put a hand on my shoulder, falling into step with me, behind the men. "The people have heard Oldenberg is coming here for the New Year celebrations, so they've swarmed like flies."

"More like vultures," Beckett muttered as Ryana released my shoulder.

My eyes widened, uncertainty coating my features and forming a knot at the base of my throat.

Ryana let loose an exasperated laugh. "It's not that crowded," she remarked, "and I can't say I blame them. Lochmere New Year's celebrations are typically grand."

"And exclusive," Grethe added over his shoulder as he and Beckett turned the corner. They pushed through the double doors of the dining hall without an ounce of hesitation, and the room came into view in an instant.

The dining hall wasn't swarming with people, as Ryana had indicated, but there were groups scattered at almost every table now. Servants in their gray uniforms ran back and forth from the shadows and what I assumed to be the kitchen beyond. Boisterous noise echoed along the wood-laden walls and ceilings, making it hard for me to pinpoint any particular area to focus on.

Grethe let out a whistle as we approached the table we had eaten at before, surprisingly empty of others, just as it had been that night. "I wonder who let slip she was coming here?"

"I think it would be fairly obvious if Gianna came here first," Ryana replied. "And us," she added, giving me yet more insight into this strange group dynamic. From the very minimal information I had gathered, it didn't appear that any of them were expected to work the event as guards, or whatever they did—something else I'd have to ask about when the time was right. This very much seemed to be an event for their enjoyment, and if Oldenberg typically celebrated the event with them, it meant that they were likely some sort of friend group. Josaphine and Gianna were Grethe's mothers, so maybe they were all related in some way?

The questions and assumptions all slipped from my mind as the chair in front of me was pulled out. Those churning grey eyes skimmed my face before slipping away from my gaze as Beckett gestured for me take a seat. I took my place, avoiding looking in his direction but uncomfortably aware of his closeness.

For Grethe and Ryana, it was obvious that we were still friends, or something like that, now that I had been given more information about my predicament. But with Beckett, we hadn't been friends to start with, so it wasn't as if I could be upset that we hadn't returned to whatever normalcy our two days of travel had been. Still, the air had shifted. He seemed more guarded, and I found that his indifference made me uncomfortable. Not that I could explain it, nor would I even attempt to ask Ryana about it.

It wasn't like he was actively avoiding me, but the jokes and the comments had all but stopped, and while they had aggravated me at the time, the absence of them now was disconcerting. I almost snorted at the irony but was blessedly kept from that display when Josaphine and Gianna strolled into the dining hall and took the seats on Grethe's other side.

"Good evening, Ashton," Josaphine practically sing-songed. "I hope your hosts have been treating you well."

Gianna offered me a curt nod from her wife's side, which was neither dismissive nor overtly pleasant, but I returned the gesture before facing Josaphine. "It's been fascinating to learn so much about the Fae," I stated, not sure what else I could, or should, say.

"What is it that you have found the most interesting?" Josaphine asked, reaching for a goblet of red wine and taking a sip as she waited for my answer.

At this point, I didn't think it wise to bring up anything about the brands, even if I was sure everyone at the table was aware, so I spoke to what I believed to be general knowledge. "In Demetros, we grow up thinking there are four elements, and we will only receive one, if any of them. Although I do find the fact that there are many with access to all four of the elements astonishing compared to what I thought I knew, I find the gifts most intriguing. They seem so random but really amazing."

Josaphine's soft smile landed on me again. "The history behind them is equally as interesting. Once you get settled more, I'd be happy to give you book recommendations on the different species of Fae. The lore is almost as fascinating as the powers themselves."

"I'd love that," I said, practically beaming before my eyebrows pinched together. "I'm sorry, did you say species?" I glanced at Beckett to see if this was information I was allowed to learn, and he offered me a single dip of his chin to confirm that it was.

"We hadn't gotten that far," Ryana stated, somewhat apologetically. She squared her shoulders in my direction as if she were preparing for a speech, and I listened on intently as I sipped from my wine.

"There are three species of Fae that we know of. The Elemental Fae, which we have spoken of, the shifters who can transform into different animals and—" She paused abruptly as servers surrounded us, dropping off plates once again laden with food. After whispering a quiet thank you to the one closest to her and placing her napkin in her lap, she turned back to me. "The final species is the Shadow Fae."

"How are their powers different than the Elementals?" I inquired, more than a little interested in the idea of shifters. Of course, Demetros had mentioned such magic in their fairytales, but I was beginning to understand that what I had viewed as myth might have just been history twisted by the spell.

"Shifters can transform into animals at will," Grethe replied in Ryana's place.

My eyes widened. "Any animal they want?"

His eyes dropped to his food as he shook his head, as my questions had embarrassed him for some reason. "No, just one type of animal. It's mostly genetic."

"People who can shift into wolves usually have children who can shift into wolves," Ryana stated before shoveling a bite of greens into her mouth.

"Or they used to," Gianna offered, surprising me when I discovered her eyes were locked on mine. Her lips pressed into a flat line. "The spell is draining so much magic that the heritage isn't necessarily being passed down like that anymore."

"That and interbreeding," Beckett remarked, startling me with his closeness. Had he scooted his chair closer to mine, or was I imagining the distance between us growing shorter?

Confusion twisted my features.

Ryana perked up, reading the question through my expression. "Shifting is a genetic ability, so the more dilute the shifter blood, the less likely the next generation will have the ability."

"But the spell is not helping," Gianna countered, sliding that green gaze that was so much like Grethe's and yet void of all of his warmth in my direction. "Even those born with the ability to shift are not inheriting the full range of—"

"And the Shadow Fae," Grethe said, cutting his mother off and earning a sharp look from her which he promptly ignored, "have the ability to manipulate shadows and compel their victims."

"They can also steal magic from other Fae," Ryana added solemnly. "They are able to borrow powers from those they bite."

I dropped the fork in my hand, and it fell with a clatter to the plate below it. "Bite? Compel"

Beckett slowly swiveled his head in my direction, those silver eyes pinning me in place. For some reason, I could already tell that whatever he was about to say would be ominous. "They are able to obtain the power of those they bite through consuming their blood. They can also control others, although their abilities range in effectiveness."

The blood drained from my face, pooling inside the thudding organ in my chest, giving all of its energy into ratcheting up my heart rate. "That's... horrible." And terrifying. No wonder Beckett hadn't wanted us to be roaming around too long after dark. "How do you protect yourselves against them?"

"I wouldn't be so concerned with that," Grethe stated. "They are mostly extinct, and none of them reside in the Light Kingdom. You probably won't ever see a Shadow Fae."

My focus remained locked on Beckett as a strange expression flashed across his features, gone in a blink. "Grethe is correct, you shouldn't concern yourself with crossing paths with them."

Even though his words were comforting, there was something so intense in his gaze that I was forced to look away, grabbing my discarded fork and attempting the task of eating yet again.

The subject was changed almost abruptly when Grethe began to ask Josaphine what she had planned for the New Year's festivities, and I tuned out their words as I forced bites of food into my mouth. I had been so excited to learn everything I could about this kingdom, but I hadn't considered asking about the dangerous aspects yet, having been more focused on my role in breaking the spell and whatever future abilities I might have. Internally, I added *monsters I might run into while walking around* to the list of topics I'd need to ask about if I were to remain here for any length of time.

"Are you ready?" It was Ryana's voice that finally broke me out of my stupor.

Clearing my throat to give myself a moment not to sound so panicked, I offered her a smile I hoped wasn't as weak as it felt. "For?"

"The pools," Grethe said, whispering as if he didn't want the others at the surrounding tables to hear.

Then my pulse skittered for an entirely different reason than the idea of the Shadow Fae. The pools, whatever that meant, were the place where I was going to have my bind released. I was finally going to get my magic.

Eighteen

After we excused ourselves from the table, Ryana dragged me to her room to lend me some swimwear while Beckett and Grethe opted to get the wine. My stomach sloshed with the wine I had already consumed as we made our way down the hallway where her—or rather her and Grethe's—suite was, a floor or so up from mine.

She held her hand over the doorknob for several seconds before pushing inside. "Blood locks," she said over her shoulder as I followed her within. "All of us have them on our doors."

"Blood locks?" I inquired, taking in the open apartment as we stepped inside, and the door was shut behind me.

Ryana had already crossed the space and was rifling through a dresser drawer. "Yeah, the Gothi set them up. It only allows those with permission access to the space. It uses blood to seal it, so the magic knows what signature to look for."

My nose scrunched. "That sounds... gross?"

Ryana only laughed off the comment, tossing the scraps of what I hoped wasn't the bathing suit over her shoulder as she continued to rummage in her drawers.

Instead of scrutinizing those further and somehow offending her, I let my eyes scan the apartment. Perhaps it was nosy, but I wanted to know what Ryana was like when she was Ryana Vissorri, not Ryana Vance.

Furniture was arranged in clusters throughout the room. There was a seating area with an overstuffed sofa facing two wing-backed chairs, centered around a crackling fireplace. All the upholstery shared similar deep green patterns that complemented the stained wood floors that spanned the entire room, making it almost feel as if we were ensconced in a forest.

On the far side, a simple bed was tucked under a large semi-circular window and adorned in a floral quilt. A pillow had been tossed haphazardly against the headboard next to a throw, crumpled on the other end, giving the space a lived in quality. There were several books in various stages of being read, piled on one nightstand, and a half-empty glass of water on the other.

Ryana stepped toward me, startling me out of my observation of her apartment, and my cheeks heated at how rude it must seem.

"Here you go," she stated, saying nothing of my snooping.

"What is that?" My fingertip pointed at the scraps of navy fabric, connected by thin strings. Bathing suits in Demetros, if that's what this even was, were typically a bit more conservative. This looked like undergarments. The kind that Jemma would prefer.

Ryana snorted. "You're a little taller than me, but it should fit." She seemed bemused, and I considered, if only briefly, that this was another joke until she tossed it on a nearby chair and grabbed a similar item for herself.

She stepped behind a screen, a beautiful piece, hand painted with a scene from the violet hued forest that Beckett and I had traversed to get here. It had me pondering if it held any special significance to the Light Kingdom or the owner of this castle.

"You can use the bathing chamber to change if you'd like," Ryana called from behind the screen over the sounds of her clothes being shed. Even though Beckett and Grethe had said they would meet us at the pools after procuring the wine, that didn't mean that they wouldn't return unexpectedly, and I didn't need either of them waltzing in to find me naked.

"Thanks," I muttered as I slipped beyond the door with the strappy garment in hand.

The bathing chamber was much like the one in my quarters, more opulent than I was used to. Just like with the room beyond, the counters displayed a lived-in quality that made me think that this place might be their permanent home.

Silver jewelry rested in a delicate dish. A man's razor leaned in a tin cup. A bar of soap, almost used to the point of nonexistence, had made residence next to a wash basin. All signs that did nothing to point toward any major differences in ways of life between the kingdoms. Within the castle walls, it wasn't difficult to believe that the kingdoms had once been connected. Nothing seemed overtly contrasting between the Fae and the humans.

Shaking myself out of my thoughts, I changed quickly, not wanting to give Ryana the impression that I had escalated my snooping to digging through her drawers. Within a minute, I emerged from the bathing chamber with pink cheeks. My arms crossed over my stomach as the cool air kissed my skin. "This feels... inappropriate for friendly bonding."

Ryana was already waiting beyond the door, another garment in her outstretched hand. "Put this on," she said. "It can be cold down there."

Graciously, I accepted the thick robe, slipping my arms into the sleeves immediately. My toes wiggled against the plush carpet. "Do you have any shoes, or should I put my slippers back on?"

She shook her head. "No need, we stay mostly inside."

My nose wrinkled, and Ryana's mouth lifted at the corners. "Come on," she said, motioning with her hand toward her door. "It's easier if I just show you."

Tugging on the edges of the robe and tightening the belt around my waist, I padded across the empty corridors next to Ryana, following her cue down stairwells and through hallways until we reached a roughly hewn archway. It looked more like an entrance to a cave than a doorway, and it was only then that I realized I hadn't even noticed the subtle shift in décor from extravagant rugs and oil paintings to cut stone and hanging lanterns.

As we slipped through the opening, a large cavern came into view before us, so much like the underground pools I had traveled through to get here that I thought they might be connected somehow. The only observation I had that indicated we were not below the ground was the large opening along the far side of the cavernous space.

Something, or someone, had blown out a portion of the cave wall, revealing the pale orb of the moon hanging amongst an inky blanket of stars, illuminating our surroundings just enough for me to see the glittering waves of the ocean beyond.

Instinctively, I stepped toward the edge of that opening until I could lean out and see, rather than simply hear, the waves crashing against the jut of rocks below. The cave was so far from the waterline, which beat against its base, that I couldn't fathom how anyone had even found this place.

A gust of salty air rustled my hair, sending a wave of goosebumps over my flesh. Just as I turned to find Ryana again, I heard a voice.

"Are you going to join us?" It was Grethe who had asked, but when my attention fell to the pool they were sitting in, my eyes locked with Beckett's. Steam billowed around him but did little to hide the exposed expanse of his chest. Water lapped along the ridges of his abdomen, a part of him I had run my fingertips across just nights before.

His face was expressionless as he watched me, and I had no choice but to blink away my focus and relocate it to Grethe, reminding myself again that I was fairly certain I didn't even like this person. Or, at least, he didn't like me. "Yeah," I replied, nervously, despite my best efforts.

Ryana had already joined the others in the pool, so I walked to where her robe sat neatly folded, and slipped my own from my shoulders, letting it drop to the ground in a less organized fashion.

Without glancing in anyone's direction, I lowered myself to the rocky edge of the pool and plopped my feet into the water. It tingled like a too-warm bath, and I sighed with the sensation.

"There is a lip on the edge," Grethe said. "It's not too deep."

Nodding, I slipped lower into the water. My foot met with the rocky ledge, and I guided myself deeper into the pool until I was seated on the bench-like structure, the water lapping just at the top edge of the bathing suit.

"Wine?" Grethe offered, holding a slightly opaque green bottle out in my direction. It was too dark for me to discern the color of the wine within, like I had been able to do at dinner.

Squinting at the bottle first, I let my gaze slide to Beckett. "Hopefully not any more everapple wine," I remarked offhandedly.

Grethe only chuckled, but Ryana scowled at Beckett. "Why was she around everapple wine? Nothing about that was in *your* debrief, Astor."

Beckett shrugged, leaning back against the edge of the pool and splaying his arms wide, resting his weight against his elbows on the stone behind him. "You sent a code dragonfire to the Barker Inn on the night before the solstice." His expression conveyed an air of *what did you expect* although he did not formally say it.

Sensing some tension in the air, I huffed a small laugh. "I saw what it can do to people, and no offense to you two," I said, pointing between Grethe and Ryana, "but I am not interested in being a Jemma-style third wheel."

Grethe expelled a deep belly laugh at my words, breaking the tension that was building in my shoulders. "You went down to the Barker Inn pub after dark during solstice celebrations?" He nudged Beckett with his shoulder. "How much of you did she have to see?"

Beckett's eyes darkened, his pupils flaring as he met my stare again, churning with something I couldn't place. "Enough."

Wrenching my eyes from Beckett's stare, I cut them over to Ryana. "I imagine if I had been down there any longer, I might have needed to pay him for the show."

Her eyes widened, and she tilted her head back, releasing the loudest laugh I had ever heard come from her lips. "Gross, Becks," she said, and she smacked him on the arm, the wet sound echoing throughout the chamber. "You were on duty."

Beckett rolled his eyes, his voice jovial and light, the exact opposite of my insides. "As you know, I was off duty and only waiting there to surprise you two assholes because I missed you."

"Not that you're ever truly off duty, but fair enough," Ryana answered with that same amusement sparkling in her stare, the one that told me that these people were way more to each other than coworkers. "But once you got the message, you didn't think to stop your escapades?"

Beckett's silver eyes widened in mock exasperation. "I was in the middle of entertaining when she walked in. It's not like I knew who she was until afterwards."

It was all I could do to keep the images of him with the women out of my mind. The way his hand slid down the brunette's ribs. The way they touched him, so brazenly. The look in his eyes when his stare met mine.

"One of the usuals?" Grethe casually asked as he sipped from the bottle I had refused to take. I followed the movement of the wine as he passed it to Ryana, anything to distract me from the images that had just filtered through my mind.

"Gabriella," Beckett replied with no further indication of his thoughts on the woman or the other one's name. It was as if he were relaying his order at a pub instead of admitting to a tryst in the middle of one.

Ryana sniffed a laugh as she lowered the bottle from her lips. "You could always find a room like a normal person."

"Unfortunately," I cut in, "that wouldn't have made much of a difference. In the Wolf Inn, Natasha practically had her way with him, with me still in the bed."

Grethe and Ryana both snapped their heads in my direction. It was kind of cute how in sync their movements were sometimes, except when they were both looking at me with alarmed expressions.

"Excuse me, what?" Ryana asked, brown eyes narrowed at me as if I had said something horribly offensive.

Beckett heaved a sigh. "They were overbooked at the inn due to the last-minute nature of our departure. We shared a room."

Ryana's icy glare shifted to him abruptly, although she continued speaking to me. "And from the sounds of it, a bed? A single bed?"

Her attention slid slowly back to me as if she wasn't quite done chastising her superior. Or friend? "Did anything happen with you two?"

A little unsure where all the tension was coming from, I made a joke of my response. "Other than witnessing his sexual escapades two nights in a row? No." Thank the Gods.

This softened her features some. Clearly pacified by my reply, she left my stare to glare at Beckett once more. Only a fraction of her contempt had retreated though. "Becks, this was a mission, and you have to be careful."

I couldn't decide if she was being a good friend, chastising him as a coworker, or simply being a mother hen.

Beckett straightened, minutely, but enough for me to register the movement as tense. "I know, Ry. I'm not some wayward kid anymore. I am aware of my duties." His steel-clad eyes shifted to me. "I was a perfect gentleman after that night, wasn't I, Ashton?"

My name sounded so wrong coming from his lips. So formal, in a way that set me on edge. "He has dutifully ignored me since we left the Wolf Inn. As per his *job*."

Ryana's shoulders dropped. "I didn't mean it like that, Ashton, it's just, he has certain *charms* about him. It wouldn't be right to take advantage of a vulnerable girl." Her eyes slid back to Beckett momentarily. "Again."

"You screw one noble girl on a horse..." I heard Beckett mumble under his breath.

Ryana scoffed, exasperated. "It took Oldenberg months to smooth over relations with that noble girl's father!"

Beckett hummed his annoyance, holding up a singular finger. "First, she asked me to." He raised another. "Secondly, I no longer escort people as part of my duties anymore because of said incident. So, I know, Vissorri," he said, obviously tired of having this argument with her. He dropped his hand only to snatch the bottle from her grip and took several deep draws from the liquid within.

When he was done, he swiped the back of his hand against his lips. "That was ages ago."

"You didn't happen to use any of your gifts on her while you were together?" Ryana asked, alarmed now.

My lungs stilled in my chest as I flipped my attention back to Beckett. It would explain my lapse in judgment in the Wolf Inn, but he had said he wouldn't do that. In lieu of Ryana's question, I wasn't feeling overly comforted by his claim. With bated breath, I waited for his response.

Beckett's jaw clenched. "I would never use my gifts on someone against their will. You know me better than that…" There was a hurt to his tone, and though I had no reason to believe any of them, I desperately wanted to trust this, even if it meant my attraction to him was all my own foolishness.

"Good," Ryana snapped, showing only a hint of her guilt for even asking him. "She is off limits to you."

Beckett raised an eyebrow. "My duties are complete, Vissorri. And regardless, isn't Ashton her own woman? Should she not be allowed to make her own decisions?"

I got the distinct impression that this was more about Ryana telling Beckett what to do rather than him actually trying to pursue anything with me. Still, I watched on with rapt interest, wondering how the power struggle would play out. After having witnessed her dedication during the challenges, my bets were on her.

Ryana's eyes contracted to slits. "You would regret it." The warning was as plain as day in her voice, although I couldn't discern why she even needed to give it.

"Obviously," Beckett remarked flatly.

That comment stung more than it should have, prompting some infinitesimal flinch on my part, which I covered up by reaching across the water to snatch the bottle of wine from Beckett's loose grip. Without making eye contact with any of them, I took three large gulps of the surprisingly sweet concoction before I turned my attention back to Ryana. "About my bind?"

There were a multitude of questions I still needed to ask before I determined if I was going to break the spell, but none of them mattered if I didn't have magic. On the same token, having access to all four elements would make it easier to return to Demetros and defend myself if Mr. Higgins proved himself to be a legitimate problem. Although after the revelation about the binds and the distrust I now had in the Elemental Queen and her Guides, I wondered if I would ever be able to return home again.

All of these thoughts flowed through me in the split second between my inquiry about my bind and Ryana shifting her gaze to me. Her features softened, and something akin to a smile lifted the corners of her lips. "Yeah, I can remove that." Her voice almost trembled as she spoke, but I had no desire to ask her to explain all the reasons why Beckett would regret me. Or why the idea of something occurring between us had made her so worked up.

Instead of looking at any of them, my gaze slid to the sliver of a crescent moon, hanging low in the night sky. "And you don't need a solstice, like the Guides? Or a full moon or something magical and nature-y?"

Ryana snorted. "They need the solstice because they are harnessing the natural magic, like witches. My gift doesn't require that."

"Right," I replied, recognizing that either her or Grethe had already mentioned this before. My nerves were getting the better of me for more than one reason tonight.

Ryana stood quickly, a genuine grin rounding her cheeks this time. She climbed from the lip of the pool, then walked toward the edge of the cliffside opening. "Come here," she said, beckoning me with her hand.

When I rose, water ran in rivulets down my body, leaving behind goosebumps in the cool winter air. Grethe held his hand out to take the wine from me, which I gave him before stepping up from the ledge and crossing the small cavern to stand in front of Ryana.

She took my hands in hers. "Close your eyes," she whispered, hers already shut.

My lids fluttered closed.

"Now, take a deep breath in and hold it for five seconds."

Again, I followed her direction, counting slowly in my mind.

One.

Two.

Three.

Four.

Five.

Ryana's grip loosened as she released me. "Okay, all done."

My brow creased as I opened my eyes to inspect my hands, front and back. "I feel no different." Disappointment sagged my shoulders. She had said it wasn't painful, but was it supposed to be so anticlimactic? How was I supposed to know if I had magic if I didn't sense it? Was I wrong to have expected more from the interaction? A tingling sensation or...

Her chuckle interrupted my confused thoughts. "You won't feel anything right away. It's why they send you home from Biltons Academy after the solstice too. It could be hours or days before it surfaces."

That made sense, but I had been hoping that somehow, whatever Ryana did could circumvent the rules set in place in Demetros. "So, what now?"

"We wait," Ryana replied, tugging me back into the pool.

"We drink," Grethe added in, his typical glee brightening his face with a grin as he passed me the bottle.

My spine rested against the rocky ledge. I pressed the bottle to my lips, and I tilted my head back to let the lukewarm liquid slide down my throat and warm me from the inside out.

Nineteen

"So, what other questions do you have?" Beckett asked, from beside me, slipping the bottle from my grasp.

I was so taken off guard by his question, and the fact that he had scooted closer to me to snatch the wine, that all I could do for several seconds was blink. The wine had warmed me up, making my head feel light and airy, and the only thing I could think to ask was, "Can you shift your ears too?"

It was a stupid waste of a question, but I had noted that Ryana and Grethe had shifted their ears to their pointed form, and Beckett had not. Based on his magic, he was elemental, and I had wondered if it was a preference or some other reason that had kept them rounded but had thought it would be rude to ask. Until now.

Beckett's gaze constricted as if he was also thinking it was a waste of a question, but all he said was, "My ears are typically pointed."

Grethe sniffed a laugh. "Beckett's being modest. His family has no human lineage, so they have to use an illusionist to make the tips of his ears appear rounded."

My nose wrinkled. "An illusionist?"

"Purebloods aren't able to shift their ears between forms because they have no human form," Ryana answered, matter-of-factly. "The

Astors would never lower themselves to taint the ancient bloodlines," she added, in a snotty accent. It crossed my mind that she might be mocking Beckett's parents, but he didn't correct her.

"They hire an illusionist full time over ears?" I asked lamely because really, what business of mine was it if Beckett's family hired people to round his ears? Regret pulsed in my veins.

Beckett shrugged, apparently unbothered by my directness. "My parents collect all sorts of valuable gifts for their collection. But the illusionist does tend to my ears when I need to go to Demetros."

"It's not just unique gifts they hoard," Ryana added from across the pool. "The power level it would take to hold the illusion that long, at presumably far distances, is also very impressive."

I wasn't really getting anywhere asking about Beckett's parents. In fact, he seemed uncomfortable now that they had been brought up, and although it wasn't my responsibility to save him, I changed the subject anyway. Turning to Ryana, I asked, "You can sense power levels, too, right?"

Ryana pulled the bottle of wine from her lips, passing it back to me as she swallowed. "Yeah, I can." There was a certain amount of pride in her tone that told me her gift might be unusual.

Ignoring the bottle for a moment, I let it rest loosely in my grip, holding it just above the water line. "Is what you do rare? Are there others like you?"

Ryana dropped her gaze to the water, her shoulders bouncing with her next inhale. "I can sense power levels from a distance, but individual threads of power through touch. There are others who share some of my abilities, but not all."

"That's fascinating," I replied, already considering what my gift might be when it finally emerged. Hopefully something as useful. "So, they sent you to Demetros to bring back people you sense are both strong and have enough elements to represent a Fae lineage?"

"Basically," she replied, her face neither smug nor concerned like it might be if I was overstepping.

I took a small pause to sip the wine again before passing it along to Beckett, then I returned my focus to my friend. "Were there any others like me in our year? I just have to wonder how common this is. We've only been separated by the exile spell for two hundred years, but how long until the Fae blood of the Demetros citizens is too dilute to even meet the spell requirements? How did I even have enough magic after all this time?"

My jaw clamped together when I realized I was rambling again, and my eyes came into focus only to find Ryana's face as white as a sheet. Tilting my head, I lowered my voice. "Ry?"

Her head shook like she was physically forcing herself out of the thoughts she was having. "Yeah?" The color did not return to her face.

Sparing a quick glance at Beckett to ensure he was going to let me continue speaking, I faced her once more. "Were there more people like me in our class?"

"Yeah," she replied. Too quickly.

Another glance at Beckett revealed that he had no intention to stop her, so her reaction was puzzling. "Like whom?"

"That Owens girl," Beckett responded when Ryana still didn't. "She's on our list to approach when Grethe and Ryana return to Demetros after the New Year."

I was surprised at not only the fact that Beckett had replied so nonchalantly, but that Ryana still looked like she'd seen a ghost. Like she was still witnessing its spectral form in front of her. Studying Ryana's face, I couldn't puzzle out what the problem was, but even Grethe had begun to avoid eye contact with me.

There was a part of me that wanted to demand that Ryana tell me what the hell was going on with her, but for reasons I could not explain, I didn't want to push her. In all the months we had spent together, I had never seen her look so scared, but I did want to know what was going on, so I kept Connally as the focus of my next question. "Where did she end up going for break? I know her aunt was planning to disown her after her branding ceremony." My tone was casual enough that Ryana should have eased out of her panic, but it only set her muscles more rigid.

"She went South," Grethe replied for her, which was more curious than Ryana's non-response.

"South?" I questioned. "With whom?" Last I heard, she was potentially coming home with Jemma for the break. Elmhaven wasn't exactly considered South of the capital, but maybe Grethe was generalizing it from our current location. That was stupid... everything was south from here and—

"Jemma and Dante," Grethe stated, almost flatly. Like he was nervous about something and was trying to mask the evidence.

As I tried to puzzle out what was going on, my face crinkled.

"You guys are being weird as fuck," Beckett remarked, giving them that same confused expression I knew I was wearing on my own features.

Beckett didn't say anything revolutionary, nor did any of his words lend themselves to where my mind went next, but in my next breath, everything seemed to click into place. Connally had planned to go on a trip with Jemma, who oddly seemed to be attached to Dante. The fact that they were going South, and my knowledge on Dante and Cade's close friendship, in conjunction with Ryana's bizarre reaction, led me to one conclusion that I desperately hoped was incorrect. "They're with Cade, aren't they?"

Pity swirled in Ryana's returned stare, her lips twisting into a frown. It was all the confirmation I needed.

An equal mix of relief and hurt filtered through my chest cavity. It was surprising to me that Jemma had just let go of trying to find me so quickly, almost as if she wasn't concerned about me at all. And to go on vacation with Connally, when we had planned to see each other at home, was so unlike her. Wouldn't she have wanted to comfort me? Make sure that I was okay?

It was at the tail end of that spiral that my brain finally caught on to the implications. Two people traveling with a known couple.

"Are Cade and Connally a thing?" I asked, my tone bitter and sharp.

It would have been twenty-four hours or less from my departure, from Cade and I breaking up, to the point where he decided to go on vacation with Connally fucking Owens. This left few hours between when I stormed from Cade's rooms, and he had chosen to go pursue someone new. Connally wasn't exactly my friend, but the betrayal from both Cade and even Jemma stung, nonetheless.

Jemma was my best friend, and regardless of whether or not I had admitted to how long a relationship between Cade and me was brewing, she was aware something had been. She knew I was excited about the solstice eve ball. And instead of being concerned for me or waiting to see if I was okay, she had taken her friend on vacation with my ex.

Tears sprang to my eyes as the remaining shards of my broken heart plummeted into my stomach, cutting deep gouges in festering wounds. It didn't matter that I was hypocrite-adjacent, as something had almost happened between Beckett and me in the Wolf Inn, because Beckett had been a stranger before the ball, but Cade had run off with a girl whom he believed to be my friend. How could he do this to me?

It had been foolish of me to be so relieved when Natasha had interrupted Beckett and me, as if I couldn't bear to have been the one to drive a nail into the coffin of Cade's and my relationship when all the while, he had been dutifully swinging a hammer behind my back.

Even though I knew that ship had sailed, that I couldn't return to a man who wasn't certain of my worth, a part of me had held out hope that we could be reconciled. That part of me had just shriveled up and died.

Beckett hummed a humorless laugh, a disjointing sound in the background of my heartbreak. My eyes snapped to his, but a hint of a smirk lined his lips. "So, Ignus boy is a power chaser?"

My brow lowered across my face. "What's that supposed to mean?"

Beckett tilted his head to the side, and I couldn't determine if I found pity or incredulity in his eyes. Like he was warring between feeling sorry for me and being astonished that I hadn't put two and two together.

With horrifying clarity, everything Beckett was insinuating clicked into place at once. Cade hadn't wanted to be with someone without power because his parents wouldn't have approved of the match.

"Don't tell me you aren't aware of how the elite in Demetros only marry for status," Beckett replied. "It's the same everywhere, power breeds with power, whether that be political or magical."

"What Beckett is so poorly articulating," Ryana interjected, "is that many of those in the higher rungs of society seek out matches in either wealth or magic to keep themselves in power. Maybe Cade was one of those people."

There was a lilt to her statement that almost made it feel like a question. An offering intended to cheer me up, when all it did was make me feel even more expendable.

My mind raced as I turned over every conversation I had ever shared with Cade Hudson, stifling a gasp when I realized that even as early as that run-in after Mr. Grupert's running session, we had discussed the power level of at least one of my parents. It seemed harmless at the time, a natural part of our conversation, but now it felt like the moment everything changed between us. That bit of information had allowed him to hedge his bets on me. Even helping me with the challenge seemed self-serving now.

A part of me wanted to believe that it wasn't possible. Cade had genuinely cared for me. He had killed for me, although he hadn't meant to. But, even if his feelings were genuine, a part of his affection had been conditional on my magic. In the end, it had the same outcome. It wasn't true love.

This shouldn't have been the thing that sent me over the edge, but the betrayal dug its nails into scar tissue that had never fully healed. My worthiness had always been in question, and this did nothing to pacify those lifelong worries. To think that someone whom I had loved had only been around me to further his bloodline was devastating.

The blood eddied from my face, and I could sense three sets of eyes on me as I sat there, numb and blinking. For the first time since leaving Elmhaven, I considered that it wouldn't be so bad not to go back right away. Maybe it would be nice to stay in the Light Kingdom for an extended period as long as my father was here.

Grethe's overexaggerated yawn reverberated across the stone walls that surrounded us. Water splashed as he lifted his arms, elbows out in a big stretch. "I think it's time for me to call it a night," he stated. "Are you ready for bed?"

I could see what he was doing, could even recognize that he was trying to help, but the last thing I wanted to do was go back to my room where I would be forced to be alone with these self-deprecating thoughts. Or worse, wondering what Cade and Connally were doing right now.

"We can walk you back to your room, if you want company," Ryana added and there was so much earnest in her stare that I almost reconsidered.

But then, my gaze landed on Beckett. The expanse of his chest was visible over the waterline, glistening with sweat or an effect of the steam. He just looked so beautiful. Like the kind of distraction that I needed.

Maybe we would bicker, or maybe he would annoy the ever-loving shit out of me, but either way, he could take my mind off of this nightmare.

His nostrils flared, and his eyes seemed to flash silver for a moment as they settled on me. "If you want to stay, I'll walk you back to your rooms." His knuckles wrapped around the bottle of wine like it was a cherished item. My gaze flickered between it and the steel glint in his eyes.

"I want to stay," I admitted, not tearing my gaze away from him.

Out of the corner of my eye, I caught the movement as Ryana's focus bounced between the two of us. "That's not a great idea, Ash, I—"

"I'm not going to bed right now, and I am an adult capable of making my own decisions," I snapped, practically repeating the phrase Beckett had used, a bit taken aback myself, unsure where the hostility was coming from.

A single dark brow raised on Ryana's forehead, her confused stare darting between us again. "Are you sure?"

A light smile worked its way to my face. "I'm not tired yet," I said at the same time Beckett said, "Yes."

Ryana clearly wanted to say more on the subject, but she pursed her lips instead. "Goodnight then." Her tone was wary, like she didn't think she was leaving me in good hands. Even though they were friends, possibly a family. It did nothing to deter my decision.

"Goodnight," I stated, offering her a grin I hoped came off as normal and light-hearted, even if I felt anything but.

Even Grethe seemed unsure as he pulled away from the pool, but he bid us farewell, and within seconds, the sounds of their footsteps retreating on the stone faded to nothing, leaving us completely alone.

Twenty

Beckett leaned back casually, like he didn't have a care in the world, pressing the rim of the bottle to his lips to steal another sip. His throat bobbed with this swallow, my gaze snagging on the movement, only drawn away from the column of his neck when I caught his lip quirk into a smirk.

"Tell me Princess, what is it exactly that you want from me?"

The question caught me so off guard that I needed several seconds to think, and when I still hadn't formulated a plan, I slid close enough to him to grab the wine from his hands. Only after taking a long draw, did I gather enough courage to even hold his gaze. "A distraction," I replied, more assuredly than I felt. Because, while the statement was ultimately true, even I wasn't entirely sure what I meant by it. Only that I needed something to make me feel less... just less.

The smirk on Beckett's face lifted. "Is that a proposition?"

My cheeks heated; my body flushed with more than just the warmth from the pool. Suddenly, the dusty bottle in my hand seemed much more fascinating than what I suspected was Beckett's mocking stare. Regardless of my assumptions, simmering under all that embarrassment was something akin to lust, bleeding through the cells in my body like a wound. A feeling I still couldn't comprehend harboring for a practical stranger, and especially not one who had been so bothersome on our journey. The man remained an enigma to me and yet...

Gathering enough bravery to face him, I trailed my gaze up his body until our eyes met. "Have you ever used your gift on me? Even now?" I asked, rather than answer his question, because I really needed to know if this ember pulsing in my abdomen was solely my own doing before I'd make such reckless confessions.

A coldness hardened over Beckett's features, his gaze turning stony. "I told you I wouldn't use that on you without your permission."

My eyes constricted in his direction. "And I am supposed to just take your word for it?"

Amusement returned to the glint in his stare, his body angling toward mine like he might strike at any moment. I should have been scared, but I wasn't. His chin lowered before he spoke, "There is one way to show you. So that you know what it would feel like if I had."

I was certain my shallow intake of breath echoed along the cavern walls. All the moisture receded from my mouth, and I knew if someone held a mirror to me, my face would be flushed with a mixture of humiliation and desire. Still, I held his gaze, adamant not to let him win this round. "Fine. Go ahead." My voice didn't even wobble as I lifted my chin.

He slid even closer, disturbing the water between us that lapped against my chest like a warning to follow the ripples as far away from this man as I could get. His head tilted toward me until our faces were only inches away, his voice lowered to a whisper. "I need you to tell me what you'd like me to do."

Gawking at him, I choked on air. "You can't be serious."

Without warning, he snatched the wine from my grip, placing the nearly empty bottle on the ledge beside us. "No more of this for you. It's making you testy."

I snorted my disdain for that statement, as I really thought wine would make the rest of this evening better. It would help calm my racing heart and make the distraction all the easier. In fact, I wasn't certain how he expected me to boldly request that he use his gift on me without the aid of the alcohol.

With what I thought were quick movements, I reached for the bottle again, only to be thwarted by a firm grip around my wrist.

With a contempt that I was certain had more to do with Cade and Connally than Beckett blocking me from the wine, I glared at him. A growl might have escaped my lips before I muttered, "What are you, my grandpa?"

For a moment, Beckett appeared confused.

Ripping my hand from his grasp, I cleared my throat, raising my voice slightly. "I'm speaking to your extreme age; in case you are also now hard of hearing."

In true Beckett fashion, he didn't flinch at my words. He simply leaned back against the ledge, grabbing the wine I had been after, taking slow, languid sips from it as if he was the most unbothered man in the universe. When the bottle left his lips, he turned to me, a smirk rising along the edge of his mouth. "And I'll remind you that you couldn't keep your eyes off of me that night."

"Which night?" I asked, before I realized what I had admitted to.

"Exactly." The smugness in his expression was a palpable thing—another entity in the pool with us—and I wanted to wipe it from his face.

Sliding closer toward him, emboldened by the slight buzz from the wine, I grinned a feline smile. "Are we really going to argue over who was about to kiss whom again?"

He shrugged, but I noted the tension in his jaw as I inched closer. It made me wonder if all of his '*is this a proposition*' was just a bluff.

"Don't worry," I said sardonically, pressing my back against the rocky ledge behind me, "I'm not going to do anything that you might regret." The final word tasted bitter on my tongue as I watched his face for a reaction, any confirmation that my suspicions were true.

Quicksilver eyes pinned me to the spot. Their intensity was almost overwhelming, even if I couldn't pinpoint any particular emotion in his features. "I'm fairly certain she was speaking to you." His voice was low, so low that it was a rumble against my chest, making me forget the meaning of the word regret completely.

My bottom lip worked between my teeth, pondering that statement.

"Why would I regret you?" Naturally, I had accumulated my own list of reasons, but I wanted to hear his take on it.

Beckett's gaze snagged on the movement of my mouth. His scarred eyebrow arched as his stare slid slowly up my face until our eyes were locked once more.

My spine straightened under the scrutiny. "I am under no illusion that you'd be waking up next to me with flowers or writing me poetry afterwards," I said in a voice that wasn't completely mine.

Outwardly, I might have seemed calm, but inside I was panicking. What was I doing? Suggesting?

Time seemed to stop around us, trapping us in a bubble without breath or movement. Without sound. Even the thundering of my own heart was near silent, muffled like I was hearing it through cotton.

"What is it that you want, Princess?" He practically purred the words.

What did I want?

In this moment, I wanted to forget Cade's lies about loving me, and I wanted to leave behind Demetros and never return, even if it was just for a few hours. I wanted to drive the nail so hard in the coffin of my past life that it could never open again.

Beckett couldn't let me down because I wanted nothing from him but his hands on my skin. Even admitting that to myself gave me a boost of adrenaline, and my heart began fluttering against the confines of my chest.

"I just want to forget about all of this for one night," I said quietly. "But..."

"You want to make sure that it's your choice and not my gift making you want me?" He said, finishing my sentence for me with such raw honesty that I needed several seconds to reply.

I nodded.

His smile turned wolfish as he closed the gap between us. The warm water of the pool lapped against my breasts with his movements. My tongue darted out along my lips; his attention drawn to the moisture lingering there for far too long to be a glance.

His words were almost a growl. "Say it."

"Show me your magic," I stated, more firmly than I meant to. "Just for a little while." I had to be sure that what I was feeling now had nothing to do with his gift.

His teeth scraped against his lower lip as his eyes trailed over my face. "Fine. But just this once."

A part of me thought I should be offended, but that piece was tucked into the far corner of my mind, buried beneath adrenaline and lust as I brace myself, mind and body, for what was about to come.

Beckett leaned forward, bypassing my lips altogether in favor of resting his mouth along the shell of my ear. "Let go and allow yourself to feel the desire you have for me."

His words seemed to snake along my skin, and as if on cue, my flesh pebbled. Heat pooled at my core at an intensity I was certain I had never felt, and my breaths became slow and shallow as I struggled to suck in air around my arousal.

"There you go," he whispered against the column of my throat. Not exactly touching me but coming close enough that his exhale danced along my skin, stalling the air in my lungs as he dipped lower and lower.

Just before he grazed my collarbone, he pulled back, face as smug as I had ever seen it. "Breathe it out so you can go back to normal. If you like, you can even go back to pretending you don't want this," he stated. His expression seemed to cool some of my burning need, allowing the pleasure to recede and my inhales to grow deeper.

"Feel better?" He asked, knowing damn well I didn't. His eyes were practically laughing at me as he roamed my body, but when our gazes met again, I was positive that I saw the same want mirrored there.

He might have pulled back his gift, but he hadn't turned off my arousal, and something about that look in the depths of those silver pools made me feel reckless. Compounded by my need to think about anything but Cade and Connally enjoying their little vacation together.

In a move that was too fast to be considered anything but aggressive, I closed the distance between us, crashing my mouth against his.

Rough hands roamed my back, gripping along my ribcage moments before Beckett scooped me up into his lap, moving me with a surprising tenderness so that I was straddling his waist with my arms locked around his neck. It felt like we had always done this. There was no adjustment period to ensure I was in the most comfortable position. We moved into place, forming to one another, and I was already melting into him.

My fingers threaded through his golden hair as I shamelessly ground against him, feeling the evidence of his own desire rubbing against my most intimate areas, pressing against that bundle of nerves that had me gasping against his lips.

Beckett used the movement to slide his tongue into my mouth. His exploration was anything but cautious and gentle. Everything about him was rough. The hand that traveled up my back and the other gripping my hip were calloused, scraping against my skin with every movement.

It was a beautiful, stunning distraction.

He broke our kiss, almost violently, his chest heaving as he leaned back to look at me. "Tell me to stop." His voice was ragged, and his full lips were already swollen. Even his hair was mussed like we had been at this for hours, and I liked seeing him so undone for once. For me.

"What?" I replied, enjoying the expression he wore, but practically ready to beg him to stay. I wasn't sure what it said about me that I had never felt more worshiped than I did in his arms, and he didn't even like me.

His gaze roamed my face, my chest, even my arms, before those bright silver eyes met mine again. Suddenly, our faces were so close that our noses touched. "Tell me to stop if you don't want this. I'm not here to take advantage of you, but if this is truly what you desire..."

He let the rest of the words fall silent as he showed me what he meant, thrusting his hips forward so that he slid the full length of himself across my center, ripping another gasp from my lips. It made me all too aware of the thin scraps of fabric that separated us, unsure if I wanted there to be more or less.

His lips pressed against my collarbone, burning a trail up the column of my throat and across my jaw. "I don't think I'm going to be able to stop myself once I start, so I need you to tell me this is what you want."

His breath against my earlobe was sensual in a way that nothing had ever been. It was astonishing that I could feel this much with someone who I had so little connection with otherwise. Maybe Jemma had it right all along. Perhaps the weight I placed on these types of physical dalliances was what diminished the pleasure.

Tipping my head back, I closed my eyes to the sensation of his lips against my skin, the stubble of his beard scraping against my pulse point as he planted another kiss at the juncture below my jaw. "And if I said I didn't want this?

My words were breathless, but I wasn't confident anymore. The need I felt for him was only building, climbing to that peak I had felt under the power of his gift.

The kisses along my throat stopped, and the muscles beneath my palm seemed to freeze in place. "Then I would stop, right now," he said assuredly.

My eyes were still closed. I couldn't bear to meet his gaze as I asked my next question. "And you pulled your magic away?"

I expected ire in his tone, but when he spoke, it was just the cool arrogance I had come to know. "I'm afraid you only have yourself to blame for this," he growled against my skin, his body tense like he was holding himself back from touching me until I gave my explicit permission.

My fingertips threaded through his hair, pulling him back gently so he was forced to look at me. "Then, no."

His eyes were pools of molten silver so bright they put the moon and its reflection in the ocean beyond to shame. "No, what?"

"Don't stop," I replied, in a whisper. "Please, don't stop."

This seemed to satisfy him, and a smirk crossed his lips seconds before they pressed against mine again. From there, it was a flurry of hands and tongues as I got lost in the depths of his attention.

My mind was abuzz with the sensation of his touch. His continued arousal evident as I rolled my hips against his, over and over again, my pleasure building with every swipe of his erection against my clit. The stroke of his tongue as he kissed me nearly to oblivion. The calloused scrape of his hands as they slid over my damp skin.

Suddenly, all my focus fell to those palms and his fingers as his thumb began to trace the edge of my bathing suit top, slipping just underneath the fabric.

My breath stilled in my lungs, and I felt him smile against our kiss before he pulled back again. This time his eyes weren't on my face at all but focused on the very same place his thumb had slipped beneath my swim top.

We both watched as he slowly, torturously, moved that finger further beneath the triangle of fabric, in tight teasing circles that almost brushed against the place I wanted him. Finally—finally—he made contact, the pads of his thumb swiping gently against the hardened peak of my breast. We both groaned as he made a second pass. Then his free hand slid from my hipbone and up my ribcage to caress the other breast in the same way.

I clenched against nothing as I wondered briefly if it was possible to come undone from nipple stimulation and fabric-covered thrusts alone. Because I felt almost comically close to falling into oblivion.

"You are a beautiful creature," Beckett purred as he rolled his thumb and forefinger across the sensitive buds of my breasts. The view was still blocked by my top, and that somehow made it even more intense, so that neither of us could see exactly what those fingers were doing. But we could both feel it.

I couldn't take it anymore, so I tightened my grip in the strands of his hair, pulling his face back to meet mine. My hips rocked against his, and we both moaned again as my core slid sloppily along his erection. Our lips crashed together, and without even a second of reprieve, his tongue slid into my mouth.

This was single-handedly the best kiss of my entire life, and that was before Beckett's thumbs slipped the edges of my swim top to the side, exposing me to the cool evening air. My nipples tightened further against the sensation.

He didn't break our kiss to look down, only cupped each breast in his enormous hands, squeezing almost lightly compared to the passion in our kiss. It made me crave so much more.

I pushed up on my knees, our mouths still melded together, and reached between us to tug at the band of his swimming trunks until he abandoned my breasts to prop himself up, lifting his hips to help me pull the shorts down his legs.

When I lowered myself back down, I adjusted my bottoms to the side so that when I returned to his lap, the blunt head of his cock was pressed against my entrance forcing a whimper to escape from my throat. The burning pleasure dancing behind my hipbones was so intense that I nearly came from the feel of his erection on my bare skin alone.

"I take the tonic," I whispered, although he hadn't asked.

He grunted some form of acknowledgement as his hands returned to me, finding purchase along my hips as I hovered there on the precipice of joining our bodies. He didn't push me in any direction, just rested his palms against me, his fingertips digging into my flesh as if he was holding himself back from simply spearing me onto him. "Are you sure?" he whispered into my ear, giving me one last chance to stop whatever this was.

My muscles almost shook as I hovered there, my core aching with a need that I couldn't quite explain. It wasn't born from feelings, because mostly what I felt for him was irritation. It wasn't the wine; I hadn't consumed enough to make me this reckless. No, it was some form of lust that I hadn't quite experienced before, possibly muddled with my desire to put everything I had learned about Cade in the background of my mind. I was surer of this than I had been about anything.

A tingling raced over my skin as I thought about what I was about to do, that step I was about to take into uncharted territory. With a man I could hardly stand most days but that somehow had the ability to make me feel like the most beautiful woman he had ever seen. Did he make everyone feel this way?

I couldn't think of that right now, and my muscles were already trembling at the effort it took to hold this back. So, rather than answer with words, I began to lower myself, stopping just before he entered me when another wave of tingles washed over my skin. It felt like the burning sensation of getting into a too-hot bath.

In fact, it was more than slightly uncomfortable.

My eyes flew open, and I broke our kiss, stealing a glance down at my arms and legs where the majority of the pain was radiating from now. From the outside, my skin appeared exactly as it had before. But inside, I felt like I had been struck by lightning, the pain building momentum as it zapped across my skin.

Beckett was looking at me quizzically, his silver eyes searching my face for whatever had caused me to stop. Not aggravation, but concern.

My body froze as another wave of pain rippled over my skin, sinking into my bones. Divots formed between my eyebrows as I looked to him for any sign of what was going on. "Are you using your gift on me again?"

It wasn't the exact same sensation as his magic, but I suspected that intense pleasure could hurt like this. It was the only explanation I had for the pain coursing through my veins.

Memories dragged me back to the day I had touched the Ice Trophy, and the resulting burn which had been similar to the way frostbite had been described to us, but magical in nature. It was why I had wanted to blame Beckett's gift, because what else could be causing this except magic?

Beckett's hands left my body in a movement so quick that I almost fell onto him without the extra support. "Of course not," he barked. "I told you I would never do that without your permission, and then I showed you what it felt like. It wouldn't hurt you like this."

I scrambled from his lap, adjusting my bathing suit to cover my body again. A panic rose in me as the stinging sensation got worse. "Seriously, Beckett," I whined, "I don't care if you did. I asked for a distraction, and I don't care how I got it, just turn it off. It hurts." My frantic voice ricocheted off the stone walls of the cavern.

Aggravation brimmed in his glare as he stood, adjusting his shorts with one hand as he reached for me with the other. "I am not using my gift on you!" His voice boomed as it met the sharp lines of the rocky walls around us.

Recoiling from his touch, I stepped from the pool, quickly gathering a towel and my robe so I could make a quick escape. The pain was almost unbearable now; made worse by the quick movements I required to don the robe.

"Please!" I begged, nearing hysterics. Nothing had ever hurt more than this.

Beckett began to climb from the pool's edge, presumably to come after me.

"No!" I screamed. "Don't touch me! You'll make it worse!"

The confusion washing over his expression was enough to make me pause, but he did nothing to stop the pain radiating from my bones. Assuming that, like elemental magic, proximity was required to hold the effects of the power, I had only one choice. If he wasn't going to turn it off, I was going to have to get away from him as quickly as possible.

Offering him nothing but my back, I ran. My heart constricted as I raced up the stone stairway and through the tunnels, taking the path that I had memorized just in case, and exiting through the correct door.

Enough distance was between us now that I had assumed it would be getting better. If it were anything like elemental magic, proximity was required to continuously use it on someone. But no matter how far I went, the ache didn't dull.

There was only one place I could go now to fix it. Adjusting my trajectory, I barreled down the hallway until I reached my destination. My balled fists banged on Ryana's door frantically, but moments later Grethe answered, shirtless, with only loose shorts around his waist.

He rubbed the sleep from his eyes. "What's wrong, Ash?" His voice was groggy, but I was too panicked to worry about that now.

"I don't know," I wailed. "I think Beckett used his power on me, and I'm having a weird reaction."

Ryana popped out from behind Grethe's back, taking in my haggard appearance. I was a sight for sure in my robe, the tips of my wet hair dripping water onto the carpet, and my face contorted into a painful grimace.

From the look on Ryana's face, I half expected a lecture, but she grabbed me by the hand, and immediately the pain stopped.

"Thank you," I panted. "Why would his power do that to me?"

She shook her head. "That wasn't his power." Her expression was no less concerned though. "That was yours, waking up."

Twenty-One

The light that sliced through the crack in the curtains was bright and buttery as I sat upright in my bed, wincing against its intensity. After Ryana had convinced me that the agony that I had felt coursing through my bones was simply my own magic coming in and not some wayward attack from Beckett, she insisted that I return to my room to rest. The retreat into my quarters came with no hesitation and I had promptly fallen asleep.

Now, in the light of day, shame festered in my gut as I recalled everything that had transpired the night before. Why had I accused him of hurting me, even after I knew how his magic felt?

Processing it alone in bed allowed me enough clarity to connect the feeling of fear and helplessness to the same sensation I had felt in the woods with Berit. One day, probably soon, I'd have to speak to a mind healer about that incident, but at the moment I had more pressing issues.

Like how my father was still missing, and despite the reassurance that the swallows—whatever they actually were—were looking for him, I was becoming less and less assured by that notion.

What if he wasn't here yet because he was too sick to travel?

What if he never returned?

What if I were forced to make a decision about breaking the spell without him?

My throat burned, threatening to overtake the pain in my temples, and I pressed my face harder into the pillow to muffle the start of a sob.

Even trying to distract myself with anything else, only led my mind to wander to what Cade was doing on vacation with Connally and why Jemma had been so nonplussed by my departure that she had gone along with them like some sort of double date.

My cries were perilously close to turning into screams when a knock sounded at the door.

I rolled over, swiping my hands against my face, then pushed myself to a seated position once more, wincing with the return of the brightness. "Come in," I called, instantly regretting the volume of my voice.

The door swung open, and Ryana waltzed in with a smile plastered on her face. "Good morning," she sing-songed, and I flinched again.

Air passed through my flattened lips. "Good morning," I groaned in return.

Ryana practically sashayed to the curtains and threw them all the way open, causing the entire room to flood with bright yellow light. The residual wine in my stomach turned sour, and I fought back the urge to vomit.

"It's time to get up," Ryana said, that same melodic quality to her tone like she might be enjoying this. It was something Jemma would have done, and I groaned again at the reminder of my supposed best friend.

With my forearm draped over my face, I threw myself back against the pillows. "I cannot go out there."

"Because you fucked around with Beckett?" she asked plainly, as if she had simply inquired over what I thought about the décor in the room.

Ignoring the pain throbbing behind my eyes, I shifted my head on the pillow to glare at her, my mouth gaping with indignation. "He told you?" My cheeks reddened under her scrutiny.

She scrunched her face up as she approached the bed, hoisting herself beside me onto the mattress. "No. You told me last night."

"Right," I mumbled, dropping my gaze to my hands as I fidgeted with the edge of the quilt. Obviously insinuating that he had used his powers of arousal on me had certain implications.

Ryana heaved a heavy breath. "Look, I'm not here to judge. Plenty of women fall under his spell."

I cringed but remained quiet.

Ryana's face was pinched with apology. "His charm," she clarified. "Either way, this cannot happen again."

Not that my abhorrent actions hadn't solidified that, but her telling me that I couldn't make that decision for myself tightened something in my chest. "Obviously," I retorted bitterly.

Ryana's eyes flared for a flash before her expression shifted to pity and her mouth curled up in a forced smile that I knew would never reach her gaze. "Oldenberg should be here soon, and then we can tell you everything."

Right. Because there were still things they were keeping from me. Secrets, even Beckett wasn't privy to. I closed my eyes again. "Then wake me up when Oldenberg arrives."

I could almost hear the grimace in her sigh. "I wish that I could let you wallow in your shame for as long as you need, but unfortunately, you're going to need food to keep up your strength."

"I'll take my food in here," I mumbled into the pillowcase.

"And fresh air," she added with a nearly motherly quality to her tone.

Groaning, I opened my eyes again. "Ry, honestly, this headache is so bad, I don't think I could make it down the hallway." That was not a lie, it just wasn't the only reason I wanted to stay in my room all day.

With a pitying glance, Ryana reached her hand out to grip my forearm. A shiver ran through my body, and then, instantaneously, the pain was gone.

"That's... You can heal too?" I asked her, astonished at how different I felt from just seconds before. Not only was the headache gone, but I already felt lighter. At least in my body. My mind was still a tangle of thorny weeds that needed to be pruned.

Ryana's eyebrows raised as if she could sense the lingering embarrassment, but when she spoke, she only answered my question. "Your headache was from coming into your magic. It was residual energy buildup from the night, and I only released it," she explained. "It shouldn't get that bad again, but if you don't figure out how to use your magic, those might continue to crop up."

My chin dipped like it made perfect sense. "At this point, Ry, I am just impressed to be able to open my eyes all the way without flinching. Thank you."

"So, you'll come to breakfast?" She asked, hopefully.

A part of me wanted to politely decline, but I was an adult, and I had to own my mistakes. If I saw Beckett, I owed him an apology, no matter how mortifying that might be. I'd just have to work on what that sounded like because *"Sorry you almost made me orgasm with dry humping and I, in turn, accused you of manipulating my arousal and hurting me,"* wasn't going to cut it.

With a fresh resignation, I shoved the covers back, sliding from the bed, only slightly less reluctant to face Beckett now that my face wasn't throbbing in time to my pulse.

Once I was clothed in another borrowed dress, Ryana and I returned to the dining hall, and I was surprised to find a small group still seated at the table despite Ryana's warnings that we were nearing the end of the breakfast hour. My eyes fell to Beckett first, who was, thankfully, preoccupied speaking with Grethe and hadn't noticed my entrance. He was seated in the same chair he always occupied. The one next to mine.

Grethe, Josaphine, and Gianna had taken the same places they had the first time we shared a meal together, leaving several chairs open, but all of them entirely too close to Beckett.

Don't be a coward, I told myself, tipping my chin skyward and crossing the room to slip into the chair to Beckett's right. From my periphery, it didn't appear as if he so much as glanced in my direction, but it was hard to tell with my focus officially only following Ryana's path around the table. Like she had a sixth sense about my intentions, Ryana hid a grin as she moved to her normal seat across from us.

Josaphine's voice drifted through my thoughts. "Did you have a good night, dear?"

I turned to face her just in time to see Grethe spit out his water. A burning heat covered my face. It was highly unlikely that the news of what Beckett and I had done, and my behavior afterwards, had reached Josaphine yet, so I composed myself, grateful that one of the servers had chosen that moment to set a plate of food in front of me.

Focusing on the meal before me, some sort of oats with fresh berries glazed in honey, gave me enough of a reprieve to pull it together.

Ryana patted Grethe on the back and muttered something unintelligible into his ear, and I pressed on as if it wasn't obvious to everyone around me. "Your son gave me a bit of wine last night, and I can't say that I reacted well to it," I replied, giving her as much of the truth as I could without enflaming the skin of my face any further.

Beside me, Beckett cleared his throat, but I couldn't bring myself to look at him. The apology that I knew I owed him wouldn't come in front of an audience.

Josaphine swatted at Grethe's arm playfully. "I expect better from you at your age," she chastised. A genuine grin split my face at the familial display.

With that same warm smile never slipping from her face, Josaphine turned to me. "I had some books on the different species of The Light Kingdom sent to your rooms just before I came to the dining hall. I hope you will find them to your liking."

"Thank you," I replied, genuinely pleased at the development and the chance to learn more about the Light Kingdom culture. "Do you have one you recommend?"

"I've always been fascinated with the shifters," Josaphine offered, glancing briefly at Gianna. "Maybe start with Wolfpacks of the Light Kingdom or Dragon Heart."

If the rolling of eyes could have a sound effect, I would have heard it moments before Grethe groaned, "Mom!"

Her head snapped in Grethe's direction. "What, Grethe? This is your heritage!"

"You're wolves?" I asked, my eyes widening. "Or dragons?" I added, even more impressed. Grethe had told me his gift was strength, but perhaps he had been trying to make sure I felt safe before he told me he could shift into something as fearsome as a wolf or a dragon.

"No, no, dear," Josaphine offered in a soothing tone. "My ancestors used to be dragon riders. It was our gift."

Not that it cleared anything up, but before I got a chance to clarify, a whine sawed from Grethe's chest. "Not this again."

Josaphine scoffed in a jovial way that told me this might not have been the first iteration of this conversation. "Dragons are your history, Grethe. We may have lost the gift, but that is no reason to balk."

"The gift was riding dragons?" I asked, pushing a few wayward blueberries around on my plate as I was far more interested in another glimpse behind the curtain that was the Light Kingdom than eating to conserve my strength. I could eat later.

Josaphine tipped her mug of tea to her lips, drawing in a small sip before she placed it back on its saucer. "We had special bonds with them that allowed us to speak to them in our minds. Because of that rare gift, we were chosen to ride them into battle."

"That's..." I paused, trying to find the right words to say. The more I learned about the magic here, the more I wanted to know. It had me almost excited about how my gift might manifest. "Did your family lose the ability because of the fading magic too?"

"In part," Josaphine replied. "Mostly it's because the dragons died out or fled after the Great Conflict."

A somberness hung heavy over our table, even as those around us continued to enjoy their boisterous conversations. "That's awful," I murmured, feeling guilty about bringing down the mood. "I'm sorry."

"Many of the dragons died during The Great Conflict," Josaphine said, her focus on the steam rising from her tea, eyes glazed over like she was remembering the horrors from that time, like maybe she had been alive. Based on Grethe's age, it was highly likely.

My chest expanded on a deep inhale, my stare pinned to Josaphine with what I hoped was an apology in my gaze. "I... I don't mean to be insensitive, but how did the humans defeat dragons? I am aware my only knowledge on the subject has come from fairytales, but I'm starting to believe they might all be real and—"

"The Dark Kingdom attacked from the North at the same time Demetros attacked from the South," Grethe replied, a sharpness to his tone that I knew he rarely carried.

At the mention of the Dark Kingdom, that third kingdom they had only discussed in passing, a certain intensity crept into the air, hanging heavier than the melancholy before. Although I didn't want to drag the mood down further, I wanted to know the truth about as many things as they would tell me. This seemed important. "The Dark Kingdom?" I asked softly.

"Their armies were led by the Shadow Fae," Beckett replied.

The sound of his voice—the fact that it was directed toward me—bristled something within me, but I still dipped my chin in a lame response. The Shadow Fae were the third species of Fae, the ones that could manipulate shadows and drank the blood of their victims to steal their power. I loathed the spike of fear that licked up my spine at the mere mention of them.

"The belief at the time was that the dark magic in the North posed the greatest threat," Grethe offered. "The dragons were sent to the front lines of the conflict raging on there, and most of them did not survive the battle."

He placed one hand gently on Josaphine's shoulder, squeezing lightly as he tried to catch her attention.

"We call that place the Dragon Fields now, to honor their fallen," Ryana added, although her attention was on her husband and his mother, concern marring her brow.

"The rest of them left," Josaphine said, her voice low and even like she was in a trance. "They did not reproduce as easily as the humans, and they went into hiding to try to recuperate their numbers, at least that was our understanding."

"So, they're not extinct?" I asked, suddenly concerned for a species that I had only recently realized was a real.

Beckett shifted beside me but did not speak.

It was Ryana who finally deigned to answer me. "We don't know. It's been decades since the last dragon was spotted."

"That's awful," I said lamely because I had nothing else to offer.

Across the table, Grethe puffed out his chest, tearing his gaze from his mother. "They might have taken our dragons, but they were punished with the same level of intensity."

My brow furrowed in a silent question.

"The Dark Kingdom lost," Beckett stated, anger bubbling in his tone for what they had done to the creatures. "Their capital was reduced to rubble by the rulers of the Light Kingdom, and their land was plunged into an eternal dark winter by a spell that suppresses them. It essentially keeps them from growing food."

A frown pulled at the corners of my mouth. That sounded horrible.

"Yep," Grethe exclaimed. "It's unlivable up there. They essentially died off."

"Oh," I replied as an unexpected pang of sadness squeezed its bony hands around my chest. Had all those people deserved that fate? Was that spell not also ravaging the lands?

I might have put a voice to those thoughts in my mind if my eyes hadn't accidentally snagged on a pair of grey thunderclouds in the spheres of Beckett's eyes. Hastily, I looked away, returning my attention to my food just as Ryana said, "That has not stopped attacks along the border, and you know it. Fae are being found drained more so now than ever before."

"Vissorri," Gianna warned, perhaps speaking her first words of the evening. She had been less than welcoming of my presence, only tolerating it after whatever debrief they had without me, but I could tell she still didn't approve of this flow of information.

A glance around the dining hall told me that everyone else had cleared out, so it wasn't that these facts were not meant for everyone's ears, as much as they were not meant for mine.

Regardless, it was on the tip of my tongue to ask if the Shadow Fae were behind the attacks, but just as I opened my mouth to speak, the double doors at the edge of the room burst open. Two people strode inside, and my skin seemed to tingle as I took them in.

The first person who came into view was a tall man who looked almost identical to Beckett in every way. Except, even from this distance, I could tell that he had dark eyes in place of Beckett's grey. His hair had clearly been blonde at one time but now held the signs of aging with silver streaks throughout. Given the knowledge of Beckett's pure-blooded lineage, I had to assume that the man before me had some considerable age on him if Beckett still looked to be in his late twenties at almost two centuries old.

The man was dressed in all black, with several weapons attached to the holster around his chest. Something about his presence made me want to shrink back, and I couldn't place why, because there wasn't a scowl or negative emotion to be found in his expression.

The woman beside him was wearing what appeared to be battle leathers. The supple brown material covered her, almost head to toe, and was adorned with ornate golden scrollwork that glistened as she glided across the room. Her knee-high boots, the same rich chocolate color, blended seamlessly into the gear.

A black tunic, with golden embroidery, peeked out from underneath the leathers, and she was draped in a rich emerald cloak that fell to her calves. Her wine-red hair was braided into a crown on top of her head with streaks of white woven through it as if someone had just taken a paintbrush to specific sections. Visually, she appeared to be in her late forties, but I couldn't be sure anymore.

She grinned as she took in the people at the table, stopping whatever conversation with the man at her side almost abruptly. "Welcome home, my friends!" she called to them, arms held out wide as if she could hug everyone from across the room.

Gianna stood abruptly, bowing her head slightly. "Oldenberg, Astor," she said, nodding to each of the individuals in turn with their name.

That name had my breath hitching in my chest as my eyes darted to the woman who I knew must be the person I had been waiting for. Oldenberg had finally arrived.

"Oldenberg," Ryana said, scrambling to her feet. "We need an emergency debrief. Now."

The woman seemed to register the use of her name and frowned, eyes scanning the group of us as if the mention of that moniker was a code for something else.

"Come with me to the meeting room and we can—" Ryana's words were halted as the woman's gaze fixated on me. Her face contorted into a grimace, and pure, unbridled anger flooded her features.

Code *dragonfire* or not, it was abundantly clear from the death glare I was receiving that I was not welcome here. Murder blazed in the woman's crystal blue eyes as she wrenched her focus to Ryana.

"What is she doing here?" Oldenberg spat. All the elation of her homecoming had been wiped away completely, not even a hint of a smile remained.

Ryana started to clear her throat, but the woman cut her off again. "You shouldn't have brought her to this kingdom. I trusted you." Her words were at the cusp of a growl.

There wasn't a thing I could do but look on in horror. Was I going to be thrown into a dungeon? Killed? I watched wide-eyed as this mysterious woman cut my friend down with a single pointed glare.

All eyes fell to Ryana as the tension unfurled in the room like a cloud of smoke. Wasn't she going to explain that her orders came from the Queen, like she had before?

Oldenberg inched closer to the table but did not take a seat and her glare remained a blazing inferno directed at Ryana's face.

For the first time since I had known her, I watched Ryana cower at the attention. My friend fidgeted with her hands in front of her as she took a steadying breath, raising her eyes to meet Oldenberg's stare head-on. Despite her bravado, there was no confidence in her expression.

"They were targeting her specifically," Ryana muttered. "They had planned to brand her Operarius before we even arrived, and once I found out, I knew I had to get her out of there. We have no idea what that brand does to those we know have power."

Ryana's voice was so meek, so timid. These interactions were nothing like what I had witnessed between her and Beckett. She seemed more than just respectful of Oldenberg, she seemed afraid.

Whatever the hierarchy was here, this all but confirmed my suspicions that Oldenberg held top position amongst this group. The lines between leader and subject were not so blurred between her and her subordinates as they had been between Beckett and my friends.

Beckett shifted in his chair to face Oldenberg. "Would someone like to explain what's going on? This girl has access to all four elements, so we got her out of Demetros. I thought that was standard protocol." He also hadn't mentioned the orders coming from the Queen, and I wasn't sure why. Maybe he didn't want to throw Ryana's mistake in her face.

Oldenberg shifted her turquoise eyes to Beckett and then back to me. Her features only slightly softened as her gaze met mine. Her voice was a whisper, which was in complete contrast with how she had spent the last several moments laying into Ryana. "I wasn't sure I would ever see you again, and I certainly didn't plan for you to find out in this manner. I thought I was protecting you."

Attempting to clear my vision, I blinked over and over, but every single time I opened my eyes, she was still looking at me. Try as I might, I had no memory of this woman. Was she talking to me or Beckett?

"I'm so sorry," Ryana mumbled, her head bowed. "I would have never brought her here if I had seen another way out of this. If you would come speak to me, I can explain everything in more detail."

Oldenberg's companion tilted his head in the woman's direction. "Do you know this girl?" His tone was curious, but there was an edge to it, a warning. In response, she flinched.

Beside me, Beckett's gaze seemed to dart between Oldenberg, Ryana, and briefly even me.

For a moment, no one said a word, and as I turned my attention back to the pair that had just walked in, the man's focus fell to me, his dark eyes roaming my face presumably for any hints of recognition.

Thanks to Berit, I knew what a predator looked like when they were scheming, and my hackles immediately rose under his scrutiny. Whoever he was, he was important to Oldenberg if he had arrived here with her, so I couldn't simply run the other way in fear of him, not when I needed information. Not when I was waiting here for my father.

My gaze slid back to Oldenberg, who was grinding her teeth together in a near-furious manner.

The man who looked so much like Beckett stepped toward her, snagging her gaze with his. "Whatever this secret is, I cannot imagine you keeping it from your generals," the man added. "You will tell me who she is to you."

Oldenberg nodded as if the man's rationale made perfect sense, even if her eyes widened as she spoke. Her azure gaze scanned the room, finding it empty save for the seven of us. When her stare slipped to mine again, tears were collecting along her lower lids. Her eyes seemed to bore into my soul, sending another wave of tingling recognition across my body that my mind had not caught up to.

She drew in an audible breath, and the battle leathers that had just made her look so fierce now seemed to be blocking her ability to fully inhale. A prison she was trapped in, as her face contorted with worry. "I hope you will understand that I never told a soul of my plans because it wasn't safe to. Vissorri was only recently brought into the mission because she was the only person who could get close to her."

"Why?" Beckett asked, incredulity in his tone, although I would never know if it matched his expression because I couldn't look at him. My stare was fixated on the woman who seemed to be speaking only to me.

Oldenberg looked apologetic, even though she had just been so furious that I was here. "I sent Ryana to Biltons Academy to watch out for you."

"Why?" Beckett repeated, this time with agitation lacing his voice.

The woman blinked, more of that regret flashing over her crystalline blue eyes with every flutter of her lids. "Because you are my daughter."

Twenty-Two

It felt like every cell in my body locked up, frozen in place. My lungs didn't expand or contract, I wasn't even sure I blinked as my mind tried to wrap itself around what this woman, this stranger, just said. Of all the impossibilities I had come to reluctantly accept over the last few days, my mother being the woman standing before me—the person I had been marching toward this whole fucking time—was not something I was willing to blindly believe.

"My mother is dead," I mumbled, perhaps I hadn't even said it out loud because Oldenberg didn't utter a single response.

Instead, the man beside her practically snarled. "You don't have any children of your own, that is why you named my son your heir." His words were muffled; it sounded like he was speaking through cotton, and I knew the problem was specific to me. I struggled to force that first breath. Then another.

Air slowly returned to my lungs in a shallow inhale. I blew out the exhale in a long stream, tilting my head toward Beckett to gauge his reaction.

Those stormy grey eyes were locked on Oldenberg, and while the same anger that the man beside her carried was not present in his stare, there was something disbelieving. Something both astonished and hurt.

"She was never supposed to come here," Oldenberg replied before pointing at Ryana. "You were under orders. You swore an oath."

The mention of the Queen's orders returned me almost completely to reality, although the effects of the shock still lingered.

At this, the man beside her practically imploded. He had already been doing a poor job at containing his rage behind his gritted teeth, but this time I heard as the snarl ripped through his lips. "You have a daughter? And no one here but Vissorri knew? She isn't even high-ranking." He jutted his finger in the space between them, narrowly missing Oldenberg's face. "For fuck's sake Anastasia, I am the General of your army. Don't you think this might have been useful?"

Anastasia. I had heard that name before. My father had used it in many of his stories of my mother.

My gasp was stifled by Gianna's response. "Even I did not know this information, Ebus," she offered, appearing hurt but still concerned for Oldenberg. Anastasia Oldenberg.

Ryana looked on the brink of tears. She bowed low toward Oldenberg. "I am so sorry, Your Majesty. I thought I was following orders by protecting her, and I couldn't leave without blowing our cover."

Everyone seemed to accept Oldenberg's word. That she was the woman who had birthed me. The person who had picked out the blue couch in our living room and painted roses on the corners of the cabinets. The woman who had left behind her boots under the chair by the front door when she died, bringing me into the world.

It was just too impossible. "My mother is dead," I repeated, although uncertainty rang in my words. "You've mistaken me for someone else," I added, more for myself than for anyone else.

Oldenberg's eyes landed on my face, glittering with the tears of remorse. "We chose to tell you that version of events. I had to leave you both behind in Demetros to keep you safe."

No. I refused to believe that my father was part of this. This was another trick. The Fae in the fairytales were notorious for playing games and striking bargains. This couldn't be real. My father couldn't have let me believe that my mother was dead for my whole life when she was here all along. I wouldn't accept that.

My mouth opened and closed like a fish out of water, but when words finally did come out, all I said was, "My father wouldn't have lied to me." It was a pitiful excuse, and I already knew it. If it were for my safety, he might have. Although the woman before me hadn't explained why this decision had anything to do with my welfare.

My statement seemed to cause Oldenberg even more pain. Her face pulled into a grimace as if the words had inflicted a physical wound. Her hand reached out for mine. "Come, let us talk in my study. We need privacy."

Her stern voice and her battle leather-clad frame demanded that I follow her command. Only, I couldn't move. I was glued to my chair, incapable of even shifting to offset the nervous energy.

Beckett's father—hadn't one of them called him Ebus—took several steps forward so that he was back in Oldenberg's line of sight. "To hell you do! This impacts everyone in this room, everyone in this Kingdom."

Beckett stood from his chair and pointed to me without sparing a sideways glance my way. "We've been searching for someone to break the spell for decades and you knew the key existed this entire time. Is that what this was? You thought you could hide her away until you found someone to take her place?"

Glancing up at Beckett added a new layer to my anguish. His face was red with anger in a way I had never seen before. I had witnessed him playful, arrogant, sensual, and even somber, but this was by far the hardest version of him to endure. There was hate sprinkled into his expression, his words, even the curl of his lip.

That wasn't even considering the actual words. The insinuation that if I were, in fact, Oldenberg's daughter, I was a key to breaking the spell. Like I was the solution to their problems. Knowing what I knew about the death sentence expected for whomever broke the spell, the insinuation that she had hid me because of it brought both extreme clarity to the decision and made Beckett's words all the more damning.

"We will discuss how this impacts the deal between our families," the man beside her growled. "Or shall I call back the armies?"

Oldenberg stiffened. Whatever her General had implied was worrisome because her skin had gone ashen. "No. This changes nothing, Ebus. Beckett is still my heir."

Her words did nothing to console him. Ebus Astor appeared to be livid.

Motion out of the corner of my eye caught my attention as Beckett's fist balled so tight his skin turned white around the knuckles.

"You know as well as I do that your word will not undo the magic of crowns," Ebus bellowed, and I watched as Oldenberg practically recoiled at his words. "As the rightful Queen by blood, your crown will pass down to your closest living relative."

It was then that it hit me fully. They had danced around it, but this was confirmation that Oldenberg and the Queen they had mentioned were one and the same. The woman claiming to be my mother was royalty.

"Astor!" Gianna barked, coming to step beside Oldenberg. "You're out of line! That is your Queen!"

Another confirmation. And if Beckett was her named heir... My gaze slid to him. No wonder he loathed the idea of my existence. If he believed this, I had just challenged his right to a crown.

Ebus leaned toward Gianna, towering over her in a clear threat. "And the army that she utilizes is my private army," Ebus countered before returning his harsh gaze to Oldenberg. "We had a deal."

Oldenberg swallowed roughly as her eyes fell back to mine. "I could renounce the throne," she offered in a panic.

With more tenderness than the scene seemed to be capable of, Gianna rested her hand lightly on Oldenberg's forearm. "You know the magic would just recognize her as your heir if you did that. She would instantly be crowned Queen, and she doesn't know the first thing about our people."

Gianna's words weren't meant to sting; they weren't even directed at me, and even though they were completely true, I still cowered at the notion that I wasn't seen as worthy of the honor.

A growl emitted from somewhere deep in Ebus' throat, and just as I thought he was about to throw Oldenberg across the room, she spoke. "We could betroth them."

Once again, the flow of oxygen into my body halted. Beside me, the air in Beckett's lungs retreated in an exhale that sounded almost painful.

I couldn't look at him. I hadn't even accepted the fact that the woman before me was my mother, and now I was being betrothed to a man who clearly hated me. Not that I could blame him.

"That's all well and good," Ebus spat, "but there is nothing that is keeping you from killing him off now that your heir has returned. I need more assurance than a promise of a union."

Oldenberg's wine-hued brows lowered. "We can move up the union," she sputtered, grasping for anything to pacify the man before her, and I had to wonder how he had so much power over her if she was the Queen. Or why she thought she could just make these decisions for me.

"That won't keep you from assassinating my son," Ebus growled.

Hurt flashed in Oldenberg's stare. "I would never harm Beckett. He is like a son to me."

Glancing at Beckett confirmed he felt the same way because while his fist was still balled by his side, his expression softened. Or maybe it was relief that the Queen's panicked plan wasn't going to come to fruition, and he wouldn't be stuck with me.

"I know a way to meet both of your terms," Ryana mumbled, almost too low to hear.

A breath whooshed from Oldenberg's chest as she wheeled around to face Ryana. "What is it, Vissorri?"

Nervously, Ryana bounced her attention between Oldenberg, me, and finally Beckett before her marbled brown eyes came to rest on her Queen again. "We can bond them."

The breath Beckett pushed through his nostrils was loud enough to convey his disdain for this idea.

"What was that?" Ebus snapped, as if he hadn't even been listening to Ryana. Like he didn't value her opinion at all.

"We can bond them," Ryana repeated, this time a bit more assured. "Tying their life forces together ensures Beckett can't be assassinated unless they both die, and the crown will pass to him as well."

Instead of finding notched brows on the elder Astor's face, his features began to loosen as if he was finally considering this deal a viable option.

Trepidation pooled in my stomach when I watched Ebus' grin turn feline as he looked to Oldenberg. "What do you say, your majesty? How much is my army worth to you?"

Oldenberg looked stricken, her skin growing more pale by the second. Marrying me off hadn't been a problem for her, but the idea of bonding me to another was clearly giving her pause. "I..." She stalled, shifting her attention to Ryana. "Can it be done?"

The bob of Ryana's throat spoke to her guilt, and she flashed both Beckett and me another apologetic look. "Yes. I sensed their compatibility this morning."

My eyes widened at the realization that she had touched me to relieve the tension headache from the residual magic buildup. Had she been reading me? Monitoring me? Was this the plan all along?

"This is good for you, Anastasia," Ebus stated through a wide, ominous grin. "If the bond protects Beckett and the girl from assassination, would it not also protect your daughter from dying while breaking the spell? We all win here."

I didn't know Ebus well enough to make any conclusions about his intentions, but his presence had set alarm bells off in my mind from the moment he stepped foot into the dining hall. If he was this eager to bond us, I wasn't sure it was a good thing.

Sliding my gaze from Ebus to Oldenberg, I searched for any sign that she was still hesitant about this union. Unfortunately, her fear from earlier had washed away, revealing relief. My fate was sealed before she even spoke the words.

"You have a deal," she stated, thrusting her hand between them in a gesture that seemed far too casual to confirm a bonding between two people against their will. While he hadn't outwardly protested, I knew from body language alone that Beckett found the idea of this union abhorrent, and the last thing I wanted to do was be stuck with someone who likened the notion of marrying me more to a nightmare than a dream.

Ebus peered down at Oldenberg's outstretched hand and sniffed a laugh. "First, I have stipulations."

I almost snorted at the audacity of the man, acting like he held the upper hand when Oldenberg wore the crown, but I watched on with rapt interest, hoping his terms would leave the Queen backing out.

The General lifted his chin, and his expression was so smug that I already hated him. "The ceremony will need to occur as quickly as possible."

Oldenberg bobbed her head, apparently having come to the same conclusion, shifting her gaze to Josaphine, who had remained silent and seated throughout this entire ordeal. To the point that I had forgotten she was there. "How soon can preparations be made?"

Josaphine's expression was stoic as she offered the first forced smile I had ever seen her wear in the Queen's direction. "We can convert the New Year's celebration into a reception, if that is not too soon."

My heart fell into my stomach as Oldenberg replied, "That is fine. Do it."

More of Ebus' teeth shone through his wolfish grin. There was far too much glee in his expression. How could no one else see this?

And he wasn't even done. His tone was almost amused as he added to the list of terms. "If she is to be representative of our family, she will need to undergo etiquette training." At his words, Ebus slithered his gaze over me, taking in my simple appearance and borrowed dress with distaste coating his features. It took everything I had not to flinch away from his attention.

"With Charlese in Falkland," Ebus added, although none of it meant anything to me.

Oldenberg dipped her chin in agreement, like she had the ability to barter a political marriage on my behalf without even asking me. My fists formed tight balls at my side to mirror Beckett's. How was this happening?

There was a brief pause where I thought the list of demands might be over, but then Ebus tacked on, "If she was recently plucked from Demetros, she will need to be trained to use her magic, so she has any hope of breaking the spell by the solstice."

My heart stopped in my chest. The summer solstice felt like a life-time away and the blink of an eye at the same time. What if they were wrong about the bond saving me? Knowing there was a possibility that I might die to break the spell was different than being given a death date. My heart rate began to climb as panic seized my lungs. "My father is on his way. I won't make this decision without him."

Oldenberg's eyes flared with an emotion I couldn't place. "She's right. We should involve Christian. I can't make this deal without him."

Air poured down my windpipe again. The mention of my father's name was like a balm on a burn, allowing me to calm down even if it was only minutely. It felt like reason and logic were finally being injected into the conversation. Once I gathered my thoughts, I might be able to argue against this plan. At least once I wasn't also trying to wrap my mind around this woman's declaration of being my mother.

"No," Ebus barked. "You make the deal now, or it's off the table. My army will be gone, and you will have made an enemy out of me and my family."

Beside me, Beckett seemed like he might protest, but Oldenberg cut him off. "Then I have two stipulations of my own."

Shock rippled over Ebus' features as his eyes narrowed to slits. "Go on."

If I didn't know any better, I would have assumed Ebus was the king and Oldenberg was his General. The dynamics here were troubling, but not as concerning as the deal being bartered in front of my eyes.

"First, I would like to be the one to train Ashton," Oldenberg stated. "Beckett can help when it comes to her using the magic more defensively."

"Fine," Ebus growled, as if even that was an inconvenience for him. "And?"

Oldenberg appeared almost sheepish as she lowered her gaze to the floor. "Her identity needs to remain a secret."

A twinkle of something I could scarcely place glittered in Ebus' stare.

"We still have enemies across the border," Oldenberg explained when he did not readily agree. "Both of them," she added hastily. "They would use this information against me, and she is not strong enough to fight them off."

My cheeks flamed with embarrassment. I might not have had the years of training like everyone else in this room, but I did know how to protect myself. My father had made sure of that.

Ebus' chest expanded as he puffed up with pride. "Luckily, she will be bonded to the most powerful Fae in the Light Kingdom." His lips curled into an unsettling smile.

Beside me, Beckett growled, reminding me that I wasn't the only person whose opinion had been disregarded in this deal. "Do I get a say in this?"

Against my will, a small whimper emitted from my mouth, and when Beckett turned his stony expression to face me, there was no emotion there to pick up on. Quickly he shifted his attention back to the Queen and his father.

Oldenberg frowned. "As my heir, I've never asked you for anything, but I am asking you now. Please keep my daughter safe."

Something shifted on his expression then, that almost looked reverent, mixed with the tinges of regret I was certain he already felt.

"This is ridiculous," Ebus stated, glare pinned to Beckett. "This is purely political, and if you are willing to plunge The Light Kingdom into civil war because your bride isn't as desirable as you wished, then by all means, let's discuss that instead of unifying our forces."

Beckett's jaw clenched with barely masked rage, and my heart splintered in my chest. Worthiness was something I had chased my entire life, and when Ebus put it like that, it was difficult to stomp my foot and demand that they reconsider. Maybe this would show the Queen that I was worthy of her legacy. Also, if this could somehow save my life...

"I'll do it," I muttered. "For the Kingdom." Ignoring Beckett altogether, I let my eyes lock with the woman claiming to be my mother, waiting for her approval.

A sad smile flickered over her features as she dipped her chin in acknowledgement. Then, that azure gaze slid to Beckett, and hope sprang in the blue of her irises.

Beckett snorted his incredulity. "When you word it like that, Ebus, I'm not sure you've left me with much choice but to agree."

It was clear that Beckett's choice would still be a no, but Ebus grinned as if it had been a whole-hearted declaration of love for the idea. "Then we have a deal," Ebus purred, thrusting his hand toward the Queen. "My son remains the heir to the Light Kingdom, and your daughter's identity will not be given to your people."

Oldenberg's palm came out to meet Ebus's and their fingertips curled around each other's hands to seal the deal without any further consideration of Beckett's point or my internal reluctance. Magic pulsed along my skin, and although I wasn't sure what that meant, it felt like something permanent had just been set into place.

Twisting my neck to look at Beckett, I hoped I would catch any of the emotions I felt mirrored on his face, but in the place where he had been standing, there was nothing. One of the doors to the dining hall slammed enough to rattle the ice in my glass, and my heart broke again.

Twenty-Three

I t hadn't even been a full day since the decision had been made to
convert the New Year's celebration into our ceremony and reception, and the effects of that ruling had already trickled throughout
the entire castle.

The staff who had been full of anticipatory exuberance, had begun
their stress laden scurrying about the halls, sprucing up every square
inch of the place in preparation. Those who had already found themselves guests of Castle Lochmere in hopes of attending a New Year's eve
party had gotten themselves automatically invited to the royal event of
the year, if not the decade. Unlike the staff, the guests were gleefully
strolling through the castle in hopes of catching a glimpse of the future
Princess of the Light Kingdom.

Beckett hadn't so much as spoken to me since the announcement,
dodging me like I was a puddle of mud he had to circumnavigate to
keep his boots clean. In turn, I avoided them all, the Queen included, as
I attempted to hide from everyone with the exception of meal times.

Luckily, Josaphine had been true to her word and supplied me with
several tomes to pass the time in my self-appointed exile. I had already
buried myself in Wolfpacks of the Light Kingdom for hours, more than
content to read the tome that felt more like a romance novel than a text

on history. The Queen in the story had been blessed with a great power and had fallen in love with an alpha wolf with no throne of his own. It was so captivating that I groaned when I heard the knock at the door, mostly for the interruption to my story, but also because I already knew what was coming for me.

While Beckett had been allowed to avoid all the wedding planning, I —as the lady of this union—was tasked with helping Josaphine with preparations. According to Ebus, this was a skill I would need to learn as the wife of the future king and thus I had been assigned the task.

Just as I expected, it was Josaphine at the door, who led me to the meeting room with an apologetic smile.

Three hours later, I rolled my neck to dispel some of the tension gathering there. Josaphine and I had been sequestered to the meeting room for what felt to my body like days as we went over the most minute of details for the bonding celebration.

She had explained what the ceremony itself would be like, which had only taken thirty minutes even with all of my questions, and the rest of the time had been spent picking out napkin embroidery, cake flavors, and even the dimness of the flames in the chandeliers.

The leather chair squeaked against my skin as I adjusted myself in the seat for the thousandth time, hoping to find any comfort that I knew would not come.

It was becoming glaringly obvious that I was out of my depth with this task, and I wasn't sure if I would ever be good at hosting events like the Astors expected. It wasn't like I had grown up planning an elaborate fairytale wedding. My daydreams had mostly consisted of the after. Of the man I would spend my existence loving and cherishing. The type of life we might live together. This façade was a far cry from anything I had wished for, so I found that I didn't care much for any of the details either. Only I didn't have the authority to bow out.

"Can we talk about flowers? What do you like, dear?" Josaphine's warm gaze met mine as she placed her hand on my arm.

Josaphine had continually, but kindly, pushed me to make decisions, and I could hardly be annoyed because she was putting forth a real effort to include my personal tastes wherever possible. Genuinely, I appreciated the gesture, so much so that I had shoved down an excess of irritation and resentment at still being locked in this room while Beckett got to avoid the worst of it. It still took a conscious effort to remind myself to be grateful for her kindness. To not take any of it out on her.

"I like roses," I stated with a grimace. "My dad has purple roses that grow in his garden that are my favorites."

Although one of the swallows had been sent days ago to check up on my father, and they had been set to return in the same timeframe as Oldenberg, no news had come from Demetros. Given how quickly Beckett and I had traveled here on foot, I had been expecting my father to have made it already. Especially considering he might have lived here at some point before my birth. The more days that passed without word, the less confidence I had in my delusion.

Even if this was a political union, and something of a magical last-ditch effort to save my life, I longed to have my father present. The idea of doing this without him, and even Jemma and Marjorie, felt wrong. We were a family, and this was the kind of thing families did together. Sadness became an ever-present weight in my bones. My dread was compounded by the uncertainty of where and how he was.

Josaphine's soothing voice brought me back to the task at hand, giving me something else to focus on besides the worst-case scenario. I had already spent so much time in turmoil over my father's where-abouts, and more importantly his health, that I welcomed the small distraction. "We should be able to procure them," she said it with a smile, like she knew something that I didn't. "Would you like to use purple as your color scheme?"

My fingers rapped against the table as I considered that, unsure if I even cared. But if my dad couldn't be here in person, I supposed the subtle reminder of him would be comforting. "Yes, I would like that."

Josaphine dropped her attention to the table, writing something down on a piece of parchment, her quill dancing vigorously as she recorded the notes.

"We still need to talk about food," she said, going down the checklist she had in front of her. There were several pages stacked underneath the one she was only halfway through. The evidence that we had only made a small dent in what appeared to be a never-ending pile was enough for my patience to finally fray.

My hand reached for Josaphine, letting it gently rest on her elbow as I looked directly into her warm, chocolate-hued eyes. "I know you're trying to include me, and I am so thankful for that kindness, but I honestly don't care about any of this. Do whatever you think is appropriate and will please Beckett's parents."

Crinkles formed at the corners of Josaphine's eyes as her face scrunched in a knowing smile. "How about I just let you know what to expect when it's all sorted out?"

This time, my returned grin was genuine. "Thank you for understanding and for helping plan this."

"Of course, dear."

On another day, I might have hugged her, but I only took the time to squeeze against her arm before I practically flung myself from the room, breathing in the hallway air and taking a moment of appreciation for my newfound freedom from the travesty of wedding planning.

My first order of business was to find Ryana. Despite my magic being awoken the night before Oldenberg's arrival, I had yet to see any evidence of power that I could wield. She had promised me that she'd help me until she left for the academy, and I had honestly wallowed in my room long enough.

Knowing exactly where I'd find her, I made my way to the game room, where she and Grethe spent most of their time when they weren't training or attending meetings with the Queen and the other Generals. All of which I had been left out of in favor of letting me plan the celebration that I had been forced into.

Halfway in a daze, I entered the open door of the game room, Ryana's voice greeting me almost immediately.

"Oh, hey Ashton! You're done early," Ryana called from her spot at the angular table.

A swath of sandy hair caught my attention, like he was a flickering fire, and I was nothing more than a bug driven by instinct to look at him. To be drawn to him even though he hated me. Beckett's jaw ticked, but he didn't look over at me, choosing instead to stare intently at something on the floor.

Grethe, ever the mediator, stepped in to lighten the mood. "Becks, you'd think you'd be in better spirits. At least you know we like the girl your parents are making you marry." His eyes rolled in a playful manner that was so Grethe it made my chest clench. "It's so hard to find a couple that you like both parts of the pair, you know? Ry and I always assumed we'd have to disown you when you married some aesthetically pleasing nitwit."

Ryana snorted, and I bit my lip to keep from doing the same. Even Beckett's mouth quirked as if he was trying, and failing, to squash his amusement.

The movement captured my attention yet again as I took in the sharp planes of his jaw and the stubble forming there, despite our access to bathing chambers. Dark smudges of exhaustion rested below his eyes. He looked... sad. It only added to my heartbreak. At least part of his disdain was warranted, and there was something I could do about that.

My eyes lingered on the corners of the frown that Beckett's lips had fallen back into, already forgetting all about my plans with Ryana in favor of fixing this mess between us. "Can I talk to you?" I asked him softly.

He finally looked my way, if only for the briefest of moments. Dark grey eyes, flashing with more unreadable emotion. "Sure," he grumbled, the muscle along his jaw flexing in a poor attempt to hide his irritation.

My fist pressed against my hip; eyebrows raised. "Alone?" My head motioned toward the open door.

Grethe snickered. "We have somewhere to be anyway," he said as he grabbed Ryana's hands and pulled her from the chair.

"But I was win—" Ryana began before Grethe cut her off.

"Talk to you later!" Grethe called as he yanked Ryana across the threshold and down the hall.

"Bye!" Ryana added just as their footsteps faded away to nothing.

Tentatively, I took one step toward where Beckett remained seated at the table, careful not to crowd him. "Look, I was trying to give you some space, but also, I don't even know what to say. 'I'm sorry you're forced into a bonding with me' seems..." I mulled it over for a moment. "It seems inadequate, and frankly, it hurts my feelings to apologize for it."

Pointedly, I stared at him, but the silence stretched on, screaming in the space between us. Hurting my head. Hurting my soul.

Finally, he blinked. The first signs of life, or at least some sort of cognitive recognition that I was still there, even if his focus remained on the pile of Ryana's discarded cards.

"I am sorry though," I offered. "I am sorry about what happened in the caves, and I'm sorry you have to marry me, of all people, after I accused you..." Cowardly, I sucked in a breath, unable to finish those words. "I know this isn't what you wanted."

A heavy sigh escaped my lips, frustration building the longer I spoke. He wasn't making this easier for me by ignoring me so dutifully. "I know I'm not what you would have chosen, and I am sorry you are stuck with me forever."

"It doesn't have to be forever," he countered.

My eyes narrowed in on his face. "Why, because you'll outlive me due to your pure-blooded lineage."

He scoffed. "You're royal, too, in case you forgot, Princess."

"Then what does that mean?"

The corner of his lip twitched almost into a smirk, although his expression was anything but amused. "It means that if we can keep the bond from solidifying, then it can be reversed."

"You're already planning to divorce me?" There wasn't anything I could do to keep the hurt from bleeding into my question.

"Not instantly," he replied. "If we stay together until the crown passes, I believe Ebus will be satisfied, and then we can go our separate ways. You can go back to Elmhaven and live whatever life you had planned before all of this."

My lips popped open. "You want to take my crown?"

"You want the crown?" he countered, one golden eyebrow lifting up his forehead.

"I—" my words lodged in my throat. No one had asked me about what I wanted in all of this. Not really. I had agreed to this union for the greater good, not out of any desire to be a Queen. But now that Beckett had posed the question, it gave me pause. "I would like to be worthy of the honor. I'd like to be given the choice."

The confession hung between us like a dense fog. For a while, neither of us spoke, but it was my voice that cleared away the silence. "I am sorry though. I know you didn't want this at all."

Beckett cleared his throat, his grey eyes flickering to me briefly before they found purchase back on the discarded cards once more. "Why do you think that?"

"You looked like the idea of marrying me was the worst thing that ever happened to you," I replied, suddenly unable to look at his face any longer, even though his attention wasn't on me. "Look, I know I owed you an apology for that night, and I am truly sorry for accusing you of hurting me, but now that we are in this for however long, I think it would be easier if we worked as allies, rather than enemies."

"What did I do to make you come to that conclusion?"

His words prompted the return of my focus to his face; his brows scrunched in confusion.

"You've been avoiding me like the plague since we were betrothed."

A steady stream of air blew from his nose, but he did not speak. He did not deny my assessment of his feelings, and something about that salted the wounds that Cade had made in my heart. I wasn't powerful enough for Cade, and maybe—considering what Ebus had said—I wasn't desirable enough for Beckett.

This wasn't the time for a pity party, but something in my chest cleaved at the idea that I would never be good enough for anyone. Especially if Beckett was already contemplating ways to get out of this marriage. It didn't matter that I didn't love him, I hardly knew him, but it still hurt.

Beckett's mouth opened and closed as if he was about to speak, considering replying to me with some rebuttal, but all hopes of that faded when his lips pursed together in a tight line. It was as if he was actively deciding to antagonize me.

Tears sprang to my eyes, and I tried to convince myself, somewhat ineffectively, that it was more about the overload of information I had received rather than being this distraught over the rejection from a man I didn't even fully like. "I know you don't want this, but it doesn't have to be bad. You can do whatever you want, you know?"

Once again, he didn't respond, so I continued brazenly. "You don't have to be stuck with me. You can go be free back in Demetros at the Barker Inn. I don't care what you do, but we are beholden to the agreement, and I really don't want to die. There is no need to make us both miserable with your pouting!" The words practically flung from my mouth like stones aimed to hurt.

Beckett's head jerked in my direction, and there was something icy lingering in his gaze. "You'd have me running around fucking other women behind your back?" His tone was as sharp as a knife's edge.

My chin jutted out in response as if I truly didn't care what he did. "Well, it wouldn't be behind my back if I knew it was happening. I just..." My voice broke, and my features softened. "I know you didn't ask for this; I'm trying to impact your life as little as possible since it's clear they, and you, truly believe I am the key to breaking this spell. I don't want to die before I see my dad again."

Quicksilver eyes scanned my face, eyebrows bunched in what appeared to be confusion. "We will be bound, Ashton. There's nothing you can do to avoid making that impactful. I'll be able to feel your emotions and you mine," he all but growled. "Do you want to feel me doing that with someone else?" This time, his stare remained locked with mine.

Ryana had done her best to explain the bonding, but there was still so much I didn't know or simply hadn't paid enough attention to absorb adequately. "You will be able to feel what I feel?" I asked, a little uncomfortable with the idea. "I didn't think it always worked that way." Even Grethe had only mentioned being able to sense an echo of emotions.

Beckett snorted a humorless laugh. "It doesn't always. But... you should be prepared for that possibility. If it develops, even with shielding, it will always be there to some extent." The aggression had already begun to retreat from his voice, although I didn't know why.

My eyes flared. Was there something I didn't realize about the bonding that he did? Like maybe our connection was a direct reflection of his power level. Ebus had called him the most powerful Fae in the Light Kingdom. Did that mean the side effects of that magical bond would be greater? If they were more intense would that mean... "Will you be able to read my mind?"

He chuckled, his first genuine smile in my direction in what felt like an eternity. "I won't be able to hear your thoughts, but your expressions give you away." The smile shifted to a smirk. "I can already read your mind."

On instinct, I took a step closer to him, my hand thrown onto my hip. Looking down, I smiled at him sweetly. "Can you tell what I am thinking now?"

One of us moved, causing my knee to brush against the fabric of his pants. Ignoring it, I watched him as he studied my face, looking up at me from his seated position, a heated intensity building as he assessed me.

And gods damn it; all I could think about after that look was the way his hands slid across my body. The way his kiss consumed my every thought. Without my express permission, my irritation made way for a lust that had me grinding my molars together in defiance. After what had happened the night in the pools, I wasn't going to accuse him of using his magic again, especially considering this burn was more of a smolder. He had been right, now that I knew what it felt like when his gift was being used on me, I could recognize I only had myself to blame for this unfortunate reaction.

Beckett stood abruptly, the new position putting our bodies close enough that I could feel the warmth radiating from his chest. Our height differences forced me to tilt my chin up to meet his gaze.

One finger caressed the line of my jaw as the deepness in his voice rattled against my chest when he spoke. "Based on the pink tint to your cheeks right now and the fact that you just bit your lip, I'd say you were thinking something very inappropriate," he said, cocking one brow upward in a challenge.

I retracted my lip from where it sat between my teeth, and my eyes widened as heat crept over my chest and up my neck. My face jerked away from his touch, but all he did in response was chuckle, low and deep.

"Relax, kitten. I can't actually read your mind." He smirked, like maybe that wasn't altogether true. He had basically just proven that, to some extent, he could read me like a book.

But, even through the embarrassment, I felt a tiny pulse of relief that the Beckett I had met in the Barker Inn was making an appearance. Maybe not a resurgence, but at the very least, stopping in for a visit. I would take that if for no other reason than bickering with him gave me somewhere to displace all this anger and confusion I felt inside. And, if we were going to be bound together for the foreseeable future, I'd rather spar with him than be ignored by him.

Beckett's body shifted slightly, putting us just a fraction of an inch closer, making me wonder if I wasn't the only one of us who held this strange attraction. Maybe we were each winged creatures made of fire, drawn to each other by some incomprehensible magic that both of us were too stubborn to acknowledge.

He leaned down, without touching me, so that our lips nearly met. My traitorous body longed to close the gap between us, remembering what it felt like to have his full attention, but I held steadfast as his smile broadened like he was laughing at some inside joke I wasn't privy to.

"I can, however, scent your arousal," he whispered, dipping his mouth to my ear. For one exhale, one warm and sensual breath against my lobe, he lingered. Long enough to send chills skittering down my spine, settling in places they had no business being.

My eyes closed as I sucked in a breath, trying desperately to prepare a halfway decent retort. Reminding myself that I didn't even like him most of the time.

Not that it mattered. When my lids opened again, he was already gone, and I was once again left gaping at the doorway in his wake.

Twenty-Four

After discovering that the window in my suite did face the front gates of Castle Lochmere, I spent most of my free time reading the books Josaphine had leant me and watching the horizon like a sentinel. It was the following day, after my escape from wedding planning, that I finally caught sight of the first hint of movement in the distance.

Based on my assessment, it appeared to be an entire caravan of wrought iron carriages cresting the hill. A sense of giddy anticipation filled me as I rushed to stand, running toward the door, astonished to find it already opening.

The second round of shock came when I saw Beckett standing in the doorway. Although we had ended our last conversation on amicable terms, he had all but returned to ignoring me and had been noticeably absent at meals. Unease tangled with surprise in my stomach as I peered around him to see if anyone else was in the hallway. "Hi. I was just about to leave."

"No, you weren't," he corrected flatly. "It would be in your best interest to avoid roaming about the hallways until dinner."

My eyes flared with irritation. "Are you confining me to my room again? I thought we got past the part where I was a prisoner."

His features relaxed some as he took me in. "You are not sequestered to your room; I was merely giving you a bit of advice." He pointed toward the window where I had just been staring, fairly certain I was witnessing my father's return to Castle Lochmere. "That horde of transports out the window is my mother."

The words deflated my previously happy demeanor. My shoulders slumped as I glanced back at the glass panes, wondering if I could force a different result by hope alone. "Are you sure?" Of course, it wouldn't be my father coming with a large group. Logic would have told me that if I had thought about anything but my desire to see him again.

When I turned back around, Beckett's hands were clasped behind his back. So formal. "I am positive. And she has brought an entourage."

I swallowed, reading into the shift in his tone and drawing my own conclusions to the hidden meaning. "And she will not like me?"

Beckett took a small step forward, not to comfort me, but to shut my bedroom door behind him.

My throat bobbed again.

"This union will solidify her son's place as heir to the Light Kingdom throne. I doubt she will have much to say against the deal Ebus and Anastasia have struck." He grimaced as he spoke, and I didn't miss the way he had so casually mentioned his father and the Queen by their first names. There was reverence in the way he said *Anastasia* that was missing from the way he enunciated *Ebus*.

My arms folded over my chest. "That's not really an answer." Not that it wasn't a typical Beckett response, but it certainly did nothing to soothe my nerves.

Beckett's silver eyes narrowed as he took me in, focus roaming over my plain garb. "Dinner will be a formal affair, and Josy will bring you something appropriate for the introduction."

So, I wouldn't be getting anything closer to a useful response from him. My stance adjusted as I plastered a smile on my face. "Anything else I should be aware of? Or did you just come here to tell me to stay in my room until dinner? And to wear a pretty dress when I come out."

A pained look crossed his features, and I immediately regretted not just sending him on his way because I could already tell this would not be a fun conversation. "I have spoken with the Queen about a matter that is quite sensitive."

I felt the muscles in my jaw flex as I raised a singular eyebrow in his direction. "And she sent you to talk to me instead of coming here herself?"

Beckett's chest expanded fully right before a long-winded sigh left his lips. "Despite what you might think, Anastasia is like a mother to me. I am not going to let a squabble impact my ability to speak to her, and she is well aware that you want nothing to do with her."

That stung, even though it was true.

"She asked me to be the one to relay this information."

The humorless laugh that tumbled from my throat nearly got lodged there. "This is not a squabble. She let me think she was dead for my whole life and—" I cut myself off before I got too emotional, closing my eyes so that I could take a single steadying breath. When I opened them, I resigned myself to being calm and rational. "The relationship between the woman claiming to be my mother and me is none of your concern. Please do let me know what she had to say."

Before he could speak, I motioned toward the wing-backed chairs. "Would you like to take a seat?"

"No," he grumbled, only adjusting his stance slightly, his arms still braced behind his back.

"Then spit it out, Astor."

His chin lowered with a jerk, but the movement almost looked like he was covering up a flinch. Neutrality returned to his features before I could grasp onto any definable emotion. "As you know, Anastasia and Ebus are planning to spin this as a love match and..." His hands began to fidget behind his back. I could tell by the way the muscles in his arms bunched and rolled.

"Today, please," I snapped.

He glared at me but continued. "Your mother suggested that we do a better job of acting as though we are in love because no one would believe that an Astor married a common girl. Much less one that was so obviously part human. Not unless it was evident that I was in love with you."

Bewilderment stole the breath from my lungs. I was already well aware of how the Astors viewed humans, but I hadn't expected the opinions of all the people to be the same. "Okay," I muttered, unsure what else I was supposed to say to the insinuation I was somehow less than because of my upbringing. "What does that mean?"

Beckett's head tilted as he offered me a pointed stare. "Physically, it should appear that we cannot get enough of each other."

My resulting swallow was so audible, I was certain it could have been heard in the hallways beyond my closed door. "Okay."

His scarred eyebrow lifted up his forehead. "We will share a room here after the ceremony. And for the entirety of our stay in Falkland."

My eyes widened. "Excuse me... where?"

"Falkland. The location of my family castle in the north. It is where you will be trained on how to harness your power and given etiquette lessons, per Ebus' terms."

Had I breathed in the time between my question and now? My lungs filled and expelled air in a shallow rhythm, my eyes darting around the floor as I pieced it all together. "And I'm expected to sleep with you? Every night?"

"You are expected to enter my bedchambers with me every night." His words drew my attention back to his face. His blank, unreadable face.

I swallowed down another wave of panic. Not that I hadn't been ready to have sex with him just days ago, but this expectation added a new level of issue I had with the agreement my mother had made on my behalf. She was stripping me of yet another choice, and this was asking far too much. "So, we have to consum—"

"No," Beckett bit out harshly, finally showing emotion that made him grimace. The return of the disgust on his face wasn't lost on me.

"You will have your own room," he continued quickly. "A suite off my main living quarters. Both here and in Falkland. It will allow us to enter my room together each night for appearances."

My focus fell to a random point on the rug as I considered this. "How does this play into your plan to ensure the bond is never solidified? Won't all that affection impact that?"

Beckett's eyes blazed with another unnamed emotion. "There will be no affection that isn't fabricated for the public," he replied flatly. "We are not going to have sex."

Confusion pulsed along my temples, and I fought the urge to press my fingertips into them. "You want me to act like I'm in love with you when people are around, but we are not to touch or…"

"Fuck," he finished for me, his voice void of the teasing I expected.

"Understood," I muttered. "We will not be affectionate in private. At all." There was a question lingering in those statements, but it felt a bit pathetic to commit to asking him if he planned to show me any tenderness behind closed doors. Were we even going to be friends, or would we live separate lives when we weren't in public?

"I'll do my best to keep everything appropriate," Beckett replied. "I'm not asking you to straddle me at the dinner table."

Heat flooded my cheeks, and I kept my eyes downturned so I wouldn't have to meet his gaze.

"And," he continued, "if there is anything you're uncomfortable with, just let me know. Tap my shoulder three times or something."

A soft laugh rumbled through my chest. "I assumed it would be obvious that you touching me wouldn't make me uncomfortable." The words were only a whisper, but I hadn't expected the thoughts to come streaming out of my mouth before I had a chance to alter them. Or at all. My teeth clacked as I slammed my lips shut and the subtle blush that had crawled over my face deepened.

The clearing of Beckett's throat drew my attention back to his face. It was obvious he was uncomfortable with my statement. "I'm sorry," I muttered. "I was trying to lighten the mood."

"Right," he replied, shifting his weight between his feet as he continued to stare at me with an undecipherable expression. "Do you agree to these terms?"

"Do I have a choice?" I snapped, already regretting my tone. The irony that he had said the same thing when Ebus had bartered for our betrothal did not escape my notice.

"You always have a choice with me," Beckett stated, his tone softening with his expression. "It will make the façade more believable, but I am not going to make you touch me. You are an adult, and you can make your own decision on it. If you refuse, we can find another way."

My lip worked between my teeth as I considered his proposition. It was nothing like the one I had made in the pool. Where I had wanted a distraction from my pain, what Beckett was asking for was likely to cause me more of it. I couldn't imagine having his attention and adoration under the watchful eye of his kingdom and being shut out each night as if I were nothing more than a coworker with whom he did shift work.

Then again, Oldenberg had seemed adamant about keeping my identity a secret, and as long as I avoided her, I probably wouldn't get to learn why that was so important. I wasn't sure if I was ready to speak to her yet, but I did trust that her decisions were borne from her desire to keep me safe.

Furthermore, Beckett was giving me a choice. Like we were actually partners. Perhaps I could agree to this as a show of good faith, and maybe we could learn to be allies after all.

"Okay," I replied softly. "I agree to your terms."

In the same way I had seen Ebus and Oldenberg seal the deal, I shoved my hand out into the space between us so that Beckett and I could shake on it.

He shook his head. "There's no need to seal this with magic. I'm not going to have you beholden to affection like that."

Not knowing what else to do with my hand, I let my arms cross over my chest. "Thank you."

A hum emitted from somewhere in Beckett's throat, nudging my attention back to his lips. "For what it's worth," he said, pausing long enough for an elongated breath. "I think you should talk to Anastasia. It would be a safe place to hide out while Onyx's court gets settled."

My lips remained sealed shut as I simply stared at him.

His head tilted. "She is the only person who can give you the answers you need," he said as the corner of his mouth lifted ever so slightly. "And we both know how curious you can be."

Offering him my best impression of a smile, I lifted my chin. "Thank you for your advice."

Twenty-Five

The idea of talking to the woman who had claimed to be my mother was agonizing for a multitude of reasons. If I chose to believe her, I was angry that she had lied to me, an action that had allowed grief to take over my life and consume me at times. On the other hand, I acknowledged that this had been my lifelong wish: to find a way to bring her back to me. Never in my wildest dreams had I considered that fate would grant that desire in such a tragic way, highlighting how little I really knew about either of my parents.

There was a part of me that recognized a portion of my desire to avoid her came from my worry at not being enough. What if she got to know me and found me lacking? Despite its painful awakening, my magic had yet to make an appearance, and I was starting to worry that it never would. Maybe Ryana was wrong, and I was powerless, and Oldenberg would regret ever bringing me into the fold.

It wasn't those morbid thoughts that propelled me toward her study door, but Beckett's words that had me gathering the courage to face her. He was right, and she was the only person here who could give me all of the answers I needed. Plus, it had the added bonus of giving me somewhere to be other than my suite, while still avoiding Onyx Aster and her entourage.

"Just knock," Beckett said as he led me to the office door. "She's expecting you." With that, my future husband only offered me a parting smile before turning on his heel and leaving me alone.

Several slow, deliberate inhales filled my lungs, my exhales pushing languidly from my lips as I attempted to steady my racing heart. After a few minutes of cycling between all the reasons I should knock, then all the reasons I shouldn't, I finally lifted my fist to the wooden boards and rapped my knuckles against the door.

Almost instantaneously, the Queen's voice carried past the threshold, light and airy, like a melody on a breeze. "Come in."

My palm curled against the cold metal handle as jiggled the knob, carefully stepping inside the room that I had been avoiding for days.

"Hello," I whispered lamely as our eyes met.

Unable to look at her for too long as she stared at me with such hope, I scanned the space. There were floor-to-ceiling bookshelves and a simple desk, all made from the same dark, chocolate-toned wood. Several alcoves in the shelves were illuminated from the light filtering through the colorful but tasteful stained-glass windows that hung on the wall above plush tufted benches. The room itself was small, but cozy. Rustic but refined. A glimpse into the personality of the woman who might be a mother to me. One day.

The Queen cleared her throat. "Thank you for agreeing to meet with me, Ashton. I know this must be hard for you."

My gaze snapped back to hers as she gestured for me to sit in an overstuffed leather chair facing her. Following her instruction, I slid into the cushion, gripping the arms to wipe away the sweat forming in my palms.

"So," she began with a neutral expression, "what do you want to know? I will tell you anything." It seemed like she might be ringing her hands in her lap, but I couldn't tell for sure.

Settling in the chair, I tried to find the most comfortable position for this uncomfortable conversation. Mixed feelings danced throughout my body in jarring complicated movements. I did not want this to be an interrogation, but I desperately wanted answers, and I warred with myself on how to best achieve my goal without ruining any chance of a relationship with the woman before me.

A deep breath filled my lungs, and I started at the beginning. "How did you and dad meet? I assume *'while strolling in the town gardens'* was a lie?" Notes of bitterness floated through the air, but the Queen allowed them without comment.

She smiled as her crystal blue eyes went glassy, obviously replaying the memory in her mind, holding it for herself just a little longer before she could give it to me. "Yes, and no. As you know, Christian, your dad, is an avid gardener and collector of flowers."

My acknowledgement came with a tight nod of my head. The corners of my mouth quirked at the thought, but I couldn't decide which direction they might land.

The Queen's gaze remained focused on the space behind me. "He used to travel all over the kingdoms for rare and unusual species. He had fancied himself a healer long ago." She chuckled like it was some inside joke they had shared—even though I had never heard that—but I couldn't even bring myself to smile. "One day, in his exploration, he had taken his boat to the island that you came here from, The Emerald Isle."

That journey felt like a lifetime ago. How had it only been days?

As she continued her story, her smile broadened. "I was coming through..." she paused, and the briefest hint of sadness breezed across her face, gone in an instant, replaced by an even brighter grin. "We all but ran into each other while on the island. He caught me before our collision threw me to the ground and it was an instant connection. I don't think we left each other's side after that for months."

My head tilted to the side. "But you are a Queen. How did that even work?"

She sniffed a laugh. "That was a tumultuous time in my life but at that point I was not the queen."

"A princess then?" I asked, then realized something else... "Are my grandparent's alive?"

Her smile softened, dipped a little, but didn't completely fade. "I was just a Lieutenant in the Light Kingdom army then. My predecessors had not named an heir, but we shared blood, I had always been a consideration."

Thinking back to the day Oldenberg had waltzed into the dining hall and changed my life, I considered what Ebus had said about the magic of crowns choosing a blood relative. Other than it reminding me of the Biltons Academy cook, Maude's similar spiel, I hadn't given it much thought at the time. "Does the crown always go to the next closest blood relative?"

She sighed. "It's a bit more complicated than that. Primarily, it goes down a single line, but sometimes that is not an option. It will not go backwards, so if I had a great uncle, it would not choose them. Probably something put in place to keep families from slaughtering each other, but it's hard to know for sure."

My brows furrowed. "So, you cannot actually select an heir?"

A bit of rueful amusement brought out a small hum from her lips, but she only shook her head. "Not unless there are no true descendants from the original bloodline." She pushed on, eager to get away from that topic. "The fact of the matter was that I had not grown up with a Light Kingdom title, and I had not expected to be Queen. When I met your father, I did not know the challenges we would face because of my lineage."

Trying to puzzle out the meaning behind her words, while respecting her privacy, was difficult. Curiosity flared bright in my mind, but I chose safe questions, figuring I could dive deeper when we knew each other better. "Dad told me you were in the Queen's Guard."

"Here," she corrected as her frown deepened. "I was a lieutenant in the Light Guard. Back then, there were only two branches of the army. Queen's Guard or Infantry. He told you what he could, I'm sure. So, you'd still know me as much as possible."

The organ in my chest constricted like it was being squeezed, pushing out all the blood. We were veering a little too close to topics I wasn't completely ready for yet, like how my entire life was a lie, so I forced out another question to steer us away from that subject. "You abandoned your duties to be with Dad, then?"

A soft laugh emanated from her chest. "I brought him back to the Light Kingdom, and he followed me to my various assignments."

My forehead crinkled with my raised eyebrows. "Then you just showed up with a baby and no one batted an eye?"

A shaky breath rattled in her lungs. It wasn't a sigh, but it was heavy with regret. "As you've been told, Fae lifetimes are longer than human ones. This all occurred before The Great Conflict."

The confusion must have been plain on my face because she followed that up with, "A few hundred years ago."

"You're Fae?" It was such a stupid question, really, because she was the Queen of Fae lands. Furthermore, why else would I be a child of both worlds if neither of my parents were Fae? Still, I had to be certain, and the braids along her hair blocked my ability to see the tips of her ears to confirm another way.

Her smile was mixed with something other than happiness. "Mostly."

"And dad?"

The woman before me looked like she was considering carefully how to answer my question. "Your dad is mostly human, but we are bonded. He has some Fae blood, or he wouldn't have been able to wield magic."

As I processed her words, my head swiveled back and forth as if I were refusing them. "I don't understand how any of this works."

The Queen offered me an understanding smile. "Your father does not have enough Fae blood to significantly extend his life, but we are bonded. Our life forces are woven together. His life is extended because of it."

"Like mine will be extended because of Beckett and his pureblood line," I remarked sardonically.

Her eyes narrowed briefly. "You are royal, Ashton. It is possible you would have an extended life regardless. At least now that you are outside of Demetros."

I considered her statement for a moment, curious as to why my location played a role in my lifespan. "Why is that?"

The Queen chewed on the inside of her lip. "The spell ensures that the Fae have normal lifespans within the construct. Aging occurs at an accelerated rate for those of us who live within it."

Initially, I wanted to ask her why this didn't seem to affect the Elemental Queen, but I was more interested in how it would impact my father and his health. "Even Dad? You're bonded though, does that help him? What other effects does it have on him?"

My inquiries came rapid fire and a small smile tugged along the Queen's lips, but she mulled over my questions for a few seconds before replying. "Your father will age like a human while living within the construct, whereas we share a lifespan when he is outside of it. Beyond our lifespan, we share power. That is why he is so skilled at... well, everything. He was originally just a wielder of water magic."

A flush crept up my throat as I considered that I might be able to utilize Beckett's gift. Then, my mind snagged on her words. A rough breath sawed from my throat as another piece of my life slid into place. "That's why Dad was so good at construction... he can access all the elements?" How had I missed him using other elemental gifts? Again, my brows pinched together. "But I saw his brand. How was he able to use magic at all?"

Her eyes scanned my face. For what, I wasn't sure. "His brand has always been an illusion. We put it there when we returned to Demetros."

"When I was born?" I surmised, treading lightly into the topic I was truly curious about.

Sunlight glinted in her auburn hair as she dipped her chin once in agreement. "The short story is that we were bonded before The Great Conflict ended. When it was over, and the spell was in place, I was officially named heir, and after some time, I took over as Queen. He was my consort."

A swarm of flies could have flown into my mouth for as long as it stayed propped open. Had my dad been a king? It was almost comical how we had lived, considering he had once worn a crown.

The Queen continued, unaware of my shock, or maybe just forcing herself to keep going. Keep relieving these memories that filled her face with dread. "We knew that a child of both worlds could break the spell, and I assumed, since my magic helped set it, that any child of mine would be more likely to be the one capable of such a feat. By then, we were aware of the effects of the magic on the land."

A sigh heavy with regret seeped from her lips. "Recognizing that it was a death sentence, we chose not to have children. We even named an heir, knowing I had no other blood relatives alive; we thought it would work."

Melancholy overtook her expression, and her gaze dipped to a swirl in the wood of her desk. "We thought we were being careful. Fate had other plans."

A pinching sensation twisted my heart, but I remained stock still as I watched her.

"Essentially, I sent myself on a mission when my predicament became apparent, and your father came with me. We set up a life in Elmhaven, knowing the bind would hide your magic from detection. Even so, I knew it couldn't last. Taking you back to The Light Kingdom would put you in danger, and visiting too often would arouse suspicion."

Her exhale was tainted with her sadness. "I originally planned to leave my life behind and abdicate my throne, but the magic of the crowns doesn't really work that way. The exile spell and the bind it put in place couldn't hide you from that forever."

A frown pulled at the edges of her mouth. "We agreed that the safest option for you was to leave you in the care of your father and have me return to the throne without you both. If I had stayed, we feared that others would put together that your lineage could break the spell, and I couldn't chance your life being forfeit."

Tears filled her ice blue eyes, which I now recognized as the same color as my own. "It was the hardest decision I have ever made. I never went back once. We didn't even exchange letters that could be traced back to you."

She choked over the words, and the burning sensation in my throat climbed higher. "I've watched over you as best I could without telling anyone who you were, but when we discovered that you'd be attending Biltons Academy, I sent Ryana there. She is the only person who knew about you."

Considering the reactions of everyone in the dining hall when Oldenberg was unceremoniously forced to admit who I was to her, I believed this statement to be true, and a part of my heart cracked at the thought of how painful that must have been for her.

Her eyes had fallen to her desk, where they remained locked on some invisible marker. "Officially, and to the others, she was sent to figure out what was going on with the brands, as her gift was perfect for such a task. The Elemental Queen announcing her intent to choose an heir was the ideal cover because that escalation meant a clock was set for how much time we had to break the spell."

By now, the frown seemed permanently etched on her face.

"So, you planned to have someone take my place?" I asked, already knowing the answer. "And none of them were able to break the spell?"

"Blood magic is the strongest kind, and as my daughter, it was almost guaranteed that your attempt would be successful since I helped set the spell," she replied, repeating some of her earlier statements with more detail. "I don't regret my decision to find another, I only lament that I was not successful. If for no other reason than that our reunion could have been under better circumstances."

As sad as I had been to lose her to death, I couldn't imagine what this time had been like for her. And, although I was still hurt over a lifetime's worth of lies, I felt that perhaps I understood it a little more now.

"I've been trying to find someone else who can break the spell since I returned," she admitted, and I knew the weight of that. Knew that it meant she had been actively seeking out those she could sacrifice in my place. It was both horrifying and endearing.

Her voice cracked with the heavy emotions that lingered in her stare. "All I've wanted since the moment I learned of your existence was to keep you safe. Even when that meant I had to leave you behind, I spent every day trying to find a way for you to come back to me."

"And Dad?" I prodded, noticing that she hadn't said *you both*.

A new wave of sadness crossed her features again. "I am not sure. The people have not forgiven him for abandoning the kingdom. We had to spin a story that explained his departure back into Demetros, and the best we could come up with was that he wanted to be with his people and chose to join their exile. It was common knowledge that we were bound, although no one but my inner circle is aware that we are mates."

My nose wrinkled. "Mates?" There was still so much about the Fae that even the fairytales didn't tell me. So much to learn that I feared I would never catch up.

A tiny hum emanated from her chest. "When two people are bonded, their life forces are woven together. When mates are bonded, it connects their souls. There is no undoing that." Her brows scrunched together. "Unfortunately, something about tethering yourselves together like that makes the bonding magic act erratic."

My head cocked to the side as I wondered when I would stop learning so much new information about this kingdom. "How so?"

Her features grew stern, almost sharp. "I am telling you this information because I trust you, but this needs to remain between us. It is dangerous knowledge."

My head inclined sharply, gesturing my agreement. This was what Ryana had meant when she said I would get full clearance. All of it. Because of my lineage.

The Queen paused for a long moment, as if warring with herself on whether she should speak. Ultimately, she must have decided to, because her eyes slipped back to mine, and she continued on. "Bonding in itself is simple. Your life forces are combined, and therefore, if one of you is injured, even fatally, the other can keep you from death as long as they are whole."

This was a repetition of information I already knew. The entire reason I was being bonded to Beckett. "But they can be killed. If the body is destroyed, right?"

She grimaced. "Yes. But with mates, since their souls are bound, death is more complicated."

I wasn't sure what could be more complicated than death itself, but I listened on with bated breath.

"For bonded mates," the Queen began, "the body of one mate could be destroyed, and they could still be resurrected through the bond. A piece of their soul clings onto the soul of their partner, allowing their body to regenerate."

Resurrection? Gasping, my eyes flared. Magic would never cease to amaze me. "That sounds like it would be a good thing."

The Queen hummed, tapping her fingers lightly against her desk. "You'd think. But it is only one of two scenarios. In the other, when one mate dies, their bonded is pulled into the afterlife instead of acting as an anchor, and they both die."

My brows pinched as I mulled over this new information. "How do you know which will happen? What makes it go one way or the other?"

She shrugged as if we were simply talking about the weather. "True mates are so rare that it is not well documented." Frustration swelled in a half-laugh, half-sigh. "As far as we are aware, we are the only mates in existence right now, and it has been many years since the last pair was recorded. Simply put, we don't know."

My teeth ground along the inside of my cheek. "So… mated bonds are dangerous?"

"Very," she replied with a shudder. "Which is why this has to stay between us. If the Dark Kingdom, or the Betrayers, got hold of this knowledge, they could use him to hurt me."

"The Betrayers?" I had not heard this name yet, and I was feeling bogged down by the ever-growing list of new enemies.

The Queen waved her hand in the air between us. "The Guides, as you call them in Demetros."

Right. Of course, they were behind the brandings, although that didn't explain fully why they were being referred to as the betrayers, but it seemed like a history lesson for another day because panic was slowly ratcheting my pulse to an alarming level. "Wait… Dad is still back there! We don't even know if word has gotten to him yet. What if the Guides already have him? Surely, they know I've run away by now."

I got the distinct impression that the woman before me was hiding her true emotions on the subject because her face was too stoic for us to be discussing the fate of her mate. "Your father was aware of the risks of remaining in Demetros. We have a network of safe houses set up there, and he knows how to go into hiding."

Her throat pulsed on a swallow, a gesture that seemed unsettling in the moment. "I have sent our best scouts to look for him. We will find him before anyone else can. Then, he will come back to us."

"So, he's not at home? In Elmhaven?" I had suspected as much, but this seemed to be confirmation that he was truly missing.

Her gaze drifted from mine, falling to my hand that was still clutching the edge of her desk. "No, but I am not concerned. I would know if he had met his end. Another benefit of the bond.

This only offered me a modicum of relief. "Can you tell if he is hurt?" I needed to know if he was suffering, as he had been when I left for Biltons Academy. I needed to be sure I hadn't left him to die.

The Queen placed her hand over her heart, eyes fluttering closed.

"There is great distance between us, but I should be able to feel if he is suffering if I reach for our bond. At the moment, it feels calm. Contented."

It was a relief in part, but I still wanted to ask more about that connection. Maybe ask her if she was certain. Before I could, a despondent countenance shifted her features from that emotionless state to something soft around the edges. "I see he gave you my ring."

My fingers gripped the band, and I began to tug it off.

Her hand darted out, her fingertips brushing against my wrist. Our first contact. "No," she commanded. "It's yours. It's spelled with protection to keep you safe. I always wanted him to give it to you if you were ever separated."

My gaze fell to the glittering orange stone adorning my finger. How many times had it protected me? Did it aid me in traveling to Eden? What kind of magic did that? And... I gasped as my brain snagged on a new question. "How would you know if you are mates?"

Her brows pinched. "We did not know until an event prompted it, but now, Ryana should be able to detect the same energy signature on others."

"And Beckett and I are not..." I couldn't even bring myself to finish the sentence. We were about as compatible as oil and water if you took away the physical attraction.

The Queen chuckled, shaking her head. "No. Ryana has assured me that you do not have the same signature as Christian and I." Her smile did not falter as her gaze landed on my own. "I would not force something as serious or permanent as a mate bond on someone. Although I would trust Beckett with your life."

The sentiment was not reassuring as she meant for it to be because, although I had technically agreed, her actions had forced me into a different kind of bond. "Right," I mumbled. "Luckily, this one can be reversed."

Her head tilted as she studied my features. "Even though the regular bond is not permanent, you should know that it is not as simple to undo as those binds on your power in Demetros. It will come at a cost."

It wasn't lost on me that she hadn't commanded that I stay married to Beckett, but she wasn't exactly trying to reassure me that I could leave either.

"What kind of cost?"

The Queen frowned. "Every bond is unique, so the price isn't always consistent. Some have lost the ability to wield an element, others have gone blind. There have been a few cases where the pair has reported untreatable, lifelong depression."

Shuddering at her words, I filed away that information for later. My fingers began to curl around the arm of the chair again, gripping tightly as my knuckles turned white. Perhaps it was possible to undo the bond, but I wasn't certain it was a viable option for me. Not with repercussions like that.

"For what it's worth," The Queen stated, "I believe that Beckett is a good man. I would not have agreed to a match that would put you in harm's way or pair you with a monster."

The words were minimally comforting, but I caught the thread of her honesty woven between them.

"It's not a consolation," she added, "But had you grown up here, this likely would have been the outcome anyway."

I thought back to the way in which Cade had spoken of his family and their expectations. How they had treated his relationships like extensions of their power, almost as if he were royalty too. The concept had seemed so foreign when I was a poor girl from a small town, and I thought those rules could never apply to me, but as I considered the Queen's words, I saw some semblance of truth in them.

If I had been raised a princess, I would have been betrothed to someone for the betterment of the kingdom. Considering Ebus' choke-hold over Oldenberg, in a twist of fate, it might have been Beckett even in that alternate universe.

"Your father approved of him," she added, as if this would sway me one way or the other over my bond.

It might not have warmed me to the idea of being bonded to a man who was already plotting ways to rid himself to me, but it did give me pause. A wry laugh spilled from my lips at the idea of the two of them chatting comfortably over breakfast. It was unfathomable. "I cannot even comprehend Christian Blake being in the same room as Beckett Astor. Beckett is..."

"There's something else you should know about your father," the Queen said, interrupting me mid-thought. The expression Oldenberg wore told me that the list of discoveries I had yet to make about my father would not end with this one tidbit of information, but I waited for her to tell me anyway.

"His last name isn't Blake."

Twenty-Six

Later that evening, I watched as Ryana's nimble fingers braided a section of hair around the crown of my head. I had already applied the kohl to my lids, and Ryana passed me various creams and balms to add pink to my cheeks and mauve to my lips. The dark powder swiped over the creases of my eyelids made my irises look like a deeper shade of cerulean than I had ever seen.

My dress was flowy and ethereal. The ensemble was made up of two distinct pieces. The first was the soft lilac silk dress that cut into a deep V, cinched at my waist, and cascaded to the floor in wispy movements of fabric. The dip in the neckline would have been entirely too revealing had it not been for the shimmering amethyst corset bodysuit underneath.

A delicate, layered golden necklace hung in thin ropes from my neck, and matching metallic bangles lined both of my wrists. Regardless of the fact that the orange clearly clashed with the purple hues of the gown, I kept my mother's ring on, prepared to put the protective properties she had promised to the test.

The entire event almost felt like a repeat of preparations for the solstice eve ball, even though Jemma, Connally, and Ingrid were all noticeably absent. That, and when I looked into the mirror, I scarcely recognized the woman staring back at me.

She looked older and could almost pass as something regal, someone born into this. The reminder that I didn't belong here only served to tighten the ball of knots in my stomach.

"Do the Astors truly hate humans?" I asked Ryana, as she slipped on her navy gown that was fitted to her body, flaring at the bottom like a mermaid's tail. The dip in her own neckline nearly reached her belly button. She was fiercely beautiful as ever.

Ryana grimaced, placing sapphire jewels into her earlobes. "It's complicated in the Light Kingdom. Many have no issue with humans, but there is a portion of the people who blame them for the wars."

My gaze slid from Ryana's reflection to her actual face as I twisted my body around. "They cannot possibly blame the humans alive today. The rebellion happened generations ago in the human lands."

A frown tugged at the corners of Ryana's mouth. "I know. I'm not saying I agree. But there are those who feel that the humans who are powerless will always seek to steal what they do not have."

I dropped my gaze to the floor. "That's ridiculous."

"They also feel like the interbreeding between species has led to weaknesses in their own species," Ryana added, her tone flat.

For the most part, I was confident that she didn't feel the same way, but I found myself searching her face for disgust or disapproval to confirm it. A sigh nearly spilled from my lips when I caught the expression I was looking for. "So, the Astors are part of that group. That believe I'm tainting their bloodline?"

Ryana grimaced, slipping her attention to the mirror again to tuck away a strand of her loose raven hair. "Ebus was eager to accept the deal because it was strategic, but I do not foresee either of them being overtly nice or welcoming to you." Those mottled eyes turned to me. "I'm sorry."

My head shook as I twisted around the ring on my finger. "It's not your fault my father is mostly human."

"Right," she mumbled, almost regretfully. "But I am the one who offered the solution, and I wanted you to know that I believe Beckett is a good man, or I wouldn't have suggested it."

Ryana was the second person in a twelve-hour period who had mentioned what a good man Beckett was, but none of them were aware of just how much he hated the idea of being tied to me. As if to punish me, my mind recalled the image of his face when I had tried to ask him if we'd be expected to consummate the union. "Beckett and I have come to an agreement about what will be expected during our brief union," I replied flatly. "With any luck, I will rid myself of all of the Astors after the summer solstice."

A flash of skepticism danced along Ryana's expression, but she quickly contorted her face into something more closely resembling neutrality. "Just be careful, Ash. Ebus is a general of the infantry for a reason. He's strategic to the point of concern, and I don't believe for a moment that taking you to Falkland wasn't part of some grander scheme of his. I just can't piece together what he's up to quite yet."

It was on the tip of my tongue to ask more about the man who would become my father-in-law, at least in a magical sense, but a knock at the door stole both of our attentions before I could voice my thoughts.

"Come in!" Ryana called, even though we were in my suite.

While I had expected Josaphine to come and bring another update around the wedding preparations, it was Beckett who stepped across the threshold instead. The sight of him practically stole my breath from my lungs. He was dressed in a fitted black suit that had evidently been tailored to the exact lines of his body.

His sandy blonde hair had been combed out of his face, highlighting the scar across his eyebrow and cheek that on anyone else might have been a knock against their attractiveness, but on him just enhanced it. Like a dangerous edge, or a mystery that needed to be solved.

Without so much as a smile in my direction, he crossed the room to me, holding out an elbow for me to grab. "Are you ready?"

While I caught him eyeing my appearance, I saw no indication of whether or not my attire met his parents' standards. "Sure," I mumbled, taking his arm. He smelled of the soap he must have used to shave his beard, the aroma reminiscent of rainwater and evergreens. The faintest hint of the night-blooming jasmine I typically associated with him remained an overlay over his natural smokey musk. I had to remind myself to breathe normally rather than soak in his alluring scent.

Once I was situated with my arm fastened around his, he tilted his head toward Ryana. "Thank you for helping her get ready for tonight. She looks stunning."

A blush crawled its way up my chest, mixing there with the irritation over the fact that he hadn't just told me himself. Like I wasn't even truly there.

Ryana lobbed him a look that spoke of her similar feelings to my own. "Beckett, you should tell her that yourself." A smile crested her lips as she began to walk toward the open door. "But you're welcome. See you both in a few!" With that, she stepped into the hall and disappeared from view.

Beckett's posture seemed to grow rigid as Ryana's footsteps trailed down the hallway. His voice reflected that strange tension. "Well, I guess we should go."

Swallowing roughly, I bobbed my head up and down. "If we have to." After my conversation with Ryana, I certainly wasn't looking forward to my formal introduction to the Astors.

A flicker of amusement twitched at the edge of his lip, crowding into his tone. "It's safe to assume you are not looking forward to this event then?"

We were still awkwardly rooted to the same spot in the room where I had taken his elbow to begin with. Instead of letting go as I wanted to, I left my hand in its place, glancing up at him to speak. "I know your parents aren't fond of my father's lineage, and my meeting with Ebus already went so poorly. I'm not exactly excited to add another person to the mix."

"I don't expect her to like me," I added quickly, "I know this isn't a typical meeting of the parents, but I don't know how to handle these situations. I know I am supposed to be some princess, but I wasn't raised to be one. The closest I came to high society was Biltons Academy."

For a millisecond, astonishment passed over those otherwise neutral features, gone so quickly I thought I imagined it. The muscles in his arm bunched as he pulled me closer, ever so slightly, and probably not enough for me to have noticed if I hadn't already been hyper aware of all the ways our bodies touched.

He peered down at me, those storm clouds for eyes catching with mine. "Just follow my lead, and there is nothing to worry about. You have plenty to offer, and they will see that."

I felt the frown twisting my lips. There was nothing I had to offer them except the crown I had barely even processed for myself. But I wasn't about to fish for any compliments from the man who had already voiced how ready he was to be free of me.

"Are *you* ready?" I asked, instead of putting a voice to any of those thoughts. He hadn't exactly tugged me toward the door either.

An unsteady sigh escaped his full lips. "I think we will both survive the night. This union is highly in their favor. I doubt they will find reason to cause trouble."

That did nothing to quell my nerves as I considered exactly how they might usually cause trouble, but whatever strange moment we were sharing had already passed as he began to move us toward the door and out into the hallway.

When we arrived at the dining hall, I was stunned to find that the room had undergone quite a transformation. Each table had been lined in deep pine colored cloth that fell to the floor and decorated with enormous floral arrangements fanned into the air with flowers in shades of purple and pink. All of it was foliage that I knew was not in season after the winter solstice.

As we passed the nearest table, I noted that the plates were bone white, rimmed in gold, and encircled in ornate floral patterns. So reminiscent of the plates at my childhood cottage that the sight nearly stole my breath, leaving me wondering which had come first.

More golden utensils than I knew what to do with bracketed the dishes, and I sent a silent thank you to wherever Josaphine was in the castle for her help in attempting to aid in my memory of how to use them. Crystal goblets full of sparkling wine had already been carefully placed to the upper right of each plate.

Instead of stopping at any of the seats, Beckett guided me toward two people, one of whom I already recognized as Ebus Astor. The woman to his right had to be Beckett's mother Onyx, except unlike with Ebus, the resemblance to her son was almost nonexistent.

She was a petite, thin woman with milky white skin and thick dark hair piled on top of her head that showed off the slanting points of her ears. Her sharp features created shadows under her cheekbones, and her lips were painted blood red. The kohl around her eyes fanned out in points, making her look as lethal as the big cats that were rumored to stalk the woods in the south of Demetros.

The judgment pouring from the Astors' cold stares led me to believe I was already starting the night out on the wrong foot. Neither of them smiled as we approached, both silently assessing me in a way that made my stomach twist.

"Good evening, Ebus, Onyx," Beckett said, nodding at each of them at the same time he spoke their names. "I'd like to formally introduce you both to Ashton, my betrothed."

Releasing Beckett's arm, I offered my hand to Ebus first as a way of greeting, but he left it lingering in the space between us. Onyx only dipped her chin in response to the gesture when I pivoted my body to face her.

"Charmed, Miss Oldenberg," Ebus sneered in a whisper as if he were the farthest thing from charmed that existed.

Beckett craned his neck to see if anyone around us might have heard before he blew an almost imperceptible breath through his nose. "Blake, father, her last name is Blake."

According to my mother, that wasn't even necessarily true, but I plastered a smile on my face to hide my grimace.

"Interesting," Ebus said, disdainfully. "I don't recall ever hearing that name before."

Of course, if my father had known Beckett, he would have certainly crossed paths with Ebus. However, considering Ebus had been around during the time of my father's departure back to the human lands, would he have really expected us to continue using the last name Oldenberg?

Regardless of all of that, no one was supposed to know my relation to the Queen so bringing it up now seemed odd. Was he trying to make the connection known, despite his deal with my mother? Rather than puzzle out what he was up to, I only offered them both a sweet smile. "My father raised me by himself and that was his last name. It would have been unusual not to share it with him."

The mention of my upbringing must have sparked more disgust on Onyx's behalf because she wrinkled her nose as if I stunk. "It's such a shame you were not brought up properly." She made the remark has if she was insinuating that I had been raised on a livestock farm with the animals.

It was becoming a struggle to remain neutral in both tone and facial expression, but I willed my mouth to hold its grin. "Lochmere is a beautiful place. I would have loved to explore the grounds here as a child."

We were dancing around my heritage, and I couldn't help but glance around, wondering who else might have heard and put two and two together.

The Astors laughed as one, sneering all the while. "Oh dear, no. This place," Onyx said, gesturing around like she was pointing at an actual pigsty, "is not the castle. The royal castle is north of here, on the coast."

Kicking myself internally for not asking more about the geography and general setup of the Light Kingdom before the Astors' arrival, I held their stare with what I hoped was a neutral expression. Thanks to Beckett, I had already been warned that we'd be traveling to Falkland on the morning following the ceremony, but I hadn't thought to ask anything further about the Light Kingdom. This was the Queen's castle, so I assumed it was *the* castle. A tinge of pink dusted my cheeks.

Beckett broke the tension, his tone full of forced politeness. "So lovely to see you both. We will have plenty of time to catch up more in Falkland, but we must greet the rest of our guests now."

A nearly inaudible, "Nice to meet you," fell from my lips as Beckett pulled me away from them and toward Ryana and Grethe, ignoring all of the people who were openly gawking at us as we passed. Not a single guest was going to be greeted.

"Hey Ashton! Good to see you," Ryana exclaimed cheerfully before adding a playful, "Beckett," in the blandest way she could muster.

Next to Ryana, Grethe chuckled, standing tall in a suit that was almost identical to Beckett's but a lovely shade of midnight blue to

Beckett's black. It was then that I realized that everyone around us seemed to be adorned in darker hues.

"Hi," I replied, scanning the growing crowd.

All the new faces, presumably the people that Onyx had brought with her from Falkland, were in black or navy. Even the Light Queen, while in something slightly more colorful, was wearing a deep amethyst gown, talking quietly to a man with distinguished gray hair.

It wasn't just the shades that spoke of a shift in fashion, but also the cuts of the gowns that caught my attention, once I was finally slowing down enough to notice. There was more skin on display than I would have expected from a formal affair. At least, compared to what I had witnessed in Demetros.

Beckett's lips dipped to my ear. "The people of the North wear much more revealing attire. My family, in particular, all have similar gifts to mine. We are a sensual people."

It seemed unusual for someone to comment on the sensuality of their parents, but there was so much about Fae culture that I didn't understand. Perhaps this was just the norm. "Your parents seem..." I began searching for the least offensive set of words I could use, but my voice stalled with the effort to be both polite and honest.

"They are dicks," Grethe said, saving me from having to lie. "And not the good kind. The small, shriveled kind."

We all laughed, including Beckett. His smile finally reached his eyes.

"They're different," Beckett said. "I believe that the only reason they had me was for a bargaining chip for a better position in royal politics. They were ecstatic when I was chosen as heir." His face dropped, his features forlorn. "I didn't know what a family could look like until I came here," he admitted softly.

Grethe clapped Beckett on the back. "It's alright, buddy, you are part of our family now. You don't need them."

One side of Beckett's mouth lifted on the edge, but the sadness still coated his features. "Thanks, Grethe."

Watching Beckett around his parents was almost heartbreaking in a way that made me feel grateful for how I had been raised. My mother might have been absent—off faking her own death and whatnot—but I did have a father who loved me so much that he would do anything for me. Including separating from his mate to give me a fighting chance at survival. It was a pity I had gone and fucked that up by coming to the one place they had tried to keep me from.

My stomach lurched at the reminder. I scanned the room just in case my father had miraculously shown up, but he wasn't there. Neither were Gianna and Josaphine, which struck me as odd.

"Where are your parents?" I asked Grethe, my stare grazing over the mingling groups as if maybe I had missed them.

"The help doesn't sit with the royals," Grethe replied flatly.

My brows pinched together. "What?"

Grethe sighed. "Gianna would be welcome as a General, but Josaphine is essentially an estate manager. She's not welcome while the Astors are here."

Grethe and Beckett shared a look, but there was no resentment in Grethe's stare. Whatever had transpired on the subject, they had already hashed out everything well before I showed up asking about it.

As much as I wanted to know more about how that worked—why Ebus was allowed to dictate who sat at the royal table at the Queen's own residence—I could sense that this was not a topic for casual conversation.

Regardless, I was prevented from asking anything at all when the Light Queen's fork tapped against a glass. "Thank you all for coming." She stood tall by the main table where we all usually sat, glancing around the room with a smile plastered on her face. "Although I imagine most of you have heard of Beckett's whirlwind romance, I'd like to formally announce that my heir, and trusted General, is to be bound to his lovely bride in a few short days."

Cheers and applause rang out across the room, but all I could think of was that she had basically referred to me as an accessory. As all eyes shifted to me, it took a conscious effort to force something resembling a contented grin to my face. Beckett's arm slid around my waist as his lips dipped to my ear. "You're going to have to work on your acting skills, kitten."

I laughed halfheartedly as the crowd continued to clap and stare at us. All I wanted to do was sink into the floor. This much scrutiny was not what I had signed up for. Especially as every single stare seemed to contain a grimace or a frown, as if I wasn't even worthy of their gaze.

When the applause ended and we were finally instructed to take our seats, I was herded to a chair at the table next to the Light Queen. Beckett took his place on my other side, his parents opposite us. Grethe was sandwiched between Ebus and Ryana, looking the most uncomfortable that I had ever seen him, struggling to stop fidgeting or adjusting his clothes. The eldest Astor clearly wasn't paying Grethe any attention, ignoring him with ease as if he simply wasn't there at all.

The table was filled with faces I didn't recognize outside of my group of friends. Under such short notice to gather the masses, the Astors had been forced to greatly reduce their guest list to those that could be housed in Castle Lochmere, but it didn't stop their entourage from filling most of the tables in the room.

As a sort of shield from my instinctual reaction to ramble, I sipped on my wine between every question pelted my way, letting the fruity flavors dance along my tongue before each reply. It was only natural that the people here were curious about me, the unknown girl who had captured the attention of the heir apparent.

"Where are you from again?" An elderly man in a navy suit asked, bushy brows bunched together on his forehead as his gaze slid over my rounded ears.

"The south." Sip.

The much younger woman beside him leaned over her husband's chest. "And who is your family again?"

"I was raised by my father in a small settlement. It's practically unknown, even in Demetros." Sip.

We weren't hiding that I was from the other kingdom, only who my father and mother were, so I tried to tell as much of the truth as I could without giving anything away.

"You said your surname is Blake, correct?" A middle-aged man spoke up from the other direction.

Based on what my mother had told me, it was safe to use this name, so I replied as honestly as I could. "It is a typical last name in the southern kingdom." The statement was only a lie, because I couldn't recall ever coming across another Blake in my travels, but these people didn't know that.

The man inclined his chin in agreement as if that made perfect sense. A common name for a common human girl.

"And where did you meet Beckett?" This question came from a much younger woman, probably closer in age to me. She had wavy raven hair that spilled over her shoulders and dark green eyes that were glaring at me like I was the dirt beneath her immaculate shoes.

Sip. "In a pub where I was set to meet a friend."

A server stepped by, dutifully refilling my wine glass, and I offered him a silent nod of thanks as he scurried away to the next empty cup.

"That makes sense," the dark-haired woman replied, "he meets lots of girls in pubs."

The woman beside her with closely cropped blonde hair leaned toward her friend. "Wonder how long this one will last?"

"He will be in my bed before the week is up," the woman replied, loud enough so that I would hear, her eyes still glued to mine.

My fists clenched by my side. It wasn't as if I was naive: I had told Beckett to do what he wanted. This arrangement had nothing to do with love, but she didn't know that. This girl, who didn't even know me, took one look at me and decided it would only take a week for him to grow tired of me.

Before I could issue a retort, Beckett's hand wrapped around mine beneath the table. When I looked at him, he was turned toward the duo who were still loudly whispering about me. "She caught my eye from across the room..." he shifted his gaze back to me, our eyes catching. "But once I captured her attention, too, I knew she was special. And once we spoke, I knew I needed to make her mine. That belonging to her was the only worthy goal I had left to achieve for the rest of my life."

My heart thrummed in an uneven beat as heat crept up my cheeks. Logically, I knew that the words were an act, but I couldn't convince my body of that. I couldn't even bring myself to look away from him.

"I have never met someone so infuriatingly captivating," he added with a grin that for the life of me felt real in every single one of the crevices in my heart.

The whispering continued, but it wasn't loud enough for me to hear over the rush of my pulse. Still staring at him, wide-eyed and breathless, all I could do was attempt a smile that I was certain looked more like a grimace.

"Well, we cannot wait to host you both in Falkland after the ceremony," Onyx said, sparing me from trying to decipher the expression on Beckett's face. "Charlese will no doubt have her hands full."

Knowing that if I turned in Onyx's direction, I would only be able to glare at her and realizing that continuing to hold Beckett's stare was doing something uncomfortable to my insides, I glanced down at my dress. Sliding my palm from Beckett's grip, I folded my hands into my lap, threading my own fingers together to avoid grabbing onto Beckett any harder. He was not a lifeline here, and his words were only for show. The more I remembered that the better off I would be.

When I was certain those hands could be trusted, I reached for my glass of wine, sparing a glance at Queen Anastasia in a fruitless attempt to get her attention. Maybe she would save me from this ridiculous interrogation? Except her focus was firmly on Ebus Astor as she spoke in hushed tones.

My gaze shifted to Ryana, who was looking back at me, but the only thing she offered was an apologetic half smile. Beside her, Grethe jerked his head in the direction of the Astors, giving me a thumbs down gesture which actually made me laugh before a frown took over again. Even though I had thoroughly questioned their loyalty to me a time or two, now that everything had been explained to me, I was going to be sad to see the two of them go.

I returned my focus to my meal and the dinner continued without too much agony, due mostly in part to the fact that I had consumed at least a half bottle of wine by myself. The Astors and their guests continued their relentless questioning and judgmental comments, but after some time, the frequency slowed, and I didn't feel like I was the sole focus of their scrutiny. I was also completely inebriated, which may have played a role in how much I cared.

When the meal had concluded, Beckett was the first to stand, gripping my arm tightly and pulling me upright with him. "If you will excuse us, I need to escort Miss Blake back to her rooms to retire."

He turned to his parents, bowing slightly at them. "Ebus, Onyx, it was a pleasure." He bent forward once more, an informal acknowledgement to the Queen, before sliding his arm around my waist and escorting me from the room.

The feel of his warm body pressed against mine and his strong, muscular hand gripping my hipbone to steady me made the heat pool low in my abdomen. Again. Involuntary flashes of his hands sliding across my skin, his fingers pinching my peaked nipples, and his perfectly wicked tongue stroking against mine bombarded my mind. Biting down on my lower lip, I leaned into his warmth as he held me close.

It was the last thing I remembered until the following morning when I woke up fully dressed, with a half-finished glass of water by my bed and a splitting headache.

Twenty-Seven

A forced smile spread my lips as Ryana led me up a flight of stairs and down another unfamiliar hallway. With the preparations for the ceremony complete, thanks in no small part to Josaphine's diligence, all that was required of me was to attend some sort of pre-bonding *celebration*.

The wrongness of that word slipped around in my mind like some sort of pollution. A dark cloud spilling through water like ink. This was no love match, and with my father still missing, and none of my friends present except Grethe and Ryana, I didn't feel much like celebrating.

We reached a door, tucked far away from any of the others, and Ryana led me inside without knocking. As a show of comradery, she laced her fingers in mine, pulling me through a receiving room lined with tufted couches and marble-topped tables. We meandered down a brightly lit passageway that boasted more fine paintings and landscapes I didn't recognize in the slightest. Until the final two.

My breath hitched as I gazed upon the first, the most lifelike depiction of Elmhaven that I had ever seen on canvas. The scene showed trees lining a riverbank, by all accounts a generic picture that could have been anywhere, except I knew that bank like the back of my hand. This was my home.

Ryana stopped in her tracks, giving my hand a knowing squeeze. "She never stopped missing you."

The words hurt more than they should have, so I turned back to the paintings and blinked a few times to keep the tears from building along the ridge of my eye. Anger was no longer the predominant emotion that I held when I considered the Light Queen, but it still simmered beneath the surface of overwhelming grief. Grief that had molded and shaped me and didn't just vanish because my mother had suddenly appeared back in my life.

My attention shifted to the second painting, clearly commissioned by a different artist than whoever had done Elmhaven. The brush strokes were peculiar, broad, and not exactly a lifelike depiction. But the scene was unmistakably the city of Fulgrande. A sparkling sapphire lake was nestled in the bowl of snowcapped mountains. Just like in the painting that had been at the top of the secret passageway that Cade showed me in Biltons Academy, this scene depicted a version of the capital city prior to the establishment of the town as I knew it. This rendition only had the castle and the academy, although I suspected it had just been an artistic choice. Then again, for all I knew, the academy might have predated the apartments and shops that lined Fulgrande's streets.

Too much time had passed when I realized that Ryana had been stalling a few steps away, waiting for me and perhaps giving me some space to reflect. "Sorry, I got distracted," I muttered, nodding to relay that I would continue to follow her.

"It's normal to miss home," she supplied, as she continued her walk down the hallway.

"Do you miss your home, sometimes?" I asked in a whisper.

A little hum expelled from her chest. "For the most part, this is home now. But sometimes I miss Iverness and even my parents." She dipped through an open doorway that led us to a balcony and my questions died on my tongue as I took in the sights.

The balcony was comprised mostly of the bright white marble that topped the tables in the entryway, threads of gold woven throughout that glinted in the firelight. Heavy wooden tables were spaced evenly before us, some of which were laden with meats, cheeses, fruits and vegetables arranged in a kaleidoscope of colors. A comically large fountain made up the centerpiece for the display, only humorous because it was overflowing with a creamy substance instead of water, which reminded me a lot of...

"Cheese," Ryana remarked with a smirk, catching my confusion.

My stomach grumbled with excitement at the same time a gasp split my face into a grin. My finger jabbed at the air in the direction of the fixture. "That is a fountain of cheese?"

A person approached from my other side. The Queen wore a tentative smile as our gazes met. "Ryana tells me you like this type of food."

Warmth swelled in my chest when I realized she was trying to make small talk. As much as her decision had hurt me, I didn't intend to hold a grudge forever, not when she had sacrificed the life she could have had with us in order to keep me safe.

I plastered a smile on my face that wasn't entirely faked. "It's an embarrassing obsession. I'll eat anything dipped in cheese." The dairy product had been a rare commodity in my kitchen growing up and every time I ate it, even more regularly at Biltons, it felt special, like something to be savored.

Oldenberg's features softened, but her stare still held a lingering sorrow, clinging to the corners of her mouth as if she recognized the conflicting emotions in my own stare. "There is so much I don't know about you." Her fingertips slid against my palm as she squeezed lightly. "I hope you give me the chance to learn."

"I'd like that too," I replied honestly.

A commotion sounded from the archway that led to the balcony as Gianna laughed warmly at something Josaphine said, the two of them staring at each other with so much love in their eyes, I hardly recognized the Queen's female General.

Oldenberg moved away from me to pull them each into equally long embraces, beckoning them to go ahead and make a plate so that we could begin.

When it was my turn, I piled my food so high that the tower of salami, apples, olives, and apricots threatened to topple as I walked. A grey-clad server scooped a heaping helping of cheese into a bone white teacup, following me to my chair so that they could place it beside my plate.

My eyes rolled at the sight of my seat, the one obnoxiously decorated with an uncomfortably large lavender bow, and I slipped into the chair, facing the edge of the balcony's parapet at the center of another long, sturdy table.

Pale orbs of purple lights floated beneath the night sky, casting a faint violet haze all around us.

Ryana took her place beside me, and I gestured up to the lights. "What are those?"

She beamed, as if the question itself was a compliment. "Grethe invented them. There is a chemical composition inside the glass that makes the flames last longer and burn purple without the constant addition of new magic."

Josaphine's warm smile appeared over Ryana's shoulder as she slipped into her own chair. "It was a passion project of his before he joined the Queen's army."

Gianna left a space between my other side when she chose her spot, placing a mostly empty plate in front of her. "He likely would have been a chemist had he not chosen the military." She spoke in a matter-of-fact tone that did not convey disappointment but elicited my curiosity all the same.

"Why did he choose the army then?" I asked, dipping a slice of salami into the cheese before bringing it to my mouth. My eyes closed as I soaked in the flavors. This was heavenly.

It was Ryana who replied, even though the question had been posed to Gianna. "Beckett."

Swallowing my bite and opening my eyes again, I twisted to face Ryana, and she continued without any prodding. "Grethe traveled a lot as a child of a General. Beckett was one of his only friends, and he wanted to stick with him."

Josaphine, who had already cleared off half of her plate during that brief discussion, smiled wistfully. "The lifestyle was just what he was comfortable pursuing. It's what he was used to. Then, he met Ryana and his decision was solidified."

None of them had to clarify that because of both Josaphine and

Gianna's positions in The Queen's castle and army, respectively, Grethe had never known another life. One of living in the same home and sharing meals around a table with just your parents. He had probably only ever called Lochmere home, a residence he had been forced to share with whoever was traveling through at the time as well.

The resulting silence was only slightly awkward and quickly shattered by the Queen's next question. "Are you ready for your surprise?"

My eyebrows lifted to my hairline. "I wasn't aware I was getting a surprise." There had been rumors about some of the events that might happen on a hen night, which I supposed this was, and I very much hoped that none of them would occur in front of my estranged mother.

Almost as if sensing that worry, the Queen chuckled, motioning vaguely to someone behind us. The orbs instantaneously went dark as shadows settled around us, the only light now scarcely supplied by the moon.

Before I fully adjusted to the darkness, loud explosions rocked the balcony, urging me to prepare to fight. It wasn't until giant shimmering flashes of light illuminated the sky in front of us that I realized what I was seeing. Fireworks.

Dad and I had seen them on a few rare occasions when work took us through the capital for the week of the Elemental Queen's coronation anniversary, but the spectacle above my head tonight far surpassed those memories.

The eruptions of light morphed into the shapes of animals. Glittering green snakes slithered across the sky Radiant red horses galloped in the other direction. A circus full of animals exploded into the blanket of gleaming stars above the sea.

I stole one glance at the other women around me, their faces lighting up in a rainbow of flashing lights with each new animal, astonishment glistening in their captivated stares. Maybe this wasn't commonplace for them after all, but something truly special the Light Queen had done just for me.

It was magical, just like everything else here. Demetros had elemental magic, but it had never felt so enchanting. Everything in Lochmere—in the Light Kingdom—felt extraordinary. I found myself captivated by the spectacle, fully planted in the moment and thoroughly enjoying the display as if my worries had slipped away into the shadows beyond.

When the sky faded to near darkness, claps and cheers rang out across the balcony. With the flick of the Queen's wrist, the orbs flickered back to their previous brightness, and when I looked down, I found that our plates had been cleared and in the center of the table sat trays covered with more frosted cakes, pastries, and cookies than five women could possibly eat.

Placing more than a few of the delicacies on my new plate, I turned to the Queen. "Thank you for that. It was lovely. I'd love to know how it works because those were not normal fireworks."

She chuckled as she selected her own dessert with delicate fingers. "That was because it was someone's gift. A manipulation of light."

My mouth dropped open. So far, none of the Fae I had met or heard of had similar gifts at all. "It was brilliant," I exclaimed. "I wish I could do something like that."

The Queen studied me for a moment before humming softly. "We will see." She had already explained that her gift was control over plants, making them grow or even inventing new species. It was the reason my father had been so skilled at gardening. The reason he had been so diligent about keeping her garden alive. But that did not mean I'd inherit the same ability.

The mental mentioning of the powers my father gained through their mating bond reminded me that I was less than a day away from my own ceremony, and despite the euphoria still weaving its way through my body from the firework display, nerves began to take over yet again. Like a non-native weed, wreaking havoc in my mind, choking out the positive emotions I had only just unearthed.

The Queen frowned, notches forming between her brows. "What's wrong?"

We had shared more than a few casual conversations over the last few days, between Ryana attempting to teach me how to use my awoken —but still useless—elemental magic, but I didn't know if I could be completely honest with her about my concerns over the bond. My eyes lifted to hers, catching the genuine worry there and knowing I needed to say something. "Will the bonding hurt?"

Behind me, Josaphine snorted a laugh. "Were you listening during any of our meetings?"

Cringing, I swiveled to offer her an apologetic smile. It had been overwhelming the amount of information she had tried to give me, and with everything going on around me, I hadn't exactly retained all of it.

The estate manager shook her head, but I sensed the playfulness dancing in her stare. "It didn't hurt for Gianna and me."

Ryana licked some stray frosting off her fingertips before she added, "Us either. It was more of a tingling."

Shifting my gaze back to the Queen, I noted the look of sadness that washed over her features. "It only hurt for a moment, but it wasn't the worst pain of my life. Nothing like childbirth." This turned the corners of her mouth up in a rueful smile.

Gianna nudged Oldenberg with her elbow. "Nothing as bad as that." Another rare grin crested the General's face.

The Queen slid her attention back to me. "I doubt it will be something you can't handle. Ryana tells me you are quite resilient."

Ryana laughed from my other side. "Yeah, you should have seen her during the challenges."

My blush crept along my neck, but all I felt in that moment was pride.

Later that night, resolved in those feelings and with a stomach full of the most exquisite meal I had ever had, I drifted off to sleep. There wasn't a nightmare to be had as my dreams were lush with secret gardens and new promises.

Twenty-Eight

ESTELLA

The man glared at Estella, the deep lines in his face scrunching with his disapproval of her responses. His hand gripped a cane, which he swung wildly at her. "I'm going to ask you again... do you have any other relatives?"

The potions they had forced upon her had been keeping her disoriented long after their visits were over, but they had not uncovered any of her secrets, even within her own mind.

They visited her day after day, asking the same questions over and over again, dosing her with the potion that kept her compliant and her limbs heavy. The only change to their regimen was that they had removed whatever spell had silenced her during her imprisonment.

"No," Estella whispered, forcing the air from her throat in a rattling noise that sounded unfamiliar even to her own ears. She massaged the column of her throat as the man, her interrogator for the day, glared at her.

She didn't understand. Her captors had known her for years prior to the war. They attended her parents' joint funeral when they didn't return from their Northern mission. Unless... "Did... my... parents... live?"

The man cackled, throwing his head back and dropping his cane in the process. "No, the King and Queen of Demetros perished in their quest to rid you of your betrothed. That was confirmed."

Estella sucked in a gasp. They had been presumed dead for many months after their departure, but the way this man spoke made it sound like he knew for certain. As if they had plotted the entire thing. She had been a fool not to have considered the connection before now.

The man prodded forward with no regard for her feelings or the crushing realization she had just made. "We just need to know if you had any other siblings. Any distant cousins?" His expression was cold and expectant, so far removed from the person who had offered her a handkerchief after the tough call had been made to announce her parents' deaths to the kingdom, even without bodies as proof.

"No," she croaked again. Positive in that. Her parents had both been only children, and everyone she held any relation to had perished in the last battle. It was possible her grandparents were still alive, but it was unfeasible for her to know with any certainty what had transpired outside of these four walls since her imprisonment.

The pathway in her mind touched too close to that memory, and instantly Estella was transported back into another waking nightmare. Flashes of frozen limbs. A blade raised high, glinting in the perfectly sunny day. The shattered remains of that woman's body piling up like rubble.

While the memory had typically ended there, whatever was awakening Estella's magic had allowed the vision to go further, making her realize that she had been shielded from so much more of the horrors of the day.

When the woman's soul had left her body, a violent gust of pure magic had thrown them all against the ground. A final act of defiance against the people who had waged war against her. The blast had knocked Estella unconscious and...

"We will know if you are keeping something from us, soon enough," the man sneered, drawing Estella from her traumatic thoughts and back to the present.

For the life of her, she couldn't figure out what they were looking for. She had answered their questions honestly, although she had no qualms about lying to them, and she was ready to be done with their interrogation.

If there was someone left, a distant cousin, or a family member sired in secret, she had never been made aware of that information, but the fact that her captors were desperate to know intrigued her. Her throat burned as she pushed out the question that she was dying to know the answer to. "Who do... you think... is—"

The man cut her off with another wave of his gnarled hand, refusing to acknowledge her words in favor of rising to his feet. "Enough of that. We will be back." With those ominous words, the man hobbled from the room.

Estella could only watch him in his slow retreat from her, waiting until the door clicked shut to release a sigh of relief.

They had been dosing her frequently enough with the potion she had come to learn was called chrysanth, that in the early days of it, she had become too lethargic and had fallen asleep in the middle of the interrogation. At some point, the decision had been made to supply her with the potion at the end of their questioning, which had the unfortunate side effect of making her forget a portion of what they talked about. She knew it was meant to keep her pliant, but at the quantity she was receiving, it was also impacting her memories of the events. When they remembered.

Tonight was one of those evenings that her captor's irritation had offered her a reprieve as the man had, once again, neglected to dose her with the foul-tasting liquid. Excitement blossomed in her chest at the same time magic tingled along the surface of her skin, as if her emotions and her powers were working in tandem to help her retain the information long enough to transcribe it.

On nearly silent slippered feet, she rushed to her mattress and pulled out the tiny notebook within, folded around a small nub of charcoal. She had found it some time ago in the room hidden behind the tapestry on the wall. There was hardly enough charcoal left to scribble down her thoughts.

Relative? She wrote, thinking of the shortest way to transcribe the ideas racing around in her mind.

Magic of crowns, she added, feeling confident that she was going down the right path. Why else would her captors suddenly care about a relative? They hadn't even asked about her grandparents, meaning they either knew something she didn't about their statuses, or they were irrelevant.

The only reason they'd be irrelevant in this matter was the magic of crowns. They would not pass backwards. Her parents were dead, confirmed by the man who had once wiped away her tears, and that meant there might be someone out there who could inherit her crown.

She didn't even care about what that could mean for her usefulness; she was too focused on the fact that this person could be the key to her escape. She just had to consider her next move carefully, and she had to find a way to turn the tables on her captors to glean more information from them during the next interrogation.

Her freedom depended on it.

Twenty-Nine

The bonding ceremonies in the Light Kingdom were nothing like the weddings I had attended in the Kingdom of Demetros. In my homeland, the bride wore brightly colored gowns with her face slightly hidden behind a stunning veil. The wealthier the couple, the more elaborate the veil, some boasting intricate embroidery and glittering gems placed throughout.

The ceremonies themselves occurred indoors in large gathering spaces. In the larger cities, old temples that had been used to worship Merè played host to the events. In the smaller ones, sometimes, barns were utilized. Either way, attendees perched in rows of seats and benches, watching as the bride was escorted down a long aisle toward the front of the gathering, where an eager groom awaited.

In The Light Kingdom, at least for bonding ceremonies, the bride apparently wore a thin flesh colored camisole dress that barely reached the upper thigh. My attire would not break from tradition, and although I was in my suite, a fire blazing in the hearth, my skin was pebbled from the chill in the air.

I rubbed my palms against my arms, trying and failing to bring warmth back into my flesh while I hazarded a glance at my reflection in the tall mirror. My hair had been brushed and styled in soft waves that cascaded down my back like a waterfall. A crown of flowers had been placed upon my head like a lively violet halo. Even though it was highly unnecessary considering how much of my body was on display beneath the thin silk, blush had been modestly applied to the apples of my cheeks. Everything else about me had been left unadorned with the exception of my mother's ring.

As if thoughts of her had summoned the Light Queen, I blinked and found her standing behind me, tears already bubbling to the surface of her crystal blue eyes. "You look lovely, Ashton." She stepped forward, pulling me into an embrace, careful not to crush the flower crown as she lightly kissed my forehead.

It was as intimate as we had ever been, but I didn't want to lose that comfort, so I leaned into the hug, breathing in the scent of roses as I sucked in a lung full of air.

The Queen pulled back, gripping my shoulders as her eyes danced along the contours of my face, and I stood stark still, letting her assess me, wondering how I measured up against how she imagined me all those years we were apart.

Nothing in her expression indicated disappointment; if anything, I caught sadness along with the lingering hints of regret. "I never thought I'd see this day." Her voice cracked at the admission as her thumb brushed along my forehead, wiping away whatever remnants of her lip stain she must have left behind.

I couldn't bring myself to open my mouth, couldn't find the words to say in that moment, so I remained silent, guilt already building in my stomach as I let her admission go unanswered.

The Queen released my shoulders, her focus shifting over to the mirror again, this time to smooth out her own deep emerald skirts. Auburn hair was piled on top of her head, braided into a crown where a genuine golden tiara rested. I let myself focus on that, rather than the hurt welling in her eyes.

The circlet was made of solid gold with seven distinct points. The center being the tallest, with the others tapering down from there. In the middle of each arch, a single blood orange diamond—matching the stone in my ring—was mounted in a halo of glittering emerald stones.

Would I be expected to wear that one day? If all of this wasn't for naught, and I didn't die breaking the spell.

"I wanted you to have this," she said, tearing me from those thoughts. A small velvet pouch rested neatly in her outstretched palm. Without waiting for me to grab it, she retrieved a golden necklace from within it.

As she tugged at the chain, a charm fell loose, revealing a sparkling blood orange diamond that coordinated with my ring, mounted in a halo of small green stones that seemed to be the match to the ones in the Queen's crown.

My eyes darted to her face, where a solemn smile rested, still speechless.

Surprisingly, her smile didn't budge as she kept her gaze on my face. "Turn around, and I'll put it on."

Twisting around, I lifted the waves of my hair to give her better access. The duology of the moment was enough to tighten the muscles of my chest and burn up my throat. It wasn't that I wasn't grateful to have a second chance with a mother I thought long gone, but I couldn't keep the feeling of disappointment at bay that Jemma wouldn't be here. Even if I was confused by her recent actions, the idea of doing this without her, was devastating. That was before I considered that Marjorie was missing too. And not least of all, my father.

I understood that Ebus hadn't given the Queen that time, and while I couldn't comprehend what was at stake to make the timeline so dire, I knew that there was much about the politics in The Light Kingdom that I didn't fully grasp yet. Maybe I didn't completely trust her as the Queen, but I had to believe that my own mother—the woman who had sacrificed a life with her family to keep me safe—was doing what she believed to be best.

She cleared her throat as her hands fell away from the clasp and came to rest along my shoulder. Her cerulean eyes slid to our reflections once more. Standing side by side like this, it was easy to see how much of her had made its way into my features. Had it hurt my father to even look at me?

Oblivious to those thoughts, her smile crinkled her eyes at the corners. "There. All good. What do you think?"

I grimaced at my reflection. "I think this slip is not what I expected."

A true laugh parted the Queen's lips, and she quickly rolled them inward to stifle the mirth. "I did mean the necklace. But it could have been worse. They used to do the ceremonies naked."

Blood rushed to my cheeks as I swallowed, unfortunately wondering if her own ceremony with my father had been like that, and simultaneously wanting to never consider that image again. "Thank you. I love it," I replied, not wanting her to mistake my silence on the matter as me being ungrateful.

The gift was truly beautiful, perhaps the nicest piece of jewelry I had ever owned. Any disappointment I felt in that moment was more to do with what—or whom—was absent, rather than any lack of gratitude.

She was my mother, in the flesh, and yet, she was still such a stranger to me that it was almost odd sharing this moment with her. It crossed my mind that perhaps she felt the same. Maybe this was just as awkward and hopeful for her as it was for me.

"I'm glad you're here," I whispered, forcing my gaze to hold hers. While I worried deeply for my father and wished more than anything that he was here for this, I couldn't ignore the fact that I did have a parent here, one I wanted to grow closer to, if given the chance.

Tears welled in the Queen's kohl-lined eyes indicating that we likely shared those same thoughts. Still grieving for a life we might have had, a relationship that could have already been established under different circumstances, but hopeful that we could get there one day.

It was in that moment that Ryana practically barged into my room before either of us could put words to those thoughts, prying our gazes apart in favor of facing her. Ryana's navy skirts swished along the floor as she approached. "I have the ring," she sing-songed. "Josaphine did an excellent job, if I do say so myself."

The Queen stepped away as Ryana approached, handing me the jewelry that I would use to symbolize my undying love with a man who was being guilted into marrying me.

Cool metal kissed my fingertips as I inspected the band. It was silver with tiny round moonstones embedded into its surface. Because I had never seen Beckett wear anything but black—and certainly no other jewelry of any kind—it didn't remind me of him specifically, but I did think it was beautiful. Placing it on my thumb, the only finger even remotely large enough to attempt to wear it, I lifted a silent prayer to whatever long-dead god would listen that I wouldn't lose it and botch this entire thing.

The Queen placed a single hand on my shoulder. "Josaphine showed you the entrance to the gardens, correct?"

"She did," I replied. There was so much more I wanted to ask or say, but with very specific timelines necessary for the ceremonies, I knew I could only stall for so long.

"Then we will see you out there," the Queen said softly, squeezing her hand against my shoulder to pull me into one last hug before they both slipped quietly from my room.

I allowed myself a single steadying breath before making my way to the gardens. It was customary, apparently, that each person entering a bonding do so—both physically and emotionally—of their own free will. Which was why I was forced to make the long trek to the gardens completely unaccompanied. A symbol that this was my choice, even if the idea of that was almost laughable. These were not the circumstances that I had hoped to enter a marriage under, but I was prepared to do what it took to keep peace. To save my Kingdom from their captors. To make my mother proud. To stay alive.

My arms wrapped around my waist as I stepped through the door that led to the outside space. All bonding ceremonies were performed outdoors, something about being closer to nature. They occurred at either sunrise or sunset, another relic of the old religion that lingered even in the Fae society. Further proof that our cultures were once linked.

In this moment, I couldn't stop myself from wishing that we had more time so that I could, at the very least, have had this outdoor ceremony in the summer. Instead, I entered the courtyard to the gardens on the last day in December, the chill in the air causing my breath to form puffs of smoke around my face.

As was tradition, my feet were bare, and each step forced the skin on my soles to meet with the near-frozen steppingstones that marked my route. With every contact with the frigid ground, an icy chill swept up my legs, which danced across my back and shoulders, leaving goosebumps in its wake. The thin silk dress did nothing to shield me from the elements, so I picked up my pace, teeth chattering the entire walk.

In Light Kingdom tradition, the guests of the bonding ceremony were standing in a circle with enough of an opening to allow me to walk through. Jealousy surged through me as I caught glimpses of thick wool and fluffy furs draped over their shoulders.

Finally, I let my eyes sweep away from the guests and to the center of the ring where Beckett was standing tall. Waiting for me, although he wasn't looking at me at all.

Beside him was a Gothi man, hired to perform the ritual. According to Ryana and Grethe, the Gothi resided over all bonding ceremonies. I had learned in passing that there wasn't really a structured religion anymore, not since the gods and goddesses had abandoned the continent, but that the magic of the ceremony had originated during the time of the immortal rulers. The Gothi were the only ones trained to utilize the texts of old.

The Gothi man before me appeared to be older than my mother, at least visually because wizards apparently had the same lifespan of humans. If I had to pinpoint an exact age, I would put him in his late sixties or early seventies. He had a distinguished beard and mustache that still retained some of its brown coloring but otherwise was predominantly grey. Long, billowy white robes covered most of his body, tied at his waist with a sash constructed from the same fabric. The only color in his attire came from the golden swirls and shapes that had been embroidered into the sleeves and belt of his garment.

To his right, Beckett was almost as naked as I felt. He was shirtless and barefoot, with a small circlet of purple flowers creating a crown on top of his golden hair, which had been effortlessly swept away from his face.

The same flesh colored silk that my dress was constructed from had been used to make him loose-fitting shorts that were borderline obscene. Although I was still shivering, despite my best efforts to exert mind over matter, he looked comfortable, if not warm, in the elements. He gave me a slight nod as my glance passed to his face, our eyes locking.

Careful not to trip, I made my way to the center of the circle, to the left of the Gothi man. He spoke in an accent I couldn't quite place. "Face each other and connect your hands."

Josaphine had made me practice the movements, so I knew what to do. My left hand landed face down on top of Beckett's upturned right, his left in the same position over my right.

Relaxing against the heat of his palms, I leaned into his touch. If my magic would have cooperated at all over the last several days, I could have kept myself warm. Instead, I tensed at every slight breeze, making me inch closer to my only source of comfort.

The Gothi man began to chant something in a language I had never heard, apparently the language of the immortals, and the circle of people around us joined in. A younger Gothi woman—her classification evident by her matching white robes—approached, carrying a tray with several jars of something that I assumed was the paint utilized in the ritual. She stood opposite the Gothi man and removed the lids to reveal a smooth golden liquid.

"You may begin," the man said, low enough for only us to hear.

As the chanting continued in a steady, slow beat, Beckett released his right hand from my left and dipped his fingers in the paint. He touched my left hand, right at the knuckle of my ring finger, and dragged his forefinger up to my shoulder, leaving a gold trail in its wake. Even while he repeated the motion on the other side, his gaze did not meet mine, and I couldn't blame him. This was entirely too intimate for two people who hardly knew each other at all.

Beckett dropped slowly to one knee and followed a similar pattern from my second toe all the way up to my hip bone, making sure to adjust the bottom of my dress as little as possible as he reached underneath the skirt.

He briskly did the same to the other leg.

The final stretch was the part that I was most nervous about. On the next collection of paint, he lowered himself on both knees and lifted my skirt up to my belly, using his head to block me from view of the guests. He swiped the gold paint between my hipbones, slowly as goosebumps pebbled my already frozen skin, this time with a sort of heat that caused my cheeks to flush. Never once had I been so thankful to be *permitted* to wear underwear.

Beckett made quick work of the last swipe in that area, from the center of the line across my hips, up to my ribcage. Then he stood, replenished his paint, and connected the marks across my shoulders. The final brush of his fingertips joined that line to the one that ended at my ribcage. His calloused fingers grazed my breasts as he drew the line down between them, and under the thin fabric of my dress to meet the golden paint there.

He still wouldn't look at me.

When he was done, it was my turn to do the same to him.

In all the times I had seen or touched him before, I had never studied his form in the way I was being given access to do today. The ridges of his muscles caused my lines to swerve haphazardly along his body, but I followed his lead, repeating those same motions, starting with his arms and then moving to his legs.

My knees dropped to the harsh, frozen ground, and I chanced a look up at him. His silver eyes, glowing like the moon, were finally peering down at me, but I couldn't read a single emotion from his neutral expression.

My heart thumped in my chest as I continued my work, sliding my hands up his shorts to reach his hip bones.

The rest of his body was easier to get to than mine, but I didn't make quick work of it, admiring his stomach and following the line of dark hair up, across the planes of his abdomen. Just below his heart, I stopped, bringing myself upright to complete the rest of the ritual. When my fingers connected the last of the lines, I peered up at him once more, finding his jaw clenched as he took me in.

It was somehow worse than his neutrality, so I averted my gaze.

"Please join your hands again," the Gothi man instructed. As soon as we had followed orders, the chanting resumed. The male Gothi let loose another series of words I could not comprehend, shouting into the fading light of the sunset.

The incantation ceased with the raising of the man's hand, and he turned his attention to me. "It is time to exchange rings."

Pulling the silver moonstone band off of my thumb, I placed it gently over the knuckles of Beckett's ring finger. It fit perfectly.

Next, Beckett produced an almost identical ring, but crafted in yellow gold, from his pinky. He slipped the band gingerly on my finger before our hands were moved back into an interlocked position. Just enough time for me to catch moonstones encircling my ring, each representing phases of the moon.

"It is time for us to bear witness to the painting of the runes," the Gothi man announced to the entire crowd, who fell silent as they watched us.

Beckett dipped his fingers into the gold paint and softly traced the shapes over each of my breasts. He took his time, and with each swipe of his hand, I felt warmer.

When it was my turn to paint his runes, I made quick work of it, trying not to focus on how the muscles of his chest felt beneath my fingertips. After I was done, our paint smudged hands interlocked again.

The Gothi man uttered another string of foreign words, and then he nodded to the Gothi woman. Again, our hands were moved apart as we were adjusted into a new position. Both of us with our right hand on the other's hip, our left hands, palms up, between us.

We were close enough that I could feel the warmth from his body radiating off him like a hearth, and in the place where his hand met my hip, heat pulsed from his fingertips. I nearly moaned at the relief from the biting cold of the evening, but I managed to keep it to myself.

The Gothi woman returned with her tray, this time carrying a single black metal dagger. The hilt was adorned with onyx-hued gemstones placed in the shape of a reptilian creature. The edge of the blade was curved and reflective enough that I could see my face in its shiny surface.

The woman handed the blade to the Gothi man, and he quickly sliced our palms, pressing the cuts together between us. Seemingly out of nowhere, the woman produced a gold chain which she wrapped intricately around our hands, wrists, and arms.

The Gothi man began chanting again, and the crowd followed suit. My skin began to tingle like it had the night my magic had awakened, presumably proof that the magical aspect of the bonding was taking effect. My breath held in my lungs as I steadied myself for whatever sensation might come next.

Beckett's hand squeezed around my side, pulling me closer so that our hips were flush. Nothing about his gaze gave me any indication of his intention, but I could almost imagine he was trying to comfort me until I caught something forlorn etched into his features.

"Now, we will bear witness to the sealing of the life forces," the Gothi man said as he folded his hands in front of his thighs, only inches away from us, staring in anticipation of the final part of the ritual.

Beckett dipped his head so that our mouths could press together. Not the passionate joining of two lovers, but a clinical, cold connection. Still, I found myself relishing the feel of his lips against mine, the smell of night-blooming jasmine, and his musk infiltrating my senses as I resisted the unwarranted urge to grip his hip tighter and pull him deeper into the kiss that I knew he didn't want.

The chanting resumed, and I wished I had retained all the words that Josaphine had relayed to me so I could understand exactly what the incantation meant.

Without warning, a burning sensation rippled across my body, causing me to flinch against Beckett's chest, although I didn't dare move away. Separation at this stage, may cause the magic binding us to falter. So, I stood there, lips pressed to reluctant lips as I felt the burn fade to a small ember, pooling in the place where our sliced palms met.

The chanting ceased, and Beckett tilted his head back to break our kiss.

The guests began to disperse as the female Gothi unwound the golden chain from our still joined hands. Our right palms remained attached to the other's hip.

She made quick work of it, but the entire time we were entwined, I couldn't decide if I was ready to be separated from the man I had just been bound to, or if I was sad to have to let him go.

Beckett clearly identified more with the first thought because the moment we were fully unwound, he released his hold on me, taking a long step backwards as if he couldn't wait to get away from me.

The shock of the sudden absence of his warmth sent a fresh wave of goosebumps across my flesh, and I twisted my arms around my waist to attempt to retain any of the heat he had donated during our ceremony.

His throat bobbed on a rough swallow as his eyes trailed over my body, lips twisting into a grimace. Quickly, he schooled his features, although it wasn't fast enough for me to miss that anguish.

With a face full of indifference, he stepped toward me, offering me his arm in a gesture that felt more practiced than simply out of the kindness of his heart. It felt like obligation.

Unfortunately, I was too cold to turn him down out of spite alone. For better or worse, we were bonded until I broke the spell, and we'd have to find some way to coexist, hopefully as friends.

My arm curled around his, relishing the return of his body heat as he led me back to the great hall in Castle Lochmere. He said nothing to me for the entire walk.

With our arms interlocked, Beckett expertly steered us to the ballroom, another one of the many spaces in Castle Lochmere that I had never seen before today. Between wedding preparations, my failed attempts at using elemental magic with Ryana, and avoiding Onyx's entourage in the halls there hadn't been much time for official tours.

The ballroom was more expansive than I had imagined, even larger than the dining hall. Long curtains of wisteria draped across the two-story arched entryway and hung in excess along the crown molding throughout the space as if it had grown there. Orbs of light floated around us like stars in the sky, shimmering in shades of lavender, amethyst, and periwinkle.

Grethe, I thought fondly to myself as I smiled up at the twinkling lights. Returning my attention to the crowd, I let my gaze sweep along the gathering people, hardly any of whom were looking at us. One silver lining of the Light Kingdom traditions was that there would be no formal announcement for the entrance of the bride and groom into the celebration space. Although, I doubted that would spare me from the lingering stares for long.

With the confidence of someone who was unbothered by his near nudity, Beckett directed us to a small table with two chairs at the front of the festivities. Our table, along with a handful of slightly larger tables, surrounded an open space that I knew would be intended for dancing like a frame.

Briefly, I wondered if we would be forced to dance for an audience as Beckett released my arm and dropped stiffly into the open chair at the table designated for us. Whatever was going on in his mind had distracted him enough that he hadn't seemed to notice me at all, so I slipped into the seat next to him with pursed lips. At least the table would hide the majority of my body from view.

Within seconds, a uniformed member of the castle staff filled our wine goblets, and plates were placed in front of us, piled high with baked chicken and various vegetables. I almost teared up, wondering yet again if the chicken dish—which smelled so much like the meal my father always prepared for special events—had been created by my dad or if his time in Castle Lochmere had inspired him to cook that specific combination of flavors. Either way, the reminder only served to deepen the ache in my chest at his absence.

In an attempt to expel the emotion, I rubbed my palm against my sternum, accidentally smearing the golden line that Beckett had so artfully traced mere minutes before. Not that something so simple could undo what we had done, but I paused all the same, wondering if there would be repercussions to disrupting the lines.

"It's not everapple wine, if you're worried about that," Beckett said flatly.

When my eyes refocused, I realized that they had been trained on the glass of wine in front of me. My cheeks flushed at the reminder of the Barker Inn and all I had witnessed there on the first night I had met —or at least seen—Beckett.

With nothing to say as a rebuttal, a terse laugh left my lips as I reached for the alcohol in front of me. The glint of the golden band around my finger caught my attention before I could lift the glass from the table. "I like the rings they used for the ceremony. They are lovely. Although I've never seen you in anything but black. Do you even like silver?" I could hear myself rambling, so I committed to bringing the wine to my lips, forcing a large gulp down in an attempt to make myself stop talking.

Beckett had yet to respond when I placed the empty glass back in its original location, but he took my hand in his, adjusting its position so that it was flat on the table. His hand came to rest on the space next to mine, silver ring glinting in the hazy purple glow of the orbs. "I designed these rings myself, so yes, I do like silver." He cocked his head to the side. "That is a strange thing for you to be concerned with, considering everything else."

Everything else. Like the fact that this was a sham of a marriage? Or perhaps the small detail of my husband seemingly being disgusted with the idea of being stuck with me. Already preparing to make this temporary...

"I didn't grow up with jewelry," I stated, scrunching my brows together, trying to focus on the rings rather than how embarrassing that admission was. "I suppose if it's something I'm expected to wear at all times, I am relieved that it is pleasant to the eyes."

Beckett's resounding chuckle was a melody to my ears, even though it was only a whisper of a sound, twinkling and fading before it could gain momentum. "Fair." He inclined his chin in the direction of my hand. "Then I am glad you like yours as well."

Taking whatever lifeline that he would give me, I dared to ask another question. "What is the significance of the moons?"

He shrugged, but I didn't miss the glimmer of some sort of shock. "They symbolize change and strength."

A snort left my nose before I could rein it in, and his eyes narrowed in my direction, all but demanding an answer to my reaction.

My head tilted to the side. "You designed rings to mark our bond that we hope will be dissolved in a few months with the symbol of strength?"

Even he smiled at the statement, although it didn't fully reach his eyes. "What can I say? I am a man of tradition."

Pulling my focus from his strangely conflicting expression, I scanned the ballroom, finding more than a few of the faces that had interrogated me at dinner over the past few days. "How long do we have to mingle?"

Out of the corner of my eye, I could see the motion of Beckett leaning toward me, shifting his mouth to the edge of my ear. "We likely have to partake in a dance or two but after that it won't be unbelievable when I throw you over my shoulder and haul you back to my room."

I swatted him away with my hand lobbing him with an incredulous glare. "You wouldn't dare."

He flashed me a wolfish grin and I couldn't determine if it was for the show or just for me. "Oh, it will be expected of me. I have a reputation to uphold." One eyebrow raised, the scarred one, as if he was daring me to call his bluff.

Since I wasn't brave enough to do that, I plucked my fork and knife from beside my plate and began to work on eating my chicken. As I chewed, I mentally calculated how I was going to sneak away from him, even though I still didn't know where his suite was in the castle.

A shadow of an approaching figure caught my attention, and I swiveled my neck to greet whoever was likely coming to offer us well wishes. Except when my eyes locked on the person, I realized it was the same woman who had made a comment about Beckett being in her bed by the end of the week.

My grip tightened around the utensil in my hand as she stilled in front of Beckett. She had never introduced herself, and it didn't appear that she would be doing so now.

"Beautiful ceremony," she said, leaning over Beckett's side of the table, pushing her small breasts up with her arms. Her dark hair cascaded across her shoulders, nearly blocking the parts of her body she had so willingly displayed. The desperation felt so reminiscent of Natasha that I nearly snorted a laugh. Except after that night in the pools, that would be wildly hypocritical of me, so I scowled instead.

"I'd love to congratulate you myself, later," she purred, still acting as if I weren't there.

Part of the reason we were expected to share a dwelling from here on out was that well-paid staff might gossip if we were apart. It was possible that someone who had been here when I arrived had informed the lady that our union was a sham. But that did not detract from the audacity it took to approach him in front of me on the night of our bonding.

Beckett cleared his throat. His obvious discomfort was somewhat reassuring. "Easy, Mollie, you don't want the Queen to hear you talking like that to me."

Whatever relief I had felt dissolved in a puddle on the floor. He hadn't exactly told her no, just not to do whatever it was she was doing in front of the Queen. The subtle difference in the words was not lost on me.

She stood straight, holding her chin in the air as if the entire exchange hadn't bothered or deterred her in the slightest. As if my interpretation of the meaning behind them was accurate. "See you around then, Beckett," she cooed before sauntering back to her table.

Internally, I cursed myself for telling him that he could do whatever he wanted because now there was nothing I could do or say about the scenario that had just unfolded in front of my eyes. Not that he owed me anything, but I had thought he'd be living his life of freedom away from me, not parading his long list of mistresses in front of me for all to see.

My fork pushed around the remaining chicken on my plate. There was no way I could eat another bite when my stomach felt like lead.

Music started playing from the corner of the room, and couples began migrating to the dance floor in front of us. The melody itself was so unlike the tunes that had been performed at the solstice eve ball at Biltons Academy. This was slower, requiring more of a sway or a gentle roll of the hips to move to, instead of the fast-paced, structured dancing of Demetros.

"Shall we?" Beckett asked me, extending a hand.

"I suppose we have to?" I countered, raising my brow.

He gifted me with an apologetic grin in response, and I reluctantly offered him my palm as I kept my face as neutral as possible so that no one would think we were already squabbling.

Beckett pulled me to the opening in the dance floor by our interlaced fingers, weaving through the numerous partners until we reached a free space. Instead of having me face him he turned me around and pulled me close, his hips pressed against my backside, my spine against his chest.

We began to sway, and I looked around at the others on the floor. About half of the couples were in the position we were, the others facing their partners, but all of them exhibited a similar level of intimacy. Whatever this dance was, the way in which I was pressed against Beckett was not inappropriate or even unexpected.

With a loud sigh of relief, I spotted Ryana and Grethe walking hand in hand toward us.

Ryana beamed as she approached. "Congrats, you two, it was a beautiful ceremony!"

She giggled as Grethe spun her around in his arms, stopping her when she was facing him. He pulled her close, and she laced her fingertips behind his neck.

To anyone on the outside, it seemed like a genuine congratulations shared between friends, but my returned smile was weak. "So, we've been told," I said flatly.

Beckett's posture shifted behind me a split second before his breath danced along my cheek. "You can't blame a girl for trying, *friend*. I thought that was what you wanted."

A chill skittered down my spine that had nothing to do with the temperature in the room. My jaw remained clamped shut.

It was Beckett's turn to spin me now, shifting my body with such ease that it probably appeared as if he had been doing it for years.

His hand slid around my hips and roughly cupped my ass, and I tried not to react. Before I could smack him away, I reminded myself that this was part of our arrangement to keep my identity a secret. It was more difficult than I had imagined because I had never pretended to be intimate like this with anyone before. In all honesty, I wasn't exactly faking my attraction to the man either.

My exhale was shaky, a perfect blend of melancholy and longing, and I was sure he could sense the tension in the way I held my body in his arms. If I could have slapped myself without drawing attention to it, I would have. Anything to regain some composure. This was a business arrangement, we were friends, he was probably going to celebrate with Mollie tonight, and I needed to get a grip and accept all of that.

"Can we leave now?" I whispered against his chest.

I hadn't been expecting him to react so quickly, considering we hadn't even mingled, but before I could remember what that might entail, I was being lifted off my feet. His palms tightened around my waist as he slung me over his shoulder, using his enormous hand to block my ass from view. Squealing in shock, I clutched at my chest, using my forearm to ensure my breasts didn't escape out of the top of my dress while I was held upside down.

"My bride can't seem to keep her hands to herself, so it is time for my husbandly duties," Beckett bellowed to the room. "Goodnight to all! Thank you for coming!"

The sound of cheers and applause swelled around us as his free hand smacked me across the ass, eliciting more than a few whistles from the crowd. I refused to raise my eyes to look at any of them, especially knowing my mother was somewhere out there. Not when the entire thing had forced a wide grin on my face, despite the humiliation of his actions.

Beckett didn't put me down when we left the double doors of the ballroom or even when he reached a deserted passageway. He carried me, thrown over his shoulder like a sack of potatoes, all the way back to his room.

"What?" he asked, feigning confusion when he finally placed me on my feet after crossing the threshold of his open door. "It was for the ruse." He blinked at me like he couldn't fathom why I'd be upset, or why my fists were immediately perched along my hips as I glared at him.

His eyes might have hidden his amusement, but his smirk gave away that he knew exactly why I was perturbed. Something told me that the entire ordeal was more about needling me than bolstering some façade that we were passionately in love.

"I didn't think that was so important until we reached Falkland," I commented before my eyes narrowed at him. My arms shifted to a folded position under my chest.

He shrugged as he walked further into the space. "You didn't tap out."

It was all I could do to keep the shock from my face because I hadn't even considered it. Averting my gaze quickly, I shifted my focus to taking in the view of his room.

Inside was an extravagant suite, significantly larger than the one I stayed in. Like everywhere else, thick rugs filled the space, in green, blue and cream patterns.

A heavyset mahogany bed was situated under floor-to-ceiling windows with dark cyan velvet bedding and a mountain of pillows. The very edges of navy silk sheets peeked out from underneath the comforter. At the foot of the bed was a long, narrow, tufted leather stool.

Bookshelves lined one wall in the same mahogany tones, full of tomes, their leather spines in various shades and conditions, but all clearly read. A solid desk, in matching wood, was placed in the center of that space. It was the only part of the room that wasn't tidy, with paperwork strewn haphazardly upon its surface.

On the opposite side of the wall, a fireplace that nearly dwarfed the bed was surrounded by three slabs of marble. Two velvet chairs, the color of a calm ocean, were placed facing the warm light of the fire. It was a beautiful room, but somehow still masculine.

"Your room is this way," Beckett said with a smirk, motioning me to a doorway on the far side of the space. I followed him down the short passageway until we reached another door, opening into a room that was clearly the sister to the one we had just left. The area was smaller, the furniture slightly less grand, but it was still decorated in the blues, leather, and dark wooden tones that appeared in the other.

He snapped his fingers in the air. "In that door," he said, pointing at another arched doorway, "is your bathing chamber. I just filled a tub so you can wash off the paint." His eyes lingered along the smeared gold lines on my skin before he cleared his throat and averted his gaze. "Josaphine had your things relocated here, so you should have clothes in the armoire. Is there anything else I can do for you?"

Before I could request anything pathetic like *please stay here with me*, I just said "No, thank you," in a barely audible mumble.

His throat bobbed with a rough swallow. "Okay then, goodnight, Princess," he said, without a hint of mockery at the title. Technically, it wasn't a joke anymore.

"Goodnight, Beckett," I replied, offering him a weak smile and hoping more than I had ever hoped that my eyes did not convey how much I wished that he would stay with me instead of leaving to seek Mollie.

If he sensed my intention or emotions, he didn't let on. He simply turned on his heel, disappearing into the passageway that connected our rooms. He closed the door behind him with a soft click and the sound of his footsteps faded to nothing as he made his way to his own chamber. Possibly beyond.

Not willing to give any more time to those thoughts, I stepped into the bathing chamber, quickly ridding myself of the flesh-toned dress and dipping into the perfectly warm water of my bath.

When I had finished bathing, I dressed in a simple nightgown before climbing into the bed. The scent of night-blooming jasmine engulfed me but didn't comfort me in the slightest. Not tonight. Reminders of him only served to torment me with thoughts of where he was and what he might be doing. More importantly, or perhaps tragically, whom he might be doing it with.

If I had a clock somewhere in the darkened room, I wasn't aware of it. Therefore, I didn't keep track of the time I spent tossing and turning, but I got a sense that hours had passed since I first lay down based on how exhausted I felt. Sometime in the dead of the night, I had given up trying to sleep in this new but familiarly scented space.

Almost on instinct, I found myself sliding from the bed and tiptoeing over to the door that led to our shared passageway, tilting my ears toward Beckett's room, and reluctantly listening for any sign that he was entertaining a guest.

When I was certain I heard nothing, I pushed the door open and made my way to his side of our tunnel. I was grateful that his door was unlocked when I approached it, and even more thankful that it swung open with minimal noise.

"Beckett?" I whispered as I approached his enormous bed. No movement came from the mattress.

Using the tufted bench at the foot of the bed for leverage, I hoisted myself onto the soft coverlet, my bodyweight causing me to sink slightly into the heavenly mattress. It was absurdly soft, and I was instantly jealous. Maybe with a better mattress, I wouldn't need to wake my husband up in the middle of the night to talk to me because I couldn't sleep.

Even the thought, the use of that word, had me rolling my eyes as I carefully crawled across the bed toward the lumpy form in its center.

"Beckett?" I whispered again, a little louder. I wasn't even sure what

I wanted, other than company. It was a little late to contemplate the reason I was here. Everything about me felt so odd. Like maybe my skin was a size too small in some places and baggy in others. It was as if my body didn't fully belong to myself now that we had been magically bound, and I didn't know enough about any of it to know if this was normal.

Could I have gone to Ryana or my mother? Maybe. But logically, I'd have to pass through Beckett's room to get anywhere else, so it made the most sense to wake him up first.

Gingerly, I pulled back the covers, shocked to find that the only thing beneath those navy sheets was a stack of pillows. My heart sank, and my disappointed exhale was a huff that echoed across the darkened room.

Sitting back on my heels, I forced myself to accept the obvious. Beckett was with Mollie, or someone, after all. Since I was the one who had given him the go-ahead, there was nothing I could do about that, besides accept my new reality.

Solemnly, I made my way back to my room and climbed into my own, less comfortable bed. Sleep never found me, and I spent the entire night tormenting myself with thoughts of them together if for no other reason than to remind myself that my place in this world was strictly to break the spell, and Beckett was only a means to keep me from dying. Nothing else mattered.

Thirty-One

Most mornings, I woke with a sense of anticipation. The good kind that left me looking forward to the possibilities of each new day. This morning, however, I had to force myself out of bed. My body and mind were exhausted after a night of restless tossing and turning. I wasn't sure how today could possibly get better, but I trudged to the bathroom regardless, knowing I'd have to endure it either way.

Cool water splashed against my face, dripping back into the basin as I stared at my reflection in the mirror. That girl appeared just as drained on the outside as I felt on the inside. Contemplating if my husband shared the same appearance for a vastly different reason did nothing to help my mood or my scowl.

Husband. The word felt thick and sticky in my mind. It was real though. We were magically bonded, married by the stars. There was no going back from that now, at least not until I fulfilled my duty to the Light Kingdom.

Beckett and I hadn't discussed a plan for the morning, but I refused to go looking for him, if for no other reason than I was worried how I might find him. So, I dressed for the day and dropped into one of the tufted armchairs that faced the windows. From this angle within the castle, I could see a salty haze permeating from the soft waves below the cliffside. My first free-flowing thought was to question if everything I had done from the moment that I signed Mr. Higgins' contract had been a mistake.

A soft knock on the door that led between our rooms halted those thoughts and alerted me to what I already knew was Beckett's presence.

"Come in," I called numbly.

Beckett waltzed into the room, and it wasn't until he stopped right along the edge of my chair that I deigned to turn my attention to him.

The signs of exhaustion that smeared across his features mimicked those on my own face. His hair was ruffled and unkempt in a way I had only ever seen it in the cave below the castle. When my fingers had caused it.

His skin had lost some of its luster, the beginnings of darkened circles barely visible beneath his eyes. We looked like quite the pair.

My molars clamped together, forcing the questions swirling around in my mind to remain locked there.

Beckett tilted his chin down, his eyes slightly out of focus as if he couldn't bring himself to truly look at me either. Maybe it was guilt, or perhaps that he hated the fact that it was me he was dragging to the dining hall. Like resentment was winning out against our alliance. "Are you ready to go to breakfast?" he asked, his tone neutral.

A silent answer in the form of a nod was all I could produce.

He made no comment about my haggard appearance and did nothing to smooth out his hair. When I placed my hand in his offered palm, he laced our fingers together and pulled me from the room.

Claps resounded in the dining hall as we entered, and I did my best to avoid eye contact with all of them. Unfortunately, it didn't keep me from spying Ebus and Onyx. Or Mollie, who appeared to also be suffering from exhaustion.

"Come join us," the Queen said, gesturing to the open seats in front of her.

Beckett pulled out my chair when we got to our normal spots, and I slipped into it, letting my gaze fall to the other end of the table rather than face my mother. A quick scan of the other attendants showed me that Josaphine and Gianna were noticeably absent.

"Well, you two both look exhausted," Onyx stated from her spot across the table, forcing me to bring my attention to her face. Her charcoal eyes, a similar shade to Beckett's this morning, were bouncing excitedly between us. A flush spread across my cheeks, and I had to will my eye contact to remain on her and not flitter over to Mollie or Beckett to check for their reactions.

Onyx's blood red lips parted in what I assumed was meant to be a smile. "Not to worry. You will have plenty of time to rest in the carriage during today's journey." Her eyes narrowed in a way that could have been knowing, if her assumptions had been correct. "You will have your own."

Heat fully engulfed my face, and I attempted to sink down into my chair, as if I had anywhere to hide. Was she insinuating that we should continue having sex on the drive to Falkland? Maybe being raised by a father who only lightly grazed upon such subjects made me a bit naïve, but it was more than slightly unnerving how freely the Astors discussed matters that I felt should be much more private.

Unfortunately, she wasn't done either. "You know, the Fae are not traditionally a very fertile people. Unlike the humans." She was hardly holding the sneer on her face at bay as she mentioned my less-than-desirable lineage.

The crimson color refused to drain from my face. "So, I've heard," I said meekly, offering her a weak approximation of a smile.

Beside me, Beckett sighed. "Mother, is this really the time or the place for such discussions?"

Ebus smirked but remained silent at her side.

Onyx scoffed at her son, pinning him with an expression I couldn't quite place. "She doesn't know the ways of our people. You should already be trying."

My jaw unhinged. Was she serious? Obviously, the Astors weren't aware that Beckett planned to make this arrangement temporary, but it was still shocking that they were already considering hypothetical offspring.

"From the looks of them, you will have an heir in no time," Ebus said to his wife before putting his own mug of coffee to his lips. His gaze lingered on me a little too long, and I averted my attention back to Onyx, whose staring turned out to be no safer.

The smile splitting Onyx's face was enough to set alarm bells off in my mind. Her grey eyes caught mine, serving only to intensify her unnerving grin. "If you hope to find yourself carrying a boy, I suggest letting him take you on all fours. It worked for us."

Certain there wasn't a shade darker than crimson that my skin could turn, I was reasonably confident that my blush hadn't deepened. Still, the humiliation was enough to make me consider leaving the table.

In reaction to my discomfort, Ebus chuckled. "There's room in the carriage. Depending on where you are in your cycle, it might be the perfect opportunity."

Beckett cleared his throat, tension radiating from him in waves. "If you don't mind, we'd like to keep that aspect of our relationship private," he said sternly as he slid his hand along my leg under the table, offering me a gentle squeeze that could either mean that I needed to remain quiet or possibly that he was sorry. Not that I could decipher him when he was as cold and stoic as a statue.

Grethe, who had joined the table in the middle of my education on sexual positions, spoke up. "Won't it be a little cold in Falkland this time of year?"

The question was just related enough to the subject that it wasn't blatantly rude, but a great segue into anything but my personal life with Beckett.

"Because of its proximity to the Dark Kingdom," Grethe added, sensing I still needed a lifeline when no one immediately responded.

No one had shown me a map, but I had heard enough about the Dark Kingdom's winter curse to know that it impacted the weather in the border towns. Tensing, I looked to Beckett for confirmation.

"No need to be scared," Ebus cooed in his best impression of a comforting tone. "Falkland is safe from Dark Kingdom advances. No one has been bold enough to attack the largest army base in the Light Kingdom."

The Queen set down her glass, and although she appeared weary of the conversation, she didn't seem like someone about to step in and save me either. "Don't fret, dear. Clothes are already being packed for you to ensure you stay warm."

"Thank you, your majesty," I muttered.

My focus dropped to the bacon and eggs on my plate, but the sight made my stomach roil, so I abandoned those in favor of picking up my coffee mug. It had the added bonus of occupying my lips so my lack of response wouldn't appear impolite.

"Yes, we will have garments available upon your arrival, so you won't freeze," Onyx said pointedly at the Queen. There was something about that exchange that I was missing, but looking at any of the Astors for answers continued to be a fruitless endeavor.

"Anyway," Onyx said, ignoring whatever face the Queen might have given her. "It has been so tedious having custom gowns made on such short notice. If only we had learned of your *lover* sooner."

Beckett only hummed in a nondescript way.

"Thank you for your generosity," I said softly, trying to acknowledge her hospitality in the most genuine way I could muster. If it came off cold or forced, she hadn't seemed to notice.

It wasn't until this moment, under the scrutinous watch of the Astors, that I questioned my mother's choice to name Beckett the heir. He was charismatic, a good leader—from what I had seen—and loyal to her in ways that I could not comprehend. However, the proximity to his parents was making me consider that there might have been a flaw in her judgment.

They were insufferable, rude, and overtly sexual in a way that appeared beyond the bounds of typical Fae culture if everyone's uncomfortable expressions were any indication. In my opinion, there were no cultural differences that should have made any of Onyx's suggestions the norm. Especially not as a breakfast conversation.

"Well, speaking of clothing," the Queen stated, "It is best if we finalize our packing and make the journey to Falkland as quickly as possible."

That was all the dismissal I needed before I sprang from the table and briskly returned to my new room. Just as I reached the passageways between our bedrooms, I heard Beckett's voice call out. "The weather will be much colder when we arrive at my parents' castle. Josaphine should have already left something out for you to change into, but if not, I can pick something appropriate."

Ignoring him, other than to gift him with a simple nod that I wasn't even sure he could see, I kept walking.

Sure enough, a thick cotton dress was laid on my already remade bed. The skirts and sleeves of the dress were a lovely shade of amaranth with a darker hue for the bodice. A ruffle of rose pink was attached to the hem of the skirts. Beside the dress was a luxurious sapphire velvet cloak lined in dappled grey fur.

When I emerged from the passageway into Beckett's room, I caught a glimpse of him fastening his own cloak around his chest. It, like the rest of his attire, was solid black. Even the fur lining his outerwear was the color of the darkest night, not a hint of brown or white to be found.

He raised the scarred eyebrow, the white line catching my attention in a beam of rogue sunlight. Everything about him caught my attention, though, so I didn't let the thought linger for too long.

Beckett's assessing stare roamed my body. "It seems Anastasia is using your attire as a thinly veiled way to get her point across."

"Excuse me?" I asked, glancing down at my dress, my cheeks flushing again. "What is wrong with my attire?"

He shrugged nonchalantly, but his expression was bemused. "Nothing. You will find your color choice unusual in Falkland. It stems all the way back to the gods and goddesses that once ruled the lands, but reds and pinks are typically reserved for the humans."

Onyx had been wearing a scarlet dress the first night I met her, so I didn't understand the offense, but I chewed on my lip anyway. "Should I change? The last thing I want to do is offend your parents further."

Beckett's hand caught my arm just as I began to take the passageway to my room to find another option. There was a smirk dancing along the corner of his lips when I turned back to him. "Do you want to please them?"

My focus slid to his hand, and he instantly released my arm.

"Not really," I admitted. "But I don't understand politics the way that I should. I'd hate to unintentionally cause some issue that could be easily avoided by a different colored frock."

Beckett shifted his weight between his feet, the smirk fading into a gentle smile. "I will not let you commit such an act. This"—he gestured to my dress—"might annoy them, but they will not retaliate over something so trivial as traveling attire."

For some reason, his words reassured me. He wasn't going to leave me to fend for myself in the viper's den. "Thank you," I muttered.

"Especially if they think that the garment will be in a puddle on the carriage floor for most of the trip," he added, evaporating whatever relief I had managed to accumulate and spilling it to the ground like a shattered glass of red wine.

"Let's go then," I muttered, ignoring the flush creeping up my chest. He was so hot and cold—shunning me one second, then making blatantly sexual references in the other—and in this moment, I didn't know what to do with that, so I kept my jaw clenched.

When Beckett and I made it to the carriages that lined the long driveway, Ryana and Grethe were already standing next to one, waiting for us.

As I approached Ryana, I forced a smile on my face. "Are you sure you have to go?"

Her head tilted to the side a fraction of an inch as a playful grin rounded her cheeks. "Somehow, I don't think the General will be pleased if I desert my mission to hang out with my friend."

Even as my stomach plummeted with disappointment, I laughed it off, reaching out to give Ryana her farewell hug.

Grethe jumped between, his lopsided grin taking up all my vision as he scooped me off the ground, spinning me around in a tight circle. "Good luck with everything, Ash! See you soon!"

Despite my somber mood, the corners of my mouth lifted as he placed me down.

Josaphine stepped forward next. "It was lovely to meet you, dear. I hope to see you again soon." Her words hit me the hardest. The possibility of my seeing her again hinged on my breaking the spell and surviving the aftermath. On still having a place in The Light Kingdom when this was all over.

Gianna was waiting behind Josaphine to embrace the dark-haired woman after my turn so luckily Josaphine was spared from having to decipher my expression, which I was certain had turned melancholy.

"You're not staying?" I asked Gianna as she kissed Josaphine's forehead.

Her green eyes met mine with a bittersweet smile. She wasn't exactly as warm as her wife, but our tension-filled relationship had relaxed significantly since my hen night. "I travel with the Queen."

Notches formed between my brows. "But you're married." It was neither a question nor a statement, but somewhere in between.

Gianna's features softened where I expected them to harden with sorrow. "I have a duty to the Queen. I am the General of her Light Guard. I go where she goes." She stood proudly with no hint of regret or resentment in her eyes.

Josaphine leaned into her wife; one arm wrapped firmly around her partner's waist. "We make do with the time we have."

"Of course," I replied, turning away to give them a moment of privacy.

Finally, Ryana appeared in my line of sight, pulling me into a gentler embrace than the other two. "I hope you know that this friendship is real. You're the first friend I've had in ages, since these two." She jabbed a thumb in the air over her shoulder to where Grethe and Beckett were locked in their own embrace. "I take my friendships seriously, Ash, so you are one of us now. We love you."

Tears threatened the edges of my vision again, but I blinked them back. "I love you guys too." Her grip on me tightened briefly before she let me go, offering me one last smile before she boarded her own carriage.

Grethe waved to us, and Josaphine, before loading in behind her, and as soon as the door shut, the transport lurched forward, taking them south.

Maybe I would have watched them disappear until they were only a speck on the horizon if Beckett hadn't spoken to me. "Are you ready?"

My gaze swept across his face, forever searching for some kind of sign as to what he was thinking. There was nothing but a masked smile curving the edges of his mouth. Reaching for his hand for the benefit of whomever might be watching, I offered him a quarter smile of my own. "I am."

Cold grey eyes stared at the hand hovering in the air between us for a brief moment before opting to place his arm around my shoulders and tuck me against his chest. His lips dusted my forehead as he placed a single kiss there, before tugging me toward our own carriage. It was fake, but I leaned into it, if for no other reason than I already missed my friends.

Beckett opened the door to the carriage, and I straightened my spine as I climbed inside, resigning myself fully to the notion that none of this mattered. Soon enough, we would go back to being strangers. I just had to make it to the other side alive.

Thirty-Two

My eyes narrowed at Beckett from across the compartment. With his head lulled against the back of the tufted leather benches, he looked so at peace. A soft snore emitted from his full, parted lips, and it made me want to strangle him for being so nonchalant about this entire thing that he could just... sleep. For being tired due to gods knew what kind of activities he had partaken in last night.

His golden hair still looked sex rumpled, and I considered shearing it as he slept so that I wouldn't ever have to see it like that again. I audibly harrumphed at that thought.

Logically, I was aware this was an overreaction. That jealousy didn't become me and had no place in this political union. But, as those sawing sounds of indifference floated to my side of our carriage, I became more and more irrational.

With no one to talk to and nothing else to do but consider all the ways I would seek retribution for my wounded pride, I glared at him with crossed arms.

As an ally, shouldn't he be preparing me for what to expect in Falkland?

My lungs filled with air as I drew in a deep breath, shaking my head to chase away the rage, although it seemed to do little good. Another rattling breath from across the compartment had my eyes forming slits at Beckett again, wondering what aspects of my power I could use to wake him if I had any control of it whatsoever.

Ice-cold water would be a good start, if I could summon it and direct it to his perfectly relaxed face.

His tunic seemed like the kind of fabric that would be easily set ablaze with the right use of fire magic.

If I had a keen enough grasp on the air, I could suck it from his lungs, causing him to wake up gasping for breath.

An unhinged grin split my face, but ultimately, I decided that even in my imagination, being awakened by frigid water was the safest option to avoid injury. As much as his snoring bothered me, I didn't really want to hurt him. Plus, even imagining the scenario was bringing me a level of joy I had thought impossible during this nearly silent ride.

My chest expanded on a deep breath as I closed my eyes, imagining with great mirth the look on his face when an imaginary bucket of ice-cold water was dumped on his head. The daydream was so vivid that I could almost feel droplets of the frigid liquid flinging against my face. Could audibly make out the sound of water splashing across skin.

"What in the actual fuck is this?" Beckett bellowed.

In a millisecond, my eyes flew open, stunned to see that Beckett's entire body was soaking wet, clothes and all. Dripping tendrils of honey hair covered part of his face.

There was nothing that could hold back my smile as I beamed with pride. "It was me!" The enthusiasm in my voice only deepened his scowl.

He shook his head like a dog, sending water droplets spraying across the carriage. His fingers stabbed through his damp locks as he attempted to push the mess out of his face and eyes. Calmly, he lifted one hand in the air and snapped, just as he had done to dry my clothes on the other side of the Emerald Isle tunnels that led us to the Light Kingdom. Except this time, nothing happened.

Confusion marred his features as he lifted the other hand and snapped again. Nothing.

His mild annoyance at my display of magic seemed to grow to full-blown irritation as dark grey eyes aimed a constricted stare on my location. "What did you do?" The words came out in a growl.

Grinning like a lunatic, my chest swelled with pride. "I just imagined dumping a bucket of ice water on your head, and it happened."

His nostrils flared as he slammed his eyelids shut, his muscles tensing under the damp tunic.

It was impossible to dampen my smile, even as my teeth clamped down on my lower lip. "Would you say it's ice cold? I need to know how well my vision worked for next time."

Beckett's lids peeled open slowly so that he could glare at me with contempt.

That only caused a snort of a laugh to peel from my nose. My hand flew up to clamp over my mouth a few seconds too late.

His eye twitched. "It's fucking freezing, Ashton. Undo it."

If I wasn't mistaken, I saw the evidence of the truth in that statement through the pale tint of blue blossoming across his lips. It was enough to force a barking laugh from my chest, my body convulsing in uncontrollable shakes. The pad of my palm swiped away at the tears from my face. "I'm sorry, I don't even truly understand how I did it. Ryana has been working with me, but we haven't been able to coax out my elemental power yet."

Silver eyes flared, but his tone remained neutral. "Just imagine my clothes dry and see if you can make that happen."

"Do I need to snap my fingers like you do?"

He glared at me again. "Give it a try." His teeth began to chatter, and I desperately tried to bury my mirth behind the furrowed brows of concentration.

If looks could kill, I would have already been dead. "Sorry," I muttered, glancing down to catch a shiver racking his body. "I didn't even think you could get cold."

The muscle in his jaw ticked. "Me either."

That was it, if I was going to take this seriously at all, I couldn't watch as his lips changed colors like a chameleon, or as his teeth knocked together underneath that grimace. It was all too comical.

Closing my eyes, I put all my focus into the water in his clothes, considering nothing but removing all of it so that he would be dry.

"I swear to the gods, woman!" he growled. His voice was a deep vibration in my chest, even with the distance between us.

When my lids flew open this time, I was astonished to see him completely naked, hands covering up his most intimate areas.

My mouth fell agape as I took in the sight of his body. The stacked muscles of his abdomen. The V shape below them that beckoned me to sweep my gaze lower. He growled as my focus shifted to his hand, causing me to quickly rip my gaze back to his.

Heat flooded my cheeks, but I did not find a smirk anywhere near his features. If anything, he looked more annoyed than before. "If you're done," he murmured through straining molars, "we need to focus on fixing this."

"Do it yourself," I snapped, more out of desperation than any real anger. "I told you, I don't know how."

"I can't," he seethed. With a resigned sigh, he glanced around the carriage, eyes fixating on the fur-lined cloak still draped over my shoulders. "Hand me that."

I frowned down at the thick, mottled fur. In a mockery of offense, I held my hand above my sternum. "But then I will be cold."

Another rumble emanated from his chest, and the vein over his left temple bulged with his vexation.

A snort rolled from my nose. "Relax, princeling. I'll give you the cloak."

My fingers fumbled with the clasp around my neck, unhooking it quickly and shucking it off easily. Goosebumps pebbled my skin at the chilly air, even in the confines of the carriage. Grasping the fur, I reached between us to pass it to him at the exact moment we came to an abrupt stop, causing me to fall forward to my knees, my face nearly missing the hands that covered his cock.

My nails dug into the edge of the leather bench on either side of his bare hips and my arms strained to keep me balanced above him, noticing entirely too late that he had removed his hands from covering his own body in an attempt to catch me.

Just as I began to lift myself up and far away from Beckett's crotch, the carriage door swung open. Unfortunately for everyone involved, Ebus Astor was the figure that darkened the doorway.

His focus fell immediately on me, his grin turning practically feral as he stared intently. "Well, well. I came to determine what all the yelling was about, but I can see you are in good hands."

The combination of the words and the fall itself left me in a stunned stupor, unable to move or form coherent sentences. Maybe I imagined the innuendo, but nausea churned my guts all the same.

Beckett moved his hand to my back, blocking my face and his own body from his father's view as I used every bit of my cognitive ability to avoid looking down. "Get out, Ebus." There was no reverence in his tone.

The elder Astor only chuckled. "Of course, my boy." He closed the carriage door behind him, but the wooden frame did nothing to block out the sounds of his sinister laugh as he walked away.

With his long limbs, Beckett reached across the compartment to flip a latch, locking us in. He peered down at me, and I instantaneously felt something warm and smoky pulsing along the walls of my chest. The sensation snaked along my skin, but it felt like it was coming from within, as opposed to the traces of magic I typically felt on the outside.

Confusion knitted my brows together as I tried to place the unusual feeling. "Is that your magic?"

For the first time that I could recall, Beckett Astor's face bloomed with a pink tint, and he tore his eyes from mine. "No."

My teeth grazed along my lips as I concentrated on the sensation. "It feels so... Oh my gods! It's your emotions, isn't it?"

He swallowed but did not answer, and I realized all at once that I was still awkwardly wedged between his knees.

With my hands still braced on the bench, I pushed myself upright and firmly to my side of the compartment, throwing the cloak in the general vicinity of Beckett's midsection. My palms slid against the fabric of my skirts to dispel the clammy sweat as I looked anywhere but his face.

Regardless of my best efforts, within seconds, I was already flickering my gaze to his quicksilver eyes, curiosity winning out over the abashment. "It's our bond, right? We can sense each other's feelings now?"

Beckett tore his focus from me, his stare glazed over and contemplative, like he was determining the right answer. His response came out too simple to reflect the turmoil dancing across his face. "Yes, I suppose so."

My palm shifted to rest over my chest, where the warm feeling had taken residence before but now had mostly disappeared. "What was that one?"

He cut his eyes to me as he covered his body with the cloak but kept his lips together, refusing to utter a word. His jaw looked almost painfully locked, like his molars might be cracking under the pressure.

My fingertips flexed over my chest. "I can feel... something. It's more of a temperature or a sensation. It's not obvious to me what it is based on location alone either."

Beckett's head tilted; his eyebrow arched. "Where do you normally *feel* that one?"

Pursing my lips, I offered him a pointed look. "I don't know without knowing what it was."

He hummed another non-response, but I would not be deterred. Knowledge was power here, and I had so little to begin with.

"Can you feel what I am feeling right now?" I asked him, glancing into his stormy gaze and schooling my features.

His eyes slid across my face for a few moments before meeting my stare again. "Not really, it's all confusing."

"Well, I am confused," I admitted. "I've been confused since the moment Ryana told me to leave Biltons Academy. Maybe even a little before that."

He inclined his head once but didn't comment or ask me any questions. Either he had nothing else to say, or he wasn't prepared to reveal anything about himself or our bond.

After a minute, I heard him sigh. "Well, it's also clear you are coming into your powers." He gestured lazily at his mostly naked body. "We've got a few more hours to the next stop. Let's practice your magic until we get there, so hopefully you can find me my dry clothes before we reach the grounds."

He smirked, some of his playfulness returning. "Or else, I'm going to have no choice but to shield my nakedness with your body so that I can make it to our room without exposing myself to the entirety of the Falkland staff."

I could have—likely should have—made mention that he had no need to use my body if he had my cloak, but instead I was consumed with the thought of him carrying me all the way back to his room. The notion warmed me all over, in certain places more than others, causing me to squeeze my thighs together.

Beckett cut his eyes at me with a wary expression. "I know what that one is because I can scent it."

Even as I felt my face flushing, I kept his stare. No one was going to teach me anything about our bond but him.

One eyebrow lifted. "You're right, though. It is in a different location than when I feel it." His tone held just a dash of amusement, but it was clear that the statement was more of a clinical assessment than an attempt to gain some upper hand.

My throat bobbed with a rough swallow. "We best begin the training then so we can save ourselves from any more of that." Regrettably, my voice wobbled as I spoke.

A smile, not a smirk, curled the edges of his mouth. "Deal."

Thirty-Three

"Where did your clothes go?" I asked Beckett after the third failed attempt to retrieve them. "It might help me figure out how to bring them back."

He considered the question for a moment. "I imagine they went to the void."

This time, I purposely sent confusion and annoyance through my stare, hoping he could feel it.

His laugh came out breathy, both corners of his mouth curling to form a genuine smile.

My eyebrows climbed up my forehead as I stared at him expectantly.

"Long ago, the different species were separate. Magic traditionally found only within one group would never be present amongst the others."

He drew in another steadying breath before he continued. "The Shadow Fae have access to something called the void. It allows them to transport bodies and items from one place to another through the part of space and time that is separate from the here and now. It's called shadow walking."

My muscles suddenly felt tense, certain no one had mentioned that aspect of their magic during any conversation about the Shadow Fae. "You said I was Elemental."

He considered this, allowing a few heartbeats of silence to pass between us. "I said you were most likely Elemental, but the Fae spent some time intermingling between the races since they came to be. It's completely possible that some long-ago relative was a Shadow Fae."

A frown twisted my lips. "They're dangerous. Why would anyone procreate with them?" I hated to generalize like that, but nothing about their magic spoke of good. Nothing I had heard anyway.

Beckett's head tilted to the side as he regarded me. "Do you believe that whole groups of people can be inherently good or bad?" He seemed to be highly interested in my response, and I felt the edges of another emotion that was not mine prickle along my skin. Curiosity?

Instead of going with my knee-jerk reaction of reminding him that it was his team that had warned me about the evils of the Shadow Fae, I considered the question. I shook my head back and forth. "No, I don't."

Thanks to my travels with my father, I had seen enough of Demetros to know that placing people in a bucket based on aspects of their personality, job, and especially heritage did little good for anyone.

"Right," Beckett said almost monotone. "Either way, my clothes are still missing, and it seems I require your assistance to get them back. Can we try again?"

"Tell me what to do," I said earnestly.

"I think it would be best if you focused on the clothes, in case you have simply turned them invisible somewhere within the carriage."

A little gasp caught in my throat. "Like a gift?" Ryana and I had been so focused on my elemental power that we didn't even discuss when or how a gift might show up. "Would access to the void be a gift, too?"

Beckett blew out a breath. "Invisibility would be a gift. However, the Shadow Fae don't appear to inherit variable gifts like the Elemental Fae. Just differences in power levels within their species' given traits." His eyes pinched as he looked at me. "I wouldn't worry yourself over it."

"But you just said that your clothes were likely in the void," I argued. "Wouldn't that mean I had access to the void?"

Beckett's fingers pressed along the bridge of his nose. "Yes, it is possible, but highly unlikely. I spoke without recalling that the monarchy has placed protections on the Light Kingdom to keep Shadow Fae magic out. So, they don't just pop into place next to the citizens and suck them dry of blood and power."

This was the second time I had heard this mentioned, but it didn't stop the gasp from slipping through my lips.

As if he could already sense my building questions, a wave of exasperation washed over his features, tingling along our connection. "I will tell you everything you want to know the minute my clothes have returned to my body. Dry."

Quickly, I slammed my eyes shut, trying to focus on the clothes even as my mind wandered to the void and what that kind of place might feel like. I pictured a cold, desolate space, with nothing but a profound sense of emptiness. Even in the vision, I felt lonely, like my time in the Cliffs of Alamance. My teeth clenched as I willed my thoughts back to the clothes and my mission of returning them to Beckett's body.

"Thank you," Beckett stated, clearing his throat. "Now, can you dry them?"

My lids cracked open, finding that while his clothing had been returned, they were still completely drenched. "Sorry," I muttered again, turning my focus to the water.

"Just focus on the element and the intent," Beckett stated, his voice softer than I expected. "Imagine a string or an orb of magic that belongs to the element and grab it. Own it."

It took many attempts with me picturing a thread of power associated with water while simultaneously envisioning it evaporating from Beckett's clothing before the liquid shifted at all. It wasn't until I snapped my fingers in conjunction with focusing my intention that his clothes were finally left dry.

Beckett palmed the fabric along the sleeves of his tunic just to ensure no moisture had been left behind. "Good. Soon, that will be second nature."

"Tell me more about the Shadow Fae," I said, rather than discussing abilities I had little faith I'd ever master.

A sniff of a laugh peeled from Beckett's nostrils. "Right," he said, the amusement fading ever so slightly from his expression. "What is it you wanted to know?"

"How does their magic work? You said they bite their victims and drink their blood, but what happens to the Fae they've bitten?"

Beckett peeled his lips back, pointing toward his cuspids. "Shadow Fae have sharpened canines that pierce the skin and allow blood to flow into their mouths. The amount they drink correlates to how long they are able to retain the power they've consumed."

I wrinkled my nose at the idea of what a full belly of blood might feel like, grimacing as I fired off my next question. "So, the power exchange isn't permanent?"

"No," he replied.

My brow furrowed. "Even if they drain the body?"

"Not even then."

Working my lower lip between my teeth, I considered this, recalling a mention of Fae being found drained along the Northern border. At the time, I hadn't fully comprehended the implications, but now... "Then why do they do it?"

Confusion filtered along his features.

"I have been paying attention," I countered a bit defensively.

He sighed away the puzzlement. "The going theory is that Fae are being drained to death to keep them from identifying their attackers."

The Shadow Fae couldn't even keep the magic they were stealing for themselves, and didn't need to kill their victims, and yet they were doing it anyway. The cruelty of that made me concerned with our destination and the proximity to the border where those creatures lurked.

"It is this type of magic that the Betrayers have found a way to harness and utilize for their own gains," Beckett stated, his tone calm and even, a sharp contrast to my racing pulse.

Not that I intended to defend The Guides whom Beckett was referring to, but there was a key difference in their methods. "The Guides are parasites, but they are not killing their hosts."

"True," Beckett replied. "The Shadow Fae who drain their victims are only doing so with the aim of killing them."

Swallowing roughly, I wrung my hands in my lap. "How would I know what they look like? Grethe mentioned the shifters look like the

Elemental Fae when they aren't in their animal form, but what about the Shadow Fae? Are their teeth the only identifier?"

Beckett watched me carefully, but whatever his eyes were gleaming with, it was not amusement. Unease snaked its way into my chest as he spoke. "Shadow Fae are typically winged, have retractable canines for feasting, but otherwise appear like any other form of Fae. Their access to the void allows them to hide the less desirable traits of their species. Like shifters."

Shock pulsed through my body. "So, there is no way to tell the difference? They could be anywhere at any time, and I have no way to know?" Panic laced my tone.

Beckett's head tilted slightly as if he were observing me again. "Calm down, please," he whispered, swallowing as if my fear was physically harming him. "Look at me."

In a trance, my eyes shifted to his. Calm grey pools silently urged me to slow my breaths and steady my racing heart. When he was certain I had released enough of my fear to truly listen to him, he continued. "Shadow magic is blocked in the Light Kingdom through a series of complicated wards. They must walk on foot across arctic lands to reach the borders, and if they were to cross, the magic would notify the appropriate channels immediately. You are safe."

This only moderately pacified my concerns. "But what would happen if I met with one of them? What should I do?" Despite my recent display of magic, I had no control over my elemental gifts. Being trained to fight in a human army seemed a bit useless compared to sharp teeth and wings.

There was a warning in his tone, as his typically stoic face twisted into concern. "You need to run."

This affirmed my conclusion, but I had to ask. "Even if I am trained to fight?"

"They can control you with their voice. Do you recall being told that they have the power of compulsion?"

In a daze, I nodded.

"Some of them require touch to enact their will, others eye contact."

Just when I was about to gasp, Beckett added, "Few can exert their power without either, just the command in their voice."

My head shook. "Why would anyone build a castle so close to the border with those creatures?"

The corner of Beckett's lip twitched. "Ebus uses Castle Falkland as a base. His arrogance is justified; the creatures of the Dark Kingdom will not attack his stronghold."

The breath Beckett released blew out a strand of his hair. "You're not going to have nightmares over this, are you?" There was some amusement lining his silvery eyes, but something else there too.

Leveling him with an incredulous glare only served to make him chuckle. "There is a whole world of creatures out there besides humans and human-like Fae, but I hardly think you want to spend the entire drive having a history lesson when we should be practicing your magic."

"Because I'm expected to uphold your family values of excellence?" I mused, feeling anything but amusement.

For a brief moment, his eyes constricted as he assessed my features, eyes roaming over my face. "Didn't Ryana or Anastasia talk to you?"

"About what?" That same panic from earlier flared back to life in my chest.

Pity. That was the emotion that twisted Beckett's features and coiled in my gut across our bond. "Your father has not been recovered at any of the safe houses. He's missing."

Of course I had known he was missing from our home, but the fact that the Light Kingdom spies hadn't found him yet was concerning. Was I too late? Had he already succumbed to his illness and perished, afraid for me and alone in some location where I would never find him? My heart constricted in my chest, the air leaving my lungs in a ragged gust.

I was still reeling from Beckett's words, flailing with the realization that all I had done might not have been enough, when the carriage came to another abrupt stop. A knock sounded on the door beside me, and Ebus' deep voice could be heard on the other side. "We've made it to the first stop. Is everybody decent?"

Beckett answered flatly. "Yes, Ebus. We are dressed." He slid over the bench to open the latch that locked us inside.

The crack in the door revealed Ebus' soulless eyes already pinned to me, twinkling with more of that malefic delight. His vision roamed up and down my seated frame as he clicked his tongue. "What a shame."

It was possible that if I hadn't just been hit with the news of my father being missing, rather than simply hiding out, I might have flinched or had any reasonable reaction to Ebus' words. As it stood, I was only capable of blinking.

Behind him, people were already scurrying to set up large canvas tents that I assumed would be our quarters for the night. The ride to Falkland could only be done in a day with a much smaller caravan so I had already been warned we'd be sleeping in the woods.

"Your presence is required," Ebus said, this time his focus on Beckett, who turned to me with an apology in his eyes.

"Stay in the carriage until someone retrieves you," Beckett stated before launching himself from the door and shutting it swiftly behind him, leaving me alone with my horrible thoughts.

Thirty-Four

Between the four-course meal that was somehow deemed necessary to Onyx's traveling requirements and the amount of time it took to pack away the tents from the night of sleeping in the woods, it was nearing lunch by the time the convoy began heading North again. For the entirety of the ride, Beckett and I had only minimally discussed my missing father because, according to him, there were no other details to glean.

The Queen hadn't made a decision about what to do next, she had only been informed of the fact that he wasn't at any of the safe houses sometime during our ceremony celebration, perhaps in the hours following my departure. It was the only conclusion I let myself draw, considering she hadn't said a word to me about it.

"Anastasia assures me that he is alive," Beckett offered. The tone was nonchalant, but his eyes pinned to me like he was seeking my reaction to that news.

It was a relief, although it did little to quell my concern that he was suffering wherever he was. I didn't understand enough about the bond or how the magic worked over distances to feel anything close to contented on that matter.

Rather than focusing on all the ways in which I was helpless, I decided to ask Beckett about the statement he had made the previous day. "What does his absence have to do with me practicing my magic?" I asked as the carriage jostled on. "If there's nothing that I can do about it anyway."

Beckett's eyes traced the trees on the horizon from the window of our carriage. "I will likely be sent to Demetros for an extraction, seeing as how a majority of my team is undercover there and cannot be recalled."

"I thought the Queen had requested to instruct me in magic. You do not need to be present for me to learn," I countered.

Those silver eyes slid to mine. "Yes, but I would not feel confident taking you with me if you do not have some basic skill level."

Tilting my head, I regarded his statement in a different light. "You want to take me with you?"

"Do you not want to come?" He responded, rather than answering the question directly.

It struck me then that he was yet again giving me the choice. Providing me agency that no one else had seemed willing to do. "I do."

"Then let's get to work."

We spent the majority of the ride attempting to usher my magic to the surface. However, with the anxiety of my father's fate looming over me, nothing had been overly effective. Even the basics, like drawing fire into my palm, seemed too difficult a task, amounting to nothing more than an ember that died out with my next exhale.

Frustration was pulsing beneath my ribs by the time we came to a stop at Castle Falkland. How was I supposed to break the spell or even rescue my father if I couldn't even summon the simplest of flames?

As if he were eager to be done with this lesson as well, Beckett reached for the handle, throwing the door open and exiting as quickly as he could. Soft pink light spilled into the cabin, and just as I considered staying inside for another hour, Beckett reappeared in the opening, offering me his arm.

Sliding from my position on the bench, I let him guide me from the riding compartment. The fingers of my free hand toyed with the edge of my fur-lined cloak, tugging it closer to my face as I swept my gaze across my immediate surroundings, taking in my first glimpse of the grounds of Castle Falkland.

A thick layer of snow blanketed the ground along the massive circle drive at the front of the property, and a gust of wind kicked up a flurry that ruffled my hair and clothes and set my teeth chattering again. Attempting to hold onto what little source of heat I could find, I pressed myself firmly against the wall of Beckett's body.

Beckett leaned toward me, dipping his lips to the shell of my ear. "Warming yourself will be part of your lessons." There was no condescension in his tone, despite my earlier failure to summon substantial flames. It almost felt comforting.

Still, my lips stayed sealed as my gaze drifted over the line of carriages around us. I already knew that my mother would not be among them, having stayed behind to close up Castle Lochmere for an extended time away. That didn't stop disappointment from settling heavily in my chest. Why had neither she nor Ryana told me about my missing father when they had the chance?

Beckett untangled our limbs in favor of putting his arm around my shoulder, pulling me close, and letting his lips brush against my earlobe. To the outsider, it certainly looked like a loving moment between a newly married couple. "I promise you that I will update you the moment I learn something new."

The promise did little to distract me from my anguish, but that wasn't his fault. He was planning to take me with him, and for that, I was choosing to be grateful. "Thank you," I muttered, allowing Beckett to pull me toward the grand entrance of his family's castle with his arm slung over my shoulder.

Somewhere within my body, in a place I felt was more the bond than myself, I sensed something resembling sadness, maybe disappointment. Was it my own? His? This connection between us was too fledgling for me to be sure. Rather than search for more answers behind those frosty silver eyes, I tore my gaze from him in favor of the lands before me.

Castle Falkland was nothing like Lochmere. It was settled toward the top of a dark and brooding expansive mountain range, each peak capped in pristine white snow. The castle was pitch black, made from some sort of obsidian or basalt. It looked as if the structure had been carved into the side of the mountain, the building and the rocky edges of the cliff blending so seamlessly that it was hard to tell where one started and the other ended.

The castle was larger than Lochmere, too, probably five or six stories from what I could see from the cobblestone walkway. I couldn't get a sense of what, if anything, sat below the cliffside. It was entirely possible that there were several more windowless chambers carved into the stone below.

The sky was growing darker by the second, but the eerie light cast from the courtyard and castle windows highlighted the shadows of smoke billowing out of the numerous chimney stacks that lined snow-frosted roofs.

The pathway we stood on was the only flat landing around. Everything else was rocky drop-offs and sheer cliffs. It was beautiful, in a dark, cold kind of way and I supposed it was home until we returned to Demetros, whenever that would be.

Soon, hopefully. If that meant my father had been found, or the Light Queen was sanctioning a mission to go look for him.

As we moved toward the castle, I took note of the fact that there were few people milling about around us, and as I took a glance at the carriages behind us, I realized that ours was the last in line. Had we arrived last on purpose?

Even Ebus was, thankfully, nowhere to be found, leaving the only people to greet us a line of staff, an assumption made from their matching uniforms. They all stood at attention, bracketing either side of the entryway with stiff, blank stares.

The uniforms were navy, so dark that they were almost black. Instead of the crest of the Light Kingdom—which I had learned was that lion, sun, and sword combination I had seen on the tapestry in Lochmere—each of their tunics were embroidered with the symbol of a dragon curved like the letter c in the shape of a crescent moon, the silver thread causing each one to shimmer with the subtle movement of the wearer.

Awkwardly, I smiled at each and every one of them, even though no one met my gaze. The only movement they seemed to muster was slight bows that I sensed were only for Beckett.

"You don't need to befriend them," Beckett whispered as he pulled me into the entryway.

I tilted my chin in his direction. "I wasn't raised to be rude."

He shook his head, a breathy chuckle brushing against my scalp.

Even my awareness of the many ways in which our lives had been so vastly different didn't stop me from wanting to say more. Someone being beneath my station wasn't grounds to be inhospitable. Then again, no one had really been below my station before.

My thoughts on the matter remained locked within my mind as my first view of the inside of the castle stole my attention. The décor was just as dark and moody as the outside of the building, save for the pristine white marble floors, which felt oddly out of place but reminded me of the gathered precipitation outside. The only spot of brightness in an otherwise desolate landscape.

The rest of the room, from furniture to draperies, was a mixture of deep shades of purple, navy, black and dark mahogany wood on repeat. Even the paintings and wall hangings were shadowy and foreboding.

When we reached the grand staircase that curled around the walls like a twisting onyx-hued vine, Beckett released me from his grasp. He continued to walk, and I followed as we ascended the steps, with only the sounds of our shoes scuffing against the stone floor to break the silence.

Several flights later, when I was sure we were relatively alone, I spoke again. "And you're positive he's truly missing. Not just somewhere you haven't checked?"

Beckett cut his eyes over his shoulder to where I trailed closely behind him. He stepped off the stairway to lead us down a passage with deep sapphire rugs that dampened the sounds of our footfalls. "As I have already told you, Gianna has sent her swallows, and they have returned empty-handed."

I couldn't decide if it was frustrating or endearing that Beckett answered me with such honesty. On the one hand, I still had very little concept of what he was referring to with the swallows, but on the other, it gave me the space to at least attempt to find out. "What are Gianna's swallows?"

There was no extra commentary or even a sideways glance that indicated my question was out of line. "Gianna is a hawk shifter, and she commands a group of other bird shifters that fly around and collect intel."

"Grethe is a shifter too, then?"

At this, Beckett drew in a deep breath. "That is a story for him to tell you, not me." There was nothing in his expression that indicated particularly upsetting background information there, so I trudged forward while mentally making a note to come back to that the next time I saw Grethe. "So, she sent birds to Demetros to search for him and..."

A hand landed on the small of my back as Beckett steered me toward a doorway on our right. Just as he had in Lochmere, his other palm stilled over the black iron doorknob. It wasn't until I heard the sound of a faint clicking noise that he turned his hand and pushed through the door, pressing me forward into the space ahead of him.

"They returned, having found no evidence of him at any of the predetermined locations he should have gone to, had he intended to return to The Light Kingdom." He closed the door behind us, then swept his gaze toward the room beyond. "Welcome home."

I allowed my focus to shift to the suite. The architecture and décor in this room were much the same as the rest of the castle. Cold white marble flooring, pitch black curtains and bedding, and deep mahogany wood adorned the space.

Across from where we entered were massive arched windows framing equally large glass-paned doors that were opened to a semi-circle-shaped balcony that was dimly illuminated by the setting sun.

Turning back to Beckett, I remained unsure of how to proceed in what was clearly his personal quarters without some sort of guidance. "Will they keep looking for him?" Mentally, I ran through all the locations that he might have gone outside of the safe houses. "I can make a list of settlements where we have friends. Small towns on the outskirts of the bigger cities. Places off the beaten path."

"They will keep looking for him, but the Queen has assured us that he is safe." His words were not coated in annoyance, although it was a repetition of our earlier conversation. He lifted a palm to his chest in the same way I had seen my mother do when discussing the same topic. "She would sense if he was not."

With that, Beckett jerked his head toward the balcony doors, offering me his arm.

His words had me considering that maybe he knew that my mother and father were mates but since the Queen hadn't explicitly said that anyone from her team was aware, I kept my mouth shut, opting instead to accept his answer until I could talk to my mother.

Beckett pushed through the outer door that led to the balcony, and I followed closely behind. The perforated parapet along its outer edge was constructed from a thick slab of the onyx-colored stone that matched the exterior of the rest of the castle. The cutouts formed various shapes of the phases of the moon. Entranced, I walked out to its edge, placing my hands along the ridge, marveling at how warm the stone felt, despite its location outside, surrounded by snow and darkness.

My gaze swept over the horizon. From up here, the landscape felt so uninhabitable. In the darkness of the early night, I could barely make out the road that we had traveled on, winding through the sharp peaks of the mountain range like a snake slithering through the woods. Although the two regions were vastly different in plant life and altitude, just like with Lochmere, the outer edges of the Falkland castle held no indication of structures or villages anywhere in the visible distance.

When I turned to my left, I made out the shape of another balcony, not quite connected to this one. A light draping of sheer fabric hung over the pergola that stretched over it, billowing in the frosty wind. Underneath the cover was what appeared to be an enormous clawfoot bathtub.

I stared at it longingly. What I wouldn't give to be soaking in that tub right now.

"What do you think?" Beckett asked, shaking me from my thoughts and drawing my attention to his overly attentive gaze.

My neck craned so that I could catch a glimpse of the lands beyond once more. "It's beautiful. Not like Lochmere," I added quickly. "It's stunning in a gloomy, pristine sort of way." It was meant to be a compliment, but I wasn't sure it came off that way.

A smile softened his expression. "I'm glad you like it; it will be home for a while, and I want you to be as comfortable as you can be here."

It was highly unlikely I'd find myself comfortable again for the foreseeable future, and I fought back a frown as I added the layer of my father's confirmed absence to the mix. If Beckett had caught the flicker of my grimace, he did not acknowledge it. "Come with me", he said, nodding his head back inside the suite, toward a small wooden door to the edge of his bedroom. "I'll show you to your room."

Thirty-Five

Beckett led me down a narrow hallway that opened into a sitting room, complete with two tufted couches and a marble slab fireplace that was playing host to the embers of a dying fire. We didn't linger, simply crossing to where another door gave way to a smaller room.

He stepped inside, giving me space to enter without having to touch him. It seemed that outside of the public eye, he didn't see any need to have contact between us. I should have been appreciative of that boundary, but the disappointment of it weighed heavily on my shoulders.

Without Ryana and Grethe, Beckett was the closest thing I had to a friend, and the wall between us filled me with a sadness I hadn't been anticipating. It wasn't fair of me to expect anything at all from Beckett, considering he had already technically married me in part to save my life, but when I was with him, I felt a comradery there that I hoped went beyond the bounds of our magical bond.

In the wake of those pathetic thoughts, I pushed my focus to the space that was apparently my bedroom now. It was smaller than the suite we had just left, but no less opulent, even if the decor was darker than my personal tastes. The walls here were covered in a paper-like cloth that resembled the black bedding draped over the four-poster bed in both texture and pattern. The shadowy hues gave the space the feeling of a cave, almost void of light despite the windows that lined one side of the room.

"This is your bathing chamber," Beckett said, pointing toward one door before sweeping his hand to another on a different wall. "That is your closet. Your wardrobe should already be inside."

Knowing we had beaten our luggage to the room, I suspected that if I peeked beyond that door, I'd find the clothing that Onyx so dutifully complained about having to have tailor-made for me. Something told me that I would not be appreciative of the garments once I saw them.

Beckett chuckled as if sensing my feelings on the subject, and it struck me that, considering our bond, he probably had. "There are a variety of garments to choose from, including pants for training, if you prefer them. Although Ebus and Onyx expect formal attire at dinner."

There was no holding back my scoff. Not even the Light Queen herself had implemented a dress code for her evening meals, with the exception of the night Onyx had arrived. What gave the Astors the audacity to do it for themselves?

"You'll find that Lochmere is not a formal residence and boasts much less rigid rules. When you visit the royal castle in Iverness, the traditions are upheld there as well."

My weight shifted to one foot as my hip popped out, and my arms folded over my chest. "Stop doing that."

Beckett arched an eyebrow. "Doing what?" The smirk that curled one side of his mouth told me he already knew.

"Reading my mind!" I bucked against the desire to stomp my foot in protest.

He chuckled, stepping toward me again. "As I have already told you, I cannot read your mind. Just the emotions you send my way and simultaneously wear so plainly on your face."

"Will we always share emotions?" My words were breathless as if the idea of that was both horrifying and intriguing all at once.

We were roughly toe to toe by the time Beckett stopped moving, his head tilted down to look at me. "Have you felt anything from me since yesterday?"

My head shook back and forth as I uncrossed my arms and let them fall to my side. "Not very strongly." I pressed my lips together in a straight line. "How?"

"I'll teach you," he promised. "Just like I'll teach you how to fill that bathtub you were staring at so longingly when we get back from dinner."

A low whine eased from my chest as my nose scrunched. "You said we had a few hours until dinner."

He reached out to the space between us, tucking a stray hair behind my ear. "I imagine it will take about that long for you to pick out a dress you find suitable in there." His head jerked back toward my closet. "Knowing Onyx, she will send an attendant to do your hair and makeup as well."

The noise that left my throat was a garbled mix between a scoff and a growl of disgust. "Don't you get some perks of being the prince? Can't you tell them we won't be going to dinner tonight?"

Beckett's tongue pressed between his molars to hide his grin. "Sorry, Princess. This was actually the Queen's orders."

At the reminder of my mother, the room seemed to plummet in temperature. I had quite a few questions for her, namely why she thought I wouldn't want to know that my father was officially missing and why Beckett had been the one to tell me.

"Fine," I muttered. "Let me go pick out a dress."

As if my resignation had summoned another presence, a knock sounded at the door connecting our rooms. A petite girl stepped into the space, her uniform dark, but missing the embroidered dragon that the other staff who—sort of—greeted us out front had been wearing.

"Ah, just as I suspected, Onyx has sent reinforcements." Beckett grinned but it only drew the corners of my own mouth down. "I'll leave you to it," he stated, waltzing away with an infuriating wolfish grin dancing along his features.

I looked at my reflection in the floor-length mirror as the attendant finished the last touches on my face. She dabbed something creamy against my cheeks to give them a rosy glow. My lids had already been colored with a smoky-hued powder and lined with the thin swipe of kohl that ended in points at the corners of my eyes.

The strands of my hair were pulled back in a twisting set of braids, giving full view of the only gown I found acceptable within my closet. The solid black dress hugged my curves all the way down to my upper thigh, where the skirt flared out in carefully sewn panels, thankfully giving me enough freedom to move my legs without waddling across the room.

A sweetheart neckline arched over my chest, dipping so low over my sternum that my belly button was at risk of becoming visible. Somehow, possibly by magic I had yet to learn of, the structure pulled my breasts up and apart at the same time. The thin straps that held the garment up didn't even dig into my shoulders, further indication that something unnatural might be involved. It seemed like a frivolous waste of power, but I wouldn't put it past the Astors to ensure their son's bride looked the part.

The attendant hurried into the closet, returning with a tray of baubles for me to choose between. Another knock sounded at the door just as I reluctantly agreed to glance down at the assortment of jewelry. Assuming it was Beckett, I turned my head toward the doorway and yelled, "Come in!"

My eyes remained trained on the glittering gems, so I didn't notice when a figure that was not Beckett came to stand beside me until they spoke.

"I was hoping we'd have a moment alone before dinner." It was the Queen's voice.

Abandoning the attendant beside me, I whirled around to face my mother, already dressed in rich violet finery.

Proportionate slivers of relief and determination coursed through my veins at the sight of her. My demand flew out before I could temper my tone. "Tell me what you know about my dad."

Her features pinched, and her mouth opened and closed in quick succession for several pregnant moments. "I did not think that the information we have received thus far warranted a conversation with you. There is no update."

My arms folded across my stomach. "Because you know that he's okay? Because of..." I peered over at the attendant who was still dutifully standing where I had left her.

The Queen plucked a golden bangle from the tray before saying, "You are dismissed." The petite girl scurried back into the closet to rid herself of the tray of baubles before practically running from the room.

My focus returned to the Queen, finding a stern expression twisting her features. "This is why I wanted to talk to you. Here, you must act as if you do not know me. We are not to be familiar within these walls, outside of your connection with Beckett."

The organ in my chest faltered, skipping a beat as I processed her words. "How am I to talk to you then? What about our training?"

Her hands lifted as she fitted the golden bangle to my upper arm. "Training will occur with Gianna and me in a private courtyard. It will not be strange that I am paying attention to the new heir to my throne in that regard."

"I just can't talk to you as my mother," I replied flatly.

Her fingertips grazed along the necklace that she had given me, adjusting the pendant until it was centered on my chest. My eyes rose to meet hers.

"We will find ways to speak in private, I promise." Her words were soft and gentle but hardly a comfort. This only solidified that Beckett was my only friend here, and he was barely even that.

My eyes flickered to the door that connected our rooms, but it was still firmly shut. "And Dad?"

The Queen nodded once as if agreeing to some internal dialogue I was not privy to. "He is safe, or I would know because of our bond. I have to assume that he has found another place to hide." There was a determination in her voice, a tone that led me to believe that she was convincing herself of the sentiment, rather than me. "As soon as we hear word otherwise, I will alert you."

"Where are you looking for him? I have ideas! I can tell you..."

The Queen's hand raised between us, and just when I thought she might place it directly over my mouth, her palm came to rest against my cheek. "Gianna has sent her swallows to search every square inch of Demetros. If he is there, we will find him."

Ignoring the shine in her eyes, I focused instead on straightening my spine. "Thank you for the update."

Her hand left my face, falling limply beside the full purple skirts of her gown. "There is more."

My eyebrows lifted as I looked to her expectantly.

The crown upon her head gleamed in the dim light of my suite as her head tilted so that she could better inspect my attire, but I didn't know her well enough to decipher what she found there. "Your training will begin immediately."

"So that I am prepared to break the spell," I said bitterly.

Something fierce flashed within her eyes. "Beckett is frequently called to regions that are not always safe, and sometimes I will not be with you either, if my duty calls me away."

I tried to make sense of the words she was saying. "You need me to be capable of protecting myself, in case I end up in a bad situation?" My thoughts flashed back to Berit. Then, the last challenge that I had lost due to my response to the unresolved trauma. Adding magic to the mix could only ensure I never ended up there, or at least never felt so help-less, again.

A light hum left the Queen's throat, not exactly an affirmation of my question. "Charlese will be educating you on the history of the continent, and Gianna and I will help with your elemental magic."

"And fighting?"

She frowned, as if she hadn't just insinuated that I'd need to defend myself eventually. "When the time comes to combine your teachings, Beckett can aid in that department."

Her response was so non-committal that I wanted to replay the conversation in my mind to ensure that I hadn't missed something. Maybe she had heard from Beckett how poorly my attempts at calling my magic forward had gone and realized it was not something to be concerned with.

Before I could ask for clarification on the matter, the door connecting my suite to Beckett's blew open, and he strode across the room in a fitted black suit that almost shimmered as he walked.

His gaze fell upon the Queen first. "Ah, good to see you, Oldenberg. Do we need to debrief on anything before dinner?" His eyes slid to me, pausing there for a moment before returning to my mother.

The Queen waved him off, already starting to leave the room. "No need. I was just catching Ashton up to speed on the plan here in Falkland."

The plan. Also known as the rules that I couldn't speak to her unless spoken to.

Queen Anastasia paused at the edge of the room, but she did not turn around. "Astor," she said calmly. Her tone was at odds with the way Beckett's body tensed at the sound of his surname.

His hands clasped behind his back; his shoulders squared to face her position, even though she wasn't looking directly at him. "Your majesty?"

Her chest rose slightly with her inhale. "The next time you are given classified information, I expect you not to share it with anyone. This includes your wife."

"Of course, my apologies," Beckett said smoothly as if he wasn't being chastised by the Queen of the Light Kingdom. Meanwhile, I had the sudden urge to cower. That or scream at her for blatantly warning Beckett against speaking to me about my own father.

The Queen kept walking through the open door without so much as a goodbye.

When it was clear that she was gone, Beckett unclasped his hands and turned to face me. "That went well, don't you think?" The smile etched into his features spoke of amusement. Like the entire thing wasn't even a concern.

The grimace on my face was not fake. "She just ordered you to keep secrets from me about my dad. I'm not sure how that's good for either of us."

He shrugged. "You know, if you really want to know the information, there's one way to get it without breaking her command."

I envied his ability to see everything as a game because in this moment, I couldn't find the humor in his words. "How?"

My mind raced as I envisioned elaborate schemes. Me, crouching in dark alcoves listening to conversations behind thick velvet curtains. It was ridiculous.

However, when my gaze landed on Beckett's face again, his expression held no mirth. "Join the army."

Thirty-Six

I openly gaped at Beckett as he stared at me with another infamously unreadable expression. "I can just join the army?"

He shrugged. "I'd recommend Special Operations personally, but..."

"And this will give me access to information?" I asked dubiously, cutting off whatever he was about to say. "Ryana seemed to think I'd have clearance anyway. Are we certain I need to do this?"

Beckett stretched his arm out in offering, momentarily distracting me from my thoughts. "Come on. You can contemplate the suggestion while we walk."

Looping my arm in his, I let him guide me to the dining hall. Sparing a glance at him, I asked, "And you're sure that she will let me?" It seemed a safe way to publicly pose my inquiry without arousing suspicion from anyone who might overhear.

Without even glancing in my direction, he nodded. "She has been concerned with your protection, and I believe this would help endear the people to you."

In other words, proving myself as a useful member of the Light Kingdom army would help the people decide I was worthy of the position I had allegedly married into.

Tipping my chin in his direction, I eyed him cautiously. "And I have the best chance in Special Operations... which is?"

"I am the General of that branch. It's all the fun secret mission stuff." There was an air of nonchalance to his tone that felt out of place.

"And you'd want me on your team?" I asked, hating how the words came out hopeful.

His eyebrow raised slightly, but he did not turn to me. "It is different than what you have been trained to do, although many of the same skills apply. Is that something you would want?"

My teeth grazed my cheek as I contemplated his question. "I want to be worthy of the position I was born into, not just have it handed to me on a silver platter because of my blood or who I married."

Silver eyes momentarily slid to mine, and I forced my attention to the hallway ahead as I finished. "If this allows me to be of some value to the Kingdom or the continent and also help in any way I can with my dad, I want to do it."

When my focus slipped back to Beckett's stare, there was something sad resting there. "Then I will help you," he said softly.

The moment was too intense, and I had to find a way to crack that heaviness. "Plus, I certainly don't want to sit around while your mother drones on about grandchildren."

It was meant to be a joke, but rather than laughing, Beckett only tensed, covering up the movement with another nod. "We can discuss it later."

He had agreed to help me, and I should have felt some triumph in feeling like I had a purpose other than to be the ornament on his arm, but his expression left me hollow as he led me up into the dining hall.

The room was alive with chatter and music, even more crowded than the ballroom during the celebration of our bonding at Lochmere.

Instead of the long tables that Castle Lochmere boasted in its dining hall, clusters of smaller tables were scattered about the room with couches and tufted chairs tucked into alcoves carved into the stone walls. Some areas already hosted groups of people, clad in their dark-hued finery, lounging lazily as if this were just an informal living room rather than a place for consuming meals.

A breath sucked through my teeth as I caught sight of scantily clad men and women wearing what I could only describe as metal lingerie. They balanced trays of food and drink as they walked slowly through the crowd, passing out whatever the guests asked of them. Perhaps the most shocking part of their attire was the collars that circled each of their necks, a thick iron ring dangling from the center.

Catching my attention on the strangely dressed servers, Beckett blew out a breath. "Ebus has a flair for dramatics and a penchant for skin."

Witnessing a similar disgust written on my face, I forced my frown into a fake smile. "Is this your parents' idea of a welcome home party for you?"

He hummed a temporizing noise. "Something like that." The amusement I thought I sensed curling his lip did not reach his eyes as he guided me toward the table that the Queen, Gianna, and the Astors occupied. Mercifully, he did not stop to greet them, only made polite bows to each of them before standing off to the side, spinning me so that I faced the majority of the crowd.

Ebus clinked his fork against his glassware to get the attention of the room. "Good evening," he called. His eyes scanned the hall with predatory observation as he waited for the people to give him their undivided attention.

His grin reminded me more of a beast than a man, the expression toothy in a way that spelled danger. Like how some poisonous animals were brightly colored, a warning hiding in plain sight, which everyone here seemed apt to ignore.

Ebus tilted his head in our direction. "We are gathered here today for a celebration. My son and heir to the Light Kingdom throne has chosen a bride. Please join me in congratulating the happy couple on their recent bonding."

As the applause rang out, my focus slid to the Queen, who was clapping enthusiastically although her mouth was set in a terse smile. Unfortunately, we were still not close enough for me to read into any of her expressions, although I longed to understand what was going on in her mind.

Beckett's hand squeezed against my shoulder as he raised the other in the air to wave at the cheering crowd. It was certainly more of a welcome than we received at our reception at Castle Lochmere.

Ebus cleared his throat, grinning at the people as if they were his subjects. "Do enjoy yourselves," he purred.

At the obvious dismissal, Beckett shifted us once more, moving us toward a shadowy corner. Tucked in one of the many alcoves was a velvet-lined couch in a deep sapphire. A fur throw was tossed over one side, and dainty accent pillows leaned against each corner as if this was simply a resting space in a cozy nook of a bedroom.

My stomach grumbled at the thought of missing another real meal. "Are we not meant to eat?"

Beckett gestured to the couch. "In Falkland, the newly bonded couples are expected to take to the couches so close to their ceremony." A smirk lifted one corner of his mouth. "You know, because we are madly in love and cannot keep our hands to ourselves."

The snort that left me was neither ladylike nor quiet enough not to garner a look from Beckett, but all he did in response was drop gracefully onto the cushion beside me.

Luckily, the spot that Beckett had chosen for us was far enough away from the majority of the guests and angled in such a way that it had more privacy, but that did not make us completely shielded from the curious stares of the Falkland onlookers.

Momentarily blocking my view of the crowd, a male server set two goblets of liquid down on the low coffee table in front of us. It took everything in me to keep my eyes trained on his face, and not his metal uniform, as I thanked him. I expected this type of attire from a brothel, not a castle, and the reminder of Beckett's comment about Ebus' taste for skin only stirred up more questions.

The goblet the server brought remained untouched as my thoughts shifted to more pressing matters. How was I to pretend to be madly in love with Beckett without being too forward? How could I let him look at me the way he had, and say wonderful things about me, while not reading into any of it? No one had ever showered me with such attention and it not meant *something*.

"Okay, Princess, it doesn't have to cause you that much turmoil," Beckett whispered, his voice calm and steady.

Before I could brace myself, Beckett had already leaned over, a palm landing on the middle of my thigh. He watched me for any sign of discomfort before he slid it down, tightening his grip when he stopped just above my knee.

Knowing I'd have to do something other than just sit there awkwardly, I rested my head against his shoulder.

"See," Beckett mused. "It doesn't have to be a lap dance."

"Thankfully," I remarked quietly. "I've never been good at dancing."

Beckett sniffed a laugh, but his gaze remained on the people before us. "Tomorrow we will work on you keeping your emotions on your side of the bond." The subtle shift in his voice was too rough and low to be irritation. Thanks to the way in which my elemental magic finally showed itself, I knew what his ire sounded like.

When I only swallowed roughly in response, Beckett continued. "It will be useful in blocking out some Fae gifts as well. We can practice between your lessons."

My lessons. As much as I wanted to know more about the culture of the Fae and the true history of our continent, I was not particularly excited about the prospect of whatever etiquette training would entail. Before I could voice such an opinion, a female figure waltzed into our alcove. I'd recognize her dark wavy hair and tanned skin anywhere.

A virtually inaudible sigh worked its way through Beckett's parted lips as he turned his head to face the woman. "Hello, Mollie. What can I help you with tonight?"

Keeping my head on his shoulder, I glowered up at Mollie, but she didn't even glance my way as she kept moving toward Beckett, stopping only when she had positioned herself between his knees.

"Step back." Beckett's voice was as cold as ice, and I could feel the spark of something crackling across our bond. Anger?

Mollie feigned confusion. "What? I thought if we were back here, there would be none of those stuffy Lochmere rules."

Rules like not touching someone else's husband in front of them? Rage practically boiled my blood.

Beckett pinned her with an incredulous stare. "No," he growled.

She shrugged and walked back out. "See you later then," she purred as she left our view.

My indignation lessened the farther away Mollie got, and I couldn't help but wonder if it wasn't just my emotions I was being influenced by. Tears welled along my lash line, and my vision began to blur ever so slightly, causing me to clamp my eyes shut.

"Ashton," Beckett whispered, "I am sorry for her behavior."

My head shook. "I told you that we were friends, and you were free to do as you wished. It's just—"

"I would not disrespect you like that." His tone was so serious that I wrenched my eyes open to look at him. The silver in his eyes flashed with some indecipherable emotion, but whatever connection had opened between us across our bond was decidedly silent.

"Can I go back to my room?" I asked, moving my attention to the pewter goblet rather than whatever I wasn't finding on Beckett's face. "I'm exhausted from the travel."

"You are permitted to leave whenever you wish, but I do think it would be unseemly to retire for the night before the meal is served."

Right. Because I was a Princess now, and this event had clearly been orchestrated to celebrate our union. My molars grazed the inside of my cheek as I reluctantly bobbed my chin, resigning myself to another awkward meal.

"But," he whispered, "If you need to leave, I will take you back." A smirk curved his lips again. "It might be quite the show, but I promise you no one will bat an eye at our departure."

Relief spilled through me. He was giving me a choice, although I had a decent idea what his show might entail. My head shook back and forth. "Thank you," I muttered just as the food was served.

"That's a no to my plan?" He asked, delight lilting his tone.

I put all my focus on the fork to ignore the smile spreading on my face. "I'm hungry anyway."

After I had endured as much of the food as I could bear, we exited the dining hall to head back to our rooms. Luckily, my feet remained firmly planted on the ground as we weaved through the hallways. The only sign of his undying love was an arm slung over my shoulder.

Instinctively, I slid my palm around his waist to rest just above his hip bone, and I leaned slightly into his chest. It felt natural, like we were supposed to be doing this, even though he had made his stance clear.

Every time his hands were on me in public, I seemed to forget the look of disgust on his face when I asked about consummating our bond. In those fleeting moments, I was apt to blatantly ignore that this would all end when his bedroom door shut behind us. It was a cruel sort of punishment for fate to offer me a friend on this journey while simultaneously making him the one person I couldn't truly find comfort in.

With my thoughts decidedly soured, our walk back was quiet. As if to corroborate those ideas, the moment the door of his suite shut behind us, he released me. Show over.

"I'm going to fill the large bathtub for you now," Beckett stated, back to a state of neutrality.

I padded down the connected hallway to retrieve the robe I had seen hanging in my own bathing chamber. When I had exchanged the gown for the garment, my skin almost hummed at the feel of the fur lining. My palms smoothed over the black velvet exterior as I tied the belt firmly around my waist.

Somewhat slowly, I made my way to the balcony, my attention drawn to Beckett before anything else. He had perched himself on the lip of the porcelain, formal jacket removed, and the sleeves of his shirt rolled up to his elbow. Through the steam billowing from the tub, I watched as he poured liquid from a small vial into the water.

My steps stopped when I was just out of his reach. "Is that something that will knock me out?"

His head slanted to the side as he regarded my expression warily.

"So that I quit annoying you over the bond," I clarified, forcing a smile to my lips.

He chuckled, briefly averting his attention to the water as he poured in the final vial. When his eyes met mine again, there was a gentleness there I hadn't been expecting. It made me wish that we could go back to that version of us from before he knew who I really was, because I couldn't tell if his kindness now was because of me, or duty to my mother. "It's eucalyptus and mint oil. I think it might help with stress."

It was almost thoughtful, but I grimaced when I caught the potential secondary meaning there. "Are you feeling stressed because of me?"

"It's nothing I can't handle," he replied, but it left me with uncertainty. When Ryana and Grethe explained that they shared emotions, I had wrongfully assumed that they were felt more passively. Like reading a book on war, rather than being in the middle of a battle. After tonight, it seemed as though we truly shared them in every sense of the word. When Mollie had stopped at our table, his anger had been my anger. So, it was reasonable that my stress would become his.

As much as I longed to ask him what he thought about the newest development in our union, the moment already felt too intimate. Me in my bath robes, and my husband preparing the water.

Beckett dipped his fingers below the suds, flicking the soapy liquid off as he stood. "It should be warm enough for you now." His retreat to the door seemed to carry a hint of reservation, which was confirmed when he jerked to a stop at the threshold.

He didn't turn around to face me, but I pushed words across the bond in my head, too cowardly to say them out loud. *Stay, stay, stay.* I just needed a friend.

Maybe he couldn't hear my silent plea, or perhaps because he could, his jaw flexed before he said, "Alright, I'll leave you to it." He walked away with his hands in his pockets, but neither his face nor our magical connection gave away any inkling of the emotions he might be feeling.

When the door was firmly shut behind him, I slipped out of my robe, dipping my body into the steaming water he had prepared for me.

A sigh of pleasure vibrated through me as my skin became accustomed to the perfectly scalding temperature, and no matter how long I sat there pondering my predicament, the water never cooled. As if Beckett was somewhere nearby, heating it. Because, of course, he was.

Instead of focusing on that, I closed my eyes and breathed in the scents from the tub, doing my best to expel all that tension so he could enjoy his night.

<h1 style="text-align:center">Thirty-Seven</h1>

"Spine straight," the woman, Charlese scolded from her perch across the table.

Instantly, my shoulders pushed back so I could hold myself more upright. We had been at this for days, and I was still no closer to being a domesticated princess than she was to being a horse.

Charlese appeared to be middle-aged, by human standards anyway, with dark hair that was streaked in grey and coiled at the base of her neck. She tutted at my new posture, then gestured toward the plate before me. "Eat."

It was a test more than a suggestion. In order to please her, or whatever similar emotion she was capable of, I'd have to select the correct utensil and then determine an appropriately sized bite for a lady of my station. It was ridiculous.

Charlese's charcoal eyebrow lifted infinitesimally as my fingers hovered over the obviously incorrect choice.

Right. Outside first.

Plucking the outermost fork from the stack, I shifted the tines to the smallest bite of egg I could muster while keeping the food in place.

She frowned, and I considered tossing the entire thing across the room, except I was starving, and I knew I had to keep up my strength if I wanted to hone my abilities in elemental training this afternoon.

Outside of my magical training, I was mostly sequestered to a classroom with Charlese, where on top of grooming me to behave better, she lectured me on the history and geography of the continent.

Charlese checked her pocket watch at what was evidently the exact moment we were meant to move onto our next lesson because she stuffed the timepiece back into her skirts and stood abruptly.

Shoveling as much of the protein as I could get into my mouth, I pushed away from the table as well, ignoring her disapproving scowl as I chewed rapidly with puffy cheeks.

"Today we will discuss maps," she stated as we resumed our normal positions in the all too familiar classroom. White marble floors, a single solid black desk with a solitary chair, and Charlese's podium were the only things in this wretched room besides a chalkboard that took up the majority of the front wall.

I was certain that the chalkboard was part of an elaborate exercise to teach me patience while I was forced to watch her meticulously draw out each letter of the words she intended to have me memorize.

Luckily today, she seemed to be giving a different type of instruction as there was no chalk clutched between her polished fingertips. Her heels clicked as she crossed the stone tiles to the board, reaching to tug on a silver ring that, when pulled, revealed a map of the continent. One where all the lands were tied together without the construct of the spell separating them.

Charlese wasn't one to encourage questions, so I listened intently as she explained the lesser-known regions to me. "This is the Amethyst ridge," she stated, pointing at a vaguely familiar mountain range at the northern border of Demetros. "It was the natural border between the two kingdoms prior to the spell and named so in part because of its indigo-hued rocks."

Just to prove to her that I was listening, I scribbled down the tidbit on my blank parchment.

"The region here," she said, tapping a finger against the land above the ridge, "was named the Amethyst Court because of the color of the stones and the violet-hued forest." She pointed a nail against the purple shaded portion of the map, "All of which was encompassed by the territory that once belonged to the Amethyst Queen."

If I squinted enough, I could just make out a thin line that denoted the border of this former court boundary.

"The entire continent was comprised of five territories." This time, she tapped on Demetros. "The Ruby court." A polished finger moved to the area where Lochmere rested on a peninsula on the eastern coast of the continent. "The Emerald Court."

Her fingertip hovered over a large city on the eastern coast of the map toward the middle, labeled Iverness. "The Diamond Court." Finally, she moved to the Northernmost territory. "The Sapphire Court." Right beneath where she pointed in bold black letters were the words, "The Dark Kingdom."

"We are here," she stated, only lowering her forefinger slightly to show me the location of Falkland Castle. Seeing how close to the border we were made me question the validity of Ebus' confidence that none of the Shadow Fae would attack us. It would take nothing for them to just step across the border and come for the multitude of Fae that lived within these walls. Feasting on everyone they found if only for a source of temporary power.

Fear zipped down my spine as Charlese continued to point to significant locations across the map, promising that we would come back to the court systems when we discussed the gifts of the Elemental Fae.

Only half listening to the rest of her spiel, I gathered enough to know that there were very few settlements in the Light Kingdom, with the majority of its residents living in Marituk, the capital city that played host to Castle Iverness, the Queen's official royal residence.

"What about over there?" I said, pointing toward the western coast of the continent. "The edge of the Emerald Court."

Charlese's eyes formed slits in my direction, even though I thought she'd be impressed that I remembered the unmarked territory. "Very few people live in the Western Lands. It is mostly home to animal populations that have been steadily growing in numbers since the demise of the wolves, many centuries ago. Most only venture there to hunt."

Demise of the wolves? It pricked at something in my memory, but I filed it away, promising I'd circle back to that later when it was less off topic. "Why does no one live there?"

Predictably, Charlese pinned me with an incredulous stare as she pursed her lips. "I am not here to satisfy your curiosity. I am here to teach you the basics. Stop asking questions and listen."

Well, at least some things hadn't changed. This was no different than my education in battle studies with Viggo Wood at Biltons Academy. Only this time, I knew to be more skeptical of the information given to me.

With my mouth clamped shut, I inclined my head to get a better view of the map as she continued her prepared lesson, giving a vague overview of each city of note.

After what felt like hours, she lifted her pocket watch from her skirts again, tugging along the silver ring at the bottom of the map to lift it back into place. "It is time for your lesson on politics. You may have a brief break to relieve yourself in the bathing chamber. You have five minutes."

After experiencing only a few days with Charlese, I knew I had to take the break when it was given or lose out completely. So, I scurried from the room as gracefully as I could, hurrying back in record time so as not to collect any more of her ire.

When I returned to my chair, she had written a group of four names on the board. My mother, Queen Anastasia, was on top, and the other three were beneath her. Ebus Astor, Gianna Alcides, and Beckett Astor, each with their titles written below their names.

"The Light Queen, Queen Anastasia the first of her name, has been our monarch for one hundred and forty-three years."

Charlese then went into a brief overview of how The Queen had been named heir after the Great Conflict, giving me a few more details than my mother had, while leaving out my father's existence altogether. In fact, throughout the entire lecture, there wasn't a single mention of a king or even a consort.

These people are the generals of the three branches of the Light Queen's military. "Ebus Astor is the General of the infantry army," Charlese stated. "It is the largest branch, comprised of a mixture of enlisted soldiers and his own personally paid units. He supplied their uniforms from his personal coffers, so they bear the crest of his family sigil. A crescent dragon."

This made me second guess the jobs of the uniformed people who had greeted Beckett and I upon our arrival at Castle Falkland, but Charlese moved on to the next name before I could contemplate it further.

"Gianna Alcides is the General of the queen's guard, called the Light Guard. She travels with Queen Anastasia and manages a smaller group that is solely dedicated to the protection of the crown." Charlese must have been referring to the swallows that Beckett had mentioned, but I wasn't going to make the mistake of speaking out again so I kept my lips firmly pressed together.

"These individuals will be seen bearing the crest of the Light Kingdom, or sometimes a simple sun." In my notes, I scribbled a little sun in the margins.

"And finally," Charlese stated, hovering over Beckett's name, "the youngest General and head of Special Operations, Beckett Astor. He earned his title approximately ten years before he was named heir to the Light Kingdom throne."

There was a sense of pride lingering in Charlese's expression, and it hit me that she had probably been his private tutor at one point as well. She lifted her chin to look down at me. "As the Light Queen has no official heirs of her own, she was asked to choose a predecessor, considering the crown would have no one to pass to without any living relatives."

Did she know who I was, or was this simply part of the lesson?

Again, Charlese pulled out that damn time piece, glancing at it briefly. With an accomplished smile, she placed the watch back. "And that is all we will discuss on the magic of crowns until we get to the ancient courts of long ago. You are dismissed for evening training."

She handed me a tome as I passed, and I read the title quickly on my way out the door. *Notable Families of the Light Kingdom* was printed on the cloth-bound cover. "This is your homework. Please read up on this during your own time, as I will mention these important members of our Kingdom during your lessons."

And that was it. With the book tucked against my chest, I fled from the room only to be led to my next lesson.

Thirty-Eight

ESTELLA

"Do you have any children?"

Estella felt the power behind the man's voice and knew it was more than just anger that tingled along her skin. She shook her head. "No, I do not. Do you?" It had been like this for days now. Her captors, her former advisors, taking turns in rotation to inquire over the same topics. Again, and again.

Perched in the armchair before her, Claudius glared at her, eyes roaming her body with disdain. "I'm asking the questions here."

Estella had learned that if she asked questions back, complied, but yet turned the tables on them enough, more often than not, they left flustered before they could administer her next dose of chrysanth, leaving her cognizant enough to scribble down what she learned.

Through her many interrogations, she had gleaned bits of information about the current status of Demetros. At this point, she recalled a spell sweeping the land, and her handing her magic over with the promise that her people would be protected, but there had been so much she had missed.

During a recent interrogation, Theondri had shifted while questioning her and an inked rune had appeared on his forearm, similar to the ones carved into her own skin. This marking was drawn in with black lines rather than scar tissue. When she had asked him what it was, he had bragged about how the Guides used natural magic to set the ink, binding the power of others to their own bodies, stealing from her people.

"We've learned a lot since those," he had said as he pointed smugly at her own arms and the white lines that kept her powerless.

If she thought about it too long, she could still feel the kiss of the cold marble on her back as the five of them pressed magically imbued blades into her flesh, hand carving the runes that marred her skin.

They had promised to keep her people safe from the spell that was going to take their powers and so she had given up hers to protect them, or so she thought. Based on Theondri's insinuation, it was very likely she had just handed her people's magic to her advisors on a silver platter.

After his confession, Estella had been forced to keep her expression neutral, as she prayed that she'd be able to transcribe what she had learned into her journal. The Guides were rarely forgetful these days, but she had gathered enough that she was almost at the end of her charcoal.

"Estella," Claudius said smoothly, drawing her back to the present. "Does the name Christopher mean anything to you?"

Estella shook her head, staring at the white-haired man with a new sense of frustration that she knew she shouldn't be showing. Of all her so-called Guides, she hated him the most because he had been the orchestrator of her demise. The champion of her agony. "No," she answered honestly.

It was possible that she had once met someone named Christopher. It wasn't an entirely unique name, but it held no sentimentality to her. She still felt like there was something she was missing, fractions of memories still out of reach, even though she believed that the main ones —the pieces of her past that made her, her— had been recovered. If she had no inkling of a recollection to the name, it was likely unimportant. Hopefully.

Her eyes slid down to the bare skin of her forearms, the flesh still disfigured with the white runic scars. She wondered what parts of her own magic her advisors had used to kill or torture the citizens of her kingdom. People she traded her freedom to protect.

"You promised that you would keep them safe," she hissed, unable to keep her ire at bay any longer.

Claudius pressed his lips together in a thin line, his displeasure evident. "I assure you that no harm has befallen your people by my hand."

She attempted to regain her composure, picking at the scarred flesh of her arm, wishing she could just scratch the surface and release her magic. Her muscles almost ached with the idea of how good that would feel. "Then why keep me imprisoned?"

Namea was poised by his side, standing behind his armchair with green eyes narrowed on Estella as if they couldn't understand how Estella would have the audacity to ask such a question.

"I don't see how else it is possible," Claudius said offhandedly to Namea, as if Estella weren't there at all. He ignored her question completely as he shook his head, and for a moment, Estella was left wondering if she imagined speaking at all.

"No one has been permitted into these rooms without the supervision of one of us," Namea insisted. "Unless you suspect Theondri or Phoebus of such crimes..."

Estella shuddered when she pieced together what they were speaking of. Surely, she would have recalled the memory of an assault, definitely the birth of a child... Although, the chrysanth had caused her to forget large clusters of time... It was plausible that they had used it on her before.

The blood drained from her face as bile crept up her throat. Instinctively her hand went to cradle her stomach.

"Of course not," Claudius spat, interrupting those horrific thoughts. "They would never betray us like that. They would not create the one thing that could bring our demise. End our solitude before we've found the one—" The Guide cut off his words abruptly, eyes sliding to Estella as if he just remembered she was present.

A pulse of magic tickled beneath a rune on Estella's arm, and she rubbed it absentmindedly as she held Claudius' gaze.

"Furthermore, he's in the dungeons in the cuffs so he can't cause much harm there," Namea replied, their face detached and unbothered.

Estella's ears pricked at the news, her fingers itching to write it in her journal, but she kept her face nonchalant as she continued to rub against the scars that climbed all the way to her shoulder. There was a man in the dungeons who may or may not be a distant relative of hers. She just needed to find a way to get to him or...

"If you bring him to me, I will tell you if I remember him," she suggested, knowing that it was a risk to show her hand like that. Perhaps her captors didn't recognize the value of blood magic, and they wouldn't realize what she was doing.

Claudius' cold eyes focused on something on the floor that wasn't there as he continued pondering some topic that Estella could already tell had nothing to do with her suggestion. He sighed heavily, blinking away whatever thoughts had momentarily consumed him. "We still have time before this is an issue."

"As long as the exile remains, the Dark Kingdom cannot reach us here," Namea added in solace. "There is very little they can do as long as the construct stands."

Estella had known about the magical exile that had been put in place at the conclusion of the war, but she had not realized until this moment that the Guides wanted it in place.

"Except..." Gnarled fingers rubbed at Claudius' eyes. "There has to be some passage between kingdoms that we have missed in our searches. No one just disappears out of thin air without a trace." He turned his hardened gaze toward Estella, and before he even spoke, she could feel his magic rising. "Answer truthfully, girl," he said, trying to force compulsion that he had already admitted he didn't have mastery over. "What do you know of the passageways between kingdoms?"

Something cool washed over her skin, but did not make it into her mind, and she had the distinct impression that her words were her own. Still, it took extreme effort to keep the condescension from her tone. "Seeing as you have held me prisoner since before the spell was cast, I am not aware of any tunnels that might connect the kingdoms in its wake." It was the truth, but she was glad he had not asked her where one might have been placed. She had her suspicions about the odd pulse of magic that originated in the North. Recharging itself once a year in a spectacular nighttime display that even the mere idea of set goosebumps along her flesh. Only once had she witnessed the *Lux Scaporum* and that had been enough.

Namea reached their hand to the curve of Claudius' shoulder. "There is no need to fret, Claudius. For all we know, there is no one alive who knows what we took from them."

Estella kept her features neutral as she devoured the information they were leaking. Clearly, they had taken something from the Dark Kingdom and were using the exile to hide. Not only that, but they believed significant time had passed. Her stomach dropped at the idea that she had been trapped for decades, maybe longer.

"I suppose if we cannot get the answers we seek through this one," Claudius stated, nodding his head toward Estella, "then we may need to employ more practical tactics."

Namea grinned, and it was the least comforting thing Estella had ever seen. "Shall I send *him* to the dungeons to greet our new guest?"

"Please," Claudius purred. "We do not have infinite time anymore."

"I will have the answers you seek before the solstice." Namea made to leave Estella's quarters but was stopped abruptly by Claudius' hand wrapping around their forearm.

"Don't kill him," the leader of the Guides warned. "We will need him alive for leverage."

"Of course, sir."

Estella didn't miss the curl of Namea's smirk, and she frowned, wondering if she had just inadvertently caused the torture of her distant cousin all because she didn't possess the information the Guides were demanding of her.

"As for you," Claudius said, turning his attention back to his captor. "Drink up."

He passed her the cold vial of chrysanth, and she drank it reluctantly, knowing there'd be no way out of it this time. Her eyes instantly grew heavy, and her vision blurred as she leaned back against her settee, watching in a hazy stream of images as Claudius left her alone again.

All she could do was try and hold onto the information she had learned today, hoping she could retain even a fraction of it for her journal.

Thirty-Nine

"**F**ocus on the individual strands of your power to coax them to the surface," the Queen commanded, watching me intently for anything to happen. "Let's try water today. I assume you are most familiar with that one."

Because of my father.

It had been a week since we arrived at Falkland, and I had yet to hear a word about his whereabouts from either Beckett or my mother. Distancing myself from those feelings of worry, I closed my eyes and searched within myself for even a whisp of the magic that I had already proven I could wield.

It was so frustrating to reach for something I knew was there and come up empty-handed and simultaneously embarrassing that my attempts were so fruitless when my mother was the one watching me. My breath huffed in irritation, and every muscle in my body locked up as I attempted to access the magic one more time to no avail.

"Let's take a short break then," the Queen suggested, pulling me over toward the bench where Gianna sat. Officially, the Light Guard General was the one training me to use my magic, but it had just been a guise to allow my mother to be here with me.

Gianna passed us each a cup of water before excusing herself momentarily.

After a few sips of her own drink, the Queen turned her attention to me. "Do you have any questions?"

There were so many unanswered questions I could ask, but I settled on ones that I knew Beckett might not be able to answer as easily as her. "Who are the Oldenbergs?" No matter how many pages I read in *Notable Families of the Light Kingdom*, the last name didn't show up once. And, if what had been told to me about the blood magic of crowns was accurate, then my mother could only be Queen if she was a direct descendant of a royal line.

A wave of shock passed across the Queen's face before her features brightened with remembrance. It was an endearing sort of expression but tinged with a grief that I was hoping would not deter her from answering me. There was a long pause, and then, "They were kind and gentle people. My mother liked to sing. My father loved to tell stories. I miss them every day."

"So..." I began, cautiously. "They are no longer..."

My mother shook her head. In the distance, I saw Gianna bow her head slightly as she leaned against a bit of the stone fencing that shielded us from view. Giving us a feigned moment of privacy. "No. They died long ago. Well before the Great Conflict."

It seemed insensitive to ask how they had perished, but I did want to know more about their role in this kingdom. "Why don't the history books mention them at all?"

She laughed a dry and humorless laugh. "My grandparents were the ruling monarchs here when I was named heir. Oldenberg is my father's name. It was my mother who was a princess of the Light Kingdom."

Replaying everything we had ever discussed on the matter, I frowned. "Was your mother not an only child? Is that why you were only considered for heir as opposed to already being named?"

The Queen's gaze fell to her cup. "My mother was an only child, but she was disowned when she married someone from the human lands."

It was almost comical the way history had repeated itself. My mother had also chosen a human consort. "But they still chose you? Because they had to?"

She nodded solemnly. "When I was quite young, I was taken to the Light Kingdom to be formally trained to take on my role. They had hoped they would sire another heir in that time, but they never did." Her gaze slipped to mine. "Onyx may be crude, but she is not wrong. Fae are notoriously less fertile than their human counterparts, and both of my grandparents were pureblooded."

A hint of mischief twinkled in her eyes. "I certainly caused them more than a bit of stress." My heart clenched at the sight, and I longed to ask her more about that part of her life. For the first time since I arrived in the Light Kingdom, I saw a bit of the rebellious woman that my dad must have fallen in love with.

A smile curved her lips as if she were recalling some cherished memory. "They passed me the crown before they died of extremely old age, but they were never aware that I had been bonded to a human. We kept it a secret, especially once we learned we were mates. They would have killed him."

Recalling the tidbit of information about how mates could either save each other from death or plummet to their demise together, I gaped at her. "What would have happened to the crown if both of you had died?"

"I'm not sure," she answered candidly. "There has always been a direct blood relative on the throne, so it would have likely passed to the next closest person in line."

Charlese and I hadn't circled back to the blood magic that ruled the crown or the courts yet in our daily lessons, but this was way more fascinating than the old pureblooded families that made up the dignitaries of the Light Kingdom. Even if I had been surprised, and a bit curious, to find Vissorri amongst that list.

"If I tell you something, do you think you can keep it to yourself? A little family secret?" The Queen's voice sounded almost playful, and there was a smirk on her face that didn't seem to fit with the serious nature of our conversation.

"Of course." I wanted anything she was going to offer me willingly. Prying information out of her was tedious and perilous. One wrong move and she'd shut me out completely.

"They had barbaric views of the world and those they deemed less appealing. There was no love lost on my end when they passed, and I would even go as far as to say that I am glad that they are gone."

Mild shock rippled across my expression.

My mother huffed a humorless laugh, dropping her gaze back to her lap. "You must think me horrible for saying that. I'm sorry. I just wanted you to know the truth about them because I doubt that you'll hear that opinion in any of those textbooks Charlese has you reading."

My palm came to rest on her leather-clad knee. "I get it," I admitted. "There was a boy at the academy who made my life hell. He was killed during an attack on me, and I was relieved when I realized he had died."

She swallowed down some rough emotion, worry dancing in her stare that she never brought a voice to. I was losing her, and I didn't want the conversation to shift to exactly what had happened to me in the woods. "What is your favorite color?" The words tumbled from my lips, a desperate attempt to hold onto whatever positivity we could gather.

Gianna's chuckle sounded from her position along the wall, but her eyes remained focused on a distant point away from us.

Even the Queen laughed. "What?"

"Your favorite color," I said again. "You have one, right? Everyone has a favorite color. Mine is yellow."

Her breath huffed in little waves. "Oh. Of course. My favorite color is green." She smiled with a sort of amusement that I sometimes saw on Beckett's face. How much of his mannerisms and speech were defined by the woman who hadn't been able to raise me?

Snatching my thoughts away from that sad place, I squared my shoulders. "Favorite food?"

This time, she fully committed to the laugh, emitting a sound I had only ever heard her make around Gianna and Josaphine. "Chocolate pudding. You?"

"I don't have a favorite food," I admitted, scrunching my nose. "Except maybe... "

"Cheese," we both said in unison. Something about that exchange gave us common ground we hadn't had before.

My grin spread wider. "Favorite holiday?"

She considered this for a second or two. "I love plants, like your father. So, I'd say spring equinox is my favorite. It's the shift from the death and barrenness of winter. When everything blooms again. A fresh start for the world, of sorts."

Was that a metaphor for her own life? For us? Instead of focusing on that, I offered her my choice. "I don't know that I have a particular holiday that I prefer, but Dad has always been enthusiastic about decorating for winter solstice."

Her cheeks rounded as she took me in. "I see that some things never change."

"Every year he seems to do it bigger than the one before," I said, gesturing with my hands. "I don't love winter, but the house is homier somehow. It smells like pine needles and cider spice, and we almost always have a fire blazing."

When I thought about our home, I always envisioned it in either full solstice garb, or I saw Dad in the summer on his knees in the dirt of the garden. Two wildly different views that both so perfectly encompassed the heart of being there.

"Still no word?" I asked, teetering dangerously into heavier topics that I did not have clearance to know. Although I had been permitted to join a few of the army exercises in the evening, I had not discussed with her the plan that Beckett and I had set forth about me joining their ranks. Officially, I was only included in the drills to help maintain my physical abilities and nothing more.

Nerves twisted in my stomach as I watched the smile on her face droop into a tight line. Apparently, today was not the day to bring up my thoughts on joining the army either.

The Queen glanced over her shoulder in Gianna's direction. The blonde-haired General shook her head. "No," she replied solemnly. "But he is well, wherever he is." Her hand pressed against her sternum again and I was left questioning the range on their magical connection, even as I recognized that I shouldn't ask.

Not knowing where my father was at the moment was excruciating but not having anyone to talk to about how much I missed him was worse. Her silence on the topic broke something within me because all I wanted was to have someone to share this grief with. Instead, I just felt even more alone.

"That's enough for today," Gianna said, her boots crunching against gravel as she came to stand by my side. "Let me escort you back to your chambers, Princess."

Recognizing a clear dismissal, I stood. "Thank you for the training today, your majesty," I muttered, letting Gianna lead me from the small, enclosed area without a glance back at the woman who was still obviously keeping secrets from me.

Forty

When I emerged from Charlese's classroom the next week, I was met with an empty hallway. Gianna was not waiting for me in her usual spot just outside the door to escort me to my elemental training, and I craned my neck to search down the passageways in either direction, only to find them completely deserted.

Charlese had already departed for the afternoon, and this was not a day I was scheduled for army exercises, so I made my way down the frequented path to the outdoor courtyard we had been utilizing for my elemental training.

Surprise filtered through my body as I recognized a familiar form, or precisely two now well-known forms. Beckett and my mother were sitting on a bench, speaking in hushed tones and sharing what appeared to be a snack. Their casual conversation sent a pang of hurt to my chest. They had a relationship that I might never have with the woman who had birthed me, and I frowned as I considered that sooner than later, I would lose him too.

Bright silver eyes snapped to mine, and he stood instantly, clearing his throat in an obvious attempt to alert my mother that they had company. Like I was an outsider.

She turned to me as well, but she did not appear alarmed at my presence. "You're early."

My footfalls crunched over the fresh layer of snow as I approached them, dropping my pack onto the bench beside my mother and ignoring Beckett for the time being. "Gianna wasn't there when I got out with Charlese."

A moment passed between the Queen and her General as they shared a tense look. My mother turned her head to the sky and squinted into the clouds as if she would find some sort of answer there.

"She was converging with the swallows," the Queen supplied.

The statement brought a frown to Beckett's face. Notches formed between his golden brows.

"She should still be back by now," my mother added, her nerves bleeding into her tone.

As if our conversation had summoned my mother's Light Guard General, Gianna swept in through a vine-covered archway. "I am sorry I am late," she said, a bit out of breath. "I have news."

Suddenly, it clicked into place. The swallows. Their concerned looks.

Wheeling around, I watched Gianna with wide, hopeful eyes, but the General of the Light Guard only flicked her gaze in my direction for a split second before returning her stare to the Queen. "Shall we go somewhere more private?"

A flash of confusion marred my mother's features for a breath until she caught on to Gianna's meaning. She turned to me, assessing me for something I couldn't place.

"She deserves to know," Beckett whispered. "It's her dad."

The Queen glared at him for a moment before returning her focus to Gianna. "Go ahead."

Gianna gave our surroundings a sideways glance. "It would be more prudent to have this meeting in your private quarters."

"Our sitting room would be the most private," Beckett offered, bringing a blush to my face for no other reason than that he had used the word *our*.

"Shall I retrieve the other General?" Gianna asked, facing my mother fully.

"No need," Beckett answered for her. "He is away on business at the moment."

Momentarily, the Queen seemed shocked by this, but she schooled her features quickly. It struck me as odd that the monarch wouldn't know the goings and comings of her generals, but I supposed that Beckett had also been in Demetros under unofficial circumstances when I met him. Our paths crossing had been coincidental.

The sentiment was quickly forgotten as Gianna hurriedly led us down the halls. Within ten minutes, we were seated along the tufted sofas in the tiny room between Beckett and my bedrooms. With me beside Beckett, as if we were truly entertaining guests.

"Please report, Alcides," My mother said to her general, switching effortlessly back into the role of monarch.

Gianna shifted nervously in her chair. "There have been two Fae found with their blood drained near the border."

Fear and disappointment lanced through my heart. "What?"

Beckett's eyebrows furrowed. "Where exactly?"

"The forest on the edges of Iredell," Gianna supplied. Charlese had shown me that location on a map. It was one of the towns that bordered the Dark Kingdom.

Beckett blew out a breath.

"The bodies were found ten minutes or so from the village from which they were reported missing several weeks ago," Gianna added.

My mother shook her head. "Ages?"

Gianna pulled a slip of worn paper from her side pocket with notes haphazardly scrawled across it in no distinguishable pattern. Her eyes roamed the sheet until the general found what she needed. "They were twins, both aged roughly seventy-three years old. No known family. Their absence was reported by their employer."

"There doesn't seem to be a pattern with age then," Beckett offered. "Sex?"

The sound of Beckett's voice next to me startled me for no other reason than it forced me to acknowledge that he was still beside me.

"They were identical twins, both females," Gianna replied.

Shifting in my seat, I browsed over at the paper in Gianna's hand like I could even read it from this distance. "What were their gifts?"

Gianna scanned the parchment once more before she responded. "They both had the same gift; they were illusionists."

"Condition of the bodies?" Beckett queried. "Other than being drained."

"Puncture wounds were found on their necks in similar but not identical locations," Gianna answered as if she were reading a textbook rather than describing a method of murder. "The distance between the wounds suggests multiple perpetrators."

The Queen exhaled deeply, her thumb and forefinger pinching the bridge of her nose. "I was afraid of this."

"What is it?" I asked, already considering that this sounded like the work of the Shadow Fae.

With her brow groomed with concern, my mother looked to me. "There have been several attacks along the Northern border where the bodies have been found in shreds, for lack of a better word." She grimaced as if recalling an image of what she had seen. "We had assumed that some of the beasts from the Dark Kingdom had attacked, looking for food. Recently, we have come to suspect it might be the Shadow Fae."

"Oh," I replied, unsure of what else to say as a fear settled deep within my gut. Beckett had already told me that officials would be alerted when they did, but the fact that they were seemingly crossing over the and the Queen didn't seem to know until after an attack was alarming. "Grethe made it seem like they were dying out. How many of them are left?"

Beckett's jaw ticked. "We all have differing opinions on the level of threat that they pose."

"Regardless," Gianna interrupted, "The frequency of their attacks is of concern. They are up to something." She turned her gaze to the Queen. "I suggest that we revisit the other bodies chalked up to animal attacks to look for similar signs of puncture wounds."

Beckett dipped his chin as if there was some unspoken agreement that this subject was his territory. "I will assign someone to examine the bodies that have not been claimed and burned."

"Thank you, Astor," the Queen replied before beginning to stand.

"One more thing," Gianna said, hesitantly, sparing me another wary glance. She had warmed up to me since my initial arrival, but it was clear to me she still wasn't confident with what could and could not be vocalized in my presence.

"It is about Christian," she said, as her green eyes slid to the Light Queen.

My breath and every muscle in my body froze.

"Go ahead," my mother said, her voice primed with the same worry pulsing in my veins.

The General of the Light Guard looked three shades paler as she released a heavy breath. "There were issues crossing the border this time, which have been resolved," Gianna stated quickly. "However, news has come from Elmhaven."

She looked hesitant to continue, and I found myself gripping the edge of the sofa, my pinky grazing against Beckett's pants. Rather than pull away, he leaned closer to me, almost as if he wanted to provide the comfort of his presence.

"We decided to double back and check the home once more in case he returned. This time we were able to recognize that an illusion had been cast over the home. Once it was removed..." Gianna swallowed with some effort as if the words were painful to release. "The cottage has been ransacked."

My gasp echoed in the chamber, and my mother's entire demeanor changed to something tense and horrified. Yet again, her hand lifted to her heart, resting there. "He is still alive. I would know if he had died."

Of course she would know. He would either be tethered to this world because of her or she would be dead too.

The General straightened, clearly more uncomfortable sharing this news than the information about the drained Fae bodies near the border. "There was evidence of a struggle and whoever had been there was looking for something, although we cannot tell if they found it."

The Queen seemed to ignore what I already suspected this meant. "So, they might have broken in after he went into hiding?" Hope filled her glassy eyes.

My mouth popped open to say something about how ridiculous that line of thought was, considering the illusion was clearly meant to hide it, but Beckett's hand curled around my own, stopping me. No, I couldn't rush into this with pure adrenaline. If I wanted to prove myself as a worthy member of the Queen's army, I needed to think and speak strategically. Even if this was about my dad.

Taking in a deep breath, I let my attention fall to the Queen, using the warmth in Beckett's hand to steady my heart. "My file at Biltons was already marked before I got there, indicating I would be Operarius."

"Explain," Beckett said softly. He couldn't be surprised by the information, so I had to assume he was encouraging me for a reason.

A rough swallow pushed down all my unwanted emotions. "It indicates that they were at least aware of my power levels. If the Guides are related to this in any way, they would have the same access to the information the headmaster and our instructors had."

Thinking of Mr. Higgins made my stomach constrict. "My botany professor was blackmailing me in order to force me to make it to the branding ceremony and become his indentured servant, but what if the entire purpose was to brand me? Neutralize me. All he said was that I had to be branded, and then he was free to take me."

The Queen's body went rigid across from me. Surely, she had heard all of this during the many debriefs over my ordeal, but as I had not been present for any of them, I couldn't be certain.

"It would make sense that they would then procure leverage to force you to return," Beckett said, from my side.

"No," my mother snapped, still clutching at her chest. "If they wanted leverage, they would have already shown their hand."

"To whom?" I asked. "They don't know where I am. The only other people I consider family are Jemma and her mother, Marjorie." My gaze shifted to Gianna. "Have they been accounted for?"

Instead of answering me, Gianna placed a hand on the Queen's shoulder. "Anastasia, it is entirely possible that this is true, in which case we need to pull more of the network to sweep for him. This is a risk to the entire kingdom." Those judgmental green eyes fixated on me for a heartbeat. "We can't lose you right now. There would be too much unrest if the crown were to pass before she's ready."

The statement felt like a swift punch to the stomach, leaving me momentarily silenced. I didn't want to lose my mother after I had just reunited with her, especially if it took my father in the process.

Beckett's hand pulsed along mine. "Ashton said she had a list of places he might have gone that wouldn't be on the network."

The Queen's face brightened in an eerily hopeful grin. "Yes, of course." Her gaze snapped to mine. "Where should we look first?"

All eyes turned to me. "We have a good relationship with the people of Estes. It's in the foothills of the Amethyst Ridge, so there are plenty of tunnels for hiding."

Finally, my mother's grip along her chest relaxed. "That makes sense," she replied, her tone entirely too light for the topic at hand. "That's why I feel contentment across our bond. He's safe in the mountains."

Beckett's glared at the Queen for a millisecond before his features cleared.

"He will be trying to keep a low profile until the dust settles, and Eden is too large of a town to just waltz through unnoticed," my mother added, that same unmerited hope sprouting across her entire face now.

No one in the room but the Queen appeared to gain any assurance with her words, but Beckett and I remained dutifully silent. Hands still intertwined.

"Of course, your majesty," Gianna finally muttered, averting her eyes from the Queen as she stood from her chair. "I will get my people on that at once."

"I will contact those in my chain of command that are close and have them scout the mountains as well as anywhere else Ashton provides," Beckett said, looking down at me as concern pulsed across our bond.

"Good," my mother replied with a smile as she stood, brushing imaginary dirt off her skirts as she shifted her gaze to mine. "Now, we must return to your elemental lessons. I'm sure you're dying to be able to fill up your own bathtub."

Confusion washed over me like a storm surge. A bathtub? Did she truly think I wanted to work on my power to fill a bathtub and not to rescue my father?

Beckett's grip squeezed along my hand again, prompting me to stand and reply to the Queen. "Please," I said, forcing my lips to part in a quarter smile. "I certainly need the practice."

"How about I take over for now, Anastasia?" Beckett offered, coming to stand by my side.

My mother's brow lowered as if she was trying to determine his angle.

Beckett dipped his chin in reverence. "Although he is safe, I am certain hearing of the home you and Christian shared being ransacked is a lot to take in. Why don't you take a break, and I can lead Ashton's training today?"

There was no mention of how my home being vandalized would impact me, but perhaps Beckett already knew me well enough to know I'd want a distraction.

The Queen pursed her lips together but ultimately acquiesced with the dip of her head. "Let me know how she does," she murmured quietly, before going to stand at Gianna's side. The two of them left the room and that was that.

"You're not worried that I need time to process?" I asked Beckett when we arrived at the clearing I usually trained in.

The corner of Beckett's lip twitched. "Would you rather go cry about it in your room?"

I scowled. "No, I would rather do something about it." Exasperated I looked down to my hands. "But I can't seem to grasp the magic like I did in the carriage."

When I peeked back over at Beckett he wasn't smirking as I anticipated. In fact, his smile was soft in a way that was dangerously close to pity. "It can take time."

"That's what the Queen said," I huffed.

"And you are trying too hard."

Another scoff eased through my lips. "Obviously not or it would be working by now." To punctuate my irritation, I threw my hands in the air.

Beckett stepped closer to me, placing his hands on my shoulders. He angled his face so he was staring right at me, forcing our eyes to catch. Forcing my world to narrow to those pools of silver. "Breathe."

I drew in an exaggerated breath. "Kind of hard to stop without dying."

He tugged me closer, close enough that his body heat engulfed me instantly. "Slowly."

With our gazes still tangled, I made myself take an elongated inhale.

"Out," he whispered.

Despite being overtly aware of his proximity, I listened, calming almost instantly.

"Close your eyes," he commanded, with all the authority of a general and all the tenderness of someone who might actually be my friend.

My eyelids fluttered closed.

"Picture the strings, or the orbs, or whatever you envisioned before." His tone was soothing, almost like I was back in the Mind and Body class at Biltons.

"Strings," I replied, doing as he asked and diving within the recesses of my mind to locate those strings of energy I associated with my power.

"Find whichever element you prefer and tug that string to the surface of your palm."

Doing as I was told, I tugged on the bright orange string of my flames.

Beckett's hands remained curled around my shoulders so when I presented my palm it was wedged between our chests. On my next exhale, I put everything I had into drawing that string of energy to my open hand, surprised when I instantly felt the warmth of my flame.

My eyes shot open, and there between us was a tiny sphere of fire.

Blinking, I peered up at him. "How did you do that?"

His eyebrow lifted. "You did that."

My gaze fell back to the ball of fire, floating over my hand like a miniature sun. "I know that, but you made it come to the surface. How do you do that?"

"The only thing I did was get you out of your head," he replied at the same moment he let go of my shoulders and took a step back. "All you need to do is keep practicing until it's second nature."

I continued to stare at the flames in amazement, pouring the little orb back and forth between my hands. "Okay," I muttered, losing some confidence in my ability to do this with any speed or finesse anytime soon.

"Oh, and Ashton," Beckett said, luring my attention back to his face. "Look around."

I did as I was told, unsure what I was supposed to be looking for.

"Do you see any sconces?"

After another sweep of our surroundings, my attention returned to the spherical flames floating before my face. "No."

"No," Beckett echoed. "Meaning..."

My eyes met his. It was obvious he wasn't going to let the question be rhetorical and I had the sudden urge to stomp my foot in defiance. Except... "I can conjure fire from nothing."

Even Beckett seemed pleased as his smirk lifted into a smile. "Ryana wasn't lying to you when she said you were powerful. You just need to harness that power. You can do this."

I have to do this, I thought, before my mind reminded me of another detail. In order to break the spell, I'd have to get control of my magic. It was part of the reason I was being given personalized lessons. The sooner I mastered my power, the better odds I had at being successful at breaking the spell. Something that might very well kill me.

The thought was so sobering that the flame disappeared from my upturned hand, and I sighed out another frustrated breath.

Forty-One

My education continued with alarming efficiency with Charlese each morning. The only shift in my schedule, or rather instructors, was that occasionally Beckett stepped in to train me in the evenings. Although it would show its face in the Queen's presence now, my magic rarely revealed any promise of grandeur when she or Gianna were present. It was disappointing considering how much I craved my mother's approval, but according to Beckett, that was part of my problem.

I had no such issues when I was with him, though. When Beckett was helping me, it almost felt as if his power was coaxing my own to the surface and I was able to call forth all four elements in some capacity with ease. Part of me wondered if it was our bond, if he was tugging on some invisible string to aid me when he was around, but I didn't want to think too deeply about that. We were still hardly allies and it wouldn't do me any good to need his proximity.

My breath formed a misty cloud in front of my face as I stood in the courtyard where we practiced, waiting for instructions. The thick leggings, sweater, and fur-lined cloak did very little to keep out the late January chill, and I glared at Beckett expectantly, urging him to get on with this lesson.

He was adorned in all black, even boasting a completely onyx-hued leather strap where his daggers were all sheathed, glinting in the afternoon sun. Just like at our ceremony, he seemed as comfortable in the winter weather as someone lounging beside a warm hearth.

My arms folded over my chest. "I'm not sure how freezing my ass off is supposed to make my magic show itself," I ground out through my vibrating teeth. "I don't even want to be out here. Why would it?"

"Ashton!" My mother chastised from her perch on the bench.

My face contorted into a grimace. "Sorry," I called to her. "I'm just not used to it being this cold." As if that was a reasonable excuse. "Don't you want to go inside?"

She frowned, and a divot formed between her eyebrows. "If I'm making you nervous, I can leave."

Quickly, I backtracked, not wanting to hurt her feelings. "No, I just want you to be comfortable," I lied. My magic had done far more when she wasn't around, as evidenced by my effortless ability to fill my tub with hot water without Beckett's aid, but I didn't know how to tell her that.

"I think I saw Gianna making her way to the turret, actually," Beckett said as he approached me. He could probably sense how uneasy I was around her through that overbearing connection.

The Queen's brows furrowed as if she needed to mull over this information. "Oh," she said, somewhat disappointedly, "Then actually I do need to go."

Torn between wanting to know if Gianna had finally returned with news of my father and my desire to master another element, I shifted my gaze to Beckett.

He shook his head. "Stay," he whispered, and I realized this was a favor to me. He would be the reason that she left us alone, not the truth I was so reluctant to give her. That no matter what I did, my magic was shy around her. Because I wanted it too much.

My mother dismissed herself with a hasty goodbye, and the minute that her form disappeared behind the heavy wooden door to the castle, Beckett spoke. "I thought you'd do better without an audience."

My cheeks heated. I both hated and loved how easily he could decipher me, attending to needs I didn't have to specifically ask for. On the other hand, it felt a little like being read as if I were a story on a page. Despite my best efforts, I couldn't completely block him out. "Thank you," I muttered.

Beckett eyed me in a way that told me he was observing my expressions again, sensing my emotions. "Why can't you just tell her that you don't want her around for this?" He stepped in, close enough to me that our foggy breaths mingled in the air between us.

"It's complicated," I replied, crossing my arms in an attempt to gain some warmth through the gesture.

There was no prodding or fanfare as Beckett stepped back, assessing me like an instructor rather than his wife. "Okay, then let's get back to work. Start with your stretches."

Groaning, I got into position. "What does this have to do with my magic?" My fingertips stretched toward my toes as I loosened my muscles.

"Everything is connected," Beckett replied, joining me in my movements. "Your body, your magic, your mind. You need to get them on the same page if you want any of this to be second nature."

My head tilted in his direction; brows raised. "So, you're exhausting my body so that my mind and magic have to get in line?"

He smirked. "I'm trying a new tactic to make this more natural for you."

Continuing the series of poses he had forced me to memorize, I blew out an irritated breath. "I still think that we should be focusing on the elements, rather than the physical aspect. I've been training my whole life to be part of the Select Guard. This is already second nature to me."

"Fine," Beckett conceded. "Pick an element."

Abruptly, my spine straightened, lifting me to my full height as a grin rounded my cheeks. "Really? Okay... fire!" It was my favorite, even with the reminder of a certain fire wielder that I refused to think about anymore.

One corner of Beckett's mouth lifted into a smirk. It was my only warning. "Catch," he called as he produced a spherical flame and launched it directly at my head.

A gasp tore through my throat as my palms instinctively went forward to block my face from the agonizing burns that I knew were coming. But then, no pain came. My eyes peeled open, revealing that not only had I blocked the flames, but Beckett's orb of fire was hovering in front of my outstretched hands.

Wheeling on him, I fumed, holding the flame out like a weapon in front of me. "What the fuck was that?"

He shrugged off my anger. "Are you hurt?" There wasn't even an ounce of concern in his features.

Tossing the ball of fire in his direction, I growled at him. "You had no way to know I could stop it!"

He dispelled the flame before it reached his face with a wave of his hand, the snow crunching beneath his boots as he stepped toward me. "Do you think I would hurt you?"

"Well..." My scowl softened. "No." If I had learned anything about my time with the younger Astor, it was that he cared for me in his own way. He had spent hours practicing my water magic with me, if only to let me fill my bathtub up alone. And while that was somewhat beneficial to him, I knew it wasn't the only reason he had done it.

His eyes constricted slightly as if he could sense the affection brewing in my chest. But then, with a tone that spoke of boredom, he said, "Produce your own fireball."

Offering him my back, I pretended to struggle to form the flame. Instead, I created a little sphere of compacted snow, utilizing my Flumen and Ignus powers to freeze little drops of water until I had created enough for the perfect-sized ball.

As if I was partaking in a battle, I flipped my stance, launching the snowball right at his face the instant I was in position, hitting my mark with a surprising level of accuracy.

In slow motion, the splattered snow fell from Beckett's face, and underneath, his features were expressionless. In a brief moment of panic, regret coursed through my body. It dissipated the moment those full lips snapped into a wide grin, and within seconds, he was hurling his own snowballs in my direction.

Squealing, I ran to the closest column, hoping it could give me some shelter from the constant pelting as I created more of my little weapons.

A deep booming laugh echoed off the courtyard walls as we chased each other around the space, spilling out into the nearby gardens, which were full of the skeletons of plants and shrubbery that littered the snow-covered flower beds.

With nowhere to hide behind, it wasn't long before we were both drenched in the remnants of our fight. It was hard to say who had even won by the time we agreed to the truce, landing on our backs in the snow in a sweaty heap. A snap of his fingers dried our clothes from the worst of the dampness.

"That counts for our exercises, right?" I asked through panting breaths.

He chuckled from beside me. "Sure, Princess. You controlled multiple elements at once, and you broke a sweat. I think that counts."

A grin split my face. That was exactly what I had done, and I hadn't even been thinking about it. Like in the carriage, Beckett seemed to attract my magic in ways that already made it feel natural. Just like being around him felt so right.

Beckett cleared his throat. "We should get going."

"I'd hate to miss dinner," I said, sarcastically.

Dinner time was both my least favorite and my most treasured meal now. The charade of our love was tedious to maintain as I walked that fine line between relishing his touch and keeping myself at a distance from the man who could never be anything more to me.

He groaned as he shifted to his side to face me. "I know it's not ideal but thank you for going along with everything."

My body twisted so that I could look at him as a snort peeled through my nose because I enjoyed his attention, no matter why it came.

"What?" he asked, a smirk lifting one corner of his lips as if he truly hadn't sensed my emotions on the topic.

I continued rolling, brushing myself off when I stood to full height. "It's nothing." Maybe there were some thoughts I could keep to myself. My palm reached for him. "Come on, old man, I'll help you up so we can get you to dinner before your early bedtime."

His silver eyes rolled as he allowed me to pretend that I was the driving force behind lifting him to his feet. He slung his arm over my shoulders, pulling me closer to him, and I nearly sighed into his warmth. "Come on, wife. Let's go put on another show."

There was a rare reprieve in early February where it seemed every one of my instructors was otherwise occupied. All three Generals had been called away for various reasons, and even Charlese had taken a few days away from lessons. Freedom was a relative term, when I wasn't supposed to know the Queen well enough to sit with her at dinner, so I found myself taking the majority of my meals in my suite when no one stopped me.

My fingers tracked along the tomes that lined Beckett's bookshelf, looking for any hint of something more entertaining than Charlese's latest homework assignment on species of shifters found in the Light Kingdom. It wasn't that the type of Fae that could shift forms completely wasn't intriguing on their own, but the text simply mentioned almost any animal could be a shifter. Squirrels, foxes, wolves, bears. It might as well have been a list of animals found in the wild.

The only thing of note in the entire book was that sometimes the shifters took on personality traits of the beasts they could shift into, and this was of importance when trying to find a compatible partner. Like this book could help my dating life.

So instead, here I was skimming over titles for the thousandth time, trying to pass my free day, which was starting to feel like a punishment.

The door to my left swung open as Beckett crossed the threshold. Surprise at his early return was only a fleeting emotion. There was nothing I could do to stop the elation swelling in my chest at the sight of him, but I did maintain my outward composure, and that was something of a win.

He shook his head, clearly sensing those emotions, and ignoring them the way he always did. "I have news."

Abandoning my quest for a book altogether, I practically ran for him. "About my father?"

His resulting grimace was the only answer I needed. "No, about your induction into the army."

This wasn't the news I had originally wanted, but it was exciting. Now that I had a better mastery over my elemental gifts, I had shifted a few of my afternoon sessions so that I could add magical training with the cadets. My primary goal remained being invited on the mission to bring my father home. If we ever found him.

Beckett sniffed a laugh like he knew exactly where my thoughts had gone. "You are getting an opportunity to go on a scouting mission as part of your training. If that is something you are still interested in?"

"Yes," I blurted out, skimming right over the irony of the entire situation. My desire to join the Select Guard in Demetros had landed me in the Light Kingdom. Now, I'd have to be inducted into the Light Kingdom army to return to Demetros.

"Great," he beamed. "Then let's go. You have seven minutes to change and present yourself to the training field."

He almost chortled as he left the bedchamber, and I scurried to locate my leathers and fur-lined cloak, almost tripping as I ran from the room to make it in the allocated timeframe.

I was out of breath and panting by the time I gathered in the courtyard with the other cadets. Some wore the navy uniforms of Ebus' infantry, while others boasted the creams of Gianna's Light Guard. My leathers paid ode to neither, in solid black like Beckett's. All eyes turned to me, and I wanted to cower under the scrutiny, but Beckett's voice bellowed over the crowd, drawing all of their attention to him.

"Listen up, cadets, we are going to partner you with seasoned members of the infantry to run a routine scouting mission along the border." Silver eyes skimmed over the group. "Get into formation."

His gaze snapped to mine, and he subtly jerked his head toward an empty space in front of him where I scrambled to get into position.

Pacing in front of the fifty or so assembled cadets, he took note of form and posture, correcting everyone who needed it before coming to stand in the front again, hands clasped behind his back. "We are going to read out the role and divide you into groups. Listen carefully because I will only say this once."

Twenty minutes later, of what should have been pure chaos, but was ultimately a smooth transition, I found myself on the back of a horse. I relished the familiarity of the sway of the animal, trailing a few cadets behind Beckett and one of his senior officers.

The animals came to a stop at a completely nondescript location, and I drew in a deep breath of crisp snow and fresh pine as I scanned our surroundings.

Beckett's voice sliced through my moment of peace. "Blake and Reed, take the western perimeter and report back in thirty minutes."

There was something pleasurable about the tenor of his voice when he was commanding his unit. Something alluring that had me biting back a grin as I nodded in his direction. Some of those emotions must have slipped the walls within my mind because Beckett roughly cleared his throat and jerked his head to the side to prompt me to move along. I was certain only I caught the infinitesimal twitch of his lip.

Another cadet in all black, steered his chestnut stallion toward the defined area we were supposed to patrol, and I followed him in near silence that only lasted for five minutes. "Reed, right?" I asked, not missing the annoyed eye roll I received as my initial response.

"Yeah," he replied, not reciprocating the question. That was okay though.

"Have you done one of these scouting missions before?"

Irritation pushed a breath from his pursed lips. "Most of us are cadets for years before we are inducted into the army or permitted on these types of exercises." He stared at me pointedly, and I shut my mouth promptly. *Message received.*

We traipsed through the woods for another few minutes with the crunch of snow under hooves as the only sound for quite some time.

It wasn't difficult to sense when we were approaching the border as the thrum of magic washed over my skin and every muscle in my body bunched with nervous anticipation, eyes frantically flitting around the surrounding woods.

A noise much like the thumping of a heart sounded in the distance, but it seemed too far away to be my own pulse raging in my ears. Suddenly, I recalled Beckett's mention of creatures that lived on the continent, all of which I had never seen. When I had asked him about them after the attack Gianna had discussed, what Beckett had explained were the things of nightmares. Wings, scales, slitted eyes, talons and claws designed to make them apex predators.

I wasn't eager to discover any of those monsters here, but if they were encroaching on the Light Kingdom lands, we'd need to report it. Just because this was a practice scouting mission, didn't mean it wouldn't be fruitful in uncovering the enemy.

"Do you hear that?" I whispered to Reed, already envisioning the worst of my imagination come to life.

He tilted his ear to the stretch of trees around us and paused for a beat. "I don't hear anything." Yanking along the reins, he twisted his horse back in the direction we had come from.

A wiser person would have just let it go and followed him, this was an exercise after all, but I got the sense that I was on to something. My curiosity burned brighter than whatever ember of fear I carried, and I moved deeper into the thicket of trees as if in a trance.

The further my horse stomped through the snow-packed woods, the darker and colder it became. The trees had grown closer together here, and strange vines had made their way between them, like curtains, blocking out much of the oddly crimson light dappling the skyline along the border.

A rustling to my right had my eyes snapping in that direction, catching only the subtle hint of a deep emerald vine with an unusual iridescent sheen. Non-threatening in nature until it moved.

Was something hiding in that cluster of underbrush?

Like an idiot, I dismounted.

Calling fire to my palms, I crept closer, noting a strange curl of the vine that hadn't been there before. The shimmer I had so obviously witnessed was gone as well as if every bit of the scene had clearly been born from my imagination. I let the flames fade away.

"Are you coming or do you want us both to be set back months so that you can finish your little nature walk?" Reed's aggravated voice sounded from the other side of my horse as he looked down at me with incredulity.

"You might not be reprimanded," he sneered, "but I cannot afford to go backwards in my training. My family is counting on me."

This I understood. It had been reckless to go after a shimmering vine in the name of scouting. "I'm coming."

Reed abandoned me before I even reached my horse, leaving me rolling my eyes as I prepared to mount. Just as my boot entered the stirrup, a twig snapped behind me, and I whipped my head to see what had caused the noise. Because I had halfway convinced myself it would be another vine or small woodland creature, I had not expected to find a Fae woman standing several yards away.

She had no uniform on to distinguish her as one of the cadets on the patrolling mission, only nondescript black fighting leathers like mine. Her attire, and something about the way she looked at me, had the hairs on the back of my neck standing to attention.

Her pale blue eyes squinted as she caught my hand slipping to my dagger out of old habits rather than strategy. "Who are you?" I demanded.

The corners of her mouth lifted. "He grows tired of waiting for you, and I'm sure he would reward me handsomely for bringing you in ahead of schedule." She moved the braided sections of her flaxen hair out of the way moments before massive wings spread out behind her back. Although I expected her to complete the shifting into a great hawk, the dark brown feathers only relegated themselves to that appendage, and the rest of her features remained distinctly Fae.

Another twig snapped beneath her boots as she approached on sure feet. There was something dark and twisted in her gaze, and I knew beyond a shadow of a doubt that she was not an ally to be trusted.

Flames had always been the easiest of my elements to control, so I called them to my palms, readying to strike her.

The horse behind me bucked wildly, snapping its reins free moments before it bolted from its position, leaving me completely stranded in the woods. Not that it mattered, if I didn't make it out of this alive.

The woman noted my change in stance, then her eyes snagged on mine. "You will drop the weapon."

I would have scoffed at that, had a slimy energy not coated my skin and my body not instantly complied, the blade clattering to the dirt. Realization dawned on me. She was not a bird shifter; this woman was Shadow Fae, and somehow her compulsion had worked on me within the wards.

She had made one mistake, though; she hadn't commanded that I not run. Just as Beckett had told me to do if this situation ever arose, I bolted, pumping my arms and legs as fast as they would go.

Her screech echoed around me as I dodged tree trunks and brambles in a retreat that felt all too familiar. Hazarding a glance over my shoulder, I spied her, far enough away that I felt some sense of safety, but close enough that I could clearly see the whites in her eyes as she pursued me.

When my attention turned ahead, I all but knocked into a solid wall of muscle. Night-blooming jasmine enveloped me at the same time Beckett's arm encircled my waist and he tugged me behind his back.

"How dare you come here," Beckett seethed, taking in the woman before us who had come to a sudden stop fifteen feet away.

Those pale blue eyes widened as they took in the warrior before her. Honestly, he did look fearsome in this moment, teeth bared and rage spilling from a vicious glare.

The Shadow Fae raised her hands into the air. "I meant no harm; I just came for food."

"That's a lie," I growled, pointing at her. "She said she was planning to take me to someone."

"You think you can take my wife as a prize to your King?" Beckett was all but snarling now. "Instead, you will be a message to others."

In a blink, Beckett's outstretched hand had produced daggers made entirely of a mottled blackened flame, which he flung at the woman in quick succession. One after the other until six blades were embedded into those brown wings, pinning her to the trees behind her.

The woman wailed in pain as her feathers caught fire, going up in a blaze so bright, I was forced to temporarily throw my arm over my eyes.

Beckett released my waist and stalked toward the Shadow Fae like he was a man consumed with mind-numbing anger. It thundered like its own drumming pulse across our bond.

The woman's screeching got louder as the fire burned away everything but the charred stumps of her appendages, and only then did she fall to the ground. The breeze carried with it the smell of burnt hair and flesh and it was enough to make me dry heave.

Reaching behind his back, Beckett withdrew the longsword from its holster, raising it above his head as he looked down at the woman menacingly. "It is a shame I cannot send you back like this for your penance, so that you may warn the others of what I will do if any of you cross the border again. But unfortunately for you, I am not that merciful."

"Please, your maj—" The Shadow Fae's words were cut off swiftly as Beckett brought the blade down over her neck, severing it from her shoulders in one smooth motion.

The head rolled on the ground, stopping only when it knocked against a fallen tree. The body fell next, the crisp nubs of the woman's wings breaking off like the end of an already smoked rolled stick. It was sickening, but even in the morbidity of it all, I couldn't bring myself to look away.

Beckett sheathed his sword along his back, then walked calmly over to the head, picking it up by the flaxen braids. "Come with me," he demanded, ice lingering in his tone.

"Where are we going?" I asked, unsure if I wanted to follow him. It wasn't fear that kept me from him; he had just proven that he would protect me, but the desire to be as far away from the head he carried as possible. It served as a stark reminder that I was not as safe as I had thought. In fact, the incident left me wondering if there were others waiting for us in the thickets.

I let my attention fall back on the Fae woman's severed head. Dark red blood dripped from the neck wound, and it was all I could do not to hurl at the sight. Although I had theoretically been trained for combat, I had never seen anything as gruesome as that.

Dark grey eyes slid to mine as he held up the head, some of the blood splattering against his boots. "We are going to toss this back over the border so that if they get any more ideas about coming for you or anyone in this kingdom, they will know the consequences."

My chin dipped before I had even processed his words, and my feet carried me to his side.

He turned, marching toward the border with a menacing glare at that invisible line, holding the severed head on the opposite side from where I stood.

"I suppose I won't be allowed on any more scouting missions when my mother hears about this," I said, adrenaline coursing through my veins and making my limbs shake in the aftermath.

Beckett halted when he reached the point where even I could feel the magic intensifying, that same strange emptiness washing over my skin. As far as I could see, it was nothing but snowy woods ahead, but he must have known exactly where the border was because in that moment, he tossed the head into a tall drift of pristine white snow.

The snow turned crimson, blood pouring from the mound like an active volcano, and I finally tore my eyes from the scene to look at him.

"We need to work on your combat skills," he said, wiping his hand against his pants.

I considered that a moment. "So, you're not going to tell her what happened?"

His eyes contracted. "I will tell her I apprehended a Shadow Fae who had crossed the border, but I can leave out your involvement if you wish."

He was giving me another choice, and I took it. "Deal." If my mother thought my safety was at risk, she would likely call off all battle related training and I refused to be reduced to a royal ornament on Beckett's side. I needed to do something.

A smile not befitting the moment curled Beckett's lips. "Good, then when we get back to the Castle, be prepared to be reprimanded by your General for losing your horse."

By the time March came around, dread was nestled deeply into my bones. Time in the snowy mountains moved in obscure ways. Some days, I felt every single minute tick by while others blurred away in the blink of an eye. It was difficult to comprehend that I had been out of Demetros for nearly three months, even harder to accept it had been over half a year since I had hugged my father.

There wasn't a single clue that pointed to his whereabouts. It was as if he simply vanished without a trace, and I was trapped here in Falkland, with no way to return to Demetros to look for him until my mother gave me the go-ahead.

The Queen remained in strict denial when it came to my father, and since no new information was trickling in, everything had stalled on that front. The only silver lining I had was that keeping the Shadow Fae attack on me a secret made it so I could continue training and honing my skills.

Beckett had been right to tell me to run if I came across a Shadow Fae, but that didn't mean I shouldn't learn how to fight them if that scenario ever unfolded again. If what the woman had said was true, someone was looking for me, and even if I didn't know why, they would likely come for me again.

Which was precisely why Beckett had taken over my training, forcing me to combine my hand-to-hand combat skills with my elemental gifts in new and arduous ways. Training with him alone wasn't the best way to hone those skills, because I knew beyond a shadow of a doubt—despite the violence I had witnessed from him— that he wouldn't harm me. It took away some of the urgency and fear I would feel during a real battle, but I could recognize the practice served to make the moves more natural. We were spending more time together outside of the watchful eyes of the court, which meant I had a bit more trust that his behavior with me was genuine and not an act.

The exercises had been working, and I felt confident that next time I was confronted with a would-be assassin, I would at least have enough wherewithal to keep my feet firmly planted on the ground and fight back. I wouldn't always have Beckett to defend me; I had just been lucky.

"What is on your mind today, Blake?" Beckett asked as he approached the courtyard.

He only used my surname when he felt he needed to appear as the General rather than my husband—or friend—so my eyes darted to our surroundings, confused to find that no one else was around.

"You may speak freely," he stated.

A sigh tumbled from my lips as if it was a weight off my shoulder to simply be allowed to be honest. Since the revelation of my true identity, I had been forced to hide so much. "Do you truly think he is just in hiding? After all this time?"

There was something sympathetic in Beckett's stare that had my stomach plummeting. But he knew who and what I was referring to without clarification. "No. In fact, I have activated a small portion of the network for more tactical operations in case an extraction is necessary."

Relief coursed through my veins despite what the admission meant. "Has the Queen said anything about this plan?" I asked cautiously, knowing I hadn't spoken to her about my desire to join the army, but hoping that Beckett had.

His shoulders sagged as he offered me an apologetic wince. "She is aware that I have activated the network, but she doesn't seem inclined to let you join at the moment. She can't see the value in it past the risk to your safety, which was the whole reason that she did all of this." He gestured to the space between us.

Of course, he was referring to so much more than our bond. My mother lying to her people about having a true heir would be a political nightmare. All of it had been done to ensure my safety, so while I understood the desire to keep me away from the conflict, it was disappointing.

"Give her some time," Beckett offered. "She will come around."

My eyes pinched in skepticism, but there wasn't anything further to do about it, so I turned away to start my stretches.

Beckett's hands moved to clasp behind his back in a gesture I recognized as preparation to share bad news. "Actually, I was coming to find you to say that I needed to cancel today's training session."

The Queen and Gianna were traveling, and neither was set to return until the Spring Equinox ball. If Beckett was ending our session, it meant I'd forego training for the day and be back in our suite with the wall of history texts for company.

"Take me with you." I blurted out. "I want to be involved."

To my surprise, Beckett smirked. "Okay."

"Just like that?"

Amusement danced in those quicksilver irises. "Are you arguing with me over something you requested?"

"No," I bit out quickly. "I wasn't expecting you to agree without a fight."

He leveled me with a serious expression. "I am not in the business of holding you back from anything you desire."

Except you, I thought to myself, keeping the words tucked behind a quarter smile. It was complicated having him be my only friend and also the person who touched me so tenderly and looked at me so lovingly, at least when we had an audience. It didn't matter that it was fabricated affection, my body simply couldn't tell the difference.

The arch of his scarred eyebrow was the only indication I had that he might have sensed the emotions that accompanied those thoughts, and I made quick work of strengthening the mental shields I had been perfecting.

He motioned for me to follow him, this time not extending his arm for me to take. "Come on, Blake, I'll introduce you to the team."

Twenty minutes later, I was standing in a much larger courtyard on a ledge that overlooked the mountain ranges beyond. It had clearly been created using earth magic, and I suspected someone with use of a fire element was keeping the surface warm because the blanket of snow that was thick everywhere else was non-existent here.

We reached a brunette woman first, her tawny skin wrinkling around her narrowed eyes. She was about my height, if not a little shorter, but it made her glare no less intimidating.

Beckett gestured between us. "Ashton, this is Shania Stephalago. We call her Steph, and she has the gift of illusions."

Steph's eyes flared wide for a moment before she offered me her hand.

"Nice to meet you," I mumbled. "I am Ashton. I'm..." The words trailed off. Everyone else I introduced myself to knew I was Beckett's bonded, and I wasn't sure how he'd want me to address him with his own team. Especially considering how much resentment people like Reed seemed to throw my way when they thought I hadn't earned my position here. The cadet had been so smug when Beckett had given me a verbal lashing in front of everyone for losing the horse in the woods.

"Ashton is my wife," Beckett interjected just as the Fae woman took my hand, her grip tightening for the smallest of moments as she offered me another astonished glance.

A weak smile crested my lips, but Beckett was already pushing me toward the next person, a slim dark complected man, with a steady hand on my lower back.

"This is Franks Axel," Beckett stated, guiding me to stop in front the man standing next to Steph. "He has a mastery over lightning."

"Nice to meet you, Ashton," Franks replied with a subtle dip of his chin. It was difficult not to stare at him as I offered him my hand because his eyes were a shade of blue so light, they were almost white.

Beckett spoke again, forcing me to drop my gaze and Franks' hand in favor of returning my attention to their leader. "Steph and Axel have both been at Wythe Academy." Beckett's expression, once again, held nothing but stoic indifference. However, both of the Fae I had already been introduced to swiveled their heads in my direction, confusion twisting their features.

"After I introduce you to the rest of the team, we will spar," Beckett added, ignoring their expressions in favor of continuing to walk me toward the next pair.

A raven-haired woman with almond-shaped eyes that reminded me of Ryana smiled at both of us as we approached. She was taller than my friend, which was not unusual given Ryana's height, but they had enough similarities that I wondered if they were related.

Beside her, a man who was actually Ryana's height, grinned. Once again, I was momentarily frozen by the sight of his eyes, but this time for a different reason. They were so similar to Jemma's that my heart skipped a beat. Nothing else about them spoke to a relation, as this man had dark auburn hair that was stick straight and a smattering of freckles across his pale skin, but the eyes had been enough to give me pause.

Oblivious to my shock, Beckett dislodged his hand from my lower back, sweeping it toward the new pair. "This is James Baylor and Eri. They have been at Chapelstone Academy in the south."

He skimmed right over Eri's gift, choosing instead to explain James'. *Baylor's*, I corrected myself internally. I was going to have to get used to referring to them by their surname if I became part of this unit.

We shook hands as Beckett added. "Baylor can distort and manipulate sound."

The skin around Baylor's unusual green eyes crinkled with delight as the noises of hundreds of stampeding horses echoed along the ridgeline around us. By all accounts, it sounded as though an entire army was charging our way.

Short lived fear had me sucking in a sharp breath and Beckett only grinned. "Now that introductions are out of the way, we need to discuss more pertinent matters."

The group of four lined up in a perfectly straight line in front of Beckett, and unease slipped into my gut as I considered where I should be standing. Beside my husband, or with a potential unit?

With a movement so subtle that I was certain no one registered it,

Beckett slipped his pinky around mine and squeezed. Although I stayed, I slammed that mental shield back into place quickly, and I swore I saw his lip twitch in response as he released my finger.

His hands came to clasp behind his back as he addressed his team. "We believe that a person of interest is being held captive somewhere in the Kingdom of Demetros. Which is why I have called you four in."

"What information can you give us?" Steph asked, still somewhat apprehensive about my presence, if her continually darting glances were any indication.

"Male. Aged two hundred and thirty—give or take a few years. Greying hair. About six foot two. Hazel green eyes." Beckett sounded off the brief description of my father, and my heart clenched. He was so much more than the amalgamation of this inadequate description.

Eri's head bounced slowly as if she were taking mental notes. "Fae lineage or gift?"

Without so much as a blink of hesitation, Beckett replied. "He is predominantly Elemental and of human lineage. He would have access to all four elements, and his gift remains unknown."

They were not outright lies, but not whole truths either. My father shared my mother's gift with plants since they were bonded, but according to my many lessons with Charlese, that particular ability was very uncommon. Telling anyone he possessed it would certainly raise a few brows, if not draw unwanted attention in his direction.

Franks—Axel—spoke up next. "When and where was his last known location?"

When silence stretched out for a few awkward heartbeats, I lifted my gaze to find Beckett staring expectantly at me.

Adjusting my posture, I swiveled my head toward the group. "Based on the state of his cottage in Elmhaven, and interviews with neighbors, we believe he was taken from that location sometime around the winter solstice." Beckett and I had discussed that possibility after Gianna's debrief and had come to the same conclusion.

Baylor tilted his head to the side. "Any known enemies?"

Nervously, I glanced at Beckett. What was I allowed to tell them about my own relation to the man without revealing my identity? He gestured for me to continue with a subtle bow, either trusting me to make the right call or trusting his team with the information if I didn't.

"A professor at Biltons Academy was blackmailing his daughter over the financial aid he provided her. She ran away so he might be seeking revenge," I offered, with as neutral of an expression as I could produce. "We have some reason to suspect that the Guides might also be looking for ways to force his daughter to return, as she missed her branding ceremony. She has not been located by either."

At that, all four of them relocated their attention down to their forearms, hidden by the sleeves of their various tops and outer layers of clothing.

"I'm just glad Ry was able to break those bonds on her way out," Steph said, eyes still locked on the place I knew the brand would be. "It was uncomfortable being blocked from my gift and the other elements."

Curiosity almost won out as I considered asking them what they had been branded with, but I ultimately decided my father's return was more important. Except one nagging thing. "How are you all here right now? From my understanding, Biltons Academy doesn't offer leave to their students with the exception of the time after the solstice."

"We are allowed to go home on the weekends," Axel explained. "It's typically impossible to get all the way here and back in such short timelines, but thanks to Steph, a mysterious illness has been plaguing the students so our absence from training won't be noted."

Steph's lips curled into the first grin I had seen from her. "The boils were a nice touch if I do say so myself. Although a pain wielder would have added more credibility."

"We have the option of partnering with mentors for healing training if we decide to do that," Eri stated, tucking a strand of her dark hair behind her ear. In the light, I caught that same violet hue that Ryana's sometimes had but was given no time to ask about it as Eri finished her statement. "A couple forged documents later, and we essentially have leave whenever we need it."

It made me wonder how many more people had slipped into Demetros and taken residence as its citizens. When Beckett and I were alone again—if that ever happened—I'd have to ask him about it.

"Without an extraction location, I can't formulate a plan, but I wanted all of you to be prepared." Beckett wordlessly handed them each a stone, flat in shape and mostly onyx-hued, with a tiny rune carved into one of its shiny surfaces. "These will be activated if you are needed. You know the meeting location for Fulgrande."

It was a statement, but they all nodded in agreement.

"Good," Beckett said, with a wry smile lobbed in my direction. "Now it's time to see how slack you all have gotten at your cushy academies."

He shot off the first round of pairings, and five minutes later, I was staring wide-eyed at Steph, who had already taken her defensive position inside a makeshift ring.

"The trick is to distract her from the illusion," Beckett whispered in my ear. "It takes a lot of focus to uphold, so if you can make her drop it, then it's just a battle of elements or hand-to-hand." With that, he nudged me forward into the ring, and I took my stance opposite the Fae.

Steph's expression shifted from jovial to downright menacing and within seconds I was sucked into an illusion that felt so real that my skin prickled with the shift in temperature in the air.

My vision scanned over a crimson sky as winged beasts floated midair, thankfully several hundred feet away. A monster, covered in rotting flesh that exposed jagged patches of torn muscle and bright white skeleton underneath, appeared before me in the next blink. Its lipless mouth opened wide in a hiss that parted my hair with the aroma of decomposing flesh and death.

Just as I was about to scream, Beckett's advice sounded in my mind. *If you can make her drop the illusion, then it's just a battle of elements.*

My eyes slammed shut, blocking out the creature before me, even if the image was burned into my memory and left my limbs trembling. I called to the delicate strands of my air, water, and fire magic and threw a blast of ice out in all directions.

A soft grunt sounded from my right, and my eyes flew open, immediately relieved to find the imaginary creatures gone. My head whipped in Steph's direction, discovering her hunched on all fours from the impact of my power.

Without a second thought, I encased her ankles in rock and soil from the ground, just in the way Beckett had taught me.

I stomped over to her location, ready to deliver another elemental blow when she peered up at me with a smile on her face. "Well fuck me. I wasn't expecting you to be so well trained."

At this, Beckett snorted a laugh. "She's been personally trained by me for the last few months."

He could take credit for my elemental training, but my fighting style had been my dad. And Cade. Brushing that thought away, I glanced back down at the woman that I had at my mercy. "Do you yield?"

"Yeah, I do, little Astor," she replied. "Now, can you let me out of these shackles?"

Virtually tripping over the name she had used, I quickly recovered enough to recall my earth magic and set her free.

Beckett didn't correct her either, and for entirely too long, we just stood there in silence until my eyes slid to his and discovered an indiscernible wrinkle along his expression.

Swallowing, I shifted my stance to face Steph, offering her a hand up. "What were those creatures you showed me?" The winged ones were too far away to see any discernible features, but the other one...

The brunette took my hand, shaking the remaining dirt from her boots as she pulled herself to full height. "Which ones?"

"All of them," I replied, nearing breathlessness at the cavalier way she regarded the images she displayed in my mind. "Are they real?"

"Oh," Steph remarked, garnering Beckett a sideways glance before she continued. "The winged creatures were Wyvern and Chryptera. The other was a Mortinam."

Balking, my eyes flared with something akin to fear. "The wyverns were listed in a tome back in Demetros, but I've never heard of the others." House Wyvern. Cade's house.

My mental fists practically punched that thought away as I let my gaze fall back to Steph, who slid her eyes to Beckett for some sort of confirmation.

It was my husband who spoke. "They are all creatures of the Dark Kingdom. Wyverns are a cousin species to the dragons. The Chryptera are Fae whose features more closely resemble a bat than a human, and the Mortinam are, for lack of a better word, living dead."

My nose scrunched at the recollection of the reek of decomposition and the chunks of missing flesh from the Mortinam with vivid clarity. I wasn't sure I'd ever be able to cleanse that image from my brain. "Was that where I was in your vision? The Dark Kingdom?"

Naturally, Charlese had touched on the spell that punished the lands in the north with a never-ending winter, but the creatures within had not been part of any lesson. There had been so many of them in the vision, I couldn't fathom why the topic had been left off the table unless their existence was one of the many classified things around here.

The brunette shrugged as if she had shown me nothing more than a spring meadow. "I assumed it would make you freeze with fear. Not freeze me." She sniffed a laugh. "Are you planning to join us for the extraction?"

Resisting the urge to look to Beckett for permission, I squared my shoulders. "I want to be there," I replied. Hope blossomed in my chest when he didn't correct me.

"Good," she responded. "I look forward to seeing you again."

"Switch off!" Beckett called, interrupting our moment for gods knew what reason. "Ashton, you are with Eri next."

Steph left the circle, and Eri stepped in, practically naked save for the scrap of fabric she held against her body.

Head snapping to Beckett for any reassurance, I only found a smile curling one side of his mouth. Was this another test?

"Ready?" the raven-haired Fae asked, drawing my attention back to her nakedness just in time to see a shimmering ripple skate across her exposed body. My eyes bulged from my head as her tanned skin transformed into ruddy brown fur, and her very bones contorted and twisted until her entire form was in the shape of an enormous wolf.

Beckett had told me Gianna was a hawk shifter, and thus Grethe theoretically had the ability to transform as well, but I had never witnessed the shift, and the vision left me momentarily stunned. "I thought the wolf shifters were extinct?" Hadn't Charlese taught me that?

Before me, the rusty brown wolf growled.

"Almost!" Baylor called out. "Which is what makes her so good at being undercover. No one suspects that any wolf shifters are left."

The wolf nudged at the ground with its massive paws, dark eyes taking me in and preparing for an attack.

Squaring my shoulders, I drew in another deep breath, glancing in Beckett's direction. "You weren't going to warn me about this one?"

Ever the picture of indifference, he had adopted a very relaxed posture. "I think you can handle yourself, and I want to see what that brilliant mind comes up with."

Sweat poured off me as I considered every possible outcome. Before I could cling to any as a viable option, the beast lunged, and I was left with instinct alone.

My eyes slammed shut as my hands raised to block the wolf's attack. Power exploded from me in a surge that left my skin overheated and tingling with electricity, and when I opened my eyes, a very naked Eri was crumpled on the ground.

"What was that?" Steph asked, staring at my hands.

My throat began to burn as I fell to my knees at Eri's side. "I'm so sorry. I just reacted."

"She's fine," Beckett whispered from his similar position beside me. "See, she's breathing."

He looked over his shoulder to Baylor. "Can you take her to the healers?"

Baylor squatted to lift up Eri's naked form and immediately carried her off the field and toward the castle.

"I've never seen anything like it. It's like she combined all the elements into one," Steph said, still hovering over where I was kneeling in the dirt.

Hazarding a glance up at her, I found that she was looking to Beckett for direction, and when I shifted my attention to him, I only found confusion that mirrored the feelings he had let slip across our bond.

"What does it mean?" I asked in a hoarse whisper. My throat burned. Had I been screaming when I let the power loose? My focus fell to my hands. "Was that my gift?"

Beside me, Steph huffed. "You're considering sending an unvetted gift into the field?" Her astonishment and complete disapproval were palpable, a heavy weight in the air.

Behind her, Axel glared at his General. "Damn, Astor, you've really got it bad, don't you?" His tone was teasing, but there was a serious edge to the notes.

Beckett abruptly stood to full height. "She would be an asset to this mission. Do not question my tactics again, or both of you will find yourself in the infantry with Ebus. You're all dismissed."

Without waiting for a formal acknowledgement, he stormed from the field, and all any of us could do was watch him with gaping mouths.

My mother returned to Castle Falkland in flurry the evening before the Spring Equinox ball. Instantaneously she summoned all three Generals into a larger meeting room. Because I had been training with Beckett when he got the command, he pulled me along with him.

The Queen eyed me warily as I entered the space, but refrained from making any further comment, which was as close as I was going to get to permission from her. Slipping into my seat beside Beckett, I scanned the crowd for familiar faces. The clean navy uniforms told me that many of the people I did not recognize belonged to the infantry, and all of them crowded behind Ebus at the table. The only person who sat by his side was as unknown as the rest of them, a middle-aged man, watching me intently with piercing blue eyes.

"Thank you all for gathering tonight, I come with news." My mother's words gave me a good reason to strip my gaze from Ebus' eerie companion. The Queen paused for a moment, allowing everyone's full attention to fall on her. "Another attack has occurred along the border at one of the smaller settlements."

To the left of my mother, Gianna's fists were clenched. "I do not understand why they insist on staying."

Surprisingly, Charlese had covered this in her lessons on geography. Thanks to my sublimely strict instructor, I knew that most of those settlements belonged to families who had been there for generations. They either feared the change or were not financially capable of making the move, despite the pressing dangers of being so close to the Dark Kingdom. But I suspected Gianna was not asking for a history lesson, so I remained mute on the subject.

"What kind of magic was sought after this time?" Beckett asked. Pragmatic. To the point. I had noticed that he didn't linger for too long on the emotional aspects of the reports, and I longed to be more like him, if only so that my mother might see I was capable of joining his ranks.

Gianna shifted her stare to Beckett; her face contorted to a grimace. "An Elemental rabbit shifter was drained. She had no gifts to speak of, but we believe her companion, a Gothi man last seen with her, was taken during the attack."

If I hadn't already been looking in his direction, I would have missed Beckett's flinch.

Creases formed between my mother's brows. "I get the distinct feeling we are missing something vital about these attacks."

Since I had only specifically heard about the illusionists who were drained and left for dead, the wording indicated there had been others who had not been discussed in front of me. My eyes slipped to Beckett, whose focus was pinned to the Queen.

My mother laced her fingers together in front of her, elbows resting on the table. "Ebus," she stated, flashing the elder Astor a concerning look. "You have lived here the longest. What are your thoughts?"

Did that mean he was the oldest, or had he occupied the North the longest?

The huff he released was so close to a chuckle, I tensed at the noise. "I tend to agree with Alcides on this matter. People should relocate if they value their lives."

My molars ground together to keep me from speaking. My attendance in this meeting likely depended on how quiet I could remain. Listening but not contributing, unless I was asked.

"It has to be about a spell, right?" My mother inquired, turning to Beckett.

His nod was slight, although his face remained locked in a contemplative frown. A faint heartbeat pulsed beside my own across the bond, but I didn't need to sense that to know he was worried.

My mouth opened and then quickly shut. There was no need to be ejected from the meeting on a whim.

"Go ahead, Blake," Beckett stated, lines still deeply etched between his eyebrows.

When I looked to my mother to confirm I could contribute, I found no glaring reason to halt. "The Gothi are required to perform and break spells, correct?"

My mother bobbed her head up and down, confirming what I had been taught. "Any witch or wizard can cast and break spells." Her eyes flared as she processed what I was saying, turning to Beckett with haste. "Do you think the Shadow Fae have found a way to utilize that magic to cast their own spells?"

Beckett grunted in response, giving himself a few precious seconds to contemplate her question further.

"Don't be absurd, Anastasia," Ebus drawled. "The Shadow Fae can't steal Gothi powers any more than they can become shifters with that blood."

My fingertips trailed along my forearm where my brand should have been if I had stayed any longer at Biltons Academy. "But they could use them, forcing them to do magic to cast spells that can siphon power."

Ebus' laugh was a bitter rumble in his chest. "And what do you know of such things?"

It was my mistake, missing the tension rising in the room, neglecting to see the subtle warning in my mother's eyes. "The Guides..." I stopped, correcting myself. "The Betrayers use symbols branded into skin with magical ink to steal powers from those with magic in the Kingdom of Demetros." This was not news, at least not between the other Generals so I didn't recognize an issue with giving it. "Could the Shadow Fae be attempting the same magic as the Betrayers?"

Something dangerous flashed in Ebus' stare, but he maintained a mostly neutral stance as his grimace contorted into a feral grin. "Magic like that would take years to hone and many magical sources to accomplish." He turned to my mother. "Surely you don't think there are enough of those rogue bandits in the frigid tundra of the North to accomplish such a task."

It wasn't even a question. Arrogance permeated from Ebus, prickling along my skin and setting me on high alert.

Either my mother hadn't recognized the challenge, or she chose to remain oblivious to Ebus' tone because her brows were scrunched, and her eyes remained focused on something on the table. "With all of this increase in attacks, I worry that breaking the spell prematurely will put the people of Demetros in danger," she confessed.

"You aren't seriously considering postponing this to a later date?" Ebus' rage-filled eyes could have bored holes into my mother's face. "Every second we wait, our people grow weaker. It's bad enough we are forced to wait until the summer solstice. At this rate, all the Fae born will come into this world powerless."

The summer solstice had been mentioned in several conversations around breaking the spell, but not lately. I had almost forgotten about the date of my potential demise and the reminder set my pulse galloping in my chest.

From the Queen's other side, Gianna spoke up, the conversation continuing on despite my rising panic. "We are not sure how much longer the wards will hold Shadow magic at bay if the spell exiling Demetros is allowed to stand. It already weakens with each passage through the portal."

Shuddering, I tried not to think about the creatures beyond the border. About the monsters that Steph had shown me in her illusion. It was not a physical barrier, but the wards were a magical one that gave me a modicum of safety.

The Queen leaned forward, and I thought for a moment she was going to find some way to calm my fears. Instead, she said, "There has to be a way to prepare them before we break that spell."

All I could do was sit there, blinking in surprise. When my mother was the Queen, she thought like a monarch, and despite the fact that I was her daughter, sitting right beside her, in this room she was focused on her kingdom.

"We've discussed this before," Ebus drawled. "We will send troops to the border in preparation for the construct to fall. Then, we will march on Demetros to quell any panic."

Even in the haze of my fear, Ebus' words gave me pause. What he was talking about didn't sound like a way to put those in Demetros at ease, but a way to conquer them.

"Furthermore," Ebus added, "There are still wards in place to prevent shadow walking across the continent. The Dark Kingdom is no more a threat to Demetros than they are to us."

Momentarily, I took a break from the concern for myself, to place it on my people, speaking up before I became too afraid of the repercussions. "If you are planning to break the exile spell, won't the wards protecting the people of Demetros also be removed? Are they tied together?"

Cold onyx eyes slipped to me, narrowing with that same unbridled malice I had seen in Berit's stare. "This is an army matter. Why are you here?"

"She is with me," Beckett replied flatly. "I value her input on these matters, and she makes a good point."

"Then tell me, Princess," Ebus drawled, "aren't your people trained in some capacity in the South?"

Warning bells chimed in my mind. "Minimally," I supplied. "But nothing like the training I have been given here, and I cannot speak to the elemental aspect of the education or quality of training outside of the capital."

"Excellent," Ebus purred as though I had been agreeing with him. He shifted his focus back to the Queen. "So, it is decided then? We will break the spell in June and bring the Demetros citizens up to speed so that they may defend themselves against any unlikely attacks from our Northern enemies."

In my opinion, that was not solving any problem at all, but my mother dipped her chin in agreement as if it had, facing Ebus with a steely determination. "Send more soldiers to the border settlements to give reassurance to the people that we will protect them." She shook her head. "There are far too many of them going missing for my liking and we must protect them."

Ebus smiled, showing off his teeth in a wolfish grin. "Of course. We can't let the Shadow Fae continue with their schemes, no matter how trivial." With that, he pushed away from the table, and all the infantry in their navy uniforms did the same, trailing behind him as he waltzed from the room.

When we were alone again, with Gianna and Beckett still present, my mother turned to my husband. "How has training been going in my absence?"

"Ashton is a natural with the elements," Beckett reported. He didn't mention the incident with his unit—when I had unleashed some strange magic on the wolf shifter—but then again, he likely wasn't supposed to let me be involved until it was agreed that I could join their ranks.

As if checking off some imaginary list, the Queen asked, "And her physical training?"

My heart swelled. Was she finally going to let me be a part of her army?

"She is keeping up with even my most seasoned soldiers," Beckett replied, and this time I felt the pride simmering along the bond.

Just like Ryana had at Biltons, Beckett had pushed me harder than ever before. I had graduated from running laps around the courtyard and instead been forced to traverse steep rock-lined trails that cut into the mountainside and left little room for error. When that warm-up—his words, not mine—concluded, we worked on my stances, sparred with my elemental power, and sometimes even trudged to the weight room, which was my own personal hell.

The only thing keeping me from completely abandoning his workouts was that he was doing them right along with me, pushing his own limits and gritting through the repetitions with the same pained grimace. This said nothing of the time I spent with the infantry and Light Guard alike, working on hand-to-hand combat, and improving my skills in weapons.

"That is good to hear," my mother replied, giving Beckett a brilliant smile. "My hope is that she never needs this, but I do appreciate the effort you are putting forth to train her."

My heart skipped a beat before it plummeted into my stomach.

What did she mean that she never anticipated me using this? Had I not been privy to classified information that only her Generals and most trusted soldiers were allowed to hear? Had I not proven myself by putting in the work, day in and day out? Was all of this for nothing?

My fists balled by my sides. Did she truly just expect me to be an ornamental bride?

"My wife has excelled at every test both I and Charlese have presented her," Beckett remarked. "You would be remiss to waste her talents."

The Queen narrowed those cerulean eyes for the briefest of breaths. "I will take that under advisement, Astor." Her glare remained locked on Beckett, and I couldn't be sure if it was a challenge or if she was considering his words. "You are all dismissed. I look forward to seeing you both at the celebrations tomorrow."

With that, we stood, and Beckett led me from the meeting room all the way to his bedchamber, where the farce of our relationship faded like a setting sun as soon as the door shut. He quickly removed his hand from my lower back, and after the smallest goodbye, I padded to my room and shut the door behind me.

Forty-Five

For as much as the equinox celebration had been discussed, I could hardly tell a difference in the atmosphere of the dining hall as Beckett, and I stepped into the space that evening.

That was not to say that it hadn't been decorated in the spirit of the holiday, as flowers and foliage covered almost every square inch of the room. Woven vines draped from the crown molding to the chandeliers, dappled in a rainbow of blooms that gifted the air with a crisp sweetness. Centerpieces adorned each table with a mixture of foliage and blossoms that seemed to have been expertly crafted. Even though my mother had not arrived at Castle Falkland until the evening before the festivities, I wondered if most of the plant life had been her doing.

My eyes swept the gathering crowd for her auburn hair, finding her on a dais sitting in a throne-like chair in front of the room wearing a stunning emerald dress that complemented her eyes. The crown she had worn to my bonding ceremony glinted from her coppery hair as she spoke to Gianna.

To her left, Ebus and Onyx were clothed in what most in Demetros would consider scandalous attire. Ebus' grey chest hair was exposed through his unbuttoned black shirt, and Onyx's dress had a similar open neckline that dashed an angled path to her belly button. This, I had come to learn, was not unusual at all for the Astors.

While many guests did wear the colors that more closely related to the spring—pale pinks and greens—just as many saw no point in changing from the typical shadowy hues that I had come to expect in Castle Falkland. Not that I could say much, as the bottom of my own gown was a shade of purple that I'd say fit better with an autumnal festival than the spring.

The amethyst hue faded into a bright aqua at my neckline, a shade that probably matched better with the summer. Neither color was particularly fitting for the season, although perhaps that was why I chose it. One miniscule revolt against the Astors' impossible expectations. The only surprise was that it was in my wardrobe at all and I had a sneaking suspicion it might have been part of my mother's quiet rebellion as well.

A smile curved my lips at the thought just as the sound of clinking metal drew my attention to the servers in the room, still clad in Ebus' preferred uniform. Quickly, I averted my gaze back to the dais that we approached. The Astors collectively caught sight of us first, greeting Beckett and me with sneers rather than smiles.

"Good evening," Beckett drawled before twisting his neck to my mother. "Your majesty," he added, dipping into a slight bow that I mimicked.

"Do enjoy the festivities," the Queen replied, wearing what appeared to be a forced smile.

Before anyone else at the dais could speak to us, Beckett steered me away, back to the alcove, where we took our usual seats.

Leaning toward him, I whispered, "Besides the flowers, how is this any different than most nights?"

A faint smirk tilted Beckett's lips. "You will see."

That sounded oddly ominous, but before I could ask another question, I heard something. The melody of a stringed instrument filled the air seconds before a flute joined in. Then percussion. Finally, a female voice floated over the crowd, layering above the instruments with a sound that was hypnotic in both tone and rhythm.

It took several heartbeats before my gaze landed on the group, but my eyes never strayed from the blue-haired woman once I found her. Although the language was not one that I had ever heard before, I felt the emotions behind every word, deeply in the marrow of my bones.

"I can sense that you like it," Beckett whispered as I blinked away whatever heavy feelings the song had elicited within me.

"It's lovely."

Beckett stood before me, offering me his hand. "Would you care to dance?" There was a flash of something affectionate in his silver eyes, but I disregarded it in favor of preserving what little self-control I had. "Of course," I replied, giving him my palm.

We stood, and he led me by the hand to the dancefloor, surrounded by pots of sky-blue hydrangea and other foliage I was sure my father could name if he were here.

Beckett's palm nestled in the crook between my ribs and hip, the other clasped with my own as he directed me through the movements with light pressure and sure feet. Surrendering my body to his ministrations, I let him sweep me along the floor. The full skirts of my gown floated around us, swishing across my feet as we moved to the melodic beat of the woman's song.

It might have been minutes or hours later when we finally broke apart to catch our breaths. Beckett walked away, promising refreshments, and I made my way back to our couch only to find Mollie perched on the cushion my husband typically took with slender arms folded into her lap.

My eyes formed slits, even as I pushed a smile to my face. "Miss McFaden," I said, using the surname I had gotten from one of the staff. The very same last name that wasn't found in any of the *Notable Families of The Light Kingdom* chapters. "How may I help you?"

Her returned smile was saccharine. "I don't need anything from you. But thank you."

"In that case," I gestured away from the couch, "would you please remove yourself from the alcove reserved for my husband and me?"

She blinked a few times in an unnatural cadence as her lips twisted into a mixture of amusement and disgust. "Actually, I was looking for the Prince."

The scoff rolled from my throat before I could stop it. "He's not here at the moment, but I'd be happy to pass along a message."

"Wonder where he got off... to?" She asked, placing particular emphasis on the words she knew would trigger me.

My nails dug into my palms, eliciting a bite of pain that distracted me from any grand ideas of using my elemental magic to throw her on her ass. "Leave," I seethed, no longer even pretending with formalities and proper etiquette. Charlese would skin me alive if she could see the way I was behaving, but I didn't care.

The giggle that left Mollie's lips only served to sour my mood further. "Can you tell him I brought him a drink?" She pointed a perfectly polished nail toward the silver tray on the low table in front of the couch. There were two fluted glasses, full of a bright pink bubbling concoction.

Focusing on the color, rather than my unchecked rage, I managed to take another deep breath. "Sure," I lied.

Finally, Mollie rose from the couch, straightening the fabric of her sky-blue dress, before she waltzed away from the alcove and—thankfully —out of my sight.

With irritation simmering beneath my skin, I stared at the bubbly pink drinks, taking my seat on the cushion so I could piece out what to do with them. Because my husband certainly wasn't going to receive them after that interaction.

It was a petty reaction, but I had suffered enough of Mollie's brazen displays. Out of the corner of my eye, I caught Beckett's approach, and before I could think twice about it, I grabbed both flutes, draining the contents of each of them as quickly as I could muster.

The drink tasted like the ripest, sweetest strawberries that I had ever consumed, blended with whipped cream and something else I couldn't quite place. The bubbles danced along my tongue and within a matter of seconds I felt warm all over.

Nothing about the drink reminded me in any way of Beckett Astor, and I let the self-satisfied grin on my face linger there as he took the seat next to me.

"What was that?" he asked me as he placed a tray of small snacks on the table in front of us.

Warmth and happiness spread over my entire body as I leaned against his shoulder. "Some pink drink that your friend brought you."

He snatched one of the empty glasses off the tray, sniffing along the rim. His eyes closed as the scent reached his flared nostrils and then instantly sprang open. "Ashton," he growled, "what did this taste like?"

Licking my lips, I tilted my head up to stare at his beautiful silver eyes. "Strawberry cake. But bubbly? It was so good."

He shifted so quickly that my head would have dropped had he not caught my shoulders. "This is important, so I need you to try to focus. Did you drink both?" Those gorgeous grey eyes scanned over my face, but I lost sight of them as my own gaze fell to his lips.

Perfect and plush.

"Ashton!" he whisper-yelled. "Focus!"

A giggle bubbled from my chest, and I was too warm and light to care. "Yep," I replied, popping the p.

His eyes formed slits. "You cannot have that much Champelle."

His grip tightened on my shoulders, and I silently wished he would move them lower. "Looks like I just did."

Worry flooded the bond, like a splash of ice-cold water against the warmth surging in my body.

Glaring at him, I audibly scoffed. "What was that?"

"We are leaving," he announced, throwing me over his shoulder the same way he had after our bonding ceremony.

When I squealed this time, it was pure excitement. Though I genuinely hoped this would end differently than that night. Images flashed through my mind, all but blocking out the faces of the people openly gawking at our departure.

"Try to keep your emotions on your side of the bond for a few more minutes. I can practically hear the ideas swirling around your mind right now," Beckett whispered through clenched teeth.

Before I could even retort with something resembling denial, his grip tightened on my thigh. "Be quiet," he said, but it came off as a plea rather than a demand, and for once, I listened to him.

By the time my mind began to wander back to memories, rather than invented scenarios, I was being tossed on the sofa in the sitting room between our suites. A glass of water was instantaneously pushed into my hand, quickly enough that it seemed it had been conjured from thin air.

"Drink," Beckett urged, and something about the fear in his tone sobered me long enough to pause.

"What is it?"

"This is water," he replied, pushing the glass against my chest. "And you need to drink it in as fast a manner as you can manage. Now."

The deep timber of his voice vibrated along my ribcage, but I hesitated when the rim of the cup reached my lips. "What did I drink?"

Beckett fell to his knees, his hands grasping my elbows, lighting up my skin with the sensation of his touch. "Please drink the water, and I will explain everything when you're acting like yourself again."

There was so much earnestness in his voice, although it couldn't relieve the tingling sensation branding my skin every place his hand touched my body. Who knew an elbow graze could be so sensual?

Reluctantly, I drained the glass of its water, and only then did Beckett back away to a nearby chair and speak to me again. "Where did you get Champelle?"

Whatever he was trying to wash away from my body had not cleared because I felt no different, giggling at my petty deed. "Mollie brought it for you, so I drank it." My chin lifted triumphantly.

He shook his head, prying the cup away from my grip and refilling it with his water magic. His fingertips only dusted along the edges of mine, but it was enough to distract me again. The idea of what those fingertips could do had me salivating.

"Drink some more water," he commanded, passing me the cup again.

Shrugging, I took another few gulps. "I don't see the issue here. I feel great. What is so bad about Champelle?"

He snorted a laugh, and the noise caught me off guard because it was such a contrast to the concern he had been conveying up until this point. "You haven't figured it out yet?" Those silver eyes cut me with an expectant look. "You are a clever woman, I'm sure you can deduce the symptoms, even under its influence."

My throat bobbed with another few gulps of water as I considered what he was saying. Taking note of my body, I recognized an elevated heart rate. Blood was pumping throughout my veins at an alarming rate that could mean poison. Except I didn't feel any of the telltale signs of that. In fact, there was a warmth all over my skin, not like a fever, but it was definitely pooling toward...

With a gasp, my eyes widened. "No," I bit out as if it changed any of the facts.

Beckett arched that scarred brow at me yet again. "No?" He leaned forward as if to challenge me, the heat from his body seeping into my skin.

The sensation had me groaning again. He hadn't even touched me, and his proximity was eliciting noises from my lips that would typically make me blush. For all I knew, I was flushed already, the heat masked by whatever was in that drink.

What I finally recognized as desire crashed across my body, and I flinched away from him. "What do I do?" My spine pressed against the back of the sofa as I attempted to put as much distance between us as possible. Except the movement had my thighs squeezing together, forming friction between my legs that was almost too much to bear.

Crumpling to the ground, I curled myself up in a fetal position, terrified to move any further. And while it was ridiculous to be embarrassed of something I couldn't help, the idea of Beckett witnessing me climax over adjusting in my seat would be so mortifying that I would be forced to leave the Kingdom by any means necessary.

Peering over at the man who had inadvertently caused my misery only had rage adding to the heat of my skin as I found him shaking in what appeared to be full-body laughter. If I hadn't been so afraid that movement would send me over the edge, I would have set his perfectly tailored shirt on fire.

As if he could sense those thoughts, his head tipped back, and his lips parted in another heart-wrenching laugh. The soft waves of his honey-colored hair bounced with his uncontrolled mirth and suddenly I wanted to grab that hair. Yank him down to me and ride his—

My teeth gritted together to force the image out. "I'm glad my traumatic experience is so humorous to you," I growled at him, interrupting my own thoughts. With that, I dropped my head and curled tighter into the fetal position.

Another snort-like chuckle sounded from behind me, but I refused to move even to glare at him.

"What would you have me do, then?" he asked, that infuriating amusement lilting his tone. "I can't leave you alone like this. You're likely to mount the next person who walks in here to tidy the room, and I won't have my staff assaulted like that."

In any other circumstance, I might have laughed, but I didn't have it in me. "I'd like for you to come over here and make it stop."

Of course, I hadn't consciously meant anything by it, but as soon as the words left my mouth, that smoky feeling washed across the bond like a crashing wave. His lust smacked right into my own so forcefully that it left me panting.

The shuffling of his feet told me he was on the move again, but I couldn't tell if he was getting away from me or coming closer, so I focused on my breathing, steadying myself until each inhale and exhale was slow and even.

Beckett dropped to his haunches by my head, and I flinched at his proximity. There was more than a hint of embarrassment buried underneath my mountains of lust, but I usually had a hard time pushing him away even when I wasn't under the influence of some sexually charged concoction.

On a normal day, I thought of us sometimes as a moth and a flame, forever feeling inexplicitly drawn to him. But, right now, my body was a swarm of the flying little creatures, and his was a raging bonfire, beckoning me closer with an almost instinctual level of need.

He cleared his throat, and I regained a portion of my senses. "I didn't mean it like that," I muttered into the plush carpet beneath my face.

He sat on the ground, crossing his legs like a child might do when they are listening to a story, but he didn't touch me. His hand remained folded in his lap as he looked down at me. "I'm sorry."

"Whatever for?" I laughed because, in my opinion, there were so many things he might be sorry for, but this was certainly not his fault.

He exhaled another laugh. "Everything."

Before I could decipher that, or even ask about it, another full glass was placed in front of my face.

Carefully pushing myself to a seated position, I curled my hand around the cup. "Are you sure you shouldn't fetch a pitcher at this rate? I'm not sure it's doing anything."

"It is," he replied, and I didn't have to ask how he knew. Apparently, my lust was receding from our bond, which was good because I wasn't sure I had the ability to try to block my emotions from him right now.

"Thank you," I muttered. Maybe for the water and possibly a little for the blanket apology.

A slice of tenderness cut across his expression. "For what it's worth, you are exactly who I would have chosen if I had been given the choice."

My focus dropped back to my empty glass, and I scoffed. It had been months since I had mentioned anything of the sort, and it hardly required a response now. "Well, you must be really worried about me. Could that have killed me?"

The edge of his mouth twitched but didn't lift fully. "No."

The empty glass made no noise as I placed it on the carpet. "So, it's the princess with her own kingdom that really does it for you? Surprising."

The resulting silence forced me to risk a glance at him. He shook his head. "No."

My heart stuttered. "Well, I am a woman, so I assumed I checked that particular box."

With his silver eyes pinned to mine, he reached over, tucking a stray hair behind my ear. Instead of dropping his hand, he slid his fingertips down the line of my jaw, gripping it gently between his thumb and forefinger. The sensation sent goosebumps across my entire body that weren't entirely to be blamed on the drink I had stolen.

"Just you," he said as if that clarified anything. "In another life, it would have been you."

The contact was a bit too much, and maybe the emotional bits too, so I pulled away, and he let me. It was so unfair for him to say that because we were in this life, and I was right in front of him. Thanks to the magical bond that tied us together, I was as much his as anyone else's.

My knees tucked against my chest, and I wrapped my arms around them to steady myself. A strange hollowness pooled behind my ribcage as the effects of the Champelle ebbed away to a dull heat.

Beckett stood to his full height, looking down at me without actually looking at me. His voice was soft as he spoke, almost remorseful. "Get some sleep. It will help."

Even though I muttered, "Okay," I didn't stand. Only listened as his footsteps sounded down the hallway. It wasn't until I heard the click of his door closing that I pushed myself off the floor and made my way to my own bedchamber.

I had no idea what I had just witnessed, but one thing I was certain of was that I would never drink Champelle again. Throwing myself fully clothed into the bed, I closed my eyes and let the gentle thumping of my own heart lull me to sleep.

Forty-Six

Weeks went by without Beckett—or me—acknowledging the Champelle incident, but I was more than happy going back to our usual agenda of pretending there was nothing going on between us. At least when we were alone. In the public we were very much faking a loving, committed relationship, and it was exhausting. The only reprieve I had, came when Beckett was sent away to whatever undisclosed location he had to travel to with the army. Something that was occurring more frequently these days.

Despite the increased army presence along the border towns, it seemed that Fae were going missing at a troubling rate. Some of them had been found, drained or maimed, but many had not been recovered. None had been discovered alive. At this point, once they went missing, they were presumed dead.

Ebus and Beckett had both been sent to assure the people, although I couldn't fathom what good it was doing while the incidents were still occurring. Either way, the evenings when Beckett was away, like tonight, were the only nights where I was permitted to miss dinner in the dining hall, and I relished them.

Dressed in silky navy shorts and a matching thin strapped top, I padded barefoot in the passageways between our rooms in search of a new book to read. Charlese's assignments were boring, but I recognized them as necessary for a woman who might one day be Queen. No matter what happened between Beckett and me, I was still the rightful Princess of the Light Kingdom, and it would be idiotic of me to stick my head in the sand and pretend that wasn't true.

But tonight, I couldn't bring myself to study any more notable families or redefined borders. My gaze scanned over the bookshelf for the hundredth time, wondering if this would be the day I found something new. Just as I began to scoff at that notion, my eyes caught on something, and my breath hitched in my throat.

A tome had been shoved behind a few others, the dark navy binding almost blending in with the ebony wood of the shelves. Pushing the other books aside, I grasped onto the fabric-bound book, pulling it out into the light to get a better look at it.

"*Unabridged History of the Immortal Courts.*" I read the title out loud like a lunatic but something about it pricked at my senses. Charlese hadn't mentioned any immortals when referencing the courts, and I instantly hoped this would read more like the wolf shifter romance Josaphine had leant me than a textbook.

Tucking it under my arm, I moved to the large, tufted chair by the fireplace, waving my hand toward the hearth to get it started again. My feet propped up on the fur-lined footstool as I cracked open the spine.

Inside were fantastical stories about the gods and goddesses who used to roam these lands, each a King or Queen of the regions that Charlese had called courts. This was the first tome that had meshed the old religion I had read about in Demetros with the history of the continent.

The book didn't offer an explanation about why the immortals had settled there in the first place, or when their reigns had begun, but it did mention that they had bestowed gifts upon the Fae who honored them.

Healing and other light magics to the Diamond Court. Shadows, siphoning, and compulsion to the Sapphire Court, storms for Amethyst, flora and fauna for the Emerald, and finally lust and love for the Ruby.

Smiling at the last one, I considered that if this was to be believed, then Beckett's family magic likely hailed from the Ruby Court, which was now Demetros. I considered the stained-glass window in the chapel-like building at Biltons Academy, honoring the goddess Merè. Hers was the only one whose name did not match the monarchs of the ancient courts. Was she the same person as Amira, or was one simply influenced by the other? Which had come first? Already entranced by yet another mystery, I decided to keep reading to find out.

A throat cleared somewhere in the darkness beyond me causing me to startle enough that I almost dropped the book to the floor. My hand flew to my chest. "What the fuck Beckett, warn somebody," I hissed, glaring at him as I recovered the tome.

He laughed through a quarter smile. "Well, I did place my daggers on my desk. I'm surprised it was the throat clearing that startled you."

He stepped toward me, neck craning to see the book in my lap. "What are you reading?"

Turning it over in my hands, I showed him the cover, letting him read the title. His eyes constricted momentarily, but otherwise, he seemed unbothered. "How do you like it so far?"

Chewing on my lower lip, I let my gaze fall back to the cover. Plain and unadorned. If it hadn't appeared magically printed, I might think it was a journal where someone had kept their personal notes. "Why do you have this? It doesn't read like history, but it hasn't felt like fiction either. Some of these names and scenarios correspond to the old religion from Demetros but they're the same as the monarchs from the courts. I was surprised that Charlese had not made the connection during any of our lessons."

Metal banged against wood as Beckett pulled a long sword from the strap along his back and let it rest on his desk with the others. Dirt, or something equally dark, was smeared over his face, but rather than heading to the bathing chamber, he walked to where I sat, taking the chair opposite mine. With nimble fingers, he began unlacing his boots. It was so domestic. "Some believe this is the account of the gods and goddesses that gave Fae our gifts. That they are the same as the royals who once ruled over these lands."

"Some?" My brow arched. "Are you one of those people?"

He watched me, searching my eyes for something that he must have found because he answered. "I am. Although it was thousands of years ago, many of the stories in that book can be corroborated with evidence in other tomes. As well as our magics. I don't believe everything in every tome is accurate, but I have been studying the texts of old for many years and I think there is a bit of truth in all of it. Warnings of what is to come..."

"Like a prophecy?" I asked, wondering why Charlese's lessons couldn't be this interesting. If I had known the monarchs had been believed to be immortal and the source of our magic, I might have cared about those borders a bit more.

Beckett raised a brow. "Are you aware of the magic of prophecies?"

I scrunched my nose. "It hasn't been mentioned in any of my lessons, so, no. Is it important?"

"There is a belief that if you speak outright about a prophecy, it won't come true."

A huff of disbelief escaped my lips before I could stop it. "Convenient," I deadpanned.

"But there are other ways to convey messages, if you know what to look for," Beckett replied. He pointed toward the book in my lap. "I've spent a lot of time reading through any tome I could get my hands on in order to find the patterns."

"Patterns?" I almost hated how enthralled I was about something that was starting to sound like myth.

He waved off my question. "It's hard to describe until you notice it for yourself and I have to be careful about discussing my predictions."

My eyes rolled on their own. "Typical."

Beckett laughed as if we shared some inside joke on the subject. "What have you learned from the text so far?" He dropped his boot on the floor beside the chair, stretching his sock clad feet out to meet the footstool that my heels were already resting on.

By now, I knew Beckett well enough to know that prying information out of him that he didn't want to give was borderline impossible, but I had learned something interesting in the book.

A grin parted my lips. "According to this," I said, lifting the book in the air, "the powers of lust and love that you and your family boast abilities for would have come from the Ruby Court. Which are human lands." Snickering, I raised my eyebrows in a questioning look.

"Are the great and mighty Astors going to claim potential human lineage?"

He actually looked affronted. "No. I doubt Ebus would consider that any more than he'd accept being called a squirrel shifter."

My laugh came out as a snort as I placed the book on the table next to the chair. "Well, then I will just have to keep reading to find more evidence to corroborate my claim. I'll be sure to present it to him at the next meeting, since he loves having me participate in those."

A little hum of a chuckle sounded from his chest. "So, what had you reading a book about gods and goddesses instead of attending the most exciting affair that is dinner at Castle Falkland? You missed out on bonding time with my mother."

Although I knew he was kidding, I answered honestly all the same. "It's lonely here without any friends, and I was hoping I could make some new ones in a book. Except all you have is history and history-adjacent fiction. Where is the shifter romance like what I read at Lochmere?"

His eyebrows raised up his forehead. "I can assure you that I do not have any *romance* novels. If you borrowed it from my shelves, it was historically relevant."

A real laugh escaped my lips. If I recalled correctly, Josaphine had been the one to lend me that specific book. "What, you don't appreciate a good romantic storyline now and then?"

The look he gave me was pointed. "If I wanted romance, I certainly wouldn't look for it in text form."

"Maybe one of your girlfriends left it behind one evening?" It was too easy to rag him on this, so I wasn't going to admit the true source.

His eyes dramatically rolled around, almost disappearing behind a curtain of full lashes. "First, women are not permitted into my bedchamber, and second, there have been no girlfriends."

My face heated, and my jittery heart left me in a stunned silence.

"But we aren't talking about me," he countered smoothly, as if he had no idea what he just admitted to me. "You are lonely?"

Well, that doused whatever warm and happy emotions I was feeling. "It's not like I know who can be trusted around here. And anyone I tried to get close to could never really know anything about me." My shoulders sagged. "It's easier to keep to myself."

His sigh was long but not exactly irritated. "Have you considered your mother?"

My nose scrunched up at the suggestion. "The woman who has asked me to pretend like I don't know her at all? No, I have not considered her." Truth be told, since Beckett had taken over most of my elemental and physical training, we hadn't spent much time together. Whatever progress we had made on our fledgling relationship had stalled.

The edge of his pinky toe knocked against mine, causing me to catch his stare again. "Ashton, she just meant in public. Why don't you ask her if you can join her in her private quarters when I'm away? That way, you aren't alone, and you don't have to pretend."

It was almost comical how I hadn't considered her before, when she was basically my only option unless I wanted to take my meals alone with Onyx. I could think of a million things I'd rather do than sit with Beckett's mother. "So, how do I approach a woman that I'm not supposed to acknowledge?"

Beckett's lip quirked upward. "The same way everyone else does. Write her an official letter requesting a private dinner."

"That easy?" My returned stare was incredulous. "Why hasn't she just asked me?"

His features softened. "You obviously didn't know her before, but Anastasia has been through a lot in the last few hundred years. Hell, she's been through a fuck ton in the last fifty alone. She lost her mate and her child."

I gasped at his mention of my mother's bond with my father, disbelieving that he knew this whole time.

His brows furrowed as he took in my reaction. "She told me that she let you know about the bond. Had she not?"

My head shook back and forth. "She has I just didn't know that you knew."

A smile quirked up his lip. "Your mother and father hand-picked me as heir. I knew them both well."

My eyes widened as I looked at Beckett, really looked at him. This man, who knew my mother more than I ever would. Who met my father years before we were bonded. It felt a little like fate, had our situation not been so tragic. "You know that she would be amenable to meeting with me because you know her like a mother, or because she told you?"

Silver ringed eyes pinched in my direction. "You do want to talk to her, right? She's not going to force herself on you after what she did. She had her reasons, but she's not going to demand your forgiveness or expect you to treat her like *mommy* dearest."

"What do you think I should do?" My voice was hardly a whisper, full of so many emotions that stripped most of the sound from coming out.

Beckett's head tilted to the side as he raked his fingertips through the messy strands of his hair. "I am not naïve enough to think I can tell you what to do and expect you to listen."

My mouth flew open on an already halfway formed retort, but he spoke again before I could get it out. "If it were me and I had a chance at building that kind of relationship with a woman as good as Anastasia, I would take it. You both deserve to have each other."

A burning sensation climbed up my throat, but I kept it at bay with a rough swallow. "Thank you," I replied, dragging myself off the chair to stand. Looking down at Beckett, I had the sudden urge to hug him, which I also pushed away forcefully. "Goodnight, Beckett."

"Don't you want the book?" he asked, a puzzled expression taking over his face that I couldn't assign a meaning to even if I tried.

Shaking my head, my feet carried me toward the doorway that led to my bedchamber. With my hand braced on the doorframe, I turned to face him. "I think I might make a real friend instead. But thank you for lending me your library." My smile spread. "However, if you happen to come across any more romantic but historically accurate stories, I will read them."

His eyes darted to the tome I had been reading. "That one has romance, but it's probably closer to a tragedy by the end."

My head swiveled back and forth as a breathless laugh escaped my lips. "Goodnight, Beckett," I called, already retreating down the hallway.

His voice was so quiet, I wasn't sure if he had even meant for me to hear. "Goodnight, Ashton."

Forty-Seven

By the end of April, the ground around Falkland Castle had finally begun to thaw. In the muddy puddles left behind by melted snow, green sprigs of grass had pushed their way to the surface in sparse patches.

The landscape was still cold and lonely, but the sun took longer to descend behind the horizon each day, giving me just enough light to glimpse a few of those rare clumps of green from my mother's personal balcony.

Beckett had been right, and all it had taken was a formally penned letter to receive an invitation to the Queen's royal chambers for dinner. This was our third night sharing each other's company, as Beckett and Ebus were away again.

The Queen and I weren't as close as she was with Beckett by any means, but the more time we spent together alone, the shorter the awkward pauses were. We were making progress, as long as I remembered not to bring up my father or my desire to join the Light Kingdom army. I hadn't even tried to broach either topic since being invited to spend this precious time with her.

The sharp edge of my knife sliced into the delicate meat of the roasted fowl on my plate, and I brought the bite to my mouth, chewing slowly around the superb flavors. The bitter taste of lemon mixed with the tang of dill layered nicely over the perfectly salted butter. The chef at Castle Falkland was as skilled, if not more, than the one at Castle Lochmere.

"So," the Queen said, having already put her own fork down for the time being. "What are you learning with Charlese this week?"

No amount of Beckett's absence kept me from my lessons with the strict, but effective, tutor the Astors had forced upon me.

"We are discussing the capital, Marituk, and the history of castle that is not part of the town, but next to it?" My words ended in more of a question, which left my mother grinning.

"Yes, Iverness. It is the official royal seat."

Picking up the knife again, I cut into a fingerling potato, practically moaning around that bite when I gracefully placed it into my mouth, rather than tossing it there with my fingers like I would have been apt to do before Charlese. "Do none of the other castles have towns near them? Josaphine said Castle Lochmere was self-sustaining, but from what I can tell, Castle Falkland also has no surrounding settlements."

Her lips twitched into something I assumed was amusement. "Too afraid to clarify with Charlese?" She laughed to herself, seemingly answering her own question before she continued. "Castle Lochmere supports itself with both food and trade but is considered part of the royal family's property. Castle Falkland is privately owned and purchases all its food because plants do not grow so close to the blight."

Even though I felt myself frowning, I was unable to shift my expression to something less troubled. Every time anyone talked about the punishment spell that had overtaken the Dark Kingdom, I couldn't help but feel sad for those who might not have deserved the death sentence that the forever winter was. Instead of voicing those concerns, I asked a question I had been longing to pose to Charlese all week. "Iverness is also close to the border though. Why is such a large town clustered around it, rather than Castle Lochmere?"

"Relations with the Dark Kingdom have only significantly soured in the last few hundred years. There have been periods of time in our history when they were our allies or at least pretending to be. It has never made sense to move such a large population over tension alone."

"And Iverness falls within the old Diamond Court border?" I asked the question without looking up from my half-eaten food. "Does that have anything to do with the location of the royal seat? Because diamonds are more precious than the other stones?"

When I slid my gaze to meet hers, she was watching me. Not quite with skepticism but with something else. Maybe pride. "The Light Kingdom was created when the Diamond Court, Emerald Court, and Amethyst Court were combined into one region, and a singular King was named. He was the monarch of his court, the Diamond Court, so when he was crowned, Iverness became the royal palace for the entire region."

I mulled that over with the next bite of potato. "Charlese hasn't had time to go into much detail about the origins of the former courts, but she has touched on some information around the history. In fact, I was reading a book the other day that said the original monarchs were gods and goddesses." Laughing to myself, I used the tines of the fork to push around the last bite of the meat. "So maybe there isn't enough factual evidence for her to teach."

"Where have you read a book on the immortals?" It was the curiosity in her tone that drew my attention to the Queen's face. There was no hardness there, only surprise.

Suddenly, I felt like I was back in the first challenge at Biltons Academy, shielding the location of the Blue Tipped Blood Rose from the instructors. My shoulders rose and fell in a nonchalant way that did not match my insides. "I can't remember exactly where I found it." The lie tasted bitter on my tongue.

The Queen hummed her response, but she did not question my statement. "My grandparents did not approve of many of the teachings of old. They destroyed almost all the copies in circulation." Her brows raised. Not in suspicion but again with that earnest curiosity. "If you find it again, bring it to me. I'd love to read the tomes. The gods and goddesses have always fascinated me."

Surprise flickered in my chest. "Do you believe that there is any truth to the stories? That the queens and kings were immortals? That the Fae gifts came from these ancient monarchs?"

I could tell by the way that her mouth moved that she was chewing on the inside of her cheek as she considered the question. "Sometimes it's difficult to distinguish myth from history. More often than not, the truth is somewhere in between the lines of the stories that have been transcribed generation after generation and the bigger-than-life persona the heroes of the books take on. There's always something lost in translation, but that does not mean there isn't something of truth to be learned from the text of old."

The way she described the topic reminded me of the history texts we had been taught from in Demetros. If the works authored about my birth kingdom were any indication of how far the truth might be buried beneath the words on page, I imagined it was possible for the Light Kingdom to have similar mistranslations and purposeful omissions in their own history.

A sigh pulled me from those thoughts, and I glanced at my mother to find her rubbing against her sternum.

"Are you okay?" I asked her, recognizing the same gesture in my father in the months leading up to my departure for Biltons Academy. A fresh wave of panic surged through my veins as I recalled just how sick he had been when I left. Was this her finally feeling the echoes of his demise?

Her smile was weak as she offered it to me. "It's nothing, just some aches and pains from..." She paused, and a guilty look flashed across her features. "Age."

No. This was all wrong. It felt like the months that my father lied to me about his own ailment. With my heart pounding against my chest, I broke one of my self-imposed rules of engagement and brought him up. "Is it dad? He was so sick when I left, and he refused to admit it and..."

"Stop, Ashton," The Queen stated calmly, and I knew I had gone too far, but I couldn't stop. Not when she was showing the same signs.

She closed her eyes against what I assumed was another wave of pain. "Your father was, and likely is, still suffering from the same ailment as I, but there is nothing that can be done about it now."

It was too late to keep up pleasant conversation, so I barreled forward with no regard for my rules. "Please tell me. The only reason I signed that damned contract was because I thought he was dying. I still think he's dying and he's out there." My pointer finger jabbed at the air as fresh tears bubbled up against my will. Almost four months of keeping my fear locked so deeply inside, and it was all coming crashing down around me at the sight of her pain.

"He's not dying," the Queen stammered, this time forcefully enough to drag me out of the downward spiral I was stuck inside. "It is a sickness caused by our separation."

My breath seemed to freeze in my lungs. "What?"

She lowered her voice, even though we were alone on the balcony. "It is something that affects mates."

Swallowing against the hard ball of emotions at the base of my throat, I languidly blinked a few times as I gathered my thoughts. "So, he's not dying? And neither are you?"

She shook her head. "No, it's just uncomfortable."

Abandoning my fork for good this time, I rubbed my slick palms against my skirts. "Why was it getting worse? Were you getting sick like he was this whole time?"

"My best guess," she offered with a casual shrug that was a stark contrast to the somber mood, "is that your magic would have naturally awoken sometime around when his symptoms started."

My jaw dropped. "And it caused this sickness?"

"There is nothing more powerful than blood magic. Even with your bind in place, it seems that with your magic simmering under your skin, his bond recognized my blood within you. But, since you were not me, it likely agitated it rather than soothed it."

A choked sob threatened to burst from my throat. "I made him sick by being around him, and now I'm making you sick?" Dread lodged itself in my stomach, pulsing like it wanted to reject all the food I had just eaten.

The Queen reached beneath the table to grab my hand, squeezing lightly. "You are not making us sick. Our separation strains the bond, and it manifests in strange ways. You are a blessing, and I would go through any level of discomfort to be sitting here with you tonight."

Even as I felt the honesty of her words wash over me, I couldn't stop the guilt that spilled into my very soul. This whole time, I had been the reason he was sick. "Do you think he's suffering now? Can you tell?"

Her hand pulsed against mine as her expression turned sorrowful.

"It seems to lessen when I travel, and it dulled after our initial separation... after a few months, anyway. So, I believe that your distance from your father right now is probably reducing the effects. The exile spell also helps block some of the worst of it."

Shoving every ounce of hope I had into that statement, I sucked in another deep breath, trying to focus on the presumed fact that he was better off with me on this side of the magical boundary than he would be if I was still with him. Or worse, branded and powerless in Demetros. I'd give anything for any indication that he was safe, but the only thing I knew, based solely on my mother's mating bond, was that he wasn't dead.

"Is that why you travel so much?" My tears crested my lash line, dragging salty lines down my cheeks. "To get away from me?"

Beckett was wrong to push us together. Maybe I had wanted a friend, but I was hurting her to do it. I'd rather be alone than cause anyone I loved any ounce of pain.

"Oh, my dear," she whispered, scooting her chair over until she pulled me into her arms. "I only leave you when I must, my darling. There hasn't been a second of a single day where I wanted to be anywhere but where you were."

She swiped the tears from my face before they could drip into my lap and held me tighter against her chest, rocking me back and forth as if I were a small child in need of comfort from their mother. And, even if we weren't quite there yet, I let her, leaning into the embrace of the only parent I had right now.

Forty-Eight

Emotionally exhausted from the previous night's conversation with my mother, I declined dinner with her in favor of hiding out in Beckett and my shared suite yet again. The books no longer appealed to me, so rather than staring at the wall and mulling over my complicated feelings, I changed my surroundings by drawing a bath on the expansive balcony.

Tendrils of steam billowed from the porcelain basin as the water slowly rose. My fingertips curled around various vials as I poured oils and dumped salts until the air smelled of lemon and verbena and relaxation.

Beckett was still gone, and after months of sharing a suite with him and rarely hearing or seeing him in the hours that one should normally be sleeping, I wasn't concerned one bit with my nudity as I dropped the sapphire-colored silk robe to the floor.

Despite being in control of and fully aware of the temperature of the water, I hissed as I submerged my body underneath the bubbles. It was borderline scalding, and my skin tingled and pricked like I was being stabbed by thousands of tiny needles. It was divine.

Sighing, I let my head rest along the rounded edge of the tub, my hair piled high above my head to avoid most of the dampness. Utilizing my control of the air, I thickened the layer of bubbles made by the various oils I had added, creating an almost solid blanket of white iridescent clouds across the top of the water.

With a flick of my wrist, the candles resting upon the iron chandelier above my head went out. Only the moonlight, streaming in through the gauzy curtains that framed the balcony's edge, illuminated the space.

My eyes drifted shut as I breathed in slowly and deeply, taking in the citrus scents emanating from the foam. For the first time in a long while, my mind was focused on nothing except the ambiance in the room that burst like the bubbles in the water when I heard a distinct male cough from the door of the bathing chambers.

Water sloshed over the edge of the basin when I twisted around to get a better view of the intruder, magic sizzling along my skin as I called it to the surface. "Hello?"

A figure stepped further onto the marble-tiled balcony and the beams of moonlight offered a glimpse at Beckett's face. He seemed nonplussed on the outside, but I caught a hint of his unease, or something akin to it, across our bond.

"I didn't mean to startle you," he stated. No smirk. No frown. Just... nothing.

Sighing out my frustration, I turned around and resumed my earlier position, except this time with my eyes open. "Welcome home, Beckett," I said tersely, even if I was somewhat happy to see him. I had been on edge for the last few days, and my mother's news about the mate bond being aggravated by my proximity hadn't quelled that in the slightest.

When he didn't respond, I added, "Why are you here, specifically?"

His face was no longer in view, but I could sense that he was smirking from the tone of his voice alone. "Well, I live here for the time being, I'm a little dirty from our latest mission, and this is my bathing chamber, so..."

My snort echoed between us. "Don't you mean *our* bathing chamber?"

And there it was. Like a glimmer of a twinkling star, a flicker of amusement shimmered across our connection. Outwardly, he remained infuriatingly silent.

My hand rose from the water to wave around. "Well, as you can see,

I have plans. But you are welcome to do whatever it was you planned to do in here. It's not like I can see you anyway." Already images of him entering the stand-up shower stall just inside the archway filtered through my mind.

He didn't tell me about his trips, and I didn't ask, but sometimes he came back a bit more hollow than before. Occasionally, even covered in blood. If he needed a bath, I wasn't going to keep him from the luxury of cleansing his skin after days on the road.

His voice was rough when he finally answered me. Almost pained. "Yes, but I can see you."

This piqued my interest, but I didn't turn around. Shrugging as if I was suddenly the carefree one, I said, "It's like you said before, it's just a body."

He hummed his reply, but instead of leaving, I heard the distinct shuffle of fabric heading toward me. His frame came into view just beside me, but I didn't flinch or move to cover my body. The bubbles did enough of that for me anyway.

Wordlessly, he knelt to the floor, so our faces were only a foot apart. His quicksilver stare pinned me in place, but his eyes never left mine, never dipped any lower.

My next breath stalled in my chest. "What are you doing?" It came out as a whisper, a shell of the confidence I had hoped to convey.

His brow furrowed; the white lines of his scar illuminated by the moonlight. "I just wanted to see you." His reply was just as soft and light as my question had been. Almost as if we were simply tiptoeing around whatever was about to happen, afraid that if it caught us and we were forced to face it, it would hastily disappear.

His gaze remained on me, but his hands began to drift, and I tracked those movements with rapt interest. His fingers curled around a cloth from the nearby metal cart and he dunked it into the water.

My eyes flicked back to his.

"May I?" He asked, gesturing at the cloth and then back to my body.

For a moment, I was frozen. Then I felt my chin dip once.

He collected the bottle of the lemon verbena bath soap and poured a small amount on the cloth, then submerged it again. Every single thought I had in the world narrowed into that small, finite space where his hand moved beneath the thinning layer of bubbles.

When he finally made contact with my skin, it was right along my ankle bone. His movements were slow and deliberate as he maneuvered up the length of my leg. The cloth was positioned in such a way that his fingertips never openly grazed against my flesh, but they might as well have been making direct contact with the way my pulse spiked.

When he reached the juncture between my leg and hip, he simply continued his movements north, avoiding my core altogether. That alone threatened to elicit a whimper from me, but by some miracle, I was able to keep my composure.

Unable to tear my gaze away from him, I studied his face, even though my thoughts were torn between those soft grey eyes and the location of that gods-damned cloth. If I didn't do something, anything, to stop this, I was going to throw myself at him and I wouldn't have everapple wine or Champelle to blame this time.

"Where were you?" I asked, the sound of my voice startling us both as Beckett's hand jerked away, popping a few more of the bubbles that blocked my body from view.

Those same grey eyes that had just been looking at me—with such adoration I almost believed it was real again—widened in shock, following the line of his arm where it still rested beneath the water. He dropped the washcloth where he had paused it against my forearm, and stood with an unnatural speed, backing away from the tub with soap-drenched water dripping onto the tiled floor.

He cleared his throat, his eyelashes fluttering rapidly as he schooled his features into that same mask of indifference that he wore so well. Except I wasn't one of the people who didn't know any better anymore, and I could feel his erratic pulse across our bond. Could sense the guilt and worry and lust that still lingered there like a cloud of ash, covering everything in sight.

His jaw ticked as if he realized the same moment that I did that our connection was still wide open, and his emotions disappeared so quickly that it felt like they had been ripped out of my body. "My apologies," he stated through his gritted teeth. "I have overstepped."

I was too shocked to do anything but stare at him as he took small, measured steps backwards. Away from me.

"It's fine," I whispered, when I really wanted to scream at him. We could be in that other life he had mentioned—and subsequently forgot the mention of—if he just gave us a shot. Instead of yelling that across the bathing chamber, I dropped my gaze to the dissipating bubbles floating like half-melted patches of snow in the water.

"If we have any hope of ending this, we cannot," he growled.

I shut my eyes against his statement. There was the reason he hadn't let this go any further. He didn't want to be stuck with me in this life or in any of the others. He might have found me physically appealing, but once he knew who I was, who my mother was, he didn't want to go there. I desperately needed to stop torturing myself with these feelings of grandeur that we might be something more. He was still planning to end this, and I needed to remember that no matter how he acted when we needed to put on a show.

By the time I risked a glance in his direction, he was already gone. Even as disappointment surged through me, I sent a silent prayer of thanks to those long-dead gods that we hadn't gone any further. I had already fallen for a man who didn't truly want all of me once before, and I refused to make that mistake again.

Forty-Nine

ESTELLA

The plush blanket of bright green grass outside her window was the only indication Estella had that it was spring. Perhaps it was already summer, and she had just lost count of the days again. Between her captor's inconsistent dosage of chrysanth, and no discernible way to tell when she had started counting, it was impossible to know for sure.

She hadn't been summoned for any appearances, but that wasn't altogether surprising, considering they knew her memories had returned, and they had given her back her voice. That didn't stop her from pacing the floor, trying to figure out what was going on beyond her doors. *Had students been released from Biltons Academy yet? Had whomever they kept in the dungeons finally succumbed to the torture Claudius had insinuated all those days... or months ago?*

A loud noise jerked her from her thoughts as her door blew open on its hinges. In its frame, Claudius glared at her, although when he finally made to move toward her, he did so with a calmness that was at odds with his entrance.

"Good morning, your majesty," he said with a curved, calculated smile. The whites of his eyes were more yellow than usual as he took in her appearance.

Estella hadn't been treated like a Queen since that last battle in the Great Conflict, and she certainly didn't believe that Claudius had been gifted with a sudden change of heart on the matter. Still, she held her smile as she greeted him. "Good morning, advisor."

He grinned as if her salutation was an unspoken agreement of compliance. "We need your assistance."

Even as her face remained on the slightly polite side of neutral, her pulse began to quicken.

Would this be her chance to escape?

Outside of the confines of the castle, her captors would have less control over the spells that had been cast to keep her prisoner. "How may I be of assistance?" she asked, with a dash of honeyed sweetness in her tone.

Maybe submission was the best tactic here.

The amount of brown and yellow teeth that Claudius presented in his returned grin was enough to sour Estella's mood. "You need to officially—magically—name an heir."

Estella's eyes flared, giving away her true feelings. "You want me to name an heir?"

Claudius scoffed, appearing almost bored even though she caught the sway in his stance. "That is what I said." He stared at her expectantly, waiting for her agreement.

She couldn't outright refuse him, but she could reason with him. "If you truly believe that I have someone of blood relation out there, then you know as well as I do that it will not work. All the spells and power sources in the world cannot override the blood magic the gods put into place."

The fact that Claudius didn't even appear surprised by her statement was more worrisome than his request. Every bit the picture of grace, the ancient man glided over to the closest chair and slid into it, waving a hand over the settee, suggesting that Estella join him.

Her legs felt like pudding as she crossed the room to sit by his side, reining in the defiance that bucked under the surface of her skin alongside her trapped magic. As soon as she was seated and facing him, Claudius spoke again.

He folded his knobby hands in his lap. "It's simple. We do not believe that the anomaly in the magic has anything to do with blood magic and everything to do with the one who was prophesied to return."

It had been so long since Estella had heard anyone mention the prophecy that she had to rack her brain to select the correct memory. But it was there: her mother pointing to a handwritten page in her notebook, explaining the signs that would appear when they had entered the second age. The recollection was still too hazy to pinpoint specifics, but she could remember thinking it was all a bit too farfetched to be real. Which was why her mother had been leading the lesson and not her tutor.

Shaking herself from thoughts of her family, Estella raised her chin, squaring her stare at the man who had trapped her here. "If that is true, as soon as I follow your instruction, you will kill me. Why would I agree to that?"

The wolflike grin that curled his cracked lips was enough to make Estella internally recoil. "I suspected you might say that. There are ways I can get you to agree."

Estella wondered if the combination of the chrysanth and the minimal control Claudius had over compulsion could force her to do something so drastic. It wasn't like they had anything else to hold over her anymore. Based on the look of satisfaction on his wrinkled features, there was something he wasn't telling her. Her eyes narrowed to slits. "And if you are wrong. If there is some long-lost heir apparent?"

Again, the man seemed more delighted than nervous at her inquiries. As if he were hoping she would ask each and every question she had posed.

Claudius' chest expanded on a gentle, lazy inhale, before he pushed out an equally lackadaisical sigh. He held up a single finger like he was teaching a toddler something very important. "One, if the person in question is truly an heir, then we have already laid the trap to rid ourselves of them." Another spotted finger raised in the air beside the first. "Two, we have contingencies for that, which will give us a better-suited direct heir."

Estella's mind worked slower than she would have liked to grasp onto the pieces of the puzzle, and Claudius spoke again before she could pose another question to decipher his meaning. "We've narrowed down the selection for heir to a handful of students from your lovely little academy."

Her eyes flared with a rage she couldn't hold back. How dare they utilize the school, that her family founded to do good, for their own perverse purposes? Her tone dripped with malice. "You can't change blood relation. If there is someone out there who is in the direct line of succession, they will wear the crown."

He clicked his tongue, shaking his head in mock disappointment. "Most of the candidates are male, and while I cannot force the blood magic to recognize another heir if there is someone else more suited, I can *make* a better candidate. I can force you to freeze."

Acid burned its way up Estella's throat as she fought back the urge to vomit. Every ounce of blood that had warmed her enraged cheeks receded into the pit forming in her stomach. Her nostrils flared with contempt. "You wouldn't." Surely, after so much time together, there was some part of him that cared for her in even a small way. What he was suggesting was monstrous, even for him.

Claudius' hands had long since returned to his lap, and he leaned against the back of the chair, the picture of relaxation. "I think we both know that I would. You were useful until the little issue with the spell caused your memories to return, and now you are a liability." He stared at her with a singular raised grey brow as if daring her to challenge his statement.

The only question she had left was why he even thought to tell her all of this information. The location of a man in the dungeons might not have been purposeful at first, but everything he had let slip today had been a tactic.

Claudius stood abruptly, looking down at her with triumph blazing in his stare. "Do rest up. We will be naming that heir soon, and then your real task begins." He swept from the room without giving her another glance or forcing her to take her chrysanth. For the first time since the dosing began, she considered that the missed dose was purposeful. He wanted her to know what fate was coming for her. He wanted her to feel the fear of that inevitability.

Shock had overtaken her limbs, keeping Estella firmly rooted to the settee, but her eyes slipped to the window, wondering if this would be the time that it unlocked. If she leapt from it, would that stranger be crowned? Would they even be a worthy ruler for her people?

There hadn't been a period of time during any of this that she had assumed her demise might be strategic, but sitting there, fresh in the astonishment of her newly learned predicament, she couldn't stop her thoughts from going there.

Estella's eyes drifted shut as she pocketed that option for a later, more desperate time. In the blackness of her mind, another image floated to the surface. A man she had been set to marry. The broken betrothal that had cost her parents their lives and set her course for this miserable destination.

Had she chosen to marry him, everything would be different. Her parents and her sister would be alive. She would have been miserable, but it would have been a price she would have happily paid over and over again to avoid any of this happening.

Guilt settled heavy in her chest, wrapping its arms around her like her oldest companion. It was clearly morning, as evidenced by the ever-increasing light in the room, but she no longer cared about time and schemes.

This was the most helpless she had felt since her advisors began carving those ancient runes into her flesh, and given their most recent plans for her future, everything seemed so bleak.

She hardly scribbled something about making an heir into her journal before she slouched down the settee, pulling a pillow under her head and curling up into a ball to cry. Everything was so hopeless.

Fifty

Cade had been on my mind a lot as of late. It was possible it was a result of the confusing feelings I was starting to have—or finally admitting to having—for Beckett. Or perhaps it was simply that as the solstice drew near, all the walls I had tried to erect between myself and whatever had happened between Cade and me, had started to crumble. It was already May, which meant I had precious weeks before I'd have to attempt the spell that would rejoin Demetros with the rest of the continent, but I hadn't gained the confidence to bring up my joining the army again.

My mother had offered me just enough classified information to make it seem like I was being included. However, as much as both Beckett and Ebus had been gone lately, I knew there was so much she wasn't telling me. Even if Beckett hadn't been giving me vague updates on what was going on, it was obvious to anyone paying attention that unease was on the rise along the Northern border. It felt like we were on the brink of war.

I stared across the table at The Light Queen, wondering how we had begun our relationship on a bed of half-truths and flat out lies, because while I resented her for keeping me in the dark about so much, I also harbored my fair share of secrets. Neither Beckett nor I had told her anything about the Shadow Fae attack during my routine patrol, or about my mishap with the Fae from his network.

The fact of the matter was that despite the distance between us, we had something in common. We were good at pretending and deflecting. Tonight, we shared a simple dinner, full of quiet conversation about uncomplicated topics which had morphed into quietly lounging by the fire with a book. The entire scenario might have been relaxing, had I been capable of such a thing while my mind buzzed with questions.

The Queen was perched in an oversized chair, reading a tome that appeared to predate the Great Conflict. Her eyes caught mine, then pinched with concern. "What's on your mind tonight, Ashton?" An open invitation to be honest. A motherly tone that she reserved only for a few sacred moments within these secluded walls.

A heavy breath parted my lips. There was so little I could actually unload on her, so I selected a topic that I knew would be safe. "Do you ever wonder if you ever really know anyone but yourself?"

Confusion filtered across her face, mingled with the undeniable twinkle of merriment. "Is this about Beckett?"

The scoff I emitted was borderline rude. "No. There was a boy at the academy, and I thought I knew him, but it turns out he wasn't what I expected."

She offered me a knowing smile. "People rarely are. But that doesn't mean they aren't worth knowing."

My lip worked between my teeth. "It's just that, I thought he loved me, and in the end it was conditional."

Her head cocked to the side as if trying to gauge how best to answer when the entire sordid story poured from my lips like it was gushing from a busted dam. It was like I had been waiting for this exact moment to occur so I could talk to my mom about boys.

For her part, the Queen listened with rapt interest, and I couldn't stop myself from wondering if this was a surreal experience for her too.

She laughed as I recounted the first day of hand-to-hand combat, where I almost broke Cade's nose. How our encounters continued to be awkward but sweet for a while afterwards.

Her brows furrowed with concern when I admitted that Cade had saved me from Berit in the woods and had been protecting me from as many of the encounters with him as he could, leading up to that second challenge.

My mother's eyes sparkled when I recalled picking out a gown at Madame Luthane's dress shop and described my dress in more detail than any of the rest of it. She hummed lightly when I mentioned that it had been paid for by someone who had yet to claim the gift, but I suspected it was Cade.

When I made it to the part of the story where I found out I was Operarius, a burning sensation gathered at my throat. Although from there, it was a much-redacted account of Cade leading me back to his rooms, the heart of the tale remained the same. Cade wouldn't risk his parents' ire to bring home a girl who had no power, and we ended before we ever really began.

The rest, she already knew, as I had been asked to recount it in great detail to Gianna once the General of the Light Guard had been informed of who I really was, so I ended my story at my departure from Biltons Academy.

The Queen's smile was tense as she looked over my face, tainted with a pity that I had hoped I could avoid from her. Even if I had told Marjorie the same thing, Jemma's mother would have given me an identical expression. It was the kind of hurt that a mother feels for her children that was painted on the Queen's face.

Her lips separated and pressed together several times before she finally spoke. "It's hard to tell without knowing him, but I will say that the pressures of being part of an influential family can be overwhelming."

A weak smile lifted the corners of my lips. "I understand."

"I don't know the boy," she added carefully, "but maybe he would have come to his senses had you not left? Turning your back on everything you've ever known isn't easy, even for love." Was she talking about her own mother, who had given up a crown to marry a human, or herself?

It was kind of her to supply some rationale that did not paint me as someone so easily expendable, even if it did not appear to be the case. "I would have considered that a possibility if he hadn't immediately turned around and taken my friend on vacation with him the very week that I went missing." Not that Connally was a true friend, but we had been roommates. If I was being honest, it was Jemma's complacency in the betrayal that hurt the most.

My mother cringed as if I had delivered a physical blow. She schooled her features quickly and reached her hand into the space between us, placing it on top of mine along the arm of my chair. "You will find the right man one day, Ashton. Then, all of this will just be part of the path that led you there." She delivered a smile that brimmed with hope.

Shrugging, I blew out a raspberry. "Maybe I will have more luck with Fae men." Quickly, I batted away the first image that came to my mind, of a General with golden hair and piercing grey eyes.

Her smile deepened, and not for the first time, I wondered if mind-reading was truly a gift, when my mother said, "You know, Beckett is a good man."

The thought sat heavy in my chest. Did she not know he was only doing this as a favor to her? That he didn't want to be with me at all? "Beckett is a good man," I agreed with her. "I'm not sure that he's the one for me though."

The concern spilling over her features gave me pause. I might have willingly opened up about Cade, but whatever was going on between Beckett and me was too new, too fresh to examine like that. It had taken me months to really dive into what had transpired with the House Wyvern leader, and I hadn't spoken to him in that entire time. At this rate, I wouldn't be dissecting things between Beckett and me any time soon.

With as much of a smile as I could gather, I let my gaze fall on my mother. "He's so old!" My tone came out scandalized, as if I had ever considered our age difference in any of the times that we had been around each other.

The crown sitting atop my mother's head glinted in the firelight as she tipped her skull back and released a full belly laugh. The sound was lovely and unburdened by my own feelings and desires. I wanted to bask in it, but the moment ended all too soon as the melody faded into a breathy exhale.

"That's fair," she conceded, and I thought for a moment that might be it. But then, "But if you do decide to move forward with Beckett, I would approve. You should just make sure that you're positive before you do. It's a big step and—"

"Oh my gods, mom!" I shouted, interrupting her before she could attempt to give me what I assumed was going to be the sex talk. It was far too late for that, and the idea of my long-lost mother explaining any aspect of the act with me went past any level of mortifying I had ever experienced. Even my dad had avoided the subject like a plague, so I learned everything, for better or worse, through Jemma Kinkaid.

The Queen's response came in the form of another head-tilting laugh.

Dubiously, I stared at her, soaking in that sound once more, unsure when I might hear it again. A light chuckle left my own lips, but it didn't capture my mood within as I said, "I don't see a future there." That was the only truth I could give her right now.

She nodded nonchalantly, unaware that the notion of that cleaved something within my chest. I wasn't in love with Beckett; I could recognize that what I had was an infatuation—a crush of convenience because there was no one else to confide in here—but there wasn't enough logic in the world that could stop me from wishing that he wanted me back.

The Queen's grin faltered for a moment, the only sign that she might finally understand all the words I wasn't able to tell her. Then, "I have some business to attend to tomorrow and I will likely miss dinner. Will you be okay?"

Disappointment unfurled in my chest, but I tried not to let it show. We had grown closer, but she didn't know me well enough to decipher the emotions on my face. Not like Beckett.

"Beckett will be back sometime in the morning," she promised, as if that changed my level of perceived safety. If they were both gone, I'd be left alone to read another chapter of *Unabridged History of the Immortal Courts*, which wasn't a bad thing. Honestly, it was starting to get good, as a secret romance between two of the monarchs had been revealed. Although the King was betrothed to another, and I couldn't see how that was going to resolve itself. Which might explain Beckett's use of the word *tragedy*.

Forcing my lips to curl upward rather than droop down as they clearly wanted to, I smiled at my mother. "Then I'm sure, Beckett, the ancient gentleman, will keep me safe."

The Queen's expression shifted to a soft smile that didn't reach her eyes. The sight had my insides twisting. "I know he will."

It was the first time I considered that she might know someone had tried to kidnap me, but I couldn't ask without risking my potion in the army. I refused to do anything that would keep me from being able to go with the team to Demetros to extract my father when the time came. The longer he was missing the more certain I was that he was being detained rather than just hiding.

On top of that, the fact that it had taken us weeks to return to our version of normalcy after my questions about the separation sickness, made me apt to keep my lips sealed on any matters that might set us back further. At this point, if the bonding failed to save me on the summer solstice, I'd be dead soon. I didn't want our last moments to be full of strife and tension.

So, I picked up Charlese's assigned book on The Light Kingdom's military history and pretended to read, even as the words blurred together in a stream of unintelligible ink stains.

Fifty-One

The next evening, back in the recesses of our alcove, Beckett had taken his seat beside me on the couch. Normally, we went right into playing our roles, but tonight, my thoughts were uncharacteristically muddled with reminders of Cade. My melancholy was only intensified by my father's continued absence.

Not a single letter from Ryana had made its way to me, and although I understood she was on a mission, I hated that we hadn't spoken. Even with all the uncertainty surrounding Jemma and her lack of concern for my disappearance, I found that I missed her too. The subtle way she'd reassure me when I needed it. The nudge to the elbow and dazzling smile she always doled out at just the right time. Without my friends, I was lonely, despite the fact that I was surrounded by people at a near-constant frequency.

The Queen and I had partaken in the sporadic dinner here and there where we traded polite and well-meaning conversation, but, for the most part, I had no friends here. Beckett was the only consistent presence I had in my life, and at least a portion of our interactions were pretend. It made it tremendously difficult to discern if our friendship was genuine.

The latest conversation with my mother hadn't gone poorly, but the topics had dredged up a feeling of inadequacy that I thought I had long since worked through. It coaxed that voice in my head awake—the one that told me that I wasn't good enough, the one that didn't blame Beckett in the slightest for not being interested—letting it rise from its slumber to taunt me.

You will never be enough.

It didn't seem to matter how much I pushed myself in training or how many of Charlese's tests that I aced, I was only destined to be Beckett's ornamental arm candy, and a temporary one at that.

Deep in the darkest pits of my self-inflicted pity party, I hardly felt the slide of Beckett's arm as he rested it around my shoulders. The gesture in and of itself wasn't out of the ordinary, but it jolted me into the present.

"Hello, wife," he whispered, as if the sentiment was just for me. A bit of endearment that might not be for show.

Glancing up at him to gauge the situation, I found his attention firmly planted on me. Silver eyes ablaze with what I swore was adoration.

"Hello, husband," I replied tentatively.

His eyes flashed as he smiled. Like it meant something.

It was a risk, as any sudden movement around Beckett was when he was like this, but I gingerly placed my hand along his thigh, sliding it halfway between his knee and the crease at his hip.

When I couldn't find an ounce of reservations hiding in his features, I dragged my hand further up before smoothing it back down toward his knee, tracing circles and fanciful designs along his leg as I went.

His breath hitched, and the muscles along his jawline ticked, forcefully squashing the smile he had plastered there for the benefit of the potential onlookers. He leaned his head toward mine so that to the outside, it would appear as if he were kissing my neck.

"What are you doing?" His voice was deep. Even at a whisper, it rumbled against my chest, and although it held some warning, there was a playfulness that mingled with that familiar smoky sensation that crept along the bond.

He wanted me too.

Recklessly, I smiled up at him. "Just working on the acting. I don't think we are believable enough." Gods, this would be the best distraction from my hollow thoughts.

My fingertips ran a trail up his thigh again, this time crossing his waistband before I tiptoed my fingers up his chest. Flattening my palm against his sternum, I tilted my body toward his so every inch of me was pressed against a part of him.

There was no resistance as I moved. No tightened grip along my shoulder to warn me to stop, and all I could think was, *finally,* as I threw my leg over his, perching myself precariously into his lap.

He didn't have to want me back, but the feel of his hands gripping my ass and pulling me flush with his chest was too good to deny, even for the potential heartbreak that it would bring. I would take whatever amount of his attention made me feel like the center of someone's universe again, even if that made me pathetic.

Tearing down the walls I had so carefully crafted, I opened up my end of the bond, letting him sense those muddled emotions and unwavering lust. As if it were all a fragile setup of domino tiles, the gate holding his own emotions at bay crumbled to the ground shortly thereafter.

The onslaught of unexpected feelings between us surged along our magical connection, causing me to suck in a gasp.

At the top of the jumble of unfurling sentiments, the overwhelming sensation of need bombarded my senses. Smokey, warm, and heady, like some sort of propellant. With no barriers between us, I let it overtake me. Igniting me from the inside out.

From my perch on his lap, with my knees settled on either side of his hips, I finally got enough courage to look down at him. The silver tint of his twinkling eyes caught mine for a breath before my lips crashed into his.

Despite the desire pulsing across our bond from both sides, his body stilled beneath me. For some reason, he didn't push me away. Instead, his tongue slid across my lips, reaching out for mine with an unexpected sort of tenderness. Like the kiss we shared right before I had accused him of hurting me with his magic. Before he knew who I was. When this was about anything but duty.

Ignoring the bitterness that twisted in my gut, I shoved those memories away, burying them so deep within myself that he would never uncover the tinge of my embarrassment. With white knuckles, I gripped his shirt in forceful fists.

My hips rolled as I ground myself into him, willing him to stop handling me with such care. If the hardness pressing against my thighs was any indication, he wasn't just after sensual kisses in a darkened alcove either. I fought against the urge to growl at him, relishing in the idea of how good it would feel to just let go. To let him worship me again and to feel deserving of that adoration.

With a new surge of recklessness, I shoved my hands between us, pushing my skirts out of the way so that we could be that much closer to the vision I had in my mind. It took mere seconds before he was groaning against my chest, and another wave of his need pummeled me from across the bond.

I was breathless, consumed so much by our kiss that I hardly let myself consider when this would end. When he would decide this was a mistake and pull back from me. Except he didn't. His hands pushed and pulled my hips to the exact cadence that I rolled against him.

Our bodies fit together like we were two slabs cut from the same stone and moved together like we had always done this. Like we were supposed to do this. Suddenly, I needed to know if he felt the same way, more than I needed the distraction of his touch.

Pulling back, I broke the kiss, planting my lips along his jawline as I slowly made my way to his earlobe. When I licked along the path that ended just below his ear, his head fell back, and another groan escaped those perfectly full lips.

It was undeniable how much I wanted him, but we needed to talk, and we certainly weren't going to take this step in front of an audience, no matter how secluded the alcove was.

"Will you take me back to our room?" I whispered, not even caring how needy I sounded. There was no space to be ashamed when I could so easily feel that his emotions mirrored my own.

Beneath me, Beckett stiffened, and before I could even lean back to gauge the shift in his behavior, everything stopped. His hands left my hips, and his mouth closed slightly in a thin line. His stormy gray eyes churned as the door to his emotions slammed shut, leaving me firmly cut off from his thoughts.

Frozen in place, I sat there straddling him, my mouth open in a sort of stunned gawking silence.

"We can't," Beckett practically snarled. At me. Like I had somehow offended him by giving in to desires I knew we *both* shared. "I thought we were in agreement on this."

It was as sobering as being buried beneath an avalanche.

Scrambling off his lap with haste, I nearly toppled to the floor, righting my posture just before I embarrassed myself further. "I'm sorry," I muttered, gathering my skirts in my hand and running.

The moment might have been considered ironically humorous—me running away from Beckett just as I had fled from Cade almost five months earlier—had it not broken something within me. I had been a fool to put myself out there again after months of Beckett telling me that this was nothing but a temporary political union. What was worse, was that I had agreed with his terms. I had stupidly let my loneliness convince me that it might be different between us.

Unshed tears stung in my eyes as I sprinted down abandoned corridors, searching for any place that I could utilize for a moment alone. Our rooms wouldn't be safe, he would know to look for me there, and I couldn't bear the thought of facing him so soon after whatever that was.

My molars bit painfully down on the inside of my mouth, an effective way to keep the tears at bay until I could reach a place of solitude. The tang of blood filled my mouth, and I focused on the iron taste, rather than my own miserable mortification.

As I rounded the corner, I saw a small room with the door ajar. Peering around the threshold, I discovered what appeared to be an office. A desk was centered in the room, lit only by the pale light of the moon. Blessedly empty.

Stepping inside, I all but slammed the door behind me, allowing myself a single steadying breath before I sank down to the floor. My head fell against my knees. Then, the tears finally broke past their barrier, falling in a silent stream. Rolling down my cheeks and dripping off my chin into the plush carpet beneath me.

"What a shame for a pretty girl like you to be crying *all alone*," Ebus

Astor said from a darkened corner of the room. He practically blended into the shadows, and although I couldn't make out any discernible features, I knew it was him by his calloused voice alone.

Blinking him into existence didn't seem to work. He only came into focus when a sconce on the wall behind me lit with a magical flame.

It was then that I could see his hand wrapped around a crystal glass, brimming with amber liquid. When my gaze finally lifted to his face, his eyes were dark, swimming over my body in a way that was more assessing than concerned. Like I was a problem he was about to have to solve.

His forward movement stopped before he reached my spot on the floor. "May I offer you a drink?" Not a hand. Not comfort. Just alcohol.

With Ryana's warning ringing in my ears, I shook my head, scrambling to my feet so that he wouldn't be towering over me. Not that it offered me an equal footing to stand. Ebus was nearly as tall as Beckett, and I still was forced to crane my neck to look him in the eyes. Something I possessed no desire to do.

My gaze drifted to the glass again.

"This will help make you feel better. Calm down some." Ebus' words sounded kind on the surface, but there was something menacing lurking below the murky waters.

Even though I was certain I didn't want the drink, in the shock of it all, I found myself nodding anyway. Thinking that maybe it would help take the edge off.

Ebus sauntered to the bar, still clad in his navy uniform, the silver buttons glinting in the dim light. He poured the amber liquid from a carafe into a crystal glass that matched his own. An A had been ornately etched into the surface, more visible now that the liquor he offered me had filled in the space behind it.

Without so much as a hum, Ebus handed me the beverage. Taking a tentative sip, I strained to mask the urge to cough and sputter as it burned my throat. Warmth traveled through my chest and belly as the unknown bitter substance made its way slowly to the pit forming in my stomach.

If he noticed my discomfort, he didn't let on.

"Let me go out on a limb and assume my son has somehow fucked something up?" His wolfish grin told me that the prospect might delight him. The wrongness of it all crept over my skin like a chill I couldn't shake.

Everywhere his gaze landed on my body felt like the caress of a ghost's touch against my arms, legs, and chest. Tangible and intangible at the same time. A whisper of fingertips. The uncomfortable feeling of a cool breath along the base of my neck.

As if frozen there by some strange magic, I couldn't bring myself to respond. Couldn't even force the air to leave my lungs. Instead, I took another sip of the drink, noting that it burned a little less this time around.

My eyes tracked his movements as he took small, measured steps around me. Like a predator closing in on its prey.

Ebus sighed heavily. "I have to blame his mother. Her influence has made him soft."

Had I not been so stiff with shock, I might have spit out the drink. Never once had I considered anything about Onyx Astor to be soft. She was carved from stone, cold and emotionless as a statue. Her sensuality might be the only thing that could be confused with warmth, but not the kind of behavior that anyone would call soft.

"Tell me what happened," he commanded, coming to a stop directly in front of me.

As much as I loathed the idea of confessing anything to the man before me, I wasn't sure how else to get out of this room. My lips parted, and the words poured out. "It's not him. It's me. I need something from him that he isn't willing to give me." The truth of that statement was enough to slap me across the face. My brow furrowed.

Ebus' cold black eyes darkened as he drank in my confession. "I can smell the desire all over you."

Bile churned in my stomach, pressing its way up my throat. His eyes were suddenly all too familiar. The same black pits that stared at me in the woods of Demetros. Red hair flashing bright in the beams of the moonlight.

Ebus hadn't laid a hand on me, hadn't even insinuated that he would, and yet I could feel my chest constricting and my lungs threatening to squeeze every drop of air from within them.

He continued, apparently oblivious to the panic brewing inside my body. "If your needs are not being met, there are those here who would be glad to help you." His voice was velvety smooth, like a purr.

It was difficult for me to distinguish Berit's stare from Ebus' in this moment, the images flashing back and forth between my eyes as if the two men were melding into one face with an amalgamation of their features blurred together. My brain was foggy and slow, and my limbs seemed to be rooted in place, but the insinuation thrust me back into those woods in Demetros all those months ago.

My heart thrashed wildly within my chest, a caged animal spurred on by its fight-or-flight reflexes. But no matter how violently the organ slammed against my ribs, I couldn't bring myself to flee or even attempt to increase the distance between us in any capacity. Like my own free will had been stripped from me.

Ebus took one step toward me, and if I had retained any cognitive function at all, I would have hurled from nerves and disgust. As it stood, it didn't much matter how incapable I was at movement because just before he reached me, the door to the study blew open.

My eyes flickered to the motion at the same time Beckett's form darkened the doorway, his features twisted in an animalistic snarl. One I hadn't seen since the day I had been attacked by the Shadow Fae while on patrol.

"Get the fuck away from her," Beckett growled. His charcoal eyes glared at his father with a wave of rage and contempt that I felt pummel me across our bond. My knees almost buckled under the weight

Ebus sucked on a tooth, taking another long sip of his amber liquid, acting as if he had not a care in the world. The only indication that he wasn't completely at ease was that he complied, taking two long steps backwards, away from me. "If the lady came to me to tell me that her needs were not being met, I hardly see how that is my fault."

Beckett stiffened at the implication, and his features shifted momentarily with the shock. "Her needs are none of your concern." He came to a stop at my side, although slightly in front of my body. Like he was shielding me from his father. Like he knew he needed to.

Ebus' sinister laugh filled the room, coating it with a fine layer of slime. The sound left my skin feeling dirty and a few degrees cooler.

"Her desire is palpable to all those around her. I suggest taking care of that, lest you find someone else doing so for you."

My horrified stare was pinned to the elder Astor as he spoke, so I didn't miss when his ebony gaze slid to me. It was charged with something repulsive, but he wasn't given the chance to address me.

"Get out of here," Beckett sneered. The two men locked eyes, glaring at each other in a silent war of willpower.

"Oh, thank the gods, you're all here already." I heard my mother's strained voice from the hallway before she entered the room with a panicked expression that didn't appear as if it had anything to do with the situation unfolding before her. In fact, she seemed not to notice anything amiss between the Astors in the slightest.

Beckett repositioned us, tucking me under the arm furthest from his father as we all faced my mother. "Your majesty," he said, dropping his chin in a subtle bow. "What is it?"

The Queen spared Beckett a glance first, but then her eyes shifted to me, swimming with concern. "They have your father."

The air was sucked from the room, spilling from my own lungs in a gasp. "What? Who?"

Then I saw it, she was blinking back tears, eyes darting between my own and Ebus, still standing a few feet away from all of us. "The Betrayers."

Beckett's arm tensed around my shoulders, and I looked up to find concern etched along his features. His focus was squarely on my mother. "What do you need?"

Ebus glided to where my mother stood. "You cannot be serious," he said in an incredulous tone. "You do not expect us to rescue the man who abandoned our kingdom for the humans. No matter who he might be related to." The last statement felt like a dangerous dare.

Rage rumbled down the bond from Beckett, but it was my mother who spoke. "They have the man who is bound to the Queen of the Light Kingdom. Like it or not, he is a liability to the crown. We will extract him before this mess causes any additional damage." I knew her coldness was an attempt to keep Ebus from discovering just what my father meant to her, but the lack of emotion caused me to recoil.

The Queen spared me a fleeting glance before her glassy eyes landed on Beckett. "We leave now."

Beckett stood at attention, straightening his spine. "Yes, your majesty. Meet you out front in fifteen." He punctuated his statement with a slight bow.

My mother reached out and grabbed my hands. "I'm sorry we must leave you, my dear. We will return as quickly as possible."

Ebus beamed from over my mother's shoulder, as if this was all part of his grand scheme. "Don't fret, your majesty. She will be in good hands here."

War drums beat with less violence than the organ in my chest. My arm snaked around Beckett's waist, squeezing tightly in a silent plea for him to save me. Hoping with all my might that he could sense my emotions across our bond, I glanced up at him, thinking, *please don't leave me here.*

Beckett wasn't even looking at me. He was staring at his father, his jaw ticked, and his eyes constricted at the man before him. "She comes with me," Beckett snarled, pulling me closer. His arm tightened around my body, like he could physically press us into one being. Even with his recent rejection, I had never felt safer. He may not want me forever, but he cared for me.

My mother's eyes pinched as she finally took in the sight, but without the context, it seemed that she hadn't quite pieced together the severity of what she was witnessing. "That is not wise," she said, in a voice I recognized as that of the Queen, and not my mother. "Her magic is not at full power. She is a liability."

That specific choice of words hit me like a slap across the face. Had I not proven myself month after month? I knew enough about magic to know that my progress was impressive. The feeling of unworthiness coursed through my veins like an ice-cold river, frothing with the motion.

For the first time I could recall, I witnessed Beckett glare at my mother with something other than reverence, and it stole my attention away from those sinking thoughts. Unfortunately, with the bond silent between us, I couldn't place the emotion his expression displayed.

"I'm calling in my favor," he said through gritted teeth as if the words alone might bring about his demise. "She joins me either as my wife or as a member of my unit."

My mother's lips pursed together in a tight grimace. Her eyelashes fluttered rapidly as she stared at him like maybe she had never truly known him at all. "This is what you want? Any favor at all and you're choosing this?"

Of course, she had offered him a favor to bond to me. And from the horrified expression on her face, I got the distinct impression she had left it open-ended and bound it with magic.

"Yes," Beckett growled. "She comes with me."

"Very well," she conceded, somewhat reluctantly. "We can discuss the terms of your favor on the carriage ride to Lochmere. We leave in fifteen."

She whirled from the room, her cape trailing behind her in a flurry of rage.

We didn't linger to see Ebus' reaction, because the moment the path was clear, Beckett scooped me up into his arms and hauled me to our rooms.

Yet again, I found myself in a state of shock, unable to move or even open my mouth to ask Beckett what had just occurred. Unfortunately, I was not so frozen that it kept me from hearing Ebus' sinister laugh echo down the hallway, even long after we had left his study.

Fifty-Two

"Are you sure you want to do this?" The Queen asked Beckett within seconds of the carriage door closing behind us.

Assuming that she wasn't talking about the mission to rescue my father but Beckett's decision to bring me along, I spoke up before Beckett had a chance. "I want to go."

Momentarily her eyes flicked over to me, before landing back on Beckett. "I asked you a question, Astor. Are you positive that you would like to use your one favor to bring your wife with you on an incredibly dangerous mission?"

The insinuation was heavy in her voice; she wanted him to choose a different path.

Beside me, Beckett's jaw flexed. We hadn't spoken at all while we changed for travel or during the walk to Falkland's front drive, so I hadn't been given any indication as to why he was taking me along. I didn't want him to change his mind. Although it seemed here, in the carriage that was noticeably not moving, my mother was giving him one more chance to.

"This is my favor," Beckett replied, his voice void of any emotion.

It was clear by her pursed lips that the Queen did not approve of his final decision, but she did not press him further. Instead, she knocked on the walls of the transport in three sharp beats. It had to have been a hidden signal for our journey to commence because no sooner had her hand returned to her lap than we lurched forward into the night.

From there, my mother—paying absolutely no attention to me whatsoever—began her debrief as if she was merely talking about the food at the spring equinox party. "The swallows located Christian in the dungeon of the castle in Fulgrande," she stated, her voice absent of the emotions I expected to accompany the statement about her mate.

"Condition?" Beckett asked, his tone much the same.

It was only at this question that my mother's focus snapped to the windows, and I caught the subtle movement of her mouth as she hesitated to provide an answer. She returned her gaze to Beckett, squaring her shoulders and placing her royal mask back on as firmly as she could. "Based on days of observation, his wounds are being magically healed on a semi-frequent basis.

I chewed on my lip as I read between the lines. The only reason someone would have to frequently heal wounds was if they were frequently being inflicted. Meaning, my father was being tortured. Tears that I tried to hold back burned my eyes. "You told me he was safe. You said the bond was calm."

Instinctively, my mother's palm went to her chest, guilt heavy in her expression. "He's in irodinam cuffs. I believe..."

Beckett shifted infinitesimally in my direction, still not making eye contact with me. "Irodinam is a metal that blocks magic users from accessing their power. It was reworked into manacles centuries ago for the use of violent prisoners."

The first crack in my mother's façade came in the form of a shallow gasp.

Compassion, or maybe empathy, rippled across our bond as Beckett continued to stare at my mother. "Anastasia, it's very likely that the cuffs, in conjunction with the exile, made it impossible for you to sense anything that was happening to him. You had no way to know."

He was trying to reassure her, but a part of me felt like he was also defending her against me, and I folded my arms over my chest. I had been the one begging them to search harder and I had let everyone convince me that I had been overreacting. A part of me hated myself for not demanding that they do more. For being all too content to play a good little Princess to win my mother's approval when I should have tried harder.

The Queen swallowed roughly, before dipping her chin once in acknowledgement of Beckett's words. "What is the plan?"

Beckett scrubbed a hand over his face, swiping away any trace the emotion that had just been there, instantly returning to the stoic General I knew him to be. "I've sent a few of the swallows ahead to alert those in our path that we will be coming through. The network has been activated as well."

An image of those stones that he had handed the members of his unit all those weeks ago flashed into my mind. I had never asked how they worked, but the thought was cut short when my mother spoke again, her finger stretched out in my direction. "And what is your plan for her?"

"She will be with me," Beckett replied, assuredly. "I will not let her out of my sight, and I will abort the mission the minute something goes wrong. She has been training with us for months. I have no doubts in her ability to perform as a member of my team."

Even though he didn't so much as glance in my direction, his praise filled me with pride.

My mother's hands twisted in her lap as she mulled over his statement, stopping only to drag her gaze to Beckett, a look of surprising authority filtering over her face. "I am permitting her to join your mission, as that is your request, but she does so as a civilian. She will not join the royal army under any capacity."

"Why?" I demanded, my nails biting into the flesh of my palms. "Have I not proven myself consistently?"

The woman who met my stare was one hundred percent Queen. "You are my subject, and I do not permit you to continuously put yourself into danger so you can prove something to yourself. It's reckless and I won't allow it."

Her words stung more than they should have, and I could feel myself building a retort when Beckett interjected. If I thought he was going to come to my rescue, I would have been mistaken. "Let's get this extraction completed and give everyone time to cool off, then we can discuss Ashton's future in the Light Kingdom. Okay?"

He didn't even give my mother a chance to answer before he turned to me, making eye contact for the first time since he found me in Ebus' office. "Get some sleep. It's a long drive to Lochmere and we aren't planning to make any stops."

As much as I wanted to protest, the moment Beckett mentioned sleep, my entire body seemed to slump with exhaustion. It was like I had been fueled on adrenaline and anxiety alone and the instant I was given permission to rest, I had no choice but to take it.

"Fine," I retorted, offering neither of them so much as a goodnight before I rested my head against the tufted edge of the seat and closed my eyes.

The next thing I remembered was being woken up by the sudden stop of the carriage. Clearly, we had ridden all through the night because as I peered out of the window, I was met with the view of the sun's early morning rays streaming over the walls of Castle Lochmere like a fiery blaze.

"We are switching transports," Beckett said, his surly voice catching me off guard.

Wiping the drool from my face, I stretched, disembarking the carriage to join my mother and Beckett on the drive.

In front of where we had stopped, another carriage had already been set up, being driven by a curly-haired man that I thought I remembered from my first visit to Castle Lochmere, although it was hard to be sure.

"Curtis here will take you two to the Violet Forest," The Queen stated, stealing my attention away from the second transport.

Whatever ire I had let fester during our earlier conversation waned slightly with my surprise over her statement. "You're not coming?"

My mother shook her head, glancing toward the front of our new carriage as she did. "It's not a good idea for me to join you. Not with both of my heirs already crossing the border."

Her statement seemed harsh until I recalled her warning about the danger of mates and the magic of crowns. What would even happen if all of us were to perish at once? I shuddered at the thought.

The Queen released a heavy sigh, stepping toward me with an

expression I couldn't quite decipher. "I know you are not happy with my decision about the army, but I do wish you well on your mission." She wrapped her arms around me, pulling me into a fierce hug. "Be safe, my darling," she whispered into my ear so that only I could hear.

"I will," I promised her. "I'm going to rescue Dad, and we can all be together again."

Simultaneously, we both pulled back from the hug, and there was a moment where I sensed the hesitation in her eyes, braced myself for the inevitability of her taking it all back to force me to stay with her in Lochmere, but the moment never came to pass.

Her focus lifted to something over my shoulder. "Bring them home to me."

"Of course, Anastasia," Beckett declared from behind me. With that, my mother stepped around me to pull him into a hug just as tender as the one we had shared.

A bitter ember of jealousy flared to life in my stomach, but it melted away when I heard my mother whisper, "And you too. Come back to me, Beckett."

Part of me wanted to look away, but I would have regretted it for the rest of my life because I would have missed the sheepish look that spread across Beckett Astor's face. A light dusting of pink settled on his cheeks. "I will."

Tears welled up behind the Queen's aquamarine eyes as she took a step back, her gaze sweeping over the two of us. "I am so proud of you both. Be safe and go well."

She reached out to me, palm cupped against the curve of my face. "I love you so much." Her tone was almost forceful, like she believed it might be the last time she'd ever say those words.

Suddenly, I was overcome with the thought of losing her all over again and although I wasn't happy with her decision, it hit me that I hadn't said the words to her yet. No matter what else was going on, I couldn't leave her like this without uttering them just once. "I love you too."

We could never make up for the time we had lost, and we weren't as close as we could be, but all I could think as I held her in an embrace was that I wanted more than anything to see her again.

Well, almost anything. With that stark reminder, I pulled back, offering her our final goodbyes so that Beckett and I could rescue my father.

As we approached the worn dock on the Demetros side of the Emerald Isle, I immediately recognized the captain as the man who had ferried us there in December. A subtle hint of glee danced in his knowing eyes, and his smile told me that he remembered me too.

"Took you long enough to spread your mom," he teased through a smile.

Somewhere behind me, Beckett snorted a laugh, the first noise he had made in what felt like hours.

Despite my cumbersome emotions, I felt myself smiling back at him. "We had to find just the right spot."

The captain offered me his hand to use for balance as I stepped down into the salt-crusted boards of his boat.

"Thank you for taking us back to shore," I added.

The older gentleman gifted me another toothy grin in response before releasing my hand and turning to Beckett. They spoke in low rumbles that I ignored in favor of finding a spot toward the bow. If I squinted toward the Southwest, I could just make out the mainland of Eden.

The boat pushed off, and within a few minutes, Beckett sat beside me. The weight of his gaze prickled my skin, but I dutifully disregarded him for the spectacular views of the glittering ocean beyond.

"Ashton, we need to talk," Beckett whispered, like he was trying to keep our conversation private despite the tiny size of the vessel.

My chin lifted into the air, but it wasn't pride that kept it there. "I don't think we do," I muttered, hoping my tone sounded more neutral than embarrassed.

He heaved a massive sigh. "As the lead on your mission, we do need to discuss the semantics of what will happen when we return to the mainland."

This caught my attention, prompting me to relegate my focus back to him. Maybe he didn't plan to discuss his rejection of me after all. "I'm listening."

His expression was in the vicinity of apologetic as he grimaced. "I can't have you going into a mission with unresolved tension between us, so we need to discuss last night."

There went that theory.

My face flamed but I had spent enough time considering what he might say that I didn't want to discuss it any further. "Are you going to tell me why you used your one favor to bring me along?"

He scoffed as if the question was ludicrous. "No."

A humorless laugh brushed over my lips. "Then, there's nothing to discuss about that night at all. I had a lapse in judgment, and you did me a favor by bringing me along. Nothing more, nothing less."

"Fine," he agreed, a little too quickly. "But we should discuss expectations for the mission."

My smile was saccharine. "Let me guess, you don't need me to pretend to be your wife anymore."

His eyes closed as another long-suffering breath left his lungs. "You are my wife," he murmured, before quickly adding, "The team is aware that this was a political union. There is no need to continue the farce of a romance."

That stung more than I would have ever admitted.

"And Jemma? My friends from Biltons? If I see them, what do I tell them about who you are to me?" Gods, there was something like accusation bleeding into my tone that I desperately needed to rein in.

The muscle along Beckett's jaw pulsed, and his eyes blew open again, only meeting mine for a fraction of a second before darting to the waves beyond. "You cannot tell them anything about the Light Kingdom's existence. Call me your escort if you wish."

My wry chuckle was void of any mirth. "Sounds good," I snapped, then clenched my jaw together so I wouldn't say anything more.

As much as I wanted answers about some aspects of the last few days, that would not be my focus now that I knew my father was being held captive. Either Beckett shared my sentiment, or simply didn't want to discuss anything important, because the two of us ignored each other as the boat crashed through the choppy waves of the eastern ocean.

After we were docked in Eden, Beckett paid the captain while I deboarded the vessel. The man looked over at me, tilting his mouth into one more amused grin before he waved goodbye. It made me wonder if I had ever been the butt of one of his jokes shared over pints in a darkened pub corner or if he was even permitted to speak of his time ferrying those who had hired him at all.

The thoughts faded into the distance as I reluctantly followed Beckett down the cobblestone streets of the port town. The sun hadn't quite begun to set in the sky, and the people mulled about the town oblivious to us, save for the occasional double-take at Beckett's tall figure by more than a few of the women. For his part, and perhaps the only thing that kept me from stomping away, was that he made no point of acknowledging them as we trudged toward the Barker Inn.

Fifty-Three

The light woke me up first. Then the birds. Their chirps were familiar in a way that I had forgotten, which made them almost new again. Tweets and calls that reminded me of home.

Home.

Bolting upright, my eyes furiously blinked away the sleep, scanning the room to take in my surroundings. There was a plain wooden bedframe and simple yet comfortable sheets. A crocheted blanket was draped over a chair in the corner. Framed dried flowers on the dresser. It came back to me all at once: I was in Skylar's apartment above the pub of the Barker Inn.

After witnessing the tension between Beckett and me the previous evening—when he stormed out of the pub to do gods knew what after depositing me on the stool at the bar—Skylar had offered me a private room in her own quarters.

The breath I had been holding eased from my chest just as another surge of overwhelming dread formed a rock at the base of my throat. Attempting to drive it away, I swallowed roughly, although it did nothing but lodge somewhere around my heart. We were going to rescue my father. Maybe not today, but soon I would wrap my arms around his neck and breathe in his comforting scent, and I had never felt such longing for anything in my entire life. I had also never been so terrified to fail at anything either.

Knowing that we had no time to waste, I made quick work of my time in the bathing chamber, hastily dressing in the new, better-fitting clothes that the teenage girl from my last visit—apparently Skylar's daughter Olivia—had left me. The navy and brown ensemble fit like they had been tailor-made just for me and weren't ostentatious enough to draw any unwarranted attention.

A messy braid fell down my back, the best I could do without a brush, and as I caught my reflection in the circular mirror over the dresser, I sighed. My hair was the least of my worries when the bags under my eyes had grown a shade darker. The bed had been comfortable, but my worry had been steep. Tearing my focus away from the tired, troubled girl in the looking glass, I waltzed from Skylar's room with breakfast on my mind.

My footsteps echoed down the hidden staircase as I made my way to the narrow hallway, which funneled me directly into the pub. Beckett's glare found me before I had even fully stepped into the room. His eyes were the color of a tempest, a sure sign that his mood had not improved in the night.

He stood, his stare still locked on mine, and stormed toward me, crowding my space in a way that set my heart galloping.

Storm clouds swirled in his eyes as he pinned me to the spot. "Where the fuck were you last night?" Pure rage swelled along the bond, and I didn't think he had any control over whether or not I felt it. There was something else there too, something unfamiliar that I couldn't quite place, but I pushed past him as if I didn't care.

Making my way to the bar, I took the first available stool I came to. Wordlessly, Skylar slid me a mug, her eyes darting between us in a way that made me think I should be taking his reaction more seriously *but fuck him*. After months of mixed signals, I was finally ready to believe his words. This was only a temporary political union, nothing more. It was high time I started treating it that way.

Beckett stopped in the space behind me, standing just out of my periphery. The lack of a visual on him didn't keep me from noticing his glare prickling along my spine, one I refused to turn around to acknowledge as I stated, "Good morning sunshine," in the most sardonic tone I could gather.

Beckett's sharp exhale blew air along the back of my neck. "You cannot just disappear like that. I am supposed to be protecting you." Even without glancing over my shoulder, I could tell that his teeth were gnashed together.

With a sigh, I gathered the mug of coffee in my hand and brought it to my mouth in elongated, unbothered motions. My sips were as drawn out as my movements, and I suppressed the urge to wince at the bitterness of the unsweetened liquid.

When I had drawn out the moment long enough, I tilted my head only slightly in Beckett's direction. "When you stormed out, I assumed you'd be busy last night," I supplied. "Considering I am more than proficient with my elements and trained in hand-to-hand combat by the General of an army, I don't understand why you'd be worried about me while *you* were off frolicking with gods knows what."

He blinked at me, disbelief flaring in his stare.

"What I think you meant to say was thank you," I deadpanned.

"Thank you?" He snarled, anger seeping into his tone.

A quarter smile dusted my lips. "For giving you a night off babysitting duty. Now, try again. This time like you mean it." With a heavy dose of self-satisfaction, I rotated my position on the stool, facing beyond the counter once more.

A low, almost indiscernible noise rumbled from Beckett's chest. "Where were you? I couldn't feel anything across the bond." His tone held notes of worry, and it lowered my guard just enough to annoy me all over again.

"I was in Skylar's suite," I replied, sliding my gaze back to him slowly. "Asleep."

My eyes remained on his, locked in some sort of unwitting silent battle, but I caught the motion of his jaw as he rolled it. "Alone?"

Deep grooves formed between my brows as I leveled him with a sharp look, brought on by the audacity of his question.

"She had her own room, just as you *commanded*," Skylar said from behind the bar, keeping her voice low enough so that only we could hear. Truthfully, I had forgotten all about her presence. Or anyone else in this room.

"But Olivia and I were also asleep in the apartment. It was a real party," she added, with a wink in my direction.

Although I expected his relief to be palpable, Beckett only issued a quiet snarl, leaning closer to me so that I could hear his lowered voice. "If you get into the wrong hands and anyone discovers who you are, it would not be safe for you anywhere. Do you understand?" His tone made it the admonition of the General rather than just the scolding of an unhappy husband.

Sensing the tension rising yet again, Skylar made herself scarce by muttering something about clean glasses before scurrying down the back hallway.

"Relax, Beckett," I seethed. "I am fine. I wasn't going around talking to strangers. I know Skylar. You know Skylar. All I did was sleep."

There was a challenge in my stare as I silently urged him to say something, anything, if my safety had not been his greatest concern. That stupid part of my brain wondering if maybe, any portion of him was torn up at the thought of me being with someone else because the idea of this being solely about my wellbeing was laughable. By now, he knew I could defend myself physically and magically.

He said nothing, but his lips curled up at one side as he grabbed my coffee and took a tentative sip. Grimacing, he slammed it back on the bar and schooled his features into perfected neutrality. "We leave in ten. Pack your things," he mumbled through the side of his mouth.

Without another glance in my direction, he turned on his heel and stomped out of the pub, coming close to knocking over a wide-eyed woman in the process. Instantly, I recognized that doe-eyed expression and those perfect curves. Gabriella, one of the women Beckett had been *spending time* with when I first arrived at the Barker Inn. Even Grethe hadn't remembered the other one's name in the recount of the night we had met, but he had known Gabriella. As if she was a regular on Beckett's roster.

"What crawled up his ass?" the stunning brunette asked me as she slid into the empty stool on my right.

Even this early in the morning, she looked amazing. Her face was bright, as if she had gotten the perfect amount of sleep. Her skin was flawless, even from this close of a distance, and not a hair was out of place on her head.

Rather than lean into my creeping jealousy, I smiled at the woman who had done nothing to earn that reaction. "Apparently me," I said flatly before holding out my hand to her. "My name is Ashton by the way. It is nice to properly meet you."

She offered me a wide grin, showing off rows of perfectly straight, pearly white teeth. "I'm Gabriella," she said. Her eyes twinkled. "You must be the reason Becks won't come to bed with me anymore."

She said it so nonchalantly. As if she were stating that she favored blue over all other colors. Unlike with Mollie, I could sense that the statement wasn't meant to be hurtful, but I frowned all the same.

A laugh bubbled up from her throat, and her cheeks pinked just slightly. "Gosh, I'm so sorry. That came out wrong."

Waving her off, I gave her a half smile of my own. "No, it's fine." My eyes pinched. "He tends to take his jobs very seriously. So, I'm sorry that my presence has put a pause on your time together."

She sniffed a laugh, her lips pursing as she struggled to contain her amusement.

"You two seemed like you were having a lot of fun together last time," I said louder than I meant to. Rambling like usual.

The pink along her cheeks deepened to a rose color. "He's a good time, and a good man," she replied with a shrug but then her eyes met mine again and there was something so genuine in her stare. "But him being on a job has never mattered before."

My breath caught in my throat before it had a chance to turn into a gasp. Even the tiniest noise might have given away too much about how those words affected me. It was a dangerous thing to think of yourself as special when you were, in fact, not.

The only thing special about me to Beckett was who my mother was, and past that, I was merely an obligation. A duty to his kingdom. We might be friends underneath it all, but he had proven to me that we would never be anything more.

My smile faltered, but I sipped my coffee as if the sentiment meant nothing to me. "He's just in a bad mood, I suppose. I'm sure next time he comes through he will be back to the fun and games you're used to."

Gabriella snorted a laugh. "I know it seems that way, but there is more to Beckett than just being the life of the party."

The fact that this woman was trying to sell me on my own husband was downright comedic. My eyes must have rolled too hard and given away my thoughts because Gabriella smacked her palm against the bar and exclaimed with entirely too much volume, "No, really. Tell her how you got here Sky!"

I had wondered how Skylar, with a teenage daughter, had ended up running an inn that was a front for the Light Kingdom's undercover operations, but it seemed like the kind of question you couldn't just ask someone. I was almost grateful to Gabriella for bringing it up for me.

Skylar sighed, and set down the glass she had been drying, draping the rag on top of it. "When I was younger, I got myself knocked up by a man in my unit."

Gabriella and Skylar shared some sort of non-verbal exchange when Skylar shook her head. "I loved him, and I thought he loved me," she amended. "We had this epic night together that resulted in Olivia, but when I told him about her, he acted like he had no memory of the evening."

"Fucking bastard," Gabriella muttered under her breath.

Skylar's head bobbed in stark agreement. "What was I going to do? Force him to admit that he had fathered a child? For what? A dad that doesn't want to be around isn't going to be the type of father Liv deserves, you know?"

"One hundred percent," Gabriella added, making me smile.

"Anyway," Skyler continued, grabbing the glass and rag and getting back to the task of drying it. "Pregnancy in the army is an automatic discharge until the baby is born, and I couldn't afford to just go lay in my bed waiting to birth a child whose father didn't want her."

A tinge of sorrow passed over Skylar's eyes, replaced almost instantly by steadfast resolve. "I kind of panic blurted out the entire story to Beckett one evening, begging for him to let me stay in the army until I went into labor..."

"Even though she would be in the unit with the deadbeat dad," Gabriella tagged on.

"And do you know what he did?" Skylar asked, facing me with a smile on her face.

I shook my head. "No."

"He set me up here," Skylar said, glancing around like it was a palace all her own. "I was able to learn the ropes from the woman who ran it before me and have help with Liv when she was younger."

"It was my mom," Gabriella interjected, making my eyes widen with shock. I had always assumed Gabriella was a resident prostitute, and now I felt horrible about that, even if the admission didn't fully rule it out.

"Gabriella has been kind enough to fill in on nights where the Inn is at capacity," Skylar stated, as if she could read my thoughts again. "I even have Liv help out occasionally, but only when it won't interfere with school."

"He should have kicked her out of the army," Gabriella supplied, "but instead he set her up with the perfect job to allow her to still be a mom."

"He gave me a family," Skylar mused, sharing a warm smile with Gabriella and I decided not to ruin the moment by asking what exactly Gabriella did to help out.

I peered over at the small clock, nestled between the clean dishes behind the bar, noting that while Beckett had given me ten minutes to head out, the story had taken up the better part of fifteen.

"I better go," I stated, "or else I might put your story about how nice Beckett is to the test."

Gabriella and Skylar snickered through goodbyes, and I left the pub with a smile on my face.

When I emerged from The Barker Inn, I spotted Beckett almost instantly. My escort was leaned up against the post in front of a dappled mare, not nearly as aggravated with my punctuality as I had suspected. The horse's black mane and tail swung around her as she idly grazed on the grass beneath her hooves, a much livelier affair than the sprigs that surrounded the muddy ground at Castle Falkland.

My eyes homed in on the animal as I approached. "What is that?"

"A horse," he deadpanned.

The slits of my eyes slid to him. "And why is there only one?"

He barked a humorless laugh. "Have you grown so used to being a princess these last few months that you are demanding your own ride? The citizens here have very little to spare, a truth that I thought you of all people might be aware of."

Air whizzed between my clenched teeth. Yes, I had instigated our fight this morning when I could have diffused the situation, but the insinuation that I didn't understand what it was like to be poor after only a few months of riches at my disposal was a low blow. "That's not what this is about," I stated as ice coated my words.

His scarred eyebrow raised in the air. "Then what is it about?"

He was calling my bluff, like I had tried to make him do back in the pub. Cat and mouse, the two of us. Sometimes moth to the flame but always circling each other in a strange dance that I was both growing weary of and stupidly craved at the same time. I needed to break myself of that habit.

"It was a harmless question, Beckett. I don't care how I get to my father; I just want to do so quickly."

He patted the horse's grey coat along her neck and whispered something that I couldn't hear into her ear before mounting the animal with ease, settling into the saddle, and holding out a hand for me. "Then by all means, Princess. Let's go."

There were no things to pack, nothing that I took with me that I wasn't already wearing so I grasped his hand in mine, my foot using the stirrup for leverage, and let him hoist me up along his back.

After pushing the hood of my cloak over my face, I tentatively slid my arms around his waist. My muscles bunched as I braced myself for some consequence of touching him again, but there were no monsters poised to bite me or strikes from an angered god. Only the ghost of my feelings and my fingertips pressing into the hard planes of his abdomen.

My forehead came to rest against his back, and I clasped my hands together in front of him, allowing myself one last moment to pretend I wasn't irritated with him. Letting myself feel how grateful I was that he had brought me along in the space where he couldn't see it.

For the smallest fraction of time, I imagined instead that he was my husband, in every sense of the word, and that we were simply riding off into battle to save my dad from the true villains of the story without all that extra baggage.

The horse lurched forward, and I pressed myself further against the wall of his back, breathing in his familiar earthy jasmine scent and keeping my eyes squeezed shut, lest the fairytale image I had of us would be burned away to ash.

We stopped for lunch and to relieve ourselves when necessary but spoke very little past the required pleasantries associated with sharing food and relaying when it was time to depart yet again.

For once, it was fine with me to bask in the quiet, and before I knew it the mountains that surrounded Fulgrande came into view.

We dropped the horse off with a nice man at a nondescript home just outside of the Northern tunnel and yet again it left me wondering how many residences were part of the network of Fae who were loyal to the Light Kingdom.

It wasn't until we made it to the tunnel itself that Beckett acknowledge me again, if only to pull the hood of the cloak back over my face before we made it to the entrance. A Demetros guard stood by the tunnel's opening, monitoring the goings and comings from the city. It wasn't altogether unusual to see police presence in the capital, but my heart rate spiked regardless as I wondered if he would somehow recognize me.

Just before we passed the man, Beckett wrapped his arm around my shoulder, pulling me against his chest and lightly kissing the top of my head. "No one will think twice of a couple," he whispered as he pretended to nuzzle against my ear.

Some of the tension in my body eased as the guard's attention moved elsewhere but Beckett did not let go. He held me like that as we wound through several side streets and alleys, growing ever closer to Biltons Academy and our friends whom we were set to meet this afternoon.

Instead of taking the road that I knew led straight to the school grounds, he veered in the opposite direction, catching me off guard and nearly causing me to trip over my own feet.

Beckett steadied me, moving us quickly in front of an entryway that, upon further inspection, appeared to be another pub. What was with this man and pubs? Although as soon as I had the thought, I realized that I probably didn't want to ponder that with any gumption.

We crossed the threshold into a lamp-lit hallway that was still darkened despite the flames as fabric coverings dimmed their brightness. The air was thick with the aroma of perfume, incense, and the unmistakable scent of salty sweat. Not the usual, just haven't taken a bath in a while kind. The carnal kind.

The sounds softy wafting down the hallways were not those of boisterous conversation, and my eyes widened as they arced to Beckett. "You took me to a pleasure house?"

The dastardly man smirked. "No one will be looking for you in here."

I tilted my head away from him so that he wouldn't catch the blush that bloomed over my cheeks. He wasn't wrong, though. Anyone who knew me at all would know that I'd never be caught dead here, much less alive and of my own free will. The establishments were legal and completely acceptable for those who chose to be there, it had just never been something I wanted to experience.

An escaped moan floating down the hall made me cringe. Not that I was a prude—or at least I didn't think I was—but I certainly had no interest in bearing witness to anyone else's pleasure who wasn't an active participant with me.

Then again... Images of Beckett and Gabriella and that still unnamed woman flickered in my mind. While it had been shocking to witness their display, had I truly been bothered by seeing it or just embarrassed that he caught me watching? A long exhale expelled from my nose, as if it could take with it the thoughts now haunting me.

Luckily, before Beckett could read into any of those emotions—or worse, comment about them—a well-dressed woman stepped into our path.

She was the definition of curvy. Every dip and bend of her body was accentuated with the perfectly tailored fabric of her red lacy dress. Dress was perhaps too conservative of a word for what she was wearing though. It was little more than lingerie and only covered slightly more skin than the undergarments might. But I couldn't stop myself from appreciating the contrast of the crimson hue against her tanned skin.

Her hair was a bright shade of magenta that fell in soft waves around her broad shoulders. The image of her immediately reminded me of the mermaids I had seen illustrated in the children's books. Like a fairytale, come to life.

"Good evening, sir," the woman purred, and it was everything I could do not to step between them like I could, or even should, shield him from her gaze.

"Lovely to see you again," Beckett replied. "Do you have a room prepared for me and my lovely wife?" He gestured toward me, and if I could hear the hint of sarcasm around the word *lovely*, I was certain the woman before us could as well.

"Just as you requested," she responded, her accent vaguely familiar in a way that tickled along the recesses of my mind.

With that, she swirled around, sashaying down the hall as we followed close behind. She stopped at an apple red door with a small painted jackelope jumping over the golden knob. The door swung open, and she gestured for us to enter, but did not follow.

Both of us turned to face her, me infinitely more lost than Beckett in this scenario.

"I will be back with your guests," she promised, exiting the room and closing the door behind her so quickly I couldn't object.

So, now I just had to endure being utterly alone with Beckett in a brothel.

It seemed that Beckett shared my thoughts, because his stare felt like some sort of charged physical contact as his eyes raked over my body. It was so out of character, especially today, that I redirected my attention to the room itself.

Everything here was lavish, obviously chosen for the sheer level of its sensuality. Coils of sweet incense smoke twisted toward the ceiling, giving the air a hazy quality. The soft glow of the dozen or so candles cast the perfect amount of light to allow the shadows along the floors and the walls to feel romantic rather than eerie.

The wood planks beneath my feet were stained in a rich, chocolate brown and the walls were covered in fabric in various shades of ruby and crimson as if they were chosen solely to honor Merè, goddess of life, who was often associated with sensuality and the color of lifeblood.

The focal point of the room was, unsurprisingly, the bed. The furniture boasted four massive posts, which barely missed touching the ceiling. The bedding was simple, albeit still luxurious. A coverlet was folded back at one end, leaving the remainder of the bed adorned in a scarlet-colored silk sheet and a collection of soft-looking velvet pillows that pressed up against the leather-clad headboard.

The mattress was easily large enough to host four grown adults, which seemed like overkill until I realized where we were and frowned.

Swallowing, I averted my gaze away from the bed only to land it on the one thing I had been trying to avoid in the first place: the cool, assessing gaze of Beckett Astor. Leisurely, as if I hadn't a care in the world, I walked over to a plain wooden chair that was on the opposite side of the room to Beckett, ignoring that look in his eyes that said he wanted to talk.

Thankfully, before his boot could even take a step toward me, the door to the suite swung wide open. The rush of Beckett's magic washed over me as he threw up an air shield to dampen the noise of our conversation as Ryana and Grethe came into view.

Ryana's eyes met mine first, widening with surprise as she rushed over to pull me into a hug. "I had no idea you were coming."

A small mirthless chuckle huffed from my chest. "Yeah, well, we haven't exactly been able to share letters or talk since you left."

The expression on her face held notes of guilt, but I waved it off. "I understand, Ry. I just didn't have a way to warn you. It was sort of a last-minute decision."

Ryana's eyes narrowed almost knowingly, but she kept her gaze on me rather than flicking it toward Beckett, where I suspected she longed to. "I cannot wait to hear that story."

Grethe's hand clapped against Beckett's back, tearing my attention to the other two people in the room momentarily. Beckett appeared to be genuinely happy to see his friend and I wondered if he had been just as lonely as me without them.

"It is really good to see you both," Ryana stated, "but I do have some questions about the mission. Care to fill me in on the redacted bits, Astor?"

My heart faltered. Had they been communicating this whole time? Without telling me?

Either neither of them noticed my confusion, or they had both shifted effortlessly into their army-dictated roles, because their focus remained on each other rather than my furrowed brows.

"It's Ashton's father," Beckett explained.

"Oh, shit, Ash," Grethe stated, green eyes wide with alarm. "I'm so sorry." Apparently, news didn't travel fast, even with the swallows flitting around Demetros so frequently.

Ryana's chin dipped a few times. "That explains her attendance, but why meet here? We were about to return to Lochmere anyway, as was the plan."

What had been redacted from their letters? Or the better question, what was in them?

Beckett shifted his stance to face Ryana. "We know he is being held prisoner in the Elemental Queen's castle."

As if they shared a mind, Ryana and Grethe seemed to tense at the exact same moment.

"Right now, only smaller shifters have been able to make their way to the cells, and as there is another prisoner, they have not shifted to alert him to our proximity," Beckett stated, giving far more information to the group than he had relayed to me.

Beckett's gaze slid over the pair. "Have any of you made progress in locating a way into the castle?"

Ryana shook her head, offering me an apologetic quarter smile before addressing Beckett again. "We've only been permitted once for the trophy, and we thought it would be a more fruitful visit, but the Guides were present, so it limited our options."

"And since then, you've..." Beckett let the question hang in the air between them, his face the picture of complete indifference.

A huff sounded from Ryana's direction. "We've been busting our asses to be named house leader," she pointed at herself then turned her thumb in Grethe's direction, "and tapped to be considered for the heir trials. As you commanded, General."

Of course, nothing at Biltons had stopped since I left. The world continued to turn, and life moved on.

Beckett's sigh was heavy as he pinched the bridge of his nose between his fingers. "We can figure something out. I'd rather not enter by force, but if we need to, we can. I don't have to tell you both that this is a highly sensitive mission."

Pushing away from the bed, Ryana straightened her posture. "Is Steph on board?"

Beckett made a gesture of agreement with his head, his stance now more upright, his hands clasped behind his back. Looking every bit the General he was, even in his civilian garb. Not that I had ever seen him in a uniform. His voice lowered to almost a whisper. "Axel, Baylor, Eri, and

Evans. I'm set to meet them this evening to finalize our plans, so *excellent* options or not, we need to move forward."

Ryana acknowledged his words with a sigh that bordered on relief. "We can work with that," she stated. "I found a map. It's old, but nothing has changed about that castle in centuries."

"Great," Beckett said. "Then we can save the strategy portion for the team meeting later this evening."

That was an interesting bit of news. The brothel wasn't the main location for all their encounters. Just the place I was being hidden.

The slight rise of Beckett's shoulders was the only indication I had that he was feeling tense. His eyes narrowed on Ryana. "Any update on the man responsible for blackmailing Ashton? Does anyone at this academy suspect anything? I'd like to make this as efficient as possible."

Grethe chuckled as if Beckett had said something funny. "No need to kill anyone today, Astor. We have it under control."

Ryana shifted her weight between her feet. "The potion held, and Mr. Higgins still has no recollection of his conversation with Ashton. Only that she left."

"That and he's been busy with the authorities," Grethe stated through a laugh.

Even Ryana smiled at that. "Turns out Berit Murdock was much more connected than we realized. They've confiscated Mr. Higgins' vineyard and even freed a few of the indentured servants they found on the premises. He's being charged with extortion, among other things."

Grethe tilted his head, his smile going crooked as well as our eyes met. "That's only what's been printed in the papers. Our intel says that he's been kept sedated under constant watch, meaning he probably hasn't been cognoscente enough to plot anything further or even mention you or your father."

"And you're sure everyone believes she's just run away?" Beckett asked through another growl.

"The Guides made it pretty believable that she left due to her classification," Grethe offered, his lop-sided grin vanished. "I don't think anyone wants to draw attention to the fact that she was targeted prior to her attendance and elemental testing so everyone is corroborating the story that she went home. No one has questioned it."

No one. Not Jemma. Not Cade. The two people who knew me the most had just accepted that I had fled in the night like a coward, just because I was named powerless.

Pain shot into my palm as my nails dug into the flesh there. There was no way that Jemma would have believed that I had just been traveling around with my dad like gods-damned royalty. It might explain why she hadn't gone looking for me initially, but that level of nonchalance implied she hadn't even tried to write to me. Hadn't asked Marjorie about me being back in Elmhaven in a letter.

It also made me question how Marjorie hadn't noticed my father missing this whole time or our cottage ransacked. My lip tucked between my teeth as I considered that. "Were you ever able to question the neighbors?"

The three of them exchanged nervous glances, but ultimately it was Grethe who replied. "Rather than interfere, we borrowed the local police report. The official story as far as the town of Elmhaven is concerned, is that the house was broken into after Christian departed for a job and that it was left in disrepair. According to their files, he is staying with family until he can afford to make the repairs."

"He doesn't have any other family," I argued. "Everybody knows that." Even as the words left my mouth, my thoughts could not be pulled away from the images of my home in shambles.

"We aren't discounting that," Grethe said, brows pinched. "We are just relaying what was in the report. We didn't see a need to question the neighbors when most of them had been interviewed by the local police."

Rubbing absentmindedly along her illusioned brand, Ryana's gaze lifted to meet mine, apology written all over her face. "We can talk more about all of that later. For now, let's keep our focus on rescuing your father."

My head bobbed in a feeble agreement, knowing she was right. Even if my cottage was destroyed, I wasn't sure I was going to be given a chance to go back there anytime soon anyway. We were set to return to the Light Kingdom once we rescued my dad.

As if I was waiting for my next set of instructions, I slid my gaze to the General.

Beckett's face was set in a deep scowl that didn't exactly instill confidence. Without even thinking, I stepped toward him, reaching my hand out like I might actually touch him. "Are you okay?"

Steel grey eyes snapped to mine, but the connection between us remained utterly silent. "I'm fine, just tired." Because I had been so dutifully ignoring him, or irritated with him when he was close enough, I hadn't noticed the evidence of exhaustion written plainly across his features. The dark circles beneath his eyes. The weariness in his gaze.

My foot stretched out in front of me, preparing to take one more step toward him, when a loud creak sounded from the doorway. Everyone's attention narrowed to the source of the noise in the open door, but my eyes widened when my gaze reached it. There, standing in the place where I had expected to find the magenta-haired woman, was Cade Hudson, staring at me with a shocked yet almost exuberant expression. Like he was happy to find me here, even if he hadn't expected to.

Those violet-flecked eyes bore into my own just as his lips parted on words that he never got to say because, in that moment, Beckett lunged.

Fifty-Five

In the timeframe that it took me to blink, Beckett had effectively shut the door and simultaneously pinned Cade against the slab of wood with a firmly placed forearm to the throat.

"Who the fuck are you and what do you want?" Beckett's nostrils flared with rage, and it reminded me so much of the version of him that I had seen in that border attack that I genuinely feared for Cade's safety.

Cade looked to me for help, his indigo eyes more white than blue as he realized how dire the situation was.

"Don't look at her," Beckett growled, pressing his arm harder into Cade's windpipe. "Look at me. I'm the one you need to convince to let you walk out of here alive."

Instinct took over, as I snapped out of my shock, and I rushed to them, yanking at Beckett's arm, scratching at his skin. "Let him go!" Cade had broken my heart, but I didn't think he deserved to die for it.

Grethe stepped in beside me, wrapping his arms around Beckett's upper body and hauling him away. The firm line of Grethe's mouth told me he was straining to remove Beckett from Cade, which was a feat considering his gift was strength.

Sputtering and coughing, Cade crumbled to the floor, trying to regain his composure. Just as I considered offering him a hand, I remembered our last meeting and his trip with Connally Owens and decided to let him suffer the consequences of his actions a bit more before giving aid. Looking down at him with a neutrality I hoped I had perfected, I asked, "What are you doing here?"

Cade pushed himself to a standing position, and without warning, he closed the gap between us, throwing his arms around me and picking me up in a full-body hug. "I am so glad you are okay," he whispered against my hair. "I've been looking everywhere for you."

A piece of my heart constricted, chipping away at my annoyance, if only for a moment. I pushed away from our embrace, glancing quickly at where Grethe was still restraining Beckett, before returning my attention to the man I once thought had loved me.

"Explain yourself," Beckett seethed from somewhere over my shoulder. "Do it quickly before I tie you to that chair and extract your answers from you. Believe me, you won't like my methods."

Cade grimaced, but his eyes slid back to mine with a pained sort of sorrow that gave me pause. When I motioned for him to go ahead, he exhaled deeply before continuing. "When they told us that you had run away because you were Operarius, I knew that a part of the reason that happened was my fault."

A growl emitted from Beckett's general vicinity, but I did not give him my attention, keeping my stare firmly locked on Cade.

Cade let his focus wander to the General behind me, but snapped back to me in a heartbeat, features softening once more. "I felt so guilty, and I had to talk to you. So, I went to Elmhaven the moment I realized you were missing. I asked around and found out which house was yours, and I went there to see you."

"Spit it out," Beckett commanded, and I noted with a backwards glance and a dose of concern that Grethe had loosened his grip.

When Cade's hands wrapped around my own, my focus shifted involuntarily to Beckett, whose glare was pinned to the place where Cade and I were joined. Annoyance swelled in my chest as I returned my attention to those familiar indigo eyes, dutifully ignoring the prickling sensation dancing along the back of my neck.

"The Ignus Guide, Claudius was there when I got there," Cade explained. "I thought he was coming to get you, but then I saw him arguing with a man that I assumed was your dad, but…" A puzzled expression filtered across his face. "Claudius attacked him. I couldn't see much when they entered the home, but when they left, the man—your dad—was being carried out by Select Guard."

We were only here in Demetros to extract him from the Elemental Queen's palace, but somehow the confirmation that he had been held prisoner that long brought a fresh wave of tears to my eyes.

Even Cade appeared devastated as he squeezed my hands. "I'm so sorry, Ashton. By the time I thought to follow them, they were long gone. I know what he means to you, and I should have gone after him. I'll never forgive myself."

Never in my wildest dreams had I considered that Cade had come looking for me. Or that the answer to my father's whereabouts had been with him the whole time. Still, I pulled my hands from his grasp. "I don't expect you to be sorry over that."

Confusion marred his beautiful face as he blinked down at me.

My head tilted to the side and a sugary smile spread across my face. "How is Connally?"

Bewilderment transformed into horrified shock as Cade made to step toward me with his hands outstretched. "That wasn't what it looked like." He flashed a glance at Ryana, and when his focus returned to me, I had already taken three steps back.

He dropped his palms to his side and sighed. "When you first left, after I knew they had taken your dad, I assumed that if anyone knew where you had gone, it would be your friends. But, considering what I witnessed, I didn't think it was safe to just ask." He closed his eyes almost as if the next part bothered him. "I am ashamed to admit it, but I inserted myself into your circle to see if they knew anything."

A mirthless laugh ripped itself from my throat. It didn't appear that Jemma had been concerned about my departure in the slightest, and the rest of their group didn't know me well enough to be useful, so I already knew he hadn't gleaned anything from that attempt to find me.

"Jemma seemed truly distraught with your absence. She wanted to go back to Elmhaven to look for you," Cade stated, and my breath froze in my lungs. "I already knew you weren't there, but I didn't want to tell her what I had seen, so I didn't. If she had known anything, she wouldn't have been trying to go back to Elmhaven."

My eyes formed slits. "Interesting. And how does whisking Connally away on vacation play into this?"

Cade became exasperated. "I was already with them when I realized they didn't know anything. It would have been rude to just leave."

A disbelieving scoff tumbled from my lips. "You were always one to care about expectations and manners, weren't you?"

The man had the decency to at least look genuinely put out. His sigh was a slow, meandering thing in the space between us. "I'm sorry, Ashton. All I wanted was to find you."

With a hardened resolve, I crossed my arms, closing myself off from him once again. It wasn't that I didn't want to believe him, I just couldn't process all he was telling me. "Why are you here?"

A grimace twisted his lips as Cade spared another glance toward Ryana and Grethe. "When Jemma and Connally proved to be dead ends, I started following Ryana. She's been meeting with Grethe a lot, and I suspected they might have hurt you. There have been too many unexplained situations at the academy. Stuff the headmaster has been keen to cover up." With that, his dark brows scrunched together.

Grethe chose that moment to burst into laughter. "You thought we were murderers?"

Even the corner of Beckett's mouth quirked with amusement, although he didn't let it curl to its full potential.

"I thought we were friends!" Grethe added through his fits of laughter.

With that, Beckett's expression went cold, but the humor in the entire situation brought a smile to my own lips. As swiftly as his haphazardly squashed smile had fallen, a frown took residence on Beckett's face. "You're Cade," he said in a half-question, half-statement. Without waiting for a reply, Beckett took several long steps toward us, closing the gap between him and Cade.

Sidestepping him, I moved between them, holding my hands wide as if I could somehow stop Beckett from advancing if he chose to. My eyes homed in on Beckett's face. "What is your problem?"

Beckett flicked his gaze over my shoulder to Cade before landing it squarely back on me. "This asshole kicked you to the curb the moment he found out you were powerless." His fingertip pointed toward Cade in an aggressive jab, as if any of us needed clarification on who he was talking about. "And now?" Beckett continued. "Now that you have magic, he's pretending that he has been looking for you this whole time? I don't buy it." His words might as well have been a kick to the gut.

"You have magic?" Cade's voice sounded from over my shoulder. He seemed curious but genuinely surprised.

"Yes," I admitted sharply, my focus still trained on Beckett.

Cade placed one hand on my shoulder. It was gentle and comforting in a way I hadn't felt in ages. "That's great, Ash."

A broad chest pressed against mine as Beckett attempted to push past me to get to Cade. "You lost the right to call her by a fond little nickname," he growled. With that, the gates to his emotions flung open, practically assaulting me with the onslaught of his rage.

Cade removed his hand from my shoulder, and I heard his boots scrape against the floor as he backed up, but I couldn't take my eyes off the man in front of me, trying and failing to untangle the emotions coursing across our bond.

Behind me, Cade's throat cleared. "Are you with him?" There was a tremble in the tenor of his voice that almost spoke of fear. He hadn't even sounded afraid the night in the woods. The night he saved me.

Without turning around, I offered a terse "No," at the same time Beckett said, "Yes."

My eyes constricted to slits, snagging on a stormy gray glare. Hadn't it been less than twenty-four hours since Beckett had informed me that we were nothing here? That I shouldn't even tell anyone about our bonding ceremony?

Shifting my head so that I could see Cade from the corner of my eye, I forced a smile in place. "Mr. Astor is my escort to Fulgrande. We are traveling together." Damn, I had gotten good at half-truths since my stint with the anonymous donor and I didn't exactly feel good about that.

From what I could see, Cade's shoulders fell. "Okay. Yeah, sure. So where have you been?"

Beckett's chest was still pressed against mine, and when I gazed back up at him, for any sign on how to proceed with that question, I was hit with our proximity. We were almost intertwined with one another, chests heaving in sync to the point that I hadn't even noticed.

Taking a massive step backwards, I felt something flicker across our bond. The feeling was unfamiliar yet fleeting, gone in a flash, and before I could chase it, I felt the door to his side of our connection slam shut with such force that a shiver slithered down my spine.

A question lingered in my gaze, but he ignored it, turning to Cade with a bit more civility than before. "Ashton's dad is still missing, so unless you have some way to enter the castle unseen to retrieve him, you need to leave. And I will trust that your..." he paused, lips twisting like something in his mouth was bitter. "I will trust that your affection for her will keep you silent on the subject of her return."

"The castle?" Cade asked, and Beckett eyed him wearily but supplied a nod in response.

Cade stood up straighter. "Then I can help. I know how to get in."

It felt all too perfect, like pieces had lined up that never would have without an exterior force. "You can?" I asked, certain he was going to explain it was a joke.

"There is another entrance to those tunnels I showed you," Cade supplied, fully facing me again.

"Tunnels?" Beckett asked, and there was a hint of surprise to his voice.

Cade's indigo eyes were plastered on me, searching my face for a glimmer of recognition. As if all of the pain he had caused me could ever make me forget. "The ones that led to our meadow?" I asked.

A sudden wave of emotion clambered across our bond, which was too distinct and recognizable to be anything other than repulsion. I rolled my eyes in response to Beckett's severe shortcomings with keeping his emotions in check today.

But when my attention fully returned to Cade, he was grinning. The sight was so familiar that my heart constricted at the warmth in his expression. It had been easy to hate him from a distance, but this close I was reminded of the man who had become my friend, and then more.

The person who had held me after Berit's attack. Who had gifted me with my very own bow. The man who I had grown to love.

"Yeah, one of the passageways we didn't take leads to the castle," Cade said. "I found it when I was looking for you."

How long had he searched for me?

"There will be time for a reunion later," Beckett snapped. Then, he stepped forward until his chest was inches from my back, and I was practically sandwiched between the two men.

"When can you show us this entrance?" Beckett asked Cade, over the top my head. From this angle, with that scowl so deeply entwined with his expression and the white scars sliced across his face like a lightning bolt, he looked so menacing. And I knew exactly what he was capable of.

Cade didn't back down, though, didn't flinch from the sheer dominance rolling off Beckett. He met his malice-filled stare with one of his own. "The Academy has released students for the summer. I'm only here to follow them," he said, pointing at Grethe and Ryana again.

Beckett growled as if his patience was wearing thin.

"I can show you now," Cade conceded. Then his eyes dipped down to me. Still the stunning shade of sapphire with those impossible, otherworldly purple flecks. His expression wasn't left up to interpretation, the way Beckett's so frequently was. I could read the adoration in his eyes as easily as if the thoughts were words on a page. "Meet me at the edge of the lake, outside of the walls, next to the tree with three trunks."

"Vissorri, Alcides," Beckett snapped. "When night falls, you will meet Cade at this location and determine if the passageway is safe."

Cade tilted his head at the exchange but thankfully didn't ask about it or why our friend's last names were suddenly different than the Biltons Academy roll call. "We can enter the academy now. It wouldn't be suspicious since Ryana is going to be house leader and Grethe is expected to still be in the dorms for heir trials." Clearly, he had been keeping up with my friends.

Beckett's iron-clad eyes arced to Grethe and Ryana. "I need to have a word with my subordinates. They can meet you after that."

"Right," Cade said, still confused about what exactly was happening. Not that I could tell him, but I was grateful he was choosing to help regardless. "See you in the dining hall," he said to Ryana and Grethe before turning his attention back to me.

Firm hands gripped my shoulders as Cade pulled me into an embrace. "I'm so glad that you're okay." With his palm cradling the base of my skull, he placed the softest of kisses to my forehead, then briskly left the room before Beckett could set him alight with sight alone.

Rage crackled off Beckett's form, and everyone in the room remained utterly still while he attempted to regain his composure. Or at least I thought that was his intent.

"How could you both be so careless?" Beckett's question didn't hold the aggression I sensed across the bond, but his tone was icily lethal and every bit as serious.

Ryana's mouth popped open. "What are you talking about?"

Grethe's smile faded into a frown.

A scarred golden brow lifted on Beckett's forehead. "You were being followed, and you didn't know. Do we need to reassess if the two of you can be on missions together in the future?"

Ryana stuttered, practically tripping over her words. "I..." She looked to Grethe for backup.

"We should have ensured that we weren't followed," Grethe supplied, standing up straight and folding his hands behind his back. "Our mission was primarily to gather intel, which we did. But," he added, under Beckett's ruthless stare, "we shouldn't have let our guard down just because the students were gone."

Grethe laid a hand on Ryana's shoulder. Judging by the way her mouth was pressed into a flat line, I gathered that these types of interactions between them were atypical.

Beckett slumped backwards into a chair, looking overall exhausted and overrun. He settled his face into his hands. "Just don't let it happen again."

Grethe nodded. "Yes, sir."

"You're dismissed," Beckett added, looking over at the pair. "Do another sweep of the academy and ensure it is safe for us to enter. Come back and we will discuss finalization of the plans before I meet with the rest of the network."

"Yes, sir," Ryana said. The pair of them offered him a dip of their chins in unison before they scurried from the room with their tails practically tucked between their legs. The door closed, and once again, I found myself alone in a brothel with Beckett.

After what felt like hours, but might have been minutes, I ended our terse silence with a question. "Can we order food here or just sex?"

Tension unfurled from Beckett's body in the same way the atmosphere changed before a lightning strike. He dutifully paced the far side of the room like it was his sole purpose in life, blatantly ignoring my question.

Clearing my throat and raising my voice again, I said, "I asked if you'd like to order food."

Without answering me, Beckett scowled and snatched a piece of parchment from the dresser, tossing it over to me with a huff. The problem with his decision was that flat paper wasn't so easily tossed, so the menu awkwardly fluttered in the space halfway between us before unceremoniously landing on the carpet.

It took everything in me to squash the smile trying to bend my lips as I walked over to retrieve it. Plucking it from the floor, I browsed the options, grimacing when I realized that every offering was sensual in nature.

Chocolate dipped strawberries, a fruit and cheese platter, mini cakes, a bowl of whipped cream—an order which could be requested in several sizes—and, of course, Champelle.

Handing the menu back to him, I sighed. "Does any of this sound good or safe to you?"

Beckett only stepped close enough to grab the parchment with his thumb and forefinger before retreating to his self-appointed corner of the room. His eyes scanned the parchment like it was an important missive. "Order whatever you want."

"You need to eat, too." Neither of us had consumed much more than the meager portions we had carried with us from The Barker Inn. Personally, I was starving.

"I'll just have some of whatever you order," he told me as he handed me the menu and found a seat in the wooden chair, a bit closer to where I was standing.

A forced honeyed smile curled my lips. "Do you want some Champelle?"

I watched his face as he failed to flatten a smirk. His eyebrow lifted as he stared at me conspiratorially. "Do you?"

It was rhetorical, but it didn't stop me from imagining a scenario where I did order it and we both drank it and... My cheeks flamed as I realized that he was still observing me, and I averted my gaze back to the parchment, carefully reading the instructions on how to order.

With the tiny lantern lit outside of our room, I returned to lean against the bed while I waited for the magenta-haired hostess to return. She entered the suite within what felt like moments in a flurry of lace and pink hair.

Her excitement was doused when I deigned to only order the fruit and cheese platter and a single serving of the mini cakes. She returned with a tray only a few minutes later, and it made me wonder if she typically acted as a servant to the rooms she managed here or if we were a special case.

She deposited the tray on the dresser, relit some of the candles in the room with a flick of her wrist and left without another word.

Beckett stood from his chair, stalked across the floor to the platter, grabbed a mini cake, and made his way to the bed. He popped the cake between his lips as he hoisted himself upon the enormous mattress, then he lay his head against the pile of velvet pillows and closed his eyes.

He stayed there, still, as if he was so unbothered and serene that he planned to take a nap. At least that was the impression I got on the outside. Our connection gave me a front row seat to his true emotions; some mix of unease and a simmering hint of rage that still lingered from gods knew what.

A long exhale blew from my nose as I collected some of the cheese and fruit on a plate, carrying my bounty to the table beside the bed. With much less grace than Beckett had exuded, I pulled myself onto the mattress to join him.

His eyes didn't even flutter like they might if he were trying not to look at me. It seemed more likely that he was choosing to ignore me, and I kind of hated that. Telling myself that the tension was bad for the mission, I trudged forward. "Do you want to talk to me about what's going on?"

One eye cracked open. "Nope," he said, but he did open the other eye and sit up a bit straighter, even if it was only to separate us further.

Plopping a grape between my lips, I gave him a skeptical look. "Are you going to talk to me at all, or are you just going to sit there brooding?"

He sniffed a laugh. "What do you want to talk about?"

My lips pressed together as I blew a raspberry with my mouth, the sound comically equine. "I'd like to talk about whatever it was that I did to make you so angry with me." He had rejected me and then treated me like a leper this entire trip. Yes, I had instigated a lot of our bickering, but as far as I knew, I was the only one with the right to be hurt and angry.

The scowl I had expected to find on Beckett's face wasn't there. Instead, it was replaced by a shockingly apologetic expression. "I'm sorry, Ashton. I haven't been fair to you or your feelings."

I worked my lower lip between my teeth. "That's not really an answer, though."

"No, it's not," he replied, and the silence between us was heavy with words unspoken and questions I feared were fated to be left unanswered forever.

Huffing a frustrated breath, I plucked a piece of cheese from my plate, practically tossing it into my mouth. My teeth chewed roughly in an attempt to expel some of this negative energy from my body. Swallowing, I let my attention fall back to my husband. "Does this have anything to do with Cade?" Granted, our spat started well before Cade walked in, but something had escalated his emotions to the point that he was struggling to block them from me. It had taken a while, but I had noticed that in times of extreme stress or a heavy dose of his feelings, he was unable to bar me completely. I wondered if he realized this too.

Cool grey eyes sliced over to me but were quickly blocked by the heavy curtain of his eyelids. Slowly, his chest expanded as he drew in a deep breath through his nose. "I'm not like you."

"Capable of feeling emotion other than irritation or amusement?"

His eyes found mine again, and there was something so hopeless there. "Good."

My head tilted to the side in confusion. "What makes you think that you aren't good? You're..." I searched for the right words. "You're frustrating at times, but you have done more to help me since coming to the Light Kingdom than anyone else. Skylar told me what you did for her. Even Gabriella was singing your praises."

I dropped my tone until I was close to whispering. "You've been my only friend for months and..." I couldn't finish that sentence.

He grunted his response.

Realizing I was getting nowhere with that, I homed in on my original question. "What does that have to do with Cade?" I pressed, crossing my arms and abandoning my plate of food.

A grumbling sigh left his lips. "He makes me want to punch him."

My mirthless laugh was breathy. "Well, we've all been there, but it only really makes sense for me. We have a history. For you..." My gaze roamed over Beckett's face. "You didn't even know him until today. Is this because he dumped me five months ago?"

"Because he had you," Beckett snapped, and then his jaw clamped shut as his eyes widened in surprise.

My lips formed an o as I struggled to regain my senses. "What?"

"Nothing," Beckett forced through his clenched teeth. "I just —"

Pulling up on my knees in the bed, I stared down at where his head rested against the pillows, a small fan of golden waves spread around him like a halo. "You don't even want me," I replied in a whisper. "Why do you care that someone else used to?"

Beckett's nostrils flared. "He still does." Before I registered the movement, Beckett was on his knees as well, towering over me.

My head tilted back, and if I could have focused on anything other than his words, I might have seen the humor in our stances. Facing off on our knees on a silk-covered mattress in a brothel. "Why does that matter to you?"

His irises had taken on the sheen of the moon, bright and open, and for a sliver of time, I thought I was finally going to get the truth from him. My heart pounded with the anticipation of it all.

Before I could get anything resembling a response, the door blew open, and the hostess entered, panting. "You have guests," she stated, gathering her breath. "I was only aware of one visitation time."

Springing from the mattress, I practically threw myself off the bed.

Beckett, having done the same, was already sauntering over to the door. "Thank you, Isla," he said in a tone that spoke of calmness and indifference. "Please permit them to the suite."

She swept from the room, and Beckett's stare remained pinned to the doorway. When it opened again, three figures emerged.

Ryana and Grethe, I had expected to see again. The person I had not been anticipating was Katarina Evans. This was certainly a day for surprises.

She threw herself at Beckett, wrapping her arms around his shoulders and practically jumping into his chest. "It is so good to see you, Astor!" she said in a tone that I had never heard her use before.

My stare jumped to Ryana, confusion furrowing my brows, but she only traced her eyes over to the distance between me and the now rumpled bedding.

Heat flushed my cheeks, but my embarrassment was abandoned quickly because in that moment, I caught Katarina smiling up at Beckett as she rested her hands on his forearms. "Excuse me?" I asked, nodding my head toward our former House Lynx leader.

Katarina finally pried herself from Beckett's body so that she could face me. The blue tip of her ponytail flicked over her shoulder with the movement, and a smile rounded her cheeks. "I wondered if I'd see you again."

My subtle blinks were the only thing keeping my fire magic firmly locked down inside my body as I offered her a honeyed smile in return, tilting my head toward Beckett. Katarina Evans had surprised me as an instructor and a mentor during my time at Biltons Academy, but none of that fondness could take away from the irrational irritation I felt at seeing yet another woman's hands pawing all over Beckett's body in front of me.

Something snapped inside me, forcing me to forget the intent behind everything we had agreed upon. "Hi Katarina. Good to see you. I see you already know my husband."

Grethe coughed to cover up his burst of laughter, mumbling "Oh, shit," under his breath.

Katarina turned to Beckett, and instead of pouting or doing any number of things I imagined her doing, her face broke out in an even wider grin than the one she had already been sporting. "That's great, Beckett! Ashton was my favorite student. I'm not surprised in the slightest that you two hit it off."

I gaped at her, maybe a little at them, catching the fact that Beckett's shoulders were shaking with laughter.

My nose wrinkled. "I didn't think you liked any of us."

With a shrug, Katarina's expression turned repentant. "Yeah, sorry about that. Ryana let us know that you were someone we needed to watch out for, but I couldn't play favorites. You already had enough on your plate."

Ryana elbowed me, startling me because I hadn't realized she had been standing that close to me. "She was mean to me, too, if it makes you feel any better."

There were a million questions circling my mind, but none of them would come out.

"She's been part of the Fae team for a decade or so now," Grethe said, and thank the gods for him. "But those of us at Biltons can't leave so..."

So, she hadn't been with the others when they were summoned to Castle Falkland.

"Beckett trained me himself," Katarina said with another beaming smile that I couldn't believe she had suppressed all those months at the academy.

My stomach soured at the thought of him training her the way he had trained me. Hands on her body, guiding her into new positions, bending her to his will. It made the hair on the back of my neck stand up.

"Not like that, Ashton," Beckett said, his tone soothing.

My gaze snapped to him, where he had taken a long step away from Katarina as if trying to placate... whatever it was I was feeling. Clearly those emotions had filtered across the bond unintentionally and I gritted my teeth as I shored up my mental defenses.

"You're not married!" Katarina exclaimed. "You're bonded!"

Beside me, Ryana rolled her eyes. "I've been trying to tell her there is a difference."

Beckett raked his fingers through his hair. "Yeah, we are." I caught the slight tint of a blush along his cheeks, and I wanted desperately to know the thought that accompanied it.

Katarina held her hand to her chest. "Well then I suppose I owe you additional apologies for the way I treated you since you're a princess now."

"Always has been," Beckett said, playfully. His smile was surprisingly directed at me, and I couldn't dampen my grin in time to shield it from him.

"Got any update for us Kat?" Beckett asked after finally ripping his gaze from mine.

Katarina sighed. "Nothing on the front of the captive but I do have an update that I think might be related to whatever the Betrayers are up to."

Beckett motioned for her to go ahead, and Katarina chose to plop into the nearest seat, a settee covered in rich crimson velvet. He followed her and I tried not to bristle at their proximity. She was harmless, and I knew I was being the unreasonable one here. I didn't even fully understand the origin of the emotions myself.

Katarina blew out another anxious breath before she began. "At first, I thought it was just one person acting alone, but students have been injured at a much higher rate than previous years. A fact that the academy had vehemently tried to cover up."

"I thought it was about the heir games," Katarina continued, "but now, I think it might have been more."

"Explain," Beckett said. A bit commanding, but still gentle. Respectful.

Katarina lifted her chin, a slight smile curling her lips. "Because I am —was—a house leader, I had access to some of the faculty areas, which I may or may not have utilized. During one of my self-appointed reconnaissance missions, I discovered missives to certain instructors asking them to pay special attention to students with more promise."

"We knew that," Ryana stated, almost defensively. I supposed this meant that they hadn't been sharing information during their time in Biltons Academy either. Interesting.

"Right," Katarina agreed, offering Ryana a sideways glance, "but they specifically asked that the instructors take note of their jewelry."

My eyes fell to my mother's ring. The one I never wore while at the academy, with the rare exceptions of our days off and the ball. Surely this couldn't have been what they were looking for.

"Any idea what intel they acquired through their observations?" Beckett's shoulders tensed as he questioned Katarina, and I could have sworn I saw his gaze flicker to my hand as well.

Katarina's shoulders slumped. "That, I couldn't locate. I assume it is with Headmaster Dracorris. It was his handwriting I saw on the missives."

Beckett swiveled his head to Ryana. "It will be up to you to determine that if the mission is still ongoing next year. Unless Alcides can get in before that." Next year. Because Ryana would be sent back to Biltons Academy to continue to uncover whatever was going on in Demetros, and I would be... dead? Magically divorced?

Grethe stood at attention, his arms rigid by his sides. "They have those of us who wanted to return home for a break reporting back for heir trials in a week. I'll see what I can uncover when I return."

"Good," Beckett replied. "Anything else?"

Katarina shook her head while Grethe remained utterly still, but

Ryana stepped forward. "Actually, yes." Her gaze slid to mine. "Cade wants to talk to you."

Another growl sounded from where Beckett was standing, whatever amusement we had shared was reduced to ash as he practically snarled. "He is permitted to say whatever it is he has to say in front of me."

Ryana had the good sense to look abashed. "He requested a moment to talk with her *alone*."

Surprising all of us, Beckett shifted his focus to my gaze, as if he were deferring the permission to me. Shocked, I just nodded numbly. It was much harder to hate Cade up close, and I genuinely wanted to hear what he had to say, if for no other reason than maybe it would bring me some closure.

With that, Beckett's attention shifted back to Ryana. "She can't leave the brothel."

"We are aware," Ryana stated. "And before you tell us no, I want to say that I trust him. We vetted him the moment he showed an interest in Ashton and based on what he did for her in the second challenge, she is safe alone with him."

Beckett raised a singular golden eyebrow in my direction.

"He saved me," I muttered. "Another student was trying to kill me, and he saved my life." Beckett should already know this, but it warranted repeating.

"Fucking Berit," Katarina mumbled under her breath.

Beckett's jaw flexed. "Then I will grant him this one favor."

"If that's decided," Ryana said cautiously, "he has rented a room this evening so that they may have a private conversation. She can meet him while you are at the meeting with the network, so that we know she also has backup should anyone come here for her. And before you ask, Isla is already monitoring all routes of egress."

When I turned to Beckett, he was an amalgamation of tension and irritation. Divots formed between his brows, which only loosened as he sighed. "Fine."

I smiled with a gesture that I knew didn't reach my eyes. Anxiety was already rippling over my body in waves. "Great," I muttered, "What time do I meet him?"

If Beckett's jaw became any more tense, it was going to snap in half. I could practically hear the bone straining to remain intact as he looked down at me. "I don't think this is a good idea."

My chin lifted defiantly. "As the cadet under your supervision or your wife?"

In a flash, his glare subsided as some of the tension in his face slackened. "As your friend."

A snort I didn't even try to hold back barreled through my flared nostrils. "Is that what this is?"

As quick as a lightning strike, hurt flashed across his features, gone before I could really be sure I witnessed it at all. Returning his face to his carefully crafted mask of neutrality, he tilted his head toward the door. "Keep the bond open," he forced through his gritted teeth, "and return here the moment you are finished."

I didn't exactly love the idea of him feeling what I felt when I heard whatever Cade had to say, but I had to admit that I understood why it was important. Not only did Beckett have a vested interest in my survival, but he had the unique ability to keep tabs on my wellbeing while he was away. To sense danger in real time. Fine," I agreed, petulance oozing from me like a festering wound.

Beckett offered me his arm like he had so many times before, and on instinct alone, I took it, coiling our appendages together in a perfectly fitted stance. He pulled me from the room, leading me exactly six doors away before he knocked just above a painted bear.

My face scrunched as I considered how a bear might fit in with the theme of sensuality and fertility around here, when the door swung open.

Cade's indigo eyes traced the pursed ridges of my lips, and a frown sprouted where there had previously been a hopeful smile. "Are you okay, Ashton?" Then his gaze slid down to where my arm was still intertwined with Beckett's, his focus snapping back to my escort faster than a crack of a whip. "I wanted to talk to Ashton alone."

The men were almost equal in height, with Beckett having only a few inches on Cade, but they stared each other down as if each of them had half a foot on the other.

My fingers dug into the fabric of Beckett's tunic as his arm tensed like he wasn't going to let me go. "You promised," I hissed.

That seemed to snap Beckett out of whatever testosterone-filled showdown he was participating in, and he released my arm from his grasp, looking down at me once more. "I will be close. Remember your orders."

Orders? I might have bristled if I didn't think he was doing his best to say *leave open our magical connection put in place during our marriage ceremony*, without alerting Cade to the existence of such a thing. "Yes, General."

Beckett's nostrils flared, and his lethal stare returned to Cade as he stepped into his space, making the men chest to chest as their eyes locked in a silent battle once more. "If you hurt so much as a hair on her head, I will hunt you down, and I will peel the skin from your flesh and feed it to my pets for entertainment as I force you to watch. Do you understand?"

The hard lines of Cade's jaw didn't release, but something in his tone relaxed as he replied. "I would never hurt Ashton."

Beckett huffed a mirthless laugh. "That is simply not true. But I am not going to make this decision for her, so use your time wisely." With that, he casually stepped away from the doorframe, gesturing for me to enter.

The moment my boots crossed the threshold, I heard Beckett say, "I will be back in one hour." Then, with no further communication, the door shut behind me with a gentle click that did not align with the irritation assaulting me across our now fully open connection. In an attempt to ignore some of Beckett's emotions, I swallowed roughly, turning my attention to Cade, who had backed away to the center of the room to give me space to enter.

"Hi," I whispered.

Cade's palm worked along the back of his neck. "I'd offer you a seat but..." His eyes darted across his room to a bed, which was the only form of seating in this significantly smaller suite. Whatever the bear symbolized, it did not denote one of the more luxurious rooms.

"Standing is fine," I supplied, suddenly unsure what to do with my hands. Crossing my arms felt too aggressive, and standing there with them loosely by my sides was awkward. Were they always this heavy and long?

Cade took a step toward me, steadfast but gentle. His indigo eyes seemed to swell with adoration as he tilted his face down to me, his hand flexing by his side like he wanted to reach out to me but thought better of it. "How have you been?"

Some of the tension in my chest broke away at his question, so innocent and so very Cade-like that it was disarming. A small laugh huffed through my quarter smile. "It's been an adjustment. How have you been?"

Worried eyes scanned my face. "I've been missing you, Ashton. Where have you been?" At this his hands clasped my arms, and he dipped his chin, so we were closer to eye level. "Are they hurting you? Are you with them against your will?"

My chuckle shook his arms as my smile cracked wide open. "No, I'm here of my own volition."

A look of disbelief shadowed Cade's expression. He wasn't buying it. "If you need me to take you away from here, I will. Give me the word and I'll run with you."

My heart constricted, burning along the cracks where I had pieced it back together since I left all those months ago. But rather than asking him why he would suddenly be willing to leave his life behind now, I only shook my head. "I don't need to run away. I'm going to rescue my father."

With his hands still curved around my arms, Cade lifted a singular eyebrow. "With the magic you have now? What element are you?"

My molars clamped along the inside of my mouth, digging into the flesh there so I could give myself a few more seconds to think because what could I even tell him?

Cade pulled me closer to him, his breath warm against my face, his honeysuckle and salt scent overloading my senses. "That right there is why I'm worried. You look anxious about something. It's reminding me of..." He trailed off but we both knew what he meant. It reminded him of how I used to act around Berit, after the taunting had gotten out of control. When his threats had become more frequent.

I pushed away from his hold, stepping just out of reach. "It's nothing like that," I said beginning to pace the small space. "I have my magic now, that's all that matters."

He tried to catch my attention, but I wouldn't meet his stare. "What element then?"

Stopping in my tracks, I held out my upturned hand, letting flames fill the air above my palm.

"Incredible," Cade replied, but his gaze wasn't on the embers of my power, it was rooted squarely on my forearm. My decidedly bare forearm.

I hadn't given my lack of brand much thought, and neither had the rest of them. Everyone else knew how to illusion themselves or they always wore long sleeved tunics and tops. The only reason the place where my brand should be was even visible was because I had rolled my sleeves when I had gotten warm back in the suite with Beckett.

Quickly, I unrolled the sleeves, covering the empty patch of skin as if I could hide what I had already revealed.

"You don't have a brand," Cade said in a statement rather than a question. His gaze slid to mine. "But you have fire magic."

Blinking, I tried to find a way out of the hole I had inadvertently dug for myself. All the while, Cade seemed to grow more and more agitated.

In two swift strides, he crossed the small space to stand in front of me once more, grasping my face in his calloused palms. His voice dropped to a whisper. "Are you truly safe? Are they experimenting on you?"

Instead of jerking away, I placed my hands over his, pressing lightly to reassure him. "Cade, I am more than fine. I can't explain where I've been or how this is possible, but I am honestly okay."

"I can't risk that something is wrong, I'm taking you with me," he declared, dropping my face in favor of grabbing my hand. He was halfway to the door, dragging me behind him, when I said, "Stop!"

He froze and spun to face me, but he did not release my hand. "Magic works on proximity, so if we leave now, we will be far enough away by the time he realizes you're gone. Maybe whatever he's done to you will wear off or—"

"Stop," I said again, this time with more force. "I am exactly where I want to be. You're just going to have to trust me."

"You either have to tell me the truth, or you need to come with me. I don't feel right leaving you with these people after you've been missing for months." The expression on Cade's face was so serious, I knew he'd throw me over his shoulder and run with me if I refused.

It wasn't that I couldn't fight him off, it was that I didn't want to. For months, Cade had been my safe place, a haven of sorts in the chaos that was my time at Biltons Academy. If he was willing to risk having to go toe-to-toe with Beckett in order to protect me, didn't he deserve some portion of the truth? Wasn't it my own history, and therefore my own truth to give? I couldn't wrap my mind around the point of being a gods-damned princess, if I couldn't make some decisions for myself.

I pressed my hand to the space between us, carefully watching his face morph from concern to confusion. There was a part of me that wasn't even sure this would work, but I had learned enough about magic to know that intent was half of the equation. "If I tell you this information you have to swear to me that you won't tell another soul." Before he could answer I added, "Who doesn't already know." I didn't want to magically tie him into never being able to speak of this again.

Without an ounce of hesitation, Cade slid his palm against mine, squeezing against my hand when he was locked to place. "I swear I will not utter a single word of this to anyone who doesn't already know."

Not a single question spilled from his lips. In fact, all I felt from him the moment before the magic took hold was the unwavering loyalty in his stare.

A pulse of power washed over my skin, telling me that the deal had been struck and sealed.

Cade's eyes widened, astonishment parting his lips as he stared at our joined hands. "What was that?"

"Magic," I replied. "It's going to force you to keep your word."

In a daze, all he could manage was a single nod as he continued to stare at our joined hands.

Sensing that he would not do so on his own, I retracted my hand, gesturing toward the bed. "We better sit."

Unlike the piece of furniture in the jackalope suite, this bed was clearly only meant for two. However, it sat higher than I was used to, which made getting onto the mattress a bit awkward. The crimson silk coverlet was smooth under my palms as I swiped them over the fabric, getting into a comfortable position against the pillows before I slid my attention back to Cade who was waiting for my explanation on his side of the bed with bated breath.

Slowly, my lungs expanded before the air whooshed out in a long exhale. "There is another Kingdom."

His eyes widened but he didn't look to me like I was crazy. He looked at me like he trusted me. Like he was soaking in every word I had to say. Like he believed me.

After that, I focused on the highlights. The spell that kept our kingdoms separate. The brands that stole magic for unknown purposes. All the lies we had been told over the years of our basic education that were reinforced at Biltons and the other academies.

Per Beckett's instructions, I left out his true title, as well as our political union, but it felt so freeing to offload the rest of it to someone like me. Someone who had believed so many of the falsities that had been woven into every aspect of our lives in Demetros. My whole life I had been skeptical, but not skeptical enough.

"And you've only come back to rescue your dad?" Cade asked softly, clearly connecting the dots. Those kind indigo eyes drifted up to meet mine.

All I could do was nod.

"And Beckett is in charge of this mission?" He said it like he couldn't believe it.

"He is."

Moving slowly, Cade leaned forward, taking my hands in his and sighing a breath of relief as if he had been starved of my touch and this was his first morsel of food in weeks. "And you're truly okay? You're here because you want to be not as some sort of bait?"

There were many decisions that had been made for me, and significantly more that I had made for the betterment of others, but this was not one of them. "I am more than okay, and I am not bait. I promise I want to be here, and Beckett is the one who agreed to take me along even though I have many years less experience and training than the others."

There was a handful of seconds of silence, before Cade surmised, "Ryana and Grethe?"

Feeling like I was treading on other people's secrets, I squeezed my hands against Cade's. "That is past what I am comfortable talking to you about. I shouldn't have even told you what I did."

Cade seemed to mull that over in his mind before eventually dipping his chin in agreement, or at least acceptance.

"This can't be what you wanted to talk to me about," I pried, tilting my head to the side to catch his gaze.

He twisted his grip on my hand so that our fingers were laced together, our knees had moved during the conversation and were now tucked close enough to touch. Inside I was warring with myself on whether to feel safe in his presence or afraid. Not that I believed he would physically harm me, but the hint of the notion that he might still have the ability to break my heart was still present.

"Can I hug you?" His voice was barely a whisper, so full of emotion that I was forced to remember the man who had been so patient with me in the meadow. Who had commissioned me my very own bow when I showed interest in the weapon. The one who had saved my life.

"Of course," I replied.

He wrapped me in his arms almost instantly. The scent of honey-suckles and salt filled my lungs again as I took in a deep breath, only stilling when Cade's lips brushed against my forehead.

He backed away, releasing me in favor of folding his hands in his lap. "I'm sorry, I just missed you so damn much."

I couldn't decide if I wanted to be elated at the statement or irritated. He only missed me because he had broken my heart. Then again, had he not done so, I might not have met my mother. Or Beckett. I might not have my magic. It was entirely possible I would be fulfilling my ten years of servitude as we spoke. The thought was sobering. "Is that what you wanted to talk to me about?"

A small frown curved the edges of his mouth. "I don't even know how to tell you how sorry I am about the way our night ended at the ball. My shock kept me from being supportive and kind, and you deserved a better reaction than what I offered you."

They were the words I had wanted to hear for weeks after I first fled, so I listened rather than push him away. Curiosity kept my attention, but fragments of my lingering ire kept my heartrate thumping steadily in my chest.

Notches formed between Cade's furrowed brows. "I meant it when I told you that I loved you that night. I never stopped."

The violet flecks in his eyes seemed to pull his irises more purple as he looked to me, heart on his sleeve. "Up until this afternoon, there was a real possibility that I'd never see you again, and it's been eating me alive with regret. And I just..."

He reached for me again, and I let him take my hand in his. "I love you, Ashton, and I need you to know that I will not botch this second chance. If you can find it in your heart to forgive me?"

An apology was a start, a pathway back to the man I believed him to be, but something was still gnawing at me from some dark corner of my subconscious. Beckett's comments flashed in my mind, and I had to fight the urge to recoil from Cade's touch. "Because you determined I have power now, so I am not worthless to your parents?"

There was a touch of something icy in my tone that Cade immediately picked up on, his eyes widening with shock. "It does make it easier but that's—"

Ripping my hand from his, I waved it in the air between us, effectively cutting him off. "So, if I were still powerless, you would have what? Apologized for being callous but ultimately still sent me on my way?" I launched myself from the bed, putting more space between us.

Cade's mouth fell open, and he ran his hands through his dark strands. "Not necessarily," he said, panic lacing his tone as he slid off his side of the mattress. His stare never left mine. "I don't know?" The fact that he said it as a question was unsettling. "This just makes it all easier, doesn't it?"

A burning sensation climbed slowly and painfully up the column of my throat. His words, while meant to soothe, had only reopened an old wound. One I thought I had moved past.

My eyes narrowed on his grief-stricken face. "Why were you looking for me, Cade? When I ran, why did you even bother coming after me if you thought I had no magic?"

A sense of helplessness overtook his expression. "I just felt so bad. I —I knew that it was my fault that you ran, and I thought something might have happened to you. I just needed to see you. I love you."

The sigh that trickled from my lips was born of profound frustration rather than relief. "So, you didn't come after me to tell me that I didn't need to wield an element for us to be together?"

His face fell, a mirror to my own despondency. "I loved you," he whispered and then shook his head. "I *love* you," he clarified. "I just needed some time to think. It is a lot to expect me to change everything that I had been raised to be. There are familial expectations that I don't presume you would understand."

That cut deep. Deeper than I thought he meant to because his eyes surged wider with horror, but it was too late for him to take it back.

"Of course not," I deadpanned. "Why would I understand obligation and duty?" He had no idea how wrong he was.

Abruptly, I began to make my way to the door. A clock was absent in the room, so I had no way to know if an hour had passed, but I was well aware of how to find my way back to my own suite. I certainly had no interest in being here any longer.

Cade's hand formed a cuff around my wrist just before my hand grazed the knob. One final stand of intimacy, one last unspoken step in the fight to keep me here. It was too little, too late.

Even if he explained himself a thousand times over—even if he led me directly to my father—he hadn't wanted me at my lowest, and I couldn't fathom giving him my best after that.

"I loved you," I said, making sure to emphasize the past-tense nature of it all. "I just deserve more than someone who loves me with conditions."

"Please don't do this, Ashton. I love you. I never stopped loving you. We can make this work." His pleas were punctuated with two tears streaming down his cheeks, and a part of me wanted to swipe them from his face and pull him into an embrace so that he would feel better. After everything, I felt like I owed him a life's debt. But, owing someone wasn't the same as wanting someone. Obligation and love rarely existed in the same plane without resentment.

Prying my wrist from his grasp, I practically threw my hand around the knob, pausing just as I cracked open the door. Just as my own heart seemed to pull apart at the seams. "Thank you for your help today," I whispered, loud enough for him to hear. "I appreciate everything you've done for me, but..." My shoulders sagged as my gaze dropped to the floor. "This is goodbye."

There was finality in my tone, and I wanted him to hear it. Needed him to realize that I didn't plan to see him again.

This time when I left his room, he didn't make to follow me.

This time, I didn't even run.

Fifty-Eight

The hallway of the brothel seemed to blur together in streaks of crimson and pink dappled light as I made my way back to the suite I shared with Beckett. Every ounce of my body was praying to whatever god would listen that he hadn't returned because I couldn't bear the idea of facing him like this.

It wasn't exactly heartbreak; I hadn't been holding out any romantic notions that Cade and I would be together again. I hadn't even considered forgiving him until I saw him today. Not once had I contemplated a world where I'd give him another chance. But he had made me hope. He had made me think that I had been mistaken about his intentions, and being proven wrong about that for a second time almost hurt worse.

The pain I thought I had released, but obviously had just buried, dug itself from the grave, coming back to life with a vengeance. It fissured something in my chest, allowing a sob to work its way through my lips that came out as more of a choked gasp.

Blessedly I ran into no one in the halls, making it to our suite in a matter of a few shaky breaths. My hand twisted around the brass knob beneath the painted jackalope, and I allotted myself a single steadying inhale before I pushed my way inside.

Unfortunately, Beckett was already there, standing only a few feet away from me, dazedly staring at the entryway. He was frozen mid-step, like he had already been heading toward the door I just opened.

"You're back," I muttered, hoping that I had wiped away the tears along my cheeks efficiently enough to remove all traces of the pathetic emotions I was feeling.

His eyes were searching, slashes forming between his brows as he perused the lines of my face. The anguish melted from his expression when our eyes caught, and he closed the distance between us in two long steps.

"Are you okay?" he asked as he pressed me against his chest, his arms enveloping my body like a cocoon.

Words failed me as I stood there in utter disbelief, only brought out of my trance-like state when fingertips began to weave through the strands of my hair, almost as if... was he petting me?

"He isn't worth your tears," he whispered in a soothing tone. My heart constricted at the tenderness he was showing me. Then it stopped beating altogether as I realized with horror that I had kept our connection wide open. He had felt every bit of the emotions I had just experienced, and he was clearly more adept at reading them than I was deciphering his.

My cheeks heated as I sniffed back the remainder of my tears and all those dismal feelings of worthlessness, shimmying out of our embrace. "I'm fine," I said, patting down imaginary wrinkles in my pants.

Brick by brick, I stacked up that mental wall in my brain, until I was confident that I had constructed a thick enough barrier that my emotions weren't crashing against Beckett like a storm surge.

"You are not fine. I can feel you." Beckett's palm pressed against his heart in the same place my mother touched when she spoke of my father. "What happened?"

It had been ages since he had been so gentle with me. So careful. I loathed the pity I saw shining behind his stare.

"How did the meeting go?" I asked, abruptly shifting the subject.

What did he expect me to tell him? That the man who told me he loved me, still wouldn't take me without magic? That because the man before me didn't seem to want me either, I was left feeling like I was the undesirable one. It was too pitiful to put into words.

Beckett stepped toward me again, placing one hand tentatively on my shoulder. "I'm here if you need to talk. Or anything. We have a couple hours before we need to leave."

Fuck him for that because it was a lie. For months, he had been dancing along that platonic line only to practically ignore me when we stepped foot on Demetros soil again. "I don't want to talk to you."

He gave me a puzzled look, the silver of his scar flashing in the dim candlelight as his brows furrowed. "Are we not friends?"

Not even trying to hide the ire in my tone, I snapped. "Is that all we are?" I was reaching. Recklessly grasping for anything to hold onto.

He stepped toward me, lifting a hand as if to grab me. "Ashton."

Recoiling from his grasp, I tucked my arms over my chest. "No. Answer me clearly for once in your life. Is that all we are?" I could visibly see the moment that my hastily constructed mental wall crumbled again, and my emotions hit him with their full force. The want and lust and need I had been bottling up for months, rushing between us like a raging river.

Where I had expected to find smugness, or even irritated resignation, I only saw fear and that gave me enough confidence to take a single step toward him. Then another until my chest brushed up against his.

A flinch accompanied Beckett's sharp intake of breath as if our contact had burned him.

There was a fleeting moment when I really challenged what this was going to prove. Maybe he just felt sorry for me? Common sense demanded that I back away, knowing that only regret could come from pushing him like this. There was a reason he didn't express his feelings for me. Like Cade, there was a justification for why he didn't actually want me. But something instinctual took over, driving me forward.

"I just need to hear the truth." My cracked admission shuddered its way through my whisper. My eyes raised to meet his.

A flash of light glimmered over his stare, brightening his eyes like the moon over a still nighttime lake. But he didn't back away.

My fingertips raked over his chest, pushing up until they wound in the strands of hair at the nape of his neck. "What is this?"

His alarmed expression did nothing to deter me from my question as I stared up at him expectantly.

His features softened minutely. "You mean a lot to many people." Then his hands were hooked along the base of my spine, pulling me closer. It was a truth, but not the one I required.

"And to you?"

He closed his eyes as if he couldn't look at me while he spoke the words. "I cannot describe what you are to me in a way that you can understand. This is ineffable."

Using the leverage of my fingertips wound through his hair, I tugged gently against him, bringing his face to mine, never losing eye contact until the moment my lips pressed against his.

The muscles along his entire body went rigid, and just as he had done before, he gripped my upper arms, gently prying me away from him. He stared down at me with a strange intensity, eyes still shining like the brightest star in a midnight sky.

With disappointment already catching in my throat, I blinked up at him as if I could find an expression other than pity there. "I don't understand," I admitted softly. "It can be that other life for just one evening, right?"

His chest rose and fell in steady movements, and although he had extracted my mouth from his, he hadn't backed away, and I felt every one of his inhales and exhales in time with my own. Those quicksilver eyes scanned my face as the subtle sensation of his emotions began to unfurl across the bond like a dense fog casting its tendrils over a lake. There wasn't a chance I could pry them all apart or untangle one from the other, and his face mirrored those conflicted feelings.

"The bond is—" he began, but I cut him off, placing a fingertip against his lips.

"I don't care if this complicates the magic or makes the price higher to dissolve it. I just need..." It was on the tip of my tongue to say *you,* but I had supplicated myself enough for one night, and I could tell that he was steadfast in his decision to reject me yet again. Now, I had to undertake the monumental task of preparing myself for the mission we were here for, while I felt so completely dejected.

Beckett watched me as I began to pull away with a sort of calculated expression that made me wonder if he was figuring out the most diplomatic way to deal with my ridiculous advances. That expression only made me want to flee, although I couldn't if I wanted to be part of the team that rescued my dad.

Tears pricked along my eyes as I made to turn away, too exhausted to shield my emotions from him, but too ashamed to let him witness the full extent of my breakdown.

A hand cuffed around my wrist, stopping me in my tracks, then immediately yanking me back against his chest. "This is about the Ignus boy."

It wasn't a question, but I peered up at him and responded anyway. "It's not." Sure, I was a little bruised from our conversation, but what was happening between Beckett and I right now was more than a rebound.

His nostrils flared again as he soaked in my words. "You will regret this," he growled, the vibrations shaking me to my very core.

Me? Regret him? "Why?" The words came out like the softest sound of falling snow. Delicate and fragile.

"The bond is—"

"Stop talking about the bond," I snapped. "You either want me, or you don't." I certainly didn't want to hear about how being with me tonight might make it harder to leave me later.

His mouth clamped shut for the heartbeats it took him to steady his breaths again. "Wanting you has never been the issue." His mouth twisted as he tried to work around my request not to specifically mention our magical tether. "There will be consequences for this decision. Ones I'm not even sure you fully understand."

"Then just say no," I replied flatly.

Beckett's nostrils dilated once more. "Tell me to go."

The cruelty of those words nearly flayed me alive. "You don't want me, but you want me to command you to leave, General?" The last word was so acidic that it burned coming out.

I lost sight of that greyscale stare as his eyelids fluttered closed. "Because I can't fight this alone. You need to be strong for the both of us."

My hand slid over the stubble forming along his cheeks, and his eyes peeled open to look to me. "Answer me honestly," I demanded. "Do you want me, too? Have all these months been an act?"

A shuddering breath expelled through his nose, and his teeth ground together as if he were fighting against the response with everything in him. "I want you too. It is not an act."

That was all I needed to hear. Not the reasons we wouldn't work—we were already fucking married anyway—but the words that confirmed everything I felt wasn't all in my head.

"Ashton, I want more than your body. I want everything with you. But—"

I was done hearing his excuses after his admission. *I want everything with you* ricocheted around my mind as my mouth crashed against his, cutting off whatever he was about to say, knowing that his resolve was fraying.

This time, he didn't back away or tense, and as his lips slanted against mine, my universe condensed all the way down to a pair of silver eyes and the heat of his body.

Beckett's hands slid down my spine, holding me in place as his lips parted in time with my own. Savoring the moment, I let myself sink into the warmth of his touch and the smoky lust caressing me from his side of the bond.

Breaking the kiss only to reposition my hands to his chest, I pushed against him until the back of his knees hit the bed, and I kept shoving until his spine was flush with the mattress.

With trembling hands, I ripped my tunic over my head. I toed my boots off and then rolled my leggings down, taking my socks with them before kicking the garments to somewhere in the abyss of the room.

Beckett remained utterly still, watching me with a sort of astonished fascination as I reached for the laces of his trousers. A muffled grunt escaped his lips as I untied them with efficient speed and briskly freed his cock, slipping my hand around the shaft, delighted to find he was already this hard for me. So soft and warm and achingly stiff.

Had we been a different couple and if this had been a parallel reality, I might have climbed on top of him and kissed him for a few more hours, just to savor the feel of his body beneath mine. But, as it stood, we were not a couple—not really—and I didn't want to give him the opportunity to change his mind again.

With his hands clamped around my arms, Beckett tugged me over him. Our chests pressed together as if we could meld into one, and with his fingertips shoved through my tangled hair, he pulled me into another universe-altering kiss.

He was everywhere. Hips rocking into mine, hands roaming my body and suddenly it was too hot and there were too many layers and boundaries between us.

A sniff of a laugh rumbled over my lips as Beckett adjusted us so that we were both sitting upright, my knees still resting on either side of his hips like they belonged there. He slid me off him, and before I could consider that he was once again changing his mind, he began to strip. His eyes were molten silver as his gaze drifted to my underthings. "Take those off."

This was actually happening. The realization had me ripping the garments off my body in the least graceful way possible. I couldn't bring myself to care, not when the heat in his stare was so palpable. Those irises glowed like a crystallized kaleidoscope of the stars and galaxies that made up entire universes. All that desire and all that power focused on me. Utterly, devastatingly beautiful.

And that said nothing of his body. Thick muscular thighs gave way to a chiseled waist and hard lines stacked up in perfect angles to construct his broad chest and shoulders. And yet, the loveliest thing I saw was his expression. Pure unadulterated lust.

His jaw clenched and his body vibrated with energy, but he didn't immediately make to put his hands on me again. "Are you sure you want this?" His tone was approaching sterile. Clinical. Like this was just a transaction.

He shifted uncomfortably, almost as if he were afraid that I would be the one to change *my* mind. Nose in the air, I stared at him defiantly. "I want you, Beckett." The words were somehow half-shouted, half-whispered and all plea.

Beckett's fingertips flirted along the edge of my stomach, tracing a long and torturous line up the center of my body, between my breasts, and up my neck until they finally settled on my chin. The callouses on his hands scraped roughly against my jawline as he idly stroked along my cheek. His eyes never broke contact with mine. "I can be gentle."

A scoff rattled against my chest. "I'm not a virgin."

"Don't want to hear about that right now," Beckett murmured as his fingertips pulsed against my cheek. "But I will be nice for you, if it's what you want."

Reaching for his hardened length, I twisted my grip, stroking him not-so-gently between us.

The corner of his mouth lifted. "Say it, then. Tell me what you want."

Gods, he was really going to make me do this again. My palm squeezed roughly as I leaned forward so that our lips were only a whisper apart. "Stop playing games and fuck me."

<h1 style="text-align:center">Fifty-Nine</h1>

It was perhaps the least romantic way that I could have made my request, but when one of Beckett's hands slid into my hair and the other gripped me along my waist so that he could pull me back into him, I didn't have it in me to be ashamed.

He scooped me into his arms like I weighed nothing, bringing me back to the silk-clad mattress and laying me gently on its surface. I raised an eyebrow at him. "I thought I already explained, I don't need gentle."

A smirk was the only warning I had before those hands reached out again, pressing my legs apart so that he could dip between my thighs. Before I could utter a single gasp, his tongue slid the entire length of my center, swirling against my clit with the perfect amount of pressure.

That mouth was going to be the death of me. A guttural moan left my lips as my fingers fisted the silky sheets by my side.

Beckett's fingertips dug into my thighs as he held me against his mouth, lapping at me like I was a delicacy and turning me into a puddle of wanton need.

"More," I breathed out in a pant. "I want all of you."

His tongue made one more swirling motion before he extracted his head from my thighs and stood to his full height. His eyes blazed as he gazed down at me, gripping my legs to yank me to the edge of the bed.

The blunt tip of his cock swiped across my slit, collecting the evidence of my desire before pressing against my entrance.

I clenched around nothing as I bucked my hips in frustration. He was so close. "Beckett," I whispered. "Please."

That was all it took in the end. Not my explicit consent or my heady demand, but a vulnerable plea.

One powerful thrust later, and we were both groaning against the awareness of our combined bodies. His fingers bit into my hip, and he stilled there for a moment, as if I wasn't the only one who had to adjust to the feel of him inside my body.

"Are you okay?" The whisper was so soft that I almost didn't believe that it had come from him.

The breathy huff of a laugh that fell from my lips was full of genuine mirth. "Not a virgin," I countered, a little more flustered than I intended to sound. "But I would be better if you'd move."

A chuckle escaped his lips just as his hips began rolling again. At a torturous pace, he pulled all the way out of me before thrusting back in. Over and over. In slow, deliberate movements that left me moaning into the arm I had slung over my face.

Beckett arched over my body, gripping my arm to pin my wrist over my head. "Keep that there," he commanded before straightening himself again.

I obeyed, if for no other reason than I was too stunned and too blissed out to move. And that was before he shifted his thumb to that bundle of nerves at my center and started rubbing tight circles that had stars flashing behind my eyes. It might have been a whimper, but it felt more like a gentle sob that escaped my lips just before Beckett's free hand clamped over my mouth, and the force of his thrusts increased.

It shouldn't have been a shock after the way he had handled me in the pools, but I still found myself astonished at how quickly I was already barreling toward that cliff. And I desperately wanted to hold onto this moment for a bit longer. "Stop," I whispered against his palm.

Beckett stilled instantly, eyes wide with horror. He began to slide out of me, his hand already retracted from my mouth, when I gripped his hips. "No, I just need a minute. It's happening too fast."

Understanding flashed across those greyscale eyes, and his hands were on me again, slipping underneath my back to gain the leverage he needed to lift me into his hold. My legs locked around his hips, and my arms snaked around his neck as stood upright and moved us across the room.

With this new angle, I could see his expression more clearly. His eyes were the first light cast upon a brand-new world, bright and open and full of the possibility of everything.

When my back crashed against the nearest open wall, he resumed those ministrations, using his grip on my hips to drive me up and down along his shaft.

The angle was deeper now, and there was no reprieve and no tenderness as he used the leverage of the wall's flat surface to pin me in place, slamming into me with a renewed sense of urgency. All I could do in that position was hold on and spread my legs just a little wider so that I could take all of him.

He dipped his chin, taking the peak of one of my nipples into his mouth. He fastened his lips around it and sucked, swirling his tongue in circular movements that mimicked the way that he had teased my clit.

My hips rolled to meet his pace, my nails digging into his back.

Kisses trailed their way over the swell of my breast, across my chest, and then up the column of my throat, lingering there for a heartbeat as his teeth scraped along my skin.

When he pulled back to look at me, his expression was softer than I had ever seen it. Despite the sharp snap of his hips, the tenderness of his stare threatened to unravel me completely, in ways I wasn't sure I would ever recover from.

As if to disarm me entirely, he crashed his lips into mine without warning. It was rough and claiming. His tongue took possession of my mouth, and in this new position, with him sliding in and out of my body and his lips sealed against mine, I felt utterly conquered.

My teeth clamped around his plump lower lip as a particularly rough thrust caused me to bite down to muffle a scream. The coppery tang of his blood was surprisingly sweet as it danced along my tastebuds, and there was no room for me to be disgusted as his groan signaled us both plummeting over the edge.

"Fuck," he growled against my lips.

Although I couldn't be certain, given the intense waves of pleasure spasming along my core, I was pretty confident that it was my voice that I heard screaming as ecstasy climbed along my spine and radiated across my overheated skin.

Beckett caught the end of my scream with his mouth, kissing me until the aftershocks of my orgasm had slowed.

Only then did he pull away from me. Our chests heaved against each other; the tender peaks of my breasts ached with every inhale that scraped them up against his skin. And yet… I already wanted him again.

To my astonishment, he didn't place me on the ground, even when he slid himself from between my legs. He simply carried me to the attached bathing chamber, filling the grand copper bathtub in the center with the flick of his wrist.

Gingerly, he lowered me into the water, climbing in after me. Strong, muscled legs framed the outside of my thighs, and as I leaned backwards to relax against his chest, the evidence of his continued desire pressed against my lower spine.

We didn't acknowledge that, didn't even speak at all, as if both of us realized the moment we did, we'd have to go back to being whatever we were *before*.

So, without a word, Beckett gingerly wet my hair, and I didn't even ask what he was doing, my question answered as he shifted to grab one of the scented soaps from a nearby tray. His fingers massaged against my scalp, eliciting a different kind of moan from my lips as I tilted my head back to give him better access.

After my hair was thoroughly rinsed with the most precise use of water magic I had ever seen, he went to work on my body, lathering up a washcloth that he dragged across my skin in careful, calculated movements. Unlike at Castle Falkland, he didn't avoid any part of me. He ran the cloth over my chest, each breast, and down, lower, until he had pressed the material against my core, delicately cleaning my most intimate areas.

Then, with very little in the way of hesitation, he left my center and began washing my legs. Disappointment blossomed in my chest, but I remained in place, not wanting to shatter this fragile moment.

When he was done, he used the same cloth to wash his own body, or what parts of it he could reach, as I remained firmly pressed against his chest. My eyes fluttered closed as I focused on the steady beat of his heart against my back, until I was certain he had finished.

Shifting slightly, testing how far he'd let me go, I twisted until I was facing him. Then, slowly, as if he were a wild animal I might frighten, I adjusted myself until I was back in his lap, knees tucked in line with his hips.

When I met his stare again, his eyes were still a mimicry of twinkling constellations. And across our bond, I could feel everything. Arousal, longing, closeness, guilt, and even sadness. I didn't want him to feel either of the latter emotions, not here with me. Not when I had chosen this.

My lips pressed slowly, tentatively, against his. A soft reassurance that I was fine, and this was *more than fine.*

His arms wrapped around my waist. *Are you sure,* seemed to linger in the way he held me.

Despite the soreness between my legs, I ground against him in invitation.

He didn't ask me if I was certain this time, only moved his hands to my hips to guide me into place on top of him. But he didn't thrust in like he had before, he just waited for me to make the call.

Steadily, I sank back down his length, and when I fully bottomed out, he aligned our faces to bring our mouths back together.

This kiss did not have the burning urgency of the previously fiery need but instead held something more precious that I was afraid to name.

My rhythm was slower this time as I rocked against him in what felt like a ballad—a gentle farewell to what we could have been. My hands cupped his face as I deepened our kiss without rushing it. The pace never picked up, and I didn't want it to. Both of us were content with this leisurely connection, neither of us ready to call it over.

Before had been satisfying in a different, more carnal way. This was a balm to my shredded heart. Which was ironic because in the morning, we would likely go back to normal.

My fingers threaded themselves in the strands of his golden hair, pulling his face back to mine. I wanted him as close as he could be, and then even closer.

The thought of that was terrifying, and I broke our kiss. My gaze found his, and his expression mirrored my thoughts. Confusion. Concern. Fear. Adoration.

I didn't balk at the sight. Instead, I continued to rock slowly against him, eyes locked, as he gripped me tighter, almost as if he feared letting me go too.

"Kiss me," he whispered, but there was a pleading behind his stare that I had never witnessed before.

My face tipped forward, slanting my lips over his in an unhurried movement. His tongue slipped into my mouth, twinning together the last remaining pieces of our bodies together.

When we fell over the edge, we did so together. Moaning against each other's mouths. Grips tightening along hips and lips and skin and hair as our orgasms rolled through our bodies like an avalanche of warmth and contentment rather than crushing snow.

Even when the last of the tremors had passed, we remained there clutching each other as if the moment we let go, we would be forced to revert to nothing. It felt like turning the hands of time back, through the stars and galaxies it had taken us to get here. It was enough to make me want to cry, but I couldn't. Emotionally, I was utterly spent.

My face pressed against the crook between Beckett's shoulder and jaw as he rested his cheek against my head. He idly stroked my back as if we had nowhere else to be. But we did.

Gasping, I shot up, and before I could even ask, he shook his head. "We still have a few hours before we head out."

The anxiety in my chest was quelled, but a new wave of panic surfaced as I realized I had broken the moment.

With the flick of his wrist, the bathwater disappeared, leaving us dry and naked in the tub. Beckett stood, his arms still wrapped around me, as he carried me into the room.

The silk sheets were chilly on my overheated skin as he placed me into the bed.

I knew it was over, but I couldn't quite let go. Patting the spot next to me, I looked up at him expectantly. "Just a little longer."

There wasn't even a hint of confusion as he slipped into the bed beside me.

Rolling, I offered him my back, glancing at him over my shoulder. Another invitation. One he took.

Beckett's body pressed against mine for the umptieth time tonight, and I marveled at the way we just seemed to fit. Despite our height differences, his body molded to mine like it had always been part of it.

It made me want to abandon the theory that we were moths and flames. Whatever this was, whatever we were made from, it wasn't different species and elements, it was the same. Maybe it came from that other life, that alternate universe where we were allowed to just be, and bits of it were scattered about the cosmos so that those other iterations of ourselves had a better chance of finding one another.

As if sensing my thoughts, maybe even sharing them, Beckett squeezed me tighter. "Just a few more minutes," he whispered against the shell of my ear.

Leaning back, I tilted my head to face him. Wanting to see as much as I could before I lost this. Lost him. "I don't want this to end."

"I know," he replied, voice going soft.

He was already slipping from consciousness, so I didn't feel like he would even hear my words as I said, "I'll see you in another life then."

Sixty

"What the fuck did you do?" Ryana's voice thundered from somewhere near the foot of the bed.

A bed. My brow furrowed. Something warm and heavy was draped around my waist, and my cheek was resting against a pillow that was entirely too firm. My eyes flew open, recalling where I was and who I was with. Then, to my horror, the exact level of clothing I was wearing.

Luckily, at some point, Beckett had draped the coverlet over our bodies, but I still shot up in a distraught state, clutching the blanket to my chest. How could I have fallen asleep knowing we had been hours from going to find my father?

It took every bit of my energy to summon the mettle that was required to look Ryana in the eyes. Except, when I tried to meet her stare, her sharpened glare was firmly set on Beckett.

He promptly adjusted us, sitting fully upright and far more alert than I was. Considering how Ryana had found us, I half expected to find some smug satisfaction in his expression, or—more likely—indifference, but I was completely blown away to discover that all the blood had drained from his face. He was impossibly still and remained completely silent as Ryana continued their strange staring contest with rage simmering in her gaze.

"What the hell is happening in—WOAH," Grethe exclaimed as he clambered through the door with two cups of coffee in his hands. He came to a halt beside Ryana; wide green eyes locked on Beckett as well. At least he had enough sense to close the door this time, lest we attract more spectators to this event.

Ryana's eyebrows were bent in the middle in a way that I hadn't even seen during the Ice Games. "You promised the Queen you wouldn't do this," she said, only slightly quieter than her earlier outburst. Was that the reason he had rejected me before? My mother made him promise to leave me alone? This was difficult to align with the words she had told me when she had all but pushed me toward him.

Discovering more secrets being kept from me was enough to boil my blood. "Can you two please keep it down?" I snapped. "We don't need to alert everyone in a five-mile radius of our location."

Ryana ignored me as her glare strengthened in both intensity and contempt toward Beckett. "Do you know what you've done? This isn't some game!" She was getting louder again, and I winced at the volume.

Her finger pointed at me, the first acknowledgement that she had even seen me at all. "She is not some conquest at the Barker Inn. She is the Princess of the Light Kingdom! You swore to protect her!"

"Clearly, this is not a game for me either," Beckett ground out through his clenched teeth. The pain in his expression was unsettling.

My focus bounced between Beckett and our friends. "Would any of you like to explain why this is such a big deal?" My free hand flapped at the space between Beckett and me while the other kept the blanket clutched against my sternum. "We are married, and I highly doubt one time is going to make it that much harder to undo."

Finally, Ryana's heated gaze slid to me, and she scoffed. "You are not married. You are bonded."

"Semantics," I deadpanned. "We both chose to be here, and I wanted this. Truly."

She blew out a deep breath, all while holding the bridge of her nose between two fingers like she was fighting off a migraine. "This really should come from you, Becks." Her voice was softer now, almost sad.

There was something I was missing. Some bit of crucial information I hadn't been given. Turning to the man beside me in bed, my gaze trailed along the angles of his face, taking in the frown curving his lips. "Beckett?" My voice was stripped down to bare bones and a shredded heart.

When his eyes met mine, it almost took my breath. They were grey, not the glowing light of the moon or stars, but the kind of desolate shade of a still body of water beneath heavy cloud cover and endless gloomy rain. The kind of weather that embodies depression and regret.

He took a breath in, and somehow, I heard an apology in it before he even began. "A bonding isn't typically solidified until it is consummated."

My eyes flared. We had discussed that early on, but I didn't understand the magnitude of his choice, of consistently pushing me away, until I caught that look in his eye. The one that told me we had just made a monumental decision, and I hadn't been fully aware of the consequences. "It only takes once?" I squeaked out.

He closed his eyes, seemingly composing himself for the rest. "Not always... not usually."

"So, it is more difficult to reverse now?" I asked cautiously. "Will it just take more from us?"

There was a desolation in Beckett's eyes as they roamed over my face. "We thought the bonding would save you but be easier to reverse if we hadn't gone any farther."

Nothing about what he was saying was new, but his tone told me I was still missing some important aspect of this. "Beckett..." I said tentatively, ignoring everyone else in the room with us. "What's going on?"

He shuddered a shaky exhale. "It would have been more difficult to reverse under normal circumstances." He paused momentarily, but he didn't wait for me to press to continue. "Now, it might be impossible." He flinched as if each word he uttered physically harmed him.

"What?" I breathed. Turning to Ryana for any form of clarification was fruitless because her stare, and Grethe's, were firmly planted on Beckett. Their glares had shifted to something closer to pity.

"I was told it could be undone at a price," I said to Ryana, who finally tilted her face to mine. "How is it no longer possible? What aren't you telling me?"

Even Grethe looked solemn in a way that told me that this was bad. Whatever he had felt in Ryana's emotions had alerted him to the grave nature of what was happening, even if she couldn't speak. That scared me.

Ryana shot Beckett a disapproving look and sighed. "It can't be undone because your bond has solidified in an unusual way." Her head shook with disapproval. "You guys are practically glowing."

Beckett shifted uncomfortably beside me, and it brought my attention back to him. There was a certain helplessness in his eyes that made him look younger, and I could almost imagine him as a sullen teenager.

I tilted my head. "Because we had sex once?"

He just blinked at me. Blink. Silence. Blink.

"Twice? I had two orgasms, and I made this permanent?" Exasperation swelled in my voice.

Not even Grethe snickered at the comment.

"That is not the problem," Ryana said. She was still rooted to the spot that she had started in. Her gaze swept back to Beckett, and then so did mine. He was staring at an errant spot on the exposed portion of the wooden floor with his head slumped.

When he finally looked over at me through his heavy lashes, guilt flooded the bond.

Guilt.

My stomach clenched.

His eyes were swimming in regret, and I hated that perhaps more than still being in the dark about whatever was happening.

"Please," I urged him. "I deserve to know."

He spoke so low that I almost couldn't make out his words. "Because our bond is a mate bond."

"What?" The bones in my neck cracked as my head whipped in Ryana's direction. "I was told there was no mate bond. That you would have sensed it!" It was my turn to yell then, with no regard for who might be standing beyond the closed door.

There was enough guilt to go around because Ryana had the good sense to look as despondent as Beckett had. "I had only been around Anastasia and Christian's solidified bond. I didn't know what it felt like or looked like before they grew closer or even before consummation."

She swallowed, almost like she was fighting back tears and that alone was enough to dampen my ire, even if it didn't relinquish her from the entirety of my misplaced anger. "The connection between you and Beckett has always been strong, but..." Her voice trailed off, and Grethe put his arm around her shoulders, looking wild-eyed and terrified.

"It's so rare," Grethe said softly. "None of us would have considered that it would have a different energy signature."

Ryana took a singular step toward the bed. "It's similar but it doesn't look like theirs. It's almost as if it still isn't fully in place. Like the threads are bright but frayed."

"You said it was solidified," I stated flatly.

She winced. "The ceremony bond is, yes. The other one... it's odd. I can't figure out why." Her eyes darted to Beckett. "You feel it too?"

His chin dipped once but he didn't speak.

"If the... other one," I said, unable to force out the words *mate*, "if it is not solidified, then it can be undone?"

Ryana's brow scrunched. "I don't know. The fact that I can even sense it makes me think... no. But we don't know enough about it. Anastasia has always been hesitant to ask for any extensive research on the topic." She didn't have to clarify why. Anyone knowing about the mate bond put my parents in immense danger.

When my eyes eventually trailed over to Beckett, he appeared to be in absolute agony. "I'm sorry," I heard myself say in a meek tone. "You didn't sign up for this."

He dropped his head into his hands and muttered, "Neither did you."

The room was silent for some time while we all processed the new information. After seconds, or maybe even minutes, Grethe cleared his throat. "We came early to bring you this," he said, holding out a pile of clothing that must have been tucked under his arm when he came in. I had no clue where he had abandoned the coffee. "Now I'm thinking we should have at least knocked."

"It's leather gear for tonight," Ryana muttered as Grethe placed the garments on the dresser, ignoring his statement. "If you're still coming."

My heart clenched in my chest. My mother hadn't come to Demetros for fear of the Guides realizing who my father was to her and utilizing that in a game of chance. Murdering him to see if the departure of his soul would drag the Light Queen with him. Now, I had a mate too.

"We will let you two discuss that, preferably while you get dressed," Grethe added, as he practically dragged Ryana through the door, slamming it behind him.

With the coverlet still clutched against my chest, I swiveled my focus to Beckett. "I... I didn't mean to trap you." My face fell against my free hand. "Gods, I'm so sorry, Beckett."

There wasn't much I—or apparently anyone—knew about the mating bonds, but I had learned enough about Beckett to figure that being staked to one woman for his entire life was not in his long-term plans. Guilt and regret pulsed like a second heartbeat in my chest.

"I knew." Beckett's whisper came out like a sigh.

Rapid blinks cleared my thoughts, but not enough to comprehend his statement fully. "What?"

His contrition was tangy and bitter across the bond. He turned to me so he could look me in the eyes. So that he could face this head-on. "I wasn't sure, but I did sense that we might be something more."

"When?" I demanded.

His focus dropped to an errant spot on the floor, far away from me. "I meant what I said, from the moment we met there was something special about you."

I shook my head. "That can't be it."

"No," he admitted. "I suppose I began to consider it a true possibility during the carriage ride to Castle Falkland."

That had been so early in our bond that I couldn't fathom how he had kept it from me for so long.

My jaw dropped, and his focus snagged briefly on my mouth before sliding back to meet my stare yet again. "When you used your magic to douse me in ice water and I wasn't able to use my magic to counteract it."

"What does that have to do with this bond?" I still couldn't bring myself to say it by name.

"I was so angry with you and my magic wouldn't let me counteract yours. Mates can't harm each other."

I couldn't recall if my mother had ever shared that detail with me. "I've been able to use magic against you when we spar," I countered.

"Yes, but you weren't angry with me." He sighed, heavy and drawn out. "Also… when we were apart for those few days, I…" he sighed. "It was uncomfortable. I thought if we didn't consummate, that we could stave off those particular side effects."

Racking my brain to recall what he was talking about, the memory of that night in the tub surfaced almost instantly. We had been separated for more days than we ever had been before. Then, he had returned home to find me bathing on his balcony. I had been irritated the whole time he had been away, testy in a way that was uncharacteristic for me. Was that the same as separation sickness my parents had been suffering from?

"So, you rejected my advances." My words came out flat. "Instead of just telling me. Or the Queen?"

He released a long-winded, anxious breath. "Yes. And I promised Anastasia I'd take care of you. She asked me not to do anything to jeopardize your future unless we were sure we wanted to be bonded for life."

My eyes widened in shock as I stood from the bed, the blanket still clutched in my hand.

Beckett shook his head. "She didn't know. She trusted Ryana's assessment."

My exhale contained the heaviness of my relief. "Then what changed? Why didn't you tell me? You didn't give me a choice."

He flinched at that. "Ashton," he breathed. "I can't give you a good excuse for that. I was hoping that I could stop it from solidifying by just staying away from you."

The stubble of his chin dropped against his chest, lowering his head in defeat. "I could feel you with Cade, across the bond. The despair. The anguish. The heartbreak, even. It was agony for me to feel you in so much pain, and I don't know how to explain it except I had to fix it."

"What?" I gasped.

His gaze moved to me again. "When you walked in, and I saw the look on your face... I couldn't deny what you begged of me. It was instinct."

My scoff was somewhere between dumbfounded and mortified. "What I begged for?" I asked. "You... you didn't want this? You just felt bad for me?" The beginnings of tears welled up along my lashes again, and I couldn't blink fast enough to force them away. Yes, I had been aware it was a possibility before, but what we had just shared hadn't felt fabricated or born from obligation. It felt so real.

Beckett's hands came out to grab my upper arms, forcing my eyes to lock with his again. "No," he rushed to say. "I want you. I've always wanted you."

He shook his head, but he didn't let me go or break our eye contact. "I should have been strong enough to stop it. I should have tried harder to explain what it meant. I just... couldn't."

Tried harder? A memory flashed through my mind, hazy and lust-filled, but... yes, he had mentioned the bond. "I stopped you from telling me," I said, a statement blending with the question in my tone.

His chin dipped again to snag my focus. "It is not your fault. You didn't know. I did."

My brain scrambled to grasp onto and file away the nuggets of information he was giving me, trying and failing to decipher all their meanings. "I want to discuss this further," I muttered. "But right now, I need to focus on my dad and getting him the hell out of that dungeon."

"Of course," Beckett replied. "We will talk when we are all safely back in Lochmere."

"Can I even join you now?" There was a desperation in my tone. Everything I had worked for, all the way back to accepting the bargain with the anonymous donor, had been to save my dad.

"You go where I go," he said firmly.

When my puzzled stare met his, he clarified. "That shouldn't be a concern if our mate bond isn't solidified. The other one could still save you."

It was with terrifying realization that I considered that the one thing that could save me from dying while breaking the spell, now could kill us both if he was wrong about the way the mate bond worked. If it was true and the lack of a fully formed tether would stave off that particular side effect, then it meant we couldn't risk getting any closer if we had any hope of making it out alive.

Sixty-One

It was the cusp of morning when the four of us emerged from the brothel. Ryana and Grethe had waited for us, but Cade had already gone back to the academy sometime in the night, and I was secretly grateful that I wouldn't have to face him too.

"They fit then?" Ryana asked, as she gestured to my attire.

"A perfect fit," I replied, somewhat monotone. To that, she said nothing more and we walked down the empty cobblestone streets in silence.

Beckett and I followed Ryana and Grethe through the thick shadows of the nearby buildings until we reached the outer wall of the academy in an area of the town I hadn't seen before. At this part of the perimeter wall, a miniature forest wrapped around the stone-clad structure, almost enveloping it in a crescent-shaped hug.

Ryana and Grethe continued to wordlessly shepherd us through the underbrush and limbs, pushing through the increasingly dense woodland until we reached an oddly placed, but overall unassuming rock. It was about the size of a horse, which in and of itself wasn't especially suspicious given our proximity to the mountains that circled the capital city. But its location deep within the forest was notable. Probably made here, or at least deposited in this spot, with Saxum gifts.

Ryana walked up to the boulder, stepped around it, and then promptly disappeared.

I quickened my pace to follow her trajectory, and when I rounded the formation, I noticed an opening of sorts in the ground beside the rock, covered only haphazardly with thick ivy vines.

Grethe nudged me forward. "Go on then," he prodded.

Dropping into the hole, I discovered the solid shelves of makeshift stairs that had been carved into the ground. This was unmistakably man-made.

Beckett followed behind me, and Grethe made up the tail as he shifted the vegetation around the opening to conceal it once more. We each produced our own small orb of fire and proceeded in the only direction that the narrow tunnel provided.

The roughhewn rock passageway was damp, and places along the wall appeared to have been dug out by hand, or small tools, rather than earth magic. All around us, I could see the evidence of what had once been a root system, likely for the forest above. Now, it was a hacked-away jumble of long-dead snaking vines.

Before long, the underground tunnel transformed into a set of mud-caked steps which Ryana, still leading the group, took without hesitation. We emerged once more into air that was fresh and crisp enough that I gathered it in my lungs in a deep inhale before taking note of my surroundings.

Even in the grey haze of the early morning, I could see the glimpses of the trees around us. They had once been ablaze with the colors of autumn but now were washed away by the renewal of spring. Recognition hit me like a punch to the soft spot of my stomach, almost winding me. It was mine and Cade's meadow.

Water bubbled over stones in the distance, and a feeling of longing spread over me as I noted the shadowy outline of my practice target. This place had contained some of my most peaceful moments during a time when I needed a sanctuary. Both the meadow and Cade had given me reprieve from the anxiety and fear that dwelled in the academy beyond.

Looking at it now, I could acknowledge the part it had all played in making me the person I had become. I couldn't linger in nostalgia, though, because it usually gave way to a spiral of wondering what I could—or maybe even should—have done differently. Blinking away those memories, I trudged forward.

We entered through the door that led into the academy, and as we reached the juncture of the tunnel systems, I heard people talking in a hushed whisper.

When the sources of the voices came into view, my focus fell to Cade, who was speaking with Katarina, surrounded by those in the network that I had met in Falkland. Eri, Axel, Steph, and Baylor rushed to greet Beckett, who emerged just behind me.

It was surprise that caught in my throat when Cade began taking tentative steps toward me, as I had thought my farewell the night before had been obvious.

"Hi," he said in a whisper as he came to a stop just before me.

"Hey," I stammered. "How are you here?" I asked somewhat rudely.

His shoulders rose and fell as if he had been asked to tag along to a market trip and not a secret Fae mission. "Your magic made it so I couldn't speak to anyone who didn't already know and when I caught Kat lurking around the halls, I tested whether or not I could tell her, and it let me."

The curveball left me speechless. He had found a way around my deal in less than ten hours. I wasn't sure whether to be flattered that he was still finding ways to be around me or irritated that he had gone against my intent as soon as he had the chance.

Sensing this inner turmoil, Cade pressed a hand to his neck. "Look, I left the brothel in a hurry last night. I needed some time to process everything we talked about and..." Those indigo eyes slid back to mine. "Can we talk?"

"Again?" I blurted out before I could stop myself.

He sniffed a laugh. "Yeah, I didn't get my fill of disappointing you last night." The edges of his mouth quirked up slightly, but he still seemed uncomfortable.

My gaze shifted momentarily to Beckett, who was too deep in conversation to make me think we were moving out immediately. Then his eyes caught with mine, for the briefest of moments, his jaw flexed before he returned his focus to Eri, continuing his conversation without even a beat of hesitation.

I shifted my stance to face Cade, squaring my shoulders. "What did you want to talk about?"

His eyes softened. "I wanted to apologize. Again. My words came out all wrong."

Nodding, I offered him a half-smile. "It's okay. Don't worry about it."

Cade sighed, long and heavy. "I don't care if you have magic or not. I don't care about what my parents think. I only paused because I'm an idiot and your question tripped me up." He raked his hands through the chocolate strands of his hair.

His head tilted back as he drew in another breath. "Kat thinks that I can go with you." His eyes returned to mine. "Back to the Light Kingdom."

A tiny pocket of air spasmed in my lungs. "So, you spill secrets from the Light Kingdom to the first person you were magically able to communicate with about it and they offer you a place in society?"

He at least had the good sense to look abashed. "I asked her if it was possible for someone who was not born there to take residence there and she told me it was possible." Cade stood up a little straighter. "I want to go."

For some reason, head tilted subtly to Beckett, and I found my husband—maybe my mate—glaring at me with warning.

Wrenching my gaze from Beckett, I returned it gently to Cade. "I think that's great if that is what you want. But don't come for me."

Cade's lips pressed into a thin line, and I watched as the column of his throat shifted with a hard swallow. "I'm not."

I offered him a disbelieving look, which he followed up with, "I've always wanted something more than the fish empire could give me. A new kingdom..." His eyes lit up with wonder. "It could be just the adventure I was looking for."

Ironic, considering he hadn't been willing to give up those things for me in December. My expression must have conveyed as much, because Cade released a harrowing sigh. "I would be going a little for you too. To prove to you that you matter more to me than my parent's expectations. My words failed, but my actions will show you that I meant what I said. I love you, Ashton."

"Cade, I mean it, you shouldn't come for me." I didn't know how to explain to him that I had a mate, who I was already magically married to, without giving away too many secrets that he couldn't possibly understand the weight of.

"I don't expect anything from you," Cade replied, that same earnest from the previous night returning to the violet flecks in his eyes. "Just let me show you—"

A throat cleared from the direction of the gathered Fae, and I heard Beckett's voice commanding the group. "It is time to head out."

Cade's body went rigid with the announcement. "I'm not coming now," he confessed. "I'm staying behind in the academy with Kat to make sure you have a clear way to egress."

Relief pummeled through me. I didn't think adding Cade to the mix of whatever was going on between Beckett and I was going to make anything less muddled. I needed time to think and this certainly wasn't it.

"Well then, this is goodbye," I replied, softly.

Cade's hand reached out, grabbing my wrist and stopping me from walking away with the rest of the network.

"I brought you something," he admitted a bit sheepishly. "I think it could help." He padded over to a bend in the tunnel, retrieving something dark from the edge of the shadows. His grip contained ebony wood, curved with the tension of a bow string, and a quiver full of fresh arrows.

"My bow!" I exclaimed, grabbing the weapon with exuberance and a broad smile.

Cade huffed a little laugh through his own grin. "Good luck out there, Ash."

"Thank you," I muttered, slinging the quiver over my back but keeping the bow between us, lest he attempt to give me a hug.

"Better head out before you get left," Katarina interrupted, and her voice caused me to jolt as if I were still her underling.

She placed her hand on my shoulder, making sure to snag my attention. "You've got this." Her reassuring words meant more than she could ever know and armed with my weapon of choice, I felt like I finally believed her.

After a brief farewell, I turned to follow the group, only to find that Grethe was the only person left. He was casually propped up against a stone wall, waiting for me. His face was somber, and I wondered if this was typical in the space leading up to missions or if it had more to do with me. "He went ahead to give you some space."

"Who?" I asked, even if my mind had already conjured the image of the golden haired general.

Grethe gifted me with an unusually pointed stare.

"Well, I'm ready now," I replied, gripping my bow tighter, unexpectedly uncomfortable with Grethe's scrutiny.

"Just a minute," he replied, reaching out to stop me from heading down the tunnel. It wasn't aggressive per se, but I stilled all the same.

Withdrawing his hand, he let it fall limply by his side, those green eyes staring at me with an intensity I had yet to witness from him. "I've never seen Beckett take to anyone like he's taken to you. You've met his parents," he sighed as if recounting some horrible memory. "Real connections aren't a thing for him. I know it might be the bond, but I can also tell he's taking this seriously."

Confusion danced along my face. "You stopped me to tell me that your friend has a crush on me?"

"No," he remarked. "I stopped you to tell you that this mate business is consequential."

At his words, my vision took in the now-empty cavern. "No one can know that," I hissed.

"No one but the four of us will," he answered, voice lowered to match mine. "It's just... I've known him a long time, and he deserves happiness. And even if he's not a shifter like me, this is just as heavy for him as if he were."

My eyes trailed along the passageway that Cade had taken, clearly missing yet another piece of crucial information about shifters and bonds. "And you think I am going to break his heart? Ryana seems more concerned that it will be the other way around."

Bright blonde curls bounced as Grethe shook his head. "She's only seen him as a wayward adult. She loves him like a brother, but I think she's always going to be protective over you and—"

"And she's only seen him be promiscuous and careless with hearts." I paused. "Grethe, I'm going to be honest with you. The only thing I can focus on right now is getting my father back. When we have returned to the Light Kingdom, then I will consider what this bond means for Beckett and me."

Grethe responded with a sharp nod. "I understand. I just didn't want you to make your mind up about him before you heard something good. He's more than just what you see on the surface. There is a heart in there, too, and it's bigger than you'd expect. It just lives more guarded than most."

Sixty-Two

As the group walked down the narrow passageways, damp and dank with stale air, I forced my thoughts to the mission.

To my father.

To his freedom.

We passed the remains of what had been a wall, piles of stone and debris clustered against the edges. Next to the largest mound was a pickaxe that made me seriously question if Cade had manually broken down the wall that blocked the tunnel to find me.

It was a dangerous game to consider that, and I quickly redirected my thoughts once again.

Beckett had already given me an overview of the plan, and the rest of the team was so in sync that they didn't even require a refresher as we gathered at the slabbed wooden entrance that signified the door to the palace kitchens.

All of our flames had been extinguished, leaving us in shadows as we waited for the signal to move forward. We were going to be broken into teams, and the only thing I was certain of once we crossed the threshold was that I was to remain by Beckett's side.

We had opted to come around four in the morning, well before kitchen staff would arrive to start breakfast and late enough that the inhabitants of the castle would be asleep. There was no ideal time to break into the residence of perhaps the kingdom's most magical people, but we had no choice.

The longer my father resided in the dungeons, the worse his health would become. No one was confident that the bond would keep a person alive if they died from starvation, as opposed to a wound. I shuddered at the reminder of Gianna's report. *Wounds that had been magically healed.*

Instinctively, my gaze turned to Beckett. Even in the dark, I could make out the hard planes of his jaw. He turned to me as if my lingering stare had somehow alerted him to my attention.

"Go," he whispered to the others in a hushed tone, and the six of them slowly crept from the door until we were left alone. A large portion of his plan revolved around securing the corridors for me, so that I could join with as little risk as possible. It was likely some result of whatever he and my mother had discussed while I slept in the carriage, but it was why we would be the last to leave the safety of the tunnels.

That, and we were the heirs to the Light Kingdom now. I pondered if Beckett had always been at the rear of a mission like this for the same reason.

Beckett stepped to me and looked down, worry slithering its way across the bond like a snake, sliding into my chest and settling there with cold scales and a looming sense of dread.

"You stay with me, no matter what, okay?" Beckett's voice was hushed, but that didn't mean I missed the command in it.

"Okay."

"I'll keep you safe," he added as if it hadn't been implied.

"I know," I replied, almost absentmindedly.

He opened the hatch, and instead of leading directly into the kitchens, it allowed passage into what must have been the castle's rubbish bin.

We skirted around the lip at the edge of the room, and I did everything I could not to hold my nose. It smelled putrid, beyond what I knew of food alone, like maybe it contained human waste. Though there was something else there, too, something far too close to rotted meat.

My heart plummeted as I searched the floor around us in the dark, scanning the piles of debris and trash for any sign of a human left behind to decompose. Would they have disposed of my dad if I took too long to return?

The smell burned my lungs with those thoughts and before I could linger on them too long, I was being pulled into the kitchen and the semi-fresh air that awaited us there.

"He's not in there, Ashton," Beckett remarked.

Feverishly, I nodded, sucking in a gulp of the air that no longer stank of death.

"Do you want to go back?" He breathed against my hair. I hadn't even realized that I was pressed against his chest until that moment.

"No," I whispered.

His eyes sharpened, and his jaw tensed. "Then I need you to get your head in the game. I can't send you in there like this." His words were harsh but valid.

With my palms flattened against his chest, I pushed away from him and straightened my spine. "I'm fine," I declared, tightening my grip along the strap that held my bow across my back.

Beckett twisted to the direction of the exit, and I got my first good look at the space. The room itself was nothing like I imagined. For one, the place felt unused, and it went beyond a simple closeout for the night. Pots and pans were piled haphazardly near a sink, still coated in food that had long since molded or rotted, waiting to be cleaned.

A thin layer of dust covered the wooden countertops. Some cabinets were left ajar, as if the room had been in the midst of preparations for a meal when the entire staff had disappeared unexpectedly.

Inwardly, I groaned. It didn't matter why this room looked like this. The only thing that was important was finding my father and getting us all out of here as quickly as possible.

Beckett ushered me into the next room and down a hallway that intel had suggested would lead us to the stairwell that went to the dungeons. There was no frill or opulence here, nothing like what I had witnessed in the entrance to the castle when we had come to see the Ice Trophy.

A bird call sounded right next to my ear, and I ducked at the approach of an animal that I would never find because it wasn't there.

"Shit," Beckett growled. "It's the signal." Panic laced his tone.

James Baylor's gift was sound manipulation, and that was the noise he had decided to use if the mission was compromised. Dread steeled over me as my stomach wound itself tightly in a tight knot. "No."

"We need to go," Beckett said as he reached for me. "This was a trap."

"No," I repeated, pulling back from him with blown-out eyes. I hadn't come this far to leave my father behind.

"Ashton," he growled but I could scarcely hear him over the frantic thumping of my heart. I whirled to the spot where a door lay in wait, a passage to my dad. Before I could second-guess my choice, I bolted through it, throwing a gust of air magic in Beckett's direction to give myself even an ounce of a head start.

"Blake!" Beckett whisper-yelled behind me, and I had only a millisecond to decide what to do when I realized that the stone steps only led up.

Taking them two at a time, I ascended the stairs, slipping through the first door I came to with no regard for who—or what—might be waiting for me on the other side.

Scanning the halls quickly for people or doors that looked like they might lead down was useless from this angle, and I could already hear the footfalls echoing from the stairwell I had just abandoned.

It was reckless, but Beckett was approaching at an alarming rate, and I needed to move fast if I was going to have any chance at reaching my dad. If Beckett caught me, he could easily physically overpower me, and I knew he would if my safety was at risk.

There were no lit wall sconces down this hallway, nothing to indicate that this area was even occupied. So, I took a chance and ran, choosing speed over stealth as my arms pumped wildly at my sides. It wasn't a matter of if Beckett caught me, but when. All I could focus on was that I needed to get to my father first.

An arched opening gave me the first glimpse of carved stone steps, and my heart lifted in triumph moments before hands wrapped around my shoulder and mouth, stifling my attempts to scream.

"What were you thinking?" Beckett seethed as he pulled me into an alcove a few feet shy of the stairwell.

My eyes filled with tears, and I blinked them away as I stared at Beckett with fury. But I couldn't answer because my mouth was still firmly covered by his palm.

"We have to go, Ashton," he breathed into my ear. "I promise we will come back for him, but it's not safe right now."

A door creaked from behind us, and Beckett's entire body froze as his eyes flared.

The voices were muffled at first but then became more distinct as people approached our hiding spot in the shadows.

"You guaranteed us the girl," a familiar male voice said, although I couldn't quite place who it belonged to. "And yet, here you are showing up uninvited and empty handed, thinking I would bargain with you?"

There was a desperate sigh. Then, "You said all I had to do was make sure she attended the academy, and I did that." It was a female, and I stilled instantaneously because I would know that voice anywhere. The voice of my childhood and afternoons by the riverside, gossiping about boys and dreaming about our futures.

It was Jemma.

My Jemma.

My lunge forward was involuntary, but Beckett pressed himself tighter against me, pinning me roughly against the stone at my back. His eyes flared with warning, and he made no move to release my mouth from his grasp.

Their conversation continued with no indication that they had heard our shuffling.

The man spoke again, his tone void of any emotion. "You assured us that she would come for her father and thus far, she has not shown."

A strangled noise left Jemma's lips. "Please... please, I did everything you asked just let him go."

She was begging for my father's freedom, so there was still hope.

The man laughed, but it was humorless. "We have half a mind to throw you in the dungeons with him."

Again, I tried to push past Beckett to get to my friend. Maybe we could help each other? The attempt was fruitless; I didn't even budge an inch. No amount of my own training overcame his sheer size and strength. His grip tightened against my hip, his fingertips rendering me immobile.

Beckett's lips grazed my ear, and in a tone almost too quiet to be heard over the rush of the blood in my ears, he spoke. "My duty is to protect you even if it is from yourself." He paused. "I will drag you out of here if it is what it takes to leave this place."

Jemma's choked cries interrupted the moment. "Please. We've done everything you have asked of us. For years. Please just release my dad. I promise I will turn her over as soon as she comes home. You know she will find me."

My mind whirred with the incoming information, my heart cleaving as it hit me all at once. Her father was alive, and she was bartering my life for his.

Another strangled wail split through the air, amplified by the bare stone lining the halls. "Please," Jemma choked out, but whatever else she tried to say was swallowed by her anguished sobs.

The man made a noise most similar to a chuckle, but far too malicious to be in the same realm as something so traditionally jovial. "You were supposed to have her wearing the charm. If you had even done that, we could hunt her down ourselves." This time, his tone dripped with irritation.

Realization had me gasping against Beckett's palm. Was he referring to the necklace Jemma had given me when she returned from her trip South?

"Give me another chance," Jemma asked through a sniffle. Their voices already sounded farther away.

A door creaked open further down the hall. "One last chance," the male replied. "Deliver the girl to us or we kill your father."

"I will," Jemma agreed, her voice equally terrified and determined.

"Oh," the man added, too casually for the conversation, "If you come here with nothing again, I will kill you."

The door clicked shut and all my resolve dissipated. I was grateful that Beckett's hand remained clamped over my mouth because it muffled the gasp that I couldn't hold back. Something shattered within me, and if the feeling could have been a sound, it would have pulled snow from the mountaintops around the capital in devastating waves.

Jemma had been more than a friend. She had been family, my sister. And it had all been a lie.

Beckett's stare snagged on my own, and even in the dimly lit alcove we were pressed into, I saw him speak to me in the blink of his eyes. An *I'm sorry* that he never said, because instead he whispered, "I'm getting you out of here."

Knowing I was now in no position to perform, I dipped my chin in reluctant agreement.

Tentatively, Beckett released my mouth and stepped back, allowing me full use of my limbs and voice. Not that it made a difference, as shock held back my words.

We took a few cautious steps in the hallway to head back the way we had come when I heard the man call out again. "Is someone there?"

Before I could register what was happening, Beckett was snatching me into the closest darkened room. As silently as possible, he shut the door behind him and pressed his ear to the boards.

I had been in such a state of shock, and Beckett so focused on the threat in the hallway, that neither of us had noticed that this was no stairwell, and while the room was pitch black, we were not actually alone. It wasn't until we heard the feminine voice that we were alerted to the other presence, but by then, it was far too late.

"Who are you, and why are you here?"

Sixty-Three

ESTELLA

With her schedule so wildly off these last couple weeks, Estella was wide awake when two figures entered her bedchamber at the brink of dawn. That, in itself, wasn't so unusual that she was concerned by their lack of formal announcement or knocking, it was the fact that both of them were clothed in black leather and strapped with weapons. Furthermore, there wasn't a Guide to be found by their sides.

Estella shoved herself up from the settee, unsure whether to be terrified or elated. Not recognizing someone these days could mean that she was finally getting her freedom, or she simply had a new attendant.

Rather than tossing her empty glass toward their heads, she decided diplomacy was the best option. "Who are you, and why are you here?" Estella's voice still sounded raw from years of being a forced mute.

The man whipped around to face her first, eyes wide with fear. There was something almost familiar about him, but within a blink, the woman turned as well, and that was when Estella's heart skipped a beat.

Those eyes.

"It's you," Estella stammered, already closing the gap between them. She'd recognize those crystal blue eyes anywhere, in any version of her dreams. No magic had ever been able to strip them from her mind.

The man before her was already drawing a dagger at his waist. "Take another step and I slit your throat." His words came out in a whisper.

They had not intended to come here, and that realization prompted fear to fall over Estella like a heavy downpour. She slid her gaze back to the woman, looking for any reassurance, but all she found there was the same mirrored terror. Now that Estella took the time to really observe her, everything was wrong.

Golden brown hair glinted in the weak flames, void of any hints of auburn.

Her stature was off, several inches too tall.

Most notably, the woman from her vision was dead, so she could not be standing before her.

The sound of sliding metal drew Estella's attention back to the man who now had the dagger held in the space between them. "Who are you?" he demanded in a tone that said he was used to holding authority.

She wanted to laugh at him. She was no more a danger to him than the empty cup she left behind. Not while she was covered in runes and powerless. The only thing she had to barter with was her name.

Her chin lifted as she did her best to look down on the man in front of her. "I am Estella, The Elemental Queen of Demetros."

The atmosphere shifted then. The man crouched down, flames flickering along his fingertips, licking along the sharp edge of his blade.

Estella noted a strange color shimmering around his fire, but she didn't have the luxury of contemplating such curiosities. Not when he was poised to strike her.

She flickered her gaze to the girl, who no longer expressed fear in her eyes. "Your majesty," the woman said, breathlessly as she sidestepped her companion to take careful, measured steps toward Estella.

A low growl came from the man's chest. "Blake."

Estella cocked her head to the side. "Do you know who I am?"

The woman continued to approach, much to the man's disdain, but he didn't raise his voice to halt her. "I have been told many stories about you, but I believe most of them were false, now." Those familiar blue eyes trailed the line of Estella's threadbare clothing.

A rumble emitted from the man's chest as the woman reached her hands out to clasp Estella, and the Elemental Queen released an accidental sigh with the tender touch. *When was the last time she had been handled with anything but roughness and demand?*

Estella shook her head. "I'm afraid I have not been acting Queen in quite some time." The prolonged contact was enough to make the Elemental Queen shiver as a tingling began taking over her hands.

The woman must have felt it too because she flinched, although she did not back away.

"What do you mean you have not been the acting Queen?" The man asked warily, voice still unnaturally low.

Ignoring the brute, Estella turned back to his companion. She looked so much like the woman who had plagued her nightmares that it hurt. "Who are you?"

The man sheathed his weapon, using his now free hands to pull the woman away from Estella and shield her behind his body. "Who she is is none of your concern. Will you let us leave in peace?"

Tears pricked along Estella's eyes. "Leave? Please take me with you. I am a prisoner here." This was the closest she had ever come to escaping, she couldn't let them simply leave her behind.

Over the man's shoulder, the woman was staring intently at her fingertips. "What is your magic?" Those heartbreakingly blue eyes shifted to Estella. "It hurts me. I felt it when I touched the ice trophy too."

"Fuck," the man whispered, almost to himself. "Fucking blood magic."

Estella's gaze raked over her rune-covered forearms, making their way to the girl before her. Blood magic could only mean one thing. "These have stripped me of my power," the Elemental Queen stated, gesturing at the white scars that littered her skin before turning her gaze back to the woman. "I cannot harm you like this. I only wish to know who you are."

The woman's brow furrowed as she took in the harshly carved shapes in Estella's arm, closing the distance between them to run a fingertip across the old wounds before flicking her attention to her companion. "We have to take her with us. Ry can undo these and—"

She never finished her sentence as a wave of pain exploded from where the two women touched, leaving them both a crumpled mess on the floor.

No longer caring about volume, the man dropped to his knees beside the woman, catching her before she fully hit the rug. "What the hell did you just do to her?"

Estella rubbed her hand against the runes, opening her mouth to protest her innocence, when she felt it. Pin prickled stinging washed over her entire body. It felt like jumping into an icy lake in the dead of winter, a moment in a suspension of time when every muscle in her body locked up.

The runic slashes across her arms began to glow, brighter and brighter, all the while burning like the white-hot flames of a forge. She screamed out, the only way to relieve some of the pressure building inside of her. Then, deep down in the marrow of her bones, something shattered. The scars remained, but the weight of them had been lifted, as if they no longer held any power. Like they were nothing at all but the vestiges of her advisor's betrayal.

The swell of Estella's magic lapped against her skin like the ocean greeting a familiar shore. It felt as intrinsic as breathing. As fundamentally sacred as freedom. For a moment, she closed her eyes to inhale that sensation, letting herself be reunited with the magic that had been stolen from her.

Then, what the man said hit her like a key sliding into a lock. Metal fitted to metal. The smooth turn of a door unlocking.

Blood magic.

Estella's eyes blew wide, and she whirled to face the woman, already pulled to her feet by her companion. "You are—"

Her words were cut off yet again as the door to her bedchamber—to her prison—was blasted off its hinges and a wild-eyed, feral Claudius stood in the opening the explosion left behind.

She turned to face the strangers, locking eyes with the woman who so clearly belonged to her in some way she had yet to discover. "Run!"

Sixty-Four

There was no time to contemplate the bizarre interactions between myself and the Elemental Queen or any of Beckett's comments on the subject as Claudius blasted his way into the suite and began his attack. I had told myself I wouldn't run the next time I faced an opponent, but there was something convincing in the woman's tone, when she told us to flee. Like I knew the best chance I had to save my father came with my escape from this situation.

The Queen, Estella, shot a blast of icy air in the direction of the Ignus Guide as she pointed to a tapestry at the back of her bedchamber. She whisper-yelled her next command. "Behind that is a tunnel to a connecting suite. Go! I'll follow you!"

I couldn't place what had drawn me to her when we entered the room, or what exactly had me ignoring the history lessons surrounding her involvement in The Great Conflict, but there had been something so intrinsic about the way I was pulled in her direction. Just like it had been with the Ice Trophy.

Before I had seen her, witnessed the phenomenon that occurred with her touch, I might have spent the rest of my days hoping to never meet her in person. Now, although the urge to run wrapped around my

518

heart and tugged me in the direction of the tapestry, I couldn't fathom leaving her behind.

Beckett had no such qualms. He hauled me to my feet and yanked me behind the tapestry and into the hidden tunnel before I could so much as protest.

The unmistakable sound of steam hissed behind us as Claudius presumably used his firepower to melt through whatever frozen shield Estella had created.

Throwing my gaze over my shoulder, I took one last glimpse at the fabled Elemental Queen, her long blonde braid whipping in the wind as dark clouds began spiraling in a halo around her body. Despite the fact that the tapestry fell back into place, blocking her from view almost instantly, that image was imprinted in my mind.

I shifted my attention to the passageway and in a few frantic heartbeats, Beckett and I emerged on the other side into a similarly sized bedroom coated in a fine layer of dust.

Beckett flicked his hand behind him, crumbling the passageway between rooms with the groan of stone as he used his earth powers to block Claudius' entrance.

Utilizing my ability with the air, I shoved a dresser against the exterior door, and Beckett turned to me with surprise. "We can't go that way," I stated, "I studied the maps Ry provided, and if I'm correct, the door is right next to the one we entered. We wouldn't stand a chance."

Trusting my intel, he scanned the room for another option. Surely the Elemental Queen hadn't pointed us in this direction only to have us be cornered unless...

Beckett seemed to draw the same conclusion I had, a look of disconcerting flashing over his face.

If this was truly a trap, perhaps we could barricade ourselves in and hope for backup or...

Without warning, Beckett pushed out another wave of air magic, shattering the massive panes of glass behind us, leading me onto an exterior balcony with a firm grip. Our boots crunched against the mangled shards of debris that littered the stone tiles.

He peered over the edge of the balustrade, wincing when he calculated the distance.

"We could cushion the fall with air?" I suggested, unsure if that was even possible. It wasn't something I had trained for, but at this point, we were running out of options.

A loud commotion from within the room alerted us both to the fact that Claudius had breached one of the entrances into the space we had barricaded.

"Shit," Beckett hissed. "Hands up, Blake, be prepared to strike. They could have any number of gifts."

It wasn't a surprise to expect multiple elements, but the confirmation that they were poaching gifts too had not been part of any meeting I was privy to. The thought of that had anxiety swelling in my chest as I kept my focus on the blown-out opening to the balcony. I had done well against the network, but all of them only boasted one special power. The Guides could have many and the realization of that made me uneasy on my feet.

Astonishment ripped over my entire body as a figure crossed the threshold that was decidedly not Claudius. Elvyina, the Saxum Guide, strode onto the balcony slowly, as if she had simply joined us for tea. Her icy white hair cascaded over her shoulders, and her black eyes fell upon me. "Yes, I can feel the power from you. You are the one we have been searching for..."

Peering over the ledge, all I could see were rocks jutting out along the border of the lake. If by some miracle we could avoid the jagged stone, we would die in that shallow water if our air magic didn't work.

And yet, Beckett guided me up onto the edge of the railing, the parapet just wide enough to stand on. He placed his body in front of mine and faced the castle just as Phoebus, the Flumen Guide, stepped into view, joining Elvynia.

"We take her alive," Elvynia stated, pointing a bony finger in my direction. "Kill him for all I care. It will be cleaner."

Phoebus grinned, the deep lines that bracketed his mouth expanding as he smiled. "With pleasure."

His hand opened in the space before him as lightning crackled across his fingers. My eyes widened with the substantiation of the theory that they had, in fact, stolen gifts too.

"When I say jump, we are jumping," Beckett whispered, low enough that I wasn't sure the Guides could hear me over the display of electric magic that Phoebus was currently twisting between his bony fingers. The sparks jumped between his knuckles like he was doing a trick. Almost as if he were toying with us before he decided to strike.

Fire licked along my hands as I called upon my favorite element. "You will only take me dead," I warned them, ignoring Beckett's command. I would not fail at this mission. I was going to bring my father home.

Elvynia's mouth twisted into a sickening approximation of a grin. "Is that so? Or will you hand yourself over when we tell you we have your father?"

White hot rage simmered beneath my skin, heating my body to an uncomfortable temperature.

"Blake," Beckett warned, "Prepare to jump."

"No," I growled, "You prepare to fight. I'm not leaving here without him." If I left now, there was no telling what they would do to him, and after the knowledge of what they had already done, I would not take that risk. There was only one way out of this, and it ended here. I wasn't running anymore.

Ignoring the fact that two of the Guides were still unaccounted for, I stepped forward, praying to those same untrustworthy gods that the remaining advisors were called away on some diplomacy trip and wouldn't show up to leave us grossly outnumbered.

"Give me your best shot," I exclaimed, taunting Phoebus instead of Elvynia. I couldn't be certain if their gifts were shared or divvied out amongst them, but one thing I was confident I could count on was that I'd have to take out the bigger threat first to have any hope of survival. I had learned a thing or two about hierarchy and strategy from the Fae during my time in Falkland. Based on that experience alone, I'd bet that if Phoebus was drawing my attention to him, Elvynia was actually the more powerful of the two. She had been the one to command him, anyway, and ranking usually went hand in hand with power.

Delight washed over Phoebus' features at my supposed distraction, punctuated by the shadows the arcing lightning in his palm created. He raised both hands over his head, then yanked them down, drawing the electricity from an otherwise calm sky.

The bolts barreled toward me, and I raised my hands, calling on my water power to create a cocoon that fully surrounded us. Beckett's magic joined mine, swirling around us in a protective layer that crackled and hissed as Phoebus' magic slammed into it. The shield did not falter.

"Drop the water on my signal," I whispered to Beckett.

"Only if you agree to jump on mine," he forced out through his clenched teeth, and I knew it wasn't just the strain of manipulating water that set him on edge.

I took precious moments to try to make him understand because I didn't know how I was going to do this without his aid. "Beckett, I will not leave here without my father and definitely not to fall to certain death over that ledge." There was a finality in my tone that he must have heard because he released a huff of a breath and dropped his chin in agreement.

"We might be outmatched in gifts, but I have an idea."

With his hands still outstretched and his grimace firmly in place, Beckett lowered his voice even farther, our swirling water turning dark and menacing as the Guides pelted more magic against its barrier. "Care to share with me?"

"Can you hold this without me?" I asked, head jerking toward our shield.

Taking the pointed look, I got in return as a response, I released my magic from the cocoon.

"Then, nope," I said, pulling the bow from my back and retrieving an arrow from the quiver.

"Fuck no," Beckett snarled. "You are not going to go up against unknown magic with that."

"I'm an excellent shot," I replied, confidently. "On the count of three, you're going to blast that shield apart just like I did in Falkland, and I'm going to shoot."

"Ashton," Beckett begged.

"They won't be expecting it, Beckett. Three."

His nostrils flared, but he held the shield, his eyes unwavering in their connection to mine.

"Two."

"Just jump with me." The pleading in his tone almost stopped me in my tracks. I had never known Beckett Astor to beg. Except...

"One."

Less than a heartbeat later, the shield exploded into a blast of water so frigid it had turned navy, and I used that millisecond to shoot true, nailing Elvynia right in the heart, in the exact location we had been taught to hit a deer to avoid suffering.

If they had healing capabilities, they'd have to stop their pursuit of us to save her, and that was the assumption I made before I let that arrow fly.

Phoebus shrieked, showing off a set of deeply yellowed teeth, some of which were missing. "You foolish girl," he growled. "He said we had to take you alive. Not intact." With the final enunciation of the word, his raised hand clenched into a fist, then swung in my direction, stripping the debris from the ground of all the metal it possessed, instantly forming it into shards that launched at us with a speed too fast to deflect.

I had counted on them acting as a unit, assumed that Phoebus would care more for saving his comrade than going after me, but I had been horribly wrong.

Had I just committed murder on a hunch?

There was no time to mull over that morbidity because suddenly I was falling. Beckett's arms wrapped around me as we hurtled toward the rocky ledge below. Darkness crowded my vision as my body threatened to lose consciousness.

"I'm so sorry," he whispered into my ear like he was saying goodbye. As if it had been his mission to keep me out of their hands, dead or alive.

My eyes squeezed shut as my arms tightened around Beckett's waist. It was on the tip of my tongue to tell him that I didn't regret our night for a moment. That maybe even a little part of me...

Out of nowhere, our trajectory changed. I no longer had the sensation of falling, but I wasn't entirely floating either. There was no pain, as if I hadn't even hit the sharp rocks on the edge of the lake at all and it made no sense.

Was I already dead?

The sound of rushing air was absent.

Every sound was absent.

There was only the impression of something damp and inky sliding along my skin.

This had to be death, and I had just been spared the suffering aspect by those long-dead gods I kept praying to.

My eyes peeled open, but all I could see was a wall of dark smoke, encapsulating us in the same way that the water shield had. It didn't hurt, but I could feel all the places where the magic grazed my skin, leaving behind the sense of something cool and almost metallic.

The smoke swirled around us until we were in a cage of solid black, devoid of any light. Then, as quickly as it encircled us, it began to unravel. First, with a crack, showing a tiny hint of orange light through the blackness. More shards appeared as the smoke unfurled, beams of light breaking through the darkness.

Then, my stomach dropped.

We were falling again.

When the smoke retreated completely, there was nothing but empty sky around us, a tangerine haze coating the clouds that streaked over the horizon. A horizon we were a part of.

Glancing down, I caught the rocky edges of a familiar sight. The unmistakable formation of the Cliffs of Alamance. This time, I was barreling toward them from above, moments from being splattered against the stone. A scream caught in my throat just as another sharp gust of air, and what could only be magic, washed over me.

The descent slowed, and the wind blew against my body in an unnatural cadence that had me shifting my gaze to Beckett. There wasn't confusion that marred his brow, as it did mine, only concernment.

Movement caught my attention behind his back. Large black leathery wings were spread behind us, and I would have screamed if my brain hadn't instantaneously put together that it wasn't one of the creatures like in Steph's visions coming to attack us. No, these wings were firmly attached to Beckett's back.

My eyes widened in horror; my body frozen with shock as I could do nothing but hold on for dear life as he gently lowered us to the ground. His grip on me lingered for just a moment after we landed before he released his hold along my waist.

Staggering backwards, I fell on my ass, scrambling to put even more space between us. "What are you?" My finger jabbed at the air toward his appendages.

The man had the audacity to look hurt by that statement. The corners of his mouth turned downward in a pained grimace. "I was going to tell you after we rescued your father."

He stepped forward, bending and offering me a hand like he was going to help me. Like I would let him touch me now. The pebbles beneath me dug into my palms as I pushed away, crawling far enough to get out of his reach.

He stilled, sensing my terror, seemingly confused, of all things.

"What are you?" I repeated, more adamantly than before, even though a piece of me already knew. "Tell me!"

The traitorous bastard took a deep breath in, then tucked both of his hands behind his back. My pulse beat a frantic rhythm in my chest as every last bit of trust I had for him evaporated into thin air. I didn't need him to tell me, but I waited with bated breath as he pushed out the words.

Dark grey eyes met mine, filled with the gloom of rainy evenings and ruined plans. "I am part Shadow Fae."

Sixty-Five

Beckett's words launched me to my feet. The bow had somehow survived our tumble from the castle's balcony and I had it loaded and aimed at his heart before either of us could expel a full breath. The Shadow Fae had been a lurking danger in the background of what I thought was the more pressing matter in Demetros. Now, I was faced with the reality that everything I knew about them might not be true either. That, once again, I had been lied to.

My eyelashes fluttered in a steady rhythm as I scoured my brain for all the information I had been given on the species. Mostly data points that *he* had supplied. My eyes narrowed to slits. "Do not get any closer to me."

His hands flew up in a surrender that I no longer trusted, his tone soft as if the inflection of his voice could possibly soothe me now. "We need to enter the Cliffs before the Guides decide to follow us. They clearly have access to the shadows."

My brows raised up to my hairline. "You said that the spells in the Light Kingdom and Demetros protect the people from shadow magic. Was that a lie?"

The mask of neutrality stayed firmly in place as he considered my question. "There are pockets where the spells blocking access to the void are useless. That balcony was one of them."

"And here," I guessed, or else he couldn't have used the void to get here.

Beckett's chin dipped once. "And here."

Slowly, my foot began to drag backwards. Thanks to my training at Biltons Academy, I knew exactly how to get back home from here. The thought stole the air from my lungs. There was no reason to return to Elmhaven. My father wasn't even there because I had left him in a dungeon to rot.

Beckett tracked the movement of my retreat with carefully measured glances, flickering between my boots and my eyes. "If you come with me, I will take you to your mother."

The arrow in my bow didn't lower, and my arms shook with the effort to hold it in place. As a backup, I called fire to my flesh, careful to keep it from burning the wood beneath my palms. "So, you can confess your crimes? Tell her about how you've been betraying her this whole time?"

His eyes darted to the space around me. "You're not safe out here..." No matter how worried he sounded, I couldn't bring myself to believe he had good intentions anymore.

"I don't know why you'd think I'd feel any safer with you," I spat. A flicker of a memory set my heart galloping once more. Reminders that the Shadow Fae—that Beckett—could likely control me with his mind if he got too close. That he might bite me to steal my magic.

Instantly, my stance faltered as I retreated, my back hitting against stone in a repeat of the same damned situation I had found myself in the last time I was in these caves. With a different predator.

This time, I wasn't being blackmailed, and my father *would* die if I didn't fight back. Changing tactics, I lowered the bow, slinging the weapon over my shoulder as I called on the elements that I had simultaneously wielded against Eri.

"We need to leave, Blake," Beckett stated in that General's voice he liked to use to remind me when rank mattered.

Defensively, my hands flew in front of me as Beckett took a single step in my direction. "It's Onyx, isn't it?" I asked, pleased when the question threw him off.

"What?"

"You are part Shadow Fae and clearly also Elemental unless you've stolen all of those gifts…" My stomach soured with the notion. Shadow Fae could only take power through blood. How many people would he have had to drain to uphold the ruse so consistently?

The skin along my face turned as white as ash. All those bodies found drained along the border. This whole time, could they have been his victims? And I had just shared my body with that monster, his lips on my skin, tainted with the blood of those he killed to deceive me. Acid churned in my guts as nausea cramped my stomach.

"Onyx is not the Shadow Fae," he clarified as if it mattered. Like his word meant something now.

Power crackled along my fingertips. "And you expect me to just waltz back to the Light Kingdom and keep a secret like this? Your people have infiltrated my mother's court, and you genuinely think I will stand by and let them?"

"Yes," he growled, finally showing a bit of his ire. "You will undermine everything I have worked for if you don't. This is bigger than us. Did you not read the rest of that book?"

I had no idea what he was referring to, but what I did understand from his statement was that I had been a pawn in his game. "Is that all this was?" I gestured between us, needing him to confirm what I already suspected. "Something you've worked for. A means to an end."

There was a coldness in his stare as his grey eyes flicked over my face. "This was an unexpected detour," he admitted, and it was enough to send me over the edge.

My power lashed out, a whip of fire and ice, brimming with whatever stones were close by, propelled by the air at my disposal, but it lost momentum and stopped just short of a solid black wall, which had erected in front of Beckett.

Then, before I could register it was happening, smoky tendrils wrapped around my arms and pinned them behind my back. So much for his magic not being able to harm me.

Beckett had the common sense to appear pained as he stepped

toward me. "Enough of that. Something is approaching through the shadows, and we need to move. I will tell you everything you want to know if you just follow me."

Magic wasn't as intuitive for me as it was for someone like Beckett who had been given access to it for decades. So, instead of willing his shirt to be set ablaze or sucking the air from his lungs, I let my rage flare by spitting square in the center of his face.

His nostrils flared as he wiped the liquid from the bridge of his nose. "Don't make me force you," he snarled.

The toes of his boots roughly collided with mine as his shadows held me completely still. His chin dipped, and his eyes were dull and lifeless as they perused my face. "Please."

I flailed against the confines of his inky restraints to no avail. "That is the only way I would ever go anywhere with you."

For a moment, anguish seemed to lance his features, but he schooled them yet again in favor of his perfected indifference. "Very well," he stated, grabbing my shoulders without loosening the grip his tendrils had on me.

Pain radiated from my right side, and we both looked down to find fresh blood on Beckett's palm. Had he done that? Was he hurting me on purpose? The wetness pooling along my lash line threatened to topple over the edge, and I scrambled to preserve my anger.

"Please," he whispered, and a part of me longed to believe that I was still safe in his arms. That piece of me was a damned fool.

Another buck of my body had Beckett releasing the wounded shoulder, but the moment of reprieve was short-lived as his hand came to curl around my throat, pressing against my jaw and forcing my focus to fall on his face.

My eyes widened as I sucked in a breath, and he took the opportunity to lock his stare to mine. His irises were so dark they were almost black, and in the dim light of the early morning sun, he looked exactly like Ebus. Like Berit. Like a monster.

"You will listen to me and not say a word," he began. The tears I had tried so hard to keep at bay began to leak from the corners of my eyes. And he wasn't even done. "You will follow my orders until I tell you that you are released. You will not scream, and you will not run away from me again."

A cold, slimy feeling slithered up my back, and when it reached the base of my skull, I felt the claws of something malevolent stroking the edges of my mind before I sensed the shift.

Suddenly, my body was foreign to me. Like I was trapped inside it, conscious of what was happening but unable to walk or even lift a hand. My mouth refused to open. The only part of myself I seemed to be able to control was my eyes, which glared at Beckett with increasing contempt.

He released my throat and had the audacity to look genuinely sorrowful. "I apologize that I had to do that, but it was for your own safety."

My mouth remained shut, but on the inside, I was screaming profanities at him that I hoped he could sense across our bond. That fucking bond.

He reached out his hand to mine, "Take my hand and follow my lead. We must hurry."

My fingers laced with his without my consent, and another salty tear fell from my jaw, splashing onto my leather vest with a plop. Beckett dragged me to the center of the cliffs, expertly maneuvering the maze with no compass or glance toward the sky, like he knew exactly where he was going.

It was lighter now, but still very early morning, and the pink haze in the atmosphere cast ominous shadows around us, highlighting the enormous wings that loomed behind him.

Black, almost iridescent leather skin stretched over the curved bones that arched from his spine. In this eerie light, I could just make out delicate veins running throughout like spiders' webs. The ends were clawed, similarly to the wings of a bat, but larger and more proportionate to his imposing frame.

Catching me staring, Beckett only shook his head and sighed heavily as if my observations were a nuisance. "You may ask your questions," he said, and I felt the magic free my voice. "But you may not scream out. We cannot risk being caught here."

Even though my initial plan had not been to cry out, knowing how useless that would be in the Cliffs of Alamance, the thought of being commanded not to enraged me. There were many things I wanted to say to the man before me, but the magic had apparently been as specific as his words. My throat failed to push out air when I tried to tell him to fuck off.

Only when I was ready to ask a question did my voice emerge at all. "What are you going to do with me?" The only silver lining here was that his magic hadn't forced me into speaking respectfully, and my tone was capable of being drenched in resentment.

His gaze slid to mine. "I am going to take you back to Lochmere. You will be safe there."

I offered him a piercing gaze. "Where does this tunnel lead?" There was no way this took us to some secret opening near my mother's southern castle. Even the portal on the Emerald Isle was based off actual geography. A passageway that led all the way to the southern tip of the Light Kingdom from the middle of the northern region of Demetros would take days to traverse, even underground. The idea of that much time without access to fresh air made me queasy.

"This passage was created by the gods and thus does not follow the rules of mortal magic," Beckett replied. "It will deposit us near the border of the Light Kingdom."

It was on the tip of my tongue to ask how he knew a god had made this passage but there was no point in continuing to ask him questions if I didn't trust the answers. So instead, I began calculating my next move, once I could orient myself and shed this oppressive, controlling magic.

It was during this quiet contemplation that I realized that Beckett had not been surprised to find us here. He knew his way around the maze without a map or compass. Meaning, the Dark Kingdom had always had access to Demetros. That was perhaps more terrifying than Beckett being a spy.

Beckett ducked into an opening in the cliffside that was barely large enough to permit him inside, especially with those wings behind him. A sudden chill pebbled my flesh as I was tugged into the cave. It was at least ten degrees colder inside, and it smelled like decay and mold. Access to my own motor function would have been amazing if for no other reason than having the ability to cover my nose and mouth would allow me to block out the stench.

Beckett produced a glowing orb of flame with his free hand, but it only served to illuminate a couple inches around us, as if the darkness was swallowing the light.

We meandered silently through the damp and dingy tunnels for what felt like an hour, but was probably minutes, before I started to see a faint blue glow. A few paces in front of us, a curtain of shimmering aqua light fell over the path. It danced and flowed like the waves of the ocean, pouring from an unmarked place in the rocky roof above.

Beckett didn't slow down, but he did turn his head slightly to ensure I heard him. "This won't hurt."

We passed through the light, and the other side was even colder than Falkland's snowy mountains. A blast of frigid air hit me in the face, and my body began to tremble, in shock from the abrupt shift in temperature. If we weren't even fully out of the cave, and I was already this cold, what would it be like when we left the safety of its protection?

Beckett placed his hand on my arm, sending a shock of warmth flooding my body. He leaned in so that his mouth was a fraction of an inch from my ear. His voice stayed low, as if someone might hear us. "You are free to speak softly and move your body as you wish but do not scream or run away from me. No matter what you see." Those oily tendrils of his magic wrapped themselves around my arms and legs with the shift in his command. "It is even less safe for you here than it was in Demetros. We will be back in the Light Kingdom soon, but you must trust me and do what I say."

Using my newly found freedom, I jerked away from Beckett. My mind was racing, and my heart was pounding in my chest like an animal trying to break free of a too-small cage.

It will deposit us near the border of the Light Kingdom.

He hadn't lied, he had just been selective with his words, with his truth. Because if we weren't in Demetros anymore and we were still headed to the Light Kingdom, that only left one place on the continent that I knew of.

"Where are we?" I asked him, my voice a whisper.

His reply was tense as he approached the mouth of the cave, gaze sweeping the skyline ahead. His eyes sliced to mine. "The Dark Kingdom."

Sixty-Six

Logic dictated that Beckett couldn't be trusted, but taking me to the Dark Kingdom seemed like a good indication that he was definitely not intending to return me to Lochmere any time soon.

My bones strained with the efforts to bolt, but his magic held me steadfast, keeping me from running away from him. There was nowhere to go but forward, by his side, as he stepped from the shelter of the cave and onto the snowcapped ledge beyond.

Behind the cloud cover, the light from the sun was faint, casting a red haze over everything it touched. As if we hadn't spent more than a few seconds in the tunnels, and the sunrise was still occurring. The curse, I recalled with a grimace, was meant to keep plants from readily growing, and thus it was always dusk here. Night fell when it was intended to, but the daylight was relegated to this husk of what it once had been, meaning I had no way to tell time in the way Katarina had taught me.

Blisteringly cold wind raced over my skin, chilling me to the bone and forcing my newly freed arms around my waist in an attempt to preserve whatever warmth I could.

Beckett was still watching the skyline for something, but all I could see for miles was an endless sea of white mountains, broken up by the jut of rock formations that looked more like claws digging their way out of a snowy grave.

Dark flecks seemed to hover in the crimson haze ahead, too large to be birds, but too far away to see anything distinguishable. Maybe they were the wyverns or the Chryptera that Steph had shown me, but now, given the man standing next to me, I couldn't rule out that they might be Shadow Fae too. Instinctively, I reached for the bow still strapped across my back.

Beckett slid his gaze to me only momentarily, catching the location of my hand before he averted his charcoal stare back to the horizon. He studied the creatures with a type of serene observation that set me on edge. His stare almost held reverence.

With an exhale that created clouds from his breath, he turned to me. "It's time to go." His hand extended into the space between us, and when I grasped onto it, knowing he'd just force me if I didn't, he tugged me against his chest.

The tendrils of darkness began twisting around us, encapsulating our bodies once more before the light disappeared entirely. We materialized more gently this time, with our feet firmly planted on the snow-covered ground. Before us was a series of ramshackle buildings that had been erected underneath rocky ledges at the base of a mountain. Beckett released me and stepped toward one of the shacks, his shadows extending into the structure ahead of him like probing tentacles.

The frigid wind whipped through my hair, and I realized that my fingertips were losing sensation. Temperatures never dropped consistently below freezing in Demetros, so Katarina had only glossed over the finer details of hypothermia in her survival course. I wasn't sure how much longer I'd have.

Beckett clapped a hand over my shoulder, sending another pulse of warmth across my body that made me shiver in delight. Then, to counteract the kindness, he pushed me forward into the closest building, shoving me over the threshold before him.

With a jerk, he shut the half-rotted door behind him, which did a surprisingly effective job of blocking out the paralyzing gusts. When he removed his hand from my shoulder in favor of dropping to his knees to dig through a cedar-lined chest, the warmth instantaneously withdrew from my body.

"This should help," he stated, standing to full height and passing me a grey fur-lined cloak. "That and just using your own magic to warm yourself up."

He hadn't specified that I couldn't use magic, just that I couldn't run, and I felt foolish for not considering it sooner. With my next inhale, I focused on using my flames to slowly heat my skin without burning my clothing. It took an extreme amount of focus to hold the energy at the perfect temperature, something I hadn't yet mastered without an urgent need, even in Falkland. Dropping the magic, I quickly gave up in favor of snatching the garment from his grasp.

"We must move quickly if we are to avoid patrols," Beckett stated, and I wasn't sure if he meant my mother's Light Guard or something belonging to the Dark Kingdom.

Numb fingers fastened the buttons closest to my neck as Beckett did the same with his own darkly hued cloak. "Which kingdom are you loyal to, Astor?"

Fur-lined gloves slid over his hands before he passed me a matching pair. "I am loyal to the continent."

"And what is that sup—"

"We must go now," Beckett interrupted, grabbing my hand before the glove was even tugged all the way on—barely giving me time to snatch my bow from the ground—and harshly dragging me from the shelter. He made to walk several paces when he stilled.

As quick as my next blink, my spine hit the closest tree trunk, pinning my bow between myself and the rough bark. Beckett sealed himself over me, covering my mouth with a gloved hand. "Quiet," he commanded, his magic dancing across my skin again, settling in my throat.

His chest heaved against mine, his breath erratic pants against my cheek. Shadows slid over our bodies, but it was different than the magic that transported us here, almost as if he were melting us into the darkness itself.

I could just make out an obscure version of the world outside of his makeshift shield. Through the tree line, I caught a glimpse of a shape of an enormous reptilian snout.

A dragon?

Beckett's power-laced command held my gasp in my throat. Not a sound was escaping my lips.

The animal that I thought was a dragon came fully into view then. Two clawed legs appeared, but no more. A long, scaly tail whipped in irritation behind its body, the end of which was adorned in deadly spikes that matched the ones that traveled down the length of the creature's back. Two enormous wings, reminiscent of Beckett's, were curled against its ribs. It was hard to tell in the cocoon, but the scales seemed to be a deep green, almost blending in with the evergreens of this forest, like it was a tactical evolution.

The animal paced the area, stopping only to lift its snout and sniff in various directions. It cocked its head to the side and stared directly at us. Its face jerked back and forth as if it was trying to piece together a disconnect between what it could see and what it could so clearly sense.

The magic didn't have to force me to be quiet any longer, I held my breath the entire time.

Suddenly, the creature tipped its head back and roared loudly into the sky, launching itself toward the hazy clouds. Even as the beating of wings faded into the bleeding horizon, Beckett and I stayed like that for several tense minutes.

When he finally released me from my hold, his sigh seemed to carry with it the weight of his retreating fear. Silver-hued eyes slid to mine. "You are free to talk but do not scream."

Goosebumps pebbled my flesh as his magic receded, leaving behind the ghost of its presence along my bones. "That was a wyvern," I stated in a breathy whisper. "They're bigger than I imagined." Steph's visions had only shown them at a distance and certainly not in a way that had given me any sense of scale. The creature had been close to the size of my cottage.

"They patrol the borders," Beckett admitted, eyes still roaming the tree-lined sky for any hint of another.

So, it was Dark Kingdom patrol he meant. But if he was hiding from the patrol, then maybe he truly was taking me to my mother.

With his palm facing up in the space between us, Beckett gestured toward me. "We have to walk a bit before we make it to the border, but I can't shadow walk this close to it without setting off the wards."

Glaring at his outstretched hand, I shook my head. "I can walk myself, thank you."

Beckett's mouth curled into that familiar smirk. "I was offering to warm you."

Revulsion passed along my features. "No, thank you," I replied as I crossed my arms.

He shrugged, as unbothered as usual. "Suit yourself."

Snow crunched beneath our boots as he headed forward, but as disoriented as I was, I couldn't tell if we were moving South or North.

After walking for ten or fifteen minutes, Beckett came to a stop next to a tree that appeared like all the others at first glance. His fingertips traced a marking of an ornate triangle that had been carved into the bark.

"We've reached the border," he stated.

Skeptically, my eyes scanned our surroundings. As far as I could see in any given direction that I swung my head, there was snow for miles. In the Light Kingdom, it would have been nearing summer, and even Falkland, where we had been just days ago, had seen the dissipation of the last dregs of winter.

Furthermore, it didn't feel the same way as the border had when we were on the Light Kingdom side. When I could sense the presence of magic. This felt steeped in wrongness, like I needed to turn around and run in the opposite direction until I found the true border.

My eyes fell to slits in Beckett's direction.

"It's part of the illusion," he said, reading my thoughts through my expression. Unless he had lied about that, too, and the Shadow Fae had access to *mind-reading* on top of their *mind control*. "From this side, there are spells that make you want to stay clear of the border."

It was unnerving how much he could glean from my expression alone. Considering that it was possible he was still reading my emotions, I built my mental walls back in place, putting all of my focus into shoring them up rather than contemplating how he had answered the question about the border magic I hadn't even asked.

Beckett shook his head, this time oblivious to my inner thoughts, his gaze on the snowy abyss beyond. "And yet another spell that is taking too much from the land."

As curious as that made me, I'd have to unpack that issue at a later time. "So, what are we waiting for?" The sooner I could get into the Light Kingdom, the better my chances were for escape. Once I crossed that border, his compulsion theoretically wouldn't even work on me.

The only sign I had that Beckett might have sensed those thoughts was the slight flare of his nostrils as he stared ahead at what he had explained was an illusion.

My huff of a laugh formed a cloud in front of my face. "Are you worried it won't let you cross now?" Maybe taunting him would get him to act rashly. If he thought I was questioning his abilities...

Cold, menacing eyes turned to me. "No one knows you are here with me, Princess. They wouldn't have had time to update the wards to block me from the Kingdom that, thanks to you, I still stand to inherit."

There was a reason he was stalling, though. "Then cross," I challenged.

"Together," he offered, extending his hand to me once more.

Rolling my eyes, I thrust my palm toward his but forced him to put forth that final effort to lace our gloved hands. Warmth spread over me as his magic flushed my skin, almost making me yank my hand back out of petulance alone.

"Let's go," Beckett stated, tugging me forward as we both walked toward what appeared to be more of the same frozen tundra.

Instinctively, I closed my eyes, bracing against the pain I expected to come when we traversed the protected border. Warm air washed over my face, and even with my lids firmly closed, I could sense the sun's light, bright and yellow, shining down on us from an uncursed sky.

"You did so good, my boy," a dark and menacing voice said.

My eyes blew open as the air left my lungs. Ebus Astor stood before me, next to two saddled horses a shade of black reserved for emptiness and nightmares.

Beckett's hand tightened round mine, and try as I might, my legs would not move to let me run away from him. From them.

The chuckle that fell from Ebus' lips turned my blood to ice; colder than the cursed winter lands we had just left. He began to pace toward us. "I knew that bond would be a benefit to our mission." Soulless black eyes slid to mine. "It only took a few months for her to trust you so implicitly."

There was a portion of my heart that held out hope that Beckett really had planned to take me to my mother. That this was all some gross misunderstanding. The thought hurdled itself off a cliff when I turned to face the younger Astor, only to find that his expression had flattened out into utter indifference. Then, one edge of his lip quirked upward. "Of course, father."

Ebus' sinister laugh pulled my focus back to him. He circled us while his assessing gaze raked up my entire body, pausing where Beckett's hand was still intertwined with mine. "Now that we have her, you'll have no excuses not to consummate the marriage. I'm sure that won't be difficult for you."

Bile rose up in the back of my throat, burning its way to my tongue.

"When you've actually completed your task, you're more than welcome to pass her along." A smirk so similar to one I had seen Beckett wear countless times flashed across Ebus' face. "Double our odds."

Beckett sneered, the first significant crack in his neutrality. "You know I don't share."

Ebus tsked before sighing.

That was enough of that conversation for me to endure. "What do you want from me?" I yanked my hand out of Beckett's hold because his magic might still be forcing me to stay firmly planted by his side, but I'd be damned if I was going to hold his hand while he discussed sharing me with his father.

Shoving all my fear to the deepest parts of myself, I squared my shoulders at the elder Astor. "You know who I am. How do you think the Queen will react when she learns that her Generals have kidnapped me?"

Fear could be one of the greatest motivators, but it seemed an inadequate force as I let my gaze flicker between the two men.

Shooting an irritated glare at me, Ebus began walking back to his horse. "You are every bit as ignorant as I assumed you'd be with your unsavory upbringing." He brushed off the defense in his tone with a sinister chuckle. "I do not care what the Queen of the Light Kingdom thinks of me."

Beckett snickered as his hand landed on the small of my back, nudging me toward the second horse. "Ebus is the King of the Dark Kingdom, he does not fear the wrath of the Light Queen."

All the blood in my body drained, pouring into the vat of churning liquid in my stomach. It wasn't any lingering effect of the cold that set my muscles trembling like a newborn fawn. "So, you're using me for ransom?" It was the only theory I had that ended with me alive.

"I have other ideas," Beckett said, grinning widely so that I could see the two elongated canines that slid down into his smile. "I've been curious about your gift. I bet I could figure it out after a little taste." His tongue darted out to slide over one of the sharp points.

"I bet she is delicious," Ebus added, eyeing my throat.

A growl rumbled in Beckett's chest, loosening the tear dangling from the corner of my eye.

Ebus laughed and shook his head. "Your mother's line was always so possessive. I see the bond has affected you in the way we always worried it would." The dastardly man rolled his eyes as if this were all some humorous joke.

"So, you understand the danger of trying to touch what is *mine*?" Beckett snarled.

This elicited another chuckle from Ebus who held his hands up in the air. "I will allow you to keep your prize to yourself," he said. "Until which time she no longer serves a purpose to us."

The tension in Beckett's body lifted his shoulders up, almost imperceptibly, but enough for me to notice. "Fair enough," he replied, with very little emotion in his tone.

Ebus mounted his horse with ease, tugging along the reins to adjust the steed in the direction we came in. "Well, if we are done here, we have business to attend to," Ebus said. "You were a bit late and nowhere near our discussed location."

Beckett shrugged, mounting the second horse but keeping his animal firmly in place. "We ran into some complications along the way."

He looked down to me, extending his hand. "Mount."

My body shook so violently that I couldn't even feel the oily magic slithering along my skin. Beckett slid back in the saddle so that when I threw myself onto the mare, I was seated in front of him.

His free hand locked around my waist as he adjusted us both to be more comfortable, and all I could do was sit there in shock and let him.

How far back had he been planning this?

Was this the reason that he had to call in the favor with my mother?

To ensure we stayed together...

The magic might not let me run away from him—possibly because it was cast in the before we crossed into the Light Kingdom—but maybe I could break its hold if I knocked him out. Most magic required a caster to be conscious.

My body began to flail, and a silent scream left my throat as I lurched forward and then snapped my head back as hard as I could into Beckett's nose.

Instead of rendering him unconscious, it only served to piss him off.

"Fuck!" he called out, releasing me momentarily to grab at his face. His compulsion did not fade, and my muscles remained rigid, unable to aid me in rolling out of the saddle.

In a flash, Beckett's arm locked itself in front of my body, his blood-soaked hand pressing against my chest.

"That was not smart," he drawled, pushing me forcefully against his him. "We won't be doing that again."

Muffled sobs escaped my lips as Beckett's mouth came to rest once more at the edge of my ear. "Sleep," he whispered.

The slick coldness of his magic covered my body and twisted around my mind for a blink of an eye before the darkness overtook me, and my eyelids fluttered closed.

Sixty-Seven

ESTELLA

It had been so long since Estella had used her powers—an exact timeframe that she still didn't know—that she had expected them to be rusty. Clunky even, like the first time she had tried to mount and ride a horse. Instead, magic flowed through her in a way that was as effortless as breathing.

Lightning tore through the air, racing for Claudius from all directions, but in his surprise, the man only thought to deflect from the front, shooting up a wall of solid ice. Her bolts slammed into the mass of the frozen shield, slicing through the magic with ease. The strikes that aimed for his back had no such barrier, though, digging into the Guide's flesh and leaving him a charred heap on the floor.

The doorway behind him was still open, but no one had come through it yet. If the sounds of crashing in the next suite were any indication, most of the backup had been sent to follow the intruders, rather than guard a Queen they all thought to be powerless.

Estella had a split second to consider what she would do next. She could run to the aid of the girl with the familiar eyes and her overprotective companion, or she could seek her freedom.

Guilt churned her insides as she made her final decision, and she took off toward the hallway, which was blessedly empty. It turned out

543

that when the kingdom's greatest secret was that the Queen was being held in a prison inside her own home, the floor she was sequestered on wasn't all that guarded.

What would her guards even do if she explained her situation to them? Did any of them know the truth? Did she even have guards considering her door had always been locked from the outside?

Her arms pumped wildly as she ignored the electricity humming in the air that had not originated from her. Without slowing down, she barreled into the back stairwell, knowing that speed was on her side for a quick escape. She just had to make it to the lower levels, through the dungeons, and out the secret passages she used to play in as a child. The ones that led to *her* garden.

Her throat constricted as she thought about all the time she had spent amongst the plants in her youth. The way the woman in her visions had meticulously grown flowers of all colors of the rainbow. Just for her. What would she think of Estella now? Running away from danger—from a potential family member—to save her own hide.

Shoving those questions aside, Estella picked up the pace, her slipper-clad footfalls sending muffled echoes off the stones she ran across. By the time she made it to the bottom, her mind was clear, and her chest was heaving.

Just as she had done a thousand times before, she pressed her hand against the locking mechanism that led to the dungeons. The Guides might have stripped her of all her humanity, but the castle knew just as well as the gods that she was the rightful heir and blood magic didn't care about politics or manacles. Metal scraped against metal as the door swung open, revealing that for once the dungeons were not empty.

Her brows furrowed because she already knew that they weren't. A man—Christopher?—was being tortured down here for information about her familial ties. She had been so surprised to see the girl with those familiar blue eyes that she had forgotten all about the relative in the dungeons, but now...

Frantic eyes scanned the cells before her. If he was in good enough health to escape with her, she would take him. Maybe that would make her feel better about leaving the girl behind. Otherwise, she had no intention of lingering in the halls any longer than she had to.

Her gaze snagged on a central cell, and she stepped forward slowly and quietly, as if the clang of metal hadn't been enough to alert the prisoner to her presence. The man in the cell had not woken up, and he lay there on the stone slab that was probably meant to be his bed, facing outward like he had fallen asleep watching the door.

Estella's breath caught in her throat, and she barely managed to stifle a gasp as she took in his features. The angle of his jaw. The slope of his nose. Everything was just as she had remembered, except the grey mottling his hair.

Dark circles smudged beneath his shut eyes, and as her gaze raked over his body, she caught telltale signs of magically healed wounds. He was skinny and frail, nothing like the man she knew before the Great Conflict, but even with those changes, it was unmistakably *him*.

"Christian," she whispered, wrapping her hands around the metal bars as her voice cracked with the emotions of recognition. Someone she knew was still alive. It was enough to begin to quell her panic until she realized that the man before her, the person she had once loved so fiercely, was on the brink of death.

THE END

Author's Notes

Thank you so much for your continued support for The Lonely Kingdom Chronicles. When I set out to write this story, I had no idea how far it would end up going and I am forever grateful that you, the reader, took a chance on this indie book.

If you enjoyed The Queen's Heir, I would love if you would consider leaving a review on Amazon, GoodReads, or the retailer you purchased it from. Reviews can be a big deal, especially in an indie space, so they are much appreciated.

If you'd like to be the first to know about the next release, the behind the scenes of my writing, and pictures of my cat, sign up for my newsletter on KathrynOscar.com, follow me on Instagram @KathrynOscarWrites or find me on TikTok at Kathryn.Oscar.Writes.

Also by Kathryn Oscar

Kathryn Oscar is the author of the Lonely Kingdom Chronicles.

Book 1: The Lonely Kingdom

Book 2: The Queen's Heir

Book 3: To Be Announced...

Available on Amazon and other major retailers and free to read through the Kindle Unlimited program.

Acknowledgments

Per usual, my first acknowledgement goes out to my husband without whom this could not be possible. Thank you for your continued support, attempting to keep up with the plot changes, and giving me the time needed to create this world. I love you more than Ashton loves cheese.

M + E, my sons, thank you for keeping me on my toes and showing me that I can do hard things (including editing in the middle of a Transformers battle). You two are a bright light in my life and the reason I push myself to do more than I think I'm capable of. I love you both forever.

To my friends, you know who you are, thank you for being the support I needed during the launch of The Lonely Kingdom and beyond. It will never cease to amaze me how much you championed this dream of mine.

Cynthia, thank you again for being a sounding board for the developmental edits of The Queen's Heir. It seems like just when I think I shouldn't be doing this, you come along with feedback that breathes new resolve back into me and my story. I'm so glad I found you as an editor.

To my critique partners and discord group, you guys are the best. I could not, and probably would not have done this without you.

Finally, my biggest thanks goes to you, the reader (realizing that some of these lists might overlap). It's because of your continued support that I feel confident to keep going. Thank you for every page read, every review, and every comment of encouragement you give me. I hope I do this story justice and make you excited for what comes next. Spoiler alert: this world is going to expand so much more and I cannot wait for you to see it.

About the Author

Kathryn Oscar is a self appointed "recovering engineer" who decided to spend time utilizing a different part of her brain to write fantasy stories in her bedroom. She lives on the coast of North Carolina with her husband and three kids—if you count the cat, which everyone including the cat, does.

When she's not writing, Kathryn can be found reading, training for RunDisney races, curating playlists for books she hasn't written, plotting books she will never have time to write, and taking care of her feral boys.

facebook.com/Kathryn.Oscar

instagram.com/KathrynOscarWrites

tiktok.com/kathryn.oscar.writes